**"LORD KOMAWARA, YOU NEED A
PROPER WEAPON TO SLAY DRAGONS**

and barbarian hordes.''

Toshaki bent over the nearby table and retrieved a lacquered chopstick. He brandished this like a sword and stepped into the guard position. "I would be honored if you would take mine."

Komawara broke free of his companions and spun back toward the Toshaki lord but, impossibly, Shuyun stood facing Toshaki, his back blocking Komawara.

"My lord," Shuyun said quietly, "that is a dangerous weapon to wield in the governor's hall."

Toshaki stood with his chopstick before him like a sword, suddenly looking unsure of himself. Botahist monks did not confront peers.

The implement disappeared from Toshaki's hand as the monk's arm became a blur of motion. Toshaki stepped back into his kinsman.

"Such a weapon should never be drawn in polite company."

Again Shuyun moved with a speed that was impossible to follow. There was a crack of wood hitting wood, not loud but strangely piercing. Shuyun bowed low before Toshaki who stared down at the chop~~st~~ ~~Shu~~yun had driven into the table.

"May your journey bring you ~~~~ ~~~~ ~~yu~~n almost whispered.

NOVELS BY SEAN RUSSELL
available from DAW Books

THE INITIATE BROTHER
GATHERER OF CLOUDS

The Stunning Conclusion of
The Initiate Brother

GATHERER OF CLOUDS

SEAN RUSSELL

DAW BOOKS, INC.
DONALD A. WOLLHEIM, FOUNDER
375 Hudson Street, New York, NY 10014

ELIZABETH R. WOLLHEIM
SHEILA E. GILBERT
PUBLISHERS

ACKNOWLEDGMENTS

Thanks to the many who have given support, encouragement, wisdom, and inspiration during the writing of these books: Don and Michael, Ian Dennis, John H., Ellen B., Jan, Jill and Walter, Margo, Kim E., Lady Murasaki, Bella Pomer, Stephan W., Betsy and Peter, Lang, Ted, Dave Duncan, Sei Shonagon, Erin, Sam, Shelley, Bob M., and David Hinton for his beautiful translations of Tu Fu.

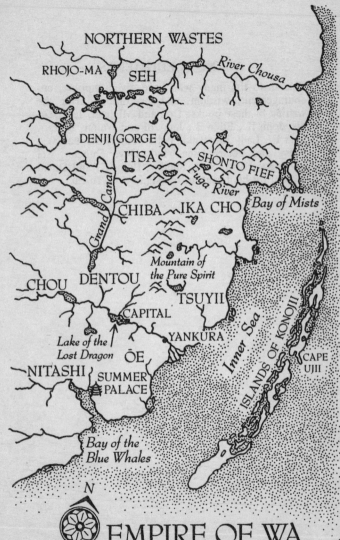

NORTHERN WASTES

RHOJO-MA

SEH

River Chousa

DENJI GORGE

ITSA

SHONTO FIEF

Fuga River

Bay of Mists

CHIBA

IKA CHO

Grand Canal

Mountain of
the Pure Spirit

CHOU

DENTOU

TSUYII

CAPITAL

Inner Sea

YANKURA

Lake of the
Lost Dragon

ŌE

ISLANDS OF KONOJII

NITASHI

SUMMER
PALACE

CAPE
UJII

Bay of the
Blue Whales

N

EMPIRE OF WA
during the Reign of Akantsu II

DEDICATION

To S.J.R. for grace and humor, always.

Rain,
Chilled by endless winter,
Runs down blue tiles
To form a bead curtain
Between our room and the world beyond.
The courtyard a small lake now

With roads washing away like ink marks
News turns to a trickle of rumors.
In far off Oe they say
Rivers have forgotten their purpose
And wander across half a province,
A shallow sea dotted by island hills.
Farmers pole wagon board sampans
Eyes red from searching
They look everywhere for their lost lives

It is a sight to pain a traveler's heart
I'm told

When asked by the Emperor
What should be done,
The Minister of the Right answered
    A generation that has not known calamity
    Will never understand the cost of war.

It is harsh wisdom
But just, no doubt

The Court Lady's Lament
From ''The Palace Book''
of Lady Nikko

One

The wind known as the Nagana blew in its season, turning the capital of the province of Seh into a city of whispers and sighs. The near empty avenues succumbed to the Nagana's invasion as it wound its way among the uninhabited residences, wrenching at shutters and filling the streets with the echoes of the city's former life—before the plague had swept the north. Rhojo-ma was a city half full of vibrant northerners and half full of the ghosts of the plague dead; only a decade gone, they walked in living memory still.

In the late afternoon the Nagana came out of the north to haunt the city with the voices of its past, and the people in the streets hurried on their way, attempting to ignore the sounds. No family had been untouched by the plague and the whispering of ghosts spoke to everyone.

By the curb of a lesser avenue, on the low wall of a bridge that arced over the canal, sat a Neophyte Botahist monk. Apparently oblivious to the life of the city, he chanted—a low, barely melodic sound that mingled with the wind echoing down an empty stone stairwell and off a nearby wall.

If he was unaware of the city around him, it could be said that the city, or at least those who walked its streets, were barely more aware of him. Their only acknowledgment, the reflex action of a sign to Botahara as they passed, but few turned their gaze to look for the source of the chant. A monk sitting by his alms cup was as common a sight as a river man at his oar.

A coin rattled dully into the monk's leather cup and he gave a quick double bow, not interrupting his chant or looking up to see who his benefactor might be.

Without warning the already cool air turned colder and the wind died to a calm. The whispering of ghosts fell to a hush. It seemed only the chanting of the young monk moved the air, and the pedestrians hesitated as though they'd suddenly forgotten the purpose of their outings.

There was a long moment of this eerie stillness, and then a deep roll of thunder shook the walls of Rhojo-ma, seeming for all the world to have originated in the depths of the earth, so substantial did it feel.

The air took on form and turned to white as hail pelted down in a sudden torrent. The staccato of ice stones drumming on tile drowned out all other sounds, but in moments it reduced its volume to a mere drizzle, then turned to rain.

At the first crash of thunder the residents of Rhojo-ma hurried to cover, leaving the monk alone on his wall, still chanting, apparently oblivious to the pelting hail despite the thinness of his robe.

The monk's recent benefactor stood under the bridge, hoping the downpour would not last and contemplating the timing of his offering with the bursting of the clouds. It was not the blessing he had hoped Botahara would bestow. He shook the hailstones from his robe, brushing the white pebbles off the shinta blossom and flying horse emblems embroidered over his heart.

Several of Seh's more humble residents shared the man's refuge, but they stood apart from him and had bowed deeply before stepping into the shelter, waiting for his invitation. Though still a very young man, Corporal Rohku was a member of Governor Shonto's personal guard and, as such, a person of some importance despite his lack of years and low rank.

The corporal's father was the Captain of Lord Shonto's personal guard and it was the young man's secret hope to bear this rank himself in his time. Even more, it was his dream that the Rohku name would be bound to that of the Shonto over generations of important service—as the Shigotu of old had attained fame for their service as elite guards to seven generations of Mori Emperors. For the time being he would have to accept a more humble position, for he was not sure that Lord Shonto even knew his name.

Beyond the shelter of the bridge, hailstones flowed down tiny rivers that ran between cobbles, disappearing before they made their circuitous way to the canal. Corporal Rohku found himself following their progress, try-ing to decide where the stones ceased to be ice and be-came part of the water. A second rumble of thunder shook the earth and, as though this were a signal, an ornate barge took form in the mist that hung over the canal. Before Rohku truly registered this, the barge faded again, reappeared, and then disappeared wholly into the clouds as though it had been only a specter of mist shaped by an errant eddy of wind.

Rain and hail forgotten, the Shonto guard mounted the stairs back to the avenue three at a time and ran out onto the bridge. So absorbed was he in trying to part the clouds with an act of will that he failed to notice the Neophyte monk was now standing at the bridge's far end staring into the fog with equal focus.

They did not have long to wait, for the barge appeared again, this time in more substantial form. It was intri-cately carved, painted crimson and gold, with banners hanging limp in the teeming rain.

One pennant did not need to stretch itself in the wind to be recognized for it was Imperial Crimson. A five-clawed Imperial Dragon would circle the sun within those folds of silk. The other pennants were unrecognizable.

Corporal Rohku waited with all the patience his young spirit could summon. A second barge, a typical river craft, appeared in the wake of the Imperial Barge, for that is no doubt what it was. Just when the young guard thought he could bear it no more, a hint of a breeze, a mere sigh, tugged at the pennants. Against a dark field, a Choka hawk spread its wings, appeared to take a single beat, and then collapsed as the fickle breeze died.

The guard was off at a run toward the Governor's Pal-ace. As he crossed the bridge, a young Botahist monk hurried past in the opposite direction though the young soldier did not notice, let alone return, the monk's half bow. There was no time to be polite to strangers. Jaku Katta had arrived—and several days before he was ex-pected.

Corporal Rohku pushed on, keeping up his pace until reaching his destination, whereupon he spent several mo-ments regaining his breath before he could give his re-port with any show of dignity.

General Hojo Masakado, Lord Shonto Motoru's senior
military advisor, knelt so that he was between his liege-
lord and the two openings to the room—screens leading
to an outer room and the balcony. It was an old habit,
one which he had developed in service to Shonto's father
during the Interim Wars. Having served two generations
of Shonto was a source of great pride to Hojo and he
often found himself comparing the two lords. Physically
they were obviously father and son, the high, broad
Shonto forehead seemed to miss few generations, and
both lords were exactly the same height and weight—
slightly more than average in both. Personalities differed,
however. The father had been more reserved and formal,
a biographer and historian of some note; his humor was
dry and intellectual. Motoru was far less formal, more
inclined to a social life, enjoying the company of those
much older and noticeably younger than himself. He had
the ability of great leaders to make everyone comfortable
in his presence.

Lord Shonto sat before a low table across from Hojo
and the Shonto family Spiritual Advisor, Initiate Brother
Shuyun, each of whom bent over the table in turn and
examined three small coins that lay on the fine-grained
wood—square gold coins with round holes in their centers.

"There is no question, Sire," General Hojo said,
"they are identical."

Shonto turned to the Botahist Brother, raising an eyebrow in characteristic fashion. Shuyun held the coin in
the palm of his small hand, staring with the ageless eyes
remarked upon by everyone who met him. Hojo reminded himself that this small monk, no larger, and
barely older than Lady Nishima, had once defeated the
most famed kick boxer in all of Wa. Despite his appearance and quiet manner, he was as formidable a warrior
as General Hojo—perhaps more so.

"I agree entirely, Lord Shonto," Shuyun said. "They
have even been struck by the same die. A small irregu-
larity can be felt along the inner edge." He turned the
coin over and ran the ball of his index finger around the
central hole. Both Hojo and Shonto did the same, with
some concentration. Shonto looked at his general and
Hojo shook his head almost imperceptibly.

"I do not doubt that you are right, Shuyun-sum," Shonto said, "though it is beyond my senses to feel this." The lord turned the disk over in his hand and realized he held the coin that had been taken from the raiding barbarian warrior. The strange dragon etched into its lustrous surface seemed to look at him with some suspicion. "Lord Kintari's dissolute son, a barbarian warrior, and now the coins Lady Nishima brings from Tanaka: 'from a trunk the Imperial Guard spirited onto a ship,' Tanaka tells us. A ship bound north. That is all we know."

They fell silent and a sudden cloudburst unleashed a torrent of hail which battered the tile roof with a clatter that would not allow quiet conversation—private conversation. Shonto reached over and opened the screen a crack that they might watch the spectacle.

Hail turned to rain and Shuyun broke the silence. "It is one of the lessons of the Botahist-trained that there are times when speculation serves little purpose, Lord Shonto, General Hojo, if you will excuse me for saying so. If we have considered all possibilities, then we must accept that we do not yet know enough. Coins come from Yankura and make their way into the desert: that is truly all we know. There are, however, other concerns which we can act upon. My teachers taught that we should begin where we may and practice patience where we must."

"Your teachers were wise, Shuyun-sum," Shonto said, surprising Hojo. He had never heard anyone but their former Spiritual Advisor, Brother Satake, come so close to criticizing his liege-lord. It was a measure of how much Lord Shonto had come to trust this monk in the short time he had been in the Shonto house. The lord turned the coin over in his hand one last time and then returned it to the table.

An almost imperceptible knock sounded on the inner screen and Hojo moved to open it a crack. He listened to a voice neither Shuyun nor Lord Shonto could hear, nodded, and pushed the shoji closed.

Lord Shonto raised an eyebrow, a gesture his staff did not need explained.

"Jaku Katta has arrived in Rhojo-ma, Sire."

Shonto reached unconsciously for the coins again but stopped himself. "Huh." He turned his gaze back to the opening in the shojis. "It would be interesting to know what the Emperor's Guard Commander could tell us of these coins."

Hojo nodded.

"Please arrange a meeting with General Jaku as soon as convenience allows. We shall see if it is true—in the dark tigers see more than men."

Even by Botahist standards the Prefect of Seh was a very old man and his age inhabited his body in manner uncommon among the Botahist trained. Monks typically remained lithe and youthful far past the age when the untrained had slipped into infirmity if they remained alive at all.

Brother Nyodo, Master of the Botahist faith and Prefect of Seh, moved so slowly that he seemed always to be progressing toward an early closure of the Form.

He set a tightly rolled scroll on his writing table and very slowly turned back to his guest; Senior Brother Sotura, the chi quan Master of Jinjoh Monastery.

"There is no brother by that name in our registry; *Hitari*, yes but no *Hitara*. Was Brother Shuyun certain?"

"Prefect, I do not think it is possible for him to make such a mistake."

"You think highly of this young Initiate, Brother Sotura. I begin to wish to make his acquaintance."

"Perhaps that will become possible at some future time, Prefect. It is the Supreme Master's wish, for the time being, that we keep our meetings with Brother Shuyun infrequent. It is important that Lord Shonto feel that his Spiritual Advisor is truly his."

"I only hope this will not lead to . . ." the monk searched for a word, ". . . to the willfulness we experienced with Brother Satake."

"That is my hope also, Prefect."

"Hitara . . . ?" the Prefect said slowly. "It is not possible that he was an imposter." It did not seem to be a question, so Sotura did not respond. "Is there not a Hitara in the Book of Illusion, Sotura-sum? I seem to remember . . ." He trailed off, a look of confusion and then dismay at his failure of memory.

"In the description of the Divine Vale." Sotura picked up the thread. "I had forgotten. *Hitara*—he who died and was reborn. The servant who served the Perfect Master faithfully when all others left for fear of the Emperor. Hitara rose from the flames of his funeral pyre: *'It was as though he stepped from the mist, and though the smoke and flames threatened to consume him, Hitara was untouched by them. He was like one arising from a dreamless sleep. When told of the seven days he had lain dead while his family mourned, he fell to his knees and offered up his prayers. And his funeral became the celebration of his rebirth and the celebration of his birth became the celebration of his life to be, for no other man had known such a miracle.'* "

Both monks fell silent at this. Rain fell on the tiles in the courtyard, washing away the hail that had collected earlier. A knock rattled the inner shoji.

"Please enter," the Prefect said, surprised that his words came out in a near whisper.

The shoji slid aside, revealing an Initiate of the faith, head bowed to the mat.

"Initiate?" the old man said, regaining his voice somewhat.

The young monk moved forward and placed a small stand bearing a neatly folded letter within reach of his superior, then retreated and waited in silence.

"Please excuse me, Brother Sotura, I must attend to this." He unfolded the crisp paper and read quickly. The Prefect nodded as though acknowledging spoken words and turned back to the attending Initiate. "He must be observed whenever possible. I will receive daily reports."

The messenger nodded, bowed and retreated from the room, the screen closing behind him.

The Prefect turned to the chi quan Master. "General Jaku Katta has entered Rhojo-ma. He comes in an Imperial Barge, making one wonder at Brother Hutto's recent news."

Sotura paused for a moment, reflecting. "The Son of Heaven has made no public gesture that would indicate that Katta does not stand in the light of the Throne. But I have found that one ignores Brother Hutto's information at great risk."

The older man nodded. "I agree, Brother. Appearances mean little in the world of the Emperor. He treats Lord Shonto as a great favorite, but only a fool would accept this as the truth."

"Jaku Katta in Seh . . . this is a cause for concern. I find this too much like the opening of a game of gii. There are too many pieces for one to see clearly. It is complicated even more with tales of alleged barbarian armies. It is as though another entire set of pieces waited to sweep onto the board at any second." Sotura met the Prefect's eyes. "We must inform the Supreme Master of these developments immediately."

"Oh, certainly, Brother Sotura. There is no question. I have only hesitated so that I may decide how much credence to give your young protégé's report."

"Brother Shuyun did not see the number of warriors that the encampment indicates, I agree, but I do not think this was a barbarian ruse. As Shuyun-sum has said, riders from Seh were unexpected there. I fear his information is horribly true, Prefect. I propose that we send word to Brother Hutto and to the Supreme Master immediately, and under both our signatures."

"I am not certain, Brother Sotura." The older man seemed to return to his former state of confusion. "It is so difficult to believe. An army of that size? How is that possible? Even the barbarians are not bred from the sand. We would appear to be alarmists at the very least if this army does not exist. I hesitate to sign my name to a report that is based on so little information."

"Excuse me, Prefect, but may I remind you that Lord Shonto does not question what Shuyun-sum reported."

The old man shook his head. "One can never know the true meaning of anything Lord Shonto says or does, Brother. He is engaged in a struggle for his life and the future of his House. If the Son of Heaven sent an army to Seh to save his Empire from the barbarians and Lord Shonto could control that army . . . consider—the balance in the Empire could be altered." The Prefect gestured slowly toward the walls as though they encompassed all of Wa.

"I do not profess to know the secrets of this Shonto's mind, Prefect, but I take nothing he does or says at its apparent value. We do have a Brother in the Shonto House, however—a trusted advisor to the lord himself.''

The Prefect's motion suddenly lost its flow and became almost stiff. ''We have had a trusted advisor in Shonto's House before, excuse me for reminding you, Brother, and he was more loyal to his lord than to his Order. We do not have verifiable evidence of the size of the army in the desert. I should tell you that this is not the first report of barbarian hordes I have heard.''

Sotura considered this for some time. ''If I send a warning to our superiors under my own signature, what will the Prefect do?''

''I will feel obliged to report that I am not convinced by Brother Shuyun's evidence.''

''Conflicting reports will certainly ensure that no action is taken. If Shuyun's information is correct, there is little time for hesitation. Little time to seek more information.''

''Excuse me for saying so, Brother Sotura, but Lord Shonto's Spiritual Advisor, for all his abilities, is a young man and new to the north. No experience from all my years in Seh would indicate that such an army could exist in the wastes. I do not feel I would be acting as my position requires to give credence to Shuyun-sum's report.''

The old man seemed to slump a little as though this rebuttal had taken all the energy of his ancient spirit.

''I fear I have tired you, Prefect. Please excuse me if I have destroyed your harmony.'' The chi quan master bowed. He rocked slowly back on his heels, a look of concern registering on his face. I'm sorry, old man, Sotura thought, but I cannot allow your fears to stop what must be done. There is more at stake than your comfortable position. May Botahara forgive me.

Lady Nishima sat before a low table looking at the design for a robe which her servants would embroider. Only moments before, as was often the case, she had a melody in her mind, a folk tune that a talented court composer had borrowed to create a composition for the Imperial Sonsa troupe. But her visitor had disturbed her harmony and the music faded away as though the musicians in her mind traveled off into the distance.

"It is of no consequence to me, cousin," Lady Nishima said, trying to keep her voice even. "Jaku Katta could arrive at my door and I would not interrupt my painting."

The mere mention of Jaku's name brought back memories she would rather have left undisturbed. She feared she colored with embarrassment, perhaps even shame, at the thought of what had happened between her and Jaku when they last met. *I went to his rooms,* she whispered to herself.

Lady Kitsura Omawara nodded in response. "I did not mean to suggest that you would be . . . pleased by the news, cousin, I am merely the messenger." She smiled the smile that disarmed the coldest hearts.

"I did not mean to be abrupt, Kitsu-sum. Please excuse me. I am thankful for your consideration in this matter." She tried a smile in return. Kitsura had not intended to cause her discomfort, after all; Kitsura was entirely unaware of what had happened between Jaku and herself. Deciding it would be best to change the subject, Nishima observed, "You seem to be very well informed, Lady Kitsura. Does Lord Shonto have this information? Or does he rely upon you?"

"I'm quite certain your esteemed father has all the information that I possess, ten times over." She looked down at her hands folded in her lap and began to turn a delicate gold ring until the design had gone full circle. When Kitsura did not look Nishima in the eye, it was a sign that she had been engaging in certain activities that she believed her cousin disapproved of. "I simply wish to keep us both informed. I have befriended certain members of your father's staff and often act as a confidante to them. After all, whom could they talk to who would be more concerned for their lord's welfare, except perhaps the Lady Nishima?"

"I am not entirely convinced that their lord would view these breaches of security quite so benignly." Nishima said this with feigned disapproval while she fought the feelings of confusion that set her heart whirling. Despite all efforts, she was afraid that these feelings must show on her face. She tried to cover this with words. "However, it is important to know as much as we can."

"I agree entirely, cousin. So much is hidden and yet everything that is important to us is in danger of being lost." She moved to the next ring, turning it a little more urgently. "Do you think it's possible that Lord Shonto could be wrong? Could the Emperor's general really be in disfavor at court?"

Nishima took a last look at the design and began to clean her brush. This would not be a brief interruption. "I do not know Lord Shonto's source of information at court, Kitsu-sum, so I cannot judge. But my father has an uncanny ability to weigh information on the scale of truth. It is worth noting that he does not speak of Jaku's present situation in absolute terms."

"This is what worries me, cousin. If Lord Shonto is right, then Jaku Katta's fall from favor and banishment are but a ploy to place the Guard Commander within our circle of trust. But if Jaku has truly fallen, and one with so many ambitions could certainly do so, then Lord Shonto cannot hope to win the Emperor's support to battle the barbarians through Jaku. This situation is of great concern. It is as you have said; so much depends on so little knowledge."

"If Jaku Katta engineered the attempt on my father at Denji Gorge without the Emperor's approval, as Lord Shonto suspects, then it is possible that our handsome general is not in favor." Nishima pushed her table aside. "It is all very confusing. Being sent north to restore order to the canal is hardly a sign of disfavor."

"Being sent to Seh as its governor would not seem to indicate disfavor either, Nishi-sum." Kitsura held her ring up to the light, examining it carefully. "It is as Brother Shuyun says; at the gii board an opponent's design does not need to be strong if you are unable to see it."

"I did not realize you discussed gii with Brother Shuyun," Nishima said, her tone registering something close to disapproval.

"Shuyun-sum has been kind enough to instruct me in the intricacies of the board . . . and to discuss matters of the spirit, also."

The two women fell silent. A distant thunder rumbled, like a far-off dragon. Rain beat on the gravel border of the garden outside.

"Nishima-sum?" Kitsura said quietly. "We must be absolutely certain of Jaku Katta's situation at court."

Lady Nishima nodded. Yes, she thought, and I must know what this man expects of me. She remembered the last thing she had said to Jaku the night she had gone to his quarters—they would speak in Seh. Now she did not know what they would say.

"I think I know how this can be done," Kitsura said quietly, "though I fear you will not approve."

Sister Yasuko held the paper up and blew gently on the ink, careful not to spread it. The dampness of the evening invaded her rooms and she huddled close to the charcoal burner and her single lamp. She blew again, careful not to spoil the fine brush work.

"There," she whispered and held the paper up to the lamp. It was a letter to her superior, Prioress Saeja.

Honored Sister:

> *In this time of great doubt, I wish I had better news. Our dear Sister, Morima-sum, shows little sign of improvement since I last put brush to paper. She has times when her crises seems to be passing, but the scrolls of the Brothers haunt her dreams still. We do not give up hope, Sister. We do not give up hope.*
>
> *The young Acolyte who accompanied Morima-sum has not fared well. It pains me to report that she left us three days ago. This was a tragedy, certainly, but nothing compared to the loss of a Sister of Morima's abilities. Our young Acolyte had her own faith shaken by the crises of Morima-sum and as she said to me; "If the way is too difficult for one such as Senior Sister Morima, how do I presume to walk such a path?" Perhaps she will return to us yet. I pray that this will be so.*
>
> *The rumor that Lord Shonto's Spiritual Advisor went into the desert in the company of Lord*

*Komawara seems, incredibly, to be true. Our
friend in the Governor's Palace tells us that
Shonto is convinced a large barbarian army will
attack Seh in the spring. We can neither prove nor
disprove the theory at this time, but if Governor
Shonto and his staff believe this, it is my opinion
that our Order should act as though there were no
doubt.*

*When I think of the suffering that a war would
bring and how it would affect our own efforts, my
heart grows heavy. We always hope calamity will
not overtake us in this lifetime, rather like
children trying to avoid difficult lessons. But they
must be learned: if not now, later.*

*Jaku Katta arrived today. It will be difficult to
place someone close to him, but be assured our
efforts will be tireless. We have a trusted friend
close to the Lady Nishima, however, and will
certainly know if she continues to correspond with
the Emperor's guard commander.*

*At this time Lord Shonto's daughter seeks her
companionship with the Ladies Kitsura Omawara
and Okara Haroshu, although the Shonto
Spiritual Advisor is also one of her regular
visitors—occasionally staying in her rooms later
than could be considered strictly proper: I know
no more at this time.*

*There have been no cases of plague reported in
Seh for several months now, for which we may
thank the Botahist Brothers even if they have done
little else worthy of praise. Chiba has not been so
fortunate, I am told. The many followers of
Tomso in that province have suffered terribly.*

*The rumor that the Udumbara blossomed
(Botahara be praised, Sister!), is not given
credence in Seh—it is a rumor all have heard
many times before—and, as you predicted, the
Brotherhood have denied it. I find nothing in all
the Brotherhood's treacherous history as
disconcerting as this denial. If an Enlightened
Master walks among us, why do they deny it? I
am cold with fear over this.*

Work on the Priory goes well and at less expense than we dared hope: Botahara watches over us. I would inquire of your well-being, Prioress, but I know the polite response. I, too, am well enough to serve His Purpose.

> *May Botahara chant your name,*
> *Sister Yasuko*

TWO

Distant hills rise up
Through an ocean of
Wind tattered cloud

Peaks become islands
In a chaos of pale crested seas

The erratic spatter of snow-melt on the undergrowth seemed to grow progressively louder. Lord Komawara tugged at the reins and moved his mare another twenty paces into the mist, stopped, and listened for the hundredth time.

Deep in the mist that had hung for days in the Jai Lung Hills it was impossible to determine the origin of sounds. They echoed and distorted and seemed to emanate from everywhere at once.

Komawara turned in a complete circle, a motion almost as slow as Brother Shuyun practicing his meditations of movement. Nothing . . . only the suggestion of mysterious forms: to his right a twisted, pointing limb perhaps belonging to an ancient pine; behind him, an outcropping of rock suggesting the face of a disapproving Mountain God.

Shifting the horse-bow to his right hand Komawara worked the fingers, cramped from holding a notched arrow for far too long. He returned the bow to the ready position and moved forward ten paces more, listening.

Years had passed since Komawara had last hunted the Jai Lung Hills—in company with his father then, when the old man still had strength to ride. Much had changed, more than he ever expected.

There were bandits in the hills now. Holdings had seen

their gates battered down in the night and only armed parties would chance the roads.

The lord stopped again, listening as Shuyun had taught when they traveled in the desert. Armor bit into Komawara's shoulder blade where the leather shirt had worn through, his left hand cramped again, his boots oozed when he walked, and his horse favored her right forefoot. If that was not enough, he was also hopelessly separated from his companions and had only the vaguest notion of where he was. A soft drizzle fell, slowly soaking into the lacings of his light armor. He listened.

Snow, heavy with rain, slipped from a tree branch and fell in a sodden pile at the lord's feet, causing his horse to shy. That, Komawara realized, was a true indication of the turmoil of his spirit—his mare had sensed it, had caught it in fact. Every few seconds the same soft thudding could be heard somewhere out in the fog.

He moved forward, then paused, straining to hear. Was that the sound of a horse, far off? The creaking of a tree distorted by the distance, by the imagination?

Komawara tried to stretch the tension out of his back and shoulders. In a fog there could be more to fear than brigands: his own men he trusted, but the local men who had joined the hunt for bandits suffered in a silence of poorly hidden fear. Men quickly lost their inner calm in fog such as this. It was as Shuyun had said, robbed of sight, every sound became a threat—even a falling lump of snow would be in danger from an arrow quickly loosed. The arrow from an ally ended more lives in battle than men would speak of.

Ten paces forward. Stop. Listen.

And then, among all the thousand imagined sounds, unmistakably, the thud of hooves on stone. His own mount pricked up her ears. Komawara jigged at the bit and pulled her nose up to his cheek.

"Shh," he whispered as though she understood. Three paces put them among a stand of long-needled pines. The lord pulled the reins over the mare's head and made her lie down, saddle and bags still in place. Automatically testing his sword in its scabbard, he crouched down, intent on becoming part of his surroundings.

Horses moving, the scrape of loose rock shifting, the creaking of leather. Komawara drew the arrow back by half. A horse stumbled and a man's voice could be heard making comforting sounds, but the words were not clear.

Where? Komawara turned his head from side to side, certain at first that the sound came from uphill, then equally sure its source was to his right.

He listened for a voice he might know. Be still, he told himself, let them pass, they would be easy to track in this snow. They'll make camp at dusk and it will be easy to find out who they are. But even as he gave himself this advice, he saw a movement in the mist not twenty paces away. A dark form in the blinding white. Moving toward him? Away? He tried to catch any hint of color, a familiar silhouette. A man on foot, walking slowly. Komawara almost stood for a better view, so surprised was he by the sight: dark beard on a face tanned to leather by relentless wind and sun, a vest of doeskin over light mail. *A barbarian!* A barbarian warrior leading a horse through the Jai Lung Hills.

Komawara sank lower as the man picked his way up the slope toward him. Behind the walker came others, their size amplified by the fog. Knowing that a man could look directly at him in this fog and see nothing, Komawara held himself utterly still. His mare shifted, he could almost feel her quiver. Do not move, he willed her, make no sound. Concentrating on stillness, he found himself controlling his breathing, forcing his muscles to relax.

The barbarians turned to Komawara's right and made their way across the slope, led by the man on foot who searched out the path between the trees and rock. Sixteen armed men and they did not have the look of the hunted.

Is it possible they do not know we pursue them? And then he felt reality waver for an instant. Cold awareness. No, there were no wounded, no riderless mounts. It was impossible that they could have escaped a meeting with Komawara's guard unscathed, of that he was certain.

The last man of the party disappeared into the fog less than a stone's throw away and Komawara let out a long held breath. Barbarians in the Jai Lung Hills! Bandits suddenly seemed an insignificant threat—a mere annoyance. *Barbarians* in the Jai Lung Hills!

The lord waited, listening as the creak of leather and the clatter of hooves faded. Looking around at the shadowless light he wondered how long it would be until darkness fell. He thought often of his companions, twenty of his guard and half as many local men, wandering somewhere in the mist. They were well enough armed, as one would expect of men of Seh, but they were not fully armored.

Komawara had made a careful assessment of the men who had passed into the fog—they traveled light—little armor in evidence and only short bows and swords. They would carry skinning knives also, they always did. Weapons well chosen for fighting in the hills. He wished Shuyun was with him for there was no telling what his powers of observation might have added.

Komawara took up the reins and coaxed his mount to her feet. He began to follow. The footing in the melting snow was treacherous to leather soles, but the young lord chose to walk all the same. The mare would carry him, she had heart enough for that, but he preferred to give her a chance to recover—and walking allowed him to examine at first hand the barbarians' tracks in what appeared to be fading light.

The occasional distorted echo of horses passing came out of the fog and Komawara soon found the trail led out onto a narrow road that wound its way around the shoulder of the hill. Although this seemed vaguely familiar to him, Komawara was still not sure where he was.

Here and there hoofprints remained clear in the snow and a closer examination stopped Komawara abruptly. He'd watched the barbarians pass and not even marked that they rode *horses*, and fine ones, too. They rode horses like men of Seh—like bandits or barbarian chieftains! The horse was not adapted to life in the steppe and desert and was replaced there by the barbarian's hardy pony.

"Barbarians," Komawara whispered. And here he was, an advisor to the Imperial Governor, separated from his companions and lost in the hills. That would be a prize for a barbarian chieftain! If they had any idea that a man with intimate knowledge of the governor's plans wandered the hills alone, they would be searching the very clouds for him even now.

The Komawara who advised a governor knew that he acted rashly, but the young lord who was born and raised to the ways of the north could not ignore a threat to his

province. It was opportunities like this that men of Seh
prayed for—poems were made of such exploits, songs
sung in the Governor's Palace and in the court of the
Emperor.

The sound of falling water echoed out of the mist, how
near, it was impossible to know. The barbarians' trail
suddenly broke out of the trees and ran onto a wider path
between the tall pines and cedars, their shapes barely
suggested in the fog.

Walking in the clouds, Komawara thought, and then
he found himself stepping onto a wooden bridge over a
narrow stream. A small pool formed upstream and feeding that a twisting ribbon of white, falling water appeared
like mist that had acquired density and weight.

A breeze stirred his horse's mane and began to move
the surrounding fog in chaotic patterns. Out of the mist
a granite wall formed above him and the smell of horses
seemed to mingle with the odors of rotting vegetation
and the indescribable smell of snow-melt.

The young lord brought his mount up sharp before her
hooves drummed on the wooden planks. Would they
make camp by the water? He backed her up five paces
and dropped the reins to the ground. The faint breeze
pushed holes in the mist—holes that opened like pupils
for mere seconds and then swirled closed. It was like
looking through a blowing curtain: a glimpse of something, then gone.

Komawara moved back to the bridge, straining to hear
above the sound of falling water. The tracks of the barbarians became confused here and Komawara realized
they had stopped to water horses at the pool. He crossed
the bridge as silently as he could and discovered the trail
leading on: there was no place to make camp.

Komawara followed the barbarians' lead and watered
his mount, drinking himself and filling his water skin. It
was growing noticeably darker now and despite the
breeze moving through the mist, visibility would soon be
left to one's imagination alone. There would no longer
be a trail to follow. Komawara realized he would have to
close the gap with his quarry or lose them in the darkness.

I have to give up this hope that my companions will
overtake me, he told himself, it slows me and fosters

indecision. He pressed on, leading his mount at a faster pace. The bow went back to the saddle and he kept his right hand free for his sword; at the pace he traveled now he would be upon someone in this mist before realizing it.

The young lord found himself wishing Brother Shuyun was with him, as he had been at Denji Gorge and in the desert. The Botahist monk did not seem to need his sight in the darkness and Komawara was sure this cloud would offer no greater challenge than the desert night. As well as possessing uncanny hearing, Komawara suspected that Shuyun could sense other living beings, could feel their presence. He senses *chi,* the young lord thought, whatever that might mean.

Despite his imminent danger Komawara found his focus slipping. He found himself wondering about the Lady Nishima and her cousin, Lady Kitsura Omawara. Since their arrival in Seh he had spoken with them only once, but he was left with a strong impression. Compared to the ladies of the Capital, even the most sought after women of Seh seemed like the unaccomplished daughters of peasant farmers. Komawara feared that, having seen women of true culture and great beauty, he would have little hope of a happy life with the match he would likely make.

Another clump of falling snow brought him back to matters at hand. He could no longer see the barbarian tracks. Darkness had become complete. Bending close to the ground and feeling lightly with his hand, he discovered that the trail had not merely been hidden by darkness—it was gone.

An owl hooted somewhere in the mist. A dark-wing rattled its bill. They must have left the trail not far behind, he thought. By Botahara! the young lord found himself almost whispering, what if I have passed close to them in the mist? He whirled around and half drew his sword without intending to, convinced that barbarian warriors stalked him. Calming his heart with an effort, Komawara listened for what he feared most: the small sounds of armored men attempting to move in silence.

Waiting without the tiniest movement until his muscles ached, Komawara decided finally that the barbarians remained unaware of him. He began to retrace his steps, counting them consciously. Five paces, then stop; listen. He searched the ground as best he could, his hands beginning to ache from the cold of the wet snow and meltwater. Five paces more.

The tracks reappeared. Komawara could feel the depressions made by many hooves in the soft mud. Following them carefully, he found a path branching off down the slope into the black curling mist.

He searched about in the darkness until his hand encountered a sapling to which he tethered his horse, hoping she would not spook when he left her. As a precaution he took his saddlebags from her back and set them out of reach of her hooves, praying that he would be able to find them again. Opening one bag he found some bread that was not yet soaked and ate, crouched in the darkness and light rain. The barbarians would be forced to make a camp nearby, he thought, they are as blind as I in this darkness and fog.

He listened. The sounds of the Jai Lung Hills surrounded him: creaking trees, meltwater running into streams. An owl called again and the lord wondered if it truly was an owl. But nothing seemed amiss; there were no sounds that rang untrue to this place nor was there an unnatural silence. The tribesmen are part of their world, even here, he thought.

Finishing his bread Komawara set off to follow the track, now crouching, now on all fours—fighting an absurd fear that he would come upon a sleeping man in the darkness, discovering too late that he had blundered into the barbarian encampment. But this was not to be. The sounds of voices came to him and then, unmistakably, the smell of smoke.

Komawara stopped again. What would he do now? If the fog lifted in the morning, he could go looking for his guard, but the barbarians might well disappear while he searched. The lord was not confident that they could track the tribesmen, especially if they did not wish to be followed. Bandits, he thought, and snorted. Bandits indeed.

He moved toward the voices. I will watch them for now, he told himself, and make decisions when I know what they will do at sunrise.

The barbarians made their camp in an opening amidst the pines, a rock outcropping on one side giving protec-

tion from prevailing winds. Even before he could see the
light, he could hear the hissing of wet wood as it steamed
and smoked on the fire. Komawara felt his hunger waken
as the smell of cooking came to him. They poach the
Emperor's deer, he found himself thinking, and almost
smiled at his reaction.

Hiding himself behind fractured rocks, the lord lowered himself to the wet ground, prepared for a long vigil
but not sitting in a manner that would prevent him from
rising quickly. He could see the barbarian encampment
now. There were two fires burning, and men cooked at
each. Crude shelters had been made of what appeared to
be the roofs of the tents the wandering tribesmen called
homes. Komawara knew this material—tough and, when
treated with the boiled sap of the tekko root, virtually
waterproof.

The men drank something which steamed in their
bowls and though they were subdued, the lord realized
they were all at least slightly intoxicated.

No one stood watch, not yet, not while the entire party
was still awake. Later, no doubt, they would place sentries, but at this point it was clear that these were men
who did not realize they were hunted.

The hunter looked on, unnoticed in the darkness; more
than a little envious of the men who drank warm liquor
and would soon be eating.

I must remain still, Komawara told himself, or I will
quickly become the hunted. He made himself follow a
simple breathing exercise that Brother Shuyun had taught
him, but his heart would not slow to a resting pace and
he realized his muscles remained knotted.

A hard, cold point pushed into the back of his neck
and a voice, heavy with the accent of the desert, whispered close to his ear; "Be very still, Lord. Be also
quiet."

The scene before Komawara seemed to disappear and
all that remained was a dark man-shape on the periphery
of his vision. The fire flared briefly and Komawara felt
sweat break out on his brow. They use fire to question
their captives, Komawara thought, before letting them
die.

Suddenly the pressure of the knife disappeared.
"Brother Shuyun sends the Kalam with message.

Friend,'' the voice whispered again. And then Brother Shuyun's servant, the tribesman who had become their guide in the desert, slipped down beside the astonished lord.

Komawara let out a long breath and then found himself almost immediately hot with anger. ''Why . . . ?'' He reached back, feeling for blood.

The tribesman shrugged. ''You see desert man in darkness, how can you know it is the Kalam? You take your sword and I die and these,'' he gestured toward the men clustered around the fire, ''hear and make hunt Lord Komawara.'' He shrugged, then turned his attention to the tribesmen and said nothing more for some time.

''How did you find me?''

''My guard are lost,'' he said, waving a hand at the darkness. Then, pointing at the barbarians, ''I find them. Find you.''

''Who?'' Komawara whispered. ''What do they do here?''

The Kalam seemed about to answer, but then he shook his head and Komawara could see him struggling with the language—missing his translator, Brother Shuyun.

''In desert . . . dragon bones. . . . '' He shook his head again, showing frustration.

''Ama-Haji?'' Komawara offered.

The tribesman nodded: he seemed surprised Komawara remembered, as though the separation caused by language somehow isolated their experiences as well. ''Ama-Haji, yes. Men of the Dragon.'' He fell silent again, searching.

''The followers of the Khan,'' Komawara said.

The young barbarian shook his head in frustration. ''No, no. The men of the dragon . . . these men,'' he said pointing. ''They come to find . . . to look. The eyes of the dragon,'' he said and pointed again.

''Ah,'' Komawara heard himself say, though he was not sure he grasped what his companion meant.

They fell silent then, turning their attention back to the barbarians who had begun to eat and continued to drink. The conversation had not grown louder and though it was punctuated by occasional laughter, it was subdued laughter.

"The message," Komawara whispered, "from Shuyun-sum?"

The Kalam nodded. "Yes." He paused as if remembering. "A warrior . . . great warrior comes—Daku Kaita."

"Jaku Katta." Komawara corrected. "General Jaku Katta."

"Yes," the tribesman nodded. "General means great warrior?"

"Yes," Komawara agreed, "very great. Is he here now? In Seh now?"

An outburst of laughter brought their attention back to the men before them.

"In Seh," the Kalam said, "yes."

"Ah." Komawara whispered, but if he meant to say more it was lost.

There was a wild cry and armored men burst out of the trees, falling on the barbarians with drawn swords. Komawara jumped to his feet and drew his own blade but then stopped and grabbed his companion. "You must stay here!" He shouted into the Kalam's face. "My men will not know you!"

The young tribesman nodded, but Komawara saw him draw his sword all the same.

There was no more time. The battle before him was pitched and though they had the element of surprise it was quickly apparent that the men of Seh were few in number. Komawara dashed the ten steps to the struggle and cut down a barbarian who was about to finish a man who had fallen. Not waiting to see if the man would rise, he leapt at another. They crossed swords briefly and then this man also fell.

A soldier in full cavalry armor, green-laced, turned on Komawara and the lord had to parry a blow before his opponent realized he was not a barbarian.

But before Komawara could find another opponent, his head seemed to explode and he found himself on his knees, fumbling with his sword, slashing his hand on the blade. The green-laced warrior jumped past him and Komawara watched him engage a man swinging a staff. Komawara struggled to his feet in time to deflect a stroke from an enormous tribesman.

The lord found himself being driven back now, his

famed reflexes and tactics dulled by the blow to his head.
A second barbarian joined in, close on his right, forcing
Komawara to parry. The larger of his opponents lunged
at this opening and he tensed, waiting for the point to
find him. But the pain did not come. Instead, the barbarian seemed to freeze and then his knees buckled as
he was run through on the sword of another tribesman.

Komawara saw the Kalam pull his blade free, but that
glance almost cost the lord his arm. The man he battled
now sensed his present state and was intent on taking the
weakened lord's life before he could recover.

Komawara found his vision blurring and kept shaking
his head, hoping to clear it. The firelight did not seem
to be helping. One second it would catch his opponent's
blade, but as the sword moved and offered a different
plane to the light it would appear and disappear, causing
Komawara great confusion. "Watch his hands," Komawara said aloud, reminding himself of lessons he had
received from his father. *In failing light watch the hands,
they will tell you what the sword does.*

Digging deep into his experience, the young lord
searched for something that would save him, for he could
not last long as things were. The man would soon find a
hole in his defense.

He overreaches, Komawara thought and changed the
movement of his retreat so he stepped back first with his
left leg. The man parried and lunged, point first at Komawara's chest. The lord swayed and turned away but
not quickly enough, and he felt the point slip into his
side through the gap in the armor under his left arm. But
even as he felt the barbarian's steel, Komawara's own
sword caught the man under the chin and it was over.
The point wrenched free of the lord's side as the man
collapsed at his feet.

Komawara was barely able to keep his feet, and his
vision narrowed to a dark tunnel.

Only a few men stood, scattered about the encampment—but they were all men of Seh, green-laced like the
one who had saved him. They seemed to be staring at
him, but Komawara did not know why. Slowly Komawara became aware of a ringing of swords to his left and
he turned that way in horror. The Kalam fought two men
in green and a third was coming to their aid.

''No,'' Komawara said, but the shout came out as a whisper. He turned to intervene and almost fell. ''No,'' he whispered again. Blood appeared on the Kalam's shoulder and quickly turned his arm red.

Komawara lifted his own sword and his vision blurred. With all his remaining strength he swung and took a sword out of one man's hands. Parrying now, he put himself between the men of Seh and his former guide.

''No,'' he said weakly, ''he is mine.''

The men before him hesitated, but none lowered their swords. They stared at him and Komawara could not read the questions in their eyes.

''And who are you that you claim this murderer as your own?''

Komawara looked at these warriors now and realized that the blow to his head had affected his judgment. These were not the locals who had joined his guard. They wore armor of good quality, well used, and laced in green. There was no family nearby that wore this color. The Kalam reached out and gripped his shoulder.

''I am Komawara Samyamu and this man is my servant.''

Other men gathered before him and Komawara realized that there was no escape into the trees now. He was barely able to stand as it was.

The men in their green lacing looked from one to the other and there were protests and harsh words in low voices. Komawara heard someone curse.

''Lord Komawara, you keep unusual company,'' the man before him spoke. He pulled back his face mask and gave a half bow, removing his helmet. A man behind him stepped forward.

''Lieutenant, I saw a barbarian cut down one of his own kind—a barbarian who was attacking Lord Komawara. It surely was this man.''

The one addressed as a lieutenant nodded his head. ''Excuse my manners, Lord Komawara, I am Narihira Chisato, late of Lord Hajiwara Harita's cavalry.''

By Botahara, Komawara thought, the green lacing—yes! The Hajiwara. The house I helped bring down at Denji Gorge. Against his will Komawara lowered his sword as he felt his arms were about to start shaking.

Blood soaked his side now and a glance told him that the Kalam was faring no better than he.

Komawara returned the man's bow with a nod. "Lieutenant. I do not know your purpose, but my own men are nearby. We search these hills for brigands. Yet the hills, it seems, are full of surprises. I wish to thank you for your assistance in bringing down our enemy."

"Even as you assisted in the fall of our lord's house?" another man said bitterly. The lieutenant raised his hand and silence returned.

"Lord Komawara, as you might imagine, the fall of the Hajiwara House has left us feeling . . . some resentment to those who brought about our misfortune. And though Lord Shonto and . . . his allies were instrumental in this, we realize that it was a betrayal by others that led to our lord's fall. We honor his memory.

"It is the opinion of those with experience in such matters that our liege-lord did not make the wisest decision when he agreed to oppose Lord Shonto. Please realize that our anger in this matter is reserved for others. Lord Shonto could not have acted other than he did. Nor could you as his loyal ally. You are injured, Sire, and though we do not understand the service of this man it is obviously your prerogative." He bowed again, lower this time.

"We will put up our swords and see to our wounded. I would look to your own injuries myself, Lord Komawara. I have some skill in this."

Although there were dark looks among some of the Hajiwara men, swords were sheathed and men turned back to the fires. Komawara and the Kalam sheathed their own weapons and then supported each other over the few steps to the fireside. The lord collapsed close to the warmth, glad of it, for he found himself deeply cold. His ears still rang from the blow to his head and he was dizzy and weak.

Beside him he heard the tribesman dry heave. He has lost blood, Komawara thought, and he felt hands begin to remove his laced mail and then cut away the side of his leather shirt. He felt removed from his surroundings, as though everything he heard and felt came from far away. Vaguely he heard a report of two deaths and found himself hoping they were not his own guard.

Sleep. Komawara desperately wanted to sleep. He tried to shake his head, but his muscles did not seem to respond. Beside him the Kalam seemed so distant Komawara wondered how he had done that when, only a moment before, they had been within an arm's length. And then there was darkness.

When Komawara awoke, he did not know where he was or how long he'd been sleeping. The bed he lay in was soft and smelled of the forest. Pine boughs, he realized, and pulled the covering of deerskin closer about him. The fires still burned and men sat close to the warmth, faces out to the darkness, swords in hand.

Hajiwara, he remembered, Hajiwara's men. On the run now, without a House. Marked by the Butto and their feud. He shook his head. Probing his side, he found it wrapped in silk and damp from a small bloodstain. Not serious, he thought, but his head still rang and the men sitting at the fire kept blurring and doubling. Bandits, he thought, brigands in the Jai Lung Hills. He fell into a troubled sleep.

The mist was as thick when Komawara awoke as it had been when he followed the barbarians. Men stirred in the camp and Komawara smelled both cha and food. The ringing in his ears had largely disappeared to be replaced by a deep throbbing throughout one side of his head, extending down as far as his shoulder. He lay still for some time and then stirred himself to sit up. This caused his vision to tunnel but he braced himself and it passed. Someone crossed to him, bending to help him rise. The Kalam looked greatly relieved as he took Komawara's arm. The tribesman helped the lord with his soft riding boots and Komawara had to shake him off so he could walk the four paces to the fire himself.

"You are good, yeh? Good?" the Kalam kept asking and smiling.

Komawara nodded and lowered himself onto a rock set near the flames. Sitting alone with the Hajiwara men had obviously not been a comfortable situation and even now men cast unfriendly glances at the barbarian. The lieutenant bent over one of the wounded, but when he saw Komawara he rose and crossed the clearing toward him.

"Lord Komawara," the lieutenant bowed and offered a cup of cha which Komawara received gratefully. "We hope you are somewhat recovered. The wound in your side does not appear to be serious, but I am concerned about the blow you took to the side of your head. Is your vision clear? Do you feel unsteady or ill?" The man stared at the lord with a look of concern and Komawara noticed the man's glance stray up to Komawara's short hair—the mark of his time as Brother Shuyun's Botahist companion. Whatever questions the man had in his mind he kept to himself.

"I'm sure I will be well shortly, lieutenant. Thank you for the care and for the attention you have shown to my guide." Bandits, Komawara thought again. Brigands.

The lieutenant waved at one of his men and food came the lord's way. He ate quietly and when he had finished and was sipping cha the lieutenant returned.

"We have been wondering, lord, what you might know of these barbarians—of their purpose."

Komawara nodded but said nothing. What goes on here, he asked himself. What were these tribesmen doing in the Jai Lung Hills? *Eyes of the Dragon,* the Kalam had said. Eyes of the Dragon?

"These barbarians are of a sect, I believe, a sect that venerates the Dragon." Komawara offered no more, waiting, hoping the lieutenant would say something that would help him understand what transpired. But the Hajiwara man offered nothing.

Komawara tried again. "You will find on their persons a gold impression of the dragon embossed . . ." He stopped as the lieutenant held out a small gold figure on a chain.

"This?" the lieutenant asked.

The Kalam made a warding sign and drew away.

"Yes," Komawara said. He took the figure in his hand against the protests of his guide. It was not the embossed coin he had seen before but a tiny figure of ornate beauty. The same dragon to be sure, the dragon of Ama-Haji, but not the primitive depiction the barbarian raider had carried.

The Hajiwara lieutenant cleared his throat. "Lord Komawara, you must realize that we have come to Seh to escape the Butto. We have not done this from fear but because we have an oath to fullfil. Please do not ask its nature for I may not speak of it.

"There were eleven of us when we crossed the border . . . now we are nine." He looked around at his companions who began to draw nearer. "We have lived in these hills for some weeks now and, as you have no doubt guessed, our actions here have not always followed the most honorable course. Of this we are not proud." He paused then as if to gauge Komawara's reaction. The lord of Seh said nothing. The lieutenant went on.

"We happened upon the barbarians some days ago," he began, but a moan from one of the wounded drew his attention. A man rose immediately and went to see to this companion. "We happened upon them by accident and we have watched their camp since.

"We did not pursue the barbarians for any personal gain but only because they are the ancient enemy of our people and because there are rumors that they grow in strength again. Yet now we find ourselves in a most difficult position, Sire." He nodded to his men who had gathered around them and two stepped forward bearing a leather saddlebag between them. They set it down at Komawara's feet and pulled open the flap.

Coins glinted in the pale light as only gold could do. An entire saddlebag brimming with gold coins!

Komawara reached forward and took up one of the coins—square, finely minted with the round hole in its center.

"Here is more money than, together, we could have dreamed of seeing in a lifetime. It is most unfortunate, however, that we should find this now, for we are men who have lost our honor. Men who are hunted, not just by the family that murdered our lord . . ." He shrugged and shook his head, started to speak, then stopped again. He shook his head once more and went on.

"This gold can never profit us, Lord Komawara. There is nowhere we could go that this past we have made will not finally pursue us. Nor is there a way to escape our own knowledge of our recent errors. Karma . . ." He shrugged. "No, this gold will only tempt us from our chosen path.

"What we wish to ask you, Lord Komawara, is that you take this gold and compensate those we have wronged.'' He looked down at the saddlebag. ''If that is not too much to ask.''

Such a plain bag, Komawara found himself thinking.

''And you will do what?'' Komawara asked, not taking his eye from the gold—more gold than his entire holdings were worth—many times more.

''As you slept, Sire, we spoke. It is clear that under any other circumstances what we did yesterday would have been considered a service to our Empire. I believe it is true to surmise that, considering this great treasure we have found, we would have been richly rewarded. But in our present situation this cannot be. There is a certain irony in this. Rather like the plight of Shubuta when he was tricked by the Goddess of Greed.'' He gave half a laugh.

''So all that is left to us is an oath that we swore when our House fell. It will guide us now.''

Komawara thought for some time, staring into the fire.

''I do not know the exact nature of this oath, though it is obvious what it must be. Do you wish to revenge yourself upon my ally, Lord Shonto, or members of his staff?''

''No, Lord Komawara.''

''Who would offer you service, lieutenant, if this oath would endanger their own House?''

''A House with the same enemies, Sire.''

''Huh.''

Komawara tossed the coins back into the bag. ''It is not within my power to release those who have broken the laws of our Empire, but as you say, you have performed a service and it should not go unrewarded. Can you swear that carrying out this oath will not endanger the purpose of my House or my allies?''

The lieutenant looked around the group. ''We are patient, Lord Komawara. We can wait until such a time as we would not endanger the Komawara House.''

The lord nodded and returned his attention to the fire. His head throbbed. Forcing himself to sit, not slump, Komawara met the lieutenant's eye. ''Then will you exchange your green for the colors of the Komawara house?''

There was a low murmur among the Hajiwara men and they gathered about the lord and their lieutenant.

"You would offer this knowing that we are hunted by the Butto and aware of our recent actions?"

"Lieutenant Narihira, I saw men fight the enemy of our Empire knowing that it would profit them not at all. You could have easily ridden by—what do you owe the Emperor? Men who would act so are men of honor, of this I have no doubt."

The lieutenant withdrew to confer with his men, leaving the Kalam and Lord Komawara to share food.

The Hajiwara men were not gone long.

"Lord Komawara," the lieutenant began, "we have weighed your words and we know that this offer is more than any of us had ever dared hope for. We were resigned to living without House or honor. Yet there is the matter of the Butto. They have sworn an oath to hunt down all of my lord's followers, sparing none. You would be standing between the Butto and ourselves and we cannot allow this."

Komawara smiled. "Lieutenant, the Butto believe they owe the Komawara a debt that they cannot repay in one hundred lifetimes. I think I can trade part of this debt for your lives . . . in return for your sworn service, of course."

"If this is as you say, Lord Komawara, then I may speak for all of us. We would be honored to wear the colors of the House of Komawara."

The Hajiwara men knelt before him and, one by one, laid their swords at his feet.

After this was done, Lord Komawara stood with difficulty. "It is good that you have proven that you can fight our enemies, for there is war awaiting us. Of this, have no doubt. In this war we must stand shoulder to shoulder with those we would consider enemies . . . or we will fall. And more than Seh will fall with us." Komawara looked at the men standing before him. Do they believe what I say? he wondered. It hardly mattered. They would believe soon enough.

"What has happened in this glade must never be spoken of. You have seen no barbarians in these hills. You must never say differently. I have rewarded you with service to the Komawara for dispatching the bandits who have threatened us, and also for saving my life. No one will question this. But the graves must be hidden so that no one can ever suspect otherwise. Likewise, you must say nothing of this gold. I do not claim it for my own but will give it to the Imperial Governor, for it was carried by these barbarians for purposes that I cannot speak of. When we arrive at my lands, you will be honored for vanquishing the bandits in these hills, and in a way this is the truth.'' He smiled.

"We must go down out of the hills now. There is much that we must do.''

Three

The ships set off in driving rain, heeled to a cold west wind, their sails reefed so small it seemed impossible that they would weather the headland. Yet they made way, if not quickly at least steadily.

Lord Shonto Shokan sat his horse on a high cliff and watched the ships pass. He raised his arm once, not at all sure he could be seen, and waved slowly. Turning his mount, he picked his way down the track that ran along the cliff edge. He didn't wish to keep Tanaka out on deck in this terrible weather, for the old man must stay at the rail until the son of his liege-lord was unquestionably lost to sight—anything less would be an unforgivable insult. After all, Shokan had ridden to the headland to see the older man on his way, paying him a great honor. Honor, Tanaka deserved—protracted suffering, he did not.

If Shokan had known, he would have been less anxious to leave, for Tanaka stood at the rail staring up at the distant rider and the streaks on his face were not all from the rain and salt spray. He looks much like his father did at that age, the merchant was thinking. And he is as dear to me.

Tanaka watched as the figure in Shonto blue waved and then turned back along the cliff, followed by three guards. So few, Tanaka thought, it's almost as if there were no danger.

The young Lord Shonto worked his way down to a stretch where the cliff path turned flat and broad and pressed his mount into a canter. He was delighted, as always, by the stallion's motion. He had brought the animal back with him from Seh, and it had survived the voyage, first by river and then by sea, without apparent harm to body or spirit.

Seh. . . . It was that province and his father's situation

to which his thoughts constantly returned. Tanaka's visit had been most unsettling, adding fuel to the slow kindling of fear that had been smoldering since his father's most recent letter.

As he had feared all along, there was more hidden in the wastelands than the proud men of Seh would admit possible. And now this news from Tanaka.

He spurred his horse up a steeper rise, hooves throwing clods of soft turf as they went. Reining in, he turned back to the sea and took longer than he expected to catch sight of the small fleet disappearing into the sheets of rain that shrouded the entire Bay of Mists. There would be no more ships setting out across those waters now until spring returned; these were tempting the Storm Gods quite enough.

Late, late in the season for such folly. Shokan turned his mount toward the Shonto Palace. Folly, he thought, there has been entirely too much folly. Sensing his mood, his guard hung back as far as duty would allow, leaving their young lord alone with his thoughts.

Reaching down a heavily gloved hand, Shokan patted the stallion's shoulder as a sudden gust whipped its unplaited mane into a tangle. His father did not believe that Seh could be held. He shuddered though he was not cold.

Did the Emperor know that all that stood between his Imperial person and the loss of his throne to a barbarian chieftain was Shonto Motoru? Shokan supposed that he did not.

If Shonto abandoned the north and fell back to the south, how long could he keep control of the army he was raising? Surely the Son of Heaven would order him to step down from his command in shame the moment he crossed the border of Seh. Shokan had not liked the tone of his father's last letter. Staying in control of the army long enough to defeat the invaders had seemed to be his father's only concern.

Wa is in danger as never before. We cannot be swayed by desires for revenge upon those who have allowed this to come about. It is not a question of losing our fief or Shonto honor—we are in danger of losing the entire Empire.

So his father had written and Shokan did not doubt it for a moment.

There would be no support from the Emperor, and the men of Seh seemed equally blind to their plight and might well remain so until it was too late. My father needs an army, Shokan thought, he needs the largest force the Empire can raise, yet that is impossible. He fought off the bitterness and anger that had been growing since his visit from Tanaka.

He tried to replace this bitterness with the feelings of affection he felt for their vassal-merchant. Tanaka sailed into more danger than winter storms. If Lord Shonto was removed from command of his army, all of the Shonto House would fall with him. Tanaka, who controlled the family's vast trading interests, would be the third Shonto retainer the Imperial Guard would seek out, after Shokan and Lady Nishima.

Tanaka was convinced that the Emperor would invite the young Shonto heir to come to the Capital for the winter social season and Shokan was certain he was right. He had been expecting the Imperial summons for days.

Of course he would stall as long as possible, but that would not be forever—the Emperor was not a patient man.

At least Lady Nishima was no longer within the Emperor's reach. This brought a smile to replace the anxious look on the young lord's face. He wondered how the Emperor would react to *that*? Nishima gone, and in the company of the woman the Emperor had himself appointed to be her instructor in the arts. Although he stood somewhat in awe of his adopted sister's charm, Shokan could not imagine how Nishi-sum had tempted the Lady Okara from her island sanctuary.

Shokan would like to see the Emperor's response to that news. The Yamaku Emperor was not patient nor did he like to appear a fool. The young lord laughed aloud. There were at least small victories to be enjoyed. Oh, Nishi-sum, how did you manage such a thing? He laughed again and spurred his horse in a wild gallop along the cliff top. Below him the sea battered the ancient cliff, endlessly: soft water against hard stone in an unequal contest.

Four

Jaku Tadamoto tried to sit calmly, without betraying any sign of the fear he felt. It was a difficult exercise. The Emperor was known to fly into rages, but in Tadamoto's experience the sovereign could be at his deadliest when he was silent—trying to contain his infamous temper. The Emperor stood, apparently examining a figure in a three-panel painting of the battle of Kyo. He held his sword of office in its scabbard before him in both hands and Tadamoto could see the Emperor's right hand flexing like an involuntary seizure on the sword's grip.

Jaku Tadamoto's sense of tranquillity was further eroded by the knowledge that the object of the Emperor's rage was his own brother, Katta. He was not certain what caused him more apprehension: the thought that the Emperor's legendary distrust would now be focused on him because of his brother's latest betrayal, or whether he feared for Katta. Certainly Katta had gone off to the north, turning his back on Tadamoto, but even so, Katta was still his brother.

The Emperor turned suddenly and glared down at the kneeling guardsman.

"So, Shonto's daughter is in league with my former Guard Commander, damn his arrogance!" He gazed back at the figure in the painting again as though it calmed him. The figure, Tadamoto could not help but notice, was impaled upon a lance.

Very quietly, Tadamoto ventured to speak. "It is difficult to say, Sire, it is just as possible that their meeting was merely coincidence."

"I am not a believer in coincidence, not when your brother is concerned." The Emperor paced back to his dais, paused to consider, then kicked a silk-covered pil-

low across the audience chamber. "And it was the Lady
Okara? You are certain?"

Tadamoto looked at the floor directly in front of him.
"It would appear so, Sire. Her staff report that she is ill
and cannot receive visitors, the same explanation we are
given at the Shonto House. The description I have received would seem to leave little doubt."

The Emperor dropped back to his cushions and stared
at the mats as intently as did Tadamoto. "And you still
do not believe he has secretly joined the Shonto?"

Tadamoto shook his head slowly. "It would be most
uncharacteristic, Sire. My brother is ambitious, I will not
deny it, but he believes that Shonto's famed loyalty is a
sham. He thinks the great lord is loyal only to his own
ambitions, all other alliances merely serve his purpose.
I think Katta-sum's distrust of Lord Shonto is
unwavering."

The Emperor shook his head. "He is your brother,
Colonel, it is natural that you trust his motives more than
others might." He looked up at the young officer in front
of him. "You, however, must decide where your loyalties
lie. You cannot serve two masters, Tadamoto-sum, be
very clear on that."

Tadamoto bowed his head to the mat and returned
slowly to his kneeling position. "My brother and I have
had a parting of ways, Sire. Katta went north on the great
canal, while I remained. . . . I am my Emperor's servant. It is my hope that my opinions regarding my brother
are not dictated by family loyalties but come only from
careful thought and concern for duty to my Emperor. If
this is not the case, Sire, please dismiss me from my
position and allow me to serve in some other way." He
bowed again.

The Emperor stroked his chin, and though his eyes
were fixed on the young Jaku, his focus was elsewhere.
When he spoke again, his voice was quieter, softer. "No,
Tadamoto-sum, I trust you. I am well aware that your
brother's actions cause you great pain and that you still
hope there is an explanation that will indicate his continued loyalty to the throne. I hold the same hope, for Katta
is dear to me." He paused. "But I cannot let my affection blind me entirely. If your brother does not soon act
in a manner that proves our hopes are justified. . . ."

The Emperor let the threat hang in the air. He began examining his scabbard.

After a moment he turned back to the young man who knelt before him. "Is there more to this report, Colonel, or is that all the bad news for the day?"

Tadamoto hesitated, offering a silent prayer to Botahara. "There is one other thing, Sire." He tried to work some moisture into a dry mouth. "It seems that Lady Nishima and Lady Okara have one other companion."

"Oh."

Tadamoto almost whispered. "It is possible they are accompanied by the Lady Kitsura Omawara, Sire."

The Emperor did not take his eyes from his sword.

"That will be all, Colonel."

"Yes, Emperor." Jaku Tadamoto touched his head to the floor and, without rising, backed from the room as quickly as concern for the Emperor's dignity would allow.

Akantsu II sat for a long time, staring at his sword of office. Insults such as this were not paid to Emperors. No doubt Lord Omawara believed his name and failing health would protect him. The Emperor pulled his sword halfway from its scabbard and then rammed it home savagely. Oh, there was nothing the Emperor could do openly—Omawara was correct in that assumption. But that would not protect the old man. Nor would it protect the rest of his House.

The Emperor thought suddenly of the Lady Kitsura, and her legendary beauty seemed an affront to him now. Such arrogance! The Emperor tightened his grip on the sword. The old families would never accept the Yamaku. This proved it beyond all doubt. There could be no other course of action if he was to preserve the Yamaku ascendancy. Once the Shonto were gone, the old families would realize their mistake . . . their many mistakes.

He turned and set his sword in its stand with exaggerated care, controlling his shaking hands with an act of will. He took a long deep breath and let it out slowly. The insult would not receive the slightest recognition, of course. In fact, he would send a letter inquiring after Lord Omawara's health that very day. He would also ask if Lady Kitsura's journey went well. A solicitous letter. Let the dying old man know what he had wrought upon his family. But the Emperor's mood was not so easily broken. Even the thought of what could be done to the Omawara brought him no comfort.

The Emperor took another long breath. He clapped his hands softly and a servant appeared.

"Send for Osha-sum," he said, "her Emperor desires her presence."

Destroying her lover's letters crossed Osha's mind when she received the summons to attend the Emperor. It will not matter, she thought. If he knows, the letters will not make a difference. Selecting robes to wear into the royal presence, an activity that could take many women several days, was comparatively easy. Calming her spirit, however, was not possible.

If the Emperor knew about her meetings with Tadamoto-sum, it would not matter that the Son of Heaven had lost interest in her . . . had not called for her in weeks. He would quickly forget that he had cast her aside without a word. That anyone would presume to pay her court would drive him to a fury, of that she was certain.

And they had been so careful! She sat down as a wave of fear weakened her limbs. What of Tadamoto-sum? Had the Emperor . . . ? She did not want to think of it. Hanging her head in her hands for a second, she tried to control herself.

No doubt this is not what I fear. It is more likely merely a good-bye—*your presence in the Imperial Palace is no longer necessary. Here is a gift from the Son of Heaven who is an admirer of your talents. It is said that Chou has need of dancers, and the air there is so healthful and pure.*

But would she be called into the presence of the Emperor for such a message? No, she thought, that is not likely. Perhaps, then, the Emperor would truly give her a gift! Perhaps he would allow her to continue to dance with the Imperial Sonsa troupe!

She thought warmly of Tadamoto. He had been so certain that he could sway the Emperor to allow her to stay in the Capital. She smiled as she rose and examined her appearance in a bronze mirror. But as she left her apartments to walk to the Emperor's audience hall, her confidence seemed to waver a little with each step.

By the time Osha arrived at the guarded double doors, she was shaking and pale. Only her years of Sonsa training forced her knees to support her.

Osha barely noticed the two Imperial Guards who opened the doors. She knelt in the doorway, casting her gaze down, even when she had returned to a kneeling position. She sat thus, in the grip of more terror than she had ever known.

"Please, Osha-sum, enter," came the familiar voice. "Be at your ease."

She closed her eyes and bowed again. What could she read in that voice? He did not hide his anger well, but she had seen it done . . . had seen him toy with someone until they believed they were safe. Then he had exploded in one of his fits of anger. Osha rose and moved forward on her knees until she was a respectful distance from the dais. Folding her hands carefully in her lap, she tried to force herself into a calm but still did not meet his eyes.

"Your dancing goes well?"

"The Emperor is kind to inquire. My dancing goes most well."

"I am glad to hear this, though Colonel Jaku Tadamoto has said as much."

She closed her eyes and fought tears. Even without looking, she knew that the Emperor sat with his sword across his knees. An urge to prostrate herself and beg for forgiveness began to pull at the edges of her rising fears.

"I value the young Jaku brother's judgment," he said as though to someone else. "It pleases me that your dancing goes well. It is a demanding path that you pursue, I understand why you have so little time for mere social occasions. Demands are something an Emperor understands only too well. Though the demands made upon an Emperor do not give us the time we would wish to pursue the things that are close to our hearts. I do not think this is so with the Sonsa?"

Osha could hear the pounding of blood in her ears—a steady rhythm of fear.

"Please excuse me," she said with difficulty, "I am not sure what the Emperor means."

"Is it not dancing that is closest to a Sonsa's heart?"

"Ah." Osha smiled as if he had said something clever.

"I understand this passion that controls you, Osha-sum. I am sometimes jealous, but an Emperor must never give in to such things." He paused. "You must dance and I must spend my days listening to ministers and counselors, though it is not pursuing what is closest to my heart. Do you become jealous when the Empire takes so much of my time?"

"I . . . the Empire, Sire, cannot be compared to dance. Dance is but a trivial thing when set beside affairs of state."

"So many would say, though I am not sure I would agree. Let us say that we both are governed by things of importance. It does not matter." She knew he stared at her, and she tried to remain calm. "It warms my heart to see you, Osha-sum. You have grown even more beautiful these last months."

"I am honored that you would say so, Sire."

"We must learn to live with the demands of our lives, Osha-sum, and take pleasure in the moments that are truly our own."

His outstretched hand appeared before her.

Her heart sank entirely now. He did not know about Tadamoto! That was not why she had been summoned. He desired her! After ignoring her entirely and subjecting her to the greatest humiliation, he wanted her!

She closed her eyes and fought back tears. The Emperor wanted her again. Was she not pleased? She thought of Tadamoto and realized that she was completely terrified of arousing the Emperor's suspicions. She dared not refuse.

"Are these tears, Osha-sum?" the Emperor asked. "Is there something wrong?"

Shaking her head, she tried to smile. "Tears do not always indicate sadness, Sire."

With effort she reached out her hand and the Emperor grasped it. She had forgotten how strong he was. As she moved forward the Emperor pulled her, almost roughly, onto the dais so that her knee struck the frame, but he did not seem to notice.

A kiss that would have seemed passionate before felt coarse to her now. His hands touched her without concern for her pleasure, failing to arouse as they once had. The Emperor fumbled at her sash, for it was not a Lover's Knot and easily undone. She had to untie it for him, helping unwind the yards of brocade.

Pushing her down into the deep silk cushions, the Emperor opened her robes. There were no words of love, no whispers close to her ear. Osha felt nothing but revulsion. With all her heart she wanted to run. Until that moment she had not known what it was she felt for Tadamoto-sum. The Emperor lowered his weight onto her, his face close to hers, his breath coming in harsh gasps.

Five

There were few people as skilled at waiting as Brother Sotura. He could truthfully say that he had only known impatience twice, perhaps three times, in his life, and on each of those occasions he had mastered this emotion almost immediately. The chamber in which he practiced waiting contained a small shrine to Botahara on one wall and an austere, but very skillful arrangement of cedar boughs and autumn slip maple on a small stand against another. These two things in themselves would have provided the necessary focus for many days of meditation, even if Brother Sotura didn't have other things to consider. And he could barely remember a time when he did not have *other things* demanding his attention.

He was more than concerned that Lord Shonto had not allowed this second meeting with Brother Shuyun to take place in the Temple of the Pure Wind. The lord had insisted that the meeting should be held in the Governor's Palace so Shonto "would not be deprived of his Advisor's counsel at this crucial time." Of course, Brother Sotura had agreed immediately—one didn't argue with an Imperial Governor, especially one whose family name was Shonto—but still, he was concerned.

Lord Shonto was known to be a very convincing man and Sotura feared the lord's influence on his former student. Shuyun was too important to Botahist interests to go the way of Shonto's former Spiritual Advisor. The Brotherhood could not afford another renegade. He smiled at the term he'd chosen. Perhaps "renegade" was too strong, but Brother Satake had certainly pursued a course of independence. And independence was not something the Brotherhood either encouraged or admired.

Private discussion with Brother Shuyun was what the

chi quan Master required, and he was not convinced that it would be possible inside the Governor's Palace. Sotura turned his gaze to the paper-thin walls. Lord Shonto was certainly not above having the conversations of his Spiritual Advisor listened to; of that he was certain. Of course Sotura did not plan to make a request of Shuyun that the young monk could not fulfill in good conscience, so that was not the reason he was concerned with being overheard. It was what Shonto might learn of the Botahist Order that concerned Sotura. Knowledge of the schisms within the Brotherhood could prove most useful to some parties in the Empire.

So the conversation with Shuyun must be private, that was certain. The young monk had seen the evidence of armies in the desert with his own eyes, and that was a crucial factor. Sotura had to have Shuyun's support in what he was about to do, although Shuyun could be spared the details and reasons. The Initiate would undoubtedly be distressed to know that his information would be used to destroy the credibility of a senior member of their faith.

Brother Sotura turned his gaze back to the statue of Botahara in its shrine with its arrangement of leaves and branches. He felt a second of confusion as though the statue gazed back at him and the look was not entirely benign. Sotura shook himself out of this state immediately.

Footsteps could be heard approaching down one of the labryinth of halls that wove through the fabric of the palace. *Shuyun.* The chi quan Master recognized the sound of the footsteps as easily as he would the boy's signature or his style of chi quan. The older man smiled until the shoji was pushed aside and then the smile was replaced by the unreadable countenance of a Botahist Master.

Shuyun bowed low to the Senior Brother as he entered the room. There were few people he respected more, and though the Botahist Brothers neither showed nor felt much emotion, Shuyun felt something close to affection for his former instructor.

"My lord's House is honored by your presence, Brother Sotura."

"As I am honored by Lord Shonto's consideration."

The two monks knelt a few feet apart on thin cushions set on the straw-matted floor. There was a short silence while Shuyun, as the junior monk, waited for Brother Sotura to speak. His patience seemed every bit as developed as his former teacher's.

"I have many things to discuss with you, Brother Shuyun, but I have spent so much time indoors of late that I wonder—is it possible for us to speak outside without inconveniencing your lord should he have need of your counsel?"

Shuyun thought for a second. "I will send a message to Kamu-sum saying that we are to be found on the Sunrise Viewing Terrace. The terrace will be most pleasant at this time of day. Will that suit your needs, Brother?"

"Perfectly, Shuyun-sum. I thank you for your consideration."

A servant was sent running with the message and the two Botahist Monks set out for the terrace. As they walked, the conversation stayed within the strict bounds of polite discourse between teacher and student. Sotura asked questions and Shuyun responded with short answers; they even laughed at a joke. To anyone listening, there would have been no hint of tension in their discourse.

The Sunrise Viewing Terrace was an excellent choice, for it was well situated to make the most of the sun while still offering some protection from the wind. The cold north wind typical of the season had relented that morning to be replaced by a sea wind that suggested spring more than the true season. The conversation, however, had a certain chill in it.

Lady Kitsura was followed by a maid and by the daughter of one of Seh's more senior military men—Kitsura could not remember the man's name or rank. His daughter was playing at the role of lady-in-waiting and though Lady Kitsura had been annoyed by this farce to begin with she admitted to herself now that the young girl had charmed her. There was something about the girl's naïveté that the woman from the Imperial Capital found very attractive, perhaps especially so during this time when everything seemed so complex, when there were so many suspected lies. The fact that the young

woman admired Kitsura almost to the point of worship
might have had some effect as well.

Now it seemed that the young woman was beside herself with excitement at the prospect of meeting Lady
Nishima Fanisan Shonto. Much to her surprise, Kitsura
found herself telling her companions that Lady Nishima
was only human, after all. The tone of mild annoyance
that accompanied these words was a bit of a surprise to
the sophisticated lady from the Capital.

Lady Kitsura walked as quickly as decorum would allow. She did not want to seem to be rushing, after all,
but in her mind she ran. Her cousin, Lady Nishima, must
be told the most recent news immediately.

The three women came to a doorway leading outside.
Kitsura had insisted they venture out to appreciate this
fine day and though this suggestion had met with some
small resistance her companions had not wanted to disagree. The truth was that the route outside would save
them several minutes. Stepping out into the bright sunlight Kitsura's two companions broke into smiles. Not
only did the sun shine, but the day was almost warm. A
gentle sea wind tugged at their elaborate robes and attempted to improve upon the studied arrangement of their
hair.

Kitsura had to shepherd her companions along or they
would have stopped to play the Cloud Game, looking for
forms in the sky, perhaps hoping that the famous lady
from the Capital would compose a poem—excited, though
somewhat apprehensive, that she might expect them to
do the same.

For her part, the great lady from the Capital felt a
slight tugging of regret that she could not stop and play
the Cloud Game or just walk in the sun and discuss nothing of importance. It was more than that though; it was
a regret that, in some inexplicable way, these pleasures
were no longer accessible to her. And this made her sad.

Bearing news to Nishima-sum was far too important
to delay with such selfish concerns, so, to the disappointment of the two young women of Seh, Kitsura marshaled
them along the covered portico.

All three of the women showed great surprise at finding two men deep in conversation on a terrace. If they
had not been Brothers of the True Faith, the women

would have been deeply embarrassed. How would such a situation be looked upon? Three young women meeting men alone outside on a winter day? Most unseemly!

It was rumored that the ladies of the Capital did such things, but the women from Seh had certainly seen no evidence that either the Lady Nishima or the Lady Kitsura acted in such a manner. They hadn't actually believed the rumors anyway, they told each other, trying to cover their disappointment.

The monks gave their short double bow and the ladies bowed in return, except Lady Kitsura who favored the Brothers with an elegant, though modest, nod of her beautiful head.

The young lady of Seh found herself committing this gesture to memory and stopped herself as she began to imitate it.

A few polite inquiries were made before Lady Kitsura suggested that they continue on their errand, assuring the Brothers that their destination had not been the Sunrise Viewing Terrace and though they were very kind to offer, there was no need for the honored Brothers to leave. The ladies must be on their way.

And so they left, though the officer's daughter could not help but notice that Lady Kitsura looked back over her shoulder as she left and caught the young monk's eye in a manner that could only be described as flirtatious. The young woman looked away, trying not to notice. But she had noticed and she was more than a little disconcerted. She found it a bit difficult to catch her breath for a few seconds. Walking more quickly now, she hoped the blush on her cheeks would be attributed to the wind.

The apartments of Lady Nishima were not as elegant as those she was used to, but she laughingly told Kitsura that they were a great improvement over their cabins on the river barge. In truth, they were quite pleasant surroundings, though both Kitsura and Lady Nishima found all the rooms in the Governor's Palace somewhat colder than they were accustomed to. When her visitors arrived, Lady Nishima was practising her harp so Kitsura and her two followers were treated to an ancient melody which wafted through the thin screens as though it echoed out of the past. The officer's daughter seemed close to tears, though whether this was due to the effect of the music or to finding herself in a social situation she had long dreamed of, Kitsura could not tell.

Informed that she had guests, Nishima put aside her instrument and rearranged her robe so that the pattern was arrayed to its best effect. The young women from Seh seemed almost to glow, for here they were in the company of two of the most celebrated women of their generation. Their friends would be envious beyond anyone's power to describe!

It was with some disappointment that they found themselves drinking cha, alone, while the ladies from the Imperial Capital retired to the balcony. They could just make out the two peers sitting on the wide railing engaged in a conversation that seemed much too serious for women who, it was said, were courted by every young man of worthy family in the entire Capital—including the sons of the Emperor! How could one be anything but constantly gay when one's life was perfection itself?

"We can hardly barge into an audience with the Imperial Governor, Kitsu-sum, we must think of something else," Lady Nishima was saying. She let her gaze wander out over the tiled roofs of the city.

"Considering what is at risk, cousin, I fear you may be paying too much heed to propriety. We will barge in on the Imperial Governor by *accident*," Kitsura explained.

"I'm not utterly confident that this type of intrigue is your greatest area of skill, cousin. We must have some reason. I do not want my father to believe I am trying to see the Imperial Guardsmen. That would be unacceptable."

Kitsura turned away so her frustration would not be seen. Not to seem rude, she leaned over and made a show of checking her companions. The two women were trying not to appear too disappointed as they drank their cha and carried on a stilted conversation.

"I fear my *lady-in-waiting* is quite disappointed not to have been invited into our company."

Nishima shrugged. "It is the life of those who wait. Did she think it was otherwise?"

"Perhaps. You know all those terrible romances young girls read, the ones where the Princess' true friend is her youngest, least well-born, lady-in-waiting."

"Ah, like my Lady Kento," Nishima offered.

"Exactly!" Kitsura laughed. "Of course you would conform to the conventions of the romance, cousin, it is why you are so adored." Kitsura laughed again and squeezed her cousin's hand.

Nishima, however, did not catch her cousin's mood. She remained pensive, withdrawn. Her gaze kept straying over Kitsura's shoulder, and finally the young woman turned to see what it was that had caught the artist's eye. The view was lovely, there was no doubt—tile roofs of celestial blue, plumes of smoke lofting up from among the buildings, and beyond this, all of Seh stretching her green-blue hills off to the west. Beautiful, indeed, but Kitsura was looking for some unusual composition or play of light that stood out among all of the day-to-day beauty, something unique enough to keep demanding Nishima's attention. Kitsura was about to ask when she caught sight of the two monks still engaged in their conversation on the Sunrise Viewing Terrace. She turned back to Nishima who looked away, a faint blush blossoming on her neck and cheek.

"We should not disappoint them, Kitsu-sum, your young ladies-in-waiting. After all, when winter has worn on they may indeed become our truest friends." Lady Nishima tried to force a smile. "I will play my harp for them and you will charm them over plum wine with a scandalous tale from the Capital."

"Which scandalous tale do you suggest?" Kitsura clapped her hands suddenly with joy. "How foolish I am! It is all too obvious! Tonight, over dinner, when Lord Shonto makes his customary offer to take me as a concubine, or maid, I shall tell him that I will prove I am worthy of consideration as a wife if for no other reason than my musical skills. You, of course, will have to accompany me. We will claim a need to rehearse, which will give our Governor several opportunities to comment on the questionable skills of musicians who, of all things, need to practice.

"Tomorrow we will arrive at the audience hall with our instruments. What gentleman could refuse two young ladies in such circumstances? Of course they will be honored that we have come to play. And Jaku Katta, I guarantee, will swoon." Kitsura broke into a smile, enormously pleased with herself. ''Well?'' she said when she received no response.

''It is not entirely impossible, though it will put you and me, not to mention my uncle, in a somewhat embarrassing situation.''

''Embarrassment may have to be suffered to defeat the barbarian hordes, cousin.''

Nishima laughed this time. ''For the Empire of Wa I will dare to suffer it, then,'' Nishima said and then she thought for a second. ''Perhaps there is a less obvious method of accomplishing the same end.''

''Nonsense. My plan will work perfectly well. Come, cousin, if you play your harp for my young companions, I will overlook your suggestion that intrigue is not one of my many skills. No, no, come along.''

One's ear for the truth, Shuyun knew, was not infallible, and after all, he was only a senior Initiate. The monk rubbed his head as though it had been mysteriously bruised.

It had been an innocent question, almost polite conversation, really. There was a widespread rumor in Seh that the Udumbara had blossomed, fulfilling a prophecy of the Perfect Master—the flowering trees of Monarta would not blossom again until a Teacher walked among men. Sotura had shrugged, saying it was a rumor that surfaced every decade. And though the senior Brother had been careful in his choice of words, Shuyun's sense for truth had wakened immediately—*he lies,* it whispered.

But even a senior Brother did not have an infallible ear for truth, so Shuyun tried to push this incident aside though it resisted this treatment strongly.

Then there had been Brother Sotura's request for a written account of Shuyun's journey into the desert—and this, too, had seemed strange. Not the request, which was hardly out of the ordinary, but the senior monk's tone—he felt some guilt over this. Shuyun found the meeting with Sotura-sum most disconcerting.

A certain sadness had come over him as he walked. Sotura-sum had always been the man Shuyun admired most, the Brother he sought to emulate—Sotura of the *butterfly-punch.* And now he found himself doubting his

former mentor—was, in fact, considering speaking to
Lord Shonto about this meeting. This was also disturbing, Shuyun realized, as though a subtle shifting of his
loyalties had taken place without him realizing. Had
Brother Satake undergone this same change? It made
Shuyun feel a pang of apprehension. Would he find himself following the path of his predecessor? Satake, it was
said, had gone so far as to request his final ceremonies
be carried out by the family he served—not by the Botahist Brothers! Such a thing was unheard of. I must keep
my awareness of what transpires in my soul, Shuyun told
himself.

He lies. The words came back to him like a whisper.
Perhaps he should speak with Lord Shonto? The monk
pushed this idea from his mind. But what was it about
Shonto that made Shuyun consider going to him rather
than to a senior of his own Order? He realized he did not
know—not yet anyway.

The young monk mounted a set of wide stone stairs
that led up from the gates. Slowing his pace only slightly,
he admired the flying horse sculptures that flanked the
first landing and then he was at the enormous main doors
to the Palace. The Palace Guard bowed as he passed—
solid men of Seh who would never think to question the
Imperial Governor's Spiritual Advisor.

Shuyun's destination was his own apartment and his
writing desk. The account Brother Sotura had requested
was required almost immediately as the older monk
planned to include it in documents he was sending to
Brother Hutto in Yankura. But having written of his journey into the wastelands in detail for Lord Shonto, Shuyun
felt this would take little time.

Several turns into the maze that was the Imperial Governor's Palace, Shuyun entered a narrow hallway that
substantially shortened the route to his rooms. At a door
that led into another corridor he stopped abruptly. Voices
from the other side confirmed what his chi sense had
already told him—Lady Kitsura and two others had just
arrived at the same door. He opened it for them, stepping
aside to allow the women clear passage through the narrow opening.

"Ah, Brother," Kitsura said, "our karma keeps bringing us into your delightful company. Obviously this must

be good karma.'' She smiled at her maid and lady-in-waiting who nodded agreement.

''My teachers told me always to turn a deaf ear to flattery, Lady Kitsura, but they did not warn me of its true power. I am, therefore, flattered.'' He bowed.

Kitsura motioned to her companions, who passed through the door ahead of her, and then she followed, tripping as she did so and falling lightly against Shuyun who reached out to steady her. She recovered almost immediately and before Shuyun could apologize she had passed on, her hand lingering on his own until the last second.

The monk stood holding the door open for no one and then realized how foolish he must look and moved on, missing the corridor to his rooms and stopping, for a second, lost. Shuyun had never had a woman so close to him, had never touched a woman who was not being treated for illness, and part of his shock was caused by his own reaction.

Flattery as a temptation, he realized, was hardly worthy of consideration compared to the softness of a woman's body. With great effort, he pushed the memory from his mind, but the thing that kept echoing back was the knowledge that this fall had not been an accident. There was no doubt of this.

Shuyun found this realization as disturbing as his meeting with his former teacher.

Six

The sculpture garden in the Imperial Governor's Palace had not been created by an artist of great note, but it hardly mattered. The raw material was so superior in nature that it had almost worked itself.

Shuyun crossed the lotus pattern terrace at the garden's edge and then paused to admire the late afternoon light that slanted low into the garden. It created shadows that gave texture to even the most featureless surfaces. Already Shuyun could feel the stones releasing their warmth to the cooling air. The sea wind fell to a breath, then gusted, then fell again in a pattern that no man could determine. It would not be long before the clear northern night began to tug at the edge of the eastern sky.

Shuyun came to the garden to meditate on the sculptures and to purge himself of certain feelings. Stopping before the Mountain Dragon, he let his eye run over the fluted sandstone. He felt a certain awe at nature's work, thinking about the several lifetimes that the elements had scoured and carved this stone. Working patiently, waiting for the day when an artist would find it.

The artist, a lady-in-waiting of a retired Mori Empress, had set the three stones together in a fashion that, when seen from the north, suggested an animal poised to strike; when seen from the south, however, it appeared to be sleeping. The low light made the effect far more dramatic than at any other time of day and Shuyun found he was able to bask in the artist's skill as though seeing it for the first time.

The voice of the waterfall drew him and he wound down the narrow path and across the foot stones toward the sound. Shuyun had been in the garden many times and knew the illusion of the cataract twisting down a mountainside was nearly perfect. The stone was cracked and sculpted in scale to an enormous cliff face and the effect was enhanced by carefully stunted trees, many the work of thirty years and more, let into ledges and cracks.

Shuyun stepped through the final copse before the waterfall and there he found the Lady Okara, paper stretched onto a drawing board on her lap, a brush held idly in one hand. She started as the monk appeared.

"Please excuse me, Lady Okara, I did not realize you were here. Please, I did not mean to interrupt your work." The painter was dressed in the plainest cotton robes and Shuyun was certain she must be deeply embarrassed to be seen so. He bowed quickly and turned to go.

"Brother Shuyun, do not apologize. I am hardly working at all. In truth, I have been sitting here weaving memories for some time." She smiled her warm smile. "Please join me, the light is changing color by the second. Have you seen?"

"Pardon me, Lady Okara—have I seen?"

"Ah, you haven't! Come, sit down, if you have the time. This will be worth the short wait."

Shuyun found a second sitting stone at Lady Okara's side and took his place dutifully. Lady Okara was not someone he knew well, but he liked her immeasurably. He often imagined that the ease he felt in her company was the way he would have felt with his own mother had he known her.

The evening sun lit the face of the miniature cliff, throwing every crevice into clear relief, the shadows stretching as the sun fell. The spray from the falls caught the light and a rainbow appeared.

"Watch the deep rose begin to change now," Lady Okara said.

Shuyun stretched his time sense in an attempt to see what the artist's eye would see. The waterfall slowed, each drop of spray catching the sun in a different way, with a different color. Indeed the rock was faintly rose hued; he had not realized this before.

"Rose to deep purple, but watch how many shades it passes through, Brother. It is a daily miracle, I should think."

"I had never seen this before, though I come here often."

Wind rustled the needles of the small pines and the light played among the greens and cast oddly elongated shadows.

"For many, the skills of brush and pigment are more easily learned than the skill of seeing, truly seeing. I came to Seh largely for this. Oh, not to see this garden, as lovely as it is, but to learn to see again."

"Lady Okara," Shuyun said, nodding toward her half-finished painting, "excuse me for saying so, but I find it difficult to believe that you have forgotten how to see."

"Ah, Brother Shuyun, it is kind of you to say so, but a good painter, an artist, does not see only with the eye. A skilled journeyman could learn to capture this scene, light and all. That, I have not lost. What an artist must seek and try to capture is the part of this setting that occurs within. What does this beauty evoke in my heart? In my spirit? A painter asks that question. The true skill, the skill that separates an artist from a journeyman, is the ability to find and express that—the part of this scene that exists within." She fell silent, as though she had begun to search within even as they spoke.

"You see, Brother, until Nishi-sum came to my home, I did not even know that I had lost that skill. Until I encountered her lovely, open spirit, I had thought the skill intact. But it was gone. I had lost it by forming habits of seeing and habits of feeling, as well. It is easily done. One can form habits in one's heart as easily as in one's day-to-day existence. Cha at dawn, a walk alone at sunset, meditation on the full moon . . . nostalgia, loss, bitterness, comfort. All of these habits shield us from the other parts of life. The journey to a new place, encountering people, considering new ideas, different landscapes, risks, excitement, joy . . . disappointment . . . grief.

"From the great palate that life offers I had chosen my colors—good colors, certainly, but few in number—and I had lived with them for many, many years. My spirit withered slowly in its habits. When Nishima-sum came to my house, I could see what this had done to my art.

"It is an odd choice to make, to dedicate one's life to a single pursuit, but if one has made that choice it would be terrible folly to limit what one can accomplish simply because of habit." She gestured with her brush. "Watch this rainbow fade. Isn't that wonderful? As though it had never been.''

She reached down and for several seconds held the tip of her brush in the running water. ''So I have come to Seh, hoping to find a way to open my heart and my spirit to the world again—hoping to revive my art. I do not know if this is possible: I am not the age of Lady Nishima, after all. But if there is a way, I must try to find it.''

They fell silent again, watching the last light illuminate the miniature mountainside. Listening to the sound of the water as it fell into the pool and then ran among the stepping stones.

Lady Okara rose suddenly. ''Please, Brother, you have come here for your own purpose. I grow cold easily and must go inside. But please, I insist. I can make my way indoors without an escort.''

Despite her words, Shuyun rose and handed her across the stepping stones before giving way to her protests and allowing her to continue on her own, disappearing down the path, her plain robes in contrast to her great natural dignity.

Shuyun returned to the falls and seated himself where Lady Okara had been. It was almost dark now, the first stars appeared. He mulled over the painter's words. The touch of Lady Kitsura came back to him and hovered at the edge of Lady Okara's words as though speaking to him in some other language. He thought of Lady Nishima and how he dreamed of her in the desert, dreamed that he was in her embrace as the Perfect Master had been in the embrace of his bride on the cliff sculpture in Denji Gorge.

All of these spoke to him in their own way.

Words came back to him. *It is an odd choice to make, to dedicate one's life to a single pursuit, but if one has made that choice it would be terrible folly to limit what one can accomplish simply because of habit.*

The illusion of the mountain waterfall was hidden in darkness now, but the voice of the cataract still spoke, reminding him that Lady Okara had opened her spirit to this wonder.

She explores the nature of the illusion, Shuyun told himself, that is her purpose. Whereas it is my purpose to deny the illusion: yet what is the nature of this thing I deny? Lady Okara opens her spirit to the world, while I close mine. Who can say who will learn more in this process? Lord Botahara did not attain Enlightenment from denial but from exploration—as Lady Okara has said—both within and without.

This thought unsettled him and all of the voices in his head added to his confusion. He began a breathing exercise, chanting quietly, then sank himself into contemplation, driving out all the voices and focusing all of his mind on the words of his teachers.

It was the habit of a lifetime.

Seven

The servant had drowned in the canal the morning before and not been discovered for almost a day. The small sampan he'd borrowed was later found floating upside-down among the flotsam in a small eddy beneath a seldom used bridge. No one was sure how the accident had occurred, but it was well known that the boy couldn't swim.

General Jaku Katta, the servant's master, was surprised by the effect this death had upon him. The servant boy, one Inaga, had not held a special position in his master's house—a personal servant—a good one, yes, but no better than one would expect in the house of so powerful a man. And yet the death was felt throughout the household.

Jaku sat alone in his cabin on the Imperial Barge and considered his reaction to the loss. The river flowed quietly by, lapping at the barge, a reminder of every poem that had ever been written with a river as an image of life. The calls and shouts of the passing rivermen broke the calm and this seemed a great offense to the general's state of mourning. Of course he was not officially in mourning—one did not mourn servants—but in his soul Jaku Katta mourned and this unsettled him, for he was a soldier and not unused to death.

Inaga had been young, that alone explained some of Jaku's reaction, but this was more than the common response to the death of a child. Inaga had possessed qualities that were rare and, though Jaku hadn't known this, they were qualities he valued highly.

Attempting to alter his gray mood, the guardsman dipped a brush in ink and poised the tip over the report he was supposed to be writing, but no words flowed. He realized he had lost focus entirely when ink dripped onto the rice paper, spoiling it completely. Rinsing the brush, he set it on its rest to dry and gave up the pretense of work altogether.

Though he told himself he had no time for melancholy, Jaku could not force his thoughts elsewhere. Inaga had qualities that Jaku had seen too infrequently. It was not common to find someone who was entirely loyal and there was no doubt in Jaku's mind that the boy had been. There had never been any doubt, not from the very first day Inaga had come to service. That was another point about Inaga—he concealed nothing—was somehow incapable of hiding anything and it seemed everyone knew that instinctively.

Katta touched the paper on which he had been writing to a lamp, letting it burn, slowly turning it to avoid the flame. He waited until he dared hold it no longer and then dropped it onto his inkstone and let it burn itself out.

It was not the boy's death, Jaku realized, it was something more. The intrigue of the Imperial Palace and in the Empire was something he had always found exhilarating, like the kick boxing ring or a duel—one was truly tested—and failing the test meant more than losing a game of gii. Failing could mean loss of everything. But somehow the death of the servant had affected Jaku's love of the *game*. It had been such a senseless death, in aid of nothing.

Suddenly the game of court intrigue seemed as senseless as . . . Jaku was not sure what. And it was this game that had brought him here—to Seh where the Emperor plotted against the Shonto House.

Does the Emperor intend this as a lesson or is it his intention that I fall with Lord Shonto? Jaku asked himself again. Certainly the Son of Heaven knew that Shonto would not accept Jaku as an ally—and Jaku was not about to join forces with a man who was about to fall—not just fall from favor.

The last flame from the burning paper flickered and disappeared, leaving a pile of smoking ashes on the inkstone. The report would have been meaningless anyway, Jaku thought, just another arrangement of words on paper in a bureaucracy weighted down with words on paper.

In a few hours he would meet Lord Shonto. He could expect no honesty there either, and certainly no loyalty. Jaku touched his fingertips together as though he would meditate. There were so many lies now that even Jaku was beginning to lose his way among them.

He had spent hours searching among all the past lies, assuring himself that he knew his path so well that Shonto could never cause him to stumble. He thought of Lady Nishima, from whom he had not received word since his arrival in Rhojo-ma. She walked the path of lies also, though he felt somehow that she found herself there by accident, not by choice.

There was no one he could think of now whom he could rely on to be honest at all times. He thought of Tadamoto-sum and the usual anger he felt was replaced by a deep sadness.

A riverman called out to another and they both laughed. Jaku rose fluidly from his cushion and began to pace the cabin, six paces, side to side. A tap sounded on the screen and Jaku gave permission to enter.

"Your audience with Lord Shonto, General," a servant whispered.

Jaku nodded. He mustn't keep the Imperial Governor waiting. No. Every act of the farce must be carried out, without exception. An audience with a governor who would soon be a ghost seemed particularly appropriate to such a play. And Jaku had no doubt that a ghost was what Shonto would soon be. There would be no rest for the lord, nor for his retainers, nor for his son. Jaku was certain of that.

And now the architect of Shonto's downfall had arrived to participate in the lord's fate. The guardsman shook his head. It had been a beautiful stroke, Jaku had to admit. He had not thought the Emperor capable of such a pure act. He wondered if the Son of Heaven thought Jaku should feel honored to be in such esteemed company. An audience with a corpse. He must dress for the occasion.

His most finely made light duty armor, the suit with the Choka hawk worked into the black lacings along the shoulder covering. A purple border with tiny silver hawks. Jaku thought it quite possible that there had been no finer armor made in his generation. Certainly, Shonto had his garden, but Jaku was not a man without means as this work of the armorer's art would attest. And Shonto would recognize the work of an artist—Jaku was counting on that.

The Commander of the Imperial Guard took more time than usual with his preparations—almost as though he made ready for a duel. Shonto was undoubtedly an adversary deserving of such treatment. Perhaps it was this thought that made Jaku choose his *Mitsushito* from among the several swords he traveled with. He opened the rosewood case with great respect and examined the weapon most conscientiously before lacing it into his sash. It was very old, almost an artifact, yet the name of its maker alone would unnerve most opponents. Jaku, of course, was too much of a pragmatist to rely on another's reputation—the sword was a beautiful weapon, not an ornament.

So like a journey to a duel did this feel that Jaku had an urge to look over at his Second as he took his place in the sampan. He even felt that strange sense of unreality; "floating on the surface of illusion," his teachers had called it.

The boatmen pushed off and began to scull rhythmically. Denji Gorge, Jaku thought. Shonto had found a way out of Denji Gorge. Bribery was the only possibility. Jaku felt himself begin to float higher and resisted with an act of will. To have men so well placed in Hajiwara's army spoke of long preparation. Unreality tugged at him again. Just how long, Jaku wondered, had Shonto known that he would be sent to Seh?

Jaku rubbed the palms of his hands on the padded armrest. What did Shonto know? Whose game was being played here? Perhaps it would not be an audience with a ghost but the ghost that traveled to the audience. Jaku looked down at his hands as though reassuring himself of their substance.

Even if Shonto was not aware of his situation, certainly he was aware of Jaku's part in the debacle in Itsa Province. Using the control of the kick boxer, Jaku forced a calm over himself. Shonto would not act openly, after all, the lord was a gii Master of some fame. No, this meeting might serve no purpose other than to make Jaku aware that Shonto had no doubts about who stood behind the attempt at Denji Gorge. That would be more worthy of him.

The Imperial Guard Commander realized that the irony of the Emperor's plan was quite complete. No doubt the Son of Heaven had divined Jaku's plans for Lady Nishima, or perhaps it was truer to say that the art of divination had not been required . . . Tadamoto had seen to that. What was it the Emperor feared? That Jaku Katta would join forces with the Shonto. And now the Son of Heaven had sent Jaku into Shonto's palace knowing full well that the Imperial Governor would never join forces with the man who had arranged for him to be trapped in Denji Gorge.

Jaku realized that, for the first time in many years, he had very few options. He had become a traveler on a path without branches, a path that narrowed with each step. So it was that he played out each act of the farce as though it had meaning. What choice was there? He had even done exemplary work ridding the Grand Canal of its parasites. Jaku laughed softly. If nothing else, he was still Wa's finest soldier.

"He is in disfavor or he has been sent north to oversee your fall, Lord Shonto. If he is in disfavor, our attempts to convince the Emperor of the true threat will not be successful. If General Jaku has been sent north to be sure there are no mistakes made and that my Governor is truly brought down, then there is a slim chance that he could be made to see the true danger . . . a very slim chance." General Hojo bowed.

Shonto nodded. He shifted his armrest unconsciously, considering what Hojo said. It was not that the general's words had not been said before, but Shonto believed that ideas, even bad ideas, in some mysterious way generated other ideas and one of those might be the truth or the beginning of wisdom. His former Spiritual Advisor had a saying that he used often: *search for the truth inside a lie*. So he searched, not that Hojo had lied, of course, but it was the same principle.

They sat in a plain room: General Hojo; Lord Komawara; Shonto's Steward, Kamu; Lord Taiki; and Brother Shuyun.

The wall paintings drew the governor's attention for a

moment—on one side of the hall a scene of the great war
with the barbarians in which his own ancestor had played
a significant part—on the other a scene among the plum
trees in spring in which Genjo, the great poet of Seh,
chanted to a rapt audience. Shonto turned back to his
advisors.

"We will proceed as we have discussed," Shonto said,
finally. "Perhaps the guardsman will tell us more than
he means to. Lord Komawara, you are prepared for your
part?"

Komawara nodded, half a bow. His hair had still not
grown back from his travels as an itinerant Botahist
monk, and he welcomed the dressing on his head wound
and wore it larger than necessary in an attempt to cover
as much of his scalp as possible. His efforts to pretend
this did not shame him were sometimes difficult to watch.

"Then we can do no more."

A guard opened the screen a crack, as though on cue,
and a hand signal was given to Kamu.

"He is at our gate," the steward reported, and all present composed themselves to wait.

Jaku arrived with two of his black-clad Imperial Guards
who stationed themselves, with Shonto's own guard, outside the entrance to the room. He knelt on a cushion that
had been set for him and bowed deeply.

Shonto nodded and then smiled. "Does the chaku bush
fare well, General Jaku?"

Jaku nodded. "I am convinced that my gardener never
tended his own children so well. The chaku fares well
and is without question the centerpiece of my garden. I
remain in the Governor's debt for such a gift."

"There is no debt between friends, or so Hakata said
and I believe he spoke the truth."

"It is my honor to introduce you to my guests." In-
troductions were made and Shonto watched carefully the
guardsman's reactions but even when introduced to Shuyun he gave no sign of what he might think or feel. Well
played, Katta, Shonto thought, gracious even to the man
who defeated you in the kick boxing ring.

"May we offer you refreshment, Katta-sum?"

Before the guardsman could answer, they were interrupted by screens sliding open to Shonto's right and then
the rustle of silk and female voices. All eyes turned to

find Lady Kitsura and Lady Nishima, followed by their ladies-in-waiting and servants who carried a harp and a flute.

The women bowed to Shonto and his guests. "Our apologies, Uncle," Nishima colored as she spoke, "It was not our intention to interrupt. Kitsura had promised a concert. . . . Please excuse us." She turned to go.

"Nishima-sum, please do not apologize." He smiled to reassure her. Certainly he would never think to embarrass his daughter and Lady Kitsura by sending them away. "I'm sure music would be welcomed by our guests. Especially music provided by players of such note. Please, join us." Shonto waved to the servants.

The ladies bowed and cushions were set for them before the dais. They were less formally dressed than the occasion demanded, as they were in the presence of guests, but even so their robes were of fine materials and matched to the layers of inner robes with the greatest care. Nishima's kimono was a pattern of snow-laden plum blossoms on a field of blue and Kitsura wore a robe of deep red bearing a flight of autumn cranes.

Although Nishima's hair was worn in a traditional arrangement, Kitsura's was most informal—worn in long cascades that flowed down her back. The ladies-in-waiting took a moment to arrange Kitsura's tresses for her hair all but reached the floor when she stood. It was not common for women to wear their hair this way except in the privacy of their own rooms or with members of their families or occasionally with trusted family friends. The effect this had on the gentlemen present was visible.

"You have met General Jaku, I believe?" Shonto asked. "Lady Kitsura Omawara, and my daughter, Lady Nishima." Servants arrived with wine and tables. The ladies' instruments were set nearby.

"Did your efforts on the canal go well, General Jaku?" Nishima asked. Shonto admired how quickly her poise returned.

"It is kind of you to ask, Lady Nishima. I believe the Grand Canal can now be traversed by unescorted women and children in complete safety."

A typically modest warrior, Shonto thought.

"That is welcome news indeed." Nishima said, her smile a bit forced. She turned immediately to Komawara

who had been slowly sinking into himself since the
women arrived. "And Lord Komawara, I understand that
you also have been making the Empire safe from brigands?"

"A small altercation in the hills, Lady Nishima. Of
little consequence." Shonto noted that Lord Komawara
only met his daughter's eye for the briefest second.

"You are far too modest, Lord Komawara." She
turned to Jaku. "Lord Komawara's men were twice outnumbered, and yet they did not hesitate. At some loss,
and with many wounded, including our brave lord, they
made the Jai Lung Hills safe for passage again." She
rewarded Komawara with a smile that seemed to speak
great admiration.

"Nishima-sum," Kitsura said, "shall we play and then
allow Lord Shonto and his guests to return to their conversation?"

Nishima agreed and they took up their instruments.
The melody they had chosen for the occasion was not in
the modern style that they usually preferred but was of
an ancient form known as "Poem Song." *Autumn on the
Mountain of the Pure Spirit* was a melody that conjured
up the sounds of the world and was thought to be one of
the most evocative songs ever written. The flute led the
harp through the first movement which captured the mood
of the leaves beginning to fall.

It was not impolite to watch musicians as they played,
which meant that the gathered gentlemen could regard
the two women in a manner that would otherwise have
been unacceptable. In the warm lamplight Kitsura and
Nishima appeared to be two figures from the wall painting come back to a time where things were more real and
mundane. With her eyes closed and her face covered in
a blush from winding the flute, Kitsura seemed even more
the ideal of feminine beauty. Shonto turned his gaze away
with difficulty and found that both Jaku Katta and Lord
Komawara appeared enraptured. At the same time Shuyun sat with his eyes closed as though he meditated—
whether it was upon the music or something else Shonto
could not know.

The melody followed the falling leaves down to a small
waterfall that became a stream winding down the mountainside among the pines. The sound of temple bells

echoed in the strings of the harp as the stream passed one of the many fanes among the mountain groves.

It was not a long piece, and when it was over everyone sat in silence for several moments. As though on cue, Kitsura and Lady Nishima rose and their servants collected up their instruments.

"Please excuse our interruption," Kitsura almost whispered. And before the men could protest, the women had retreated the way they had come.

The room seemed as empty as a bell after it has been rung. The men sat quietly, each lost in his own thoughts and the feelings the music and the presence of the women had stirred. Shonto finally broke the silence.

"All official business should have such interruptions. It provides the proper perspective from which to proceed." He looked at each member of the group in turn, holding each of their gazes for just an instant, and then he nodded. The audience began.

"General Jaku, may I begin by expressing the thanks of the government of Seh for what you have so recently accomplished on the Grand Canal. We are all in your debt and owe much to the Son of Heaven who sent you on such a worthy enterprise." He nodded to Jaku again.

"Do you plan to stay long in Seh, General? We could plan some fine hunting and other entertainments, which your officers may also enjoy."

Jaku paused before answering. "I have completed my work on the canal sooner than anticipated, Lord Shonto. As I have no orders as of yet, I had hoped to offer some small service in your military efforts. It would be an honor to serve with such a renowned general."

"This is better news than I had expected, General. It would be an honor to have your counsel." Shonto smiled broadly. "If this is indeed your intention, Katta-sum, then I would happily share what little I have learned of our situation here."

Jaku said nothing but composed himself to listen.

"Only this morning I have finished a long report to our Emperor detailing the situation we have found in Seh. Although this is a report for the eyes of our ruler I feel that, as you command the Emperor's Guard, I may speak to you with complete confidence.

"As you no doubt are aware, there is a disagreement

among the lords of Seh regarding the barbarians and their intentions and also about their numbers. On both sides of this debate stand men with many years of experience and proven wisdom. As you might imagine, this made deciding between the two arguments difficult. I have always believed that the direct approach is best whenever possible. We decided to send men into the desert to find out what we could.

"The only people of the Empire who can travel north of the border of Seh are the healing Brothers, so Brother Shuyun, accompanied by Lord Komawara disguised as a Botahist Brother, went into the desert." Shonto turned to Komawara. "Perhaps, Lord Komawara, you should tell this tale."

The young lord nodded and, as agreed, told an abridged version of his journey into the desert, saying nothing of the Kalam, or the cult of the Dragon and its shrine. Shonto watched the Imperial Guard Commander's face throughout, but Jaku betrayed nothing. When Komawara finished, he bowed to Lord Shonto.

"Please, General," Shonto said, "I'm sure both Shuyun-sum and Lord Komawara would answer any questions you might have."

"I must have time to consider this information further, Lord Shonto. Please, continue, it is a most intriguing tale."

Shonto took a long drink of his wine as though the talk of the desert had caused him thirst. "As you see, General, I am much more concerned with the situation in the north than I was when I set out on the Grand Canal." He shook his head and then looked up and caught the guardsman's eye. "Do you know anything of the barbarian Dragon Cult, General Jaku?"

It was a minute reaction, but Shonto was sure Jaku hesitated as though surprised.

"I have not heard of it, though dragon worship is not uncommon even within our Empire, Sire."

"Huh." Shonto looked thoughtful for a moment. "Perhaps that explains it." He was silent for a moment. "I believe that we are about to encounter a threat the likes of which we have not seen since the day of Emperor Jirri. And this will not be a threat that confines itself to Seh, for though the men of Seh are brave and skilled in the arts of war, they are few in number as the plague destroyed most of a generation here.

"The situation is complicated by other factors. It is my belief that barbarian raids on Seh fit into someone's design, someone within our Empire. Their purpose I leave to your imagination. For this reason the true threat will not be understood until it is perhaps too late."

Shonto stopped and looked at Jaku expectantly.

"Lord Shonto, I am not sure what you suggest, but certainly no one within the Empire would be foolish enough to betray us to the barbarian. Why would anyone do such a thing?"

"I was hoping, General, that you might tell me."

Jaku drew himself up to his full sitting height. "Lord Shonto," his voice showed signs of an effort toward control, "you come close to suggesting that I am party to a treason."

Careful, General, the lord thought, you speak to the lord of the Shonto. I will accuse whom I please. He nodded to Kamu who signaled an unseen attendant. A screen slid open and two of the Hajiwara men, now in Komawara livery, entered carrying a black, ironbound trunk on a pole. They set this on the mat before the dais and at a nod from Komawara they opened the lid and spilled the contents onto the floor before the Emperor's Guard Commander. A cascade of gold spread like a landslide across the floor and came to rest, glittering in the lamplight. An Emperor's ransom in gold coins!

The two Komawara guards retreated, and as they did so a third man entered. The Kalam, dressed in his barbarian clothing, came and sat between Lord Komawara and Shuyun.

When Jaku raised his eyes from the fortune that had been spread before him, his face seemed utterly changed. Perhaps it was the light reflected from the coins, but his skin had grown pale and appeared to be drawn taught over rigid muscles. The sight of the barbarian caused him to stop as he began to speak.

Lord Shonto caught the Tiger's eye again. Now you wonder what I truly know, Shonto thought. You even wonder if I know your part in our beloved Emperor's plot. "By the middle of the summer," Shonto said, his voice hard, "the Empire of Wa will have been overrun

by an army the size of which has not been seen in a
hundred years. Everything we strive toward will be destroyed utterly. Anything that gives meaning to the life
of General Jaku Katta will have been rendered meaningless. . . . Everything you value—family, your command,
lovers, estates—will all become the prerogative of a Khan
who will sit upon the throne of our Empire. And he will
distribute what is left of your life among his lieutenants
and chieftains." Shonto stopped to let his words have
their effect.

"Akantsu," Shonto said, using no title or honorific,
"does not understand what he has done. In his mad attempt to bring down the Shonto House, he will bring
down his Empire and blacken the name of Yamaku for
all of history.

"I am prepared to mount a force to take you into the
desert, General Jaku, so you may see with your own eyes
the things that Lord Komawara and Brother Shuyun have
seen. I will spare no effort to convince you that the barbarian threat is real, for if we do not gain Imperial support before spring we cannot stand against the force that
will come out of the desert. Without your influence at
court, General Jaku, the Empire of Wa will fall."

Jaku reached out and took up a handful of coins, but
he did this without sign of desire or awe, as though it
was a fist full of sand he held. He let the coins run
through his fingers, ringing as they fell back into the pile,
the sound echoing in the silent room.

Picking up a single coin, Jaku turned it over, examining it as though the meaning of gold had just become
clear to him, and its meaning did not bring him comfort.

He turned his gaze on the Governor's Spiritual Advisor. "Brother Shuyun, on the soul of Botahara, do you
swear that this story of what was seen in the desert is
true?"

Komawara almost rose from his cushion. "You cannot
ask him to commit a blasphemy! It is against his . . ."

Shuyun reached out and grasped the young lord's arm
and he stopped in mid-sentence.

"I cannot speak as you ask, General Jaku, but may my
own soul be bound eternally to the wheel if what Lord
Komawara has said is not truth. There is little doubt in
my mind that the picture Lord Shonto has painted will

come to be if the Empire does not rise to the defense of Seh. The army we saw in the desert was as real as the coins you see before you and the warriors more numerous.''

Jaku gave a nodding bow to the monk and looked back to the coin in his hand, turning it slowly over and over. ''I cannot guarantee that the Son of Heaven will heed my words, Lord Shonto. In certain endeavors our Emperor does not listen to the sound of reason. I will, however, do what I can. Certainly the Emperor will believe that this is only a ploy to gain control of a large force and that I have fallen victim to your cunning. Or the fact that I am convinced by your words may suggest treachery more than it will suggest an accurate military assessment.'' He placed the coin carefully back in the pile. ''A way that we could strengthen our case would be to convince a certain lord in Seh of the danger to the Empire.'' He hesitated. ''But I am concerned that revealing his name might bring about his own demise, and that would certainly put assistance from the Son of Heaven out of reach forever.''

Shonto shifted his armrest again. ''If I were to invite this lord to the palace and display the contents of this trunk to him, do you think you could assist us in convincing him of the true danger to Seh?''

Jaku nodded. ''I believe I could help make the argument convincing. Again I stress that if I reveal his name, revenge must not be sought against him. This could damage our cause beyond any hope of repair.''

''General Jaku,'' Shonto said, ''the Empire has been brought into great danger through the rivalry of its Houses. If we are to save Wa, all such pettiness must be put aside.'' He turned to his Steward. ''Kamu-sum, invite Lord Kintari and his two oldest sons to come and hear the Ladies of the Capital play.'' He turned back to Jaku and raised an eyebrow. The Black Tiger nodded.

Each rhythmic sweep of the oarsmen sent the fine craft gliding along the silent canal. The speed of his boat often brought Jaku great pleasure; when he discovered an empty stretch of water he would exhort his boatmen to greater and greater speed for the pure joy of it. This evening, however, he seemed unaware of his crew's efforts.

Jaku Katta had absolutely no doubt that the Supreme Master of the Botahist Order could look him in the eye and lie as easily as he chanted the name of Botahara. He was equally convinced that Brother Shuyun was as incapable of this as his former servant had been.

Despite all that he felt about the Botahist Brotherhood and its meddling, he knew that this boy-monk had somehow remained pure, untouched by the hypocrisy of his Order. How else could one explain the feat that Jaku had witnessed in the kick boxing ring? The boy had deflected a blow without actual physical contact! Jaku had felt it.

Even though Jaku had long worn the humiliation of that defeat and the years of anger that it had caused, he knew that Initiate Brother Shuyun was not another Botahist hypocrite. . . . What the boy was Jaku could not be certain, but his suspicion caused him both awe and fear. Shuyun, he sometimes believed, was a child touched by Botahara himself.

Jaku considered what he had heard in his audience with the governor. The barbarians were no longer pawns in the Emperor's plot. The tribes had plans of their own, it seemed—were under no one's control except perhaps this Golden Khan. Should he tell Shonto what he knew about this one? Perhaps. He would see.

Jaku looked out at the thoroughfare that edged the canal. Like most of the streets of Rhojo-ma, it was almost without traffic. By the Gods, if he joined Shonto he would come to war with the Emperor. Akantsu would never be convinced that his barbarian chieftain had escaped his control. Never, never, never.

Jaku rubbed his temple. To join Shonto was probably a decision to commit suicide, there was no doubt of that. Yet only Shonto could save the Empire. That was also beyond doubt. And if the Empire was saved? What then?

Jaku thought of the Lady Nishima, sitting before her harp. Was it possible that there was another solution? What if he truly became worthy of Shonto's daughter? If Shonto won the coming war, the Yamaku would fall. Who would Shonto put on the throne?

Perhaps, perhaps, perhaps. . . . Perhaps Shonto could escape the Emperor's trap. Shonto, Jaku was beginning to believe, was capable of anything. He thought of the trunk of gold and this brought him back to the question he had considered earlier. How long had Shonto known?

The canal slipped by and before Jaku realized it he had arrived at the Emperor's Barge. Absorbed in thought, the Commander of the Imperial Guard sat in his sampan. His boatmen waited without sign of impatience.

The path has grown too narrow, Jaku thought, I have no choices left. If Wa falls to a barbarian chieftain, it will be as Shonto says—the Jaku will lose everything. He shook his head. When there are no choices, one should not be frozen in indecision. The Empire must be defended. One cannot play gii without a gii board.

Jaku almost bounded onto the deck of the barge. Bowing guards fell back in surprise. Their commander laughed at their reaction. He mounted the steps to the upper deck as he tackled the question of how to raise an army. He considered any number of lies he could tell the Emperor, all of them far more plausible than the truth. But some part of him balked at this course, and he found this reaction somewhat strange as though it belonged to someone else and appeared in his personality entirely by accident.

Eight

O sha knelt before a low table and, in the soft light of a lamp, went through the ritual of choosing between two perfumes. As each bottle was unstopped, she would take great care not to breathe while a dab was placed on her forearm. This would be allowed to evaporate appropriately before the delicate fragrance was inhaled. Although the entire ritual was enacted with eyes closed in apparent concentration, in truth, it was a sham. Osha could not truly focus her attention on the scents and she let her arms fall to her sides with a sigh—an act of resignation or despair.

Before she had opened the perfume, Osha had sent all her maids away so that they would not distract her, but the truth was she wanted to be alone to tie her sash. She looked at the gold brocade but could not bring herself to take it up.

The women had left with some reluctance, running a last comb through her long hair, rearranging the hem of a third under-kimono so it would be properly displayed. Although Osha was very careful not to reveal her feelings to her servants, it still made her sad that they were so unaware of her situation. Osha shook her head sadly. They were excited to see the Emperor's renewed interest in their mistress, believing that this would make her happy.

Finally settling on a scent of ground conch shell, musk, and summer tulip, the Sonsa dancer carefully washed the other scent from her arm before dabbing tiny droplets behind her ears and on her wrists. Osha was circumspect in her use of perfume, unlike many of the women in the court. As a Sonsa dancer she believed that beauty resided in movement—all else was unimportant.

The ritual completed, Osha took the long brocade sash

that she had chosen to offset the pale green of her robes and laid it across her lap. Until this moment she had done so well, but suddenly her spirit sank like a stone through water. Taking deep breaths she mastered this moment of weakness. Sonsa dancers were trained to such control. Slowly winding the yards of fabric around her waist, Osha imagined that she bound her emotions inside with each turn.

A shoji slid aside somewhere down the hall and several sets of footsteps could be heard through the rice paper screens. The voices of Osha's maids were quiet but, all the same, projected a note of urgency. Osha stopped the winding of her sash and cocked her beautiful head to listen. It was not urgency that she heard, it was *protest* and the footsteps were those of a man or men.

Immediately the dancer imagined the worst. It was an enraged Emperor coming to confront her with her infidelity. The shoji to her chamber banged open and Osha started as though struck. Tadamoto stood in the opening, tall among the protesting servants.

Collecting her wits, Osha waved the servants out and Tadamoto entered, dropping to his knees a few feet before her. The resolve he had shown forcing his way to her rooms disappeared and he slumped, staring down at the floor. He raised his eyes to hers as though he would speak, but no words came and his gaze returned to the floor.

Nor could Osha find words for the turmoil that Tadamoto's arrival had sparked. They sat in silence for several minutes before Osha managed to form a few words.

"Tadamoto-sum," she whispered, "you must not, you . . . you place us in the gravest danger."

Tadamoto shook his head. The pain he felt was brushed in broad strokes across the features of his scholar's face. Yet he did not speak.

"Tado-sum," Osha whispered again, "I could not tell you." She reached out to take his fine-boned hands, but he pulled them away and left her, half reaching out to him. She covered her face then and silent tears glistened on delicate fingers. "I thought he was finished with me. It was my dream that, in time, he would . . . not care about us." She pushed small fists against her eyes. *"We have been so loyal!"*

Tadamoto reached out as though he would comfort her but stopped.

"I wanted to tell you, Tadamoto-sum, but there are no words to describe the confusion in my heart."

"How?" Tadamoto said at last. "How could you let this happen?"

Osha emerged from behind her hands now, tears still shining in her eyes. "Tado-sum," she said so quietly he almost did not hear. "What did you imagine? Did you imagine that I could make a choice? That we have a choice?"

The young officer said nothing and she reached out to take his hands again, and again he pulled away.

"You could have chosen to refuse," he said, his voice colder than he intended; it was almost a hiss.

When Osha answered, her voice sounded calm, with a touch of distance in it. "And what would have happened then?" When he did not answer she continued. "Could a member of the Jaku family visit me secretly in a monastery in Chou or Itsa Province? What would the Emperor say to that? I would have lost everything, Tadamoto-sum, my dance, my life here in the Capital, and I would have lost you also. Do not deceive yourself. If I am sent to the outer provinces, it would be the end for us. There is no place where we could run, Tado-sum. You know this to be true."

She reached out and took his hands now and he did not resist. "What other choice is there?" She tugged his hands gently, but still he would not meet her eyes. "Speak to me."

"Osha, Osha-sum. You cannot. . . . You cannot." He was unable to finish.

"Our only choice is to never see each other again. Tado-sum my love, I cannot make that choice. Can you?" When he did not speak, she went on. "He will tire of me soon. There is no doubt of that. As soon as he has recovered from this slight by the Omawara girl, he will have no more need of me. If you want to truly help, find a girl of high birth who is ambitious for her family and a great beauty as well. I am nothing to him, truly." She paused. "And he is even less to me. Tado-sum?"

He looked up at her now.

"I know this is terrible, but. . . . Please, I would not do this thing if it were not for us."

Osha pressed herself into his arms and he responded, pulling her close against him. He could feel the struggle as she tried not to sob. Life was so unfair to her, this tiny girl trapped by talent and beauty, and yes, by ambition, too. Tadamoto buried his face in her hair. The delicate scent of her perfume was the greatest blow of all.

When he had gone, Osha sat staring at the lamp on her perfume table, watching the flame sway and dance to the will of imperceptible currents within the room. Taking the brocade in her hands she finished winding it and tied the Lover's Knot with barely a second's hesitation.

Later, in the chambers of the Emperor, Osha tried to focus on an image of Tadamoto. The Emperor was lost in his passion and held her tightly to him as he moved. To her horror, Osha felt her breath begin to come in short gasps. She heard a moan of pleasure, and the voice that uttered it was her own!

No, she thought, *Jenna, Jenna, please . . . let me be.* But the voice cried out again, uncaring in its own pleasure.

"No, Jenna," Osha whispered under her breath. "Oh, no. Oh . . ." But the protest was lost in a cry of passion that heeded no voice but its own.

Nine

Narrowing
High above Screaming Monkey Gorge
The footpath jags up
Into the Sacred Mountains

When one walks among clouds
The way becomes as insubstantial
As a strand of moonlight

"Verses From a Pilgrimage"
Initiate Brother Shinsha

Shuyun came easily to the Fifth Closure and altered his pattern. He had been practicing this same exercise now for several weeks though he had yet to achieve the results he desired. Jaku had tried to strike him thus: Shuyun moved through the complex pattern of punches and deflections as though the Black Tiger had returned to fight their bout again. Shuyun closed his eyes and concentrated on his memory, trying to find the same reaction in himself, trying to achieve the identical state.

Again he felt close, but yet it eluded him. Without hesitation he began the Fifth Closure and continued, practicing the broadening of his focus that would eventually include his entire musculature, the flow and precision of his movements, breath, and his meditative state. Far off, a rapping entered his realm of consciousness. A pause and then it came again. Three punctures of his meditative state that echoed endlessly through his altered time sense.

He interrupted his exercise and stood calmly for a moment, adjusting his sense of time. The tapping came again, though they seemed short quiet raps now.

"Please enter."

The shoji slid open to reveal a Shonto guard kneeling in the opening.

"Corporal?" Shuyun crossed toward the open screen so that any interchange would be as quiet as possible. The Governor's Palace had too many ears by far.

"Excuse this interruption, Brother but you left instructions for this situation and Kamu-sum confirmed them."

Shuyun waved this aside. "Please, Corporal, do not apologize."

The guard gave a nodding bow. "On the Grand Canal you were visited by a young Botahist nun—Sister Tesseko?"

Shuyun nodded.

"A young woman is at our gate claiming to be this woman, though she is not dressed in the robes of her Order. She has requested a meeting with you, Brother Shuyun. Kamu-sum confirmed that you had left orders to interrupt you were this young woman to come again. She is waiting in the Spring Audience Hall. I hope we have acted correctly, Brother."

Shuyun hid his surprise. "You have, thank you, Corporal. Please inform Sister Tesseko that I will join her in moments."

There was not enough time to bathe, so Shuyun settled for washing in cold water and changing his robes. Acolyte Tesseko . . . He remembered her well—young, tall, the bearer of unsettling news. He had often wondered what had become of her charge, Sister Morima. Had she survived her crisis of the spirit? There was more than concern for the nun's spiritual well-being at issue here; there was self-interest also and Shuyun knew it.

He finished dressing and left his chambers, passing down the halls quickly though somehow without seeming to hurry. The Spring Audience Hall was a small, simple room with a low dais, painted screens depicting spring in the mountains, and a simple shrine to Botahara set into a tiny alcove in the wall. The shrine was no doubt what had led the guard, or perhaps Kamu, to choose this hall for their meeting—that and the fact that the room was so seldom used.

Guards knelt on either side of the double wooden doors to the chamber. They bowed as Shuyun approached, and with a quiet knock of warning they pushed open the doors.

Sister Tesseko looked up as Shuyun entered and her face seemed to register terrible grief. If not for a lifetime of training, the strength and immediacy of the woman's pain would have drawn all of his attention, but as a follower of Botahara he was more affected by the fact that she sat with her *back* to the Shrine of the Perfect Master.

Shuyun stopped and gave the short double bow of the Botahist trained. "Acolyte Tesseko, your visit honors me, as it does the House of my Lord." He knelt a polite distance away.

The nun bowed. "I am no longer called Sister Tesseko, Brother. I am Shimeko, now." She bowed again. "I thank you for your kind words, though I realize that, in truth, I have broken all convention and exhibit the worst possible manners coming here unannounced."

"Shimeko-sum, I am honored that you would trust me enough to come without sending word, as I asked you to do when we traveled together on the Grand Canal. Please, be at your ease." Shuyun paused to gauge her reaction, but she did not meet his eyes. "May I ask, how fares our Sister, Morima-sum?"

The young woman shrugged. "She has shown some improvement, Brother, though not as much as the Sisters had hoped." She shrugged again.

There was a silence then, and Shuyun had an opportunity to study Shimeko while she stared down at the grass mats. She was dressed in the plainest cotton robes, like the wife of a poor merchant, and she covered her head with a rough woolen shawl. Her face was careworn and Shuyun thought she looked older than she had when they last met. There were other signs of great strain, for she was thin and her skin was mottled and lifeless as though her diet had been very poor for some time. Shuyun was concerned.

"Are you well, Sister?" he asked quietly.

She seemed to consider this for a second, a sad smile almost coming to her lips. "I am no longer a *Sister,* Brother Shuyun. I . . . I find I must keep reminding myself of this." She fell silent again, then looked up and held his eyes for an instant. "The Way," she said, returning her gaze to the floor, "is difficult. I–I had not the strength."

Shuyun nodded slowly. "Ahh," he said almost under his breath. "Is there some way that I may serve you, Shimeko-sum? Please do not hesitate to ask."

The conversation was punctuated by a long silence then. "Brother . . . Brother Shuyun, I have come to beg that I may be allowed to take service with you." She put her hand to her mouth as though she would stop it from causing her more embarrassment.

Shuyun put the tips of his fingers together as in meditation. "Shimeko-sum, what you ask is not possible, I am sorry. This is not my decision to make. And certainly it would not be proper for a young woman to serve me. It is out of the question." Shuyun watched her as he spoke but could not be sure of her reaction, for her face was partly hidden by her shawl. "Shimeko-sum? Why do you ask this?"

She shrugged, tugging with one hand at a strand of grass from the floor mat. "I believe, Brother Shuyun, that you are a pure spirit, untainted by the . . . present state of the Botahist Orders."

"You believe the Sisterhood is tainted, Shimeko-sum?"

She stopped playing with the strand of straw, covering it with her palm as though this would somehow repair the damage. Her voice dropped to a near whisper. "I believe both of our Orders are corrupt, Brother Shuyun. Excuse me for saying so."

"I see. Is this belief related to Sister Morima's crisis, Shimeko-sum?"

Lifting her hands she found that magic had not occurred. The straw remained as it had been. She nodded. "Yes, Brother. That and other things."

"I do not wish to pry, Shimeko-sum, but, in truth, I wonder what has occurred that caused you to turn your back on Botahara."

She shrugged. "I . . . I have not truly turned my back, Brother." She seemed to struggle for words. "I am no longer sure how to serve the Perfect Master. I feel that those things which I learned from my teachers have been . . . tainted, debased in some way. To worship the Perfect Master in such a way . . ." She shivered visibly.

"This must be wrong, Brother," she said, her voice suddenly gaining clarity. "It must be."

"You make strong statements, Shimeko-sum. Did Sister Morima speak of her concerns specifically? Again, I hesitate to pry."

"As you know, Brother, Morima-sum suffered a crisis of the spirit. She is

inced that the scrolls she saw at the Ceremony of Divine Renewal were not the scrolls of Botahara. I am not sure what evidence convinced her of this, but Morima-sum is a scholar of great repute, Brother. I do not doubt her assessment." She folded her hands in her lap now and closed her eyes as if searching her memory.

"Because of Sister Morima's crisis, she has spoken to me of things that I should otherwise never have heard. She did not seem to care, Brother. It is my understanding that the Sisters have methods of collecting information, even from within your own Order. They seem to believe that the Sacred Scrolls have disappeared. That the Brotherhood searches for them secretly." She opened her eyes and met Shuyun's own. "Though Sister Morima believes the scrolls have not been in their possession for a long time, perhaps hundreds of years."

"I see," Shuyun whispered. "The Scrolls of Botahara are guarded night and day by the Sacred Guard of Jinjoh Monastery. It is inconceivable that they could be stolen, Sister."

"*Shimeko,* Brother, *Shimeko.* The Sisters seem to agree, Brother Shuyun. Some do not believe they were removed by men. They believe it was divine intervention."

"Shimeko-sum. This can hardly be the belief of the Senior Sisters."

She shrugged. "It appears to be, Brother, Morima-sum reported this to me as though it were commonplace. And there is more." She began to worry the loose straw again. "No doubt you have heard the rumor that the Udumbara has blossomed?" The straw broke free of the mat and she began to weave it through her fingers. "It is not a mere rumor, Brother Shuyun. Sisters witnessed the blossoming before your Order closed the grounds of Monarta. It is beyond all doubt, Brother, the Teacher who was spoken of is among us."

"I have discussed this rumor with a senior member of my own Order," Shuyun said quietly. "He assures me that this is not the case, Shimeko-sum. Why would he lie to me? Why would my own Order deny the rumor?"

"The Sisters ask this same question, Brother. It is an issue of grave concern to them. It is thought that the Teacher is as yet unknown to the Brotherhood, and they cannot proclaim him. If they admit the Udumbara has blossomed, as the prophecy was written, and they cannot bring forth the Teacher. . . . As you see, Brother Shuyun, the activities of the Botahist Orders seem to reflect a self-interest that I find repugnant. I apologize for the insult that is implied, but I cannot help but speak the truth, Brother, please excuse me."

"I value the truth, Shimeko-sum, but it is not always easy to discern or to accept." Shuyun fell into a long silence and was finally brought back to awareness when Shimeko cleared her throat.

"Please excuse me, your words have given me much to consider." He tried to smile. "I come back to the question of how I may serve you, Shimeko-sum."

"But it is I who have come to serve you, Brother Shuyun." Suddenly she prostrated herself before him. "I ask this most humbly, Brother."

"Please, Shimeko-sum, sit as you were. Do not do this." He looked around in acute embarrassment as though afraid someone would come in and see them. "This is most unseemly. Why are you doing this?"

Shimeko spoke from her position, prostrate on the mats. "Brother Shuyun, there are some in the Sisterhood who believe that you may be the Teacher who was spoken of. I wish to serve you."

Shuyun rocked back on his heels. What could possibly make the Sisters believe such a thing? "Shimeko-sum, I assure you, if I were the Teacher I would not keep such a thing secret."

"Awareness is often preceded by accomplishment, Brother."

"In truth, Shimeko-sum, my own faith is not unassailable by questions and doubts. Shimeko-sum, rise up," he ordered and the young woman complied. She rose to a kneeling position, the texture of the straw mat marking an intricate relief on her forehead.

She obeys her Teacher, Shuyun realized, and this un-settled him more than her words. *You stopped a blow without it touching you.* It was like a whisper in his mind. *Brother Sotura was not even aware that such a thing was possible. Senior Brother Sotura!* It cannot be true, he told himself, my faith is so easily shaken, doubts grow in me like weeds. I cannot be the Teacher—I may never be a senior Brother if I continue as I am now.

"Brother," Shimeko said flatly, bringing him back to the world. "I have nothing, no coins, no roof, no walls, no skills, no family. If you send me away, I shall live in the street, and though I have no compunctions about beg-ging, I have no experience of this life. I will live outside your gates, Brother, until I am given some task or until I am driven away. I do not know what else I can do."

Shuyun sighed. He believed she would do exactly as she said. Botahara have mercy on her; a lost one. "Your calligraphy is presentable?"

"I am told it is sufficient, Brother. I acted as Morima-sum's secretary often."

"Would you object to serving a highborn lady in the same capacity?"

"If she is within your household, Brother, I would accept gratefully."

"I serve within *her* household, Shimeko-sum." He paused, thinking. "I can promise nothing, Shimeko-sum, but I will inquire." He shook his head. "And please, we can have no more displays of . . . this kind. I am not the Teacher, I assure you."

"If that is your wish, Brother Shuyun."

"Come, I will find a maid who will take you to the kitchens for now. You have not eaten in some time?"

"Three days only, Brother." She tried to favor him with a smile. "I—I thank you, Brother Shuyun."

"Yes, but no more of this. You must promise."

She started to bow but turned it into a nod.

Ten

Lord Shonto's steward, Kamu, wove his way unsteadily down the hallway. He held a lantern ahead of him in his only hand and occasionally used his elbow against a post to regain his balance. Guards bowed smartly as the old man passed. Despite his appearance—gray hair in a tangle, robes obviously thrown on and belted in the most haphazard manner—Kamu had once been a famed swordsman and the young men among Shonto's guard treated him like a legend who had descended from some Great Beyond to walk briefly among them.

The old steward careened down the hallway like a ship with a broken rudder, bow lantern swinging. Four of Shonto's Personal Guard watched the doors to their lord's chambers—solid doors, not screens. The four bowed as Kamu approached and hands went to sword hilts.

After speaking the password, Kamu was forced to set the lantern down to give the accompanying hand signal. The force with which the lantern made contact with the floor indicated the steward's level of annoyance.

The senior guard tapped on the door and a viewport slid open. Quiet words were exchanged and the night guard, one of the few allowed into the lord's chamber while he slept, slid the port closed.

Kamu left the lantern on the floor as he waited. The viewport slid aside again and the senior guard nodded, stepping aside as the door opened.

Passing through the small entrance hall that acted as a guard room, Kamu entered an inner chamber. A lamp flickered on a small table, casting a weak light in the almost empty room. Kamu had barely knelt when Shonto entered the room, looking only slightly less disheveled than his steward.

The lord nodded in return to his retainer's bow but did

not take the second cushion. Instead he placed his back against one of the deep lacquered posts and crossed his arms, waiting.

"Excuse this . . ."

Shonto held up his hand and the steward stopped in mid-sentence. "Despite our apparent youth, Kamu-sum, I believe we are too old for such formalities, under the circumstances. Please, speak directly."

Without a hint of a smile, Kamu began. "The Kintari, Sire. . . . They have fled."

"Huh." Shonto rubbed his chin.

"I have taken the liberty to awaken and inform your advisors, Sire. I've tripled the guard around the palace."

Shonto started to speak, but the night guard appeared in the doorway.

"General Hojo and Lord Komawara, Sire."

Shonto gestured to allow them entrance.

The sounds of doors and rustling clothing. By their dress, both Hojo and Komawara had also been caught unaware. They bowed to Kamu and their liege-lord.

Shonto said, "The Kintari have refused our hospitality, General Hojo."

Hojo nodded.

"Most unfortunate. All of them, I suppose?"

"It appears so, Sire," Kamu answered. "We will know in a few hours."

"We should take precautions, but I don't believe this means the Emperor is about to move against us," Shonto pulled his robe closer. "His plan is more subtle than that."

Kamu waved his arm in a sweeping gesture that seemed to take in all of Seh. "I believe, Sire, that the Kintari are less important than what this incident tells us. They were warned, there can be no doubt."

Shonto paced across to the opposite post, then back again. He looked up at Hojo.

"I agree, Sire. They must have had knowledge from within the Governor's Palace. Unless it was a sudden loss of nerve, and I consider that unlikely. Even the Emperor does not choose the fainthearted to carry out his treachery."

"I have also had word from those who watch our new ally. A messenger came to Jaku's barge about the same time as we received word of the Kintari. Apparently this caused quite a stir aboard the Guard Commander's barge. Jaku is on his way to the palace as we speak.''

Shonto nodded. "Lord Komawara, if you were Lord Kintari, where would you go?''

Komawara pressed the bridge of his long, thin nose. ''The quickest escape would be down the river, but once the sea is reached they will find few ships willing to risk the winter storms: it seems unlikely that they would make such a choice unless utterly desperate. The Grand Canal is the most easily searched, despite the numbers of craft that would be involved.'' He looked around the room, meeting each set of eyes in a manner he would never have done a few months before. ''If everything we believe about Lord Kintari is true, I would seek them in the desert, Sire.''

''Ah.'' Shonto gave half a laugh. ''How far ahead of us do we think they are?''

Kamu and Hojo exchanged glances. ''We are not yet certain, Lord Shonto,'' Kamu said. ''Their servants may have been keeping up a pretense for several days, though no more than three or, perhaps, four.''

''Excuse me, Sire,'' Hojo said quietly, ''we should also consider what this may say about our friend in the Imperial Guard. Jaku was well aware of our intentions; he received a message just as we did. Could he be the ear in our midst?''

''Jaku's loyalty will always be in question. It is only comforting to remind oneself that the Emperor must be haunted by the same question.'' Shonto stretched his arms high. ''Morning is too near for a return to sleep. Please, join me for my meal.'' Shonto clapped and a servant appeared. He gave quick orders and then began to pace again, an activity his retainers had seldom seen him indulge in.

Before servants arrived with the meal, the night guard again interrupted, whispering to Kamu.

''Brother Shuyun and General Jaku have both arrived, Sire.''

''Ah,'' Shonto said to those around him. ''As in all good tales: mention the spirit by name and he appears.'' Shonto crossed to the small dais upon which his sword sat in its stand and took up a place on the cushion, pulling an armrest closer in a familiar gesture.

Shuyun appeared, his tonsured scalp and simple manner of dress allowing him to arrive looking as he always did. Oddly, Jaku, who had the farthest to travel, was impeccable in his black uniform.

The monk and the general bowed as their stations required.

"I set out as soon as the news reached me, Lord Shonto." Jaku seemed very calm, Shonto thought, despite the fact that he certainly knew he would be under suspicion—someone warned the Kintari.

Shonto looked around the group. "I trust, General Jaku, that you learned of this independently?"

Jaku nodded. "I do not, however, know where the Kintari have fled or when they first disappeared. It would seem, Lord Shonto, that the Kintari must have learned of this from someone within the Palace or within my guard. I have very tight security among my own officers, Sire."

"I do not doubt it, General. More blows through the walls of this ancient maze than winter winds. Such things are inevitable in this situation."

Servants brought a light meal and tables were arranged for Shonto and his guests. As though no matters of greater weight had been discussed, polite conversation flowed seamlessly until the servants had left and Shonto gave his guard orders to secure the chamber. The discussion went from the best time of year to hunt various game birds back to the issues at hand without a sentence of transition.

Shonto sipped his cha, then set the cup back on his table, turning it slowly. "It appears that the palace is not about to be stormed by forces loyal to our enemies. The suggestion that the Kintari were warned is no doubt true. Perhaps our hopes that the Kintari would become allies in our attempt to gain the Emperor's support were vain."

Shuyun gave a half bow before speaking. "If the Kintari could have been convinced of our intentions, they may well have become the support we hoped. We will not likely know this now. We must find support without them. The men of Seh and the Emperor both need to be convinced of the truth of our discoveries in the desert. It

is a pity that we did not return with evidence other than
words.''

"As Brother Shuyun says," Jaku added, "I have been
convinced by words and the belief of the witnesses. Not
everyone will think as I do. I have composed my letters
to the Emperor and certain of his counselors. As you are
aware, the court functions according to an elaborate, unwritten system of debt and payment—the coinage is favor. If one understands the workings of the court and has
given credit to many, one can collect accordingly. In the
Palace they say: it is improper to ask the Great Council
of the Empire to add a wing to your home, but it is quite
possible to have the Great Council offer to build such a
wing.

"I am not a great lord nor do I hold high position, but
I will call in what credit I may have given. We shall
see." Jaku tugged at the corner of his mustache. "If
there is no support forthcoming from the Emperor or the
men of Seh—what will we do?"

Hojo nodded. "It is the very thing we have debated
these past months, General Jaku."

A gong sounded and somewhere in the darkness the
guard changed. The night guard appeared in the doorway
and signaled Kamu. All was well.

"It has been our hope to convince others of the true
threat, General Jaku," Shonto began, "but as you have
said—this may not be possible. When the barbarians cross
our border in the spring, the men of Seh will rally to our
support . . . too late, unfortunately." The lord rearranged several objects on his table as he gathered his
thoughts. "We will make these final attempts to gain the
support of the men of Seh and the Emperor, but we cannot plan as if these attempts will succeed. It must also
be realized that to gain the support of the Emperor but
not the men of Seh, or the reverse, will not be adequate.
Our needs are great.

"If we have not gained the support we need, our concern will no longer be the defense of Seh but the defense
of Wa. We will attempt to raise an army as we move
south. It will become a question of how many men of
Seh will be willing to follow, for they will form the heart
of our army."

"Sire!" Komawara blurted out, "you will abandon

Seh. . . ." Suddenly aware of the naïveté of this statement, Komawara reddened noticeably, adding to his embarrassment.

Shonto's tone remained calm as he answered. "I do not wish to abandon Seh, Lord Komawara, but to throw a tiny force at a vast barbarian army will accomplish nothing. If our tactics are prudent and our courage does not falter, we may slow the barbarian advance long enough to allow an army to be raised in the south. I am the Governor of Seh, Lord Komawara, and would not consider such a course if it were not for the grave danger to our entire Empire. If the men of Seh and the Emperor will not act to secure the borders or to protect the Empire, then we must act in their place.

"I believe, Lord Komawara, that the people of Seh will be largely safe from the barbarian threat due to our retreat. This Khan cannot have an army large enough to hold Seh and pursue us south to the inner provinces. If Botahara smiles upon us, the barbarian army will pass through Seh like a wind, pulling only a few leaves from their branches."

In the long silence that followed, no one met the young lord's eye. "Excuse my outburst," Komawara said evenly. "I bring shame to the Komawara House. Please excuse me." He shifted his sword in his sash. "There is one other question that I must ask at risk of again appearing naive. What will happen if the barbarians wish only to conquer the province of Seh, and we allow them to take it without a fight?"

Shonto nodded. "It is as we have often asked, Lord Komawara. This would probably fit the designs of some. Then Shonto and all who support him will be brought down. We still believe that if the barbarians only desired Seh they would have taken it in the autumn when surprise was assured. We all will gamble our lives on this assumption . . . be certain you believe it."

Komawara nodded. "I will risk my life to save Wa, though I would rather it were Seh I hoped to save. Still, for me there can be no choice."

"Truly, Lord Komawara," General Hojo offered, "there can be no choice for any of us."

"Kamu-sum," Shonto said, "we must begin to gather the craft needed to take us south and make preparations to destroy all others. Leave no boats for the barbarians. Begin an inventory of river boats at once.''

The steward nodded.

''We must consider ways to raise an army as we pass south. Who can be won to our side? Once we cross the border of Seh, the Son of Heaven will try to remove me from command of the army. Who will be sent to do this? General Jaku, perhaps your knowledge and contacts at court could answer this?''

Jaku nodded.

''Much to do. We will make our last attempt to win over the lords of Seh at the Celebration of the First Moon. Lord Komawara, I will have to prevail upon you to describe your journey into the barbarian lands again.''

The cool, first light of a northern morning glowed through the unshuttered paper screen and cast the shadow of Jaku Katta's large hand across the paper. The brush hovered in the air, as it had often in the last hours. The soft bristles seemed to contain only ink and no words.

Again he dipped his brush.

My dear brother:

> *It is with some difficulty that I write to you, not only because of the nature of our parting, which I regret deeply, but I have arrived in Seh to discover things that neither of us had ever expected. I do not know how to convince you that the words I write are true but I must find a way, Tadamoto-sum. On the souls of our father and mother I swear that every word is true. The fate of Wa depends on your ability to recognize the truth—seldom has so much depended on the heart of one man.*

Eleven

It was a small entertainment arranged for the high-ranking residents of the Governor's Palace and for those who frequented Seh's court—perhaps seventy people in all.

The evening's entertainment was provided by a wrinkled, elderly man who moved with the stooped carriage of someone who'd spent his life toiling in a rice paddy. His threadbare robes, sewn in the country style, did nothing to deny this impression, though in truth this man had once been a respected scholar, holding appointments at the Hanama court where he was renowned for the quality of his verse. Long ago he had retired to seclusion in the far north and only the promise of a concert by the Ladies Nishima and Kitsura had lured him out this night—that and a suggestion that Lord Shonto might provide him with a cask of a certain rare wine.

The old man, one Suzuku, sat on a raised platform built to resemble a balcony and behind this a silk hanging bore a sunset and far off, a V of geese winging south among crimson clouds. Skillful arrangements of dried leaves and cedar boughs symbolized the autumn, just as the flying geese were the common symbol for letters or messages.

The old man's voice had no doubt lost much of its power and timbre to the years, but his great refinement of speech and the beauty and richness of the language he used more than made up for it.

He would speak softly, the meter of the verse as subtle as the rhythms of rain, and then he would break into a chant, strong cadences driving the images like drumming drove dance.

Earlier in the evening Lady Kitsura had played without the accompaniment of her cousin, who was not in attendance, but if this had initially been a disappointment it was soon forgotten. Kitsura Omawara could hold the attention of the most critical audience without assistance. She had taken her place among those listening, now, and seemed hardly less the center of attention there. In contrast, the gathered peers of Seh, guard officers, ladies-in-waiting, and members of the administration seemed like a gathering of the dull and the gray. It was not just the refinement of her dress and manner that set Lady Kitsura apart, it was as though life flowed more strongly in her veins and gave her the ability to find pleasure and delight where it escaped others. She easily stole the hearts of all men present and gained the grudging admiration of the women.

Among those in attendance, General Jaku Katta had the most difficulty concentrating on the verse. He hoped to speak with a certain lady, and carried a poem in his sleeve that he thought might melt some of the coolness of her manner. Although he realized it was absurd, he felt like a suitor scorned to find that Lady Nishima was not present. He tried to turn his thoughts elsewhere and redoubled his efforts to focus as Suzuku began a new poem.

> *Autumn in Tu's brocade hills*
> *Leaves find a death of such beauty*
> *A man's sad end pales*
>
> *Poems seek out the unsteady hand*
> *Words dropping from the brush*
> *Like leaves.*
> *Still awake at first light*
> *Eyes red as the sunrise*
> *Letting no leaf escape*
>
> *Ink falls, drop by drop*
> *Yellow of weeping birch*
> *Crimson of blood-leaf.*
> *I send poems south with passing geese*
> *But who is left to receive them?*
> *So many leaves adrift*
> *On this chill wind*

Up here it is better to forget early days
It is enough to ache from damp mornings
To ache from memories too
Is more than a man can bear

Outside my open room
A small cloud
Tangles in the ginkyo's branches
So white against the endless blue.
Searching among a lifetime's clutter
I find my worn inkstone

What words will come now?
What wisdom will I speak
To frightened trees?

The evening's last poem read, the gathering broke into small, informal groups and plum wine flowed as smoothly as gossip. Jaku found himself in the company of several of Seh's most well-born young ladies.

"It is a shame," said the youngest of the women, "that Lady Nishima was not present also. I had so looked forward to hearing her harp and had hoped she might trade a poem-sequence with Suzuku-sum."

Jaku could not have agreed more, though he said nothing.

"General Jaku," said another, "you must have heard Lady Nishima play at court?" She tried to hold the general's gaze as he answered and was disappointed that he looked away so quickly.

"Oh, many times. Not four days ago I heard Lady Nishima and Lady Kitsura play here in the palace. They complement each other perfectly, as you might imagine." He was immediately embarrassed—a short time in the north and he was already playing the fool's game of trying to impress the provincials.

As he spoke, Jaku's eye was drawn by Kitsura as she broke away from a disappointed group of young men and made her way across the hall. There is no doubt, Jaku thought, the rumor that she spurned the Emperor had made her even more desirable. Despite the fact that he had come hoping to meet another, Jaku could not help but feel excitement at Kitsura's presence.

Lady Kitsura stopped briefly to speak to Lord Komawara and Jaku shook his head. Komawara, he remembered, had made a fool of himself in Shonto's chambers the morning before. It was bad enough he had not realized that Shonto might be forced to abandon Seh but to reveal his ignorance so blatantly exhibited the poorest judgment. Jaku was surprised that Shonto allowed the boy into his councils. Strange.

Jaku's attention was drawn back into the conversation as he was asked to comment on the most current fashions in the Capital. He was forced to disappoint them, explaining that Lady Kitsura dressed in a more timeless style and was not a follower of the latest fad. The conversation then drifted into a discussion of the relative merits of silks from Oe and Nitashi. Lady Kitsura again caught the general's eye. She had finished her conversation with Lord Komawara, and as Jaku looked up she motioned to him with her fan.

Waiting for an appropriate break in the conversation, Jaku excused himself, inflicting a second disappointment upon the young women from Seh. Lady Kitsura had retreated to a quieter corner and stood fanning herself slowly, though the room was not overly warm.

The guardsman bowed as he approached and she nodded from behind a ginkyo leaf shaped fan, jade and silver combs catching the light as her head bobbed.

"I hope you have come away inspired by Suzuku-sum's verse, General. Were his poems not exquisite?"

"Certainly, Lady Kitsura, but not less so than your playing. I feel doubly inspired."

She nodded at his flattery, and lowered her fan enough that he caught a glimpse of her famous smile. "I am sorry Nishi-sum could not be present. My poor description will not do justice to the evening."

"Lady Nishima is well, I trust?" Jaku said as matter-of-factly as he could.

"I am certain we need not be overly concerned, it is kind of you to inquire."

She did not offer to convey his concern to the lady herself, as Jaku had hoped she would.

A gong marked the hour of the heron and the crowd seemed to thin noticeably in response.

"The evening has flown, I must make my good nights.

If it is not too much to ask, General,'' she reached a
small hand out from behind her fan and he found a tiny
fold of paper in his palm, ''would you read this before
leaving? I would be in your debt.'' Her eyes seemed to
plead with him over the edge of her ginkyo leaf.

''I am your servant, Lady Kitsura.''

''You are so kind, General.'' A brief touch of her hand
on his wrist and she was gone, leaving the guardsman to
catch his breath.

It was several minutes before Jaku could find a moment alone. He opened the intricately folded letter with
great anticipation—she had not been able to erase him
from her mind after all! The disastrous meeting on the
Grand Canal came back to him and caused him a second's discomfort, but he made his fingers continue. Why
would Lady Nishima put her fine hand to paper if she
was not still intrigued?

He read:

My Dear General Jaku:

*I find myself in the awkward position of having to
ask a favor. Is it too much to ask that you meet
me this evening? My servant will await you until
the hour of the owl at the door to the Great Hall.
If this is not possible, please, no explanation is
preferred.*

Lady Kitsura Omawara

Lady Kitsura! Jaku pushed hard against the post that
hid him. The depth of his disappointment shocked him.
He had so expected to find a poem from Nishima-sum.
Lady Kitsura? He could not imagine what favor the Omawara daughter could need of him. No doubt he would
soon find out. At the very least, he could now easily ask
that Kitsura deliver his own letter. She could hardly refuse.

Jaku said his polite good nights as soon as he could.

As Kitsura had written, a servant awaited him at the
Great Hall—an older woman whose accent, even in the
few words she uttered, was noticeably from the Imperial
Capital. Jaku knew—it was an accent he's spent some

time acquiring. The servant took a route through seldom used halls until they came to a door like many others.

A soft knock was answered by a woman's voice and for a brief second Jaku found himself hoping this had all been an elaborate ruse arranged by Lady Nishima so that they might meet secretly.

It was not to be so. The opened door revealed Lady Kitsura sitting in the light of a single lamp, its golden light heightening her complexion.

"General, I am honored that you would come." She smiled, no fan now to hide her beautiful face.

"Lady Kitsura, it is I who am honored." He knelt upon the second cushion that had been set, closer to hers than he expected.

"May I pour you plum wine, General?"

"Thank you, Lady Kitsura. If I am not being too presumptuous, please call me Katta-sum."

Kitsura held back her long sleeve as she poured wine into the small cups. "I would be honored." She passed him his wine cup. "Please, call me Kitsura-sum, whenever the situation allows."

Jaku gave a half bow. Polite conversation followed. Discussion of the night's poetry, the customs and manners of the people of Seh, and even a little gossip. More than once they found cause for laughter. Such formalities completed, Jaku broached the true subject of their meeting, hoping to save the lady embarrassment.

"If you will excuse my boldness, Lady Kitsura, is there some service I might perform for you? I would deem it an honor to do so."

Kitsura took a small sip of wine. "You are kind to inquire, Katta-sum." She set her wine cup back into the small table and turned it as though examining the quality of porcelain.

"As you are no doubt aware, I left a most awkward situation in the Capital. Unlike many families, my own would not argue my decision. . . ." She looked up at him, her face suddenly troubled. "Yet now I fear the repercussions of that decision—not for myself, General—but I fear for my family. My own decision was perhaps too selfish."

"You acted according to the dictates of your heart, Kitsura-sum, a woman of integrity could do nothing less.

Is there some task I could perform that would relieve some of this apprehension you feel?''

"Truly, you are kind," she said warmly, a sense of relief apparent in her tone. "I am concerned that my family could be in a delicate position. I am not sure . . ." Her voice became so small that words ceased to come.

"Perhaps I could draw upon my friends in the Capital, particularly in the court, to find out if there is reason for worry, Kitsura-sum. Would this be of service to you?"

"Oh, yes, Katta-sum, very much so!" She reached out and squeezed his large hand. "But please, enough risk has been taken for me. Do nothing that would jeopardize your position. I could not bear it. Will you promise me this?"

"Lady Kitsura, it would be an honor to take any risk on your behalf but, truly, what you ask is no cause for concern, let me assure you."

"You are kind, but you must be careful. I would not forgive myself if anything untoward should result."

"Your spirit is burdened with enough concerns, Kitsura-sum," he laid his fingers gently on her arm, "do not add this to what you carry." He removed his hand and took a sip of his wine. "Is there anything more I may do?"

She hesitated for a time before looking up, a slight blush apparent on her beautiful face. "I wish to send a message to my family, but I fear that it might be intercepted. I'm certain Lord Shonto would do this, but . . ."

"Lady Kitsura, say nothing more. I can send a message to your family in complete secrecy. Tomorrow, if you wish it."

"Katta-sum," she said, a tiny tremor of emotion in her voice. "I am in your debt for this kindness. I don't know how I can repay you."

"There can be no debt in such matters. Please do not concern yourself with such things."

"Katta-sum," she took his hand in both of hers now, "there is debt and I will not forget it. Is there nothing that I might do in return?"

He felt a soft tug on his hand, so soft he wondered if his imagination toyed with him. And she did not release his hand.

"If I may ask such a favor, Kitsura-sum," Jaku said, with obvious difficulty, "would you convey a letter to your cousin, Lady Nishima?"

As though all of her features had frozen, Kitsura paused but then, almost immediately, she recovered. Sitting up, she reached for her wine cup though she did not drink from it but only held it with both hands as though she suddenly did not know what else to do with them. "Certainly . . . General, though it seems a small thing indeed."

"It may seem so, but it is I who am in your debt now." Jaku produced the letter from his sleeve, slightly misshapen from the hours of neglect.

Slipping it into her sleeve Kitsura reached again to pour wine.

"Please, Kitsura-sum, I have duty awaiting me."

"Excuse me, General, I did not mean to detain you."

With a bow and a promise to send a trusted guard for her letter, Jaku Katta slipped away as quietly as the cat he was named for.

Kitsura sat for some time without moving. Never had she been so thoroughly rebuffed. She had expected him to fail this test, had wanted him to. And he had asked her to convey a letter to her cousin!

"Uncouth, common soldier!" Kitsura whispered.

For a second she felt anger toward her cousin but then realized how absurd this was. By Botahara, she thought, Jaku must be truly smitten with Nishi-sum. What a disaster that could mean.

* * *

Canal's end,
We have traversed uncertainty

A maid interrupted as Lady Nishima contemplated the poem's next line.

"Excuse me, Lady Nishima, Brother Shuyun inquires of your well-being."

"Ah, how thoughtful," Nishima dipped her brush in water. "Please offer him cha."

Pushing aside her table Nishima quickly straightened her robes.

The maid appeared again. "Brother Shuyun, Lady Nishima. Cha will be served immediately."

The servant bowed as Shuyun entered and in turn he bowed, Botahist style, to the daughter of his liege-lord. Though she knew full well that Shuyun was small of stature, hardly taller than she was herself, Nishima was always surprised when she saw him. In her mind his presence was larger.

"Brother Shuyun, please be at your ease. It is a pleasure to have your company." Nishima smiled.

"I came to inquire after your well-being, Lady Nishima, not to interrupt." He nodded to her work table.

"Notes to myself. I was filling time, Brother, nothing more."

Shuyun knelt on the cushion set for him. For a second he met Nishima's eyes and she wondered, as she often did, if it was great wisdom or great naïveté that dwelt in those large, dark eyes. She often wondered if it was this ambiguity that touched her.

"You are well, Lady Nishima?" Shuyun said in his soft voice. A voice that always seemed to suggest intimacy to her. "I grew concerned when the poetess did not attend Suzuku-sum's reading."

"I am well. Despite Suzuku-sum's reputation, one does not always feel the desire for the company of many." In truth she thought Suzuku's reputation was somewhat greater than his talent.

Shuyun nodded. Servants arrived with a cha service and laid out the utensils with some care. Their mistress was very conscious of detail and they did not like to disappoint her.

"And how fares the Shonto Spiritual Advisor?" Nishima asked and smiled.

"He fares well enough, my lady. In my Order we say; *well enough to serve His purpose*. The Botahist trained do not ask for more than that."

Nishima nodded and checked the heat of the charcoal burner that warmed the cha cauldron. "Perhaps we should all learn to ask less for ourselves and more for others, Brother. In my *Order* we say; I fare well, thank you—meaning, *I am well enough to enjoy all of the pursuits that I hold dear, whatever they may be*." She kept her eyes cast down, fussing with the cha preparations.

Shuyun seemed to consider this for a moment. "Excuse me for saying so, Lady Nishima, but there is a ded-

ication to duty among many of your *Order* that is worthy
of recognition and praise. The Shonto are renowned for
this."

Nishima nodded. "It is true among fewer than one
would hope, Brother, though certainly in reference to my
uncle it cannot be denied."

With great care she ladled cha into bowls and offered
the first to her guest.

"This bowl must be for you, Brother," she said, as
etiquette demanded.

"I could not, Lady Nishima. Please, this bowl must
be yours."

Though this was the proper response, the sincerity of
his words stopped Nishima and she found herself staring
into his eyes again, trying to read what lay behind the
words. The monk looked away and she collected her wits.

"Your presence honors me. Please, Brother Shuyun."
She held out the bowl and he took it from her hand with
surprising gentleness.

As though there had been a lapse, a moment of too
much familiarity, Shuyun's tone became formal. "A
matter has recently arisen, Lady Nishima, about which I
require advice." He sipped his cha, looking away.

"Brother, if it is possible to repay some of the debt I
feel to our Spiritual Advisor, I would not hesitate to do
so. Please, what is this matter?"

Nishima watched him take a calming breath before
speaking. "While I traveled with Lord Shonto on the
Grand Canal, a young Botahist nun approached me for
advice. A Sister with whom she traveled was unwell and
there were no others of her Order to refer to. I shared
what knowledge I could and told her she might ask for
me at any time. I have often wondered since if the Sister
recovered but have had no way of knowing. Earlier today
this same young Acolyte came to our gate, asking to
speak with me. As I had given orders to allow this woman
access, and Kamu-sum remembered this, she was not
sent away."

He paused to sip his cha.

"This all seems most irregular, Shuyun-sum. Please
go on."

"This young woman has left the Order of the Botahist
Sisters—it seems she has suffered a confusion regarding

her faith. It is my hope that she will return to the Sisters but until such time needs some way to live. She is Botahist educated, Lady Nishima, and has been a secretary to a senior member of that Order. It occurred to me that there might be a place for her in the Shonto household. Even more specifically, I wondered if you or Lady Kitsura, or perhaps Lady Okara might have use for someone of such talents?''

Nishima stopped to ladle more cha, obviously considering this.

''It is difficult for me to say, Shuyun-sum. There is no question that our flight to Seh has left us with a very small staff, and no secretary. This girl, is she intelligent?''

''I would say yes, Lady Nishima.''

''Huh. Is it not unusual that she would seek you out, Brother? What explanation could there be for this?''

''Perhaps what she considered to be an act of generosity—my assistance to her on the canal—stayed in her memory, Lady Nishima. It seems entirely likely that, outside of the Botahist Sisters, she knows no one else.''

''The Sisters take an interest in the events of our Empire, Shuyun-sum, do they not?''

''They do, my Lady.''

''Is it not possible that this young woman has been sent to us to that end, Brother? The Shonto are often the objects of such scrutiny.''

''I believe, in this case, Lady Nishima, that this girl is truly what she claims.''

Nishima sipped her cha and regarded Shuyun, who sat looking down, as politeness dictated. ''You have an ear for truth, Brother Shuyun?''

''So my teachers believed, Lady Nishima. Though it should be remembered that this ability is never infallible.''

''How unfortunate.'' Nishima swirled her cha leaves as though she would change the message written there. ''I would be pleased to assist a seeker who has lost her way, if I can. Please have her sent to me and I will see what she seems suited for.''

''I thank you, Lady Nishima. I do not think she will disappoint you.''

Nishima smiled. There was an awkward silence. Shuyun finished his cha, but before he could excuse himself Lady Nishima spoke again.

"How do you recognize truth, Shuyun-sum, what is it that informs you? More cha?" As she said this, she poured cha into his bowl.

"Well, perha . . . certainly. Thank you." He took up the full vessel and sipped.

"I am unable to explain, Lady Nishima, I apologize. I simply know."

"It is a feeling, then?"

"Perhaps. It cannot be described but only named."

"It is most intriguing, Brother. But do those who are raised to the Botahist Way know feelings, Shuyun-sum? Are feelings not part of the Illusion?" Nishima found a small crease in her robe that she smoothed.

Shuyun considered for a few seconds. "Botahara taught that feelings were illusory, yes. It is written that our desires trap us in the world of Illusion."

"Then you are not troubled by feelings, Brother Shuyun?"

"I am not so enlightened, Lady Nishima." He gave a small, almost embarrassed, smile. "Even the Botahist trained have feelings—one does not allow them to rule one's actions, however."

Before he could protest, Nishima ladled more cha into his bowl.

"You resist them, then?"

"I'm not certain that *resist* is the proper description, Lady Nishima."

"You do not resist them?"

"Followers of the Way order their lives according to the principal virtues, not according to their desires."

"But Brother, when a follower of the Way feels desire, or any other emotion, do they resist it? Did not Botahara teach that resistance was folly? I find this concept difficult."

Shuyun set his cup on the table and placed his palms together, touching his fingers to his chin in thought. "When one has traveled far enough down the Sevenfold Path, one does not feel desire, Lady Nishima. Until such time we practice meditation, we chant, and we learn focus. Certainly duty and desire are not always compatible,

Lady Nishima, but, as you have said, the Shonto choose duty."

Nishima nodded slowly. "Though I often wonder at what cost, Shuyun-sum," she said softly.

Shuyun looked away as though some detail in the room begged his attention and what Nishima said had not been heard. "I have not seen Lady Okara for several days," Shuyun said evenly. "Does she fare well?"

Nishima smiled at the sudden change of subject. "Well enough to serve art's purpose, Brother. I often wish I could say the same."

"I have heard Lady Okara speak of your art in the most flattering terms, Lady Nishima," he said, his voice losing its edge of formality. "She speaks also of your artist's soul. It is my impression that she is somewhat envious."

"Oh, certainly she is not!" Nishima felt her face flush with pleasure at Shuyun's words—even a fan would not hide this.

"Recently she spoke of her quest to learn to see again. It seems Lady Okara believes that over the years she has developed habits of being and feeling that act as a wall to the world and prevent her from seeing. But she does not seem to mean seeing the world, she means seeing within. 'The part of the scene that exists within,' were the words she used.

"It is Okara-sum's belief that you have the open spirit of the true artist, Lady Nishima, and she traveled to Seh with you in an attempt to recapture this. Perhaps you are her teacher, Lady Nishima."

"Lady Okara is my teacher, Shuyun-sum, make no mistake. I have been blessed with brilliant teachers."

"It is said that a child learns wisdom from the parent, but the truly wise parent learns joy from the child. Do not be confused by appearances; a wise teacher learns from the student, always."

"And what have the esteemed Brothers learned from Initiate Brother Shuyun?" Nishima asked suddenly and watched his reaction closely.

Shuyun shrugged. "I do not know, Nishima-sum, I do not know." He opened his hands in a gesture that seemed to indicate emptiness.

"We know only those things which we allow ourselves to know," Nishima said.

A troubled smile appeared on the monk's face. "That is Botahist teaching, Nishima-sum."

Nishima gestured with her hand as though she encompassed her entire life, and her long sleeve swept gracefully through the air. "I have been blessed with brilliant teachers."

"Brother Satake?"

Nishima nodded. There was an awkward silence while Lady Nishima prodded the coals in the burner, causing them to spark to life.

"My Order guards its teachings with a certain jealousy, Nishima-sum," Shuyun said at last.

She nodded again, poking distractedly at the coals. "Give me your hand, Shuyun-sum," she said suddenly, and she reached out and took his hand and placed it palm out against her own. Regulating her breathing with some skill, she pushed. Shuyun resisted for the merest fraction of a second and then pulled away slightly. When he pushed against her own hand there was almost no resistance. Shuyun could feel the chi flow. Chi in an uninitiated woman—a peer of the Empire of Wa!

Lady Nishima took his hand in her own. "As impossible as it may seem, there is much in common in our experiences, in our lives, Shuyun-sum."

"Brother Satake broke his sacred oath," Shuyun said. He felt his focus wander as he said this. Even though he had suspected Brother Satake had broken his oath, the shock of proof was great.

"He lived by his own oath, Shuyun-sum. His teachers could have learned much from Brother Satake, but they were mired in their own ways, their own habits."

Gently Shuyun removed his hand from her own. "Please . . . excuse me . . . I must go." Without further ceremony Shuyun rose and walked out like a man in a daze.

For a long time Nishima sat staring at the door where Shuyun had disappeared. Then she shook her head as if to clear it. Reaching for her writing table, she prepared her brush with exaggerated care. She read the lines she had already committed to paper and then continued.

> Canal's end,
> We have traversed uncertainty
> To arrive here,
> Purity and desire
> Tangled

She could find no words to complete her thought.

Shimeko sat with her eyes cast down while Lady Nishima examined her brushwork in the dim morning light that filtered through the screens of her chambers. The former Botahist nun sat without movement as she had been trained to do and nothing in her appearance betrayed the confusion she felt. Was she truly going from serving a respected senior Sister to the service of this pampered aristocrat, barely older than she was herself?

"It is a fine hand, Shimeko-sum, strong without being plain." Nishima nodded toward her, half a bow. Setting the paper aside, she smiled warmly at the young woman who sat before her. Shimeko sat with her shawl pulled tightly around her face, hiding her cropped hair.

"You will excuse my curiosity, Shimeko-sum, I can't help but wonder why you would seek service with the Shonto. I do not wish to pry into your reasons for leaving the Sisterhood, but life in the Shonto House will be very different."

Shimeko spoke without raising her head. "Do you wish to hear the truth, my lady?"

"Always," Nishima said, the word coming out clipped and controlled.

"I did not come to your gate to seek service with the Shonto. I came to offer my service to Brother Shuyun." She sat looking down, her expression unchanging, her tone even.

"I see. May I ask why?"

"I believe Brother Shuyun is a pure spirit, Lady Nishima, untainted by the machinations of his Order."

"Huh. Then you take service with me against your will?"

"No, my Lady, I will gladly serve the household that Brother Shuyun serves."

"I see. Will you be able to make the adjustments necessary, Shimeko-sum? You do not have to treat me with this level of deference, I am not a senior Sister who demands utter humility from others.''

"Please excuse me, Lady Nishima.'' She raised her eyes and met Nishima's for the briefest second. An attempted smile showed some potential. "If someone will instruct me, I'm certain I will learn.''

"We could find you a teacher, Shimeko-sum.'' Nishima glanced at the page of brushwork again. "You are a scholar?''

"I was only an Acolyte, my Lady. An Acolyte cannot call herself a proper scholar. My accomplishments were modest compared to the Sisters I served.''

"I see. Could you go to the Palace Archives and find information for me?''

"If the information is there and somewhat ordered, I am confident I could, Lady Nishima.''

"Good. This is what I want to know. On the canal did you see the fane of the vanquished Brothers? The one called the Lovers?''

"My Lady, it endangers the spirit to look at such things,'' the young woman said, casting her gaze down again.

"You did not look, then?''

The former nun struggled for a moment and then she shrugged, her cheeks coloring a little.

"Well, it is not necessary to look. I want to know what the scholars have written about the sect that inhabited that fane. Scholars, mind you, not members of any Botahist Order. Certainly the Imperial historians could not have allowed such a thing to pass without comment. Are you able to do this without compromising your beliefs?''

"My beliefs, Lady Nishima?'' She traced a circle on the floor. "Yes, I think so.''

"Excellent. I would like this information as soon as possible, thank you.''

Shimeko sat, her posture and expression unchanged.

"You may go, Shimeko,'' Nishima said.

"Thank you, my lady.'' She bowed in the Botahist manner and backed toward the door without rising.

"Shimeko?''

"Yes, my lady?''

"You know that servants are seldom addressed as sum?''

The former Sister paused in her retreat. "Brother Shu-yun calls me Shimeko-sum, my lady," she said simply.

Nishima considered this. "Then I will call you Shimeko-sum also."

Twelve

Sister Sutso hurried down what seemed an endless hallway until she found the door she had been looking for. Pulling her robe closed at the throat, she pushed open the door that led out into an unlit courtyard. A cold wind swirled about her, pulling wildly at her robes and whistling among the pillars. An occasional drop of rain was smeared across her forehead, though due to the wind they did not seem to fall from the sky. Almost running, the secretary to the Prioress found the door she was looking for, despite the complete darkness, and pushed into a second hall.

Pulling up the hem of her robe, she ran up several flights of stairs, surprising a group of Acolytes who had never seen such undignified behavior in a senior Sister.

Another long hallway, then a shortcut through the Archives of Divine Inspiration, another hall and then the great stairway. There, one flight down, went the Prioress, Sister Saeja, her sedan chair carried by four Acolytes.

Sutso descended the stairs and only slowed her pace as she came up beside the chair. She controlled her breathing with great discipline so that it seemed she had not hurried at all, perhaps had come upon the Prioress by accident.

"Prioress," Sutso said, bowing as low as the situation would allow.

The old woman's eyes seemed to appear out of the wrinkled folds that were her eyelids. She nodded and closed her eyes again as though conserving her strength.

"Is there anything I can do, Prioress?" Sutso asked, pitching her voice in tones the old woman could still hear.

"There will be no change of plan," came a soft whis-

per. "Continue with our preparations. There is so little
time."

"Do you have commitments I am unaware of?" Sutso
asked.

"No, child," the ancient head moved from side to
side, "but this is not unexpected. Since Morima-sum's
time of testing, they have been gathering like the carrion
eaters they have become. I remain this still only to draw
their attention from things of importance." Her face
creased in a smile and her eyes flickered open, eyes full
of humor.

"Why do they call a council now?"

"They hope to tire me, child, that is their true purpose." She smiled again. "Sister Yasuko's letter. They
have learned that there are events outside of their narrow
world that could adversely effect their dearest ambitions.
Seh is on everyone's lips suddenly, replacing talk of
Monarta."

The chair wobbled slightly and then the bearers recovered. The Prioress held out a thin hand. "Give me your
hand, child. I do not want to slide down the grand stairway alone."

Sutso took the frail hand in her own. Botahara protect
her, she prayed silently. So much is dependent on this
woman, so much.

At last they came to the bottom of the stairs, to the
relief of Sister Sutso, and then to the Chambers of Council. A gong was rung as the Prioress approached and the
large doors swung open, the Door Wardens carved into
their panels seeming to gesture entrance. A last squeeze
of the Prioress' hand and Sutso stopped short of the
Chambers. The bearers returned almost immediately and
the doors were closed, no one to enter until the Council
was over. She stood a moment, staring at the doors, and
then hurried off. There was so much to be done.

Lamps suspended by gold chains hung from the lacquered beams and flamed impressively, casting shadows
into the deepest corners of the room and the highest
reaches of the ceiling. The floor of polished woods reflected the light like a bronze mirror and the twelve Senior Sisters who knelt there seemed almost like some

mysterious part of the structure, positioned in two straight lines as they were.

The Prioress sat, propped on pillows in her sedan chair, facing her Council. The lines were not drawn clearly in this arrangement: of the twelve Sisters four, including their leader, were of the Sister Gatsa faction; five, including the Sister who sat in Morima's place, supported the Prioress; and the remaining three were called, when they were not present, the *Wind Chimes*—those who swayed this way and that, making sounds according to the direction of the wind. As one would expect, the Wind Chimes were both courted and despised.

The Sisters bowed their heads to the floor and rose, waiting impassively.

"Who called this Council?" The Prioress asked the ritual question.

Sister Gatsa spoke in her refined aristocratic voice. "This Council was called by the collective will of the Twelve, Prioress."

"Then let the will of our Lord, Botahara, be done through word and deed."

Signs to Botahara were made and silence reigned as each woman present prayed to the Perfect Master for guidance. A gong sounded softly and the Council began.

"Who will speak for the Twelve?" the Prioress whispered.

"Sister Gatsa," the women answered together.

The Prioress nodded to Sister Gatsa, conceding the floor.

Sister Gatsa drew herself up to her considerable sitting height before beginning. "Prioress, honored Sisters, there is news from the Province of Seh that is of grave concern to our Order. There are reports that a large barbarian army makes ready to assault the Empire's northern borders. Does our Order have information about this situation?"

A silence ensued. The Prioress sat looking at her Council who, as was proper, did not meet her gaze. Only Gatsa would dare to do that. It occurred to the Prioress to wonder who in the Priory in Seh had managed to find a copy of Sister Yasuko's letter. Most annoying.

"I have received information from Seh that would indicate this is true, Sister Gatsa," the Prioress said at last.

There was a minute shifting of position as though in discomfort among some of the council.

"Excuse my presumption, Prioress, but should not the Council have been informed of this?"

"In time of war," the Prioress said so quietly that she forced the others to lean forward to hear, "the Prioress has authority to act without the Council. It has always been so."

Gatsa nodded, her face not quite masking her pleasure. She had sprung her trap. "In time of war, Prioress, this is true. But war has not yet come and there is much that should be done in case a calamity should befall us. There is much that we all should do."

"A fine point, Sister," the Prioress said. "Shall we put it to a vote?"

Sister Gatsa hesitated noticeably. She had expected to request this herself. "If the Council so desires, Prioress."

The Prioress smiled her beatific smile, unsettling Senior Sister Gatsa even further. Of course, the Prioress knew she would lose—she could read her Council that well. But after the Wind Chimes had gone against their Prioress once, they would be less willing to do so on each subsequent issue, especially when the true nature of the situation was made clear to them. Today they would ring to the words of Prioress Saeja, the old woman was certain of that.

"Let the proceedings begin," the Prioress whispered. Yes, let them begin. In three hours she would have approval of everything she had already begun. Let the vultures gnaw on that. She smiled again and closed her eyes to wait.

Thirteen

The Great Audience Hall of the Empire of Wa was the largest chamber in the known world and considered to be a marvel of both art and engineering. The rows of pillars that lined the central hall were each carved from a single iroko tree and lacquered to a deep sheen. Rafters soared in elongated curves up into the tiered roof structures and light filtered down from on high without an identifiable source. So polished was the marble floor that it reflected images and light as faithfully as clear, still water.

At the farthest end of the hall the dais seemed to float on this unrippled surface. Three steps of the finest jade led up onto the dais, the blocks joined so seamlessly that the steps appeared to have been carved of a single, massive block of green-blue stone. Behind the dais, seven painted panels showed the Great Dragon in flight among stylized clouds above a landscape of rugged beauty—ancient Cho-Wa of the Seven Princes. The Princes themselves sat their gray steeds at the foot of the Mountain of the Pure Spirit about to create the Seven Kingdoms that would one day become the Empire of Wa.

Below the center panel sat the Dragon Throne of Wa carved from a single block of flawless green jade.

Upon the Dragon Throne sat Akantsu II, Emperor of Wa. His voluminous ceremonial robes flowed over the carved stone, reaching almost to the floor, where a small cushioned stool protected his feet from contact with the earth. His sword of office stood in a silver stand to one side, and it was apparent to any who knew him that he missed its feel and hardly knew what to do with his hands without it.

The Ministers of the Left and Right sat in their appropriate places, before the dais to either side, while down the length of the Audience Hall the Great Council of State was arrayed: Reminders, Major and Minor Counselors, and the senior Officials of various ministries. They sat in rigidly defined rows, dressed in their state robes that created a most pleasing pattern of color and form, each man a tiny island on the unbroken, liquid surface.

Behind the senior officials sat functionaries of high rank, scribes, and bureaucrats, and behind them stood the ceremonial guards—generally younger sons of favored peers—dressed in ornate armor.

On the first step of the dais knelt the Major Chancellor who governed all proceedings, listening carefully to the whispered comments of the Son of Heaven and proclaiming these to the Great Council.

At the moment all sat listening to a senior Counselor who spoke in glowing terms of the recent efforts to rid the canals and roads of brigands. Several minor decrees, that had been issued almost after the fact, were singled out as showing great foresight and the senior Counselor bowed in the direction of the officials responsible for these—members of his own faction, as everyone present knew.

While the great statesmen of the Empire involved themselves in this activity, the man who had convinced the Emperor to embark on this program sat quietly in the ranks of the minor functionaries. It would be out of the question that Colonel Jaku Tadamoto would ever speak on such an occasion or to such an august assembly, yet in his sleeve rested a summons to the Emperor's private chambers. He would meet alone with the Son of Heaven later that same day—something many of the senior officials present had never done.

The Council carried on, largely ceremony, for, in truth, real government took place elsewhere, in less impressive chambers with far fewer involved. Jaku Tadamoto waited patiently, trying to keep his mind focused on the conversation, not for the content but for what it told him of the shifting alliances within the council. Even so his gaze shifted and he found himself contemplating the Dragon Throne, remembering the history, or perhaps myth of the ancient seat of power. He turned away before the Emperor might notice his gaze, but the image stayed in Tadamoto's mind.

It was said the artist Fujimi had cleansed his soul through fasting and prayer for seven days before locking himself in his studio with the untouched stone.

Fujimi's apprentices gathered outside the doors while the Master toiled. The sounds of stone being worked would go far into the night and whenever they stopped the apprentices could hear the Master chanting in a language none had heard before. In the early morning of the twelfth day all noise ceased—no sound of stone being polished, no chanting . . . stillness. By midday the apprentices' concerns were such that they appointed their most senior member to knock on the door and call out the Master's name. Three times this was done, but there was no answer and still no sounds came from within. They waited.

By sunset it was decided to break down the doors to the studio. With some effort this was done. The shattered doors swung open and the setting sun illuminated the throne shining as though it had its own light within. A dragon flowed around the seat and back of the throne, a dragon so real, so alive it seemed to have turned to stone in mid-flight.

The apprentices stood in awe until the light of sunset faded and then, remembering their purpose, lit lanterns and began searching the building. The Master could not be found. All the doors were securely locked from within, yet Fujimi was gone, never to be heard of again.

Taken to dwell among the gods, some said. Murdered by the Great Dragon for stealing her soul and encasing it in stone, said others.

When the final ceremonies were completed and the Emperor and senior officials had left, Tadamoto rose and returned to his chambers without retinue or fanfare. In the privacy of his own rooms he removed a letter from a locked box and held it a moment as though the thought of opening it caused him pain. With some care he unfolded the paper on which he had written a deciphered version—the letter in his own hand noticeably more elegant than his brother's original.

Moving to a nearby screen, Tadamoto opened it a crack to catch the gray winter sunlight that a covering of cloud did its best to obscure.

My dear brother:

It is with some difficulty that I write to you, not only because of the nature of our parting, which I regret deeply, but I have arrived in Seh to discover things that neither of us had ever expected. I do not know how to convince you that what I have learned is true, but I must find a way. Tadamoto-sum, on the souls of our father and mother I swear that every word I write is true. The fate of Wa depends on your ability to recognize the truth—seldom has so much depended on the heart of one man.

There is no doubt that beyond the border of Seh a barbarian army of unprecedented size waits to invade in the spring. I realize that this defies the common wisdom that says the tribes are diminished, but the common wisdom is false, have no doubt. Seh is not prepared for such an attack and will fall within days.

The chieftain who has gathered the tribes and will lead them across our border is a formidable man, familiar with the situation in Seh and not unaware of the plots within our own court. You realize, I am sure, that the Emperor will not send troops to support Shonto. The barbarian chieftain knows this also, I am convinced.

The barbarians will not stop once they have swallowed Seh. They have a force that will allow them to push into Wa. If we begin to gather an army now, it is possible that the barbarian advance could be stopped in Itsa Province or perhaps Chiba. If the Son of Heaven cannot be convinced of this, the Emperor will lose his throne to a barbarian chieftain, and this will be one of the lesser evils of such a defeat.

It is difficult to be here in the north knowing my own part in all of this. If the men of Seh realized what destruction this feud will bring, I would certainly not be allowed to live. Yet the men of Seh do not even realize that the enemy sits on their border and such is their arrogance that they will not listen to Lord Shonto Motoru. You would

*think that the Shonto House had not once made
great sacrifice to rescue Seh from the barbarians.*

*I realize the Emperor will think I have sided
with the Shonto, but a way must be found to
convince him. Above all, you must not lose your
place close to the Son of Heaven or there will be
no voice of reason in the entire court.*

*Tadamoto-sum, it is a task of enormous weight I
charge you with, and I confess I do not know how
it can be accomplished, but the future of our
Empire depends on you now. All we can hope to
do in the north is slow the invasion—there are not
enough men in all of Seh to do more.*

> *I remain your Servant,*
> *Katta*

Tadamoto let the letter fall to the mat where he knelt.
It was so impossible! If what Katta said was true, and he
had trouble convincing himself that it was so, then the
Empire was almost certainly lost. Tadamoto knew Akantsu II as well as any man and he did not believe for a
second that the Emperor could be convinced that Katta
had done anything but joined the Shonto. That Fanisan
daughter and Katta's interference with her . . . that was
the seal on his fate. It was all so impossible.

Tadamoto reached for the letter, read a few lines, then
let it drop again. He shook his head. Katta, he thought,
knew what words to use, it had always been one of his
gifts. Tadamoto had never heard his brother swear by the
memory of their parents, no matter how desperate, he
had never done that. Somehow Katta had known that this
was the one thing he could do that would shake his brother's certainty. Could he be telling the truth?

He slumped against the frame of the opening and
looked out into a fine curling mist, letting the cold air
wash across his face. Wasn't it just like Katta to get himself into an impossible situation and then expect Tadamoto to get him out of it! Botahara save him—save us
all. He was an impossible man. But was it true? If it was
and he refused to believe, then Tadamoto would bear
some responsibility for the calamity that would ensue—
because he could not believe in his own brother. He

rolled his head against the cool wood of the frame. Katta, Katta, Katta. Why do you always demand so much of me? How can I be loyal to you and loyal to my sworn duties?

A gong sounded the changing of guards. He must make himself ready for his audience with the Emperor. As Tadamoto began his preparations, his mind went back to Osha. Osha in the Emperor's embrace. Both of their lives were terribly at risk now, Osha was correct in this. Still the question echoed over and over again: what kind of man was he that he could continue to advise this Emperor? Advise him, *comfort him*, knowing that he allowed the woman he loved to act as a common street harlot with this same man? What kind of man was he?

Tadamoto never wore armor into the presence of the Emperor, not even his lightest duty armor. He felt it was a ridiculous affectation and the fact that Katta had done it often had always bothered him—embarrassed him, perhaps, would be closer to the truth. Tadamoto wore his black uniform with its dragon insignia and the marks of his rank but no more. Even this was less ornate than it easily could have been.

It was the courtiers' obsession with signs of rank and favor that drove the young Jaku wild. What pettiness! *Could functionaries of the third rank wear a gold sash? Could officials in the Ministry of Ceremony wear the peaked cap?* It was obvious to Tadamoto that the honorable officials who governed the Empire of Wa were far more concerned with the hierarchy in the palace and signs of rank than with the governing of the land.

Realizing how angry he had become, Tadamoto tried to calm himself. It was this situation with Osha and the Emperor that was affecting him so. He was an advisor to the Emperor—it was important that he put emotion aside.

As acting Commander of the Imperial Guard he was whisked through to see the Emperor with less formality than even the most senior officials. After his morning in the Great Council, he took some satisfaction from this. He knelt before the entrance to the Emperor's chamber and waited to be announced.

Bowing his head to the mat, Tadamoto waited until the Emperor deigned to acknowledge him.

"Colonel Jaku," the Emperor said, "be at your ease."

Jaku rose to a kneeling position and moved forward to within a respectful distance of the low dais.

"Thank you, Sire."

The Emperor nodded. He was studying a scroll and seemed barely aware of Tadamoto. "You have received a letter from your brother, Colonel?"

"I have, Emperor."

"But not from Lord Shonto?"

"No, Sire."

The Emperor looked up from his scroll and picked up a letter from a small table. He set this before the dais, nodded at it, and went back to his reading.

Stretching as far as he was able, Tadamoto got two fingers on the letter and retrieved it. So, he thought as he began to read, this is the hand of the famed lord. It was a strong hand of the older style.

Sire:

> *As I have recently written, the transition of governments in Seh is complete and I have been able to devote myself to the problem of the barbarian raids. This situation has been found more complex than one could ever have suspected.*
>
> *As there seemed to be no agreement among the Lords of Seh regarding the extent of this problem and due to the consistent rumors that a new Khan had risen to power among the tribal peoples, it seemed the best course to gather my own information directly. To this end I sent highly reliable men into the wastes, secretly. After journeying as far as the desert they came upon a recently abandoned encampment that had contained seventy thousand warriors. The men sent into the desert were experienced in such matters and I do not doubt their estimate is true. This army had since decamped, but one branch of it was observed and consisted of forty thousand armed men, many on horseback.*
>
> *It is clear that there will be an invasion as soon as the spring rains have ended. I believe that*

*more than Seh is in danger from this attack. At
this time I am sure that in all of Seh there are not
twenty thousand men of fighting age and only half
of these are trained in the arts of war. It is
possible that all of Wa could be under threat.*

*I believe, Sire, that the Empire has not faced
such a threat since the time of Emperor Jirri. If
we do not raise an army by spring, Seh will fall
and a barbarian army will come down the path of
the great canal.*

*I have spoken to General Jaku Katta concerning
this issue and I believe he concurs with my
assessment. I cannot stress enough the peril the
Empire is in.*

> *I remain your servant,*
> *Shonto Motoru*

Tadamoto looked up at his Emperor who continued to
read.

"What is your response to this, Colonel?" the Emperor asked, still not looking up.

"It is similar to the letter I received from Katta-sum,
Sire, though a less emotional appeal." Tadamoto
weighted his words carefully. "It is difficult to know from
this distance precisely what is occurring at the other end
of the Empire. For that reason I hesitate to dismiss this
information entirely."

The Emperor looked up from his scroll. "What would
you advise, Colonel?"

"It seems most prudent that we seek outside corrob-
oration of this information. We should send someone
whose loyalty is beyond question to Seh, Sire."

"I had such people in Seh, Colonel Jaku."

"Excuse me, Sire?"

"They disappeared at almost the same time your
brother arrived in the north. Gone."

Tadamoto swallowed hard.

"Coincidence seems to follow your brother, Colonel,
it does not fill me with confidence."

Tadamoto said nothing. The Emperor stared at him for

some seconds and though he did not wish to do it, Tadamoto looked away.

"Write to your brother. Tell him that we will make him the Interim Governor in Seh when Shonto falls. But if he sides with Shonto . . . he cannot be saved. Tell Katta-sum that my anger has passed, he may return once the task is complete. But above all find out what truly transpires in the north—your brother certainly will know." The Emperor set his scroll aside and shifted to face Tadamoto. "We will answer Governor Shonto's request for support. I will send my son, Prince Wakaro, north to Seh before the spring in company with a force of Imperial Guards—an honor guard only, but that need not be stated. We will charge him with assisting Lord Shonto in his task."

The Emperor played with a stack of Imperial reports. "It causes me grief to do this, Colonel, my own son but . . . he is not fit to rule." The Emperor shook his head, a slow gesture. He glanced up at Tadamoto for the briefest second and left the younger man to wonder if it was truly anguish he had seen written there. "He is not fit . . . so few are." The Emperor's head sank down and he stayed like that, face hidden for many minutes. "It is a difficult role that I play, Tadamoto-sum, sometimes . . . very difficult."

Tadamoto nodded. "Hakata said that Emperors are always alone, Sire. When difficult decisions are made, it is sadly true."

The Emperor nodded. "Yes," he almost whispered. "That will be all, Colonel, thank you."

Tadamoto bowed and began to back away, but as he reached the door the Emperor spoke again.

"Tadamoto-sum?"

"Sire?"

"Please, have Osha sent to me. Thank you."

Jaku nodded and backed out. Once outside he rose and walked with great calm down the hallway.

Why do I feel nothing? his thoughts echoed. Why nothing? He seemed to walk suspended in a place where the emotions did not dwell, a place of pure intellect where all thought was cold, disinterested. It would have been frightening, if he could have felt fear.

There is no hope for my brother—*governor* indeed. If he returned to the Capital while Akantsu lived, Katta would die. And Osha. . . . The Emperor was destroying everything they felt for each other as surely as he would see Katta dead. And Jaku Tadamoto was his most loyal advisor. He heard himself laugh, high-pitched, half strangled. He could not feel fear at that either.

Fourteen

The archivist who bore responsibility for administering the records of the Province of Seh was surprised to find a young woman requesting access to his domain—a secretary to the governor's daughter, no less. He was even more surprised to find that this young woman, Shimeko-sum, was not only educated but a great admirer of the order he maintained in Seh's archives. He had seldom felt so appreciated and found himself wondering why his own daughters did not have such inquiring minds.

Shimeko applied herself to her task with practiced discipline, determined to make a good impression on her new mistress but also because it was work she was familiar with, and in such alien surroundings there was some comfort in that. It was fortunate, for she found little comfort in the history of the Sect of the Eightfold Path.

The story told by the Imperial Historians was very different from what she had been taught in her own studies. As objective as she tried to remain, still, she had found it distressing. And now this well-bred young lady wanted Shimeko to relate all that she had learned to her. How was she to do that?

Carefully gathering her scrolls and papers together, Shimeko set out for Lady Nishima's chambers. The halls of the Imperial Palace were an astonishing maze, but to Shimeko's Botahist-trained memory they were barely a challenge. Several of the Priories in which she had lived were at least as complicated.

As she made her way toward Lady Nishima's apartment, she was aware that people often turned and watched her pass. She supposed that failed Botahist Sis-

ters seldom took service with Great Houses though she
really did not know and, in truth, it seemed unimportant
to her.

To gain admittance to the wing that contained Lady
Nishima's rooms Shimeko had to give a password and a
hand sign, which reminded her that she had once mem-
orized a Shonto hand signal on the Grand Canal. It
seemed so long ago.

A servant went off to announce Shimeko to her mistress, and she worked to control her nerves as she waited.

Lady Nishima was still haunted by her conversation
with Kitsura. Jaku Katta had readily agreed to use his
sources within the Imperial court to find out if Kitsura's
family were in danger. To Nishima's surprise he had even
agreed to have a letter delivered secretly to the Omawara
family—both acts that the Emperor would find deeply
suspicious if he were to know of them, and there was
every chance that the Emperor would know.

Did this mean that Jaku had truly fallen out of favor at
court? If so, then her uncle's belief that Jaku could help
secure the support of the Emperor was entirely wrong
and most dangerous.

All of this she found disturbing news. She touched the
folded letter Kitsura had delivered from Jaku and tried to
control her anger. Such presumption! To have made ad-
vances to Kitsura and then to ask her to deliver a letter
to Nishima! One expected more, even of an Imperial
Guardsman. She shuddered. How close she had come to
making a fool of herself. How very close.

There was no doubt that Jaku Katta was an opportunist
of the worst order. And now there was a great possibility
that he was no longer in the Emperor's favor. All that
remained was to hear from Kitsura's family to see if indeed Jaku had risked delivering the message. Did he really believe that Kitsura Omawara had no way of sending
letters secretly to her own family?

He expects so little of us, Nishima thought, not for the
first time. With some effort she pushed Jaku from her
thoughts.

It had been three days since Nishima had asked the
former Botahist nun, Shimeko, to research the cult that

had dwelt in Denji Gorge, and she had been consumed with curiosity the entire time. Shimeko was on her way with the results of her efforts even now. Nishima found it difficult to maintain her tranquillity.

Fortunately, she did not have to wait long. A servant tapped on her door and announced Shimeko.

"Ah, yes. Please, bring her to me."

The young woman was shown in and knelt, bowing, Nishima noted, in the plain fashion rather than in the style of her Order.

"Shimeko-sum, I trust you have been given quarters and some instruction as I requested?"

"I have, Lady Nishima, thank you."

"Is it more difficult than you imagined? Life beyond the priory?"

Shimeko shrugged. "It is not as different as one would expect, my lady. It is a small world contained within its own walls, seldom encountering the world beyond. In this way it is much the same. In other ways," she shrugged again, "it is not so similar."

Nishima nodded. "How went your search of our archive?"

"It is a small archive, Lady Nishima, as one would expect of an outer province. References to the Sect of the Eightfold Path were, therefore, few." She began to arrange her documents on the mats in front of her.

"Most of the written works of the Sect of the Eightfold Path were destroyed during what the historians refer to as the Inter-temple Wars. Much of what is now believed is undoubtedly conjecture. As you suggested, the Imperial Historians of the time—the reign of Emperor Chonsosa—made their dutiful records.

"The fanes beside the Lake of the Seven Masters were built after the time of our Lord, Botahara. References in the travel journals of Lord Bashu indicate that followers of Botahara had made their dwellings there as early as one hundred and sixty years after the Passing. It may be true that originally the sculptures were not meant to be dwellings but were only adapted to this function when the Botahist Sects began to war. Excuse me, Lady Nishima, do I speak only of things already known to you?"

"I confess to a poor memory for history, Shimeko-sum. Please, continue."

Shimeko looked back at her papers. "After the Passing, several different branches of Botahist teaching developed and these flourished according to the support of different Houses or even the Emperor. Large grants of land were often made to the temples and these, it is said, became the source of considerable wealth. This wealth was coveted by different Houses and by rival branches of Botahist doctrine—by the Emperor himself in some cases. This led to the Botahist fascination with the arts of war. They defended their possessions ruthlessly."

"At this time Botahist monks went about armed and some of the temples supported large armies. They rivaled the Emperor for power and often were able to make demands of the Great Council of State that the government dared not refuse. But the temples warred among themselves, and during this period many Botahist sects were destroyed, including the Sect of the Eightfold Path."

She looked up. "This differs from my own teaching, Lady Nishima. I was taught that the sects were destroyed by overzealous followers of the rival temples and also by the Emperor." Having said this, she returned to her papers.

"According to the histories, the Botahist temples weakened themselves during the Inter-temple Wars and finally the Emperor Chonso-sa, recognizing the opportunity, crushed the remaining sects. He limited the size of the Botahist estates and forbade the Botahist monks to carry arms."

Pausing for a moment, she pointed to three rolled scrolls. "These histories are written here, Lady Nishima, if you would care to read them yourself."

"I may look at them later, Shimeko-sum. I am curious, what did these Brothers believe? What was their doctrine?"

The former nun looked back down at her papers.

From what Nishima knew of the Sisters' training, this reference to written material was entirely unnecessary—the Acolyte's memory should have been close to flawless. Most curious.

"They believed in the Seven Paths to enlightenment, Lady Nishima." She hesitated. "They believed also that the act of physical love was the Eighth Path . . . you call them Brothers, Lady Nishima, but it seems there were Sisters also.''

"How very strange. Do we know the nature of their beliefs, Shimeko-sum?'' Nishima said with studied casualness.

"The scholars do not agree on this, Lady Nishima. It seems likely that the sect's doctrine was akin to the ancient Shodo Hermits' belief that the path through the Illusion lay in overcoming the senses. Unlike the Sect of the Eightfold Path, however, the Shodo Hermits did this through the experience of pain." Shimeko took a long, involuntary breath. "It is said they achieved levels of focus through meditation while undergoing what could only be described as torture. They would never cry out or show the slightest signs of pain no matter what was done to them. Indeed, it is believed that the Shodo Masters could turn the agony into any feeling they desired, and it would be of equal intensity. The followers of the Eightfold Path may have believed something similar, though they substituted pleasure for pain."

Lady Nishima suppressed a shudder.

"It is all written here, my lady," Shimeko said, looking down at her gathered scrolls.

"Yes. You said the scholars did not agree?"

Shimeko nodded. "There are other thoughts. One school believes there is evidence that the sect believed the soul was divided into halves that could only be united through the act of physical love. Another thought the Sect of the Eightfold Path believed that denial of the Illusion was futile, one found one's way through it like a person groping through fog. They wrote that the followers believed one must experience the falseness of the Illusion to see beyond it and desire is the essence of Illusion. There are other scholars with other thoughts, but these represent the main schools of belief, Lady Nishima."

"I see." Lady Nishima sat, lost in thought and then she met her secretary's gaze. "And what were you taught in the priory, Shimeko-sum?"

Shimeko looked down. "Only that the Eightfold Path was a heresy, my lady. Acolytes needed to know nothing more than that."

Nishima nodded. No doubt this was true.

"Will that be all, Lady Nishima?" Shimeko asked flatly.

Nishima smiled. "I thank you for your efforts, Shimeko-sum." She straightened a fold in her robe. "There is something else. . . . Before I left the Capital, it came to my attention that a senior Sister of your Order . . . your former Order, had taken an interest in one of my maids. Before this was known, the Sister had managed to learn some few things about myself and my House. Why would they have this interest in me, Shimeko-sum?"

Shimeko opened her hands. "You are Shonto, Lady Nishima."

"That would be all?"

"I do not know, Lady Nishima, but it is certainly enough."

"You know nothing of the Sisterhood's effort to spy on the Shonto?"

Shimeko sat in silence for several seconds. "I know, my lady, that senior Sister Morima, with whom I traveled to Seh, had come to observe your Spiritual Advisor."

"Brother Shuyun." Nishima said unnecessarily.

"Yes, my lady."

"Why?"

Shimeko sat staring at the floor for some time. "Within the Sisterhood it is the belief of some," she said in a whisper, "that Brother Shuyun is the Teacher who was spoken of. The Udumbara has blossomed in Monarta. I know it is said to be a rumor but it is not. Sisters have seen it."

"I see," Nishima said, surprised by the flatness of her voice. She looked at the young woman who sat before her, staring at the floor, almost huddled into herself, unable even to look up. She is in the grip of some terrible inner battle, Nishima realized. "Do you believe Shuyun is the Teacher, Shimeko-sum?"

The woman seemed to draw into herself even more. "Brother Shuyun says he is not, Lady Nishima." She shrugged, tried to speak, then her shoulders moved again like a weak convulsion. "Perhaps . . . perhaps he is not. I do not know."

The two women sat for some time, the distance between them a vast gulf of experience, belief, and desire.

"That will be all, Shimeko-sum," Nishima said at last, "I thank you."

Fifteen

S now fell on the night of the Celebration of the First Moon—the substance of clouds floating to earth, layering Seh with white, like the Plum Blossom Winds of spring. Snows were neither frequent nor extreme in the Province of Seh and for that reason were greeted as pleasant novelties, relief from the winter rains. The First Moon Festival proceeded without pause for the weather.

The people of Seh gathered in the villages and the Manor Houses of their liege-lords where the rites and festivities took place. By far the most elaborate, if not the largest, gathering was held in the center courtyard of the Imperial Governor's Palace. Many of the peers of the northern province had accepted invitations and the fact that several of these lords represented the military power of Seh was not incidental.

The governor watched the celebrations from the top of the covered stairs that led from the Great Hall down into the courtyard. Shifting about occasionally in his unfamiliar state robes, Lord Shonto sat in the place of honor and managed to appear captivated by the scene. Below him on the stairs sat the Ladies Nishima and Kitsura, senior officials of the Council of Seh, several lords of high rank, and various guests of note, Lady Okara among them. Those who did not sit with Lord Shonto in comparative comfort, stood under parasols in throngs about the courtyard. Above them, strings of lanterns cast a pleasing light on the long silk robes and illuminated the slowly falling snow.

Dressed in costumes of fox and bear and owl, children performed a dance to the music of flute and drum. It was a more complex dance than one would have expected of their age, very stylized and rigid in its movements, yet it was not marred by a single misstep. The performers approached their roles with the utmost gravity, apparently unaware that this was certainly the least serious part of the ceremony.

Earlier in the evening Botahist monks had performed ancient rites in observance of the First Moon and to ensure a bountiful and harmonious year—burning incense to the four winds and chanting the prayer for spring rains. Once that had been done, however, the celebration took on a more festive air. Many-colored silk banners stirred in response to the occasional breath of wind as did the fine robes of the men and women present. Perfume mingled with the scent of burning oils and the pungent odor of charcoal, stirring themselves together as though the courtyard were a giant perfumer's bowl.

The children's dance ended and Lord Shonto, in his official capacity, congratulated the performers as though they were the finest Sonsa in all of Wa. Gifts were distributed, and the dancers bowed their thanks in great style.

Servants hurried about with cauldrons of steaming rice wine, for no one could be without rice wine for the first glimpse of the moon. Anxious eyes kept looking skyward, hoping that one of the breaks that appeared occasionally in the clouds would position itself propitiously, but their attention could not remain there.

A sudden burst of flame signaled the entrance of the dragon, as one of Seh's finest dancers appeared in the elaborate costume. Lady Okara had taken a hand in the design and her efforts, coupled with the skills of the dancer, created a stunning effect. Long of tail, the blue-scaled monster slithered most convincingly from shadow to shadow to the delight of man, woman, and child. After several attempts the dragon captured the moon, a silvered disk illuminated by lantern light. Attendants snuffed many of the lights then, casting the courtyard into partial shadow.

Far off, a conch sounded a long, lonely note muted by the falling snow. The dragon slithered on, gloating over its prize. Again the note, closer this time. The dragon pricked up its ears but then went back to its exploration of the courtyard, darting suddenly at a group of children who fled, screaming.

A long, sustained note came from over a nearby wall. The dragon stopped in its tracks, turning dramatically. Fire licked from a strategically placed pot as though it were the breath of the dragon.

Backlit under a great arch, Yoshinaga, the Seventh Prince, appeared, leading his gray war horse. The dragon began to thrash its tail and sway back and forth.

Leaving his mount behind, the second dancer drew his sword and entered the courtyard. Battle ensued—dragon cunning and claw against courage and steel. The dance itself was ancient of form though visitors from the Capital were surprised to see that, in Seh, some liberties were taken.

Wooden drums beat out an ominous time. The climax of the battle took place as Yoshinaga, wrapped in the dragon's tail, drove his sword into the dragon's soft breast. The dragon fell upon him and with his last strength the Prince tossed the disk of the moon out into the darkness.

Everyone turned now, for if all had been timed correctly the crescent moon should rise over the wall in that instant. A soft glow in the cloud began to grow and then, through a small tear, the moon appeared to sighs of relief and raised cups of rice wine. Eyes returned to earth in time to see the spirit of Yoshinaga, now clad in a flowing white robe, mount his gray steed and ride off into the night. The dragon was gone.

The performance at an end, the gathering began to move inside except for those few who remained on vigil hoping to sight a falling star—said to be Yoshinaga riding across the heavens—a sign of good fortune for those who witnessed it.

The celebration broke into many groups and spread through three halls. Music and dance and poetry and endless talk were the evening's fare and there was no one to complain of too rich a diet.

Lady Nishima planned all her activities so that she might avoid contact with General Jaku Katta, and so practiced at this skill was she that the General was beginning to realize that, as a tactician, the lady showed more subtlety than he had ever aspired to. Once, when he had been close to speaking to her, Nishima had drawn

him into a discussion with several of Seh's least interesting conversationalists and then abandoned him there,
without the skills to make a polite escape as she had
done.

With her practiced eye, Lady Nishima noticed that a
number of prominent lords had disappeared, as had
most of Lord Shonto's senior advisors. She turned toward the governor's dais and found her father slipping
out through an open screen followed by personal guards
and Initiate Brother Shuyun. She offered a silent prayer
to Botahara.

There were perhaps a dozen and a half men gathered
in the room, dressed in their finest robes and seated on
silk cushions. Shonto sat before them on a low dais and
to his right and left knelt the Major Chancellor, Lord
Gitoyo, and the aging Lord Akima, Minister of War.
Kamu, General Hojo, and Brother Shuyun, as the lord's
senior advisors, sat nearby, while General Jaku and Lord
Komawara were barely farther away.

Facing the dais were the lords of Seh's most important
Houses, each sitting with the kinsmen and senior members of their staff. Prominent among them was the Lord
of the Toshaki House accompanied by his eldest son and
Toshaki Shinga, general of Seh's standing garrison.
Shonto knew of Lord Toshaki by reputation only and was
surprised by the man's apparent youth. Toshaki had seen
at least seventy First Moon Festivals in his time, yet he
seemed like a man whose gray hair and beard had turned
long before their time. Lord Toshaki was aware of his
status in Seh, and though there was no greater distance
between him and the others, he sat apart all the same. If
Shonto was any judge of such things, Lord Toshaki would
allow his kinsman, Toshaki Shinga, to speak for him.

Of the province's other major Houses, Lord Taiki Kiyorama came accompanied only by his senior officer and
he bowed lower than required to Shuyun and Kamu in
recognition of their service to his son who had come near
to losing his life in the palace garden.

Lord Ranan was another matter. The Ranan House had
been the right hand of the Hanama Emperors in Seh for
two hundred years and had enriched themselves accord-

ingly. To say they were resented in the north would be an understatement of considerable proportion. Nonetheless, they were wealthy and still held power in the province, if not the favor of the Emperor that had nominally passed to the Toshaki.

It was this group that Shonto needed to win to his cause if he were to raise an army. Lord Taiki was already preparing his forces, but the rivalry between the Toshaki and the Ranan did not bode well for an alliance.

Shonto nodded to Kamu who turned and bowed to the gathered lords and officials.

"Lord Shonto Motoru, Imperial Governor of the Province of Seh."

All present bowed as their rank required and returned to the sitting position.

Shonto nodded in response and sat quietly for a moment, surveying the gathering. "The Shonto House is honored by your presence, Lords of Seh. The ancestor for whom I was named rode into battle with your grandsires and great grandsires." Shonto reached back and took a sword from its stand. "This is the sword my grandfather presented to the Emperor Jirri—legends now—yet this sword rode into battle in an Emperor's hands, and Seh retained its borders." He paused and looked around the group again.

"My Emperor has charged me to end the barbarian raids across the border into Seh and to this end I have focused my efforts. It became apparent that we needed to inform ourselves of the situation in the wastelands. To accomplish this we chose the most direct course—we sent men into the desert to look with their own eyes."

A small shifting of men in the room, eyes meeting for an instant, then all attention returned to Shonto.

"What we have learned will be related to you and no doubt you will find it as disturbing as I have. We enter a time of great decisions where our actions will affect the course of the history of our Empire. Let it be said by future generations that at this time we were filled with the wisdom of Hakata and the spirit of Emperor Jirri.

"We must speak openly, my lords, for the guarded spirit and the hidden intentions will bring us down as surely as a barbarian sword. I would know your thoughts,

Lords of Seh, if you will honor me with them.'' Shonto fell silent for a moment, but before he could proceed a cousin of the Ranan Lord bowed to Shonto and spoke.

''In this spirit, Lord Governor, I would ask of rumors that whisper throughout Seh.'' He was an older man, obviously chosen for his habits of speech, for he sounded like an old scholar though he looked as hardy as an old peasant. ''The people ask; where are the Kintari? And it is said there is a barbarian in your service.''

They were bold questions put in a manner more direct than should have been used with an Imperial Governor, not to mention a lord of such note, yet Shonto could see the approval of the men of Seh.

''Lord Ranan,'' Shonto's voice was low, ''I should like to ask the same question of the Kintari. . . .'' He laid his sword across his knees. ''As to the barbarian, we shall speak of him now, if you will consent to hear of the journey into the desert?''

The lords nodded and Shonto continued.

''As it is difficult for men of Seh to travel in the barbarian lands, it was with some risk that we did so. The only men of our Empire who can travel into the desert with any hope of living should they encounter tribesmen are the healing Brothers. For this reason my Advisor, Brother Shuyun, traveled across our border. He was accompanied by Lord Komawara, also dressed as a Botahist monk.

Turning to Komawara, Shonto nodded and the lord bowed. His wound no longer required binding and all of it but a small purple mark on his temple was hidden by newly grown hair.

''Brother Shuyun and I traveled into the steppe at the time of the Field Burning Festival,'' Komawara began, his voice stilted but strong. ''Although we saw increasing signs of barbarian patrols the farther into the wastes we traveled, we met no tribesmen for many days. At the spring of the Brothers we found signs that barbarian tribesmen used it as a camp, though they were not there at the time. One can only surmise where they might have been.

''We traveled farther into the steppe, indeed we approached the edge of the desert itself. As we did so, we were trapped in a draw by a band of tribesmen but, due

to the skills of Brother Shuyun, we were able to overcome these brigands. We questioned one—Brother Shuyun speaks their tongue—and found that they were of a
tribe that hid from the Khan, refusing to join the chieftain's armies.

"As we were convinced these men did not raid across
our border, it was agreed that one of their number would
guide us in return for the lives of the others."

Again the lords exchanged glances but said nothing.

"This is the tribesman you have heard rumors of, Lord
Ranan. Our understanding of the tribes' customs was imperfect and we did not realize that this one barbarian had
traded his life and honor for the lives of his kinsmen.
That is why he is with us still. He is honor bound to
serve Brother Shuyun and cannot be released from that
now."

"Barbarian honor?" General Toshaki smirked. "A spy
in your midst seems more likely, Lord Komawara."

"I have placed my life in this barbarian's hands on
more than one occasion, General. I am still alive. He is
more than honor bound, as the barbarians understand it.
He is truly frightened by the chieftain called the Golden
Khan, believing this man will bring destruction down
upon the tribes and their way of life."

"He shows wisdom in this, at least," General Toshaki
said to half-smiles from the other lords.

Komawara continued his tale, saying nothing of the
dragon shrine or the gold coins. The lords of Seh listened
with apparent politeness until Komawara described the
encampment of the army they had found in the desert.

"Excuse me, Lord Shonto, Lord Komawara," Akima
interrupted. "But it is difficult to imagine a barbarian
army that has more men than the total population of barbarians has ever been. How can you explain this?"

"As I am unaware of the last Imperial census of the
barbarian tribes," Komawara said acidly, "I cannot answer you, Lord Akima. When were these figures com-
piled?"

"My lords," Kamu interrupted, "before we begin to
discuss what is and is not possible, it may be best to hear
what Lord Komawara and Brother Shuyun have seen with
their own eyes."

Both Akima and Komawara gave half bows toward the dais.

"We left the encampment following the trail of the force that made its way toward our border. We were a day catching them. From a rise we were able to see a barbarian force of no less than forty thousand men. It was clear daylight—there could have been no mistake. This army turned east, it is believed to winter with the tribes of the steppe. Having seen this, we returned to Seh as quickly as our mounts would travel." Komawara bowed to Lord Shonto and the gathered lords and then sat rigidly silent.

"I thank you, Lord Komawara. I honor you and Brother Shuyun for this journey undertaken in our time of need." Shonto turned to the gathered lords. "As you see, the situation is one that requires decisive action. Now is the time for questions and discussion, my lords."

No one spoke. Shonto wondered who would be chosen as the voice of this group and watched the silent selection with interest. Finally, General Toshaki Shinga bowed to his governor. So, Shonto thought, the Toshaki will lead here.

"This is a delicate situation, Governor Shonto. We have been asked to speak our thoughts, but I for one do not wish to offend anyone present by arguing their beliefs . . . or calling their judgment into question."

"General Toshaki, in Shonto councils we speak our minds openly—to do otherwise could bring us to the greatest disaster. I have asked you all to share your years of experience and wisdom. If this requires that you disagree with me or any of my staff, so be it. Please, speak as you would in your own council."

Toshaki bowed. "The estimate of the size of this barbarian army seems beyond possibility, though I would hesitate to question what Lord Komawara and Brother Shuyun have seen with their own eyes," he added quickly. "Is it possible the barbarians war among themselves?"

Shonto turned to Shuyun who gave his double bow.

His voice was a surprise in this company, soft and quiet as though he felt no need to force his opinions on anyone. "It is the opinion of the tribesman Lord Komawara has spoken of that the Khan has every intention of invading Seh in the spring. The tribes that oppose him are small in number, Lord Toshaki, and scattered. They are no threat to this Khan. I can conceive of no other reason to gather an army of such size except to war upon our Empire."

"Excuse me, Brother, if I have difficulty believing one can hear truth from a barbarian," General Toshaki said evenly.

Shuyun's face did not change, though the hue of Komawara's skin seemed to darken.

The kinsman of Lord Ranan bowed now and Kamu acknowledged him.

"Sire," the younger man said with a note of respect, "there is yet another question that we would ask." Reaching into his sleeve, he removed a small leather pouch which he opened with some care. Retrieving something from its interior, he passed it to a Ranan officer who in turn moved forward to give this to Kamu.

The Shonto steward placed the small object on the dais before Lord Shonto who barely looked down.

"Yes, Lord Ranan?" Shonto said. Many eyes strained to catch a glimpse of what lay glinting on the dais.

"Coins such as this were taken from a raiding barbarian in my lord's western fief. You will see a strange dragon form on its face. What do these signify, my lord wonders? To our knowledge there has never been gold found among the barbarians before."

Shonto reached out and pushed the coin with the tip of his sword. "Let the others see this," Shonto said quietly and Kamu retrieved the coin, handing it to Lord Akima.

"What you see, Lords of Seh, is a talisman of the cult that is linked to this Khan who has risen among the tribes."

"You have seen these coins before, Lord Shonto?"

Shonto nodded. "Other raiders have carried them."

"There seems to be a great depth to your knowledge, Lord Shonto," the senior Ranan lord said. His voice was deep and rich and carried weight among the voices heard so far. "Do the barbarians mine gold, then? Or shall we

assume it has been stolen from some source we are not
aware of? Some lord's secret treasure?"

Shonto contemplated this for some seconds. "The gold
comes from Yankura, Lord Ranan, that is all we know.
How it makes its way into the desert is unclear. What
purpose it serves is also a mystery."

One could almost hear the snow falling in the courtyard. The senior Ranan Lord looked at his palm as though
he would read his next words there. A lamp sputtered, a
drop of condensation finding the flame.

"Do you suggest that someone in our Empire pays
some form of tribute to the barbarians, Lord Governor?"
the Ranan Lord said, his voice suddenly quiet.

"It is a likely explanation," Shonto answered calmly,
as though what he said was not an accusation of high
treason. Whom the accusation was aimed at no one
needed to ask.

Ranan nodded. The coin had reached General Toshaki
now.

"The purpose of this cult," General Toshaki said, "is
it known?"

"It seems to give legitimacy to the Khan, General."

"How is it that we have learned this, Lord Shonto?"
Toshaki asked.

Shonto nodded to Komawara.

Komawara bowed rigidly. "The Kalam, the tribesman
who serves Shuyun-sum, he has spoken of the dragon
cult. Also, when we traveled in the desert, we saw the
shrine of the dragon."

General Toshaki looked at the senior member of his
House who gave the smallest gesture with his hand.

"Lord Komawara," the general said, taking his cue.
"There is another rumor that has been whispered in
Seh." The edges of his mouth curled in the slightest
smile. "It is said that you saw the remains of a dragon
on your recent journey. Can such a thing be true?"

Hojo interrupted, ignoring the general and looking directly at his Toshaki master. "Rumors, Sire, are often
smoke without flame." And he smiled also.

The senior Toshaki lord held Hojo's gaze for a few
seconds, then he visibly dismissed him, turning to Komawara. "Lord Komawara, on the honor of your family,

do you believe you saw the remains of a dragon in the desert?''

Komawara hesitated, darting a glance at Shonto. "I saw the skeleton of a large beast, Lord Toshaki.''

"A large beast, Lord Komawara?'' he asked, as though addressing a child. "What nature of beast?''

"A beast that resembled the dragon embossed on the coin, Lord Toshaki.'' Komawara kept his voice even.

General Toshaki shook his head, looking down as though he hid a smile. Then he spoke suddenly. "One dragon, Lord Komawara, or forty thousand?''

Stifled laughter was heard around the room.

"One beast, Lord Toshaki. One only.'' Komawara said too quietly.

Toshaki nodded toward the young lord, almost a mock bow.

The senior Toshaki lord gestured his kinsman to silence.

"This situation we have heard described is of consequence to the entire Empire. General Jaku, does the Son of Heaven prepare an army as we speak?''

"That is our hope, Lord Toshaki, though we do not yet know,'' Jaku said fixing the older man with his cold gaze.

"Ahh,'' the lord said, looking away. "Lord Shonto, this is a grave matter. I wish to take council with my kinsmen and advisors.'' He bowed to Lord Shonto.

Lord Taiki spoke without warning. "Lord Toshaki, Lords of Seh. I tell you in all truthfulness that if we do not begin to prepare an army now, we make a decision to surrender Seh to our ancient enemy. It is not the epitaph I would choose for my tomb.''

There was a short silence.

"My lord wishes to consult his advisors, also, Lord Shonto,'' the junior Ranan lord spoke into the silence.

The council was at an end. With great dignity Shonto nodded to those around him, rose and left, carrying his own sword.

Shortly after the Lords of Seh had gone, Shonto returned to speak to his staff. Jaku and Lord Akima were not present. Komawara, Lord Taiki, and the Major Chancellor, Gitoyo, were the only outsiders. Shonto seated himself on the dais and regarded the men around him. *"Blind are the sighted and deaf the hearing . . . only those who look within will find truth."*

Shuyun made a sign to Botahara at this quotation.

Shonto shook his head slowly. "General Hojo?"

"It would appear that the Lords of Seh believe you are to be the victim of a hired barbarian army, an army paid in gold by our revered Emperor. No doubt the lords of Seh believe that you try to raise an army in your defense. They cannot believe the Emperor would endanger part of his Empire to bring down the Shonto. There will be no support coming from these men. Lord Toshaki, I think, will do nothing that has not been ordered by the Emperor. And Lord Ranan, though he hates the Yamaku, will take no unnecessary risks to thwart their Imperial ambitions. The minor houses, even if they could be convinced, would make little difference."

Shonto nodded. He gestured to the others and each man in turn nodded agreement. Shonto clapped his hands loudly.

"And the Emperor's support? Truthfully?"

"It is entirely dependent on Jaku Katta. But in all honesty, I think it is unlikely. After Denji Gorge, it seems the Emperor has reason to distrust his Guard Commander—it takes very little to earn the Emperor's distrust. The rumors that Jaku has fallen from favor may have truth in them. Katta-sum may not even be sure of his own situation."

Shonto looked at Kamu.

"I agree, Sire. We may hope for the Emperor's support, but we should begin to take the actions we would take if it were not forthcoming. We dare not wait."

Shonto sat contemplating this like a man considering a move at gii—and like a gii Master he showed no sign of being affected by his situation. It gave his retainers hope.

"Lord Komawara," Shonto said warmly, "you could do nothing but tell the truth. It could not be helped. I regret this deeply, but tomorrow we meet to plan our retreat from Seh." He pulled the sword that was the Emperor's gift partly from its scabbard. "Kamu-sum, start-

ing now we will have no one but those present in councils
unless I order otherwise. We give up this pretense—the
government of Seh seems to be made up of informers.
No guards but our own around our chambers.'' Shonto
slid the blade in and out of its scabbard.

"We have one other move that we can make in this
game before retreat and cover. Kamu-sum, prepare a tract
that says the Government of the Province of Seh is paying
gold for the service of armed men. They will not come
in time, perhaps, but they will come as we move south.''

The Major Chancellor, Lord Gitoyo, bobbed quickly.
"Sire, Lord Governor . . . the Emperor demands his
taxes. We dare not delay longer. There is certainly not
enough gold to raise an army.''

"Huh.'' Shonto examined the flawless metal blade.
"We must not keep the Emperor waiting for his taxes.
That would be unthinkable.'' He smiled at those around
him. "Entirely unthinkable.''

Komawara gave a deep bow. "There is one other action we could consider, Lord Shonto.''

Shonto nodded.

"The springs closest to our border in the steppe—they
could be poisoned as winter ends.''

Komawara returned to the festivities, though his heart
wanted to be gone. An urge to race a horse with a great
heart across the hills took hold of him, as though he
could leave what he felt behind. *His own countrymen,
northerners, were surrendering Seh to the barbarians!* When
the Khan swept across the border with his army, *then*
these men would be ready to fight—when the only sen-
sible course of action would be to retreat as Lord Shonto
planned. They would all die so it could be said that they
did not abandon Seh, despite the odds. The bravery of
fools. . . .

Pulling his thoughts away from this problem, he
searched the gathering for a glimpse of Lady Nishima.
She had spoken to him earlier and he had alternately felt
delight and despair ever since. Her robe of rich blue with
its pattern of snow falling on the Mountain of the Pure
Spirit was nowhere to be seen. Despair.

Lord Toshaki's eldest son, Toshaki Yoshihira, surrounded by a group of laughing kinsmen, rose from a low table. He spotted Komawara as he gained his feet and stopped. Breaking into a grin, he made a sudden extravagant bow and then rose, his face flushed from drink.

"Lord Komawara," he enunciated with the care of a man who had drunk his limit, "it is my hope that in future first Moon Festivals that Prince Yoshinaga slaying the dragon will be replaced by Lord Komawara *meeting* the dragon."

Toshaki's cousins showed some concern at this insult and their laughter was subdued. Komawara had a reputation as a swordsman that was respected.

"Perhaps it could be replaced by Lord Toshaki discovering foolhardiness in a wine cup," Komawara said evenly.

Suddenly Shuyun and Lord Gitoyo's son were beside him. "There are more important fights than this, Lord Komawara," Captain Gitoyo said quietly.

"Listen to your friend, Lord Komawara," Toshaki slurred. "You must save your courage for the barbarian hordes."

Komawara felt restraining hands on either of his arms. "I would not have the blood of a fool on my sword," Gitoyo whispered. "Come away from this. You of all people do not need to prove bravery."

Komawara gave way to the pressure on his arm and began to turn away.

Toshaki bent over the nearby table and retrieved a lacquered chopstick. He brandished this like a sword and stepped into the guard position. "Lord Komawara, you need a proper weapon to slay dragons and barbarian hordes. I would be honored if you would take mine."

Komawara broke free of his companions and spun back toward the Toshaki lord but, impossibly, Shuyun stood facing Toshaki, his back blocking Komawara.

"My lord," Shuyun said quietly, "that is a dangerous weapon to wield in the governor's hall."

Toshaki stood with his chopstick before him like a sword, suddenly looking unsure of himself. Botahist monks did not confront peers.

The implement disappeared from Toshaki's hand as the

monk's arm became a blur of motion. Toshaki stepped
back into his kinsman.

"Such a weapon should never be drawn in polite company."

Again Shuyun moved with a speed that was impossible
to follow. There was a crack of wood hitting wood, not
loud but strangely piercing. Shuyun bowed low before
Toshaki who stared down at the chopstick Shuyun had
driven into the table.

"May your journey bring you wisdom, Sire," Shuyun
almost whispered.

Toshaki stood staring at Shuyun for several seconds,
his face contorted and unreadable. Then, realizing that
his supporters retreated, he turned away and disappeared
among the crowd.

Shuyun stood watching the young lord's retreat, then
he faced his companions.

Komawara's gaze was fixed on the point where Lord
Toshaki had disappeared. He looked at Shuyun suddenly
and he shook his head. "You should not, Brother," he
whispered. "Such things are beneath you."

With a nod to Gitoyo, he turned and went off in the
opposite direction Toshaki had taken. The people present
became a blur of colored silk and the sounds a low roar
in which nothing could be distinguished. Komawara
trembled with anger.

*I have become the object of ridicule among my own
countrymen,* the lord thought. *And despite all that I have
done, my province will be put to the sword and the torch.*

He stumbled out beyond the row of pillars toward the
doors. And there he saw Lady Nishima in serious conversation with General Jaku Katta, of the Imperial Guard.
She faced toward Komawara as she spoke, but she did
not see him, that was clear.

He stood for a moment looking at this scene and then
passed through the great doors into the courtyard. Like
Yoshinaga, he disappeared into the night.

It had not been easy for Lady Nishima to slip away;
she was, after all, the governor's daughter, but she was
becoming experienced in such matters. The sounds of
music and conversation from the hall were barely muted
by the pillar she stood behind yet it would be difficult to

leave the hall entirely without passing out into a cold night.

She tapped a closed fan into the palm of her hand in what looked like impatience but was really a disguise for anxiety. After she had successfully avoided Jaku Katta all evening, he had sent her a poem that he knew she could not ignore.

She had struggled to read in the poor light:

> *Season of cold hearts*
> *No warmth from the white robe,*
> *Snow upon the shinta leaves.*
> *Who knows how deep the frost shall reach?*

> *There is something you must hear*

Nishima's heart raced. Some part of her hoped that Jaku would prove to be honorable and this hope unsettled her. Surely it was the worst foolishness. Look how he had acted so recently with Kitsu-sum! She was about to return to the gathering when a dark form appeared down the row of columns. Though it required some effort, Nishima waited with what she hoped would be an appearance of calm.

Jaku walked toward her, his strong, graceful form appearing and disappearing as he went from light into shadow into light again. Finally he stepped into the same shadow that Nishima occupied. Gray eyes almost seemed to glow in the pale light. Jaku bowed deeply.

Nishima nodded. "General. . . ." She was about to pursue a polite course of conversation but caught herself. "What is this matter you have written of, General Jaku?"

If Jaku felt this was an insult, he did not show it.

"It is something that should be spoken of in more private surroundings," Jaku said, his voice low.

"Perhaps it should be spoken of in the presence of my uncle," Nishima said curtly.

"This is information for your ears, Lady Nishima. It is to show that my intentions are honorable, though I fear that they will be misunderstood as they have been in the past."

"You wrong me, General—I was not aware that your intentions had been misunderstood." Nishima waved her fan open. "What is this information you speak of? The night grows cold, General Jaku."

Jaku nodded, looking over his shoulder quickly. "I am concerned, Nishima-sum," he met her eyes for a second, but when she did not react to him dropping her title he went on quickly. "I fear the Emperor will not respond to my plea for troops: the intrigues of the court are beyond imagining and difficult to untangle, even while living in the palace. The webs spun in the Emperor's court are such that I risked much to have written as I did, for myself and my family."

"Do you suggest, General, that the Emperor will not respond to your letters as you hope?"

Jaku hesitated. "It is a possibility, Lady Nishima."

"Huh." She waited.

After it was apparent she would say no more, Jaku went on. "The Emperor's support is desperately needed, I know, but if it cannot be obtained, Lady Nishima, I will not return quietly to the Capital." Again he searched her eyes. "I will warn my family and remain in Seh to do what I can. Though it is said by some that Jaku Katta takes only the course of greatest opportunity, I will fight beside the Shonto though I will gain the enmity of the Son of Heaven."

Nishima looked away. A man stepped out from behind a pillar not far off, hesitated, and then passed through the doors leading to the courtyard.

"Tell me, Katta-sum," Nishima almost whispered, "will the Emperor send troops to us? Is there no hope?"

She watched the guardsman as he considered her question.

"I am not without influence at court, Nishima-sum, but others may hold sway—while I am here. It is . . . it is possible that my voice will not carry, it pains me to say."

Nishima nodded sadly as she looked down at the floor. "And this mad design to bring down my father, you took no part in it?"

"Once I had learned of it," Jaku stepped closer and lowered his voice, "I took some time to speak, it is true. My loyalties were tested . . . until I spoke to you at the Celebration of the Emperor's Ascension. My shame that I did not speak sooner."

Nishima's fan stopped in the middle of its sweep. A warm hand touched her cheek and she pulled away. Looking up she met Jaku's gray eyes, as impenetrable as cloud. Turning away she walked back into the bright hall.

Sixteen

Nishima unfolded the letter for the second time and read the single poem.

> *Season of cold hearts*
> *No warmth from this white robe,*
> *Snow upon the shinta leaves.*
> *Who knows how deep the frost shall reach?*
>
> *There is something you must hear.*

Nishima's thoughts whirled as though the Nagana blew through her mind, swirling everything into a tangle. Jaku had lied to her. She was more sure of this than she was of her own name, and far more sure than she was of her feelings. Although she would not have evidence until letters arrived from Kitsura's family, there was no doubt. Jaku Katta was no longer in favor at court. It was all a pose. She wondered again if her father truly relied on the guardsman to gain the Emperor's support—for in reality, Jaku's efforts would almost certainly insure the Emperor's refusal.

And Jaku had been involved in the plot to bring down her House. No doubt he hoped to raise the other Great Houses against the Emperor who had brought down the Shonto, or perhaps it would just be a quiet murder in the Imperial Apartments, and then place Nishima Fanisan Shonto on the Dragon Throne . . . destroying her life in every way.

And yet, and yet. Nishima had pulled away at Jaku's touch . . . not because this brought her no pleasure. A single touch of his hand caused her body to betray her entirely. She found herself wanting to believe him, or worse yet, knowing what Jaku was and not caring. No, she could never allow him close to her again. He was worse than an opportunist, he was without honor. To bring down those she loved and pose as her savior! She pulled his letter from her sleeve and tore it deliberately into shreds. Childish but satisfying.

A bell sounded far off, muffled by the few inches of snow that covered Rhojo-ma. It was almost morning and she had not slept, still wore formal robes under the lined over-robe she had donned against the cold. She plunged a poker into the charcoal burner and rearranged the coals to let the air flow through. A wave of warmth reached out and Nishima pulled the fine silks of her robes close, pushing her hands into the sleeves.

Nishima lay down on the cushions and closed her eyes, but sleep was not near. She examined the room she had been given. A pleasant place, almost bare but for her writing table, a small stand bearing an arrangement of winter flora, and a three-section painted screen displaying scenes of a spring party under the plum blossoms. A thick rug made by the tribes was set squarely in the middle of the straw-matted floor and on this her cushions were arranged. Three lamps washed the room in warm light, reflecting off the lacquered beams and posts.

A simple place, without the clutter some people preferred. When very young Nishima's true father had once taken her to the home of the Shonto vassal-merchant, Tanaka. A lifetime of trading had burdened him with the most unbelievable collection of furnishings. Cabinets and trunks, chests with drawers, and, most surprising to her, Tanaka owned *chairs*. She had never sat in a chair before. Nishima had a clear memory of climbing up into one of these elaborate oddities to perch, swinging her feet, pretending she was a princess. The idea of being a princess had not seemed frightening then.

Nishima closed her eyes again. Her thoughts became lost in other images; Jaku Katta's animal eyes, a dark wooden box of tiny drawers each containing a child's treasure, the view from Lady Okara's terrace, the sound of spring rain on tile, the touch of a man's hand on her breast. Nothing that could be remembered when she awoke to early morning light.

She was *cold*! The charcoal had long since given up its heat. She sat up awkwardly, not allowing her hands out into the frigid air. A servant peered in through a crack in the screens.

"There is a warm bath waiting, Lady Nishima."

"May Botahara chant your name," Nishima said and her servant bowed.

She felt like ice as she slipped into the steaming water and expected to bob to the surface as she had once seen a block of ice do as it slipped from the shore into the moving river.

I will never be warm again, she thought, *or at least not until spring.*

Nishima came back to the question that she had asked herself most of the night: should she tell her father about Jaku's situation at court? And if so, how would she present this information so that it would not seem she doubted his abilities. It was a delicate situation. Her uncle indulged her terribly, she knew, but his knowledge of the intrigues of the Empire was vast and his ability to gather and sift information was legendary. Nishima wondered at her own temerity venturing to advise the gii Master.

He has so much to consider, she told herself, *and Jaku has an interest in me that I have been able to use to my father's advantage. I wish only to help. I am only another source of information and what I have to say he can weigh as he does every other report he receives. Presented as information only I'm sure he will not take offense.*

By the time feeling had began to come back into her body, Nishima had decided to wait a few more days and hope that Kitsura would receive a message from her family. It was slim evidence, but it would strengthen her argument at least somewhat. She could also fall back on a ploy of her youth: go see her father and test his mood before proceeding.

Shuyun waited with his usual ease. It was early morning, just barely light, but it often seemed to the monk that Lord Shonto slept as little as the Botahist-trained. He had been summoned to his Lord's chambers by a half-awake servant—the First Moon Festival of the previous night had taken its toll on the palace staff.

Despite the calm that he displayed, Shuyun was anxious to complete his meeting with his liege-lord so that

he would be free to attend to another matter: Lord Komawara had not been seen since the incident with the
young Toshaki lord the night before.

A guard entered the room and bowed to Shuyun. Lord
Shonto would speak with him.

The Imperial Governor of the Province of Seh sat upon
a cushion this morning, not a dais, and he seemed absorbed in peeling a piece of fruit. He nodded in return
to Shuyun's bow and bobbed his head toward a second
cushion.

To Shonto's left a second table stood, a lacquered chopstick embedded vertically in the top.

"I begin to wonder if this is an odd dislike of tables,
Brother Shuyun," Shonto said as he worked at his fruit.
The lord turned his head to regard his Spiritual Advisor
and raised an eyebrow before returning to his task.

Shuyun gave a half bow. "I was concerned that Lord
Komawara would injure or perhaps kill the son of a man
you would hope for an ally, Lord Shonto."

"Huh." Shonto nodded. "Lord Komawara should not
need to be restrained in such circumstances. Toshaki was
very insulting?"

"According to my understanding of the ways of Seh
he could hardly have offered more offense, Sire."

Shonto finished peeling and began to break the fruit
into pieces. "It is not likely that Yoshihira would have
behaved so if he had thought his father was planning to
come to us." He popped a piece into his mouth and
chewed with some concentration, eyes closed. "It is hard
to know which of the two was more foolish." He opened
his eyes and smiled. "Ah, well, youth will find foolishness in the house of wisdom. Perhaps, in the future, it
might be possible to find some less conspicuous way to
deal with such a situation?"

Shuyun bowed. "I apologize for acting in this manner."

Shonto waved his hand. "I regret not witnessing it
more than I am concerned for the effects on young Toshaki's reputation."

"I could demonstrate this as we speak, Sire, if you
wish."

Shonto held up his hands. "We will let the furnishings
live in peace for while, Shuyun-sum, I thank you."

The monk nodded.

"Lord Komawara has not been seen this morning, I understand?" Shonto began eating a second piece of fruit.

"I was told the same thing, Sire."

Shonto did not answer immediately. "I will have him found if he does not appear by midday. We need his knowledge of the desert. As Lord Komawara suggested, I will send parties into the wastes to poison the nearest springs. This is an arrow that will have to be aimed perfectly. We must send out men before the Khan's army moves but not too soon or the springs will run themselves clean before the barbarian army comes to use them.

"Tactics of delay," Shonto said popping another section of fruit into his mouth. "Not to be mistaken for tactics of desperation."

Seventeen

Lord Komawara Samyamu turned his horse off the road into a narrow path through snow-covered trees. The day was gray, windless, cast over with snowclouds that stretched from horizon to horizon with monotonous uniformity.

So still was the day that the horse's breath appeared in the cold air and floated there as unmoving as the clouds overhead. Cries of birds and the creaking of trees penetrated by frost were muted by the snow so that they seemed to come from far off. It was early morning: the first day of First Moon.

Hunched down over his saddle, Komawara was glad he had not been so foolish as to ride out without dressing for the season. He had slipped out of Rhojo-ma in the darkness, eluding his own guards who still would not forgive themselves for becoming separated from their lord in the Jai Lung Hills. They would not be pleased.

Breaking out of the cover of the trees, Komawara pulled his mount up. His destination: the crest of a low hill north of Seh's Capital which afforded a view of the city and surrounding countryside.

In the middle of a lake skimmed with ice and snow, Rhojo-ma clung to its island—a complex geometry of white walls and sloping roofs stacked into a structure of labyrinthine beauty. Tears appeared in the covering of white where the snow could not retain its hold, and here tile of celestial blue showed through. The single bridge to the shore spanned the distance in a series of delicate arches, too fine, it almost seemed, to win a struggle against gravity.

Beyond the city, the countryside of Seh rolled away to the south where it disappeared into the clouds. Komawara's vantage was not high enough to give him the view he would have preferred, but even so the land was beautiful under its cover of snow. Stands of trees huddled along ridges and hilltops, forming patches of gray in a landscape of white. In a distant draw he could see the signs of a village, feathers of smoke pulled up toward the cloud.

Komawara dismounted and dropped his reins to the ground. Walking further up the crest, he stopped and steadied himself against the bole of a tree. The wound in his side made itself felt at this motion, but he ignored it.

So soon, so soon . . . it will all be ruins, the lord thought. My home, my people. And I will be retreating down the Grand Canal, trying to defend other provinces and the throne of a traitor and criminal.

The sun tried to break through a weakness in the cloud, throwing part of the countryside into sudden relief as shadows appeared. A few snowflakes drifted down from the branches above, and Komawara was reminded of the robe Nishima had worn at the celebration—snow falling on the Mountain of the Pure Spirit. But more than that he remembered her tall, perfect form as she stood in the shadow of a column whispering to Jaku Katta. There was no doubt, she had looked directly at Komawara and did not even realize who he was. I am not worthy of her notice, he thought bitterly. Her attentions to me indicate good manners, nothing more.

He looked down at his snow-covered boots. In Seh they were the proper thing to wear: unadorned and well worn. They seemed shabby to him now, the footwear of a country lord.

"It is what I am," he said aloud. "I can be nothing else." He looked out across the familiar vista. "A country lord—and not even that, for soon I will lose everything." He hit the tree twice with the heel of his gloved hand as though testing for soundness, and the sound echoed through the still woods.

His encounter with Toshaki Yoshihira the previous evening came back to him. It would have been somewhat satisfying, he realized, to take a sword to that one. It would be the last thing Komawara would lose—his ability with a sword. Perhaps all he could hope for now was an opportunity to prove his worth in battle. It might not impress a lady from the Capital, but it was within his grasp.

Komawara began to search under the snow with his feet. He would make a fire and sit a while before returning to Rhojo-ma. He could not bear to give up Seh just yet.

Eighteen

The snow that had fallen during the First Moon Festival was only a memory by the time Second Moon appeared. Winds had blown in from the sea, bringing comparative warmth and what seemed like endless rain. The frigid cold had been replaced by a pervasive dampness, and though the nights were hardly warm they had not the same raw edge evidenced a few weeks before.

Spring came early to Wa, even in the north. By Third Moon the rains would moderate and by Forth Moon the Plum Blossom Winds would sweep in like a sigh.

Nishima sat alone in her rooms, trying to concentrate on the poetry of Lady Nikko. Though she turned the scroll and her eyes passed from one character to the next, it seemed they did not penetrate beyond her eyes.

There had been no response from Lady Kitsura's family, and this weighed on her more with each day that passed. Unable to proceed as she had planned, Nishima found the decision to put off discussing her suspicions about Jaku Katta with her father was turning into a decision not to discuss her suspicions at all. She had been so certain the night she had talked to Jaku, but that certainty seemed to be fading with each day that passed. What would she tell her father, that she had suddenly developed truth sense? If a letter came from Kitsura's family, indicating that Jaku had sent Kitsura's message, perhaps this would strengthen her resolve.

But what if Jaku had not had the letter delivered as he promised? It was most confusing. Of course there was always the chance that the letter had been intercepted. If that were the case, and the letter had fallen into the hands of the Emperor, then Jaku would certainly be out of favor now, whether he had been previously or not.

I will wait, she told herself, Satake-sum invariably said that impatience would be my undoing and though I often thought he teased me, I begin to believe he did not say this entirely in jest. I will wait.

But she did not wait well and was aware of it. "Tranquillity of purpose is as far from my nature as Enlightenment is to the toads," she said to herself.

Nishima began to reread the poem she had just finished, for not a word of it had registered. The lamp wick needed trimming, but she didn't want to disturb the servants . . . nor be disturbed by them. The rain fell with such force that it seemed like gravel clattering ceaselessly on the tile roof, but rather than find this constant rain oppressive she welcomed it—as though it somehow insulated her from the outside world. It was a comfort.

A tap on the screen that led to her room was hardly welcomed, yet Lady Nishima made some effort to speak in a pleasant tone. "Please, enter."

The face of a maid appeared in the opening. "Brother Shuyun returns a book of poetry, Lady Nishima. Do you wish to speak with him?"

"Oh, indeed," Nishima's tone was suddenly no longer forced. "Please, invite him in."

Shuyun entered a moment later, the grace of his Botahist-trained movements delighting her as much as any dancer's. There was not the slightest self-consciousness in his motions, yet she knew there was total awareness. He knelt on an offered cushion and gave the Botahist double bow.

"Brother Shuyun," Nishima favored him with her most disarming smile, "I hope you have found the works I have given you enlightening or at least diverting."

Shuyun nodded. "The poetry of Lady Nikko is enlightening for me, certainly. My education has consisted largely of Botahist texts, Lady Nishima. Lady Nikko's poetry tells me much of the world I now live in."

Nishima gestured to the scroll she had been trying to read. "She wrote so much and all of it equally illuminating, I'm sure."

They fell into a second's awkward silence.

He has not come to return scrolls, Nishima thought, and that realization shattered her natural command of

social situations. Looking up at his ancient, childlike
eyes, she searched for an answer to her confusion, for a
reaction to what she felt. But when he met her eyes,
Nishima looked away, afraid of what her own gaze would
reveal.

"Shuyun-sum, I. . . ." She swallowed involuntarily.
"I did not understand what I did when Satake-sum taught
me. I was only a girl. . . . It was not my intention to
give offense to the Botahist Order. When Satake-sum told
me they were secret teachings, I thought they were secret
between Satake-sum and me." She paused. "I can apologize, Brother, but it is not possible to forget what I have
learned."

"Lady Nishima, my reaction was not shock at what
you had done. I pass no judgment on your actions. It was
Brother Satake's oath breaking that affected me so
strongly. I am the one to apologize if it seemed that I
blamed you."

Nishima glanced up again but his eyes appeared as
always—filled with impenetrable calm. She tried to smile.
"Satake-sum was a man of great curiosity, Shuyun-sum.
To find out what a woman could learn . . . though I began at too advanced an age to ever achieve the mastery
that you display, Brother."

Another awkward moment. The rain continued, like a
frame around the silence in the room.

"Curiosity, Satake-sum told me, was not encouraged
within your Order," Nishima said tentatively, as though
afraid she breached a sensitive subject.

But Shuyun only nodded.

Nishima pulled her robe closer. Gathering her nerve,
she pressed on. "I understand, Shuyun-sum, that there
have been differing Botahist teachings in the past? Those
who dwelt in the fane on the Lake of the Seven Masters,
for instance."

"It is so, though the one true Way still guides us,
while the others have disappeared."

"I wonder—did the sect that dwelt in Denji Gorge not
believe they followed the teachings of the Perfect Master? Were their beliefs not interpretations of the words of
Botahara?"

Shuyun shrugged. "Their beliefs were heretical, Lady
Nishima."

"Ahh," Nishima looked down at her hands. "It seems difficult to judge their beliefs when no one is sure what those beliefs were."

Shuyun took a long breath and let it out slowly. "Others have judged the doctrine of the Eightfold Path, Lady Nishima. It does not need to be done every generation."

Nishima nodded though it hardly seemed like a nod of agreement. "Do you ever wonder, Brother? Are you entirely sure of your path? I question my own—often."

Shuyun touched his fingertips together as though he would meditate. "My teachers warned that the world beyond the monastery would test my faith, Lady Nishima." He paused, deep in thought. Then, softly, "I did not realize how hard this testing would be."

Nishima nodded but did not answer immediately. The rain on the tile seemed to respond to the sadness she felt in the room. Perhaps all ways were difficult.

A tap on the shoji interrupted Nishima's thoughts. A kneeling maid opened the screen a hand's breadth. "Lady Kitsura calls, my Lady."

Nishima hid her annoyance with enormous care, well aware of how sensitive a Botahist Initiate was to tone of voice.

"How kind of her to call. Please, ask Lady Kitsura to join us."

Nishima smiled as her cousin entered, but Kitsura's air of excitement quickly gave way to embarrassment. She was dressed in an unpatterned silk robe in a shade of peach that was matched with only a single under-kimono. Her sash was a silk scarf quickly knotted and her hair was worn long. It was clear she had not expected to find male company in Nishima's apartments.

"Excuse me, cousin, Brother Shuyun. I did not realize you were here, Brother. I apologize."

"Kitsura-sum," Nishima smiled, "please do not apologize. Our discussion of the spirit will only be more interesting with your participation. Please sit with us." She gestured to other pillows and Kitsura took her place though she did not seem at all sure this was the proper thing for her to do.

"Brother Shuyun and I had just been discussing the development of Botahist doctrine." Nishima looked over

at her cousin and realized that with so few robes the
shape of Kitsura's breast was hardly hidden. Glancing at
Shuyun, she wondered if he noticed this himself. If desire was the nature of Illusion, how was he so unaffected
by it? Nishima looked back at her cousin. Men were usually all but overcome with desire when in Kitsura's presence—Nishima had seen it many times. She was aware
of being somewhat jealous of her cousin's effect on the
men of the Empire.

"Ah, Lady Nikko," Kitsura said, bending over to retrieve the scroll. As she did so her poorly belted robes
opened, and Nishima was sure she had seen Shuyun's
eyes drawn in that direction for an instant.

Shuyun bowed suddenly, "Lady Nishima, Lady Kitsura, please excuse me. I have other duties that call me."
He bowed again, responding politely to the women's expressions of regret. The screen closed gently behind him.

Nishima smiled at her cousin, a rather sheepish smile.
"Plum wine?" she asked.

"Now that I have ruined your evening," Kitsura said,
"coming to your rooms dressed like a street woman."
She pulled her robes closed at the neck.

Nishima laughed. "You did have a most surprised look
on your face when you saw Brother Shuyun." She
laughed again.

"Well, I was hardly expecting you to be entertaining
a gentleman. Your maid admitted me so readily. Had she
said that Brother Shuyun was here, I would never have
come in—dressed like this. Really, you should speak with
that girl."

"Kitsu-sum, you would be beautiful dressed as a street
sweeper."

"Well . . ." Kitsura looked embarrassed, "that hardly
means one is allowed to appear socially, half-dressed!"

Nishima laughed again. She seemed rather pleased
with Kitsura's discomfiture.

"But I have not told you! I have just received letters
from my family. Jaku Katta did have the message delivered!" Kitsura's eyes shone with excitement. "It is information your father must have. Certainly the handsome
Guard Commander is no longer in favor at court. He
would never have dared send a message to my family

otherwise—especially as he did not know what my letter contained. There can be no doubt.''

Nishima nodded her head. "No doubt at all," she said quietly. "You are quite right."

Nineteen

W ord reached the acting Commander of the Imperial
Guard within minutes of the discovery. Jaku Tadamoto hurried down a hall and turned into the grand
corridor that connected the palace proper with the Palace
of Administration. Like much of the Island Palace this
had been built on a scale barely approachable by mere
humans—broad and high-ceilinged with a polished stone
floor that shone in the soft winter light.

In the distance he could see a party of officials moving
at a pace inappropriate to their station. Peaked red caps
denoted at least two Senior Ministers and the robes of
the others indicated officials of high rank. In the midst
of this group a sedan chair was being hurried along, but
it appeared to have no occupant. Tadamoto increased his
pace. An Emperor too impatient to ride as his station
required was never a good sign.

Tadamoto attached himself to the rear of this silent
party and matched its pace without a word. The Minister
of the Left, puffing to keep up, gave him a barely perceptible nod. The silence of the party hung in the air,
poised like a sharp blade.

Guards and officials and courtiers knelt with their foreheads to the floor as the Emperor passed. The Palace
would be alive with rumors within minutes—try to control the flow of gossip when the Emperor behaved like
this!

They entered the Palace of Administration and turned
into another hall. The shuffle of feet on stone, the breathing of the rushing officials, robes of silk and brocade
sweeping along the floor, conversations dying abruptly
as the Emperor came into view.

Another hall, smaller now, some confusion about a
door, and then a large room in the core of the ministry.

Tense, chalky faces turned toward the entering party and then foreheads were pressed to the floor. A small, iron-bound chest stood in the center of the room and, with the bowing officials surrounding it, Tadamoto had the fleeting impression that it was an object of veneration. He pushed past the sedan chair bearers and nodded to guards to close the doors.

The Emperor paused, holding his sword in both hands. "This is the chest?"

Nods from several quarters. Stepping forward, the Emperor lifted the lid of the chest with the tip of his scabbard so that it slid off and fell to the floor with an ominous clatter. He leaned forward to look in and stepped back as though the contents offended him. Glancing over his shoulder, the Son of Heaven saw Tad-amoto and nodded.

"Colonel," the Emperor waved his sword at the chest.

Tadamoto stepped past the frightened officials, staying a respectful distance from the Emperor. He rounded the chest and peered in, closed his eyes for a second, then reached down and removed a small brocade bag—the sin-gle object the chest contained. Untying the cord with trembling fingers Tadamoto emptied the contents into his palm. A dozen gold coins, square, with round holes in their centers.

The Emperor spun around looking at the gathered of-ficials, most of whom stepped back in obvious fright.

"And there was nothing taken from this chest? It came exactly thus from Seh?"

Heads bobbed. "Exactly as you see it," a senior offi-cial offered, "though with seals unbroken." He was an old man whose voice quavered terribly. "The theft must have taken place on the canal, though the Imperial Gov-ernor's own troops were the guards."

The Emperor tapped the edge of the chest with his sword, raised the scabbard suddenly as if he would strike the edge, then stopped himself. "Find them," the Em-peror said to no one and, turning, scattered the officials before him.

Tadamoto stood for a moment, looking down into the empty chest. His gaze drifted back to the coins. He pushed one with his finger to uncover another—it bore the mark of a strange dragon.

''Colonel,'' the Minister of the Left said, his voice jarring in the silent room, ''these guards were best found quickly.''

Tadamoto thrust the bag and coins into the old man's hands and stormed out. In the hall beyond he broke into an undignified trot. There was no doubt in his mind that there had been no theft. The chest and its contents were a message from Shonto—a declaration of war. Tadamoto had not received confirmation yet, but it was rumored that Shonto had published a tract offering gold for the service of armed men.

Civil war was all but inevitable. And what of this barbarian army? If Jaku told the truth, it would be more than civil war; it would be the war that ended the Empire. He went from a trot to a run.

The Great Audience Hall of the Empire was lit by only a half dozen lamps, spaced around its great perimeter, and the small light they provided appeared to be drawn into the hall's vast darkness. It gave the chamber an eerie feel and distorted one's sense of the space and distance. Tadamoto stood just inside a door to one side of the dais, waiting for his eyes to adjust. He could hear the sound of footsteps. They seemed to come toward him, then stop, then retreat again. Someone muttered—words he could not understand.

Staring into the gloom, Tadamoto was finally able to make out the silhouette of a man moving before the dais. He was unsure of what to do. After waiting in the dark for some minutes longer Tadamoto knelt down where he stood and waited until the footsteps approached and then stopped again.

''Emperor?'' he said quietly.

The unmistakable sound of a sword being drawn from its scabbard.

''Sire? I have come with my report as you wished. It is Colonel Jaku.''

''Tadamoto-sum?''

''Yes, Sire. Please excuse my intrusion.''

''You are alone?'' The voice came out of the dark.

''Yes, Sire.''

''Get up,'' the Emperor commanded.

Jaku bowed to the darkness and rose to his feet.

"Come along," the voice said.

Tadamoto walked toward the sound. The Emperor's form materialized in the poor light. Tadamoto could see him returning his sword to its scabbard.

"Walk with us, Colonel." At this the Emperor turned and started down the hall, his pace deliberate if not hurried. Halfway down the length of the great chamber the Emperor broke the silence.

"The Shonto guards are not to be found?"

"This is so, Emperor. It seems very likely that Shonto's most senior retainers have slipped away also, though appearances are being kept up faithfully at their residences. I have failed. . . ."

"The gods take them!" the Emperor interrupted. "I did not truly believe they could be found. They did not steal Seh's taxes—their lord did."

Tadamoto nodded. They came abreast of a lamp and he could see the Emperor's face, strangely distorted by the half light. The eyes hidden in dark holes and the forehead standing out like a deformity. The young guardsman looked away.

This man touches the woman I love.

"I had hoped to avoid civil war," the Emperor said softly. "I had so hoped to avoid it.

"Of course, Shonto will drive the Empire into this war. I should have realized." His voice was sad as though he spoke of an errant child.

She spends her nights in his arms.

"We will have to raise an army now. If Shonto tries to split the Empire and establish himself in Seh, we will be forced to go north to fight. If the lord chooses to come south, we will let him come to us. Either way the Empire will pay a great price."

They strode on until they came to the massive entrance doors where the Emperor changed course abruptly and started back toward the dais.

I have let this occur, frozen into inaction.

"Are preparations complete for sending the Prince north?"

Tadamoto fought the rage that swelled inside him. "They have been complete for some days, Sire," he said tightly.

"Then he shall drag his feet no longer. Send him off even if you must use force."

Tadamoto nodded again.

"And the Omawara. We watch them with great care?"

"Both by day and by night, Emperor."

"Do not let them slip away, Colonel. I will have plans for them yet."

They walked in silence to the foot of the Dragon Throne and then turned back. Half the length of the hall passed beneath their feet with nothing but the sounds of their footsteps and the hiss of the Emperor's brocade robe along the stone. Occasionally the jeweled scabbard the Son of Heaven carried would catch the dim light, and it seemed he almost brandished it as though at an enemy.

"Sire . . . ?" Jaku struggled to collect his thoughts.

"Speak your mind, Colonel," the Emperor said with some impatience.

"Excuse me for saying so, Sire, but perhaps we play this game too openly." He took a deep breath. "If we locate Shonto's retainers and they are taken by Imperial Guards, no matter how carefully disguised, the Empire will soon know. We risk dividing the Great Houses." Tadamoto glanced at the Emperor, but it was impossible to read his face in the low light. "There are other courses. We could announce that we raise an army to send north— the situation in Seh is not critical, but it is not what we originally thought. Of course, we will keep this army here under our control until we see what Shonto does. It will be a message for Shonto's allies."

Tadamoto could see the Emperor nodding. "But what of this gold we have received from Shonto?" The Emperor turned toward him in the dark. "You understand its significance, Tadamoto-sum?"

"I do, Sire." They walked a few paces more. "We could send a message to Shonto saying we are confused by this. Certainly the Imperial Treasury should contribute to the efforts against the barbarians, but this action of Shonto's staff is foolish in the extreme. Could not the Governor look into this matter and tell us his province's needs?"

The Emperor considered this. "Ah, Tadamoto, this is wisdom. Why do my other counselors not advise me so?" The Emperor slapped his palm with his scabbard. "We will do as you suggest, though Shonto's retainers should be found if it is at all possible. I'm certain Tanaka could provide a wealth of information, and not just about his lord.''

They had walked the hall's length and returned now to the foot of the throne.

"What of your brother? Has he written in return to your letter?''

"It may yet be too soon, Sire.''

"Ah.'' The Emperor paced across the foot of the dais and then stopped.

"Begin to raise the army. My son will leave for the north immediately . . . to assist Shonto until our entire force can be made ready.'' The Emperor mounted the steps and disappeared into the total darkness surrounding the Dragon Throne. Tadamoto heard him settle into the cushions.

"Prepare a letter for our governor,'' said the voice in the darkness. "Tell him that we are confused by the action of his staff. Say we prepare an army as quickly as we can. Let him wonder what we plan, let him lie awake and wonder.

"Colonel,'' there was real warmth in the Emperor's voice now, "I shall reward you for this, reward you richly. Tell us your desire, Tadamoto-sum.''

Tadamoto knelt and bowed, his spirit sinking as he did so. "To serve my Emperor,'' he forced himself to say, "that is my desire.''

This man. . . .

"You are a man of honor, Tadamoto-sum, but I'm sure something can be found that will be worthy of you. We shall see.''

Tadamoto sat on the lowest step of the dais, brooding in the darkness. The Emperor had gone, leaving the young officer in a turmoil.

Osha, Osha, he thought. He had not seen the dancer for several days, had been unable to face her, though he could not say why. It was one thing for him to be avoiding Osha, but now he began to believe that she was avoiding him as well.

We have come to this, he thought, two people who felt and thought as one.

Damn him! May all evil take his soul!

Tadamoto stood and walked along the step a few paces, then sat again. If nothing else, an army would be raised. If Katta had written anything near to the truth, then Tadamoto would feel he had done what he could. The Empire would not be entirely unprepared. And if Katta joined the Shonto in an attempt to overthrow the Yamaku . . . ? Tadamoto put his face in his hands.

"Osha-sum," he whispered, and the sound disappeared into the dark hall without an echo.

Twenty

The Imperial Governor's Palace was a riot of preparations and though most of the people involved, beyond Shonto's own staff, thought the governor was mad, they were not allowed to let this feeling be reflected in their work. Shonto's retainers made sure of that.

Shuyun found himself with little to do, for he had no specific responsibilities other than to advise his lord when required. Lord Shonto's staff were masters at logistics, so advice from an Initiate Monk, who owned almost nothing and had moved only twice in his short life, was highly unnecessary.

The day was comparatively mild, but a strong wind blew out of the west, whipping up and pushing at Shuyun where he moved along the top of the palace wall. He had walked the perimeter of the Imperial Palace atop its various sections of wall and through its towers for no other reason than to be out in the air after all the hours spent in the palace during the winter. Though it seemed to indicate lack of Enlightenment, Shuyun could feel his spirit lift with each step.

The Palace sat atop a low rise on the city's eastern edge, the highest point on the natural island that formed the anchor of Rhojo-ma. Much of the rest of the city sat upon manmade islands built on a rock shelf that lay just under the lake's surface. The palace's position hardly offered a high vantage, but it afforded some views that were worth contemplating and Shuyun had stopped at each of these.

Below, Shuyun saw two guards in Shonto blue who looked up and pointed in his direction, then one of them began to make his way at a trot toward nearby stairs.

Lord Shonto must have sent for his Spiritual Advisor, the monk thought, and increased his pace.

"Brother . . . Shuyun." The guard puffed to the top of the stairs, holding his sword hilt as he ran. "There has been a missive left for you." He bowed. "My corporal was not sure of its urgency, so he sent me immediately."

Shuyun gestured down the stairs. "Please, I will follow."

They did not have far to go, for the guard led the way to a nearby gate that opened into the streets beyond the palace—quiet streets. Guards bowed as the governor's Advisor approached and the few pedestrians who passed by stepped aside. Inside the gate house the corporal the guard had spoken of bowed low to Shuyun.

"Excuse me for interrupting your contemplation, Brother, but I thought this might be of importance."

The corporal's name was Rohku; Shuyun had met his father during his brief time in the Capital. He took from a table what appeared to be a scroll wrapped in plain gray paper and handed it to the monk.

Shuyun nodded his thanks. It was not a missive, certainly, for there was no stamp of his Order upon it.

Corporal Rohku bobbed in a second bow—the story of Shuyun's confrontation with the young Lord Toshaki had made its way down through Shonto's guard, and it brought even greater respect to the monk. "It was delivered by a Botahist Brother."

Shuyun turned it over and found a wax seal with a name-character impressed in it.

Hitara.

Shuyun felt his time sense stretch as though he practised chi ten, yet he did not.

"How long ago?" Shuyun asked, his mouth suddenly dry.

"Moments, Brother Shuyun, only moments."

"Did you see the direction he set out in?"

"Toward the market streets. . . ."

Shuyun placed the scroll in his hands. "Guard this," he ordered and then was out the door at a run before the corporal could protest.

"Follow him," Rohku snapped. "He is not to leave the palace without an escort."

The young guard set out at a run but was soon outdistanced by the small monk. By the time he reached the market streets, Shuyun was lost from sight.

Shuyun ran.

"A Botahist Brother? Did he pass?" he yelled at a peasant leading a mule. The man nodded and pointed down a narrow side street. Shuyun ran on, increasing his pace.

At the next meeting of streets he asked again and was directed left. Then right. Then up a flight of stairs and across a bridge. Coming to a small square, he was stopped by the many streets and stairs and alleys.

An old man sat on a step, working at a strap on an ancient sandal. "A Brother," Shuyun panted, "did he pass?"

The old man tugged away at the strap, looking off into the distance as he did so. After several seconds of contemplation he nodded.

"Which way?"

Without taking his eyes from the point in the distance or deigning to look at his inquisitor, he answered. "I am only a poor old man, Brother, do not ask me to point the Way."

"I have no coins, old man, but I will see you receive coins aplenty if you answer my question."

The old man smiled. "The Way, Brother is not so easily found." He paused to concentrate on his task for a second. "And I am not a teacher."

Shuyun went to speak again but realized what he should have seen immediately—the man was blind. Looking around at the many alleys and stairs, Shuyun shook his head. There was no one else to ask.

"Who shall I ask if not you, old sage?" Shuyun leaned against the wall to catch his breath.

"That is the worst of it, Brother. Until the Teacher comes, there is no one." He managed to free the broken strap suddenly and explored the damage with twisted fingers. He did not like what he felt. "Tell me your name, Brother."

"Shuyun."

The thin smile appeared again. "He who bears. What is it you carry, Brother Shuyun?"

Shuyun sat staring for a moment—he had once been a scholar, this shriveled old shadow of a man. Only a scholar would know the origin of his name. He looked down at the man's feet. His other sandal was as much a ruin as the one he held in his hands.

Shuyun slipped quickly out of his own footwear and put these in the man's hands. "To aid you in your search for the Way, old sage."

The man ran his fingers over the soft leather, his smile returning. Shuyun turned back the way he had come, bare feet over cold cobbles. He had not gone three paces before the old man spoke again.

"If you do not know what it is you bear, Brother, you risk taking the wrong path."

Shuyun looked over his shoulder. The old man sat, gaze still fixed on a distant point, stroking his gift.

"I bare my feet, old sage, and pray to Botahara to guide them."

The old man smiled now, rocking back and forth like a child. He laughed gently.

As he walked back to the palace, Shuyun was met by an anxious young guard whose great relief at finding his lord's Spiritual Advisor unharmed was visible. When the guard realized that the monk walked barefoot, he immediately tried to give him his sandals and was somewhat disconcerted when Shuyun refused.

Returning to the palace gate, Shuyun retrieved his scroll from Corporal Rohku and retired from the bustle to his own rooms. After an insistant servant had bathed his feet, Shuyun was able to be alone. He retreated to his balcony with the package, broke the seal with great care, and unwrapped the scroll, holding his breath as he did so, much to his surprise.

The scroll was new, doing away with Shuyun's most irrational expectation—Shimeko's words had affected him more than he realized. The paper was plain, common in fact, a dull shade of yellowish-brown, and the brushwork, though perfectly executed, was unremarkable. He read.

Brother Shuyun:

*I regret that we will be unable to speak, but it is
my hope that everything you might ask will be
answered here. I have come recently out of the
desert and do not know when I shall be able to
return.*

*The army that you searched for in the north is,
even now, approaching the border of Seh. The
brave men of Seh who rode into the desert to
patrol beyond your borders have been returned to
the wheel, may Botahara protect their souls.
Although the Khan's army is near, it will take ten
days to reach your border, such is its size. Over
one hundred thousand follow behind this Khan,
Brother, and they are well armed.*

*Once across your border the barbarian forces
will take another six days to reach Rhojo-ma. It
appears they will enter Seh north of Kyo. There is
so little time, Brother.*

> *Lord Botahara took out his sword and shattered
> it upon a great stone. His armor he sank into the
> rushing river and his war horse was set free to
> run across the hills.*
> *"In the struggle that comes," He said, "such
> weapons will be as the toys of children."*
> *Saying this, the Lord left his army and walked
> down from the mountain. And so began the
> struggle for the souls of men.*

May Botahara smile upon you, Brother,

Hitara

Shuyun sat for a long moment, looking out over the
roofs of the palace. The wind still blew, pulling the
clouds into long ragged banners. He unrolled the scroll
further, hoping there would be more and something soft
fell onto his knees. Looking down, Shuyun closed his
eyes and began to pray. As he did so, tears ran onto his
cheeks though he did not feel them. He chanted the long
prayer for forgiveness and then the prayer for thanksgiving. Yet he still dared not open his eyes.
When finally he looked upon this gift, he thought his

soul would swell until it spread across the sky. His fingers trembled when he reached out and took Hitara's gift into his hands. A simple white blossom, five elongated petals tinged with purple, as soft and supple as if it had just been plucked.

"Botahara be praised," Shuyun whispered. "The flower of the Udumbara."

Twenty-one

Shonto rolled the scroll with great care as though it were very old and rare. He sat near a screen partially opened to the cool day and, like the others present, Shonto still wore outdoor garb. Preparations for the move south were in motion and Shonto had walked the quay to see some of this firsthand. It was the lord's way to have his presence known in times of difficulty.

Shonto seemed more grave than usual though one could hardly detect any effects of the burdens he bore or the work he had been doing. It was part of the lord's persona—his apparent youthfulness was due less to his appearance than to his manner, his exuberance. But today the exuberance was muffled under a layer of seriousness.

"It is beyond question, Shuyun, you have no doubt?"

The monk nodded. "Though this man is a mystery to my Order, there is no doubt that he is a true follower of Botahara. I am convinced that what Hitara has written is true."

Shonto looked to General Hojo Masakado.

The general did not hesitate. "If this information is not true, I am at a loss to know what purpose such lies would serve. It is my counsel, Sire, that we should act as though Brother Hitara's information is beyond doubt."

Shonto nodded, then turned to Kamu.

"I agree, Lord Shonto, though I would feel more at ease if we knew more of this Brother from the desert." Kamu threw up his hand in resignation. Of all Shonto's senior staff, Kamu was affected most by the preparations that they engaged in. His age was beginning to tell. Yet he went about his work with customary efficiency and though he seemed to be aging daily, there was never a complaint.

Shonto turned to Komawara next.

"I do not claim to have a truth sense, Sire, but I met Brother Hitara in the desert and I do not believe for a moment that he would lie to us. The guard's description fit Brother Hitara perfectly and, like General Hojo, I can't imagine that giving us such information, were it wrong, would benefit anyone. Even the barbarians would rather we stayed in Seh where they could easily defeat us. We have only a few days, Sire, I think we should act immediately.'' Komawara bowed.

Shonto looked over at Nishima.

"Certainly we should act, Sire, but I don't think we can leave Seh before the barbarians have crossed the border. I do not mean to tell you your duties as governor, but we cannot abandon the people of Seh entirely.''

Shonto considered this. "We can begin our move down the canal, though some may stay behind until the true situation is realized in Seh. A small group can still easily outdistance a large army.'' Shonto bowed to Nishima, then turned to the Imperial guardsman. "General Jaku?''

The presence of Jaku Katta at this council was a mystery to everyone but Shonto who had invited him. It was doubly a mystery, for Jaku had not been told of Brother Hitara in the original story of the journey into the desert. Perhaps it was not such a surprise to Jaku that he had not been told everything—he had lived in the Emperor's Palace after all. The Guard Commander bowed formally.

"Lord Shonto, I agree with Lady Nishima. We cannot begin to move our forces south until the barbarian threat is realized by the people of Seh. I am forced to admit that this is a matter of pride as well as prudence. If we leave now, we will be seen as either mad or cowardly. If we leave after the barbarian army has been seen for what it is, our actions will be viewed differently by the lords of this province. As I say, it is a matter of pride—I am a soldier, please excuse me.''

Other men in the room nodded. Pride was at issue here with all but Shuyun and perhaps Lady Nishima, though none had spoken of it.

Shonto nodded thoughtfully. "Lord Komawara, what do you think your countrymen will do when they see the scale of the barbarian army?''

The young lord considered for a moment; he had embarrassed himself in Shonto's council in the past and was taking some care not to repeat this. "I fear that fewer men than we would hope will follow us south, Lord Shonto. The Taiki prepare as we speak but, as General Jaku has said, pride will dictate the actions of many. Some will stay to fight, though they will understand the futility."

Shonto pulled his armrest closer. "Kamu-sum, the tract that you distributed—when can we expect to see some response to that?"

Kamu did a mental count of days. "Soon, I would expect, Sire. The lure of gold is great. Armed men from Itsa and Chiba provinces should be making their way toward us as we speak."

"Send recruiting officers and staff down the canal," Shonto said, "as soon as you can—tomorrow if it is possible. Have them begin work in a station south of Seh's border. Then have them move in seven days. We will keep them ahead of us. Put a responsible man in charge of this, we do not want a stream of soldiers joining our flotilla and slowing us as we move. Camps must be created in strategic places for these men. It will mean thinning our ranks, but we'll have to assign officers to the recruits—we need to have them ready and useful. General Hojo, it will mean promotions for many junior officers—see to it."

Kamu and Hojo bowed.

Shonto stared out the open shoji for a moment.

"There is other news." Shonto reached out and moved Hitara's scroll as though its angle to the light was not quite correct. "I have received word from the Emperor." Shonto said quietly. He looked up at the others. "The Son of Heaven writes that an army is being raised for the defense of Seh."

Shonto seemed to enjoy the response of the people present or perhaps he made some secret assessment of those present by observing how they responded to the unexpected.

Lady Nishima stared openly and with some degree of contempt at Jaku Katta, thinking to herself that he had again proven himself incapable of telling the truth.

Kamu was not the first to recover, but he spoke first. "Si-Sire, did the Emperor not receive his empty tax box?"

"The Son of Heaven has asked that I look into this matter. The governor's staff, the Son of Heaven suggested, have acted in a most foolish manner. Certainly Seh must retain some of her revenue for defense, but. . . ." Shonto shrugged. "We are asked to prepare a document describing our exact needs. Our failure to remit our taxes has been overlooked. So, as requested, we will prepare a report for the Emperor explaining our military needs."

"What will we tell him?" Hojo asked.

"The truth." Shonto smiled. "Does that shock you, General?"

Everyone, including Hojo, laughed.

"General Jaku, perhaps you can explain the significance of the Emperor's decision."

Jaku bowed. "I had begun to lose hope myself, Sire. My friends at court could not prevail in the council to have an army raised to defend Seh. You can imagine why. This army the Emperor writes of is intended to defend the Capital from the army that Lord Shonto raises—the tract offering to pay gold to armed men must have caused a great deal of discussion. The Son of Heaven fears other Houses joining with us.

"The Imperial force is not being prepared to fight the Khan, but it is an army nonetheless: who will control this army once the true threat is apparent, that is the issue."

Shonto's staff bowed toward Jaku.

"It is some sign of hope, General Jaku. At least the Empire will not be entirely unprepared. How large a force does the Emperor gather?"

Jaku opened his hands. "This is not yet clear. I hope to know soon."

Shuyun bowed to his liege-lord. "Undoubtedly the Emperor's force will be large enough to counter Lord Shonto's army—that is the threat the throne perceives. If it is to our advantage that the Emperor raise a large force, we could assist our cause by exaggerating the number of our own soldiers."

Komawara almost grinned. "Brother Shuyun, you surprise me. Is this what one learns from the writings of Botahara?"

Shuyun responded as though no one present smiled.

"I have recently tried to broaden my education, Lord Komawara. I have heard it said that the lie no one doubts is spoken by an honorable man. We may tell a great lie and be believed."

"We will begin to move our people south the day the barbarian army crosses the border," Shonto said. "We are a laughing stock for gathering so many river craft . . . but that will change soon enough. Boats will transport what forces we have faster than the barbarians will ever ride. And rafts handled by men who have lived their lives on the desert will be slow—especially when they find the canal locks impassable. Plans must be complete to burn all other craft in Seh and also to keep the canal open ahead of us. Once the news of the barbarian army passes us on the way south, we will be dealing with thousands fleeing toward the inner provinces. We cannot have our progress impeded."

Jaku Katta bowed quickly and not as low as he had previously. "I have left garrisons of Imperial Guard along the canal, Lord Shonto. We can use them to open the waterway before us."

Shonto nodded. "Good." He considered for a moment. "The Emperor sends his useless son north with what will no doubt be a small guard. The Prince will be a nuisance, I'm sure, but we will treat him with proper respect. Who knows what part he may yet play."

"Certainly he will never make a hostage," Hojo offered. "The Prince is not dear to his Imperial father. The Emperor may be hoping we will send him to his end fighting barbarians." The general considered this. "And perhaps we should."

Shonto nodded. "Too many will find such an end, Masakado-sum, and I will wish it on no one."

Twenty-two

Beacon fires flare
From hill to tower
To hill
Like sparks escaping the brazier
In a tinder dry house

L ord Komawara stood at the window in the top of West Tower, watching. At intervals around the horizon he could see beacon fires blazing with a distant urgency. By morning the news would have spread to the remotest corner of the province.

It was a cold evening with a harsh wind, but the lord did not seem to notice. He had been standing in the same place for more than an hour, and though he felt numb to the center of his soul it was not from the night.

They come, he thought, *they come.*

His mind seemed to have no focus, starting down one path to veer suddenly into another. Thoughts of his retainers making their way up into a stronghold in the mountains were lost to images of riders, relaying from the northern border, racing to Rhojo-ma with news of the barbarian army. Could it be as large as Brother Hitara wrote?

A fire blazed to life on an eastern hill, and then, far off, another.

Lord Toshaki sat upon his horse outside a small inn. In the background a narrow river flowed and the light from the almost full moon wavered on its surface—liquid moonlight rushing off into the night. Toshaki's son, Yoshihira, sat nearby on the stump of a pine tree, his horse cropping some poor, winter grass beside him. Neither man spoke. Their guards sat upon horses or stood at intervals around the clearing without sign of either impatience or intent. Warm light from the inn reflected off lacquered armor here, a helmet there. A cold wind jostled among the pines, making them sway and creak.

The moon drifted west. The innkeeper came out with cups and a cauldron of steaming rice wine, but his suggestions that the lords would find the night less forbidding inside were politely rebuffed. The horsemen waiting in the dark felt that the wildness of the night gave their vigil a certain purity.

The sound of horses at the gallop. A guard stationed up the narrow road came into sight and whistled. Toshaki's son vaulted into the saddle and joined his father.

Men burst out of the inn and disappeared toward the stable. These were men Toshaki had spoken with earlier—retainers of Lord Taiki Kiyorama, though they bore the flying horse emblem of the Governor of Seh on their surcoats. They reappeared almost immediately with three saddled horses and spent a moment checking girths and bridles in the light from the inn.

Three men on horseback broke out of the trees and pulled their mounts up before the inn, horses in a lather, driven to their limits. A crowd appeared on the porch, talking among themselves. The riders were off their exhausted mounts, taking a moment only for drink before setting off on fresh horses.

Lord Toshaki and his men rode up then, half surrounding the messengers.

"What news?" Lord Toshaki's son called. "How large is this army?"

The three riders looked up to see who questioned them, and at a whisper from one of the Taiki handlers the men went back to their drinks, handing bowls to servants to be filled a second and third time.

Young Toshaki rode closer now, blocking their path. "The Lord of the Toshaki asks the size of the barbarian army," he said with some anger.

One rider, a young captain, swung into the saddle, his horse stepping sideways, catching the excitement of the men. "Does your lord wish to measure the size of the force he has spent the winter raising against the size of the barbarian army?" he asked with little show of respect. "Go back to your gii board, young Sire, we do the governor's bidding."

Toshaki spoke now, riding up beside his son, the wind whipping his long hair out of its ring. "We will all fight together now, despite the past. We are men of Seh, tell us what it is we face."

The captain rode forward, working to control his mount as it tossed its head, ready to run. His voice was pitched low and taut with anger. "You will bow at Lord Komawara's feet and ask for forgiveness, lord," he said to Toshaki's son. "That is the size of the barbarian army."

The messengers spurred their horses then and pushed through Toshaki's guards. The riders disappeared into the darkness where the trees tossed like confused seas driven before a great storm.

The morning after beacon fires appeared, the first riders bearing the reports from the frontier officers arrived in Rhojo-ma. By first light a great human stream was flowing into the provincial capital from the nearby countryside and villages. It was inconceivable to these people that Rhojo-ma could fall, and so they came, bearing everything they could load into carts or carry on their backs or drag.

It was late winter and still cool, but the skies were a clear northern blue during the days and filled with stars at night. Those who had experience with the movement of troops prayed for the rains that would be common at this time of year. Rains would slow the invasion, could even bring it to a halt for some time. The horizon was studied with an intensity that was unprecedented, but there was no sign of cloud.

The reports from the frontier officers came to Governor Shonto and he shut himself up with his staff for most of a day. They waited for the major lords of Seh who would arrive late that evening. For the first time in two generations a Council of War had been called by the Governor of Seh.

The fisherman stood with his family on the muddy edge of the River Chousa and watched the flames change his life forever. Smoke and steam from wet planking plumed up in great clouds, racing toward the heavens, an offense

to the purity of the sky. Tugging at the flaming hull, the
river lapped the shore and passed on, bearing a slick of
oily soot. The fisherman's wife sobbed and shed bitter
tears, holding their two small children close, but the fisherman stood looking on without a sound, a deep sadness
in his eyes.

Downstream, toward the bend in the river, he could
see another boat pulled up on the bank and put to the
torch. The governor's soldiers rowed on. The fisherman
could see them searching the mouth of a tributary over-
hung with willows, a guard standing up in the boat parting the curtain of branches with his sword.

The fisherman's burning boat heaved now, as though
some part of it was alive and in agony. This drew his
attention and for a second he looked as though he would
join his wife in tears. But this passed and the sadness
returned. The flaming pole of a mast toppled slowly to
the bank, hissing where it touched the wet mud. More
ribs buckled and the boat settled even farther onto its
side.

Turning away, the fisherman went to the pile of goods
tossed up on the bank and half covered by a patched
sail—everything he now owned in this world. He pulled
aside the sail and dragged a net out from under a chest.
There were wooden floats somewhere. War or no war,
people would need to eat.

Shonto sat in his own apartments, writing by the light
of two lamps. His brushwork was deliberate, though not
slow. The silk and brocade robes of the Imperial Governor were a bother to him, especially now when his
armor laced in Shonto blue had been readied. He dipped
his brush in ink and wrote:

Shokan-sum:

*I pray this reaches you. I will send men down the
river and along the coast, hoping they will find a
boat to carry them through the straits. With all of
Seh running before barbarian armies, it will be a
miracle if they find a way.*

*The barbarians have crossed the border and
will arrive at Rhojo-ma within six days. I will*

*retreat down the Grand Canal, hoping to slow the
barbarian advance long enough that Akantsu can
raise an army. Of course the Emperor will remove
me from my command if he can. Look to yourself.
I will control the army as long as I am able, but
there is no way to know what will occur—the
Yamaku will have time to consider their course of
action with some care.*

*Look to yourself. If this war is lost, our lands
will mean nothing. Do not waste time or men
defending them.*

*Nishi-sum stays with me and is a great comfort
and help. Often she speaks of her concern for
you.*

*I have sent word to the Capital and to Yankura.
It would be best if Tanaka were with you, but if
this is not possible do not be concerned—our
merchant is ever resourceful.*

May Botahara protect you.

Shonto signed this, folded it carefully, and sealed the
letter with his stamp. It was very late, the middle of the
night had passed. He rose and walked to the door.
The Council of War awaited him.

The Great Hall of the Governor's Palace held perhaps
a hundred men in all and though they were men used to
the uncertainties of life in the north most of them showed
some signs of the deep shock they felt. Shonto had seen
the look before in swordsmen—the split second when they
realized they had made a mistake from which there was
no recovery, and so waited for the inevitable touch of steel.
Shonto watched with great detachment as the gathered
lords bowed. For each man present the governor knew
there was a number and that number represented how
many armed men they could raise. For some of the lords
the number would be less than fifty. Komawara's forces
consisted of three hundred and fifty men, and he had
mortgaged his future to raise that number. The major
lords might raise a thousand men, perhaps two thousand
for Toshaki and Lord Ranan.
Fifteen thousand men in all was the estimate of Hojo

and Komawara. Add to this the thirty-five hundred men that Shonto had brought with him to Seh. To face a barbarian force of almost one hundred thousand.

Shonto nodded to the assembled lords. The lamps flickered around the hall and the scent of burning oil almost covered the odor of riders—so many had arrived barely in time for the council. It was readily apparent that this was not the Imperial Capital where such an assembly would be dressed in clothes of unequaled finery. Many of the lords of Seh wore hunting costume—practical for riding and ease of movement—clothing one never saw anywhere inside the Imperial Palace grounds.

Without prearrangement, the men present arrayed themselves according to their earlier beliefs: Shonto's advisors and allies aligned themselves to the governor's right, apart from the others who sat in rows facing the governor's dais. Shonto looked over at Komawara who knelt stiffly among his allies. It is a moment of vindication, Shonto thought, no one has suffered as Komawara has. Yet Komawara hid anything he felt behind a mask of earnest concern.

Off to the left the governor noticed the Toshaki Lords sitting near the Ranan—hardly a natural alliance—their only bond the fact that they had all recently been utterly wrong. Yes, Shonto thought, there will be few moments in Komawara's life as gratifying as this.

Shonto nodded to Seh's Major Chancellor, Lord Gitoyo, who bowed and gave a signal to someone unseen. Outside the hall an enormous drum boomed, twelve even beats, echoing across the city and the lake long after the drumming had stopped.

Lord Gitoyo bowed again and pulled himself up to his full sitting height so that his voice would reach the back of the hall. "The Council of War of the Province of Seh has been called. The Imperial Governor, Lord Shonto Motoru, has summoned you. Are there any who would dispute the Imperial Governor's right to lead us in time of war?"

Some few shook their heads, but most indicated their answer with silence.

"Until the state of war is declared past, the commands of the Imperial Governor, Lord Shonto Motoru, will be the law of Seh above all but the word of our Emperor."

The gathered lords bowed.

The Chancellor fell silent, waiting. Shonto nodded and the Chancellor again drew himself up. "The reports of the frontier officers have been received and what they have written shall be made known to you. Lord Akima. . . ."

The old man who had for so long tormented Komawara about his "foolish" opinions, unlike the rest of the men present, did not look like he was about to taste steel for his own foolishness—he looked like the blade had slid home as Gitoyo spoke.

Akima gathered himself together to speak, but his voice emerged small and old. "The reports from . . . from our northern border are grave indeed. A barbarian force crossed into Seh west of Kyo before sunset yesterday. This force consists of cavalry, soldiers, bowmen, and train. The combined force . . . the combined force approaches one hundred thousand fighting men." He could not go on then for some seconds, but it was hardly noticed. Some of those who had believed this number to be rumor were as shaken as Akima.

With a visible act of will Akima continued, forcing some strength into his voice. "I am assured by Governor Shonto's staff that this barbarian force will take six days to reach Rhojo-ma—its apparent destination. This force is well armed and horsed, with a supply train large enough to support an extended siege." Akima finished reading and let his hands fall back onto his knees. He met no one's eyes but seemed to stare out to Seh's distant border. "And I would not listen to reason," he said with what sounded like disbelief.

"Lord Akima," the Major Chancellor whispered almost sharply.

Akima seemed to come out of a daze, and he bowed toward the dais. He returned to a kneeling position, but his face could not hold the rigid impassivity of the other lords despite his efforts.

Shonto looked out at the men before him. They did not seem like men of great pride in that moment, but he knew this was deceptive. How many could he convince to follow him down the Grand Canal? That was the question. Proud northerners, none afraid to die. Let their names be sung in the ballad of a great battle, that would be reward enough for them—especially now. Seh was about to fall because they had known too much to listen to others and now they were proved wrong.

Shonto reached over and took his sword off its stand, laying the scabbard across his knees. Seh would have been lost if they had listened to him the first day he had arrived: Shonto knew this to be true. The barbarian army was overwhelming. How to convince them to abandon Seh to save the Empire? That was the true task.

Shonto took a long breath and began. "Lords of Seh, we have often debated the extent of the barbarian threat . . . that debate has come to an end. Those who argued that the barbarians were not a threat believe that their lack of foresight has brought us to this situation, but they are wrong. If we had begun to prepare for this war the day I became your governor, we would still not be able to meet the army that rides toward our capital. One hundred thousand barbarian warriors." He let the number hang in the still air of the Great Hall.

"Without the support of the Emperor and all of Wa, we cannot mount a force large enough to counter the barbarian threat. Rhojo-ma is a strong city, but force of numbers will tell even in a siege. One hundred thousand attackers and only fifteen thousand defenders. Despite the bravery of the men of Seh, it would not be a battle long enough to allow the rest of Wa time to raise an army. And that is what we must do . . . slow the barbarian advance long enough that an army can be raised.

"This Khan who has gathered the uncounted tribes of the desert—he could easily have taken an unprepared Province of Seh in the autumn. But that would have given the Empire a winter to raise an army. Seh is not the prize the Khan desires. With an army of one hundred thousand he seeks the throne of Wa." Shonto looked out over the hall, trying to gauge the reactions of the northern lords, but he could not read their faces. It was too much for them to take in all at once—too much for them to lose at one time. "Yet I am certain that we can save the Province of Seh." Shonto paused to let his words have their effect. "The Khan must reach the inner provinces before a force can be raised to stop him. If there is no army to fight in Seh, the Khan will not linger here but will push south. He has no choice. To move a force of that size the length

of the Empire will take many weeks—and that army must
be fed. We can slow his march south, there are ways.
There are places that will allow the few to battle the
many. If the barbarians can be defeated in Chiba Province or Dentou, Seh will bear the marks of the barbarians' passing less than other parts of Wa.''

Yes, Shonto thought, he could see that he was being
heard, by some at least. ''I will take my forces, and those
who will follow me, and set out south. All other craft in
Seh will be put to the torch. It is my intention to slow
the barbarian march south and to destroy everything that
an army could use for sustenance. When the barbarians
have gone far into Wa, they will be very hungry indeed.''

Shonto glanced over at Hojo who gave an almost imperceptible nod.

''I cannot command that you follow me. The course
of honor will not be the same for every man. By sunrise
I wish to know your choices.'' Shonto rose and left the
hall as the attending lords bowed.

The Kalam appeared after a quiet tap on the screen
leading to Shuyun's rooms. The tribesman dressed in
Shonto livery was a sight Shuyun had trouble adjusting
to, though not as much trouble as many others. It had
been decided that the Kalam should be dressed like this
for his own safety—the times dictated it. Emotions ran
high among the men of Seh and it was not for them to
make a distinction between a member of a hunting tribe
and a follower of the Khan.

The tribesman executed a bow that was a credit to his
blue livery. Shuyun did not need to be told the reason
for the interruption—there was only one thing that could
make the Kalam blush: Lady Nishima must be calling.

''Yes?'' Shuyun said.

''Lady Nishima,'' the tribesman said, mangling the
''sh'' even more than usual.

Since he had first seen Lady Nishima, the Kalam had
believed that she was a great princess and he still seemed
to think that the distinction ''Lady'' was a foolish tech-
nicality.

It was very late for a visit from Lady Nishima, but no
doubt few had slept in the hour since the Council of War.

''Please tell them to enter.''

A moment later Nishima appeared in the opening and stopped as though unsure of herself. Shuyun knew by the sounds of her footsteps that she came unaccompanied by servants or ladies-in-waiting and he was surprised.

In the light from the lamp Lady Nishima seemed so slight standing in the door. This evening she did not display the imperious air that so impressed Shuyun's barbarian servant. Instead she seemed fragile, vulnerable. Large dark eyes looked out at him and Shuyun was not sure what it was they asked, for certainly there was a question there.

"No one sleeps, Shuyun-sum," she said softly. No apology for the interruption and indeed, Shuyun felt it unnecessary.

He gestured to the cushions, "Please, Lady Nishima, like everyone else I have been sitting wondering. . . ."

Nishima retained her customary grace, despite all, and lowered herself to the cushions as lightly as a dancer. She pulled her robes close at the throat and looked around the room. "You have no charcoal burner?"

Shuyun shrugged. "But I am not cold," he said rising to his feet and disappearing from the room through another screen. Returning almost immediately, he brought a thick quilt and gave it to Lady Nishima. She smiled her thanks and wrapped herself in Shuyun's offering.

They did not speak for some time. More than once Shuyun thought Nishima would break the silence, but something stopped her. It almost seemed that what was occurring in the Empire was too momentous—defying the power of words to describe. Shuyun felt that everyone was in such turmoil that they could not find a place to begin discussing what they thought and felt.

Nishima looked up at Shuyun almost shyly. "What is everyone else doing, I wonder?"

"This," Shuyun said quietly. "Sitting in rooms alone or with others, saying very little."

Nishima nodded, it seemed true somehow. Rearranging the cushions, Nishima curled up and propped herself on one elbow. A hanging lamp went out and began to smoke, but neither seemed to care. Reaching for the remaining lamp, Nishima said, "May I?" Shuyun nodded and she turned the lamp low. She lay down, folding her arm under her head, but her eyes remained open.

"If the Yamaku fall . . ." Nishima began, her voice small, almost childlike. "If they fall, someone must ascend the throne." But it was not a question, and the lady did not look to Shuyun for an answer. She stared at the flame of the single lamp for a long time, drawing Shuyun's attention there. When Shuyun looked back at his guest, her eyes were closed. Not wishing to wake her, but feeling it was improper to be in the same room while she slept, Shuyun started to rise.

Nishima stirred then, coming half awake. Reaching out, she took his hand in both of hers and settled back, her forehead against his wrist. She slept.

I must leave, Shuyun told himself, but even so he did not move. Nishima's soft hand in his own held him more strongly than any oath and he struggled with feelings he barely recognized.

Eventually Shuyun stretched out on his cushions, resigned to the fact that Nishima would not let go of his hand. He lay so that they were head to head and willed himself to sleep so that he would be rested for his duties in the morning.

A bell sounded the hour of the owl and Shuyun heard Nishima moving. Her hand slipped from his and he felt the air stir and the warmth of the quilt descended on him. Footsteps crossed to the screen but there was no sound of the screen opening. A few seconds passed and then the footsteps returned. Shuyun felt Nishima squirm in under the cover, pressing softly up against his back. Her arm encircled him and she searched until she found his hand, pressing it. Breath like a caress on his neck.

Shuyun could feel Lady Nishima struggling to control her breathing, but this passed. They lay close like this, neither of them sleeping for some time. Nishima finally gave in to sleep, exhausted from worry, no doubt, and Shuyun lay awake, feeling her soft breathing, the warmth of her hand in his and something more that he could not name.

Botahist training told Shuyun that Lady Nishima had reached out to draw him into the Illusion and he felt as though he did not resist as he should, felt himself stepping into a cloud of desire and tenderness and emotion that no Botahist monk should know. The path upon which he should walk was becoming lost in the same cloud.

* * *

Rohku Tadamori, formerly Corporal Rohku, now Captain, looked down at the camp of the barbarian army in the first light of day. It was at least five rih off, but from his vantage atop a cliff he had a clear view and it chilled him to the center of his heart. He had been sent to assess the possibility of raiding the barbarian train—a large army on the march was an unwieldy thing and often easily harried.

Rohku handed the reins of his horse to one of his men and bent over the cliff edge to look at the corner they had seen from below. It was almost a chimney, stone shattered into uneven blocks. Sixty feet below there was a ledge with a good sized bush growing on it. From Rohku's vantage it looked possible.

He turned away from the cliff and began to strip off his armor, handing each piece to a Shonto guard. He pulled warmer robes on then and a surcoat and then strapped his sword to his back. When he was done, he nodded to his guards and turned back to the cliff.

Two of Seh's best trackers assisted him over the edge so he would not disturb the sod that clung to the cliff top. Reminding himself of Shuyun and Lord Komawara's feat in Denji Gorge, he began to climb down, stilling his fear of the height. Concentrating on each step. Above him he heard the sound of the trackers hiding the signs of his party.

The Khan's army would pass directly below him here. Only a few hundred feet would separate him from the barbarians. It would be the closest look they would have at this force.

Though much of the rock was loose, he reached his destination without mishap. The ledge was half sheltered from above by overhanging rock which formed a natural cave behind the bushes. He settled himself to wait. It would be at least two days until the entire barbarian force would pass—and then he would be in barbarian lands.

Daylight ceased to be a welcome sight in the province of Seh, for it meant the Khan's army was on the move again, drawing closer to Rhojo-ma. Shonto's senior staff were so aware of this that when the conversation paused

they seemed to be listening for the sounds of an army
drawing near. The lords of Seh had made their decisions
and Shonto met with his staff to decide what would be
done now.

General Hojo held the tally scroll in his hands. "Ten
thousand armed men, most on horse. Combined with our
own men we will field thirteen thousand, five hundred
men in all."

Against one hundred thousand, was left unsaid.

Shonto nodded to Hojo to continue.

"We do not yet know how possible it will be to attack
the barbarian train, but it seems unlikely given the size
of their force. Lord Toshaki Hirikawa and Lord Ranan
have chosen to remain in Seh, though they have commanded their sons to join the governor's forces. The lords
who stay are determined to stay in Rhojo-ma, hoping to
slow the barbarian advance by several days. If the Khan
can be convinced that Rhojo-ma is well manned, he will
be forced to waste time preparing a siege and making
rafts—an activity barbarian raiders may not be masters
of. Death in battle, Sire, it is the penance for their error."

Shonto shook his head. "Huh." He tapped his thumb
on his armrest. "It is unfortunate that they put their pride
before the safety of the Empire. A glorious death—their
glorious deaths—is preferred to a retreat. A rearguard
action that does nothing but provide others time to raise
an army and perhaps perform the great deeds." Shonto
banged his hand on the armrest, but his face displayed
no anger. "It cannot be helped. There is little time to
mount an assault on the enemy train before it reaches
Rhojo-ma. Our own assessment of the barbarian force?"

"Will take two more days, Sire, if all goes as
planned," Hojo said.

Shonto turned to Kamu. The old steward knelt as rigidly as a bronze figure, yet Shonto could detect a tremor
in the man's frame, a sign of the effort being expended.
"Kamu-sum, are preparations for our departure complete?"

The steward bowed stiffly. "Our first boats are on the
canal now, Lord Shonto, clearing the way. I have seen
to my lord's craft personally."

Shonto nodded. "I will wait until we have our own assessment of the barbarian force. General Hojo, speak with Lord Toshaki and Lord Ranan—if they will sell their lives, be sure they are sold dearly."

Shimeg nodded. "I will wait until we have our own assessment of the enemy's force," General Hong said, "and then he said, he sure that

Twenty-three

A faint rainbow appeared above the western mountains, forming a high, pure arc across a tumultuous sky—ragged clouds trailed dark ribbons of distant rain.

There was no sign of rain where the newly appointed captain, Rohku, lay—concealed on a ledge high above the broad valley. In fact the sun shone on what seemed to be a pleasant, early spring day. Unfortunately, Rohku's cave looked north and no sun came to warm his hiding place. Although the rock was both hard and cold, he would not chance movement for many hours to come. It was early morning, the second day of his vigil.

The perimeter of the barbarian camp lay not far to his right and stretched back up the valley in the direction of the border. Rohku's initial shock at the size of the Khan's forces had been replaced by a growing sense of despair. *One hundred thousand men.* Since the plague had swept through the north, the entire population of Seh numbered barely more than that. Once Rhojo-ma alone had contained one hundred and forty thousand people, but now it boasted only half that number.

How can they be so many? the guard asked himself again. It was a question without answers: the question that had led the lords of Seh to ignore all warnings about barbarian invasions.

Rohku wasn't sure which was more disturbing—the barbarian army by day or by night. The fires in the barbarian camp had been beyond counting. The fires in their camp! How could they be so many?

Patrols had left the encampment before dawn. Rohku had not been able to see them, but he had heard them pass. The Khan sent out both large and small parties. Perhaps thirty men to a small patrol and more than two hundred to a larger group. It was a conservative strategy;

the small groups would travel farther afield but would be able to retreat back to the larger patrols should they encounter Seh's warriors in any number. And Rohku found this, too, unsettling: such a vast army willing to risk so little. It was not the bravado he had been led to expect from barbarian warriors.

The army of the desert had come awake like a dragon, a slow ripple passing from head to distant tail. The head aware and moving before the extremities had even quivered. The dragon was on the hunt, now, snaking slowly across the landscape like a great worm.

The van passed below Rohku, riders on fine horses, well armored in the style of the Empire and carrying swords and short lances. Rohku could see bronze helmet ornaments flashing in the sunlight, but he could not distinguish their shapes.

Banners waved their colors in the breeze, displaying characters and symbols that Rohku did not recognize. Banners bearing the shapes of animals; a running horse, a winged tiger, the blue desert hawk, a coiled viper. Prominent among them were standards of gold silk bearing the shape of a strangely twisted dragon.

Behind these warriors came a vast cavalry mounted on the ponies of the steppe though among these men rode captains or chieftains on horses.

This sight forced Rohku to control his anger: where did the barbarians find horses except among the men of Seh and he knew that the raids could hardly have brought the tribes so many fine animals.

The cavalry were not outfitted with the consistency of the vanguard. They had not the well matched armor and elaborate helmets, but that hardly mattered. Their arms were more than adequate and appeared to have seen use. By the time the Khan's cavalry had passed, the sun was at its zenith.

The faces of the tribesmen were far enough off that they were hard to distinguish, but Rohku could see that this army was made up of men of all ages—from boymen to seasoned fighters of the age of Lord Shonto and older. None looked frail; life in the wastes saw to that. It was a hard testing ground, and the tribes had their own rites of passage. The weak, no matter what age, found no place at the fireside.

After the passing of the cavalry came bowmen and foot-soldiers, marching so close they ceased to appear human, as though a nest of ants had spewed its contents onto the valley floor. A great moving mass bristling with pikes and spears—and even these men were armored and wore helmets.

A sea of banners followed the foot soldiers and behind these rode turbaned men dressed in gray. There were rumors of these men in gray—it was said Lord Komawara and Brother Shuyun had seen them on their journey to the desert and that they guarded the skeleton of an ancient dragon. The Shonto guard caught himself straining forward for a better view and pulled back. The gray men were few in number and passed quickly, followed by what looked like an honor guard wearing armor laced in black with crimson and gold. Rohku could see the backs of these riders now. Imperial Crimson, he realized suddenly—*they wore the colors of the Emperor of Wa.*

A chieftain rode among them, a man upon a great bay horse—a horse that would have been the envy of a lord of Seh. His armor was crafted in the style of the Empire but worn with the high boots favored among the tribes. Even from a distance, Rohku's practiced eye told him that an artist of the armorer's art had created this suit—armor worthy of an Emperor. Rohku shook his head as he watched the man pass, armor laced in Imperial Crimson with trim and sash of gold. This barbarian chieftain wore a helmet crested with high plumes of deep red which bobbed and swayed as he rode. Rohku leaned forward again, a sudden realization shaking him: the Golden Khan rode before him dressed as an Emperor of Wa. Rohku pressed his eyes closed for a second. The men of Seh believe they are about to fight for control of their province, yet Seh is the smallest of this barbarian's concerns, he thought.

Inside the circle of the Khan's guard, Rohku saw other chieftains riding and though none wore the Crimson, they were finely outfitted in laced and lacquered armor with surcoats of wolf and tiger skins. These men talked among themselves and laughed as though they were on a hunt or riding for pleasure. Down the length of the great column riders passed and reported occasionally to a chieftain near the Khan.

A pebble bounced on the ledge before the Shonto

guard, and he pulled back against the cold stone. He
stopped breathing. A trickle of dirt scattered across the
moss. Something or someone, was on the cliff above.
Had he just been muttering to himself?

Voices came down to Rohku now. Despite being raised
in the south it was a tongue the guard recognized—he
had heard Shuyun speak it to his barbarian servant several times. Horses now and more men. *May Botahara
protect me.* Rohku tried to push himself into the rock,
hoping no part of him could be seen. With great care but
little expertise the captain had studied his ledge—hiding
a footprint in the moss, being sure he snapped none of
the bush's branches. He hoped that a barbarian tracker
would not be able to see signs of his passing from so
high above, but he was not convinced this would be the
case.

The reputation of the barbarian trackers was legend
among the men Rohku had met in Seh, and this made the
young captain slowly unsheathe his dagger. The ledge
would be too small for a sword. The Shonto guard's left
leg was asleep and he knew that it would not respond if
needed quickly. He offered a prayer to Botahara.

Another pebble bounced on the ledge and more talk
drifted down to him. If only he had taken the time to
learn some of this language from Kalam!

The sound of hoofs seemed to echo through the stone
and then grew fainter. There were no more voices. Rohku
lay without daring to move for some time, realizing that
he would do exactly this if he wanted to take a man hidden on a ledge: ride away and let the man believe he was
safe, taking him when he was unprepared.

Something in the long line of barbarians drew the
guard's attention. Within another circle of the Khan's
guard Rohku was amazed to see women. They rode like
the men of the desert, though Rohku could see hints of
fine silk being worn under robes of rougher material.
There were perhaps a hundred women, their heads
wrapped in bright scarves that covered all but their eyes
and foreheads.

And thus they go to war, Rohku thought, how amaz-
ing.

Late afternoon came, the clouds scattered across the
sky grouped for an assault on the expanse of blue and the

day turned gray. Rohku began to shiver. He ate some
food and drank water from his skin, but not having room
to move was making him very cold. It would be at least
another day before he could leave his ledge and he began
to wonder if he would be able to manage the climb up.

Following another group of armed riders came the supply train. The barbarians did not seem to have carts or
wagons, so everything came on the backs of ponies and
mules. Darkness came before the train had passed and
the man of Wa spent the first part of the night listening
to the sound of the barbarian flutes wafting up from in-
numerable campfires.

A soft rain fell, but Rohku's prayers for a downpour
were not answered.

Shonto sat on the railing of the balcony outside the
governor's personal apartments. The day was fine, hinting at warmth to come. Billowing white clouds scattered
themselves against the great expanse of spring blue sky.
It would be a day to lift the heart—if the heart were not
burdened with other matters.

Shonto could see the long line of people being forced
to leave the city, so many of them only newly arrived.
There were no boats to carry the population of Rhojo-
ma and animals of burden were being taken for the war,
so the refuges were forced to flee on foot. They crossed
the long bridge to the shore and then made their way up
a low hill to the crest where the road divided. About half
the people chose to go south toward the inner provinces
while the rest turned east toward the sea. One could almost see them hesitating at the top—suddenly unsure of
their decision.

It is a gamble either way, Shonto thought. His own
course was already set—to leave as he'd come, along the
Grand Canal. And that was a gamble, too.

Shonto read Lord Toshaki's letter for the second time.

Lord Shonto,
Imperial Governor of the Province of Seh:

    It was your own ancestor who said; "The way
a man dies is as important as the way he lives." I
honor his memory.

Having realized how poorly I have lived, I will take more care with my death. When this is delivered to you I will have returned to the wheel. I have chosen this course to erase my shame and because I am not worthy enough to die beside my comrades fighting the barbarians.

You see, Lord Governor, I have conspired with my Emperor to end the life of one Shonto Motoru. No doubt the design is known to you, though perhaps my part is not clear. Send Lord Shonto north with express instructions to end the barbarian raids—an impossibility of course—especially when the barbarians are being paid to raid across the border by the Emperor. You would have failed, Sire, it was inevitable. I would even surmise that the situation could have become worse.

You would be removed from your appointment and ordered back to the Capital—or so it would be said. In truth I was to remove you from your position by force. The Emperor would claim that you had refused to return to the Capital to face the consequences of your failure. In your desperation you tried to establish yourself in Seh. The Emperor's loyal subject, Lord Toshaki, however, would not allow this—saving the Empire from civil war. Among other rewards I would become the Governor of Seh, as would my son after me.

I have betrayed Seh, the people of Wa, and neither of these I intended. I admit to my part in the plot against the Shonto House: I did not intend to assist the barbarians in their invasion. Like the rest of the lords of Seh I did not imagine the barbarians could mount such a force—can still hardly believe it. Even as you struggled to save my province, I worked against you.

I give my oath that my son, Yoshihira, knew nothing of this, and so I have commanded him south with your army so that our House might continue or that he might find an honorable end. It is my hope that you will allow this. My countrymen will believe that I have chosen this

*course to pay for my errors: I would not allow an
army to be raised in Seh nor would I listen to
reason. It is my hope that you will let them
continue to believe this. In return I will give you
information. The man who devised and guided
this plot against you is in your midst: Jaku Katta
planned every detail of your fall, Lord Shonto.
Why he is here now I am not sure—you have
heard the same rumors as I.*

> *At the gii board
> It is not possible to sacrifice
> Honor for position.
> I take my place on the battlements.
> The plunge as cold as steel
> As soft as ashes.*

> *Lord Toshaki Hirikawa*

Shonto looked off at the long straggling line of humanity that wandered up the side of the hill. So sad.

Was it true that Toshaki's fool of a son was innocent?
Perhaps. Certainly Toshaki Shinga was party to this
plot—there could be little doubt of that. But Toshaki
Shinga had chosen to stay in Rhojo-ma—where he commanded the garrison. That was a life put to better use
than his lord's! The fool should have stayed alive long
enough to die slowing the barbarians' advance.

Shonto rose from his position and returned inside. He
had shed the official robes of the Governor of Seh that
morning and was dressed more comfortably now—ready
to travel. Prodding the coals of a charcoal burner to life,
the lord went to toss Toshaki's letter in but stopped himself. No, he would save this—it might be of interest one
day—historically at least.

The last inhabitants of Rhojo-ma trickled out of the
gate and set out across the bridge. Bells rang from many
towers throughout the empty city—the gates were about
to be shut for the last time. Shonto stood on a quay that
would soon be on the lake bottom—such was it designed.
Far off he could see men beginning to work on the single

bridge that spanned the distance to shore. It, too, would be under water within the hour.

Toward the north end of the quay, Shonto could see Lord Toshaki's son surrounded by his retainers. Word had spread about the old Toshaki's suicide—a plunge off the battlement into the depths of the lake. The lord had worn full armor. It was an odd suicide—one that indicated great shame. Nonetheless, Lord Toshaki had been a man respected in Seh and there was obvious concern for his son among those present, though, as northerners, they were equally concerned with his pride. All expressions of concern were therefore kept within bounds strictly defined by an unwritten code which said: *young Toshaki is a warrior and lord of Seh, therefore he is strong. All expressions of regret will be offered formally—the Toshaki do not require comfort. This is a matter of respect only.*

Shonto's senior staff continued to work nearby, attending to the thousand details that would allow an army of thirteen thousand, plus a few thousand others, to move south at speed. The barbarian army could travel five rih in a day, but the canal would carry Shonto much faster than that.

Men cut away the branches of an ancient lintel vine that clung to the stone around the city's gate. This seemed like a sign of things to come to Shonto, and he looked away.

A delegation appeared at the gate. Guards pushed through, heavily armed and bearing banners. The lords of Seh had arrived—the lords who would remain behind. Most of the older generation had chosen to pay their penance by defending Rhojo-ma—an endeavor whose outcome was as certain as the night following day. Five thousand warriors stayed with these men, chosen for this great honor: to die with their lords in a battle that could not be won.

A crier preceded the fated warriors.

"Make way! Make way! Make way for the lords of Seh. Make way!"

The fools of Seh, Shonto thought, brave fools.

As the senior member of the most important House, Lord Ranan led the delegation. He bowed as he approached Lord Shonto and the lord returned this with a deep bow of respect rather than the nod his position allowed.

"Our preparations go as planned, Lord Shonto," Ranan said with an air of importance. "We will be ready before the Khan's outriders appear."

Fool, Shonto thought, *arrogant fool*!

"You are to be honored, Lord Ranan, as are all who prepare for Rhojo-ma's . . . defense."

Ranan bowed again. "It is our intention to slow the barbarian force by as many days as our strength will allow. May those days be well used, Sire."

Everyone on the quay bowed to those who would remain.

Shonto was about to step back toward his boat when a tunnel opened up in the crowd and the young lord of the Toshaki stepped forward. Bowing quickly to Shonto and Lord Ranan, the young lord turned to Komawara whom Shonto had not seen arrive. Members of Komawara's guard stepped closer to their lord—the Hajiwara men, Shonto realized. Though they wore the Komawara colors, deep blue and black trimmed in gold, the former residents of Itsa retained a length of shoulder trim in Hajiwara green. "Lord Komawara," Toshaki began with great formality, as though he repeated a speech carefully rehearsed, "I once suggested that you would need a proper weapon to fight barbarian hordes." He reached his hand back to a retainer who laid a sword in a scabbard across the lord's palm. Bringing this around, he held it in both hands as though it were a treasure. "This blade belonged to my father, Toshaki Hirikawa. It was made by Toyotomi the Younger and gained great renown in the Ona War. This blade has been in the Toshaki family for seven generations and has proven its worth in many battles against the barbarians. It is my hope that you will accept this as a mark of my respect. Among the lords of Seh you were the first to realize our position though so many of us argued against you." He offered the sword now with a slight bow.

Komawara seemed frozen in place and for a second Shonto thought he would refuse it. But then Komawara bowed and reached out, taking the blade from Toshaki in a gesture almost equally reverent.

When he spoke, Lord Komawara's voice was tight as

though he choked back emotion with difficulty. "This is a great honor, Lord Toshaki. I hope that the hands of the Komawara will wield this with even half the skill of your ancestors. If so, it shall be a blade of great fame indeed."

Toshaki bowed again, and at a gesture from Shonto his senior staff began retreating to their appointed boats. We are at war, Shonto thought, there is no time to sit and drink wine and fabricate lies about the great esteem our ancestors felt for each other.

, As the boats pushed away, Shonto walked back to the quarterdeck. Sails were raised, luffing and snapping, until the helmsmen fell off the wind and the sails were sheeted home. Shonto saw Nishima wave from a nearby boat as did Lady Okara and Lady Kitsura. A sailor pointed, and Shonto looked up in time to see the Shinta Blossom at Rhojo-ma's high tower quiver and then come down. Seconds later it was replaced by the Flying Horse of Seh.

A line of boats tacked into the breeze, heading toward the mouth of the Grand Canal and the first set of locks. Shonto's boat found a place near the end of this line, for in the campaign to come the command would need to be in close contact with the retreating rear. A strange thought.

Lady Nishima leaned against the rail, glad of its support, for she felt a weakness in her will that was disturbing. Despite all of her prayers, war had come. As they cleared the end of the city, she looked off toward the north. Barbarian armies would appear there in only a few days. All of her other concerns seemed petty and trivial now. People would die—and not just from battle.

She thought about the people of Seh setting out south and toward the sea. Not all of them would escape, nor would they understand their danger. They would try to hide themselves, hoping the storm would pass by without harming them. Her father had left a small force behind, hidden somewhere in Seh's hills for this very reason. Its only purpose was to be sure nothing would be grown where the barbarians could find it. They would raid upon and quite possibly be forced to kill their own people.

Leave nothing for the enemy, her father had ordered.
Which meant nothing for the peasants.

A report like strange thunder echoed across the lake
and Nishima turned in time to see the first span of the
bridge collapse into a cascade of white. For the briefest
instant a rainbow appeared in the spray, but then the waters rushed back together like a healing wound. Rhojo-ma's
tie to the land was gone.

Around the south end of the city a funeral barge appeared, covered in the white flower of the snow lily. The
light breeze picked up the petals, strewing them like a
wake on the calm water. Lord Toshaki, Nishima realized.
The barge set off with purpose toward the lake's south-
western end as though its destination had never been in
doubt. Nishima raised her hands to cover her face but
realized what she did and stopped herself. Instead she
made a sign to Botahara and offered a silent prayer.

The boat suddenly began pitching in the waves created
by the falling bridge. Nishima clutched the rail until the
water was calm again and then made her way quickly
below. In the privacy of her small cabin Nishima took
out her writing implements and prepared ink in what was
almost a ritual.

> *Our boat of gumwood and dark locust*
> *Her paint scaling like serpent's skin*
> *Sets forth into the throng of craft*
> *On the Grand Canal.*
> *Uncounted travelers,*
> *Uncounted desires*
> *Borne over blue water.*
> *Only the funeral barge*
> *Covered in white petals*
> *Appears to know its destination.*

Twenty-four

An abandoned stable, recently refurbished for the presentation of plays, had been commandeered by Shonto's recruiting officers. The thatch leaked in places when rain and the west wind joined forces and there was still an unrecognizable odor in one corner, but otherwise it suited well.

Two officers sat behind a large, low desk upon what had been the stage. On three sides men knelt in more or less straight rows. In the light from hanging lamps they seemed to be of one type, but upon closer inspection it became apparent that they were of all ages, sizes, accents, experience, and temperament.

Despite this, they had one thing in common. They were warriors without Houses and though some had actually been raised to the way of the sword, many were the sons of merchants or farmers who had broken with their families to take up this life. The men who gathered in the hall had all passed a test of skill with both sword and bow. Those who failed had been sent elsewhere—all men would find a place in the war to come.

Of the hundred or so who had passed the test of arms, most seemed to be without serious criminal records. The senior recruiting officer, a Shonto sergeant, looked at his list and pointed to a name which his assistant called out. A man of perhaps forty years rose and crossed the room to kneel before him. Like most of the men in the hall, his clothes were rough, though, unlike many, his were clean and bore the marks of expert mending. He was a large man, well formed, his face hidden by a dark beard. What wasn't hidden had been darkened by time in the sun and lined with deep creases, especially across the forehead and in the corners of the eyes.

"Shinga Kyoshi?"

The man nodded, a half bow.

"Your weapons are in order?" the sergeant asked.

The man nodded again. "Complete armor and sword. I-I have no bow." A deep voice.

The sergeant nodded. There was a note by this man's name—he was very good with a sword, apparently. "Your sword," the sergeant said holding out his hand.

The kneeling man hesitated for a second, as though not sure of the request, but then drew his blade and handed it to the officer, pommel first.

It was a fine weapon, beautifully balanced and honed to a perfect edge. The sword guard was a small work of art—a lacquered scroll of sea shells over polished bronze. The maker's name on the blade was *Kentoka,* undoubtedly a forgery, but it was a well crafted weapon nonetheless—not what you would expect from a wandering soldier. The sergeant fixed the man with his gaze—a gaze that melted strong young men. "It says here that you are from Nitashi."

The man nodded.

"I'm from Nitashi," the sergeant said. "You don't have the Nitashi way of speaking."

"It has been many years, Sergeant."

The officer continued to stare. He would wager that if he looked in the man's armor chest he would find new lacing in some neutral colour.

He returned the man's sword. Stared for a few seconds more, then looked back to his lists. He pushed a scroll across the table and held out a brush. "See the quartermaster," the sergeant said. The man signed his name, bowing low and hurrying off.

Looking at the man's signature, the recruiting officer hid his reaction. That was the third man the sergeant had seen in the last two days who he believed had served the Hajiwara—and this one had been an officer! He shook his head. If there were too many more, he would have to consider turning some away. There were the Butto to consider.

"Ujima Nyatomi!" the officer's assistant called.

Another bearded man hurried up and knelt before the sergeant who leaned over his reports.

"Ujima Nyatomi?"

The soldier nodded. If the sergeant had looked up, he

would have noticed that this one was older than the last, and less powerfully built.

"Your weapons are in order?"

The man nodded again.

"Your sword."

The man placed the pommel in the officer's hand. The sergeant looked up from his list, eyes widening. This was a sword indeed! It came into the hand like a dream. The handle was covered in the skin of the giant ray, then wrapped in blue silk cord, and the sword guard, the sergeant suddenly realized, was formed in the shape of a shinta blossom!

The sergeant looked up at the man kneeling before him. Before he could begin to react the man spoke. "My armor is of similar quality, Sergeant, and I have bow, lance, and horse as well." He shook his head almost imperceptibly.

The sergeant returned the man's sword then and searched his lists. Pushing the paper and brush across the table he said, "See the quartermaster."

The man signed, bowed quickly, and hurried off. Another name was called, but the sergeant did not register it. He had just enrolled Rohku Saicha, the Captain of Shonto's guard, into the lists of the army of Seh. He wondered how many others had escaped the Capital. He smiled in spite of himself.

The flotilla had entered the Grand Canal and immediately slowed to what seemed like a walk. Kamu knew that progress south would not compare with the speed they achieved passing north—there were too many refugees on the canal and the number of boats used by the retreating army was greater. Still, an army of one hundred thousand could hardly make better than seven or eight rih a day over level ground.

It would take the barbarians over three lunar months to reach the Imperial Capital by land. With fair winds the river craft could often traverse the distance between Seh and the Capital in less than thirty days—half that time if they had crew enough to travel both day and night.

At our present speed, Kamu reminded himself, we'll travel twice as far in a day as do the barbarians. Shonto's fleet had left at least two days, probably three, before the

barbarians would reach Rhojo-ma. It was a significant
lead.

Kamu's cabin was a riot of paper, scrolls stacked in
holders like firewood, sheets of paper and letters in carefully laid out piles, none without a paperweight. Folders
of paper, rolls of paper, notes written on scraps, rice
paper, mulberry paper. There seemed to be no end of
this valuable commodity. And every piece of paper bore
information Kamu could not lose. He found himself
occasionally daydreaming about a small thatch house
beside a river in some quiet range of hills.

A knock on the door was followed by Kamu's assistant, Toko, entering bearing a folder that seemed to contain more paper. In the months since the attempted
assassination in Shonto's garden this young man had
proven to be an invaluable assistant. Oh, he had much to
learn, there was no doubt of that, but he learned well and
seldom made mistakes twice.

Kamu raised one eyebrow at his assistant in an unwit-
ting imitation of Lord Shonto.

"Requests for passage or to join the flotilla, Steward
Kamu," Toko said quietly. He had not lost the ways of
those who served. The boy was still almost entirely un-
obtrusive—silent of movement, and quiet of voice.

Kamu nodded. He pointed with a brush. "There will
do."

Toko placed the folder on the appointed pile and then
stood quietly. Kamu realized the young man was waiting
to be noticed, which almost made the old warrior smile.

"Toko?"

"Steward Kamu," the young man started, his tone revealing a lack of certainty, "several of these requests are
from members of the Botahist faith. I was not sure if I
should let them wait."

"Huh." Kamu considered the column of numbers in
the report he read. "How many, precisely?"

"Two Sisters and five Botahist monks—one claims to
have been a teacher of Brother Shuyun."

"Ah, yes—Soto . . ." Kamu trailed off.

"Brother Sotura, I believe, Steward."

Kamu squinted to make out a figure. "Yes, I have met
him. Give them quarters somewhere well out of harm's
way. This is an army at war—not an Imperial Progress."

Toko nodded. He quickly opened another ledger, made entries, and then was gone.

Kamu shook his head. It isn't an Imperial Progress, the old steward thought, may Botahara protect us.

Dusk and rain. Young Captain Rohku was stiff with cold and lack of movement. He stopped climbing and tried to control a persistent tremor in his left leg. If one of his men had not thought to bring a rope, he realized, he would never have been able to climb up on his own. Five more feet, then stop. Water ran down the corner he climbed, making the rock as slippery as ice.

He moved again and his feet came off their hold—he fell. For the third time the rope held him. Flailing until he felt the rock under his feet and hands again, Rohku leaned his cheek against the cold stone. Perhaps fifteen feet remain, he told himself. It would be shameful if he had to be pulled up by his men. This thought gave him some strength and propelled him upward.

There were barbarian patrols close by, so silence met Rohku when he clambered over the cliff edge. He sat on a stone and ate a little cold food. Something warm to drink was what he wanted, but a fire could not be risked even if they could find enough dry wood. Finally, nodding to one of his men, Rohku rose stiffly and went to his horse. It took every bit of strength he could find, but he mounted without assistance. There were men of Seh present, it was important that he keep their respect.

A long ride awaited them. First a report to Rhojo-ma, then onto the canal. They would catch up with Lord Shonto's fleet within three days. Rohku had a great deal to tell. A great deal indeed.

Tadamoto found the Emperor walking near the Dragon Pond. A flower viewing had been arranged, for the blossoms of late winter and early spring were pushing up toward a sun that showed signs of warming. Although the Emperor was ostensibly in the company of members of the court, he walked off by himself and none dared interrupt his sullen mood.

Tadamoto looked over the gathered courtiers and noted with some satisfaction that there were a number of young women of great beauty who had recently come to court.

May one of them catch his fancy, Tadamoto thought—it was almost a prayer.

But then among the pure young faces and elaborate robes Tadamoto saw Osha. She was watching him with a look of such sadness that he almost wept at the sight. *Osha, Osha. . . .* To Tadamoto's eye there was a great depth of spirit reflected in her face, while the faces of the young women around her seemed almost like masks painted with only a single, vague expression.

Tadamoto's step almost faltered. Tearing his gaze away before anyone should notice, he continued on toward the Emperor. It was a familiar exercise now, closing off his emotions. Tadamoto often thought of himself as some spiritual hermit who had developed this control through meditation. He could make himself feel nothing almost at will. When he knelt before the Emperor, he was as devoid of feelings as a stone.

The Emperor nodded and then beckoned to Tadamoto to rise and walk with him. The colonel hesitated, casting a glance toward the gathered courtiers who pretended not to watch. A lowly colonel being invited to walk with the Son of Heaven—that might raise an eyebrow or two.

They moved slowly away from the others, the Emperor pausing to look at a spray of snow lilies that clung to the shade of a chaku bush. A few more days of sun and they would be gone.

It was a warm day for the time of year. A breeze so gentle it barely rippled the surface of the Dragon Pond felt as sensuous and delightful as a lover's secret touch. A sky, bright as a ringing bell, bore a smattering of clouds like echoes and overtones in the midst of clarity.

"You have something to report, Colonel." The Emperor continued to look at the snow lilies. Let the courtiers wonder what they discussed, there would be no clue from the Emperor.

"I do, Emperor. We have finally managed to get officials into Ika Cho Province. Lord Shonto Shokan has disappeared with a force of significant size, perhaps four thousand men."

"It is a difficult trick to perform—to disappear with so many. We don't know how this was done?"

"It seems that the Shonto son may have taken his force into High Wind Pass, Sire."

The Emperor nodded. "It is early in the year to attempt the pass. Is it possible that he could win through?" The sound of women's laughter pealed across the water.

"It is thought unlikely, Emperor. The snows in the mountains were substantial this winter." Tadamoto almost turned his gaze back to the courtiers but caught himself. "I find it strange that he did not go north to Seh by ship. Certainly the storms would be no greater risk than attempting the mountains."

The Emperor plucked a snow lily and examined it closely. "The High Wind Pass would bring Shokan to northern Chiba, yeh?"

Tadamoto nodded.

"Huh." The Emperor handed the blossom to Tadamoto. "For your honored wife from the Emperor, Tadamoto-sum." The Emperor gave him a distracted smile. "Set men to watch the western end of the pass. If he were not Shonto, I would say a prayer for his soul but. . . ." The Emperor shrugged and walked on, leaving Tadamoto scrambling to bow, clutching his snow lily.

The voices of several hundred women raised in a melodic chant seemed to emanate from the floor and the walls. The Prioress reclined in her litter, eyes closed. It was impossible to tell if she slept or simply lay listening in a state of total concentration, for there was only the merest movement of her breathing. Sister Sutso hesitated to approach her.

From the nave below, the singing soared up into the rafters where a balcony perched like a well hidden nest. The room that opened onto the balcony was one of the Prioress' favorite retreats and her staff preferred not to disturb her there.

Sutso decided it would be better to wait and took a step toward the balcony. The Prioress did not move, but her voice sounded almost inaudibly over the chanting.

"Sutso-sum?"

"Yes, Prioress."

The old woman did not open her eyes or move in any way at all. "I believe our singers become more inspired with each year," she said in a voice that seemed dry and withered.

The Prioress' secretary came and knelt at the side of

the litter. "I agree, Prioress. I feel closer to Botahara even now."

"It is the height, child," the Prioress said and a beatific smile spread across her wrinkled face. Sutso did not laugh, she dared not, even though she was quite sure the Prioress intended humor. No, this ancient woman was as close to perfection as anyone Sutso had ever met. In the presence of the Prioress one did not act in any way that could be interpreted as disrespectful.

"You have something weighing on your mind, Sutso-sum." It was not a question.

Sutso nodded though her superior's eyes remained closed. "I wrote to Morima-sum, as you instructed, but I am concerned. There has been no response."

Still, the Prioress could lay so utterly still. "Morima-sum will not fail us, Sutso-sum, do not concern yourself. Much goes on in Seh. Writing a letter may not seem as important to her as it does to us. Wait a little yet."

Sutso nodded again. She bowed and started to rise when the Prioress spoke again.

"You are concerned about the coming war."

Sutso sank back to her knees. "Everyone is concerned, Prioress. It is not like the Interim War where all concerned were followers of the Way. The barbarians will not treat us with respect. Our Sisters will be in danger."

The Prioress' large dark eyes sprang open and she studied her secretary for a moment. The eyes closed again. "If the men who fought the Interim War had truly been followers of Botahara, there would have been no war, Sutso-sum." She fell silent for a second. The chanting suddenly became slow and gentle. "The Empire is vast. This war will be like others—parts of Wa will suffer terribly while other regions will be entirely unaffected. It saddens me. . . . Until the Way is truly followed, there will always be wars. We have made every preparation we can. Let wars be the concern of others. Our concern is the Teachings of Botahara." She smiled again.

"But think, child, the *Teacher*—in our own lifetime! It is a miracle beyond imagining. We can spare no effort, even if the Empire collapses around us. It has been one thousand years, child—forty generations! The Teacher . . . we must find the Teacher. It is the reason for our being."

The collective voice began to grow, it reached up like hands in prayer. It touched Sutso with its beauty and a tear appeared at the corner of one eye. She reached out and touched the sleeve of the Prioress' robe so softly it seemed she caressed a sleeping child.

Twenty-five

Spring's first swallows
Glide down from winter's sky
They soar across rivers,
Finding joy in every turn.

Twilight lingers like a lover
Unable to leave,
Unable to say what is in the heart

From the Palace Book,
Lady Nikko

The chambers of the Empress Jenna. Jaku Tadamoto sat on the ancient bed of the Empress herself and wondered if Osha would come—it had been so long. Perhaps she had been unable to leave her rooms without being seen or had been intercepted by some agents of the Emperor's. Or, worst of all, she had been summoned by the Son of Heaven. Because this disturbed him the most, Tadamoto's mind filled with images of Osha in the Emperor's embrace.

Did she respond to his touch? The image in his mind showed Osha driven to heights of passion she had never known with Tadamoto. He began to feel like a fool for waiting.

The lantern Tadamoto had used to guide him sat on the floor casting a faint circle of light out into the large room. They had spent their first night together here. It was Tadamoto's hope that returning to this place might allow them to recapture things felt in the past.

Running his long fingers across the sheet covering the bed, he had a clear recollection of touching Osha's breast for the first time, here, on a warm autumn night.

For some weeks now they had been avoiding each other, but seeing Osha among the courtiers by the Dragon Pond that afternoon had affected him in a way that he could not explain. Suddenly he was desperate to see her—would not eat or sleep until he spoke with her.

So he sat wondering if he was making a fool of himself—wondering if Osha was lost in pleasure in the Emperor's arms even as Tadamoto sat pining for her. And yet he could not make himself leave.

An impulse to do something took hold of the young colonel and he went to the screens opening onto the balcony and pulled them aside. He was not concerned with being seen this high up in an unfrequented section of the palace, for even if someone did notice him the reputation of the Hanama chambers being inhabited by ghosts would be all the explanation anyone would require.

Tadamoto stood looking out over the impossibly complex curves and planes of the palace's roofs lit by a waning crescent moon. It seemed so tranquil. It was difficult to imagine that Wa was about to be shaken by war, for Tadamoto was certain that was about to happen. A civil war with the Shonto against the Yamaku or the barbarian war Shonto and Katta warned of: but war either way. Less than a decade since the Yamaku ascendancy and already war seemed to be flickering to life, like a fire that had only disappeared temporarily into the earth.

Pacing the perimeter of the room made Tadamoto realize how little control he felt and he forced himself to sit and be calm.

The screen leading to the room slid aside a few inches and Tadamoto started. Osha! He could not really see her in the dark, but he was so familiar with her size he knew this could be no one else. She slipped in through the crack and pushed the screen closed behind her. Leaning against the wall she stood regarding him. In the darkness Tadamoto could not see her eyes and this unsettled him. He felt he needed to look into her eyes to know what whispered in her heart.

Osha favored him with a nod and then crossed to the open screens, her movements slow and deliberate as though her life force had been reduced to a flicker.

She does not glide, Tadamoto found himself thinking. Silhouetted against the night Osha seemed very beau-

tiful to him—perfect, in fact. Small and extraordinarily
delicate. He could almost feel the warmth and softness
of her skin. Beyond Osha the sky was not black but the
deepest possible blue. Banners of cloud so distant they
seemed to be in the heavens reflected a hint of moonlight. And the stars lacked definition, as though seen as
reflections in dark water.

Osha turned and leaned her back against the frame of
the opening, her hands clasped behind her. "This room . . ."
she began, her voice flat, "it brings me deep sadness to
come here."

Tadamoto sat, suddenly awkward, his hands on his
thighs. "Yes," he said, "I thought it would be different."

Osha took a deep breath as if she would speak but then
let it out slowly. She turned and looked out at the night,
not seeming to care that the air was cool. "My heart . . ."
she began, "my heart is in ruins, Tado-sum, and I do
not know if anything can survive the wreckage." She
almost seemed to fall back into her former position.

There was a long silence and then Tadamoto braved
the question that tormented him. "Do you love the Emperor, then?"

Osha looked down at her feet, shaking her head slowly.
When she raised her face Tadamoto could see her cheeks
shining with tears in the starlight. "I do not love him."

Tadamoto nodded; it was a gentle motion, heavy with
resignation. He seemed so weighed down with sadness
that it stopped him from moving—and so he sat on the
bed, slumped as though something inside him had collapsed. The sound of Osha crying pained him even more,
but he could not rise to go to her. Even when she sank
to her knees and buried her face in her hands, he did not
move.

Twenty-six

The canal runs thick with rumor
Overflowing its banks
Spreading to the four directions.
Intrigues and betrayals
Flood into the countryside
Banishing truth to the rooftops

Lady Okara Haroshu

A young officer gave the orders which were carried
out by stone-faced soldiers and dismayed peasants.
Everything that had been planted in the early spring was
destroyed. Winter's remaining hay was piled in the yard
and set to the torch, going up in a blast of heat. The
blaze was fed stores of seed and grains and the farmers'
carefully nurtured seedlings. The soldiers were determined to leave nothing for the barbarians. And nothing
for the villagers and peasants either.

Shimeko could see it written in each peasant's face:
*but we will starve. Is it better to be murdered by your
own people?* The sight of this had been more than she
could bear, so she had set off, avoiding the road used by
the fleeing peasants. I am a servant of the family that
turns them from their homes, she had said to herself, and
it was not a thought that brought her comfort.

Shimeko had been forced to walk some distance up the
canal to find a place where she could be alone and not
be an unwilling witness to the destruction. Part of the
fleet had stopped in this valley to "create the desert" as
she had heard one soldier say, and Lady Nishima's boat
had been unable to pass.

Under the branches of a willow that hung over the canal, Shimeko set out a grass mat and made herself com-

fortable. The fine curtain of willow branches was covered with delicate green buds and would be in leaf in mere days. Boats from the flotilla had been moored against the opposite shore, and she could see them busily taking aboard cargo from the surrounding farms. *Leave nothing for the barbarians.*

A family sailed past in a small river boat, the sail filled by a soft breeze from the east—the Plum Blossom Wind it was called, and it was eagerly awaited by the people of Wa. And though it invariably meant warmer days and planting and the blossoming of cherry and plum and apple, this year it was not being celebrated. At least not in the wake of Shonto's army.

Shimeko could see the looks of anxiety on the faces of the man and woman in the river boat. He looked up at the sail and then off to the east. Her years in the monastery told her that he was praying for the wind to hold. All boats had been ordered to pass ahead of the flotilla or be destroyed.

A kingfisher dived into the boat's wake and came out of the water in a flash of iridescent green. It darted off with its prize, disappearing into the branches of a willow.

In the privacy of the bower she tried to meditate, but after several minutes she gave this up. It seemed even that comfort was lost to her. Taking a comb from her sleeve, she ran it through her still very short hair. Lady Nishima had told her that in little more than a year she would be able to put her hair up in such a manner that it would be impossible to tell how long it was. This is foolish vanity, she told herself, but continued to comb as though the action would hurry the course of nature.

Shimeko found herself wondering again about Lady Nishima. It was difficult to dislike her, Shimeko found, though she had been prepared to. And certainly the rest of Lady Nishima's staff adored her. Even so, it seemed odd to Shimeko. Lady Nishima was so young and had not spent the years of discipline and denial senior Sisters had—and yet she was renowned throughout the Empire for her accomplishments.

Shimeko shook her head. Certainly Lady Nishima was a harp player of great skill and her hand was one of the finest she had ever seen. No doubt her social discourse was charming and witty, but they were only social con-

versations. Shimeko tossed a pebble out into the water.
In her former world, Lady Nishima would have been a
senior Acolyte, no matter what her accomplishments, and
many years away from becoming a senior sister. Yet in
the world of Wa, Nishima was something of a sensation
though barely more than a girl.

Shimeko tossed a second pebble after the first, gaining
the brief interest of a kingfisher that hovered over the
rings where the pebble had disappeared.

This interest that the Lady Nishima showed in Brother
Shuyun . . . Shimeko was beginning to wonder if it was
entirely proper. The former nun was aware that she had
little experience of the world, but even so—the way Lady
Nishima brightened when Brother Shuyun appeared, it
was difficult to mistake. If Brother Shuyun is the Teacher
who was foretold, then this situation with the Shonto
daughter was most unseemly.

Shimeko remembered searching the archives for Lady
Nishima and this brought to mind the sculpture of the
Two Lovers—an image she found most disturbing.
Though, if truth were told, it was an image she had had
difficulty taking her eyes from when they had waited in
Denji Gorge. She had found herself drawn to it more than
she would ever admit.

Is Brother Shuyun the Teacher who was spoken of? she
asked herself again. If there was only some test she could
perform . . . but she knew of no such thing.

The day wore on until she felt it must be time to return. She had been given leave only to stretch her legs,
not to disappear for an extended period.

Rising, she rolled the mat and found her way through
the curtain of willow wands. A few steps brought her
back to the path which ran along the top of the raised
bank. Plum trees were planted here and she could see
that only a few days would bring them into bloom—an
event awaited with great anticipation by everyone in Wa.
An image of lines of refuges passing through the plum
tree orchards came like a sharp pain.

Some distance off, coming toward her, Shimeko could
see a large peasant woman wrapped in cotton robes and
shawls. And she had so hoped to avoid the refugees who
had been turned from their homes. But then her head

snapped up again. It could not be! That walk, Shimeko was sure she could not mistake it.

The woman came closer and raised her covered head. "Sister Morima?" Shimeko said.

The senior nun nodded, her face contorting in a brief, forced smile. Before she realized what she did Shimeko bowed as Acolyte to senior Sister. But then she rose slowly and forced herself to look the older woman in the eye.

"This is a pleasant surprise, Sister," Shimeko said.

Morima nodded again. She waved her hand to the side of the track and they turned and took a few steps among the plum trees. "Do not be surprised, Tesseko-sum, the Sisterhood releases few entirely."

Realizing that Morima labored as though from great exercise, Shimeko laid her mat on the grass and helped the nun sit. She knelt on the mat facing her, fighting an impulse to take on the posture of humility.

"Thank you," Morima wheezed. "A moment." She sat regaining her breath and then she tried another smile— marginally more successful.

"The Sisters will not release even me, and I have lost the Way almost entirely." She stared at Shimeko who finally had to look away.

"Is the path you follow easier, child?" she said in a voice full of concern.

Shimeko shrugged. "I do not yet know, Sister."

Morima nodded as though she understood. "You appear well enough." A genuine smile this time. "And you will have a proper head of hair very soon."

Shimeko colored at the mention of this. "I must be getting back, Sister Morima, I have duties."

"Do you, indeed?" Morima said. "May I speak briefly, Tesseko-sum?"

The younger woman nodded. "I am Shimeko now, Sister—Shimeko."

Morima tried to smile again but failed. "The Sisterhood has sent me to speak with you. They advised me to come dressed as a peasant and to claim that I had left the Order also. They want information about Lord Shonto's Spiritual Advisor and anything they can learn about the barbarian war and the intrigues within the Empire."

The senior Sister looked up at her former charge and

shrugged, apparently embarrassed. "It is the worst foolishness. You might think they would become tired of lies
and intrigues, but that does not seem to be so." She
reached down and tightened her sandals. "I must be getting back myself, now that I have fulfilled my duty." She
rose with some effort and stood looking down at Shimeko.

Shimeko could not hide her look of confusion. "That
is all you have to say, Sister?"

"Yes, child." The older woman wiped her forehead
with the tail of her shawl.

Shimeko nodded though she was not sure why. They
remained as they were for a moment—an echo of their
former lives: the younger woman kneeling, the elder
standing.

"Morima-sum?" Shimeko said suddenly. "You have
met Brother Shuyun. Do you think it is possible that he
is the Teacher?"

Morima thought for a moment. "I cannot say, child."

Shimeko pulled up a blade of new grass and twirled it
slowly. "Brother Shuyun claims he is not. Is it possible
he could be the Teacher and not be aware of it?"

Morima shook her head. "I don't know, Shimeko-sum.
When did Lord Botahara know that he would become the
Perfect Master? It seems possible that Brother Shuyun
may not know."

Shimeko nodded. "I am concerned . . ."

Morima cut her off with a gesture. "Take care in what
you say, Shimeko-sum, I do not know what I may yet
repeat to my Sisters."

The young woman nodded slowly. She rolled the mat
with exaggerated care.

"Go," Morima said, "I will wait a while." She met
the former Acolyte's gaze. "And may Botahara walk beside you."

On impulse Shimeko reached out and the two women
squeezed hands. Shimeko turned and hurried back to the
path.

The river craft that Shimeko traveled on with the ladies
from the Capital lay where it had been despite her worst
fear that it had gone off without her. She nodded to the
guards as she came aboard. A maid passed her as she
scrambled down the steps to the cabin.

"Lady Nishima has gone ashore, walking with the other ladies, Shimeko-sum."

The young woman sat down on the bottom step, deep in thought. She felt vaguely uncomfortable for having talked to Sister Morima. I should not have done this, she said to herself, I cannot serve two masters nor do I wish to. She thought a while longer, then rose and retraced her steps.

She had noticed Shuyun's barbarian servant on the boat moored just down the bank, a place he would not have been without his master. Approaching the guards of this craft, she gave a password and the appropriate hand signal.

"Is Brother Shuyun aboard?" she asked.

The guard nodded.

"Will you ask if I may speak with him? I am Shimeko, Lady Nishima's secretary."

The more senior guard nodded and his companion hurried off. Shimeko nodded to the tribesman who served Brother Shuyun. He paced the deck, looking off toward the destruction taking place in the fields, then down at his feet as he resumed pacing.

The guard returned in moments. "Shimeko-sum, please," he gestured toward the boat ramp. "Brother Shuyun will be only seconds."

Shimeko went aboard and saw the barbarian crossing toward her. They had met once or twice in the palace in Seh and she had been struck by his devotion to Brother Shuyun. The sight of him dressed in Shonto livery she found quite incongruous.

The Kalam waved at the fields as he approached her. "Bad, yeh? A bad thing." He shook his head vigorously in case she did not understand his use of the language.

Shimeko nodded. "It is a very bad thing. Very sad."

The tribesman nodded agreement, obviously happy that he had been understood.

Shuyun appeared from a hatch behind the barbarian and the Kalam bowed low. Shuyun gave the Botahist bow in return, to both the Kalam and Shimeko.

"We speak," the Kalam said with some pride, nodding toward Shimeko.

Shuyun smiled and said something in another tongue.

The Kalam bowed to both Shuyun and Shimeko and returned to his pacing.

"Shimeko-sum, it is a pleasure to see you. How do you fare in your new position?" They walked across the deck and stood by the rail where their voices would not carry to others on deck or on the bank.

"Well, Brother. I thank you again for your efforts on my behalf."

"Lady Nishima has said that you are becoming an invaluable member of her staff. Consider this as a compliment of high order."

Shimeko gave a half bow.

Polite conversation continued for some minutes. Cha was offered and refused. The weather was commented on. The nearness of the plum blossom season was noted and the lengthening of the day came under some scrutiny. Finally it was appropriate to go on to other matters.

"Is there some way that I may serve you, Shimeko-sum?"

Shimeko shook her head slowly and Shuyun nodded, waiting for her to speak.

"Brother Shuyun . . ." she began. "Brother, I was approached today by Sister Morima, the nun I served on my journey to Seh. She came dressed not as a Sister but in lay clothing. Sister Morima freely admitted that she had been sent by the Sisterhood." Shimeko paused, overcome by a sudden need to swallow. "She had been sent to ask me for information or to persuade me to become an informant—it was not clear which. All of this she admitted. Her Order wanted to know anything I could tell about the barbarian invasion, the intrigues of the Empire, and you, Brother." She hesitated. "I thought you should be told of this."

Shuyun nodded. If he found this news disturbing in any way, he did not show it. "Do you know what specific information she was looking for, Shimeko-sum?"

The woman gestured with opened hands. "I did not inquire further, Brother, nor did Morima-sum pursue the matter. It almost seemed that she was performing a duty so that it could be reported done. I do not think it was a true attempt to enlist my assistance."

"Huh. This interest in me I find most strange, and the

interest in the Shonto House . . . What did you say to her?''

"She did not try to impose on me, Brother, so I did not need to argue or even refuse. We spoke briefly. When Morima-sum thought, erroneously, that I was about to speak of the matters she mentioned, she cautioned me that my words might be repeated to her Sisters.''

"Might be repeated?''

"That is what she said, Brother.''

"Most strange.'' He gazed down into the waters of the canal. "Is there more I should hear?''

She shook her head.

"I thank you for speaking of this, Shimeko-sum. I am not sure what I shall do, but it is possible Steward Kamu may wish to speak with you also.''

She gave a tight nod.

"Most strange.'' Shuyun said again.

Twenty-seven

The Plum Blossom Winds
Spread leaves and flowers among the hills
Laughter and song echo from
The Hill of the North Wind,
Harp and flute from
West Wind Hill.

The valley between the Hills of the North and West Winds became the center of focus for a disturbing meditation by the men of Seh. Barbarian patrols had appeared there the evening before and again that morning. Now everyone watched, waiting without talk for the barbarian army to show itself.

General Toshaki Shinga stood at a narrow opening in the north tower and looked toward the point in the landscape that had become the morbid fascination of everyone in the city. The rhythmic sounds of sword polishers working drifted up to him.

It is too fine a day, the general thought. He leaned out and looked down the wall to the water lapping at its base. It is a strong city, Toshaki told himself, but it was not built to be defended by so few.

Silence had invaded the city more completely than any army could. Toshaki could almost feel men waiting. The gap between the hills drew his attention again.

A small barbarian patrol could be seen among the budding trees at the base of the Hill of the North Wind. They had not moved from that place since first light.

Two boats swung to anchors off the lake's northern shore, waiting for the last scouts returning to Rhojo-ma. Toshaki wondered what choice he would make if he were out on patrol. Would he return to the doomed city or would he strike out, hoping to catch Lord Shonto's fleet?

He pushed on the edges of the opening, rocking back and forth on his heels. It was the waiting that was the worst.

The men remaining in Rhojo-ma had received a detailed description of the barbarian army from a Shonto captain. Toshaki shook his head. That had been the strangest intelligence he had ever received for, rather than assist them with their strategy, the report had destroyed all hope. The sheer numbers in the barbarian army reduced their defense of Rhojo-ma to absurdity. The sole purpose of the men in Seh's capital now was to convince the Khan that the army remaining in Rhojo-ma was too large to leave at his back. If the barbarians spent several days mounting an attack across water, Shonto would have a few more days to raise his army. *A few days,* Toshaki thought, *we sell our lives for so little!* At least it would be an honorable death.

Watches were changed on the city's walls as the men of Seh began to create the appearance of a large force. *The Scarecrow Army,* someone had named it, winning a forced laugh.

Toshaki was making an inspection of defenses when the vanguard of the barbarian army appeared between the hills. Banners as numerous as the blades of grass came down the valley, fluttering in the spring breeze. Slowly but inexorably the riders spread across the plain north of the lake. Only when they had established a perimeter of two rih did the leading edge of the army stop but, behind this, the barbarians continued to spill out onto the plain. Tents began to appear almost immediately and horses were staked out to graze. There was little to indicate that this army feared attack. With the colored banners waving and the tents beginning to appear, the scene almost looked festive.

Barbarians on foot and on horseback came out to the edge of their camp and stood staring at Rhojo-ma, then they would return to their camp to be replaced by others who would then be replaced by others again.

When the sun set, the barbarian army was still arriving. Just as the dusk descended, the first tree was felled and dragged to the shore of the lake.

Twenty-eight

The dinner conversation had faltered badly and each attempt to fan it back to life had ended in silence and embarrassed smiles. The news that the Golden Khan's army was poised to strike Rhojo-ma destroyed everyone's tranquillity and purpose.

Attempting to collect their wandering thoughts in music, Ladies Nishima and Kitsura played the harp and flute for Lady Okara. Though famed for her gracious manners, Lady Okara found it difficult to concentrate on the music of her young companions and it showed in her face. In truth, the players kept losing their focus, resulting in a less than inspired performance. Lady Nishima, especially, seemed to be elsewhere.

A clatter from the deck of the river barge was enough to destroy their focus altogether and the music lost its rhythm and failed. A dull thudding of footsteps passed over their cabin and then back again. Traveling in the dark often led to emergency maneuvers and even these did not always prevent groundings.

"It is nothing, I'm sure," Lady Okara said, and gave them an encouraging smile.

Neither Nishima nor Kitsura showed any indication of continuing and, after a moment's hesitation, set their instruments aside with apologies.

"Even though we have known what was occurring for many months, I still find it difficult to believe that war has begun," Kitsura said.

"Yes," Nishima said quietly. "So many men in Rhojo-ma. It is a foolish waste for the few days we will gain." She rubbed her hand down the frame of her harp. "I'm glad that our Lord Komawara is not among them."

Kitsura nodded and then she smiled. "I've grown quite

fond of him. It seems a very long time since we met at
the Emperor's celebration."

Lady Okara shifted her pillows and reached for her
wine. "He seemed so young then." She shook her head
sadly. "It is difficult to believe this Lord Komawara is
the same young man. He has become very grim."

The conversation faltered again and finally Kitsura and
Nishima bade their good nights and left Lady Okara in
her cabin. The barge they traveled on now was markedly
different from the one that had carried them north. This
one was larger and far more elegant—not a cargo-carrier
with a few cabins aft but a boat designed for passengers
from Wa's wealthier class.

At the door to Nishima's cabin they hesitated to say
goodnight and when neither of them seemed ready to
sleep, Kitsura was invited in. Nishima's cabin was lit by
a single hanging lamp which cast a warm glow on the
rich woods of the walls and beams. Being in the stern
the cabin had actual windows rather than ports, though
these were all shuttered but one. Spread over the straw
mats were two thick wool carpets made by the tribes.
Nishima always tried to bear in mind something the Kalam had said about the tribal people—they did not all
support the Khan. In her mind her rugs were made by
those tribes that hid themselves from this new chieftain.

"Oh, Nishi-sum," Kitsura said to an offer of wine. "I
have had enough for one evening."

They sank onto cushions and back into silence. The
coolness of the night was just starting to find its way into
the cabin, so Nishima called a maid and asked for a charcoal burner.

Kitsura held her hands close to the heat when it came.
"It is a sign of spring, Nishi-sum. The heat from this
burner is not immediately stolen by the darkness. It may
even warm the cabin." She flashed her incomparable
smile.

Nishima nodded. Kitsura was not one to remain sad,
no matter what the circumstances, and she could never
bear to see her cousin anything but cheerful. But Nishima
could not pretend happiness; any smile she summoned
would be entirely artificial. Kitsura fell silent for a few
seconds before she spoke again.

"Do you wonder what part Jaku played in the sudden

decision to raise an Imperial Army? He claims it was the
influence of his friends at court, but . . ."

Nishima opened her fan and looked at the pattern of
plum trees in blossom. "I think our test told the truth,
Kitsu-sum: he is no longer in favor at court. I do not
think Jaku would align himself so closely with my father
if he were at all concerned with the Emperor and what
he might think. No, he is ever the opportunist—when the
Emperor decided to raise an army to protect himself from
any designs the Shonto might have, General Jaku stepped
to the fore and claimed credit. I do not trust him, Kitsu-
sum. I do not trust him at all."

Kitsura shrugged. "Still, he is a handsome man. . . ."

"You are impossible." Nishima said, and though her
tone was meant to be mock dismay she did not quite
carry it off. "Jaku Katta is so embroiled in plots that it
is a wonder he knows who to tell what lies to."

Kitsura smiled tightly. "We all plot, cousin. For some
reason those of us from older families think we have a
right to plot, while those who have only recently risen
step beyond social conventions when they do the same."
She shrugged.

Nishima did not know what to answer. "I made the
mistake of allowing myself to be drawn by his appearance, Kitsu-sum, but I was acting in a very foolish manner."

Kitsura regarded her cousin, who stared at the pattern
on the charcoal burner. "You have not developed another
interest, have you, cousin?"

Nishima glanced up, then went back to her examination of the burner. "No, of course not. I simply feel that
I was foolish in my regard for Jaku Katta."

"Huh." Kitsura produced a brush and began to comb
out her long hair. "We will pass the fane of the Lovers
again—in a few days if we do not pause. A fascinating
thing, don't you think? It would be interesting to know
more. I regret that I did not look into the archives while
we were in Seh."

Nishima carefully smoothed a crease in her robe.
"Yes, it would have been intriguing, I'm sure."

The silence returned. The sounds of water lapping and
bubbling past the hull. A tap sounded on the door, making them both start.

"Please, enter." Nishima said.

Shimeko's face appeared as the door opened. She bowed quickly. "Brother Shuyun calls, Lady Nishima."

Nishima was not quite able to hide her pleasure at this news. "Ahh. Please, ask him to join us."

Kitsura nodded to her companion and started to rise. "I must be going, cousin."

"Kitsu-sum, I'm sure Brother Shuyun would welcome your presence."

As she said this, the door swung open and Shuyun stepped past a bowing Shimeko. Kneeling, Shuyun bowed and as he did so Nishima noticed Shimeko perform a sign to Botahara as she pulled the door closed.

Kitsura and Nishima nodded to the monk.

"It is kind of you to visit, Brother. I am having difficulty convincing Kitsura-sum to stay. . . ."

Kitsura favored them both with her most disarming smile. "Please, cousin, Brother Shuyun, I have other matters calling me. I regret missing your company," she said to Shuyun, then nodded again. "If your duties allow you time for gii, Brother, I would be delighted to have your company." She nodded to Nishima. "Cousin." Kitsura slipped out, opening the door herself and giving a final smile as she left.

The sounds of the river craft's progress seemed to fill the cabin.

"I received a message from Lady Okara." Shuyun said quietly. "She was concerned that the news from Seh had affected both you and Lady Kitsura most adversely. I came to inquire of your well-being."

"You are kind, Shuyun-sum, and Lady Okara is most considerate." She gestured to the windows. "It is difficult to remain tranquil when war has returned to Wa. So many men remained in Rhojo-ma. It is a tragedy, certainly. To provide us with a handful of days . . ." She shook her head. "It is like the coming of the plague. You look around you and ask 'who will live and who will die'? I'm certain it haunts everyone equally." She looked up and tried to smile. "Do not be overly concerned, Brother, the shock of it beginning—becoming real, will soon wear off."

Shuyun nodded. "It is a sad truth, Lady Nishima. The

shock of war wears off. Perhaps if it did not, fewer wars would be undertaken.''

A look of pain flickered across Nishima's face, but she recovered her poise immediately.

''And you Shuyun-sum, how do you fare, now that war is with us?''

Shuyun thought for a moment. ''When I traveled in the desert, the monk I met there . . . he said that war brings no soul to perfection. The suffering to come—it is difficult to imagine that it is the karma of so many to suffer this way.'' He fell silent, looking toward the stern windows.

''I am a follower of Botahara, yet my Order has instructed me to support Lord Shonto in all of his endeavors—for the good of the Brotherhood which preserves the teaching of Botahara. So I go to war also.'' He looked up and met Nishima's eyes. ''It is not the place of a Spiritual Advisor to burden his charges with his own conflicts. I apologize.'' He bowed low.

Nishima reached out and caught his sleeve as he bowed. ''Shuyun-sum, please, do not apologize. Outside of this room I must be Lady Nishima Fanisan Shonto—I have great obligations to my uncle and our House. I confess that I find this role taxes me to my limit at times. If I did not have some place and someone with whom I could speak openly. . . .'' She shrugged. ''Your role is as difficult, I'm sure. It seems to be true that our lives are fraught with contradictions and I am honored that you would speak of these to me.'' She gestured with a sweep of her sleeve. ''This room feels like a haven in which I do not have to play out my role of Lady of a great House. In truth, Shuyun-sum, I feel less need for a Spiritual Advisor and more need for a friend.''

She took his hand. ''What happens in this room is between us and no one else. I would not speak of it even to my liege-lord. Be at your ease, Shuyun-sum. It is my hope that here the Lady and the Advisor may be only Nishi-sum and Shuyun-sum. Nothing else.'' She tugged at his hand as if she would draw him closer and he seemed to become stiff and awkward.

''It is difficult, Lady Nishima,'' he said formally, ''to forget that I am a Brother.''

Nishima stared into his eyes until he looked away. ''It

is not easy to forget that I am the daughter of two great Houses. I have been trained to always be thus.'' She bowed formally, returning to a kneeling position, her posture relaxed but erect. The look on her face spoke of lack of involvement with the world around her—the pose of the sophisticated aristocrat. Then she broke into a smile.

"And you, my friend, are always so." She performed a perfect imitation of a Botahist double bow and then returned to the kneeling position, hands on her thighs, her face an impenetrable mask of serenity. She let out a long controlled breath as though she would enter a meditative state.

So perfect was her imitation that Shuyun was at first shocked and then he broke into a grin.

"There!" Nishima said in triumph. She moved quickly to his side, still facing him. "I have just seen the true Shuyun-sum." She took his hands and his smile was gone as quickly as it had come. "Please, do not disappear again," she said in a small voice.

Shuyun's face almost seemed to flicker like a candle, wavering between the mask of a Botahist Brother and the expressive face of the young man that Nishima had just caught a glimpse of.

"This discomfort you feel in the presence of women, Shuyun-sum, it simply has to be overcome."

He started to protest, but before words formed she reached out and pushed him, almost toppling him over.

"Ahh, a point of resistance! Your teachers would be most disappointed." She slipped into his arms and buried her face in his neck. "This is the comfort I need. The comfort of a friend," she whispered. "And you, Shuyun-sum, must learn comfort in the company of women. I will be your teacher in this."

They stayed thus for a moment and then Nishima spoke again. "Breathe as I do," and they went through a breathing exercise designed to relax the muscles.

"The night we spent together—I could feel your resistance, as I can feel it now." She pushed against him with her body and again there was a second of resistance. Pulling away, she stood quickly and blew out the hanging lamp. She took his hands then in the dark, a hint of light coming in the stern windows. "Promise me you will not leave?"

Shuyun hesitated and she squeezed his hands until he nodded. She disappeared into another part of the cabin and returned almost immediately. In the dim light she rearranged the cushions and spread a thick quilt over them. She turned to Shuyun who sat like a stone.

"Lady Nishima, I . . ."

She took both his hands again. "There is no Lady Nishima present and all Spiritual Advisors are henceforth banned from my chambers. You, Shuyun-sum, are welcomed."

He followed as she gently pulled until he was in the hastily made bed. She joined him, pulling the quilt over them both. Taking his hands between her own she said, "The object of tonight's lesson is to attain a state of tranquillity in the presence of a woman." She reached out and squeezed the muscle in his shoulder which was a knot of tension. "You must begin by relaxation of the muscles. You do know how to do this?"

He nodded.

"Begin," she instructed and felt him control his breathing, sinking into a meditative state. After a few moments she pushed herself into his arms again. She was wearing only a single robe of the thinnest silk and when Nishima came close to him she felt the tension return. "Do not let my presence destroy your tranquillity, Shuyun-sum," she whispered in his ear. "I intend to let your presence enhance my tranquillity." She took a long deep breath and released it like a shudder. "Your arms are around me, but your hands float in the air. You cannot possibly be relaxed like this . . . That is better."

They lay close in the dark for a long time, neither speaking nor moving. Then Shuyun felt soft lips kiss his neck and Nishima whispered in his ear, her words as soft as a sigh.

"We come soon to the Faceless Lovers."

He nodded.

"Lord Botahara knew women?"

He nodded again, more slowly.

"And yet he attained perfection. . . . Meditate upon that if you will not sleep." She kissed his neck again, then he felt her breathe herself to sleep.

Shuyun lay awake for some time thinking of the image carved into the wall of Denji Gorge and then he, too, forced himself into sleep.

Later Nishima awoke, feeling Shuyun's warmth close to her. They were of a size in height, but the years of training had given his muscles a tone that could not be equaled and yet he did not have the massive physique of the kick boxers she had seen. She turned carefully, trying not to wake him but was unsuccessful. Gently pushing her back into his chest, she felt him stir.

"Shh, sleep," she whispered. She took his hand in the dark and kissed it softly. Holding it for a moment as though making a decision, she guided his hand through her open robe to her breast then held it there firmly. Stifling a small moan, she began a breathing exercise. That is enough for this lesson, she thought, I will certainly frighten him away. Thinking this she pressed his hand tighter. The burbling of the boat passing through calm water was like the music of delight itself, joyous, irrepressible.

When the watch changed, Nishima awoke again, warm, languid. Shuyun's hand still caressed her breast and she felt her entire body flash with heat, her breathing became urgent. She started to control this but then felt Shuyun wake in response to her own state. His hand moved on her breast and she turned toward him, shrugging her arm out of the sleeve of her robe.

Pushing as close to him as was humanly possible, she began kissing his neck, then his cheeks and the corners of his eyes. He reacted by pulling her closer, so close that she could not move.

"Nishi-sum . . . I cannot. . . ." He started to pull away, but she would not release him.

"No, Shuyun-sum, please . . . stay a while. I will feel I have acted terribly if you go. I will never forgive myself."

He stopped trying to pull away and they lay rocking each other gently until both found their breath again. Nishima made no attempt to replace her robe but lay in the circle of Shuyun's warmth.

He ran his fingers slowly up her spine and she found herself focusing on this touch as if nothing else in the world mattered. Heat seemed to radiate from his hand.

Slowly his fingers went down her back and she willed
him not to stop. Pushing his palm flat against the base of
her spine, she felt the chi flow, like a glowing warmth,
like a tiny branch of lightning.

And then the chi flowed out from his hand and Nishima felt it touch the center of her desire. She could not
catch her breath. She smothered a moan, fighting not to
let him know what she was feeling. As though it had a
will of its own, she felt her body push closer to Shuyun's.
The lightning branched from his hand.

Burying her face in Shuyun's chest Nishima moaned
uncontrollably. She began to convulse, his hand almost
unbearably hot on her back. Shuddering for what seemed
like moments on end Nishima finally lay, unmoving, in
Shuyun's arms.

Botahara save me, she thought, did he feel nothing?
Could I have felt the skies open while he felt nothing?

Before the darkness disappeared, Shuyun slipped out
onto the deck, finding himself a place to sit among the
cargo. He had left Nishima sleeping, using his Botahist
training to move silently. And now the cold air and infinite night were an almost painful contrast to the warmth
of Nishima's cabin, the warmth of her presence.

Shuyun began a silent prayer for forgiveness but lost
the thread of it almost immediately. What is to become
of me? he wondered. For what I have done I should be
stripped of my sash and pendant and turned out of my
Order. He brought a lifetime of training to bear on the
chaos he felt within, but the turmoil resisted the attempt
to impose order.

Shuyun sat as though in meditation, but in fact his
mind was filled with an image of the Lovers in Denji
Gorge—features beginning to appear on the two faces.
This was mixed with a strong memory of Nishima in his
arms, lost in a pleasure so overwhelming that it was like
a moment of great discovery.

Twenty-nine

In the midst of the vast sprawl of the barbarian encampment a single plum tree had blossomed, appearing like a lone act of defiance, a statement poetic in its purity. The cloud of white blossoms floated just above the tents and teaming thousands as though the land itself had unfurled its standard.

It was early morning on the second day of the siege of Rhojo-ma, though not an arrow had been loosed nor a sword drawn other than to test its edge. A fast boat sailed along the lake's northern shore out of range of barbarian bows. Toshaki Shinga wished he were in that boat himself. He desperately wanted to look into the faces of his enemy, see them for what they were, though he could not explain this impulse.

The barbarian rafts lined the shore and the men of Seh waited. The wind was not terribly strong, but it would gather its reserves intermittently and send a great gust down the lake and this might be what was stopping the expected attack. *They wait for the Plum Blossom Winds,* was the phrase Toshaki heard again and again; it was said with a note of scorn.

The men who sailed along the shore had reported that there were pirates in number among the barbarian warriors. It was an indication that the barbarians were capable of better preparation than the men of Seh had wanted to believe—the second time the barbarians had been underestimated. Toshaki wondered about this Khan—where did he come from and how had he gathered so many?

A young man recently given an officer's rank appeared at the top of the stairs to the tower from which Toshaki observed the plain. He bowed quickly.

"Lord Ranan reports that the fleet is in readiness, Sire."

Toshaki nodded. "We must be patient. The barbarians gather their nerve slowly." Looking back out at the enemy's army, Toshaki said, "The signals are understood."

"They are, General."

"Good." He nodded a dismissal, and the officer returned the way he had come.

Horsemen came and went from the barbarian camp, usually in patrols of some size. No doubt they had realized by now that the army of Seh had retreated south. And how many do they think remain in Rhojo-ma? Toshaki asked himself. The men in the city had been entirely true to their Scarecrow Army ruse and perhaps that explained some of the hesitation the barbarians were showing.

A boat set out from the shore toward the city. Toshaki had to look twice: a boat! They had found a boat that Shonto's men had missed. A flag of truce flew from a staff at the bow and, as it approached, the general could see that it was manned by experienced oarsmen. Pirates were among the barbarians, indeed. Toshaki could see their brightly colored turbans. The enemies of Wa had formed an alliance of the unholy—not a follower of the Perfect Master among them.

The city's own boat changed its course to stand within arrow's shot of the pirate's craft, holding that position until they approached the walls.

Toshaki turned and yelled for an aid. A young soldier appeared immediately at the stairhead.

"Go to the signalmen," the general snapped, "have them signal our patrol boat. If this strange craft attempts to round the city, they must take it at all costs."

By the gods, Toshaki thought, we can't have them seeing everything we prepare.

But the boat made no attempt to round Rhojo-ma, continuing toward the tower Toshaki had made his command position. Realizing what they did, the lord made his way down the flights of stairs to the top of the wall.

As the boat pulled closer, Toshaki could see a single
man sitting in the bow not handling an oar. The lord
squinted.

"That man in the bow," Toshaki said to a young bowman standing at hand, "can you see him?"

The bowman focused for a second. "I can, Sire."

"Is he a barbarian?"

The younger man shook his head. "He is not, Sire,
nor is he a pirate. He is dressed as a man of Seh might
dress."

Toshaki took hold of the stone wall, leaning out over
the water. A gust of wind pushed the bow of the boat
off, and the steersman fought to put them back on course.
Five strokes closer, then ten. A muttering began down
the wall and progressed from man to man. Toshaki turned
to his aid.

"Some say this is Lord Kintari, General."

Toshaki turned back to the scene before him. By Botahara, it could be. The general thought Shonto had done
away with the Kintari clan.

Lord Ranan appeared at his elbow followed by several
other senior lords. "Lord Kintari," Ranan said, "reincarnated as himself. May Botahara be praised." Even
Toshaki smiled at this.

"Reincarnated as a traitor, I think, Sire," said another
and there was a quiet nodding of heads.

The boat came close enough for shouted speech. The
steersman turned it head to wind and the oarsmen held
that position. The man in the bow stood, and if there
were any still unsure of his identity the doubt was buried
now.

"Lords of Seh, I come with a message from the Great
Khan of the tribes." Kintari paused as if time were
needed for his words to be fully understood. His voice
sounded small against the noise of the wind and the
waves lapping the stone wall. Kintari was so close that
Toshaki could see the man's robe ripple in the breeze,
could make out a strand of hair in a streak across Kintari's forehead.

"He is without sword," Ranan said quietly and Toshaki nodded.

"Your numbers are known to the Great Khan, my

lords. You cannot hope to stand against the force of the tribes. What will you gain by this futile defense? Did your Yamaku Emperor send an army to protect Seh? You give up your lives for an Empire that will not even notice you have done so." He paused again.

"The Yamaku care only for their own ascendancy. They are not Emperors of Wa—they do not govern, they divide the Empire against itself and rob from all. You will give up your lives for blood-suckers?" His voice rose on the last word, and it echoed from the buildings.

"I know you, lords of Seh. You are brave men—all of you—but your sense of duty is misplaced. The Khan has come to bring down the Yamaku, not to destroy Wa. The Khan is a man of greatness, lords—greatness the like of which we have not seen since Emperor Jirri rode upon this very plain.

"You are invited to feast with the Khan, lords. You may know for yourselves. The Yamaku have bled Seh for ten years. The Khan will bring us peace and wealth as we have never known. Those who ride with him will be great men in the Empire to be. Consider this army." He pointed to the encampment. "Among one hundred thousand only the Khan and a handful of others are men of culture. When the Yamaku are brought down, the Khan will need men of skill and knowledge to govern the new Empire. If you are those men, how can it not be an Empire of justice and culture?

"A feast, lords, not a trap—for you have already trapped yourselves. What word shall I take back to the Great Khan?"

There was a second's hesitation as men looked from one to another, questions in their eyes.

"Bowman," Toshaki Shinga said quietly.

"Sire?"

"Silence that traitor."

An arrow flashed, appearing in Kintari's heart as though it had sprung from there. The lord did not move to clutch his pain but slowly toppled over the side like a falling tree. The pirates set to their oars in a frenzy, pulling to get beyond bow range, but no arrows fell among them.

Lord Kintari was left bobbing, facedown, in the small

waves that broke the surface of the lake. The pirate's craft, under its flag of truce, raced to the far shore where the oarsmen ran it up on the bank as though arrows were aimed at their hearts.

Toshaki looked down at the floating lord. There was silence on the wall.

"It was a better death than he deserved," Lord Ranan said so that all might hear, "but it was the best that could be managed." He bowed to Toshaki and nodded to the bowman, then turned and started back to his duties.

A shout echoed across the lake, as powerful as distant thunder, and Toshaki looked up to see rafts being pushed out onto the waters.

"Give the signals," Toshaki said calmly to his aide. "It begins."

Along the wall he saw men make signs to Botahara and then, in a warrior's ritual, they tightened their helmet cords.

Toshaki loosened his sword in its scabbard and mounted the stairs to his tower, pulling his helmet tight as he did so. There would soon be little he could do, but he would try to give some direction to the defense while it was still possible.

There must not have been enough pirates to man all the rafts, for many were paddled by barbarians under the tutelage of screaming, gesturing pirates. On at least one raft Toshaki saw a fight underway, swords flashing.

Fools, the lord thought, come a little further.

The vast flotilla moved slowly toward Rhojo-ma, the cumbersome rafts colliding and hampering each other. Against all efforts the crosswind blew them off to the west and soon they were strung out, paddling into the wind and trying to make their way crabwise toward the walls.

Toshaki almost laughed. In an attempt to send the greatest number of men against the city, the barbarian chieftains had built too many rafts and now they became their own enemy. At least one raft had broken up, leaving terrified tribesmen clinging to the logs, armor trying to drag them under.

Boats appeared beyond the east wall of the city, towing makeshift rafts piled with shattered furniture and straw floor mats. The men of Seh were not strangers to the water and their operation was executed with a precision that would have made a naval officer proud. Positioning their craft quickly upwind of the enemy, the men of Seh fired the rafts and cut them free.

Toshaki hit the stone with his fist. The barbarians on the windward rafts saw what bore down on them and stopped paddling, which sent their craft into the rafts behind.

A gust of wind fanned the fires into hot blazes and pressed the fire rafts down on their victims. The barbarian flotilla lost all way then as men on the windward craft jumped to the rafts behind. The fire touched the first barbarian raft and flaming straw started to blow free.

Toshaki saw men in flaming clothes and men falling into the waters to slip beneath the surface with barely a struggle. The fleet blew east now, all chance of making the walls of Rhojo-ma gone.

Someone pounded up the steps behind him and an out of breath Lord Ranan appeared at his side.

"Ah, Admiral Ranan. Your squadron has done well."

"Who thought it would become a naval battle, General?" Ranan said with obvious satisfaction. "And the men of the desert make poor sailors." A bitter laugh forced its way out from behind his face-mask.

The remains of the barbarian flotilla ended up on the west shore of the lake. Most of the logs were new cut and too full of spring sap to burn, so the fire rafts did less damage than one might have hoped.

"We have given Lord Shonto the gift of another day at least," Lord Ranan said. "May his army swell by a thousand men."

Toshaki turned to his aide. "Order our patrol out again. I want to know everything the barbarians do."

Ranan leaned his back to the wall and opened his face-mask. "I wonder what they will do? Is it possible they might dare this again?"

Toshaki shrugged. "We will soon have the measure of this Great Khan. If he cannot take an almost undefended city in a few days, he will be no match for Shonto Motoru. The great lord is a gii player of some fame. He will never let this upstart catch him where mere force of numbers can win the day.''

He turned back to the north. In the midst of the barbarian army the plum tree swayed and released a flurry of petals to the wind.

Thirty

The flotilla carrying Lord Shonto's army south sailed by night, trailing a wake of terrible destruction. Word had spread quickly down the canal and the people of Wa fled before Shonto's fleet as though it were the barbarian army itself. In places the canal choked with the boats of refugees and when this slowed the progress of the flotilla, soldiers were sent ahead to clear the way. Everyone in the flotilla had seen the results of this earlier in the evening. They had passed the still smoldering hulks of half a hundred craft, stranded on the canal banks.

I feel as though we follow on the heels of war, not precede it, Brother Sotura thought. He stood at the aft rail watching the following-wave pull a ribbon of moonlight along their wake. Just at dusk he had heard the sound of a flight of cranes passing over and it had saddened him in a way he could not control.

It was a night of great beauty. The Plum Blossom Wind pushed the river craft along the waterway like a gentle, guiding hand, and the scent of budding trees and opening flowers perfumed the air. In so steady a wind and a section of canal free of hidden bars, the sailors on watch had little to do. A charcoal fire smoldered amidships and the sailors cooked and brewed cha and lounged about the deck talking quietly, awaiting their turn as lookout or at the steering oar.

A sailor approached Sotura, offering the senior Brother a bowl of cha which he accepted with a nod. He sipped cha and watched the night landscape slip by. The constellation of the Two-Headed Dragon appeared above the calypta trees lining the bank, and the breeze murmured in the branches. It was night rich in beauty.

Steps approached, not the barefoot slap of a sailor, but a studied gait. Sotura turned and saw a woman walking toward him. She seemed at first bent and tired, but the Botahist Master could see that this was not a statement of truth: she was neither. The moonlight outlined the familiar shape of a square jaw.

"Sister Morima," Sotura said quietly. He bowed. "I am honored to find myself traveling in your company."

She was dressed in the yellow robe and purple sash of her Order though over that she wore shapeless robes of gray and brown, her head wrapped in a shawl. She nodded in return and leaned against the rail as though she had just expended great effort.

Sotura thought she was thinner than when he had last seen her—at Jinjoh Monastery where she had come for the opening of the scrolls. To an untrained eye, her clothing would have hidden this change.

"You keep close watch on your protégé, Brother Sotura, one would think his judgment was in question."

It was an insulting statement and doubly so, for the nun had shown the worst manners, refusing to respond to his polite greeting.

"Shuyun-sum seems to be watched by many, Sister, which is the true question."

"Huh," Sister Morima blew the syllable out like a sharp exhalation. "True questions," she mused. "Tell me, Brother, do you not have true questions now that the Teacher has arrived and is not among your senior Brethren?"

Sotura turned and looked back at the boat's wake. "You listen to rumors, Sister. I am surprised."

"The blossoms were seen, Brother," Morima hissed in a low whisper, "touched by my own Sisters. Touched! Do not play the fool with me, Senior Brother Sotura."

He shrugged. "Believe as you will, Sister."

"That is the conclusion I'm coming to, Brother." She fell silent then, and only the wash of boat slipping through water was heard.

Sotura looked over at the steersman, but the man was too far off to hear and too well mannered to notice.

"Do you wonder, Brother, who Shuyun-sum was in his past incarnation? A child of such accomplishment was not a merchant or a lord. It is not possible."

Sotura shrugged. "As you are aware, we cannot always know."

"With the unaccomplished, perhaps," Morima answered but carried the thought no further. She turned also, leaning over the rail and joining her hands. "It must be difficult for you, Sotura-sum; the blossoming of the Udumbara, Sacred Scrolls that are missing or worse, the coming of the Teacher you cannot find, and a young protégé with an ear for the truth." She paused looking down into the dark water. "Lies cannot come easily, even to the seniors of your Order. What will you say when Shuyun-sum asks of these things?"

Sotura stood away from the rail so that he looked down at the woman. "It is rumored, Sister," he said icily, "that you have had a crisis of faith. I will pray to Botahara to guide you." A stiff bow and he was gone, leaving Morima at the rail.

The monk made his way to the bow where he sat in the lee of the gunnel. It was as far forward as he could go and yet he still felt the lies that pursued him close behind.

Thirty-one

The entire line had come to a halt for perhaps the hundredth time that day. Lord Shonto Shokan looked down the draw at the horsemen strung out behind him. Like their lord, they had long since dismounted to lead their horses. Shokan stepped to the right for a better view and plunged through the softening crust up to mid-thigh. He cursed.

They were completely surrounded by mountains now, above the snow line and into an area that, each afternoon, became truly frightening. The guides had signaled a stop and gone ahead to assess the danger. They had lost thirty men to avalanches already and Shokan wanted to lose no more. Of course, this was quickly becoming a moot point. Could they go ahead at all? That was the question they asked now.

Willing himself lighter, Shokan tried to pull his leg free and step back onto the crust. His other leg broke through and he sat down, sinking to his waist. He cursed again and then laughed.

The night before they had debated leaving the horses, hoping men could win through where horses couldn't. With care, men could travel in the mornings when the surface of the snow was still frozen from the bitter cold of the mountain nights.

A boy ran lightly up the line of men, earning Shokan's envy. When we have no more food, perhaps we will all run as lightly as this one, Shokan thought. The child dropped to his knees on the crust before his lord and bowed. Shokan nodded for him to speak.

"Sire, Lord Jima's men have reached the end of our line, but the snows caught seven and swept them into the gorge."

Shokan made a sign to Botahara. "Can they go on?"

The boy hesitated. "Lord Jima says they are prepared to proceed, Sire."

Shokan nodded. This might be as far as they went this day though it was barely midday. With some effort he stood and looked up the draw. There were perhaps twenty men above him and then the track of the guides disappearing over the curve of the endless snows. Movement caught his eye and he turned quickly. Yes! he was certain this time.

"I saw it, also, Sire," the boy said, his tone tentative. He had just spoken to the great lord without being requested to do so.

Shokan did not seem to notice. He pointed up at a ridge line above them to the south. "There?"

"Yes, Lord Shonto."

"Huh." They had started appearing on and off two days before. It was considered good luck to see one of the Mountain People, so men had begun keeping a lookout. Down the line he saw others pointing.

Turning back, he looked up the slope. Certainly it is not possible, he thought, we will have to leave armor and all the horses behind. He looked at his stallion, the horse he had brought from Seh, and shook his head sadly. They would butcher the horses for all the meat they could carry; there was no other choice. He smiled at the child.

"Tell Lord Jima that I await word from the guides. We will not move until then."

The boy bowed low, rose, and jogged off. Thirty paces away, he plunged through the snows up to his chest and had to be rescued by a wallowing rider.

Thirty-two

The ruin of a treed hillside
Wounds the heart.
Plum Blossom Winds
Whisper across still water.
Spring's gentle arrival
Lifts the eternal spirit

Lord Akima

Lord Ranan and Lord Akima stood at the wall on the city's eastern extremity and watched the building of a floating bridge. The barbarian army had spent a day skidding logs from the western end of the lake, where they had been blown after the first failed attack. The arrival of the Plum Blossom Winds had precipitated this tactic, and the men of Rhojo-ma looked on with something approaching approval: it is what they would have done in the barbarians' place. With the breeze at the barbarian army's back, it would be impossible for the men of Seh to position fire rafts upwind.

The floating bridge grew by the hour, reaching out toward the walls of Rhojo-ma. The last sections of the bridge were being readied near shore. When done, these final sections would be easily floated into place, connecting the shore to the wall of Rhojo-ma with a causeway wide enough to allow fifty men abreast. It was only a question of when this would be done.

"There are too many sections, look." Lord Akima pointed to the north and south of the floating bridge where work was going on at an astonishing pace.

Lord Ranan watched the activity briefly and then nodded. Teams of horses kept arriving with planks torn, no doubt, from nearby barns and houses. These were being used to tie the bridge together and provide a relatively even footing for the attackers. "They must plan to make the bridge wider at this end. I would do the same." It was the ultimate approval of anything the barbarians did: *I would do the same.*

Akima looked over his shoulder at the position of the sun. "They might finish while there is still light."

"But they will not attack until dawn—when we will have the sun in our eyes. That would be my choice."

Akima nodded.

Most of the men who remained in Rhojo-ma were concentrated on the defense of the city's eastern end now, drawing them away from the more easily defended Governor's Palace and inner city. Lines of retreat to the western end had been prepared through the city—bridges destroyed, streets blocked. Only a man who knew the route could move quickly from east to west and that route was the most easily defended. Even so, the men of Seh were preparing to hold the city's eastern end for as long as possible.

Lord Ranan bowed suddenly. "Please excuse me, Lord Akima, I have matters that must be attended to."

Akima bowed and watched the man go. "How the great have fallen," Akima said to himself. Ten years earlier the Ranan had been the virtual rulers of Seh—Imperial Governors generation after generation. And now here was the senior lord of that House—a general at the fall of Seh's capital.

How we pay for our mistakes, the old man thought and turned back to the eastern shore for a final look before attending to his own duties.

The sound of the barbarian flute-pipes echoed across the water in the night. It was a melancholy air played in the strange scale of the desert tribes and it did nothing to raise the spirits of the men in the city. A night attack was unlikely but not impossible, so large numbers of men stood watch and others stayed in the recently abandoned buildings nearby.

Boats had been sent out from the city to patrol the lake to be sure the barbarians did not move their bridge in the dark. An attack at first light on some other quarter of the

city would be a disaster. The men of Seh were too few
to be spread around Rhojo-ma.

Other boats were readied after the moon set, but they
had their own purpose. Men, armed and armored, went
aboard these boats in number. In complete silence they
pushed off, setting course by stars and the barbarian fires
on the shore. The light evening breeze bore them along,
barely rippling the sails as they tacked. It was a difficult
exercise, for the boats could risk no lamps, so there was
a very real danger of being separated or colliding.

Fires set in sand burned at intervals along the floating
bridge, and they illuminated the span from one end to
the other.

A torch on the wall of the city was extinguished, and
the boats turned toward the agreed upon fire on the
bridge. There was not enough wind to give them speed,
so the helmsmen aimed the boats directly at the floating
span and ran their bows up on it, snapping anchor lines
in the process.

A shout went up immediately from the barbarian
guards, and the sound of swords shattered the peaceful
evening and stilled the playing of flutes. Torches came to
life among the attackers in an attempt to fire the bridge
planking.

Lord Ranan reached the top of the wall and found Akima and Toshaki there ahead of him.

"It does not burn," Ranan said.

The noise was fierce now and men appeared at all the
stairways, believing the siege had begun. In the light of
the fires, barbarians could be seen pouring out along the
floating causeway. Torches were kicked into the water
though here and there the planking burned feebly.

Out beyond the point where the attack had been aimed,
a watch fire burst apart and men could be seen spreading
the burning wood across the float. Suddenly there was a
tearing sound and the outer watch fires began to drift
toward the walls of Rhojo-ma.

"They have broken it!" Akima said. "Look!"

A cheer went up from the walls of the city, but the
sound of swords continued. Bowmen strung their weapons then, ready for a section of the bridge to come covered in barbarians and hard-pressed warriors of Seh. So

slowly did the section of bridge move that men's arms began to grow tired holding arrows at the ready.

The sound of clashing swords stopped abruptly and the shouting of the barbarians fell silent also. On the section of bridge that had been broken free, flames began to spread as the dry planking caught. It drifted on like that toward the wall of the city, a long torch illuminating the area for more than a rih. Barbarians standing on the end of the now truncated bridge could be seen clearly in the orange light. A small boat under sail passed by the burning raft—a patrol boat, no doubt looking for survivors.

The men of Seh watched as the burning hulk began to break up as it drifted near the city. Signs were made to Botahara. The first defenders had died, and the attack slowed by half a day.

Morning came, a clear spring day. Another tree had blossomed on the hillside north of Rhojo-ma. General Toshaki stood at the wall, looking at the scene. He tried not to think of the funeral barge that had born his lord across the lake only a few days earlier, for it had been white with blossoms also.

The sound of the barbarian army preparing their siege echoed across the lake, ruining the perfect stillness. It would be only a few hours now. Toshaki loosed his sword in its scabbard for the hundredth time. The men on the wall around him were silent. There was no need to discuss plans and strategy—their intent was not that complicated.

Captain Rohku stood on a hill south of Seh, hidden by brush and trees that had not been taken by the barbarians for their great floating bridge. He wondered how he had been chosen for the function he now performed. Perhaps being the first to report the arrival of Jaku Katta had started it. Rohku knew that events of even less significance had set men off on a life's endeavor. Whatever it was, the young captain had become the watcher—the witness.

It had been Rohku who had hidden on the ledge and watched the army of the desert pass. Having reported all he had learned from that to Rhojo-ma and sent reports on to Lord Shonto, he had been given sealed orders. And

now he and a few of his company were to be witnesses
to the fall of Seh's capital. No doubt what he saw would
tell Shonto and his staff much about the barbarian army
and its leaders, but Rohku did not relish the duty. As
foolish as he thought the lords of Seh were, he did not
want to watch them die.

Much had happened in the dark the previous night
though it had been difficult to know what. The men of
Seh had obviously staged an attack on the bridge and
cut a section of it free, setting it to the torch. Rohku
had watched the flaming raft as it spun slowly, breaking up before it reached the wall of the city. It was
impossible to tell what had happened to the men of
Seh. They had seen only barbarian warriors in the light
from the burning bridge section which had led to much
speculation. His companions had finally agreed that
most or all of the men from Rhojo-ma had escaped in
boats, but Rohku was sure they didn't really believe
this. The attackers from the city, the captain thought,
lay on the bottom of the spring cold lake, weighted
there by their armor for all time—may Botahara protect
their souls.

The last section of the span that would connect the
barbarian army with the walls of the island city had been
warped out to the bridge's far end where preparations
were being made to move it into its final position. The
Shonto guard looked around to make sure his men
watched the woods behind and not the drama that unfolded on the lake.

A guard appeared at Rohku's side just as he turned
back to his duty.

"Another barbarian patrol passes to the west. They
should appear below us." He waved off to their left.

Rohku nodded. Barbarians were exploring the surrounding countryside with great determination and this
resolve was showing occasional results. More than one
patrol returned with some hapless resident of Wa in their
midst. Not everyone had left quickly enough. By now the
Khan would know where Shonto's army had gone.

The barbarian patrol appeared as had been predicted—
this one without captives. Watching them ride past,
Rohku had to admit that they were fine horsemen. If they

handled the sword and bow as well, they could make a formidable army.

"Captain," one of Rohku's men pointed.

The final section of bridge was beginning to move. Using ropes and poles, the pirates and barbarians began maneuvering the makeshift structure into place. With the Plum Blossom Wind still wafting in from the sea, there was nothing to struggle against but the inherent momentum of the raft itself, and they had enough men a thousand times over to deal with that. Slowly it moved, so slowly there was not a ripple in its wake.

Barbarians holding shields over their heads began to make their way out to the section's far end, guarding against a foray by the men of Seh. Arrows arced out toward the bridge as it came within range of the strongest archers, but the barbarians knelt down and shields gave protection.

Looking quickly toward the shore, Rohku saw the banners of the Khan close to the shore where the bridge began. Warriors in red were stationed there on horseback, and the Shonto captain assumed the barbarian chieftain was there, inspiring his warriors to perform great deeds.

When the bridge was almost under the city walls, a shadow appeared on the waters like a passing cloud, but it was a cloud of arrows. Realizing that he held his breath, Rohku tore his eyes away to be sure his guard watched behind, for he would need to give his full attention to the battle now so that he could give as complete an account as possible to Lord Shonto.

As the bridge bumped against the wall, Rohku saw the men of Seh swarm down the wall on ladders and ropes at the same time as the vanguard of the barbarian army started across the last section. The barbarians who guarded the bridge's end were pushed back almost immediately, much to Captain Rohku's satisfaction. Those will be their strongest fighters, he thought, and yet they could not stand against the men of Seh.

The barbarian army and the men swarming out of the city met in the center of the bridge, and a great shout went up from both sides. The sound of steel ringing on steel echoed across the valley like the sound of an enormous bell.

* * *

Toshaki turned command of the city over to Lord Akima and grasped a rope, lowering himself quickly down the wall. The floating bridge heaved as his feet struck, swaying and jerking like the deck of a ship. Men dropped to the bridge around him; they were the third wave of men from the city and would replace those falling where the opposing sides met.

Despite the number of barbarians, the Khan could not bring his great force to bear, for the causeway to the city would only support fifty men abreast. The second wave of men from the city had won another hundred feet, not pushing the great column of tribesmen back but driving them into the lake and cutting them down where they stood.

Toshaki turned and made his way among the fallen, the deck slick with water and blood. He drew his blade as he went, not looking at the faces of the dead and wounded. He did not want to know who had fallen. As he came up behind the wall of men fighting, he saw men of Seh poised, ready to cut as much of the bridge away as they could if the barbarians began to push them back. It was their intention to drive the barbarians as close to the shore as could be done and then cut the bridge away, forcing them to build again.

We are five thousand strong and we will lose five hundred in this very hour, Toshaki thought, how long can we carry on such a defense?

Thinking this, he threw himself into the fray, cutting down a barbarian in a single stroke. After that it was as if he had lost consciousness—a lifetime of training took hold and he fought on without his mind grasping what truly occurred.

A barbarian tripped and Toshaki felt his boot take the man in the ribs, knocking him into the cold waters. He felt a blow to his shoulder and registered vaguely that he might be wounded. He slipped and fell hard and found himself jerked to his feet by a young giant he did not recognize. He fought again.

He fell back to rest, and others took his place. Forcing himself up before truly rested, Toshaki returned to the battle. Arrows whistled overhead and suddenly the men of Seh began to win ground again. He tripped over a barbarian, dead from an arrow in the throat. The smell of smoke. A huge warrior knocked him down with a shield, but a man of Seh stepped in and took the blow while yet another felled the giant. Those men wore Toshaki colors, the lord realized afterward.

The sound of fire crackling and hissing. Again Toshaki fell to the rear to rest. The men of Seh were being driven back now. Toshaki turned to look for his reinforcements and saw the bridge behind him in flames, beyond the fire men of Seh had severed the span and maneuvered their section away.

We are cut off, some part of Toshaki's mind informed him. He looked back at the battle raging and realized that they were all exhausted and falling. Forcing himself to rise, the lord moved to the platform's edge. He would not chance capture; the waters could take him but never the barbarians.

> *A lifetime*
> *To discover a single truth.*
> *A solitary white petal*
> *Drifting on the wind*
> *Comes to rest on my breastplate*
> *More beautiful*
> *Than all the works of man.*
>
> *Lord Toshaki Shinga*

Thirty-three

Brave heart
Contemplating the plum trees blossoming
Against the infinite blue

From "Poems Written in Old Age"
Lady Nikko

Along the banks of the Grand Canal willows and calypta trees began to unfurl tiny, embryonic leaves
adding yet another scent to the complex perfume of
spring. Rushes appeared, straight and green, in the growing shade of the trees, and the banks were newly grassed
and awash in spring flowers.

Shonto sat on a low platform placed on a high point
of the bank. A silk awning in the blue of the Shonto
banner protected the platform and a fence of silk hangings bearing the shinta blossom created an enclosure,
giving the lord privacy in all directions but east, toward
the canal. Boats of armed guards patrolled the water before the enclosure, forcing all traffic to the opposite side.
Other guards were posted around the enclosure and beyond them another ring of armed men both on foot and
on horseback.

Nishima watched her father as her sampan approached.
*In the midst of war he has set himself in a place where
he can truly appreciate the changing season.* Her boat
hissed to a stop in the mud, its bow barely on shore, and
guards hurried down to pull it up far enough that disembarking would not be difficult.

Nishima looked up again and saw that her father was
deep in conversation with a senior military aide. She
nodded to the guard who had assisted her and walked a
few paces along the grassy bank looking at the spring

flowers. The last of the snow lilies were spread there in the shade of a great calypta, but a few days of such warmth and they would be gone until the next season.

She picked a tiny purple flower not recognized, reminding herself to ask Lady Okara what it might be. An aide of Kamu's hurried down the bank toward her, and she looked up to see Shonto smiling at her as though they had not met in a long time.

On the platform a cushion had been arranged for her and Nishima slipped out of her sandals. She bowed to her father and he surprised her by bowing low in return, a large grin appearing.

"Lady Nishima," he said in mock formal tones, "your presence honors me."

"The honor, Lord Governor, is mine entirely," she answered.

Shonto waved to a servant. "Governor is no longer a title I claim. When our esteemed Emperor learns that I have abandoned Seh and travel south with an army, I will have achieved a new office—that of Rebel General."

Nishima's smile disappeared. "It is a frightening thought, Uncle."

Shonto continued in the same tone, not showing any of the signs of distress that his daughter displayed. "Not at all, Nishi-sum. Think of all the great men of history who have borne this same title: Yokashima, Tiari, even our beloved Emperor's own father. My only concern is that my accomplishments will pale in such esteemed company." He reached out and touched her arm. "Do not be of barren heart, Nishi-sum, the Shonto are in the best of company."

A servant brought cups and wine, placing them on a small table. Waving him away before the wine was served, Shonto proceeded to pour the wine himself, surprising his daughter for the second time.

"You are in a bright mood today, Uncle. I wish I could feel as light of heart in our present circumstances." Nishima started to refuse the offered wine, as was polite, but Shonto took her hand and curled the fingers around the cup, squeezing her hand gently. She laughed.

"Hakata wrote that, as he grew older, spring became more beautiful and more painful each year. I, personally, have reached the age where spring is more beautiful but has not yet begun to cause me too much pain. Perhaps in a few years you will be able to appreciate the spring as I do. War cannot be helped now, but there will be beauty in spite of it. The truly brave soul will find time for beauty in the midst of the most terrible destruction.''

"Lady Nikko," Nishima said. "Though I believe she meant that the truly brave hearts would see beauty at the hour of their death.''

"Poets . . . why must they all be so dramatic?'' Shonto gestured toward a branch of the plum that grew down to eye level, not an arm's length away. "See these blossoms? I have been watching them all morning. They prepare to open. They gather their resolve as we speak. Their opening will be an act of singular beauty, more lovely than the blossoms themselves. In the midst of all that occurs, we will sit here and observe. It will be a test of the bravery of your heart.''

Nishima nodded and they both shifted their cushions to face the emerging flowers. They stayed like that for more than an hour, side by side: a tall, willowy young woman and the strongly built older man. Despite this contrast in their appearance, there was little doubt that they both focused on the same thing.

The plum blossoms unfolded in the sun. "As slowly as the timid heart," Lord Shonto whispered at one point. A quote from another poem and the only words either of them spoke until a flower had spread its petals like fragile wings. A bee came then and thrust its head into the flower, emerging covered in pollen.

The two renegade aristocrats turned away then, Nishima holding back her sleeve as she poured more wine into their cups.

"There is one other matter, Nishi-sum, that I hesitate to speak of.''

Nishima nodded, recognizing seriousness in her father's tone.

"The river people have a saying: 'A whisper aboard ship is a shout upon the land.' Keeping secrets aboard a boat is a difficult thing.'' Shonto looked down into his cup, turning it slowly, then up at the plum blossom again.

Nishima nodded, sipping wine into a suddenly dry mouth.

"Brother Shuyun is a magnetic young man, but he is a monk who has taken a sacred oath. A heart can be broken against more malleable things, Nishi-sum, I have seen it."

Nishima gathered her nerve, not quite certain whether she heard disapproval or concern in her father's voice. "Satake-sum had taken this same sacred oath, Uncle, yet he did not live according to its letter, as we both know."

Shonto nodded. "He remained a monk despite his independent spirit. Shuyun-sum—what will become of him?"

"Do you fear to lose your Spiritual Advisor, then?"

Shonto considered this. "Shuyun-sum would always be invaluable, there is no question of that. I feel little need of a guide to the words of Botahara—I can read them myself. That is not my concern.

"You are a lady of a Great House, Nishi-sum, and though I have often spared you the responsibility that comes with your position I may not be able to continue to do so in the future. This war will require sacrifices of everyone—perhaps even of you. You may not be able to choose your own course, Nishi-sum, any more than I chose the path followed now."

Nishima nodded stiffly. She looked out over the canal at the trees blowing in the soft breeze, wafting their spring greens like new robes. A guard stood up in one of the patrolling boats, looked off to the far bank. Years ago Nishima had trained herself to remove such things as guards and walls and strong gates out of any scene she viewed, but she knew this was only an act of the imagination—they had not gone away.

She swallowed with difficulty. "Your words are wise, as always, Uncle. I thank you."

Shonto nodded, half a shrug.

"Uncle, there is something I have not spoken of. Kitsura-sum asked Jaku Katta if he would have a letter conveyed to her family, which he agreed to do. Kitsu-sum received word from her family that this letter arrived. This would seem to indicate. . . ."

Shonto held up his hand. "Kitsura-sum has already informed me of this. It raises another question of the Guard Commander's claims."

Nishima suppressed her annoyance at her cousin's in-

terference. "I believe Jaku Katta is no longer in favor in
the Emperor's court, Sire."

"Huh." Shonto looked down at his cup. "I agree,
daughter, but I am not sure who this young Jaku sup-
ports—Tadamoto—is he loyal to his brother and family
or is he loyal to his Emperor? It appears to have been
Jaku Tadamoto who convinced the Emperor to raise the
army. Does the younger Jaku intend that army to fight
barbarians or to fight Shonto, and perhaps even his own
brother? It is a curious puzzle. For the time being, at
least, Jaku Katta has little choice but to side with the
Shonto and hope the Yamaku do not stand. He plays out
the charade quite admirably, I think."

Nishima picked up her cup but did not drink. "I confess that I no longer find much to admire in the Guardsman,"
Nishima said softly.

Horses were heard coming to a halt outside the compound and General Hojo appeared at the opening.

"I must excuse myself, Uncle. Please give my regards
to General Hojo."

Shonto nodded. "I thank you for viewing the plum
blossoms with me. It added another facet to the beauty
entirely." Shonto bowed again to his daughter as he had
when she arrived. She bowed as her position required,
slipped into her sandals, and made her way down the
bank.

The boatmen pushed out into the slow moving current
and began to scull toward Nishima's barge.

But Uncle, she thought, I have discovered the rarest
beauty in the midst of terrible destruction. If my heart is
truly brave, can I turn away?

Guards cleared a way through the long line of refugees
strung out along the south road. It seemed a last indignity for these people. They had been turned from their
homes, crops torn from the fields, livestock taken, feed
stores set to the torch, and any food they could not carry
confiscated to feed the growing army. And now they were
being forced to stand aside for the lord who had failed
to stop this alleged barbarian army in Seh where such
things should be done.

Yet when Shonto and his company rode past, the refugees bowed low, displaying nothing of what they felt.

They were fatalists in a manner that a person of action like Lord Shonto would never understand. Karma dictated that they would occasionally be the victims in the machinations of the Empire. It had always been so and would never change—unless one progressed, perhaps becoming a monk or a sister of a Botahist Order.

Passing on horseback, Shonto was saddened by the endless procession of villagers and peasants, some leading ox-drawn wagons, others carrying everything left to them on the backs of mules or on poles slung across their own shoulders. It affected him, but he knew what he had said to Nishima was true—everyone would make sacrifices in this war. There would be few exceptions.

They crossed a stubble field, damp from the spring rains but firm enough for horses. Another group of riders waited on a low rise and Shonto could see the banner of the Komawara House—the mist-lily against a night blue background. Komawara bowed from his horse as Lord Shonto approached while his men dismounted and bowed properly. Shonto noticed the trim of green lacing on two of these men—the Hajiwara Komawara had found in the Jai Lung Hills.

"This is the place?" Shonto asked.

Komawara nodded.

Spurring his horse, Shonto gained a few feet in elevation and then turned to look west toward the hills, trying to gauge the height of the undulating land.

"This entire plain has been under flood many times," Komawara said, coming up beside Shonto. "Six years ago there was a sea here sixty rih wide. We can dam the canal and defend the dam. This defense could last many days. Once the dam is burst the land will still be impassible for days until it dries."

Shonto nodded as he looked both east and west again. "What of the Canal? It will have no source of water, yeh?"

Hojo pointed off to the south. "Ten rih away the river Tensi joins the canal. There will be no difficulties once the fleet has passed that point. The section of the canal from here to there may be shallower than usual, but . . ." He shrugged.

"And the roads through the hills are narrow and perfect for ambushes," Komawara added with satisfaction.

"We can hold the barbarians here for many days, I think." The young lord rubbed his sword hilt and Shonto realized this was not the weapon Komawara usually carried. The Toshaki gift, the lord realized.

"General Hojo, Lord Komawara, begin planning the tactics to be used in the hills. Lord Taiki will take responsibility for seeing the dam built and defended. We will move the fleet south immediately." Shonto gestured to the line of refugees. "These people must be clear of the area by this time tomorrow." He looked around again as though weighing the plan one last time. "We will see what this Khan can do when he meets the unexpected."

Thirty-four

The first swallows had returned to the north that day, and the wood vibrated with the excitement of birds calling and courting. Rohku Tadamori held his horse by its bridle and watched the city of Rhojo-ma. The Flying Horse Banner of the Province of Seh had come down from the high tower of the Governor's Palace and the gold banner of the Khan with its strangely twisted dragon had appeared in its place. The dissonant sounds of horns and clashing of metal had echoed across the water then. Rohku's horse nudged his shoulder, pulling at the lacing of his armor.

Seh had fallen. For the first time in the history of the Empire the province had been taken by the barbarians. And Rohku served the man who had allowed that to happen. Though not a man of Seh, the captain felt the loss all the same.

Smoke curled up from the eastern end of the city, but there were no signs that the rest of Rhojo-ma was being put to the torch. If anything, the smoke was diminishing.

Five thousand men, Rohku thought, may Botahara rest their souls. It was impossible to say how many barbarians had fallen. More than five thousand, Rohku thought, many more. He looked out at the floating causeway that connected the shore and the eastern edge of the city. Beneath the waters lay uncounted warriors of both armies. The fighting had been hard.

The barbarians had not shown themselves to be brilliant tacticians, but they had not exhibited any lack of resolve either. The Khan had thrown wave after wave of men against the walls of Rhojo-ma, spending as though he had endless resources, and in the end this had won the day.

Rohku made a sign to Botahara and mounted his horse. He looked back at the city again.

Now we play gii, he thought, struck by how cold this seemed to him—but it was true. Who would learn the most from this first encounter? Who would come to the board next time armed with greater wisdom? He prayed that he could provide his lord with all the information they would need. The good name of his family depended on such things.

Thirty-five

Soldiers were neither numerous enough, nor skilled in the work, and in the end, peasants were pressed into the effort as well. Poles with baskets hanging from their ends proved more effective than oxen and carts when loading and unloading were considered. Shonto's advisors in this matter soon realized that stopping the flow of the canal would not be enough—the dam needed to stretch from higher ground further back from each bank to create the depth of water required. The volume of water flowing into the new sea was simply not great enough to backup sufficiently due to a mere constriction. Near the forming dam, workers dug away the bank to allow the blocked waters quicker access to the lowlands beyond.

Imperial messenger boats had been confiscated for the war effort and they plied back and forth to the north bringing news and moving observers. The word had passed to most now—Rhojo-ma had fallen and this news cast a shadow of desperation over the men who built the dam. Suddenly the war seemed real and the odds truly impossible.

There was as yet no news of the barbarian army moving south and, predictably, there were some that speculated the Khan had already achieved his goal. The victory in Seh would be consolidated and all this dam building would prove a fool's work.

Rhojo-ma had stood for five days. Five thousand against one hundred thousand. Though no one would ever truly know what had happened inside the city's walls, poets and writers of songs would not hesitate to fill in the missing details.

Ten days had passed since Shonto's fleet had left the northern city and in that time they had not traveled far. Creating the desert in their wake took time.

Captain Rohku Tadamori stood on top of a section of the new dike and watched the teeming workers. His report would have reached Lord Shonto by now, but his presence would still be requested. There would be questions not answered by his report.

Riders came up the rise toward him, wearing night blue and black. Lord Komawara Samyamu himself pulled his horse up before the young guard.

"Captain Rohku?"

Rohku bowed. "Captain Rohku Tadamori of Lord Shonto's guard, Lord Komawara."

"Lord Shonto would have you join him." A horse was led forward and the young captain mounted.

"It is a ride of several rih, Captain. I have not eaten today, would you share a meal with us?"

"The honor, Lord Komawara, would be mine entirely."

Motioning for Rohku to ride at his side, Komawara turned his horse and set off.

Passing the lines of workers, both men and women, coming from the stone and gravel pits, Rohku was astonished by the numbers who toiled. They passed an old man who sat on the ground in the grip of a fit of coughing. A young girl bent over him, obviously frightened. A soldier rode down the line toward this pair. Seeing the rider, the girl reluctantly tore herself away from the old man, tears appearing as she went. Rohku turned away.

"We have little time." Komawara said softly. "The rains this spring have not been great, so it will take many days for the waters to gather." He said nothing for a moment but then spoke again. "It has been said that we have created a desert in our wake, but now we will create a sea. I am told, Captain, that the barbarians proved to be poor sailors so perhaps seas will serve our purpose better than deserts."

Rohku kicked his foot free of a stirrup and shortened it as they went. "The lake surrounding Rhojo-ma proved an excellent defense. If it had not been for the pirates, the siege would undoubtedly have taken days longer."

"Pirates!" Komawara exclaimed, proving again that he was from the outer provinces. "I had not heard there were pirates." Komawara looked at his companion in

amazement. "Brother Shuyun and I saw no pirates among
the barbarians."

Rohku found his now properly adjusted stirrup. "I am
sure that is true, Sire, but there are pirates in the Khan's
army now."

"This Khan, he has built an army out of impossibili-
ties." Komawara could not get over his surprise. "Pirates!"

"It would indicate that my lord was correct, Sire. The
Khan has enlisted pirates so his army can follow the great
canal south to the inner provinces. It seems the barbarian
has considered the possibilities with some care before
embarking on this endeavor."

Komawara nodded. "I agree, though I suspect it never
occurred to the Khan that the army of Seh would not
stand and fight. Once the army of Seh had been defeated,
the canal would take him easily and quickly to the undefended center of Wa. Lord Shonto has done the unexpected," Komawara said with satisfaction. "The canal
will prove a difficult road indeed."

Komawara raised a hand to stop. "This seems a likely
place for a meal, Captain, would you agree?"

Rohku nodded. They were on a low hill, the first of
the range that lay to the west of the canal. Below them a
large plain stretched north toward Seh, black soil ready
for planting—though it would bear a crop of weeds this
season.

They dismounted and a bamboo mat was rolled out for
the lord and the man he treated as a guest.

"As you say, Lord Komawara, I am sure Lord Shonto
will slow the barbarian advance to a crawl. If only the
Emperor will raise the army we need."

Komawara smiled. "Yes. It is the one instance where
we may pray the Emperor's spies are alert. Once they
have seen the barbarian army, one would hope the Son
of Heaven will respond accordingly. Though we may be
in Itsa before that happens," Komawara said with a show
of frustration.

A small fire was lit and food was laid out for the two
men. Rohku was unused to the company of lords—even
minor ones from outer provinces—but Komawara was so
natural and likable he soon found himself put at ease.

War, the Captain thought, may break down more walls than one would expect.

"You have served the Shonto long?" Komawara asked, trying to carry on the polite conversation he believed Rohku would expect. Rohku was obviously too young to have served anyone long.

"Not long, Lord Komawara. My father is the captain of Lord Shonto's personal guard," he said, trying not to show any sign of pride.

"How is it that I have not met him?"

"He stays in the Capital performing duties for our lord."

"Ah. And you are also a captain."

"Recently promoted." He waved to the north. "This war has already seen many a junior officer receive ranks that would otherwise be years away."

"You are modest, Captain. Lord Shonto would not have sent you to watch the barbarians and witness the battle of Seh if he did not hold great respect for you."

Rohku shrugged, coloring almost imperceptibly. "You are too kind, Lord Komawara. I myself wonder if any number of lieutenants will not find themselves generals before many months have passed—such is our need.

"Lord Shonto is off in the hills somewhere?" What Shonto did and where he was at any given time was not considered a topic for general discussion, especially now that war had come, but there was no one within hearing and Komawara seemed at ease with Rohku—he might drop a hint at least.

The lord waved to the west. "We make plans for defending the hills. Perhaps Lord Shonto will explain."

Rohku nodded. Pressing the point was out of the question. He looked off to the west. The barbarians might try to skirt the new lake, and then there might be opportunities for ambush.

"Perhaps," Rohku said, "I will take a more active roll in the near future."

Komawara nodded as he ate. When he spoke again, he seemed quite serious. "What you have just done, Captain Rohku—witnessing the battle of Rhojo-ma—I would have found this a most difficult duty." He gave a nodding bow. "You are to be commended for this."

Rohku did not look up as he spoke. "At the battle of

Rhojo-ma I watched, Lord Komawara. I did not lay down my life.''

"Exactly," Komawara said softly.

The conversation failed then and they ate in silence. Finishing the meal, they set out into the hills, the conversation stilted until Captain Rohku commented on the quality of Seh's horses and then it flowed like a steep river.

They found a road among the hills and followed that, riding out of the direct sunlight into the trees robing themselves in new leaves. Shonto guards blocked the way until Komawara gave the password and they continued on, encountering more and more riders in blue as they went. Finally, Lord Shonto stood before them in a clearing surrounded by guards and officers. Conspicuous among them was an ill-dressed soldier, unarmored like the senior military men, though armed. He carried a sword in Shonto's presence.

Komawara and Rohku waited beside their horses until General Hojo waved them forward. The ragged man turned and then a smile flickered across his face. It was Rohku Saicha, the young captain's father.

The two monks sat on mats that had been placed in the bow of the river boat. The fair wind of the season moved them south, if not at great speed, with a consistency that saw the rih pass in surprising numbers. A rain shower had blown over earlier, but the sun soon dried the decks and only the occasional droplet from steaming sails indicated that there had been rain at all. Plum and cherry trees flowered on the banks and where there would normally be gay parties out under the boughs to observe the blossoming, frightened refugees streamed south instead.

Brother Sotura was glad that he could speak to his former student in privacy—only the tribesman in Shonto livery stood nearby and he was not close enough to overhear. The sailors had little to do and, as they followed a boat with deeper draft, there was no lookout in the bow nor did anyone sound the bottom, but out of respect for the Botahist monks they confined their idling to midships.

"These events are unsettling, Shuyun-sum," the senior Brother was saying. "So many people torn from their homes. Already there are hungry and, with such numbers on the roads and canal, disease is appearing. I spend time as I can now with the sick, but there are more every day." He shook his head. "I have written to Brother Hutto in Yankura, but it will be some time before our Order can respond to a situation that grows worse as we speak."

Shuyun touched his hands together, rocking back and forth slightly as though nodding agreement. "I have asked Lord Shonto if I could assist you, Brother, but he will not spare me, though often I have little to do. Every precaution is taken to isolate the sick from the army and Lord Shonto's staff. Even our meeting was difficult to arrange. I regret this."

"It cannot be helped, Shuyun-sum. Your part is to advise Lord Shonto so that the interests of our Order are represented among the powerful of Wa. Now that the situation gathers momentum by the hour, your role is even more crucial."

At this Shuyun stopped rocking.

"We do our best to prepare for this calamity, Shuyun-sum, but it is difficult. The future is uncertain." Sotura caught the eye of his student. "If we knew more of Lord Shonto's intent, we could act to assist him and to preserve our Order so that Botahara's word would not be lost."

Shuyun examined his palm, rubbing it slowly. "My lord hopes to slow the barbarian advance so that an army may be raised to defend the Empire."

Sotura paused for a second as though he had suffered a small insult and was unsure how to respond. When he spoke, he had lowered his voice. "No doubt, Brother Shuyun, this is true but the Yamaku still sit upon the Dragon Throne and we could do much if we knew what Lord Shonto . . . thought about this situation."

Shuyun shrugged. "In truth, Brother Sotura, I do not know."

"Perhaps it would be useful to find out."

"My lord gives me the information he feels I need in my capacity, Brother. I do not presume to ask for more."

"As his loyal Advisor it might be to your lord's benefit

if you spent time informing yourself of the situation in the Empire and of your lord's intent.''

Shuyun blinked.

''Jaku Katta is another question, Shuyun-sum. Does he truly have Lord Shonto's confidence?''

Shuyun watched a sampan drift past, carrying men in Shonto blue. ''Did not Botahara say, 'Do not trust truth to a liar.' ''

Sotura nodded. ''The guardsman is an opportunist of the worst sort. Trusting him would be an error indeed. Does he still seek the company of Lady Nishima?''

''Perhaps. I do not know,'' Shuyun said slowly.

''Maybe she has seen him for what he is and has another interest?''

Shuyun shrugged. ''The personal lives of my lord's family . . .'' Shuyun threw up his hands.

Sotura nodded.

''It is a crucial time, Brother Shuyun. Much could be lost in the coming struggle. We must be vigilant. The True Path must be protected and we are its chosen protectors.''

Shuyun stared at the chi quan instructor until the Master became uncomfortable.

''Brother Shuyun?''

Motioning to the Kalam suddenly, Shuyun leaned toward the tribesman and spoke in the man's tongue. The Kalam gave a proper bow and hurried off.

''There is something you should know, Brother,'' Shuyun said quietly. ''It will make many things clear to you. We must wait for my servant.''

The Kalam appeared a moment later, bearing a brocade bag containing something small and angular. Giving it to Shuyun, he retreated to his former station by the rail and stood silently.

With great care Shuyun slid a plain lacquered box out of the bag. He set the box carefully on his knees and unlatched it. ''There is a matter we have discussed before, Brother Sotura. Let me show you what I have found.'' Saying this he opened the box gently.

On the lining of green silk lay the blossom of the Udumbara. The breeze touched it and the petals moved as though still fresh from the branch.

It was not possible to tell from Sotura's face if the

older monk was overcome with joy or deep sadness. He did not move for some time and then, almost tenderly, he reached out, but as he did so Shuyun withdrew the box, closing it sharply. The young Brother's face was very cold.

"I will not trust it to you, Brother," Shuyun said firmly.

* * *

I fear that our young protégé is following the path of Brother Satake—I regret to say that Shuyun is not inclined to provide the information we seek about his liege-lord. The change in him is remarkable considering the short time he has served the Shonto House, but there are circumstances we could not have foreseen. Shuyun has in his possession a blossom from a tree at Monarta. I do not know where this has come from, but if it was Lord Shonto's desire to undermine the Initiate's loyalty to our Order he could hardly have chosen a more effective ploy. This situation will be difficult to retrieve now, especially as Lord Shonto controls my meetings with Shuyun and allows far fewer than I request. How Shonto came by a blossom from the Udumbara is a mystery—one can never underestimate this man. Although Shonto's situation in the Empire does not appear to be secure, I hesitate to say more. The Emperor may yet discover that circumstances are not what he believed.

As to Shuyun I am not yet certain what should be done—he was always a perfect student in the past. Some action must be taken soon or he will have turned so far from the light that he will find it difficult to return.

Sotura stopped writing suddenly. He wondered what the Supreme Master and Brother Hutto would decide about Shuyun. *We have been caught in a lie by one who believed what he was taught about lies. The deeper reasons for our decision cannot be seen by a young Initiate, no matter how talented—all he will see is our hypocrisy. The Teacher has come and we deny it. How can Shuyun but think we act from motives that are less than pure? He has not stepped off the True Path—we have pushed him. May Botahara forgive us.*

Sotura picked up the letter, read through the first few lines by the light of his lamp, and then very slowly crumpled the paper into a ball. He was not certain that any action his superiors took with the willful Initiate would not drive this young man further away. Even I have begun to distrust my superior's judgment, Sotura realized, and he made a sign to Botahara.

The monk remembered the interview with his former student. Even sitting as far as I was, Sotura thought, I could feel the strength of his chi. I have never known its like.

Thirty-six

The hunting party followed a winding road down the hillside, riding slowly in the spring sunshine. It had not been a successful day as the tiger the villagers claimed to have seen could not be found. The Emperor was disappointed. They had shot some game birds, certainly, but when one has set out after tiger, pheasant is a poor substitute. Still, it was a beautiful day and Akantsu II, Emperor of Wa, was coming out of his sullen mood.

Many varieties of cherry and plum flowered along the roadside and scattered their petals like a snowfall across the soft ground of spring. It would not be long now until the Plum Blossom Wind would perform the feat it was named for, stripping the trees of their petals and carrying them aloft until the wind seemed laden with blowing snow.

The rivers, too, would be covered in fallen blossoms, for the people of Wa loved to plant their flowering trees along the waterways—the sight of the perfect blossoms borne toward the sea was symbolic of Botahist thought. Over the centuries so many poems had been written about the Plum Blossom Winds that it was said nothing new could ever be written about them—though that stopped no one.

The Emperor rode a gray mare of the same line as the animals used in the Ceremony of Gray Horses. Unlike the Hanama who seldom hunted, the Yamaku men rode and rode well. Perhaps a family that had won its way to the throne only a decade before was not yet willing to give up the skills that had brought them their victory, so sword and bow and lance and horse were thought of as essential disciplines in the Imperial family. Akantsu was a fine horseman and skilled with a sword, though his sons, under the influence of the Empress, had never achieved the mastery of their father.

The Emperor's hunting garb was plain by the standards of the lords of the inner provinces, though it bore trim in Imperial Crimson which more than made up for its lack of style. As he had hoped to meet a tiger that day, the Emperor's garb incorporated a certain amount of lacquered and laced armor, although light and incomplete by battle standards. A dragon-crested helmet swung from the saddle, and the Son of Heaven carried his own sword in his sash—not the ancient sword of office but a blade that had seen many battles and duels.

It was well known among the courtiers that when Akantsu wanted to show displeasure to one of the many officials who attended him he would sometimes invite them on a hunt. It was invariably quite unpleasant, for few of the higher officials rode, having spent their entire lives caught up in the functions of the government and court—and, of course, in the Capital, as in much of Wa, one usually traveled by boat. The Emperor reserved this treatment for officials who had done something mildly annoying. To cross the Emperor seriously would mean postings in the outer provinces or far worse.

Today there were no victims in the party. A distant cousin from Chou rode near the Emperor though they spoke little. The Son of Heaven's earlier mood had quickly curtailed attempts at conversation.

A dark feathered hawk floated across the road, disappearing into the cloud of white blossoms and when the Emperor turned his eyes back to the road he saw a column of Imperial Guards appear around a bend, led by Jaku Tadamoto. The Emperor's men made way for their acting Commander who dismounted quickly and bowed before his ruler.

"Colonel." The Emperor smiled, much to the relief of his party. "Your arrival was foretold. Only seconds ago a hawk I believe was a Choka passed before us." He turned to his cousin. "Almost an apparition, wouldn't you agree?"

His cousin, Lord Yamaku, a small man perhaps a dozen years older than the Emperor, most definitely agreed. He nodded his head vigorously. More than anything else, Lord Yamaku resembled a successful merchant. He had that wealthy, ill-bred manner and dress that bad taste damned many with in the Imperial Court. Not that the man's taste was glaringly awful, but among people whose standards were strict and whose imagination was limited he stood out like a farmer in a Sonsa troupe.

"The Choka hawk has proven to be well chosen, then," Tadamoto said. The Emperor had given the Jaku House the symbol, raising their status considerably among the new Houses.

The Emperor smiled again. "It is kind of you to ride out to meet us, Colonel. I intend to stop at the shrine for the view. Would you accompany us?"

"I would be more than honored. May I ask, Sire, how went the hunt?"

A cloud drifted across the Emperor's face, but then a wan smile replaced it. "I believe the tiger we hunted today was mythical. Or a master of subterfuge. We had beaters out for several rih and managed to move nothing. And Lord Yamaku had so wanted to use his new bow."

"I am sorry to learn this, Sire. Tigers make poor subjects, sometimes—ignoring their duties, leaving without being dismissed, and eating perfectly dutiful subjects. I don't know what can be done about them."

The Emperor laughed. "Yes, this one is said to have eaten a loyal woodsman. A beastly thing to do when I have any number of courtiers and officials I could willingly spare. Most inconsiderate." He laughed again and the others nearby, deeming the Emperor's mood changed, laughed as well.

Turning off the road they followed a trail out onto a rounded promontory where a small shrine to the plague-dead stood. Knowing the Emperor's opinions on the matter, no one made signs to Botahara. They passed on to the lookout point where the Emperor and his party dismounted.

"String your new bow, cousin," the Emperor said pleasantly. "Tadamoto-sum is an appreciator of fine weapons."

An archery contest was quickly organized among the officers of the guard using Lord Yamaku's bow. Much laughter accompanied the Emperor's suggestion that an officer donate his very stylish hat for a target. This was fixed to a nearby tree and the Emperor took up a seat on a rock, flanked by Tadamoto and his cousin as judges.

Lord Yamaku did not join the contest as it would have been very impolite for anyone to best a member of the Imperial family and Tadamoto was the guard Commander, so a similar etiquette applied.

Each contestant shot three arrows and though not every one found its mark, the hat was soon well ventilated indeed. The archers could not be said to be remarkable in their skill, but they were well matched so the contest was close and therefore more enjoyable for all concerned.

Once the contest had drawn everyone's attention, the Emperor turned to Tadamoto. "I trust you did not ride all this way to view the blossoms, Colonel?" he said quietly.

Tadamoto nodded. "I have received a report from the north." He searched for the right words. "It is a disturbing report, Emperor."

The Emperor nodded. He watched a young officer make a shot and applauded the result. Leaning over, he spoke quietly to his cousin who bowed quickly. The Emperor nodded to Tadamoto and the two men rose. All present dropped to their knees until the Emperor was several paces away.

Walking to the lookout, the Emperor leaned against the railing that protected the foolish from the steep drop. Behind him the land stretched off to the Imperial Capital and the Lake of the Lost Dragon. The river wound its way toward the sea and as far as Tadamoto could see the landscape was decorated with flowering trees. Even the distant Mountain of the Pure Spirit seemed to be covered in a haze of white.

"Colonel." The Emperor nodded for Tadamoto to continue.

"I have a report that Lord Shonto has left Seh and proceeds south on the canal accompanied by an army."

The Emperor nodded calmly as though he had not just heard an announcement of civil war—civil war with the Shonto.

"A missive has arrived bearing the seal of the Governor of Seh. I broke all protocol and brought it with me, Sire."

The Emperor nodded again. "There is more?"

Tadamoto nodded. "Reports have been received that a large barbarian army has crossed the border of Seh. I do not consider these substantiated at this time, however."

"The missive?"

Tadamoto signaled one of his guards, and a small box was brought forward. Opening this, Tadamoto removed the official letter and, to the guardsman's surprise, the Emperor reached out and took it directly from the Colonel's hand. Looking at the seal, the Emperor broke it and opened the letter with no show of haste. He read.

Tadamoto pretended to admire the view. It was impolite to look directly at the Emperor for more than a few seconds and, under the circumstances, Tadamoto thought even a few seconds might not be advisable.

The Emperor lowered the scroll. He looked off at some unseen distance for a moment and then handed the paper to Tadamoto. "Read this," he said, his tone mild.

Sire:

A barbarian army has crossed the northern border of Seh, an army of one hundred thousand armed men. Their immediate objective appears to be Rhojo-ma, but I do not believe this army plans to finish its campaign in the provincial capital. As the entire force available in the Province of Seh is less than a quarter the number in the invading army, I do not feel we can stop the barbarians from advancing into Itsa Province and then further south.

Our decision, therefore, has been to leave Seh and move our army down the canal, resisting the invaders as we go. If all goes well, I believe this will give the Empire until midsummer to raise the force necessary to combat the barbarian army.

Five thousand men of Seh stayed to defend the city of Rhojo-ma, hoping to give the main force time to cross the border and begin the recruitment. This we will do.

I regret to say that I do not think this barbarian force can be countered successfully without assistance from the Imperial Government. I do not

*expect to be able to raise enough men to meet the
threat to the Empire even by the time we reach
Chiba Province.*

*We can say little yet of the skills of this
barbarian army and its commanders and will
report as soon as more is known. Certainly, the
tribes are led by the Golden Khan who flies a
banner of gold bearing a dragon of crimson. I
believe, Sire, that this chieftain has designs upon
the throne of Wa.*

*Those who have followed me in this move south
are brave and industrious men and I have faith
that we can slow the invaders' advance, but an
army must be raised to meet this threat,
preferably in Chiba Province. We destroy all
crops as we go, but once the barbarians have
reached Chiba, this will become more difficult and
if they cross the border into Dentou it will be
impossible. They will also be within striking
distance of the Imperial Capital.*

> *I remain your Majesty's servant,*
> *Shonto Motoru*

The Emperor had no compunctions about watching
Tadamoto's face as he read and the young man found as
he finished the letter that he was being stared at.

"He makes no mention that it was his sworn duty to
protect the borders of the Province of Seh."

Tadamoto nodded, not needing to ask who "he" referred to.

The Emperor turned and looked out at the view, his
hands resting lightly on the rail. For some moments he
stood like that in silence and when he spoke he did not
turn his head.

"We did not think he would be able to find the support
for a civil war—not in Seh. He fails to mention how large
a force accompanies him south?"

"That is true, Emperor."

"A significant oversight in the former governor's report. It is not possible that Motoru has raised the force
he needs in Seh." This did not seem to be a question,
so Tadamoto said nothing. The "thunk" of arrows strik-

ing wood punctuated the silence. "How goes the raising
of our army, Colonel?"

"Well, Sire, but I will redouble our efforts now."

The Emperor nodded. "We will do more. We must
prepare a plan to meet Shonto's army—somewhere beyond the Capital. There is no telling who will flock to
his banner once he enters Dentou Province." The Emperor fell silent again. "Where on the canal is my useless
son?"

"He has not yet crossed the border into Chiba Province, Sire." Tadamoto brushed white petals from the
small dragons embroidered over the breast on his uniform.

The Emperor's shoulders went stiff. "Not yet in
Chiba?"

"Yes, Sire."

The Emperor snorted. "I will send a letter to the
Prince in my own hand: an Imperial directive to proceed
north with all haste and relieve Shonto of the command
of the army. He is then to stop any barbarian invasion he
is able to find and send Shonto to the Capital under guard.
How do you think the former governor will react to that?"

"To do anything but obey the son of the Emperor, Sire
. . . would be a foolish mistake."

"Yes, but it would do away with this pose of protector
of the Empire. He will be a rebel and called one."

Tadamoto nodded even though the Emperor looked out
toward the Capital.

"Have you heard from your brother, Colonel?"

"I have not, Emperor."

The Emperor rubbed his hands slowly along the railing. "We might hope that he stayed in Seh to *defend
Rhojo-ma*. All who accompany Shonto support a rebel."

"He shames the Jaku House, Sire. We will turn our
back to him."

The Emperor nodded slowly. "I believe this matter
should be discussed immediately in the Great Council.
We will have the Empire know that Shonto has abandoned his duties in the north and comes south with an
armed force. It is not this ragged Khan who has designs
on the throne. If we had only kept that Fanisan daughter
in the Capital!" It was the closest thing to an expression

of anger the Emperor had made, but when he spoke again
his voice was calm. ''She will not sit upon my throne,
Colonel, nor will Motoru stand behind it.'' He turned
now and looked directly at Tadamoto. ''So we must raise
a great army, Colonel. My father fought the Shonto and
won—I intend to do the same. But I will not be so generous after my victory.''

Thirty-seven

Shokan lay still in the darkness wondering what one
felt when overcome by the cold. Did a person simply
sleep and not wake? Or was it painful or frightening? If
one still felt the cold, was that a sign that one was closer
to life than death? Cold was what the young lord felt:
deep, pervasive cold. The bones of his legs ached with
cold and in his feet there was no feeling at all.

With some effort the lord pulled his mind away from
this avenue of thought and tried to consider the coming
day. He had held a brief council with his staff that night,
huddled in a circle in the dark, no fire to offer warmth
or even cheer. Hard choices had been discussed and decisions made. Destroying the horses had weighed heavily
on everyone; unfortunately, no one had offered an alter-
native that would allow the group to continue. It had
been a fool's hope that the snows would not be deep in
the pass so early in the season, but then there had been
few paths open to them. Bringing the horses was a risk
perhaps not everyone had understood.

Shonto Shokan had made the decision to destroy his
stallion himself, though certainly it was not a task a lord
of a Great House should even consider. Still, he felt this
situation was of his own making and could not ask another to perform the duties his poor decision had made
necessary. This kind of thinking was a trait of the young
lord's that drove his father mad. The senior Shonto even
went so far as to blame their former Spiritual Advisor,
Brother Satake, for encouraging this trait, saying it was
good education for children but the worst foolishness for
the lord of a major House. Shokan almost laughed aloud
at the memory. It was his impression that Brother Satake
had quietly defied everyone; may Botahara protect him.

There had been no wood for fires that night and the

sky had remained perfectly clear, allowing the bitter cold
of the mountains free rein. The eastern sky was barely
gray behind the white peaks that loomed above, but that
was enough to have men up and moving, trying to restore
circulation, praying the sun would not tarry and the sea
wind would bring them warmth. It was a great irony that
by night they huddled together in teeth-chattering cold
while by day the sun burned their faces and had them
stripped down to their lightest robes.

Shokan pushed his cover aside and turned onto his
back. He had been rolling over at regular intervals all
night trying not to expose one side for too long to the
bitter chill that seeped up from the snow—not a restful
night. He was hungry and worried about their food supplies. Horse meat would take them some distance, no
doubt, but they were still many days away from the western end of the pass. In a purely foolish act they had, to
a man, fed some of their precious grain to the horses the
night before—a last meal—but the lack of fires to melt
snow had meant no water. There was no doubt that the
horses would soon be dead without any assistance from
their reluctant riders.

Forcing himself to sit up, Shokan felt the chill wind
that still swept down from the peaks. He stayed sitting
for a moment, beating his hands on his arms and shoulders. The snow would be frozen into a steel-hard crust
now, a surface that would support a man's weight with
ease, but it was also steep, treacherous ice and had led
to the loss of many of their party.

From up the gulley Shokan heard the measured rhythm
of footsteps as the guides moved higher. The previous
day they had made a stairway while the snow was soft
and now they climbed up to its top where they would
continue by cutting more steps in the hard snow. It was
a slow, laborious process.

Shokan thought again of their limited food supplies,
wondering if he led his retainers to a futile end in some
frozen pass. My father needs every armed man he can
find, he reminded himself. Every risk is acceptable.

Looking up at the mountains, Shokan thought of the
vast valley that lay on their opposite side down which ran
the delicate ribbon of the Grand Canal. It seemed very
far away, almost unreachable.

A single peak above caught the light of the rising sun and the young lord felt a great relief. Around him he could make out the shapes of men and horses. Shades of gray began to take on color and shapes definition.

"Sire?" a voice whispered.

Shokan turned to his guard who pointed up the slope. Not far away, half a dozen bearded men crouched down on their heels and watched, their faces impassive. Mountain people. . . .

Shokan turned to his guard who stared openly, unaware that his lord regarded him. Moving with great care, Shokan found the small platform he had stamped out before the snow froze and got unsteadily to his unfeeling feet.

Though he half expected them to start like deer and bound off, the crouching men made no move. It was the worst manners, but Shokan found himself staring like his guard. Mountain people! He could not hide his surprise.

The men crouching before him were dressed so completely in furs and skins that nothing showed but weathered faces. At their belts they carried long knives, almost swords, and, on their backs, bows of an almost pure white wood. As he had read, these men had deep blue eyes, like one sometimes saw among the southern barbarians.

Slowly, Shokan extended his hands, palms out, all the while searching his memory for words he had heard Brother Satake speak in the mountain tongue—but none came. His father had said that Shuyun spoke their language, and Shokan wondered if this was not uncommon for a Botahist scholar.

Turning to his guard Shokan said, "The Botahist monks often know the mountain tongue—pass the word down the line to anyone educated by the Brothers."

The mountain people looked on as Shokan extended his hands, but there was no reaction visible—it might have been his private morning ritual for all the response it received. He tried gesturing to the snow nearby and smiling in invitation, but the men crouching in the snow did not move. Both parties were soon reduced to staring at each other in silence.

After this had gone on for some time, Shokan noticed a movement higher up on the guides' stairway. Another

group made its way down toward the snowbound lowlanders.

As this second party arrived, the first group turned and
bowed stiffly. The object of this show of respect seemed
to be an old, leather-faced man in a worn hooded robe
gathered at the waist by a silk sash of faded purple. What
animal had contributed its coat to this old man's warmth
Shokan could not say, for the fur was unknown to him—
deep gray with tips of silver.

The old man continued right past the bowing mountain
people and stopped about three paces beyond Lord Shonto's guard who had been unable to move quickly enough
on the treacherous footing to stop him. Shokan gave them
a signal to stand ready but do nothing for now.

The old man stood, arms crossed, hands buried in the
sleeves of his robe. His face was as impassive as his
companions' though his eyes were the color of a sky
washed with a high mist. The mountain race seemed to
be smaller than the people of Wa though Shokan suspected they were broad of shoulder under their layers of
fur.

The old man pointed at the Shonto lord. "Name," he
said, not inflecting the word like a question, though Shokan assumed it was meant to be one.

"Lord Shonto Shokan. And you?"

The old man did not respond, but among his companions there was a whispering. Shokan was certain he heard
the name of his father's Spiritual Advisor spoken more
than once, as impossible as it seemed.

"Brother Shuyun," Shokan said. "Do you speak of
Brother Shuyun?"

After a moment the old man nodded his ancient head
once, his expression never altering. It was such an odd
movement, Shokan was not sure the man's head had not
simply fallen forward and then been returned to its upright position. It hardly seemed an expression of agreement.

With a quick motion the old man pointed up the slope.
"Fight," he said with some animation.

Shokan was not sure what this meant but obviously
some response was desired.

"Shu-yung fight!" the man said with more urgency.

"This is hopeless," Shokan whispered to his guard. "What does he mean?"

"Tribes . . . fight, shu-yung," the man said, and pointed up into the mountains again.

Tribes; the word struck the lord like cold wind. He nodded slowly, still far from certain. He was not even sure that nodding meant agreement to these people. Shuyung, the old man was saying, a word so close to Shuyun in their odd pronunciation that to Shokan's ear it was barely different—a slight ring in the last syllable, that was all.

The old man's face split in a smile then and he broke into his own tongue, speaking so fast that the men listening could have easily been convinced it was all a single long word. He smiled again. "Fight tribes, shu-yung," he said with some finality. Turning to his companions he spoke again, and Shokan was almost certain he heard the word *Yankura*.

A man detached himself from the others and ran easily up the slope, causing the men of Wa much envy.

"Yankura?" Shokan said. "Yankura?"

"Yan-khuro," the old man enunciated slowly, as though he corrected a child.

"Yan-khura. Yul-khuro, yan yul. Shu-yung," he said, and then, as if for good measure, "fight."

Shokan nodded and smiled. Am I agreeing? he wondered, and if so, to what?

Pointing at Shokan's horse with that same quick motion, the old man spoke in his tongue again, then shook his head. Holding his hands together as though he held a bowl, he made a drinking motion and then pointed at the horse, his face suddenly sad.

"Sire," Shokan's guard said quietly, "above us."

A small army of fur-clad mountain dwellers descended the slope, many down the stairway but as many walking directly down the steel hard snow without losing their footing. Shokan realized he stared openmouthed, but then it was a wonder indeed.

"What will happen now?" Shokan heard someone say. He gave a short laugh.

"I don't know." Despite a lifetime's training in suspicion, the lord somehow knew these people meant them no harm. "I don't know," he said again.

The mountain people passed by Shokan with barely a nod and a half smile, but the horses were another matter. These were objects of great admiration. Shokan was afraid the numbers of people milling around would spook the animals, but it quickly became obvious that the mountain dwellers were well versed in the handling of animals and undoubtedly horses, too.

The old man came a few paces closer to be heard above the noise of his people. He spoke a few words in his own tongue and then pointed at Shokan's horse. "No fight," he said quietly. Then pointing at Shokan's saddle bags and assorted gear. "Shuyunal." He gestured to his people. "Shuyun." Then he pointed up the pass and gave his odd single nod.

Shokan copied the gesture, then turned to his guard. "Find the boy. Have him tell everyone to offer no resistance to these people. We will leave them the horses and they will assist us over the pass . . . I think."

Shokan turned back to the old man, but he had turned and was trudging slowly up the stairway.

"Shuyun," a voice said beside him. Shokan turned to look at a beardless, smiling child. Tapping his chest, the child smiled again. "Shuyun," he said.

"Ah," the lord said. This is Shuyun? But then he realized the same word was being repeated up and down the line. Two others were fitting the pole to Shokan's armor box and lifting it easily to their shoulders although the lord knew it contained suits of both heavy and light armor as well as other arms and assorted pieces of gear for repairs.

The smiling child beside him began to collect the lord's belongings, and a guard quickly moved to intervene.

"No," the young lord said. "I will allow it." He began to roll his own bedding, though rather clumsily.

"Shuyun," he heard someone say down the line, and then again and again as though it were a chant.

To Shokan's surprise the mountain people led his party back down the gulley, making steps for the lowlanders as they went. He feared that there was a great misunderstanding and the mountain people were returning the lowlanders to the valley they had escaped, but he decided to wait a bit and see what would happen.

As the party came out from the shade of the great stone peak, the sun hit them and Shonto saw signs being made to Botahara by his men. They smile now, the lord thought, but in only a few hours the snow will soften and then the dread will return. They had seen what happened as the softening snow began to lose its hold, seen it come thundering down in great, white waves.

Looking over his shoulder, Shokan could still see the horses—surrounded by admirers. He hoped they were not to suffer the same fate at the hands of these people that they were about to at the hands of their owners. His foot slipped, but he recovered quickly. This was no place to be looking about or admiring the scenery. The footing was treacherous and would be until the sun had done its work.

The great coastal plain appeared around a corner, stretching off to the sea lost in a mist. The lowlands seemed green and warm and welcoming from this height and Shokan felt an urge to return. But there was no returning. Imperial Guards would be waiting below and had no doubt taken possession of the Shonto fief. There was only the mountains and whatever lay on the other side, if he were fortunate enough to see the western slopes.

Unlike his retainers Shokan carried no weight but his sword, and even so he did not go as lightly as the mountain people who bore the heaviest burdens. The lord had watched with fascination as the mountain people made up their loads, rigging these to be carried by a single strap across the forehead. The smallest mountain dweller bore twice what the largest lowlanders could carry, and with ease. Altitude was said to rob a man of his breath and Shokan did not doubt it now.

Before the sun was high they had come down around the peak to the south and here they dug down through the snow bank of the trench that formed on either side of the gulley, leaving a wide gap between the snow and the rock. Water ran in the bottom of the trench now and water skins were filled. A brief but slippery scramble took them up to a ledge as wide as a man was tall. The sun had melted whatever snow had lain here and the rock was dry and almost warm to the touch.

There was no talk. The mountain people seemed little

inclined to chat as they went, and the lowlanders needed
every bit of breath just to keep the pace. The height may
have had something to do with this silence, for though
the ledge only sloped up slightly the floor of the gulley
widened and sloped away so that they were higher with
each step. The lowlanders crowded the rock wall and
tried to keep their gaze fixed ahead, which meant all but
a few missed an astonishing vista.

The ledge narrowed here and there, enough to make
the passage of certain sections a test of nerve. Shokan
knew that Shonto guards would go into battle, no matter
what the odds, without hesitation, but heights were a different matter. Slipping off a ledge was hardly an honorable end. Of course, none wished to be seen as cowardly
before their fellows or the son of their liege-lord, so much
effort went into disguising fears. Still, Shokan was sure
that he had seen men famed for their prowess on the
battlefield traverse the more difficult sections with far less
confidence than some of their younger and less fearsome
companions. It almost made him smile.

Where the ledge narrowed to nothing, wooden walkways appeared to bridge the gaps and these were constructed in so flimsy a manner that all the lowlanders said
a prayer for the protection of their souls before crossing.
Shokan wondered how they bore the weight of snow or
if they were reconstructed each spring. So poorly engineered did these walkways appear, the fact that they had
no railings went almost unnoticed. To everyone's surprise they did not collapse.

By late afternoon the long snake of humanity had
wound its way around to the south, and the ledge ended
in a saddle between two peaks. They began to descend
again, at first on soft snow and then, as they came into
the shadow of the southern peak, on hardened crust.

Steps were cut again and the party slowed accordingly.
The valley widened and the west-moving sun found its
way down to them again, making the snow heavy. In
compensation, trees began to appear with greater and
greater frequency, raising hopes for fires that evening.

A stream appeared out of nowhere and wound its way
down the valley. Looking into the running water, Shokan
could see rocks and earth and realized the depth of snow
was much less than he had expected.

Suddenly the mountain people came to a halt on a small bench and with smiles and nods and gestures made it clear that this was as far as they would go that day. As camp was made, Shokan tried to estimate numbers. His retainers numbered thirty three hundred, remarkable when one considered the losses they had suffered to the snow slides. There were easily that number of mountain people, whom his own men had begun to call "dwellers" or even "the Shuyuns" which they thought funny. Close to eight thousand people.

Shokan hoped he would be able to describe this to his father one day. Eight thousand people over the most impossible terrain and they had covered at least twelve rih, maybe more. It was astonishing—it was more than astonishing; it was impossible!

The dwellers surprised the lowlanders again by starting the tiniest twig fires to brew cha and do some meager cooking. These they fed constantly with dried grasses and moss and dead needles from trees. They had reacted with horror when the Shonto men had begun to cut down trees for proper fires and Shokan had quickly ordered this stopped.

The lord had to admit that despite the fact that a terrible war was perhaps already under way across the mountains he found his own situation fascinating. Almost nothing was known about these people, and here they were, chatting away cheerfully beside him.

There was so little room in the encampment that everyone was in the closest proximity. Shonto's men had, naturally, kept a suitable distance from their lord so that he might have a semblance of privacy, and this area had quickly been filled with the dwellers, who did not seem to have much concern for rank unless one were a wizened old man in rather bedraggled furs.

Shokan's guards were not terribly comfortable with this, but the lord reasoned that they were entirely at the mercy of these people who could easily have murdered him before now if that was their intention. The lord resolved not to worry though it was obvious that his guard could not reach the same resolution, for they watched the dwellers near their lord and exchanged the darkest looks.

Using his hands and an art for pantomime that would have given Lady Nishima cause for pride, Shokan tried to discover the words for common things—fire, trail, food, drink. It was more difficult than he might have expected and caused much laughter.

The greatest reaction came when the lord tried to learn the words for man and woman. He was so obviously surprised at discovering the boy who carried his belongings was in fact a young woman that he thought the laughter would never stop. And the poor woman, it seemed, would be teased forever, but she took it well enough and didn't seem to hold him responsible for his own ignorance.

Darkness came with a suddenness that was almost startling. Despite attempts to stay awake and pry as many words as possible from his fireside companions, Shokan fell asleep. The last thing he heard was the dwellers singing softly in high, thin voices—a sound both eerie and oddly comforting.

It was much later, in the middle of the night, that Shokan awoke with a start. He took a moment to sort out his memory of the evening from his dream and then convinced himself what had startled him to consciousness had been part of a dream, nothing more. Laying back down, the lord tried to banish the feeling he was left with, but with little success. In his dream the dwellers' song had been a Botahist chant, translated into the mountain tongue and modified to suit the dwellers' ideas of music. It was strangely disturbing to him and he lay awake for some time, unable to shake the emotions the dream had evoked—unable to shiver away the feeling of cold.

Morning arrived long before the light. They were on the west side of a mountain now and the sun would not find them until past midday. Shokan had begun to believe that the dwellers were people of infinite patience, but as preparations were made to set out this was proven wrong. "Ketah," he learned, was the word for *hurry*. If *Shuyun* had been the refrain of the previous day, *ketah* had taken its place. The highly trained fighters of the Shonto guard were bullied and badgered and hurried until Shokan feared there would be an incident, but frayed tempers were kept in check and in remarkable time the company was on the move again.

Shokan took his place behind Quinta-la, the woman he

had caused so much embarrassment the night before. A
small scene with his guards had ensued when Shokan
insisted on carrying some of his own belongings, but he
had prevailed and now carried a load, dweller style,
which he was certain would soon disconnect his neck
from his shoulders. Before him walked a much smaller
woman carrying three times his own load; her step was
light and sure. It made him smile.

If Nishi-sum had been able to bear three times as much
as he, there would have been nothing to do but throw
himself on his sword—a warrior had a certain pride. But
the fact that this child could carry more than he could
ever hope to bear caused him nothing but amusement and
delight.

I have been transported to a strange world, he thought,
like the stories read to me as a child.

The work of carrying a load and matching the pace of
his guides soon warmed Shokan and hunger replaced the
feeling of cold, for they had started out having taken
neither drink nor food. There was no indication that the
dwellers planned to stop for a morning meal and inns
seemed sadly few.

The lord wondered idly if his retainers suffered the
soreness of leg that he felt. It was obvious that Quinta-
la knew no such discomfort. And this made him smile
also.

There was perhaps one thing that saved the lowlanders
that morning—they were taller than the mountain people,
so the steps that were cut in the hard snow seemed quite
close together to them. Even this small step down soon
had thighs burning from the effort for every step down
meant taking the extra weight of the carried load. Fatigue
caused a few slips, but none of these became disasters.

By noon the leaders of the party had reached the snow
line and soon only the deepest shadows still sheltered
patches of white—the oddest effect; white shadows. The
ground, however, was wet from days of snow-melt and
this offered its own hazards to footing. Sometime after
midday the sun worked its way down among the peaks,
warming the walkers and illuminating the view. Shokan
was impressed with the size of the valley—broad and long
and green. Still-frozen lakes like pieces of jade strung
together on a bubbling stream lay in the valley bottom.

As the party made its way down, the trees grew larger and less twisted. The scent of pine on the breeze was strong.

The way became a road of rock suddenly, wide slabs of stone set as though they had once been a perfect avenue but shifted by frost and time and neglect. Shokan pointed at this and made the gesture that he believed meant a question, but all he received in reply was a string of unknown sounds and a smile. He looked at his guard captain who had come up beside him.

The captain shrugged. "It is either a giant's road or a natural formation, Sire, and I must admit I prefer neither explanation over the other."

And this delighted the lord also—he realized he preferred it to be a mystery. They walked on with ease along this broad avenue.

What the lord had believed was mist ahead he was becoming convinced was actually smoke. Gaining the attention of Quinta-la, he pointed ahead. She spoke one of the dozen words Shokan knew—the one he believed meant fire.

"Well, yes," he said, "but does that fire signify anything? Food, perhaps?"

The young woman broke into her childlike smile and rattled on in her own tongue, gesturing off at the distance as she did so.

"Ah, I suspected as much," Shokan said, as though he had understood every word. "Will there be baths at this inn as well as fine meals?"

Quinta-la answered without a second's hesitation.

They carried on this preposterous conversation for some time, talking in turn, as though there were perfect communication. Both laughing and gesturing like children.

Shokan did not see the faces of his men nearby, or he chose to ignore them, but they kept glancing at him as though he had taken leave of his senses. Only the guard captain found the exchange amusing, and he was careful not to show he was listening.

The inn turned out to be a small village, though anyone from the Empire would have had a different image in mind if given the word village as a description. It sat upon what amounted to a hill on the north side of the valley and was almost one rambling building made of a gray-white stone and roofed with a simple dark tile. Stone walkways and walls connected all the various wings and alleys, and courtyards filled in the spaces that were left.

Shokan could not guess how many people lived in this place, but shutters opened and smiling faces appeared at windows to watch the arrival of the lowlanders. It was almost as if it happened all the time.

Thirty-eight

When faced with an overwhelming force there is only one possible response: limit your opponent's ability to bring such power to bear. Make them place pieces that will hamper their own attack and you will have enlisted their pieces in your own defence. Position becomes the essence of survival, the only hope for winning.

Writings of the
Gii Master Soto

S huyun rode along the rise in the late afternoon. The shadows of the plum trees stretched across the ground, twisted into impossibly elongated shapes. The blossoms had not yet begun to fall, but there was a dusting of white on the ground—a sign of what was to come.

To the monk's right lay the sea that had been created by Lord Taiki's dam; its surface rippled like the scales of a dragon. It was impressive in its size. Shuyun stood in his stirrups for a better view. To the east he could not see the shore that lay somewhere beyond the old canal banks, but then there had been extensive areas of marsh there—lands that resisted draining.

If not for the odd tree growing out of its surface and the top of a meandering stone wall, it would have appeared a natural lake—one that had known these shores for a thousand years, not mere days. Too new for dragons to have taken up residence, Shuyun thought. But even so it seemed a likely dragon pond. Crows screamed over the bloated form of a dead horse lying half submerged in the middle of the sea—a result of the Khan's attempt to march his army through the waters.

In many places the water would only be inches deep,

but the soil underneath was so soft it would turn to impassible mud with the least agitation. Extricating horses and men had taken an afternoon, and more animals than the one Shuyun could see had broken legs.

So the Khan had done as was expected, skirted the sea to the west through the hills. As Shuyun topped a slight rise he could see, in the distance, the van of the barbarian army making its camp for the night. The gold banners of the great Khan himself fluttered in the Plum Blossom Wind. Shuyun often wondered about this mysterious barbarian, wondered what Hitara could have told him of this man if Shuyun had ever caught up with the monk in the streets of Rhojo-ma. Shuyun shook his head—Brother Hitara was himself a great mystery.

The men the monk could see were only the tip of the army of the desert. The largest part of the Khan's force would be spending the night on the road that wound through the hills. It would not be a comfortable night despite clear skies and the promise of warm breezes. Lord Shonto's archers controlled much of the forest that bordered the road and even in the dark an army of one hundred thousand would be an easy target. There would be no fires for the barbarian warriors that night nor much rest either.

Shuyun's guard whispered among themselves, and the monk realized they thought he came too close to the army of the desert. He stopped for a last look at the scene, offering a prayer to Botahara to protect the souls of the men who would soon be lost here.

A soft zephyr brought the scent of plum blossoms to the monk and the sigh of wind in the trees. The sounds and the perfume reminded him of Lady Nishima, and he felt his memory stir. With an effort he forced his mind back to the present.

Much of Lord Shonto's plan had resulted from an observation Shuyun had made over cha—a quote from the gii Master, Soto—and Shuyun felt the weight of that.

A council had been called to decide how best to take advantage of the change in geography they had initiated. The argument had gone thus: the barbarian force was virtually limitless; to pass the sea that had been created by the new dam the army would have to march to the west through forested hills; the way through the hills was

narrow and winding; if barbarian patrols discovered an
ambush in the hills the Khan could muster unlimited
numbers of men to destroy it; if the barbarian patrols
simply disappeared in the hills, the Khan's response
would again be to send in large forces; a serious defense
of the road through the hills was possible but the result
inevitable, and the cost in lives would be great. Therefore, what was the purpose of the exercise?

The resulting decisions were largely dependent on timing for their success, timing and several tenets of the gii
board. Once a player is certain he perceives his opponent's plan, does he continue to search for other threats?

Shuyun turned his horse around. The sun would make
its daily plunge into the mountains soon, and he had several rih to ride to the boat Shonto was using as his command position. The plan was set, the forces had been
committed days ago. There was nothing to do but wait.

A single encounter with a barbarian patrol in the darkness would put the entire exercise at risk. Fortunately,
the softness of the ground allowed horses to pass in relative silence and barbarian patrols were either few or
concentrated elsewhere.

Jaku worried that they would not arrive at the canal
with enough men to perform the task entrusted to them—
it would be easy to lose half the company in such darkness. Even recent breaks in the cloud cover which had
begun to provide some starlight did nothing to relieve the
Guard Commander's growing pessimism. To his right
Jaku could make out Lord Komawara riding easily, setting the pace. Perhaps it was this that soured the general's
mood—command of the company had been given to Komawara Samyamu, not Jaku Katta.

Even in this low light Jaku could see they were skirting
the northern edge of the small sea that had been created—putting them uncomfortably in barbarian controlled lands. The Khan's army was camped on the road
through the hills where they awaited morning. When the
sun rose, the barbarian army would hurl their massive
numbers against the makeshift defenses around the newly
built dam. It was the prayer of the men of Wa that the
Khan believed he knew his enemy's intentions and saw
no traps nor surprises.

The plan, as it had developed, was simple. A false ambush had been set on the road through the hills and this had been discovered by a barbarian patrol. A significant skirmish ensued, resulting in the ambush failing, though at some loss to both sides. A spirited defense of the road through the hills had then been staged by Shonto's forces, led by General Hojo. Two days it had taken the barbarian army to force its way through to within striking distance of the dam. And now almost the entire barbarian army was stretched along the single narrow road, unable to move quickly either forward or back.

The supply train for that army, however, was borne by rafts moored against the canal bank to the north of the sea, waiting for the army to open the canal. Of course, the barbarian chieftains had not been foolish enough to leave the supply train untended—five thousand barbarian warriors stood guard—but it was perhaps the smallest guard such a valuable objective would ever have.

Shonto had gambled, leaving Komawara and Jaku hidden north of the lake with a force of eighteen hundred men, hoping they would not be discovered, hoping the barbarians would do exactly what they had done with their supply train.

Komawara's force had waited in utter silence for several days until a single rider had come from General Hojo bearing the orders to attack. The general had fought a wily battle on the road through the hills, offering enough resistance to convince the barbarian it was a true defense but keeping losses to a minimum. And now the barbarian army was strung out along a twelve rih road with their command virtually isolated at the southern end. A small force under the command of Rohku Saicha would fall upon the northern end of the barbarian force at dawn, their objective to cut off all assistance to the supply rafts.

Jaku admired the plan and had made some suggestions himself though it had been Shonto who had outlined the original idea to his staff. No one could say that the Shonto were timid! It was a bold plan in conception and required execution in the same manner. So why put this bumbling child in charge of the most crucial element? Jaku worked to control the anger caused by this slight. The coming fight would require absolute focus.

They skirted the perimeter of a wood now, staying on

the edge of the shadow, giving the company as much camouflage as possible while providing enough light to find the way. Earlier a soft rain had fallen and found its way under Jaku's armor—just enough water to make him cold and uncomfortable—and the light breeze was not helping matters. The general kept working his left arm as he rode, keeping it limber and warm, knowing that being wet coupled with a cool breeze could slow his muscles considerably. He was surprised others did not do the same.

Lord Komawara pulled up his mount to be sure the entire company was collected and then sent two riders ahead. An open meadow about half a rih across stretched out before them. Low walls of stone divided the area with a pattern of erratic dark lines, creating a hundred fields, irregular in both shape and size.

The two riders crossed the open area, losing shape as they went until they became a single, black shadow moving over the starlit field. No one spoke while waiting, but the sounds of horses shifting and rolling bits broke the stillness. One of Jaku's guards dismounted to tighten his girth—the thud of a knee against a belly and a sharp exhalation of breath.

The black shape of the two riders appeared again, returning, moving over the dark landscape that played tricks on the eyes. The black shape divided and became two riders who approached Komawara and spoke so quietly that Jaku could not hear the words.

The young lord nodded and then turned to Jaku. "We move, General," Komawara whispered. "Please signal your guards."

Beyond the field lay the last hill before the canal. A stand of ginkyo coming into leaf whispered with the sound of wind among the branches. The plan was already agreed to, though men would be sent out to survey the barbarian position to be sure it had not substantially altered. They came into the shadow of the hill and Komawara dismounted, crouching down on his heels without word or signal. His own men followed this example and after hesitating, Jaku did the same, his guards copying their commander.

In name they were Imperial Guards, but it was to Jaku Katta they owed their allegiance. Rumors that Jaku defied

the Emperor to be on the canal with Shonto or that their
commander was no longer in favor at court meant little
to them. Without question, they would follow Jaku into
battle and lay down their lives for him. Jaku Katta was
the great warrior of his time and to fight at his side meant
more to these men than the favor of a thousand Emperors. None of them doubted that after tonight Lord Komawara would defer command of any future raids to
General Jaku. He would see the Black Tiger in his true
element.

Komawara signaled and eight men rode off into the
night.

As the sound of horses moving over soft ground died,
the company fell silent. The voice of the breeze in the
ginkyo sounded like a complex form of music, varying
its tempo, falling to whispers, then rising to crescendos,
the pitch and timbre altering with a subtlety no instrument would ever duplicate. One could listen for hours
and never hear the same pattern repeated.

Having made himself aware of what constellations rose
and set closest to sunrise, Jaku watched the stars against
the horizon. The rotation of the heavens seemed to have
slowed that evening, for the stars appeared to hang utterly still with only the blowing clouds giving an illusion
of motion.

The riders began to reappear in pairs, whispering with
Komawara as soon as they arrived. Jaku desperately
wanted to know what was being said and felt that as a
general of some reputation he should be kept informed,
but he was certainly too proud to ask.

The star Jaku had picked as the signal to move touched
the earth at a distant point, and the general stopped himself as he started to rise and signal his men. Komawara
made no indication of being ready to move. The last riders arrived just as Jaku was losing patience. Komawara
rose to talk with these men, nodding and asking the occasional question.

He turned and signaled to Jaku who did not respond
well to being treated like a retainer whether this country
boy was a peer of the Empire or not. As a professional
soldier Jaku knew that a battle was no place to discuss
such things, so he crossed to where Komawara stood,
holding his face-mask open.

"The barbarian defenses are unchanged, General Jaku." Komawara said, his voice far calmer than the guardsman expected. "There is movement in the barbarian camp, but I am prepared to follow the plan as we discussed it: surprise appears to still ride in our company." Komawara smiled. "The novelty of limitless supplies of firewood does not seem to have worn off—there are more than enough fires for our needs. Is your company ready, general?"

Jaku nodded.

Komawara clamped his face-mask closed and tightened the cord on his helmet. Riders mounted horses and the company split into two: Jaku leading his guards north and Komawara turning south. A hint of gray appeared over the ginkyo wood as the men of Wa rode off.

Komawara kept his horse at a canter, fighting a strong desire to race ahead—Shuyun would be pleased to learn that he was gaining patience. Eighteen hundred men attacking five thousand was not much to the lord's liking, but he knew that there were several factors in their favor. The men guarding the supply rafts were cut off from the body of the barbarian army and in unfamiliar lands, which must weigh upon them to some degree. The hope was that a surprise raid at dawn would disguise the number of attackers and perhaps send the barbarians into a panic. Even if they recovered from this fairly quickly, much damage would already be done.

They skirted the wood, keeping in its shadow. Komawara glanced up at the sky with concern. Darkness would begin to draw back soon—not too soon he hoped or the impact of their attack would be lost. They began to round the southern end of the hill then, and the lord increased his pace slightly without meaning to. In a moment they would be in sight of the barbarian position. Komawara loosened his sword in its sheath.

Another tenth of a rih. There was gray in the sky now, and Komawara could make out objects at some distance if not in detail. As they passed a large willow, the fires of the barbarian encampment appeared suddenly. Drawing his sword with some care for its edge, Komawara spurred his horse into a canter.

It was only a matter of time now. Sentries would cer-

tainly hear them even if they had been staring at a fire
and ruined their night sight.

Even as this thought passed through the lord's mind, a
shout sounded in the camp and was quickly taken up by
others. Komawara heard his voice screaming, as blood-
curdling as any dream he'd had of barbarians attacking,
and his company joined in the cry, trying to make nine
hundred sound like thousands.

Aiming for the southern end of the barbarian position,
the lord could see men milling around, though what they
did was not discernible. Few will be armored, he found
himself thinking. His company began to split as the bowmen who would stay outside the camp and send their
arrows into the enemy ahead of Komawara's attack moved
left. A third group would try to fire or otherwise destroy
the supply rafts.

Although there was some attempt at a low wall of logs
and dirt on the perimeter of the barbarian position, it was
sparsely manned and Lord Komawara's mount cleared
this as though not carrying a rider in full armor.

His personal guard had come abreast of him now, determined not to let their lord be the first to throw himself
against the barbarian defense. The light was growing rapidly, and Komawara could see barbarian warriors struggling to push rafts away from the bank while others
prepared to defend them. Almost none had made it to
horse and those that had were without saddles.

Picking a swordsman on foot, Komawara spurred his
horse to ride the man down. The barbarian stood his
ground and raised his sword and just as Komawara was
about to turn aside to spare his mount and engage the
man, the barbarian's nerve broke and he turned and ran.
A single stroke brought the man down and Komawara
rode on.

It was the lord's intention to push into the barbarian
camp until resistance stopped them, creating as much
panic as possible among the greatest numbers. If the gods
smiled on them, the separate attacks on the encampment
would roll the ends of the barbarian position up before
them until they met in the middle, sending the panicked
tribesmen running toward the cover of the ginkyo wood.

An arrow lodged in the lacing of Komawara's shoulder
piece and he found himself hoping it was not from his

own men. Although some stood and fought, the raid was
having its desired effect—many more were running,
abandoning the rafts as they headed away from the river,
nonswimmers to a man.

Whistling-arrows were falling among the barbarians
ahead of Komawara now, adding their eerie screams to
the din. A half-dressed rider made for the lord suddenly,
sword and helmet glinting in the dim light. The darkness
on the man's hand and arm turned to red as he came
closer.

They clashed with an impact that shocked the lord, but
his larger horse sent the other staggering. The barbarian's
blade had severed Komawara's reins, but he had been
born in Seh and his horse responded to pressure from his
knees as quickly as to its bit. Before the other could collect his horse under him, Komawara struck, aiming at
the man's wrist and then watching the horror on the barbarian's face as he realized this was a feint. The sword
Toshaki had given him cut true to its reputation and severed the man's leg above the knee, the point cutting into
the horse's side. The man's mount jumped sideways and
threw him half off, so that he clung to the mane. It was
an ugly stroke, aimed only to maim, for Komawara would
not risk ruining his edge on the man's helmet. The barbarian fell under the hooves of his own horse and the
lord of Seh passed by toward another, a foot-soldier with
a lance. One of the Hajiwara men took this man before
Komawara had time to raise his sword.

Fighting went on everywhere around him, but the lord
found himself, for the moment, unopposed. He stood up
in his stirrups, surveying the scene. Rafts burned behind
him and on others he could see the supplies going into
the water. It was a rout of some proportion, he realized
with satisfaction. Clouds of smoke billowed up to the
north and he thought he could see black-armored riders
in the melee ahead.

Quickly collecting the riders around him, Komawara
threw himself against the barbarians again. Daylight was
full when he realized that beyond the knot of barbarian
warriors before them Imperial Guards did their work.

Behind his face-mask, Jaku Katta was grinning broadly
when Lord Komawara appeared before him, the stump
of an arrow in his shoulder piece. The two commanders

pulled up their mounts in the midst of chaos. A riderless horse galloped between them and disappeared into the melee. Resistance had been broken.

Komawara waved his sword toward the base of the hill behind which they had hidden that morning. "They will collect their forces there," he shouted over the noise. "The barbarians will soon realize how few we are. Gather every man you can and we'll carry the fight to them once more." He gestured now to the rafts that his men swarmed over. The barbarians had managed to cut loose more rafts than he had hoped and these floated slowly in the current. Others had simply been abandoned at their moorings and not yet dealt with by his men. "We need more time to complete this."

A shout went up then and Komawara realized it came from the barbarians gathering under the ginkyos.

"There, Sire." One of Komawara's guard pointed to the south. A host of mounted barbarians were rounding the base of the hill, banners waving.

Komawara looked back at the work progressing on the rafts.

"It is a patrol only," Jaku said quickly, "no more than a hundred men." He pointed his sword toward the barbarians at the hill's base. "They hope it is reinforcements."

"Sound the call," Komawara shouted to his guard. He looked back at Jaku. "What have your losses been?"

Jaku waited as three long notes from a conch echoed across the field. "I cannot say, Lord Komawara."

The lord looked around the field, strewn with both barbarians and men of Wa. "Nor can I, General."

Men began to ride to Komawara's banner, and the lord wheeled his horse to face them. "Corporal, your company will join General Jaku in an assault on the forces gathering there." He pointed toward the men at the base of the hill.

"General Jaku . . ." A shout from the barbarian horse patrol, echoed by the men who were forming ranks, cut off the lord's words. The sound of galloping horses came to them. Komawara shouted as he turned his horse. "General Jaku, engage the barbarians who are reforming their ranks. My company will prevent these horsemen from joining them."

Komawara spurred his horse and waved his men to a gallop, aiming to intercept the horsemen before they reached the others. Banners waved and pipes shrilled. The shout from the men of Wa caused a visible hesitation on the part of the barbarians struggling to prepare an assault of their own. Most were without horse and armor, though they outnumbered the riders of Wa almost three times.

Jaku Katta quickly marshaled his own men and the company given him by Komawara and sounded the charge. It was his intention to drive directly through the center of the enemy, thwarting any attempts to fight in an organized fashion. If the barbarian formed solid ranks, the advantage of being on horseback would be seriously reduced.

The initial charge broke the front of the barbarian warriors, but in the ensuing fighting the tribesmen showed greater resolve and their superior numbers began to tell.

A sword blow to a foreleg brought Jaku's horse down and the kick boxer jumped clear. On his feet immediately, Jaku found himself surrounded by barbarians. He jumped over a stroke aimed at his leg by the same man who had taken down his horse and dispatched the man as he spun toward the attackers at his back. This display of skill caused a second of hesitation and Jaku used this to cut down two near-boys and jump clear of the circle.

Without men on all sides the fight would be different though Jaku was not sure how long he could maintain this situation. He parried a blow and kicked the man under the chin, engaging another as he did so, but each time a barbarian fell another took his place. An Imperial Guard on horseback was desperately cutting his way toward his commander, but just when Jaku was convinced he would win through, an arrow took the guard through the face mask. He slumped over the neck of his mount which bolted into the fray.

It is an honorable end, Jaku told himself, deserving of a song. Pressed on all sides again, Jaku knew he was fighting to stay alive from minute to minute. A rider in darkest blue drove his horse into the barbarian warriors at Jaku's back sending them sprawling, and before the barbarian could recover the Guard Commander vaulted onto the rider's horse. The two men fought their way

toward a group of Imperial Guards on horseback, hard
pressed on all sides.

Komawara spotted an officer and gestured to him as he
continued to fight. A moment later the clear note of a
conch lifted over the battle. It was the men of Wa who
would retreat now.

Joining the Imperial Guards, Jaku grabbed the reins of
a riderless horse and managed to calm it enough that he
could mount, barely touching the ground as he moved
from one horse to the other. The men of Wa began to
fight their way free of the battle, one knot of riders joining another, then another until they gathered enough force
to push toward clear ground.

Once free of the fighting, Komawara turned his mount
to assess the situation. Most of the barbarians still fought
on foot. In their midst a few riders swung their last
sword strokes. An urge to attempt a rescue was swallowed down quickly—Komawara had an entire company
to consider.

The men of Wa who destroyed the supply rafts had
been caught by the barbarian assault and boarded rafts,
pushing out into the canal where they tried to protect
themselves from arrows while poling the rafts toward the
dam. There is nothing to be done for them, Komawara
realized. Their situation is probably better than ours.

Jaku stopped beside him. Komawara opened his face-
mask and let it hang, conserving the energy it took to
hold it. "We ride north and west, General. If we can
make the hills, we may be able to rejoin the main army.
Our work is done here." He pointed with his sword.
Perhaps a third of the barbarian supply rafts had been
fired or their cargo turned into the canal.

Jaku looked at Komawara, his gray eyes striking behind the black lacquered face-mask. It appeared he was
about to speak, but Komawara nodded to him. "Gather
your company, General. We must be far ahead when these
barbarians recapture their horses."

Calling over an officer, Komawara turned and spoke to
him. The conch sounded again and the banner of the
Komawara House was raised aloft on a lance where it
fluttered in the breeze.

"We must ride, General. Any wounded who cannot

keep the pace are to be left behind without horse.'' The young lord wheeled his mount and set off at a slow canter. To the west the ginkyo wood was already alive with crows and blackbirds.

Thirty-nine

Colonel Jaku Tadamoto considered the idea of *fortune* as his sampan swept through the Imperial Capital. Fortune, both *good* and *ill*, seemed to be holding sway in his life just when he thought he had taken control of it. Were he a more devout Botahist, Tadamoto would never view his life in such terms. Rather than *fortune* he would believe in *karma*, and would think the sense that one was in control of one's life was merely part of the illusion. But he had not been a devout follower of the Perfect Master since his childhood, so he was beginning to believe in fortune, both good and ill.

The young guard officer pulled aside the curtain and contemplated the world beyond. The city lay silent in the darkness, almost peaceful—although, as acting Commander of the Imperial Guard, he knew that was without question an illusion.

He let the curtain fall back into place. It would be foolish to risk being seen; for all he knew Lady Fortune might not be smiling on him at that moment and some informer of the Emperor's, returning home after an evening of drink, might chance to see him. That would be ill fortune indeed.

One could never be sure of the favor of Lady Fortune. She was more fickle than any woman, more volatile than the Emperor. Tadamoto believed it unwise to rely on her.

Fortune had certainly favored Tadamoto that evening but, at the same time, it had been the worst possible fortune for the man he journeyed to meet. No, perhaps that was untrue. The guards who found the man could have reported their discovery through official channels and the Son of Heaven would have been informed. That would have been much worse.

As a retainer of Lord Shonto, this man was the object

of an Imperial search—Shonto himself had defied Imperial orders and betrayed his duty as Governor of Seh. He was a declared rebel now, a general in charge of a growing and illegal army. All of the rebel lord's senior retainers had disappeared like phantoms before the Emperor's guard could reach them. Only one had been apprehended, and that was due to fortune only: misfortune. This unfortunate man had his river junk go aground on a shifting sand bar outside the Capital. A boat bearing Imperial Guards had stopped to offer assistance and the response of the crew had raised suspicions. A subsequent search led to the man's discovery. Good fortune for Tadamoto, ill for Shonto's retainer.

Some important questions plagued the colonel; *did what appeared to be fortune have significance? Were there powers beyond that moved the pieces on the board to some end Tadamoto could not discern? If so, what was the meaning of this 'discovery?' and what was Tadamoto's part to play?*

He pulled the curtain back and watched the city slipping past. If all was controlled by some unseen power, did it matter what choices he made? Did he, in fact, choose any of his actions?

"I waste my time," he whispered to the night. Who can know the truth of this? Perhaps there is no such thing as fortune but only coincidence. Either way I must blunder along not knowing, doing what my instincts tell me is correct, for now that the Empire is thrown into chaos the intellect is giving way to instinct.

Instinct had brought him here. Fortune or coincidence would dictate the results.

The sampan glided to a silent halt beside stone steps and boatmen stepped ashore to hold the craft in place. A man appeared at the top of the stair and whispered. One of Tadamoto's guards leaned close to the curtain. "The way is clear, Colonel."

Tadamoto moved quickly, coming ashore with a grace that would have seemed more appropriate to his famous brother. Light duty armor had been chosen by the colonel for this meeting, not because there was any foreseeable danger, but the helmet visor shaded his eyes well. Tadamoto's green eyes made him immediately recognizable and there were times when that was not desirable. Even on a night this dark he was not willing to take chances.

He crossed the stone quay to a small guard house. The doors opened immediately and Tadamoto found himself facing a bowing officer of the Imperial Guard.

"Captain." Tadamoto nodded. "You have spoken with him?"

"Only in an attempt to establish his identity beyond doubt, Colonel." He paused, then almost smiled. "He asked for a chair. We have treated him according to your orders."

"How many men know of our guest?"

Doing a quick mental tally, the captain, a man twenty years older than his acting commander, answered formally. "Nine, Colonel Jaku. We have kept him well hidden."

"None of these men can leave this compound. Keep them to themselves until I order otherwise. I will speak with him."

They climbed a set of stone stairs and walked down a dimly lit hallway. Outside a heavy wooden door stood two guards. They bowed when the officers approached and at a signal from the captain one unbolted the door.

As he stepped into the room, Tadamoto held up a hand to the captain. "I will speak with him alone, Captain, thank you."

A single lamp set on a low table illuminated the tiny room. The floor was covered with grass mats and in one corner bedding had been neatly folded. An expensive hat sitting on the table cast a shadow like a boat under sail. On a wooden arm chair sat a large man, well dressed, calmly regarding his visitor and making no effort to rise.

Tadamoto nodded. "Tanaka."

The man shrugged and opened his hands as if to say, *I would deny it, but what good would that do me?*

Tadamoto continued to regard the man. He realized that if he sat he would be staring up at his prisoner, as though he sat at the foot of a throne. Sly old fox, he thought. Stepping back, he leaned against the door frame. The older man did not seem to be made at all uncomfortable by this examination; he sat calmly returning the colonel's gaze. The younger man reached up and removed his helmet, tucking it under his arm.

"You are a merchant," Tadamoto said suddenly, "so I have come to offer an exchange."

The man nodded. "You have captured my attention, Colonel Jaku."

The green eyes, Tadamoto thought. The guardsman nodded. "I wish to be told everything you know about the barbarians; this Khan and his army."

"You spoke of an exchange, Colonel?" Tanaka said dryly.

"The Emperor does not know you have been found. I will not hide you from the Son of Heaven, for it would mean my life if your capture became known. When I report your capture, the Son of Heaven will want to know everything about your lord's intentions and his holdings. You will be required to divulge these things. In return I will protect you—the Emperor, as you know, is neither patient nor refined in his methods. If you fall into the Emperor's hands, I think you will answer all these questions even if you don't wish to, and the process will be far less pleasant than the one I propose."

Tanaka nodded sadly. "You ask me to betray my liege-lord and his House with an impressive casualness, Colonel."

Tadamoto walked across the bare room, looking down at the floor. When he returned to the door, he put his back against the jamb again. "Let us be open, Tanaka." He paused, choosing his words. "Civil war has all but been declared. If the Yamaku win this war, your lord's holdings will mean nothing—there will be no Shonto to inherit them. If Lord Shonto wins, all of his holdings will be returned to him. Either way your betrayal will hardly matter. If I can give this information to my Emperor, he will be satisfied, at least for a while, and it is unlikely he will want to question you himself." Tadamoto kicked at the floor. "For myself, I need to know what transpires in the north. This Khan, does he truly pursue Lord Shonto down the great canal?"

Tanaka regarded the young man for a moment. "And if you are told that he does and that the Empire is threatened and you also learn, if you don't already know, that the Emperor has played a part in bringing this about, what will you do with this knowledge, Colonel Tadamoto?"

Tadamoto stopped kicking at the mat and looked up. The merchant was obviously less afraid than Tadamoto had anticipated. He is used to trading and knowing the value of what he offers, the guardsman thought. And then Tadamoto realized the truth. Tanaka believed Tadamoto kept him hidden so that he could acquire the Shonto wealth for himself. "I am not certain. Be assured, however, that my loyalty is to my Emperor."

"That is why you have me hidden from his view and why you have offered me this exchange?"

Tadamoto looked away for a moment. "If this Khan comes to take the throne, I must convince the Emperor to prepare for that war and forget this feud with the Shonto. But I must have proof."

"You have your own sources, I am sure. What do they tell you?"

"I ask this question of you, merchant, in fair exchange." And then he added, "I tell you in truth that I do not share my Emperor's hatred of your lord's House."

"Perhaps, Colonel, I should be the one offering the exchange." Tanaka leaned forward in his chair, putting his palms together. "My liege-lord cannot hope to defeat the barbarian without an army. You raise an army to defend the Yamaku against the Shonto, but the threat comes from beyond our borders. The man who controls the Imperial Army will decide if Wa stands or falls." Tanaka looked up at the younger man; it was an appeal. "As you are the man raising this force and the acting commander of the Emperor's Guard, you are the man most able to seize control of the forming army. Would you not rather have the histories say that Jaku Tadamoto saved the Empire than Jaku Tadamoto followed his Emperor, loyally, in Wa's destruction."

"Treason, in either act or word," Tadamoto said coolly, "is a serious crime in our Empire and I view it as such. You are aware of the penalty."

"Treason . . ." Tanaka said, ignoring the threat. "It was treason to pay gold to the barbarians to raid into our Empire, Colonel Jaku."

Tadamoto turned slowly, trying not to show any response to this last remark. Raising his hand to knock on the door, he said, "All of the Shonto holdings. I will have paper and brush brought to you. And I must know Shonto's intentions.''

''I am only a vassal-merchant, Colonel, do you really believe I am party to the plans of Lord Shonto Motoru?''

''You have known him longer than anyone. He calls you sum—I know this.''

Tanaka seemed to struggle for a moment before speaking. ''You have a reputation as a historian, Colonel, so you are aware that the throne of Wa has been within reach of the Shonto many times . . . yet they have always refused it. Imperial dynasties come and go, the Shonto have seen many. If one wishes, without doubt, to eliminate one's House, ascend the Dragon Throne. Every Imperial Family falls within a few generations.''

Tadamoto raised his hand to knock again. ''All of his holdings, to start with.''

''I will need a table and another lamp.''

Tadamoto nodded toward the table at Tanaka's feet.

Holding his hand up the older man said, ''This high, and a second lamp.''

Tadamoto rapped on the door which was immediately opened by the guard. The colonel stopped as he was about to step out. ''If you will not assist me, merchant, I cannot help you.''

Forty

Despite the season and weather, the entire situation seemed very familiar. Lord Komawara walked his horse through the forest in the hills west of the man-made sea. Unlike his time in the Jai Lung Hills, the day was warm and filled with the sounds and scents of spring.

War seemed of no concern to the animals of the hills. Birds sang their mating songs and hawks and falcons hunted without regard for the long line of warriors that snaked through the trees.

Thirteen hundred men had survived the attack on the barbarian supply rafts and the several skirmishes that followed. Rohku Saicha must have performed his task admirably, bottling up the enemy army on the road, for no barbarians came to the rescue, allowing Komawara and his force to escape. Pursuit by barbarian warriors from the supply rafts had been tentative at best; they were not willing to risk the rest of their supply train by leaving it undefended. Jaku and Komawara had easily beaten back these attempts and then had led their men into the hills.

Lord Shonto's archers had controlled the hills since the barbarian army had started down the road, and though many of the bowman were gone now the barbarians were still quite reluctant to venture far from their road.

From out of the foliage ahead one of Komawara's several guides appeared, trotting at the pace they never seemed to vary. The lord was sure these men could run like that all day without signs of strain. The man stopped, leaning on his bow, waiting for Komawara to approach. A huntsman by trade, he was typical of his type, tall, lean, and sinewy. There was an air of the forest creature about

this man. Even now the lord realized that the guide had
stopped where anyone but Komawara would find him hard
to see among trees and bushes.

Bowing quickly the man almost whispered, "There
is a glade with a stream and new spring grass less than
a rih distant. It will be a good place to refresh the
horses." Looking around with the air of a wary animal
he went on. "There are signs of barbarian patrols coming into the forest ahead. They are small in number,
however. If we see them, we will make them believe
Lord Shonto's bowmen are still here in force." A smile
flashed and was gone. "Tomorrow we will be through
the hills, but the danger will be greater then, for a time.
The barbarians control the lands immediately beyond
the hills, now. We will need to have rested horses to
travel quickly. If Botahara smiles upon us, we will be
back with Lord Shonto's fleet in three days." The smile
flashed again.

"What of Captain Rohku?" Komawara asked. "Is
there no sign of him?"

The man looked down as he shook his head. "None
yet, Sire, though there is no reason we should cross the
captain's track. The hills," he waved at the trees, "spread
over many rih and it is no doubt Captain Rohku's intention to avoid detection."

Komawara nodded. "Lead us to the glade, then. Our
horses are in need."

They pressed on. Komawara called a retainer forward
and sent him to check on the wounded—so many had
been victims of their injuries since the retreat. A second
man he sent down the column to inform Jaku Katta of
their pending rest. The Guard Commander stayed close
to his men and showed great concern for the injured. It
gained him much respect and loyalty.

Despite the losses Komawara did not think they had
spent lives unwisely in their raid on the supply rafts. It
had been impossible to destroy the entire train with such
a small force, for there had been many more rafts than
Komawara had believed possible. Still, they had acquitted themselves well. Even Jaku Katta had paid him a
compliment when the attack was over, not something Komawara had expected.

After Komawara's force had reached the relative security of the hills, he had listened with some surprise to
the reports of the men who had destroyed rafts. Much
that the rafts carried was not grown in the desert: grains,
rice, corrapepper, dried fish. Many of these foods could
have originated only on the islands of the southern barbarians, which unsettled Komawara. Despite the common pejorative, these two races had nothing in common.
Komawara would have guessed them barely aware of each
other's existence—two non-seafaring peoples separated by
a wide ocean. Impressive what gold and the ships of pirates could obtain—if, indeed, it had been pirates. He
remembered Lord Kintari.

The sound of running water mixed with the sound of
the Plum Blossom Wind, wafting through the trees. The
forest was more than half pine here, mixed with plane
trees and slip maple. The scent of the trees was strong.
Unfolding leaves waved in the soft breeze, dappling the
sunlight where it touched the forest floor. The paper white
of birch trees appeared and beyond them Komawara could
see the sun green of spring grass. It was a bigger pasture
than Komawara expected and spoke of itinerant herds-
men; there was likely a hut concealed nearby.

The huntsman stopped at the edge of the glade until
he received a signal that the lord never heard. "It is secure here, Lord Komawara. There is grass like this on
either side of the brook, both up and down stream. It
will mean spreading your company out but there is pasture enough for each horse."

"The woods are free of barbarians, you are certain?"
The huntsman nodded.

"Then we will do as you suggest. The animals need
to graze or they will never manage this last sprint you
speak of." He turned and gave the command.

One of the Hajiwara men who had taken service with
Komawara took his lord's horse and led it off to drink
and feed. Komawara walked across soft grass to the
stream and bent stiffly to drink and fill his water skin
before the creek was muddied by horses. He jumped
heavily to the other bank, feeling the weight of his armor
as he landed.

Finding a fallen tree on the far side of the glade, Ko-

mawara sat and pulled his helmet off. He ran a hand
through his hair, much of which had grown back since
Shuyun's ministrations in the desert. Sweat and the weight
of his helmet plastered it tightly to his brow and the lord
suddenly longed for a bath.

The coolness of the air and the warmth of the sun were
like the differing flavors of a complex wine, opposing but
complementary. Slipping down to the ground, Komawara
leaned back against the log, closing his eyes against the
brightness of the sky.

He was not sure how long he rested like that, nor if
he even slept for a second, but suddenly he was aware
that the sun no longer warmed him. A cloud, Komawara
thought, but then the sound of a man clearing his throat
reached him. His eyes flicked open almost involuntarily.

"General Jaku."

The guardsman bowed. "Excuse me for interrupting
you, Lord Komawara."

"Do not apologize, General." Komawara struggled
into a more upright position. "I managed to fill my wa-
terskin before the hordes, General Jaku, please." He
proffered the water to the guard.

Jaku nodded and accepted the water. Returning the skin
to Komawara, the guardsman sat down on the log and
followed the lord's example, pulling off his helmet.
"Three days, I have been informed? Do you think Lord
Shonto will have moved his fleet again?"

The lord pulled a burr off the lacing of his armor and
rolled the spines gently between his forefinger and thumb.
"It seems most likely, General. The barbarians move
slowly, but Lord Shonto will not risk his army. It may
be the Empire's only hope."

"It is sadly true," Jaku observed dryly. "Though the
Emperor raises an army, it is impossible to predict what
he will do with it—and I know the Emperor." Jaku produced a square of cotton and wiped his face and neck
with it.

The same huntsman Komawara had spoken to earlier
appeared out of the trees twenty paces off, looked around
and then spotted the lord. Trotting over, he dropped to
his knees and bowed so as not to stand above the seated
peer. When he spoke, the man's voice quavered slightly.

"Sire, we have discovered . . . something of great concern." He gestured to the forest behind him, words failing him. "Close by."

Komawara glanced at Jaku, questions unspoken. Signaling to his guard, the lord waved the huntsman on and he and Jaku fell in behind. Walking through the spring woods filled with the sounds of birds Komawara felt suddenly cold. He did not know what had been found, but the huntsman's reaction was not reassuring.

As the tracker had said, it was not far. The perfume of the spring forest was replaced by a sudden stench and flies buzzed up, agitated by the presence of people. The huntsman stopped, saying nothing. At his feet lay a corpse, belly down, stripped naked, its head severed. Stubs of three broken arrows protruded from the throat and shoulder.

"There are more," the huntsman said, making a sign to Botahara.

"Who?" Komawara whispered.

Shrugging the huntsman stepped away, covering his mouth and nose. "Not barbarians, certainly."

Twenty feet away lay two men who had been felled and mutilated also. The grass and bushes nearby had been well trampled, perhaps by a struggle. A horse without saddle or bridle was found, its head twisted at an improbable angle.

Several of the huntsman's company could be seen searching the bush, stopping now and then as they discovered another corpse.

"Captain Rohku's company," Jaku said quietly to Komawara, "or some of it."

Komawara nodded. "No doubt you are correct. This man wore armor often." The lord pointed to familiar marks on the man's shoulders. He waved the huntsman over. "Hide men behind us. Be certain we are not pursued."

The huntsman nodded. "What shall we do for these?" He waved at the ground around him.

Komawara turned in a slow circle, examining the area. "Leave them to the forest."

"Sire," the man started to protest but was silenced by a cold stare.

"There will be many more like these before this war is over, and we will not be able to perform ceremonies for one in a thousand." He looked down. "May Botahara have mercy on their souls."

Forty-one

Though he waited to speak with the Emperor of all of Wa, Jaku Tadamoto had not yet decided what he would say to the Son of Heaven. Perhaps the glimpse he had caught of a woman leaving the wing of the Emperor's apartments had unsettled Tadamoto more than he realized, though he was not at all sure it had been Osha. The woman had appeared briefly down a long hall, her hair in an elaborate style, ornate robes of canary yellow—a color Osha despised and the Emperor loved. But she had moved with such ease. . . .

Tadamoto felt like he was drowning in deep sadness, unable to focus his will sufficiently to stroke to the surface. Things of the greatest import hardly drew his attention. What would be said and left unsaid in this audience with the Emperor was crucial, he knew, yet that knowledge did not seem to galvanize his energies. Despondency was what Tadamoto felt, and his famed intellect did not seem able to exert control over his other faculties.

Through the screens Tadamoto could hear the Emperor's voice as he spoke to some official. From where Tadamoto waited, he heard brief silences in which, presumably, the official spoke and this made Tadamoto wonder if he was equally quiet when addressing the Emperor. It was a strange thing to listen to, as though half of the dialogue was silence.

Tadamoto turned a scroll he carried, examining it carefully as though he would suddenly be able to assess its impact in the meeting to come. Would the Son of Heaven respond as the young officer hoped? If the Emperor's greed was caught by the information in the scroll, he might forget to ask when the Imperial Guard had found Lord Shonto's vassal-merchant—if the answer was not already known. Why have I played this foolish game with this merchant? Tadamoto asked himself.

The Emperor's voice had not responded to the silence now for several minutes, and Tadamoto made a last attempt to focus his will. A secretary appeared and bowed to the guard officer, saying nothing. Rising, Tadamoto followed the old man through a bare anteroom. Double screens opened onto a terrace tiled with small stones and shards of porcelain forming a lotus blossom pattern. Beyond was the view north across the Dragon Pond toward the Mountain of the Pure Spirit.

Kneeling before the screens, Tadamoto waited to be announced. It was done so quietly that the officer did not hear. The Emperor's mood must be dark.

At a signal, Tadamoto moved forward on his knees across grass mats that had been laid over the stones. On a small dais at one end of the terrace the Emperor sat under a silk awning. To his left the view stretched out toward the far mountains and to his right stood a small ornamental cherry, ancient despite its size and famous for the perfection of its shape. The Emperor tapped the tip of his sword on the edge of the dais, staring at neither view nor blossom—he scowled openly and his eyes were not focused on anything another could see.

Tadamoto touched his forehead to the mat.

"Be at your ease, Colonel," the Emperor said, irritation lodged in his tone like a thorn.

Tadamoto returned to a kneeling position feeling anything but at ease.

"I am told the raising of our army proceeds apace, Colonel." The Emperor gave a slight nod.

Tadamoto bowed in return. "The reports of Lord Shonto's force would indicate he has fewer than twenty-five thousand men, Sire. Our force will equal that very soon."

The Emperor nodded. He still tapped the dais with his sword. "Once Motoru reaches the inner provinces it is impossible to say who will join him. We must be prepared to face all manner of treachery, Colonel, or we will not even have the luxury of time to regret our mistakes."

"Recruitment continues, Emperor. I'm confident we will raise an army of adequate numbers."

"And no experience!" the Emperor shot back.

Tadamoto froze for a second. "We are training now, Sire," he said quietly.

"At least our army will be no less battle ready than Shonto's."

Tadamoto pressed his eyes closed for an instant, then glanced out over the Dragon Pond and back to the mats in front of him.

The Emperor fixed the young scholar with a hard stare. "You have a scroll for me, I see."

Tadamoto nodded.

"Not more news of pending disaster, I trust?"

Tadamoto lifted the scroll with both hands. "A complete, detailed list of all of the Shonto House holdings and properties."

The Emperor stopped tapping the dais.

"We have taken the Shonto vassal-merchant into our custody," Tadamoto said evenly.

"Tanaka?" the Emperor said with more than a trace of disbelief.

Tadamoto gave a half bow, keeping his eyes cast down. Leaning forward he set the scroll on the edge of the dais though the Emperor almost snatched it from his hands.

Breaking the seal with a thumbnail, the Emperor unrolled the paper and held it up to the light so that it hid his reaction. When he appeared again, his face was creased with delight. "This rebel general was once a very wealthy lord." He waved a finger at the scroll. "Astonishing that his merchant could hide so much wealth!" He let the itemization fall back into his lap. "You are to be complimented, Tadamoto-sum. I will see that you are given," he paused to think, "a fortieth of the Shonto wealth as a reward. But what else has this merchant said? What of Shonto's plans?"

Tadamoto nodded, as though acknowledging the question though he was trying desperately to gather his thoughts. "I—I am honored by your generosity, Emperor." He bowed low. "It is difficult to be sure what Tanaka knows about his lord's intentions, Sire. I have spoken with him now on several occasions and I am not convinced Shonto has been as open with Tanaka as we had believed."

The Emperor set the scroll aside and reached for his

sword. "Perhaps a less gentle method of inquiry would produce the results we require, Colonel."

"I . . . I hesitate to do so, Sire. I would rather gain his confidence and convince him with arguments." An idea. "After the war is over, Tanaka will have no liege-lord. He would make a valuable addition to your staff, Sire." Tadamoto gestured toward the scroll. "Imagine what such a man could do to increase the Imperial fortunes."

The Emperor raised an eyebrow at this. "Is this possible? A Shonto retainer?"

"This list is an example, Sire—which, by the way, was done entirely from memory. Tanaka agreed to create this itemization after I had convinced him that such an act would not affect Lord Shonto, no matter what the outcome of the civil war. He is not a warrior, Sire. One can appeal to his intellect and see some result. It is also well known that he enjoys the trappings of wealth himself. Many a lord would be happy to live in this vassal-merchant's home. When there is no Shonto House," Tadamoto shrugged, "where will Tanaka's loyalty lie?"

The Emperor looked out toward the Mountain of Divine Inspiration, lost in thought. "If you can win his willing service, Tadamoto-sum, I will double your reward, and more. But we cannot let him hide behind this." The Emperor gestured to the scroll. "We desperately need to know what Motoru plans. Be certain this merchant is hiding nothing."

Tadamoto bowed. Wealth . . . Tadamoto thought, enormous wealth . . . on the eve of civil war. The irony threatened to make him laugh. "I will spare no effort, Sire, be assured."

The Emperor favored him with a controlled smile. "Is there more that I should hear, Tadamoto-sum, or will we stop now, while the gods smile upon us?"

Tadamoto hesitated for a second and saw the Emperor's face darken as he did so. "I have had reports from the north, Sire. Lord Shonto dammed the canal and flooded a large plain north of Fuimo. A barbarian force was certainly following close behind the men of Seh at that time."

The Emperor stared hard at Tadamoto for a moment and then rose suddenly, causing the younger man to flinch

visibly. Crossing the terrace, the Emperor descended a
set of stairs. When all but his head had descended out of
sight, the Emperor turned and nodded toward Tadamoto
to rise and follow.

Waiting on another terrace, a level below, the Emperor
stared off to the north and when Tadamoto caught him
he set off again, Tadamoto in his wake. They descended
another flight of stairs which put them on the lawn that
ran down to the edge of the Dragon Pond. The Emperor
walked toward the eastern wall of the Palace where a
complex hedge-maze stood, planted generations past and
renewed and altered over the centuries.

The Emperor stopped before the entrance to the maze,
waving Tadamoto ahead with his sword. "Colonel."

Tadamoto stepped into the maze, not sure what was
required of him, his mouth drying quickly. He walked
down the path, the fall of the Emperor's step close behind. The maze branched both left and right almost immediately and the guardsman continued straight, not
knowing if he should have chosen one of the other paths.

"Have you been through the puzzle before, Colonel?"

Tadamoto shook his head, but before he could speak
the Emperor went on.

"It is a most ingenious maze. Unlike others of the type
it does not give up its secret easily. In fact, few find their
way to the center. To unexpectedly arrive back at the
beginning is the common experience or at one of the
several gates which lead out. Turn right, Colonel."

Tadamoto obeyed, walking slowly and fighting the urge
to look back at the Emperor.

"From whom did you receive this information about
the barbarian army, Colonel?"

"Spies working in the north, Sire."

"Ah. Stop where you are and look carefully around
you."

Tadamoto did as he was told. The stone pathway was
somewhat wider than a man was tall, bounded on both
sides by high, dense foliage. There was a blind-end visible ahead and a branch-left perhaps six paces away.
Turning further, Tadamoto found the Emperor watching
him, all traces of his earlier lightness of spirit gone.
Reaching right with his sword the Emperor thrust the tip
of the scabbard into the hedge.

Looking at the spot the Emperor indicated, the guard realized that there was something out of place there and a more careful inspection revealed a low, impossibly narrow passage, well camouflaged.

"A gardener's secret," the Emperor said quietly. "You will have to push your way in."

Tadamoto parted the branches with care and bent low to enter. It was surprisingly dark in the passageway, the density of the growth admitting little light. Sounds of the Emperor parting the branches behind kept Tadamoto moving despite the tightness of the tunnel. Sunlight appeared ahead and the officer pushed through into another stone pathway running between the hedges.

"Turn left," the Emperor said before he had emerged from the passage.

Tadamoto set out again at the same pace and again the Emperor's footsteps followed. Another gardener's tunnel, and then left, then right and again right. They were at the center of the maze. The hedges formed a circle a dozen paces across and in the center of this lay a round, jade pool, flashes of gold and crimson sunfish like visions of flame in the depths of a mirror.

The Emperor sat on a stone bench carved with Imperial Dragons, his sword across his knees. Tadamoto hastened to kneel, the stones digging into his knees.

The Emperor stared into the green water of the quiet pool. "You see, Colonel Jaku, uncounted people have tried to unravel this puzzle but, in truth, only a few have ever managed to stand where you are now and look into the Jade Mirror. Ministers, princes, court ladies, great lords, famed generals . . . so many have failed. Yet the humble gardeners of the palace all have been here, often. They know how to go directly to the heart of the puzzle." The Emperor pointed the tip of his scabbard at the young officer. "It is the secret of all great men, Tadamoto-sum.

"If there is a barbarian army, I believe it is in league with Shonto or is of little consequence and Shonto draws it along behind him as an excuse to invade the inner provinces. This half-breed Khan cannot threaten the Empire of Wa with a ragtag army of hunters and herdboys. You have had your confidence in this matter shaken by your brother. This impairs your effectiveness as a counselor to the Emperor.

"Cut through to the heart of the matter, Colonel, so you can set it aside. We have war in sight—it gathers on the northern horizon like a winter storm. Your entire focus will be called for." The Emperor stood and walked to the opening in the hedge. "The place where you sit, Colonel is so difficult to reach most believe it impossible. Wander without focus for even a short time and you will find yourself on the outside. May the gods guide you, Colonel Jaku."

Forty-two

Rohku Tadamori was growing used to being referred to as captain though he had now twice been confused with his father and that he would never grow used to. There was a vast difference between a mere captain and the Captain of Lord Shonto's Personal Guard—and only a true provincial would not be aware of the distinction. Still, he was proud of his new rank as he was of his father's status. His dream of the Rohku family achieving fame for their service to the Shonto did not seem as remote as it once had, especially now with war at hand.

The young officer rode along the canal bank through a grove of flowering plum trees. The spring winds were just now starting to coax the petals of the plum blossoms free, carrying them aloft and scattering them across the green countryside. The wakes of the passing river boats disturbed the petals as they landed on the canal and the Plum Blossom Winds turned them into sails, stranding them on the western bank.

Behind Rohku Tadamori rode a small company and the young captain realized that he had achieved a certain level of recognition since he suddenly warranted a guard. He shook his head. Perhaps now that war was upon them, he would have a chance to prove himself in battle as his father had. A few days earlier Rohku Saicha had led an attack on the barbarians in the hills. Despite his recent recognition Tadamori was not senior enough to know any details of his father's duty—that would come with time. Worrying was something that Tadamori had been taught not to indulge in, but his father's company had not returned and those who knew had begun to whisper. He focused his thoughts elsewhere.

Functioning in the capacity that had somehow become his own, Rohku Tadamori had been sent south down the canal as a lookout. The boats had grown so numerous that it was becoming impossible to pass to the front of the fleet by sampan in any reasonable time, so he had chosen to ride. Perhaps the fact that it was a perfect spring day and he preferred horses to boats had entered into the decision also.

Although the Grand Canal ran virtually straight throughout most of its sections, the area it passed through now was strewn with outcroppings of gray stone, making a straight line impossible. So the ancient engineers had routed the waterway among them as though providing travelers with the most aesthetic views had suddenly become their purpose. This allowed Rohku to go across country, cutting off great loops of the canal and saving much time and distance.

Rohku and his guard had not passed half the ships in the great flotilla so far and yet they had been on horseback half a day. A small stream met the canal and Tadamori dismounted to let his horse drink. Others did the same. There was no sense of urgency in this assignment, and though his men did not know what his orders were they had soon realized that he did not rush. Conversation had started among the riders, uncommon among Shonto's guard, who took their duty very seriously. A beautiful day such as this even lightened the spirits of the warriors.

"There is a mess for you," one of the guards said, pointing down the canal.

Around one of the giant rock towers came an ornate river boat, fighting not only the current of the canal but also the current of events. Barges from the south-going flotilla pulled up to the bank to let the river boat pass. Rohku could not distinguish the crests on the banners, but the color was impossible to mistake—Imperial Crimson. Prince Wakaro had arrived, not appearing out of the mists as had Jaku Katta, but in the full light of a fine spring day, forcing his way north against a torrent of refugees swept before the coming war.

Even at this distance Rohku could see the people on the bank and on barges bowing as the Prince's boat passed. Rohku ran up to the top of the bank and watched for a moment, then trotted back down and mounted his horse. There was nothing more he needed to see.

Turning quickly, Rohku spurred up the bank followed
by his guard. At the top he paused to get his bearings in
the strange countryside and then set off across the country at a canter. Lord Shonto would want to know this
immediately.

Although official greetings had been sent and the
Prince had made it known that he wished to have Lord
Shonto attend him immediately, still nothing of significance had occurred. The Prince's flotilla carrying personal staff, his small court, and an honor guard of black
uniformed Imperial Guards sat moored to the east bank
of the canal while Shonto's own vast flotilla passed by on
its way toward the inner provinces.

On the bank opposite the Prince's retinue, a silk pavilion had been erected surrounded by a fence of banners
laced to bamboo frames. The Emperor's banner, the five-
clawed dragon on crimson, wafted from a staff before the
enclosure and beside it Prince Wakaro's own banner of
dragon and crane, also on crimson, though bordered in
gold. Shonto's blue banner waved there, also, as did the
Flying Horse of the Province of Seh. Armored men in
Shonto blue stood guard and there was a ring of several
hundred yards which only specific Shonto retainers were
allowed to enter.

On the bank before the pavilion a dock had been built
so that people of rank might disembark from boats with
some semblance of dignity. A sampan of the most common variety wobbled down the canal to the stroke of its
single oar. Aboard this craft were three guards in armor
with blue lacing and an old man, formally dressed, sitting with one hand in his lap while the other sleeve of
his robe creased and rippled in the breeze.

The sampan made a careful line to the elaborate barge
that bore the Imperial Prince. Steward Kamu was left
waiting on the boarding platform for some minutes, but
eventually an Imperial Guard officer came to the head of
the stairs and bowed.

"The Prince will speak with you now, Steward
Kamu," the officer said.

They still bow, they continue to use my title, they are
not as confident as they pretend, Kamu thought. With
some care he ascended the stairs to the main deck and

then a second stairway to an upper level. There, on the stern, protected by a yellow awning, sat the Imperial Prince, Yamaku Wakaro, listening to a lovely young woman who played the melody of a spring dance on the harp.

Kneeling immediately, Kamu waited, listening. The woman was not the equal of Lady Nishima, in either beauty or in the skill of her playing, but she was certainly more than competent and the composition was well matched to the day.

The Prince did not seem to notice the presence of Lord Shonto's representative but concentrated his attentions on the young musician. Sitting on cushions around the stern of the boat sat several richly dressed men and women of similar age to the Prince. None were immediately recognizable to Kamu, but he was well informed of who fluttered about the flame of the Imperial Prince and though they were not individuals entirely without virtue, there was not one among them who it could be said was marked for great things. Another Imperial dynasty that had achieved mediocrity in three generations.

A second song was called for and plum wine was served. Kamu knelt unmoving on the hard deck controlling his not insignificant temper. Occasionally he glanced up at the Prince. He decided His Imperial Highness favored his mother in appearance, round of feature, yet fair. Large, wide-set eyes with long lashes drew the attention and would, no doubt, be the talk of the young women at court. The Prince kept teasing the corner of a long, spindly mustache. Like his mother, the Prince had a shock of white hair on his left temple, distorting the symmetry of his face.

Finally, after the second song and some idle conversation and laughter, Kamu was summoned forward. Bored with their charade, the old man thought.

Bowing, the steward waited with every indication of infinite patience.

"Steward Kamu," Prince Wakaro said, his voice slightly nasal. "I trust you have come to arrange the surrender of Lord Shonto and to pass the control of this upstart army over to my Guard Captain."

Kamu gave a half bow as though of compliance. "The edicts you bear from the Son of Heaven would certainly not be ignored, Sire. As we are at war, however, Lord Shonto is anxious to give a full report of the military situation before the Prince takes command of the army." Kamu bowed again.

"Tell your lord that the military situation is no longer his concern. I am more interested in his compliance with direct orders from the Emperor."

Kamu nodded to the pavilion on the opposite bank. "Lord Shonto is a general of great skill, Sire. Given your experience in these areas, it might be prudent to speak with him, Prince."

Wakaro raised an eyebrow, a flash of anger was replaced by a smirk. His followers became very quiet. "Your insolence has earned you a particularly small, dark cell for the brief period remaining to you, Steward."

Kamu's deferential manner did not change. "Certainly, Sire, this will be as you wish, but this must wait until after your meeting with my lord."

"There will be no meeting with your lord, you old fool!" the prince exploded, slamming his armrest.

Kamu nodded. He shares his father's temper if little else. "Perhaps, Sire, I might suggest that you look behind you," Kamu said softly.

Wakaro's eyes widened at this and his flash of temper seemed to burn down to coals. Others of his party glanced aft and Kamu heard them curse under their breath. Hearing this the Prince turned. On the deck of the boat behind, formerly awash in the black-laced armor of Imperial Guards, stood men in armor of blue. As the Imperial Prince turned, they bowed and then returned to position as if they were his own guard.

Wakaro turned and regarded Kamu. Before he could respond to what he had seen, the old steward spoke quietly.

"As we are at war, my lord is concerned with the Prince's safety. He has provided you with his own personal guard. I trust the hour of the dog will not be an inconvenient time for this meeting?"

"To threaten the son of the Emperor of Wa is a crime that will not be forgiven," the Prince said, his voice not sure enough to bear the weight of the threat.

Kamu could not help himself. He shrugged. "There is no threat, Sire. Only concern that you are fully aware of

the situation you inherit.'' Without waiting to be dismissed, Kamu bowed low, rose in the Prince's presence,
and walked with great dignity to the stairs and then down
to his waiting boat.

The sampan carrying Prince Wakaro crossed to the
small dock where it was met by Shonto's steward, who
bowed low, greeting the Prince with proper formality.
Accompanying the Emperor's son was the senior officer
of his guard and another young man of similar age to his
royal highness. They ascended the bank to the enclosure
between rows of bowing, blue-armored guards. Under
the awning of the pavilion sat Lord Shonto and his senior
military advisor, General Hojo Masakado.

All bowed accordingly as the Prince approached. A
small dais had been provided for Wakaro and cushions
set for his counselors. Taking his place, the son of the
Emperor sat and glared at Shonto with undisguised anger.

''Do not wait for me to speak,'' the Prince said
quickly. ''Despite this dais and the formal homage, there
is no question of who controls this situation. Enjoy it
while you may,'' he added, the Yamaku temper flaring
briefly.

Shonto favored the Prince with a smile of great
warmth. ''I apologize most humbly, Sire. If we were not
at war, I would never have presumed to use such measures.''

''I am not aware of any declaration of war, and I
receive news from the Island Palace daily. Refusal to
comply with the Imperial Edicts will be considered an
act of treason, *Governor*.'' He spat the word out. ''It
does not show great wisdom to erode your already ten-
uous situation.''

Shonto spoke quietly. ''Refusal to learn what is known
of the enemy you will face when you take control of the
army could not be considered great wisdom either, Sire.''
Shonto smiled again. ''As the Empire is under great
threat, I did not feel such a mistake could be allowed.''

The Prince eyed Shonto. ''What will you have me do?''

Shonto favored the Prince with the look a tolerant parent gives an unreasonable child—amusement and affection mixed with sadness brought about by the knowledge

that children will insist on learning difficult lessons for themselves, though their conclusions will hardly be startling. "The barbarian force is not far behind, not as far as we would like it to be, at least. If you can be ready at sunrise tomorrow, General Hojo will accompany you personally so that you might view this force and make your own assessment and plans." He nodded to Kamu who reached behind him for a scroll. He laid this within reach of the Prince's guard.

"This is an accurate assessment of the barbarian force. General Hojo will certainly be able to answer any questions you might have as he is familiar with every aspect of our efforts and has recently engaged the vanguard of the barbarian army in a significant skirmish."

Silence followed. The Prince finally nodded, moving his head as though he suffered from great exhaustion. "As I have little choice, I will go view this great barbarian army. May I assume my guard captain will be allowed to accompany me?"

"Of course, Sire," Shonto answered. "Take the advisors deemed necessary, by all means. I personally will be interested in the opinions of the Prince and his staff when they return."

Shonto nodded to Kamu who gave unseen signals and wine appeared. "Excuse me for not asking, Prince," Shonto said, lifting his cup. "The Emperor is well?"

Forty-three

*Upon first awakening, for the briefest of moments,
one believes in the dream.*

Brother Hutto
Seventieth Primate of Wa

Prince Wakaro wore the black-laced armor of an Imperial Guard officer, though under a surcoat bearing
twin silver dragons and a trim of crimson. A dark bay
stallion was the Prince's favored horse, and though it was
a powerful animal General Hojo suspected that it had
been chosen to complement the Prince's attire.

And the silver-trimmed black saddle and bridle . . . !
These earned many a glance from the other riders who
favored tack that showed signs of use. Such a saddle and
bridle would be a prize to attract a barbarian's attention!

Hojo turned back to the scene that stretched out before
them. It had taken some time to find an appropriate place
from which to view the passing barbarian army. Lord
Shonto had insisted that the Prince should never be at
risk—not an easy requirement to fullfil in such times—
but this hill was as secure as could be found. Unfortunately, what it gained in security it lost in proximity.

Far off to the west the Grand Canal wound across the
landscape, shining like a bronze ribbon in the late afternoon light. Rafts were being pulled along this ribbon of
molten metal, their dark shapes distorted by their own
shadows. Along either bank moved the army of the desert, like an enormous herd of unknown animals wandering in search of new feeding grounds.

Prince Wakaro said nothing though he repeatedly
glanced over at the captain of his guard as if he tried to

read the officer's response. It was a small, but telling, gesture.

"It is possible to go some short distance closer, Prince, if this would help in the estimation of the army's size," Hojo offered calmly. He was not seeing the barbarian army for the first time. He had fought them, in fact. To the general they were only men, not some ominous, unknown entity. They fought and made mistakes, felt fear, and even bled, just like any other men he had known.

The Prince looked over to his captain who shook his head. "We have seen all we require, General." He looked over at the western horizon. "It will be dark soon enough. Perhaps we should return."

General Hojo nodded, signaled his guard, and turned back the way they had come. *That will take some of the arrogance out of the whelp,* the old fighter thought—and *to think this boy's father began all of this; paid gold to this Khan to help bring down the Shonto House. Has this young Prince wondered why he was sent to Seh? Let him ponder that,* Hojo told himself. *If nothing else can shake his imperial confidence, that should.*

It was a curious aspect of the natural world and Lord Shonto had often wondered about it. The willow trees that lined the canal bank had branches that hung down close to the water, like green robes swaying in the breeze. Yet, from even a short distance, it appeared that all of these branches stopped the same distance short of the water, as though a gardener had trimmed them with great care. *Surely it is only an illusion,* the lord thought, *but it appears to be so. Tree after tree all with their long, flowing wands grown to the same length.*

The canal bank slipped past, the spring winds still hurrying the river boats south. A haze of petals floated on the waters among the reflections of passing clouds, and other petals took to the wind like a flight of butterflies. Spring in Wa was disappointing no one, at least as far as weather was concerned. Shonto sat on the upper deck of his barge, watching the scene pass.

Unlike his Spiritual Advisor the lord did not wait well, but one did not hurry an Imperial Prince nor demand that they arrive at an appointed hour—by definition, the appointed hour was the precise time the Imperial party made its appearance.

It was surprising enough that Wakaro came to Shonto, for a Prince need never wait upon another. There was little doubt that this act was a message—the sight of the barbarian army was a convincing argument—but what the Prince would be willing to do in the coming war remained a question.

"Sire," Kamu appeared at the stairway, "the Prince comes."

Shonto nodded. It had been decided that the lord would meet the Prince as an equal, not kneeling at the stairhead as the Prince came aboard—and this, too, was a message. The Yamaku prepared for war against the Shonto, had tried to do away with the Shonto House altogether; there were certain truths that each House would have to live with now. One was that the Shonto would no longer recognize the Yamaku claim to the Dragon Throne. This did not mean that Shonto would treat the son of his enemy with disrespect, but he would not credit him the full regard reserved for the son of a legitimate sovereign.

An elegant white boat shot past, controlled by skilled oarsmen. It turned easily and brought up beside the platform at the bottom of the boarding stairs. They were not within Shonto's sight, but he could hear voices and footsteps on the stairs.

Two attendants and two Imperial Guards preceded the Prince onto the upper deck and knelt to either side while their master ascended the stairs. Everyone on the deck, with the exception of Lord Shonto, bowed low.

The Prince wore a robe the color of the summer sky embroidered with a pattern of plum trees in blossom. In his sash he carried a sword in a black leather scabbard adorned with the dragon and crane. Crossing the open deck, Wakaro nodded to Shonto and took the cushion to the lord's left. Shonto returned the nod and gestured for a cushion to be set for the Prince's Guard Captain. Kamu and General Hojo approached and took places on their lord's right.

"Have you traveled the canal before, Prince Wakaro?" Shonto asked, not waiting for the Prince to open the conversation.

"Not so far north, Lord Shonto," he waved a hand

toward the shore. "It passes through some of the most
beautiful scenes in the Empire, I am certain."

Shonto nodded, looking out over the landscape. "I
agree. Years ago I traveled south from Seh. It has changed
little." Shonto looked down in slight discomfort.
"Though we will not say that after the barbarians have
passed." The lord looked up at the young man before
him, his question unspoken: *Now that you have seen the
truth of the world, young Sire, what have you to say?*

Wakaro could not meet the lord's gaze for more than
a second. "I now realize, Lord Shonto, why you so . . .
strongly advised that I increase my understanding of the
military situation. Let us say no more about it." The
Prince rubbed his palms together in a slow circular motion. "I have read your report, as has my Guard Captain.
Though I have not received thorough training in the arts
of war, I realize that this Khan and his followers are a
great threat to the Empire and to our Emperor. My Guard
Captain concurs with your staff's estimate of the army's
size. There is no doubt that the resources of the entire
Empire must be utilized to combat this threat." He
looked up now, regarding Shonto with the look of one
who has resolved to tell another the hard truth.

"I am not certain that the Emperor can be convinced
of this threat, Lord Shonto." He looked out over the
canal, brushing back a wisp of white hair. "The Emperor
believes that you proceed south with the intention of
overthrowing the Yamaku House." The Prince shrugged.
"I cannot say what your intentions are, Lord Shonto, but
certainly the choice you have made to retreat south with
so small a force and allow the Empire time to raise an
army of defense was the wise choice. Though I am certain it was a difficult decision."

The Prince shifted on his cushion. "It is my shame to
admit that my assessment of what happens here will hold
little sway over the actions of the Emperor." He paused
for a second and Shonto wondered if this was pain the
young man felt, but the Prince's face showed little sign
of emotion. "It is likely," Wakaro said at last, "that any
report I send will be disregarded. Many an Imperial
Prince has plotted to overthrow his father. The Emperor
will believe that I have joined you, Lord Shonto, unaware
that I am loyal to him, despite all." The Prince paused

again, looking down at his hands. "I am unsure how to proceed. . . ."

Shonto nodded. "It is a difficult situation, Prince Wakaro. My own staff have discussed it endlessly. Allow me to say that the Shonto interest is the safety of Wa, nothing more. As you can see I have already sacrificed everything to that end. *Rebel General* I am named, yet the subject of every Shonto council is: how can the Empire be preserved?

"The Emperor must raise an army. It is the only answer. I have gathered as many men as we will likely see, yet the total of our forces is not a third of the barbarian army. As we speak, an army is being raised in the Capital, though it is not an army for the defense of Wa. What will happen when we reach the inner provinces and the scale of the barbarian invasion is seen?" Shonto regarded his young companion. "I fear it will be too late, Prince Wakaro. We must have a plan—now—a plan and an army large enough to meet this threat from the desert."

The Prince nodded slowly, looking down at the wooden deck. "I can send a message to my father describing what I have seen and urge him to send officers he trusts to assess the situation for themselves. I can also travel south by fast boat and speak to the Emperor, though I may find retirement to a well-guarded estate as my reward. But even so, I would do this. As you have, Lord Shonto, so would I risk all to preserve the Empire."

"I think a message to the Emperor is appropriate," Shonto said quietly. "Even if it does not change the Emperor's mind, it must cast some doubt on the counsel he has received. As you say, it may be unwise to travel to the Capital yourself, especially as you have orders to take control of my army and send me south under guard." Shonto looked over at General Hojo as though remembering an earlier discussion. "General Hojo's report could be sent along with your letter though I think it may be wise to say nothing of the size of our own army. Let the Emperor wonder how many men we have gathered— perhaps he will raise a larger army if he is unsure."

A silence fell for a moment. Along the shore refugees appeared again and after a morning of seeing very few it was a doubly sad sight. The Prince brushed back the strand of white hair again, without thinking. "Then, for now, I will accompany your flotilla and offer what assistance I can. If you will allow it, I will fly my banner beside your own, Lord Shonto. When we reach the inner provinces, perhaps I will be the bridge between the Shonto and the Emperor."

Shonto bowed to the young Prince who rose suddenly. "Please excuse me, I will write to the Emperor immediately. Will you see that this letter goes to the Palace?"

"Certainly, Prince Wakaro. I thank you for your counsel. Perhaps there is hope yet, if the Yamaku and the Shonto can join to defend Wa. . . ."

The Prince gave a half bow and, followed by his retinue, descended the stairs to the lower deck.

As the white boat passed, the Prince nodded toward Shonto and then the oarsmen dug in and sent their craft shooting ahead leaving a whirl of white petals spinning in their wake.

Kamu bowed to his lord, his face drawn and serious. "I have received word from Brother Shuyun, Sire. He has spoken to the Brothers at the nearby monastery and there is no doubt—plague has broken out among the refugees. The numbers are small and it is hoped the Brothers isolated them quickly enough to stop the disease from spreading. I have given permission to use one barge to transport the victims. The Botahist monks will man it and tend the sick." Kamu made a sign to Botahara—uncharacteristic for him. "May Botahara protect us all. We need do nothing more for now, but if the disease spreads among the population moving south we will have a calamity, for the Brothers may not be able to deal with the thousands who would become ill. Brother Shuyun has suggested that Senior Brother Sotura could be asked to oversee this problem."

Shonto nodded, thinking for a moment. "Brother Shuyun has taken no risk of infection himself?"

"I spoke to Shuyun-sum of your concern in this matter, Sire, and he assured me that he would employ all necessary precautions."

Shonto sat turning his cup slowly and looking out at the people moving along the canal bank. "We cannot afford to assign many river craft to transporting the sick." He shook his head. "Have Brother Sotura take charge of this matter. If the plague finds its way out among these people," he waved a hand at the canal bank, "thousands may die before the Botahist monks are able to control the disease. We would have been better to leave them in their homes, barbarian army or no."

Shonto turned back to Kamu. "Once this becomes known among the refugees, there will be a panic that will itself cost lives. We have no more men to police the travelers." He looked down into his cup. "Let us see what happens. If the diseased are isolated, the problem may grow no worse."

A silence fell over the men on the deck for a moment. Memories of the plague years were still strong among the people of Wa. No family had been untouched by the wave of death that swept through Wa. And then the Imperial family had become ill and the war began. It was all too familiar.

"Excuse me for asking, Lord Shonto," General Hojo said, interrupting everyone's thoughts. "I do not understand why my lord did not allow the young Prince to speak directly to the Emperor? The fact that the Prince would take such a risk would light his story with a flame of truth. Men often will take great risks when they believe they are the bearers of an important truth, as though the purity of their knowledge will somehow shield them from the malice and ignorance of others. The Emperor may have been given pause to think."

Shonto nodded. "It is possible, one can never know what will impress the Son of Heaven. But if the Emperor did not believe his son . . . ?" Shonto signaled a servant for wine. "If the son stays with us, what will Akantsu think? That I have offered the Prince the hand of my daughter and the throne of Wa—two things of inestimable value, neither of which the Emperor will ever offer. If the Emperor loses a civil war, a Prince who is wed to a daughter of the Shonto, a bearer of the Fanisan blood, would be the most likely to ascend the Dragon Throne. There is more to overthrowing an Emperor than winning a war. One must have a suitable claimant or even the winning side can faction." Shonto smiled. "The more threatened the Emperor feels, the larger will his army become."

The lord shrugged. "And who can say, perhaps the

Prince's letter will make the Emperor wonder. If the Son of Heaven sends officers north to assess the barbarian army, they will see what the Prince has seen.''

"The board," Hojo said, dryly, "has become too complex."

Lifting the wine cup that was set before him, Shonto raised an eyebrow. "For the time being, General." He drank, then set the cup on a small table. "The exchange of pieces begins soon."

Returning to the flotilla had become more difficult than Komawara had expected. They had met a barbarian patrol as they emerged from the hills and somehow one of the tribesmen had escaped. After that they had been hunted by barbarian companies and forced to fight more than one running battle. Of the eighteen hundred men that had attacked the supply rafts only a thousand remained. There had been no further signs of the company led by Rohku Saicha and Komawara was not sure if this was propitious or cause for sadness.

"Sire," a guard interrupted Komawara's train of thought. The lord sat with his back against a tree, looking out over a field surrounded by tree-clad hills. Grazing horses were guarded here, and Komawara thought how lucky the animals were—his company had not eaten since morning the previous day and his stomach occasionally complained loudly.

"Sire, the guides have found the flotilla. We may reach it by late afternoon."

Komawara nodded, it was all the reaction he felt he had energy for at the moment. "The scouting parties?"

"They report that the barbarian patrols keep their distance from Lord Shonto's fleet, Sire, we have not seen sign of them all this morning." The man paused and then said with some pride, "The patrols the men of Seh ride keep the tribesmen wary."

Komawara nodded. "Tell General Jaku that we must ride again. Has our position been reported to Lord Shonto?"

The guard shook his head.

"Send someone ahead to inform Kamu-sum of our position." Komawara heaved himself up with some effort.

"The patrols have one other thing to report, Lord Komawara."

The lord had begun to turn away but stopped.

"It appears that a large party is separating from the main body of the barbarian army."

"How large?"

"Perhaps twenty-five thousand men."

Komawara nodded, looking down at the ground for a moment. "Six men will carry this news directly to Lord Shonto. Give them our strongest horses and remounts also. Tell them to ride their horses to death if need be. Lord Shonto must know of this immediately."

Komawara signaled for his horse. *The barbarians cannot let Lord Shonto continue to deprive their army of food—not after what my party has done. This smaller force will set out to catch our own army and engage it or drive us south at such speed that we cannot continue to empty the lands before us. This Khan has finally awakened.*

Forty-four

Fourth Moon floated free of the tree, sloughing off a robe of copper and wrapping itself in pure silver-white. Ladies Nishima, Kitsura, and Okara sat on cushions laid out on a carpet spread over the quarter-deck. So bright was the moonlight that the pink of the cherry blossoms and the white of the plum could be distinguished as the trees slipped past, their blossom laden shapes hanging like clouds over the dark canal bank.

At the request of Lady Okara, Nishima had played her harp, a subtle melody known as "The Lovers' Parting," though in the southern provinces it went by the name "Traveling the Spring River."

This done they had begun a poem-series, each composing a verse in turn. Nishima had been given the honor of both the first and last verses in recognition of her poetic skills.

> *"Fourth moon,*
> *Ten thousand broken hearts*
> *Line the banks of the spring canal*
> *Strewn among the plum petals."*

And then Lady Okara had taken the wine cup that went to the composer of the next verse.

> *"Blossoms as white as lintel vine*
> *Drift south against flowing waters.*
> *How do we return to houses*
> *Their gateways crumbled?"*

The cup passed to Kitsura.

> *"Last autumn's leaves*
> *And spring flowers*
> *Are whirled up into clouds*
> *On the backs of cool winds*
> *Like the lifting of one's heart."*

The cup returned to Nishima who took the required sip and then sat holding the cool porcelain in her lap, thinking.

> *"A flight of cranes*
> *Passes in silence*
> *Along the river among the clouds.*
> *Ten thousand hearts rise up,*
> *Taking flight toward an unseen lake*
> *At the foot of an unnamed mountain."*

When the poem was finished, the three women sat in silence contemplating the moon and the passing scene. After a suitable time had passed, Kitsura raised her flute and played a soft air that spoke to the mood like a well-chosen quotation. When she was finished, a bamboo flute answered from the canal bank, the unseen player offering a melody none had heard before but which matched the music of Kitsura perfectly.

"That was a spirit speaking to us, I am certain," Lady Okara whispered, and the other women nodded.

Conversation ceased for some time and then Lady Nishima rose, her smile failing even as it formed. "It pains me to leave your delightful company," she said, "but I must sleep or I will be of no use to my uncle. It has been a perfect evening, Oka-sum, cousin." A half bow and she retreated toward the companionway.

Kitsura started another song but could not keep her focus and stopped. "I fear this war has affected my cousin in ways that are difficult to understand. Her artist's spirit is too open and in times such as these. . . ." She did not finish.

Lady Okara nodded. "May she never learn to wall her spirit off from the world—though it causes her heart to break a thousand times."

The fires of a refugee camp appeared on the bank for

the next half a rih and then there was only the landscape
lit by moonlight, the calyptas and willows, in full leaf
now, silhouetted against the stars. Intent on not disturbing the women who sat contemplating the moon, the
watch changed in near silence.

"I have heard no word of the company sent to raid the
barbarians' supply train," Kitsura said suddenly, and
though it was entirely out of place to discuss such things
at a viewing of the moon, such breaches of etiquette were
becoming more and more common.

"Yes, and I am concerned," Okara answered, not
seeming to notice or perhaps care that it was not a suitable topic for the occasion.

"Lord Komawara has grown very grim, don't you
think? Far more than even the senior members of Lord
Shonto's staff—though of course they have seen war before. Still. . . ."

Lady Okara sat quietly for a second. "There is much
that has happened to our young lord of Seh. It gives me
sorrow to see him change in this manner, but I would
expect little else. He has lost the estates the Komawara
have held for generations, Seh is occupied by barbarians
who no doubt burned the beautiful city of Rhojo-ma. And
though Lord Komawara has regained the respect of the
men of his own province, the months of ridicule have not
been forgotten, and . . . there are other things as well."

"Other things, Oka-sum?" Kitsura asked.

Shrugging, the artist pulled her over-robe closer.
"Please, say nothing of this, but I believe Samyamu-sum
has been spurned, Kitsu-sum, and after all that has be-
fallen him Lord Komawara feels there is nothing left to
him. Such a feeling can lead to terrible recklessness, I
fear."

"Spurned," Kitsura said in a whisper, her interest obvious. "Who do you think?"

Okara shrugged, not meeting the other woman's gaze.
"I thought it might be the Lady Kitsura. . . ."

Kitsura gave a small laugh. "Certainly not. There
were, however, several lovely young women who frequented the Governor's Palace in Seh. There is no shortage of possibilities. Do you think it was because Lord
Komawara's views were thought to be so peculiar?"

Okara shrugged again. "Perhaps."

"Huh," Kitsura touched her fingers to her chin in contemplation that looked almost like prayer. "All the other men I am aware of are smitten with Nishi-sum. . . ." The young woman sat up. "You don't think it was Nishima-sum, do you? She certainly said nothing to me."

"I do not know, Kitsu-sum. I only mention it as a possibility. I know nothing for certain."

Kitsura rubbed her hands together, imitating a character in a play. "I must find some way to have Nishi-sum tell me," Kitsura said, obviously already plotting. "Poor Lord Komawara. My lovely cousin will break ten thousand hearts before she settles."

"I must say," Lady Okara spoke sharply, "this rivalry between yourself and Lady Nishima is something you will both regret."

Kitsura stared dumbly. She had never heard Lady Okara say anything that was not entirely pleasant. What rivalry? she thought. With my dearest cousin?

Nishima lay in her cabin awash in the moonlight filtering through the open window. She had changed out of the elaborate robes she had worn against the cool evening and a maid had laid out her bedding. Although Nishima had been able to participate in the viewing with some focus, this had suddenly disappeared and she had excused herself before the others guessed the turmoil that possessed her.

It had been several days since Nishima had spoken to Shuyun, had not even seen him except once at a distance. The monk was avoiding her, there was no doubt, and this caused her great anxiety.

In a sense Nishima felt she was engaged in a struggle for this young man's spirit—a lifetime of Botahist training and doctrine on one side and whatever charms Lady Nishima had to offer on the other. And the longer he was away from her the more likely it became that training and comfortable habit would be victorious. Even now she was certain the monks had won their pupil back, even if they did not know that they were in danger of losing him.

Nishima was surprised at how little guilt she felt from playing the temptress—drawing the devoted away from the path of the spirit. It made her question her own goodness. Certainly nothing could be more improper than this affair she was engaged in, yet her heart did not care and it was her heart that had taken control.

The pain she felt at this thought was almost physical, so deep inside that she could not find its center. For some time she lay in this state and then forced herself to follow one of the several exercises that Brother Satake had taught to force her spirit away from such turmoil. And this finally brought a fitful sleep.

A stair creaking brought the young woman awake as surely as the sound of someone entering one's room. After the noise of the telltale stair tread Nishima heard nothing at all and knew that the only person who could move that silently was Shuyun. She sat up, wrapping the quilt around her, every sense alert, but there was no other sound and her door did not ease open as she hoped.

For several minutes the young woman sat, struggling with her fears and desires. Then the need to know what transpired in the heart of this young monk won out and she almost jumped up, throwing a robe over her thin sleeping garment, forgetting a sash.

She opened her door a crack and watched the corridor and the stairs that led to the deck, dimly lit by a shaded, bronze lamp: nothing stirred. Though she did not have the skill of Shuyun, Nishima did have Brother Satake's training and her motions exhibited the harmony of movement and balance that allowed the Botahist-trained to move with almost no sound.

At Shuyun's door she paused to listen, but when she heard nothing she pushed it open and stepped quickly out of the light of the corridor. Shuyun sat up in the bedding spread over the straw mats, the moon lighting the planes of his cheek and brow.

"Lady Nishima?"

His voice was a whisper, but even so it carried tones of formality and distance. Nishima felt her heart sink. A pace from the bed she knelt and found she could not speak.

"Lady Nishima, is something wrong?" Shuyun asked.

Distance, words as cool as the spring river. I cannot win him with weakness, she thought, I must be strong. I must find the aspects of myself that drew him before.

Despite her resolve her voice was small and shook slightly. "I had not seen you in some time, Shuyun-sum. . . ." Words ceased there and finally she could only shrug and fight tears. It was as she had feared—habit and training and doctrine had argued in her absence. What could she do now?

Shuyun stared at her and though it may have been merely a trick of the light, his face, normally devoid of emotion, seemed to mirror her own confusion and sadness.

"I do not understand the ways of the heart, Lady Nishima," he said quietly, his voice utterly calm.

Shaking her head, Nishima heard herself whisper, "No one does." A second of silence and then with difficulty, "I only know that my heart is breaking."

Shuyun's lack of experience would no longer stop him from offering comfort to a woman whose heart was breaking. Nishima felt his arms encircle her and she pulled him close, burying her face in his bare shoulder. Neither moved for some time, as though afraid motion or words would somehow signal acceptance of the changes they both sensed coming.

"I have a memory from my childhood," Nishima whispered, "perhaps my earliest memory. I was crying, I can't remember why, and my mother held me as you do now."

"My first memory is singing a child's chant with my fellow neophytes. I have no memory of my family."

"Were you that young, then, when you came to the Brothers?"

Shuyun shook his head. "When you are very young, the teachers have you perform exercises where you imagine your mother's face changing—from round to sharp, or long to round. Soon you can no longer remember her true appearance. It is the first lesson that we live in the illusion."

"It seems a terrible thing to do to a child," Nishima whispered.

"Perhaps." Shuyun put his mouth close to her ear. "There is something you must know." Pulling away slowly, he held up a hand. "Place your palm against mine."

Nishima did so.

"Push."

Beginning slowly Nishima applied pressure, controlling her breathing, feeling the slight tingle of "inner force" through her hand. Shuyun stared at her with great earnestness all the while. Suddenly Nishima found her hand being forced back, not quickly but steadily. Only when this steady pressure had stopped pushing her back did Nishima realize that there was moonlight falling between Shuyun's hand and her own. She faltered and withdrew her hand, staring openly.

"Brother Satake did not tell me of this," Nishima whispered. "I . . . would not have thought it possible."

Shuyun shook his head. "There is no record of such a thing being done before," Shuyun said, his voice so filled with awe that Nishima found herself moving away as though the monk was suddenly something to be wary of.

"Are you the Teacher, then?" she whispered.

Shuyun shook his head, almost a tremor, and shrugged, looking down at his hands. "I do not know. Certainly this confusion I feel is not the Enlightenment the Brothers describe." He met Nishima's gaze and she felt he asked her, silently, to reach out to him, and despite her discomfort and questions about the nature of this man she could not refuse.

Gently, Nishima pulled the quilt aside and slipped into the bed beside Shuyun. They lay in the moonlight, close, in each other's arms—too much to be said, neither able to find words to begin.

The sounds of the boat swaying and rocking through the waters were all around them and the moonlight arced slowly across the cabin. The entire effect was one of strangeness—a room that moved and hissed and burbled, cool pure light illuminating the cabin, bright enough to cast shadows. It was as though they had been transported to some other realm where the laws and forces of nature were unknown.

Nishima felt Shuyun's finger trace the shape of her ear, his touch so light. Down the curve of her neck and she realized she was holding her breath. Out along her shoulder, pulling her robe back. She felt the soft silk slide across her breast and then the soft warmth of Shuyun's skin against her own.

Brave heart, Nishima thought, *what beauty we have found.*

Lord Shonto Shokan awoke in a small gray room, a thin line of daylight finding its way through a crack in the window shutter. Early, he thought, it must be very early. The furs he slept under kept him warm, but the stone walls drew all the heat out of the air and the lord's breath was visible. He rolled over again and was startled by pain in his back and neck. Carrying a load, dweller style, had asked much of him.

A night's sleep uninterrupted by the cold: Shokan had to admit that he was not meant to live high in the mountains. He could not bear the cold.

Unwilling to face the air in the room and unable to think of a pressing reason to rise, Shokan lay in his furs wondering about the people who had found him—rescued him was perhaps more accurate.

In some ways they were not unlike the people of Wa, the lowlanders. The mountain dwellers' dress and habits differed, there was no question, but there was a familiar focus of duty among these people which reminded Shokan of the retainers on the Shonto fief.

There appeared to be no aristocracy here, though the elders were accorded a level of respect that was impressive. But even their lives did not compare with that of a pampered member of Wa's peerage—his life, for instance.

If Shokan were to characterize the greatest difference between the mountain dwellers and his own people, it was in the dwellers' seemingly consistent ability to find delight in virtually everything. More than innocence, this was a quality of joy and spontaneity that was seldom seen in the Empire of Wa—a world smothered with rigidly structured etiquette, formality, and ceremony. Even his stepsister, Nishima, who flouted the rules of her station almost without regard—and with impressive impunity!—did not share the spirit he witnessed in the dwellers. He realized he was somewhat jealous.

The door opened a crack and Shokan was not sure whose face appeared in the dark hall beyond. The door was pushed open by a foot and Quinta-la appeared. In her hands she bore a covered wooden tray and the smell of food permeated the cold air. She set this on what appeared to be a low, round stool and went directly to the window, speaking as she went. There was no way to be certain, but Shokan had the distinct impression that this young woman was scolding him. Unfastening the latches she flung the shutters open and sunshine flooded the room, warm sunshine, and the young lord was not sure that the outside air was not warmer also.

Quinta-la squatted down on her heels and gestured to the food and smiled.

Shokan said the word he hoped meant "eat" and received a delighted smile and a torrent of dweller language, not a single word of which he recognized.

When he had eaten, every bite watched with apparent interest, Quinta-la rose and gestured to the door, speaking as she did so.

"I would love to stroll in the sunshine in your lovely company, Quinta-la," Shokan responded, "but it is improper for you to be here and certainly very improper that I should dress in your presence, so. . . ." He waved her out, smiling so that she would not take offense, and when this did not work he rose, wrapped in a fur, and guided her out the door which caused much laughter, but then many things he did made her laugh.

Dressing quickly the lord went out into the hall where Quinta-la crouched down against the wall.

"Ketah," she said and jumped up, waving down the corridor. She walked beside him, her pace forcing Shokan to hurry, yet, except for the speed at which she walked, she showed little sign of being rushed. She smiled at Shokan when he looked at her and seemed to be walking quickly out of excitement or perhaps sheer pleasure, but not because there was pressure to be somewhere.

They left the building by a very substantial wooden door and crossed a stone courtyard to ascend a set of narrow stairs. In the shade between the building and the high wall the air was frigid and occasional patches of ice appeared on the stone treads.

As they reached the top of the stairs, and another of what seemed to be an endless number of courtyards and terraces, a shout went up and in seconds a swarm of children appeared, converging from all directions. Round faced, with perfect, white smiles they were a contrast to the quiet, decorous children Shokan was used to encountering. They ran in circles around the stranger and his tiny guide or pranced along beside Quinta-la tagging on to her hands and clothing, laughing and jabbering and letting go the occasional shriek, apparently for sheer joy.

They crossed yet another stone terrace toward a wide set of steps, just high enough that Shokan could not see what lay at the next level. As they came closer to the stairs, the children became more subdued and then fell completely silent. A few at a time they began to drop behind so that the adults reached the foot of the stairs alone. There Quinta-la stopped also, her face uncommonly serious.

Shokan looked back and the children stood watching him, big eyes unreadable to his outsider perception, their smiles gone. Quinta-la nodded, the strange gesture of the head falling forward then jerking up. Waving her hand at the steps, she tried a reassuring smile though it was so forced it did anything but reassure.

I have no sword, Shokan thought. He had left it in his chambers out of respect and trust for the people who had saved him, for they did not carry swords in their own village. It is a groundless fear, he told himself, a thought without honor. The dwellers are not treacherous.

As there seemed to be little choice, he bowed and turned up the stairs, watched intently by his strangely mute audience.

Though he was not certain what he had been expecting, what greeted him at the top of the stairs did not fullfil those expectations. A round terrace surrounded by a waist-high stone wall. In its center a stunted tree lifted twisted branches against the background of white mountains and the broad valley.

The scene was so dramatic that Shokan almost did not notice the tiny figure sitting on a stone bench, looking out across the valley. A woman dressed in long robes of dark colors belted with a faded purple sash. She turned as Shokan stood regarding her, unsure what to do. A gesture, not unfriendly, to join her.

If this woman was not the sister of the old man Shokan had met when the mountain dwellers first approached him, then the lord would feel his powers of observation had deserted him entirely. Tiny and wrinkled, her face looked out from the folds of a rough woolen scarf of faded blue.

"You," she said in a thin but surprisingly deep voice, "are Lord Shonto?"

Shokan hid his surprise, for she was the first dweller he had encountered who spoke his language, and almost without accent it seemed. "I am." He bowed.

She motioned for him to sit and he took the other end of the bench to the one she occupied, her knees drawn up in a posture much like a young girl's. "I expected you to be older," she said.

"I am Lord Shonto Shokan. Perhaps you mistake me for my father, Lord Shonto Motoru?"

"You are the son?" she said. "I expected you to be younger."

The lord smiled. "I was not told your name or title; excuse me, I do not know how to address you."

"Alinka-sa," she offered. "I am," she paused. "I do not know your word . . . an old-one."

"Elder," Shokan offered.

She gave the dwellers' peculiar nod. "Elder. I am, perhaps, *the* elder. I am the voice of my people."

"You speak my language very well."

She shrugged, offering no explanation. "May I ask what led you to be in the pass before the snows had melted?"

"We were attempting to make our way to Chiba, the province on the western side of the mountains."

Alinka-sa did not hide her look of displeasure at this answer. A few seconds of silence followed and then Shokan went on.

"There are events in the Empire that led us to attempt this crossing of the mountains too early. There is a war beginning or perhaps it has already begun. It will take place beyond the mountains." He nodded west.

Silence followed while this was considered. Unlike the

rest of her people, there was no sense of lightness in
Alinka-sa. Hers seemed a personality devoid of humor
or joy.

"Why does the Emperor allow the army of the Alat-
an, the desert tribes, to move south on the canal?"

"It is a long story, Alinka-sa."

She looked at him sharply. "Perhaps there are things
even a lord of Wa does not understand. The Shonto name
is ancient and honored, but my people saved you and all
of your company: your debt is great, Shokan-li. How it
will be paid is yet to be decided. What part you play in
the events of the world will become part of the decision."

"You will not allow us to continue through the mountains?" Shokan did not hide his shock as well as he
hoped.

"What will become of you, Shokan-li, has not been
decided. The world beyond our valley is large. Some play
parts larger than others. Perhaps you should pass through
the mountains to the battle beyond. But it is also possible that you should stay with us, preserving the Shonto
House through a time of great turmoil. This cannot be
decided easily."

Shokan nodded. "You are a Seer, then?" It might explain why Quinta-la and the children were afraid of her.

"I do not understand this word," she said bluntly.

Questioning an elder, the lord was beginning to suspect, was not acceptable. "The situation in the Empire,
Alinka-sa, is difficult to explain and much that I would
tell you is conjecture only." He took a long breath. "It
began this summer past when my father was appointed
Imperial Governor of the province of Seh. . . ."

There seemed to be nothing else to do, so Shokan began the tale. Slowly at first, and then the words began to
flow more easily. He told her of the Emperor's plot and
what he thought it meant, the coins Tanaka had found,
his own time in Seh. The sun had traveled a good distance across the sky before he was done. During the entire telling, Alinka-sa did not ask a single question.
Occasionally her eyebrows would rise or she would give
the dwellers' nod of the head, but she never interrupted
Shokan's story.

Even when he finally finished, the old woman did not speak but stared off across the green valley floor.

"The tree with the fan-leaf, what is it called?" she asked suddenly.

"Ginkyo?"

She nodded. "Alinka means ginkyo in my tongue. This tree does not grow in the mountains and is something of a legend among my people. They believe that the leaves are quite large and that the ladies of Wa simply pluck a leaf from the tree whenever they need a fan. Though I often told my people the truth of this, after some discussion they decided that, in this matter, I was not well informed." She gave the tiniest smile. "My mother was like you—she became lost in the mountains and was saved by the people of this village. When my father died, my mother went back to Itsa and we lived for some time in Wa before returning here."

She looked over at Shokan, meeting his gaze. "For this reason I know your language and something of your ways, strange as they are to us. Some of your story was known to me, though much was new. Great tragedy is about to shake Wa and this saddens me." Alinka-sa looked away again.

"Tell me of this monk who serves your father," she said, not looking at Shokan.

The lord hesitated before speaking. "The people who brought us here used his name often—Shuyun. Why was that."

Obviously controlling her annoyance Alinka-sa answered. "Shu-yung, it is a word in our language: it means bearer, those who carry. To the ear of an outsider the word meaning to bear would be indistinguishable from the word meaning bearer. Tell me of him."

"I have never met Brother Shuyun, in truth. It is said that he is very advanced in the skills of the Botahist monks. Both my father and my sister have written of him in very flattering terms. That is all I know."

She nodded. "My people will guide you through the mountains. You will leave at sunrise." Alinka-sa rose to her feet with an ease that one would not expect in one so aged. Standing, she was eye to eye with the young lord.

"But why have you decided this? I am grateful, certainly but what has made your decision?"

Very gently she reached out and touched his cheek. "Quinta-la will accompany you to the lowlands. May Botahara go with you." She turned and crossed the terrace, disappearing down the steps.

Forty-five

The sky was as confused as a lover's heart. Clouds torn and buffeted by conflicting winds rolled overhead, moving against a background of higher clouds, striated like sand revealed by the tide.

It had rained earlier that day and threatened to do so again. The wind was steady from the east though it had blown from every point of the compass that morning, making the rivermen curse under their breaths.

Shuyun knelt before his liege-lord, waiting. They sat on the deck of Lord Shonto's barge which was moving south at its best speed. Dipping his brush in ink, Lord Shonto added three characters to the letter and then waved for his secretary who had servants remove the writing table and all of its contents. Turning to his Spiritual Advisor, the lord smiled.

"You have heard the news of Lord Komawara, Shuyun-sum?"

"I have, Sire. Botahara protects us."

Shonto nodded. "It is good that He does. Perhaps you do not know that Rohku Saicha has returned to us also, though his losses were even more severe than those of Lord Komawara and General Jaku." Shonto hesitated and his face showed a trace of the strain he no doubt felt.

"The Khan has done the correct thing. Driving us south will give him the possibility of food by summer. If he is wise enough to put the peasants he captures to work rather than to the sword, his army will not starve." Shonto pulled an armrest closer. "This smaller barbarian army will soon be beyond assistance from the larger army. . . . If our own force were not so small, it would be an opportunity." He fell silent, lost in the great game of gii that he played.

Shuyun sat quietly waiting. The monk was aware that

he felt a growing sense of disquiet as he sat before his liege-lord—the father of the woman with whom he had so recently spent the night. Not that Nishima was not of an age to make her own decisions in such matters, but Shuyun could not believe that Lord Shonto would be pleased by such an alliance.

I am torn in every direction, the monk thought. There was a part of him that felt closer to Shonto and the lord's purposes as he moved further from the faith of his own Order. As though the concerns of the world became more real as the ways of the spirit became more confusing. Yet he was a Botahist monk still and he had spent the night in the embrace of his liege-lord's daughter—certainly an act that would shock anyone who lived in the Empire of Wa. Although Shonto did not pry into Lady Nishima's affairs unduly, was it possible that the lord was unaware of what was taking place? Shuyun thought it unlikely and thus the discomfort.

Shonto focused on his Spiritual Advisor suddenly. "You have a report for me, Shuyun-sum?"

The monk nodded, pushing his feelings into one corner of his being. "It appears that we have isolated the plague for now, Sire, though I think we will see other cases yet. The refugees are frightened, but this has resulted in them moving south more quickly—a good thing. We have placed the barge for the sick at the front of the fleet and it flies a plague banner. All the Imperial Guards in the Empire could not clear the canal more quickly than the sight of that terrible flag. There has been only one more death, may Botahara protect her soul." The monk made a sign. "I pray that the situation does not grow worse, Sire. Brother Sotura is a man of great skill—he has the present situation well in hand."

Shonto nodded. "I wish to be kept informed of this matter. If plague finds root in our army, it will not matter if the Khan is followed by one man or one hundred thousand—our army will be reduced to ghosts." Shonto waved at the mouth of a small creek hung with willows. "Master Myochin will no doubt hear of our approach. He will not be pleased at the prospect of leaving his home." Shonto shook his head. "We all hope for peace in our old age. . . . It will be some time before we see peace again, Shuyun-sum. Even if this Khan can defeat the armies of Wa, holding the Empire will be another matter entirely. Children born today may find their way into this war before it is over, though I pray it will not be so."

Forty-six

The Stone Ship appeared to float in its own reflection in the middle of the Lake of the Autumn Crane on the western edge of the Imperial Palace. It was largely carved of marble though jade had also been employed by the ancient artisans—uncommon materials for a ship. In truth, it was no boat at all but a small island of stone blocks carved to form an elaborate, somewhat fantastic ship though to a small scale.

Over the centuries the Stone Ship had been the favorite retreat of many an Emperor or Empress and had only fallen into disfavor with the recent dynasty. It remained, however, an ideal place to find peace and to carry on conversations that one did not want overheard. Perhaps it was this that had brought the Emperor out to the Stone Ship.

An awning of spring green had been spread for the Son of Heaven and he sat on silk cushions attended by only a single secretary who stood on the bow, signaling the shore for anything Akantsu requested, occasionally scurrying back to the stern at a nod from the Emperor. So that the Son of Heaven could spend a few hours in this blessed isolation an entire retinue of officials and servants and secretaries waited on the shore, kneeling patiently—only the most senior members involved in conversation. To maintain this company a kitchen had been constructed behind a screen of willow trees, and runners stood ready to hurry to the Palace to retrieve anything or anyone the Emperor might request.

Swallows and kingfishers crossed the lake, weaving intricate patterns, and ducks cut vees into its calm surface. Jaku Tadamoto watched three swallows chasing a downy white feather, one picking it out of the air and rushing off, then dropping it for the others to dive at. This may have been a struggle for possession of nest material, but it looked for all the world like a game, and the acrobatics of the players were impressive.

Tadamoto was being sculled across the Lake of the Autumn Crane's calm waters in one of the elegant craft used by officials of the Island Palace. As was often the case, the young colonel came to his audience with the Emperor carrying written reports and scrolls, not all of which bore good news.

As well as official writings Tadamoto also carried, hidden in his sleeve, a letter from Osha. It was a conciliatory letter, full of apologies for offenses she had not committed, washed in sadness, her pain tearing at his heart. They must not give up, she had written, their love would survive if only they believed it would. So he tried to believe.

Tadamoto also tried to push this letter out of his mind as it would undoubtedly affect his ability to serve his Emperor—something that could not be allowed now that civil war was all but upon them.

The sampan came alongside a stone dock built in the shape of the platform one found at the foot of a ship's ladder. Tadamoto mounted the steps to the "deck" where the secretary greeted him with a low bow. Crossing to the quarterdeck on his knees, Tadamoto bowed at the foot of the stairs and waited to be acknowledged.

The Emperor pored over a long scroll, completely absorbed. The ruler's robe of yellow embroidered with a flight of cranes among clouds created a disturbing contrast. Although his garb was perfectly appropriate for the season—light of spirit—the Emperor's face was drawn and pale like that of a man who had not known a night of peace in many, many days. Tadamoto kept his eyes cast down, concentrating on the wood-grain that had been carved into the planks of the stone deck.

Letting his arms drop, the Emperor laid the scroll across his legs. "Colonel."

Tadamoto bowed again.

"Let us begin with your news. My patience has worn away to nothing and pleasantries have become most unpleasant. What do we know today?"

Tadamoto unrolled a small scroll—notes for this audience. "Shonto's flotilla is three days north of Denji

Gorge, Sire, and has increased its speed considerably in the last few days. The first refugees have crossed the border of our own province and they will begin to arrive in the Capital in numbers within a few days. I have detailed officials and guards to deal with this influx.

"Our own army has reached twenty-five thousand in number, Sire, and will be thirty thousand before the next moon." Tadamoto lowered the scroll. "I have reports here, Emperor, if you wish to read them." He tapped the pile of rolled paper. "I estimate that Lord Shonto could be within the border of Dentou within fourteen days if he continues to travel at his present speed. There has been a report that Shonto's fleet is preceded by a barge flying the plague banner. This report has not been substantiated and even if it proves true it would appear to be a ruse to keep the canal open before Shonto's fleet. Nonetheless the rumor precedes the flotilla like a bow wave."

The Emperor shook his head. "Shonto would think of such a thing. It is entirely without honor but effective, no doubt." The Emperor lifted the scroll he had been reading. "I have received my own reports. Prince Wakaro has sent this, a complete report of the military situation prepared by Shonto's staff. My son claims to have seen a barbarian army of one hundred thousand and it is accompanied by a letter written by the captain of the Prince's guard—a man we selected together, Colonel. He, too, claims to have seen this army." The Emperor set the scroll aside. "My son is not a warrior and easily duped, but from the captain of his guard I expected more. It is most curious."

Tadamoto nodded. "Excuse me, Sire. . . ."

"Speak, Colonel, this is no time to be shy."

"At your suggestion, I sent the most reliable men I have north to assess this situation. According to their count—they saw the barbarian army with their own eyes—the force pursuing Shonto is no more than thirty thousand and perhaps less. Shonto's own army appears to number between twenty and twenty-five thousand, a significant number of these being Imperial Guards. Alongside the shinta blossom fly the banners of both Prince Wakaro and my brother Katta. It grieves me to bring you this news, Emperor."

The Emperor looked toward the white walls of the Island Palace as though he meditated upon their form. But his breathing did not exhibit the controlled rhythm of meditation and his hands would not lie still on his knees. "Betrayed," the Emperor almost whispered, "betrayed by my own son and by the man I treated as a son." Picking up his sword, he laid it gently across his knees. "Is this army in league with Motoru, do you think?"

"My own men believe there have been real battles with the barbarians though reports that Lord Shonto scorched the earth as he passed south appear to be unfounded. They saw no evidence of this. So it seems unlikely. There truly is a barbarian invasion but not the hordes some would like us to believe."

"Two invading armies, one on the heels of the other." The Emperor toyed with his sword. "Betrayed by my own son," he said again, his voice filled with disbelief and pain.

The son you sent north to share in the fate of Lord Shonto, Tadamoto thought.

Forty-seven

The barges almost never stopped now and though it meant the countryside was left untouched by the devastation formerly wrought upon it, it also meant that Shimeko could not get off the boat to walk on the bank. This made it very easy to avoid Sister Morima and all of the influences from her former life. But she was shut up on the ship among people who were very different from her—the three ladies from the Capital and their attendants. It was difficult for her.

The Plum Blossom Winds filled the air with clouds of petals from the plum groves planted along the canal. When a gust came, standing on the deck of the boat was like being in a warm snowstorm, so thick were the petals in the air. The canal was almost a white waterway and the decks of the ships were constantly needing to be swept clear, for a rain shower would render a petal-covered deck dangerously slick.

Shimeko had given up brushing the petals from her robe despite the fact that on the deep blue they were very apparent. The robe had been a gift from Lady Nishima, one of the lady's own, no doubt, and though it was a cast-off it had obviously been worn infrequently for the silk was as new as the day it had come from the loom. Having seen the size of Lady Nishima's wardrobe, Shimeko was not surprised that signs of wear would not be found on the lady's clothing—and Lady Nishima often complained that she had left the Capital with hardly anything to wear!

Shimeko smiled. Such a statement would have offended the former nun only a few weeks before, but now it only made her shake her head and laugh. The Lady Nishima Fanisan Shonto was difficult to dislike and, despite having been raised in the greatest luxury, could not be said to have been spoiled by it. She was a Lady of a great House, there was no doubt, but Lady Nishima was a person of substance and accomplishment and depth. Shimeko could not dislike her.

Shimeko turned away from the rail, leaning there with the breeze at her back. Pulling her shawl down onto her shoulders, she enjoyed the feeling of the wind blowing through her hair; though it was still short by the standards of lay-women, it was longer than Shimeko had ever known it.

The decision Shimeko made was a difficult one. Although she had found Lady Nishima admirable in many ways, there was this other matter which the former nun found very disturbing. Shimeko was almost certain that Lady Nishima had more than once spent the entire night alone with Brother Shuyun.

The young woman looked off at the white-capped mountains rising along the western horizon. Having little experience of the world, she did not know how such news would be received by the population at large. What would Lord Shonto think of such a thing? Sister Morima always claimed that the Brothers were entirely corrupt, but Shimeko never suspected she had meant corrupt in ways such as this. And Brother Shuyun! To think that many of the Sisters hoped he was the Teacher who was spoken of.

A vision of the Faceless Lovers carved into the cliff of Denji Gorge came to her. This was the subject of Lady Nishima's curiosity. Shimeko brushed petals from her robe unconsciously. Was it possible that this sculpture was not a heresy? Was Lady Nishima aware of things that Shimeko was not?

Sister Morima had also claimed there were things written in the Sacred Scrolls of the Perfect Master that were not included in any copies of these texts—things the Brotherhood wished to keep hidden. Botahara had taken a bride, everyone knew that, but when had he attained Enlightenment? That was the question that had once caused a war. The bride was not spoken of in the writings of Botahara and his disciples only mentioned her in passing. Shimeko shook her head. Despite having left the Sisterhood and rejected its doctrine, she still found Lady Nishima's relations with Shuyun disturbing and a part of her feared this might be jealousy.

There had been a night when Shimeko had heard Lady Nishima cry out and though the former nun would admit she knew little of such things, a cry of ecstasy was difficult to mistake. Her own body had responded to this sound in a manner that was surprising and her imagination had . . . well, it had not been under her control.

A servant appeared at the head of the companionway and, seeing Shimeko at the rail, crossed to her.

"Lady Nishima awaits you, Shimeko-sum," the woman said.

The young woman replaced her shawl, nodded her thanks, and proceeded to the stairs, controlling her nervousness with care.

Bowing at the door to Lady Nishima's cabin, she entered at a smile from her mistress.

"Shimeko-sum, it is a pleasure to see you." Nishima gestured to a cushion. "You are well, I trust."

"I am well, Lady Nishima. It is kind of you to ask."

"Are the petals on the wind not a most impressive sight today?"

Shimeko nodded. "I have just come from the deck." And then she realized that not only were her robes covered in petals, but it appeared a small snowstorm had focused its efforts around her. "Please excuse me, Lady Nishima." She was obviously dismayed. "And all over your gift to me."

Laughing with great delight, Nishima reached out and touched Shimeko's hand. "These blossoms complement the robe beautifully. As for this," she waved her hand at the petals on the mat, "I would like nothing better than to have my chambers covered in plum blossoms, like the floor of a grove. Would that not be charming?" She laughed again.

Shimeko smiled, not quite reassured.

"I was told, Shimeko-sum, that there was some matter you wished to speak of?"

Nodding, the former nun gathered her courage. "It is not my intention to appear ungrateful for your favor, Lady Nishima; serving the Shonto House has been a great honor. There appears to be a matter that has arisen which is more suited to my particular skills. I have come to ask if I may be released from your service so that I might tend to the sick aboard the plague ship.'' She bowed when she finished and kept her eyes fixed on the floor.

For a moment Nishima did not respond but only looked at the woman who had come to be a trusted secretary. ''I regret to hear that you wish to leave, Shimeko-sum, for your skills are far beyond those of anyone who has served me in the same capacity. Will the Brothers allow you to assist them? Is there not a certain antagonism to the Sisterhood, not to mention great secrecy about the ways of healing?''

''As you say, Lady Nishima, the two Botahist Orders are not allies, but I am no longer a Sister and Brother Shuyun has said that the Brothers' need is great. I may assist and learn little or nothing of their secrets, I am sure.''

''And you would be in no danger from this illness?''

''Certainly not, Lady Nishima. I am no longer a Sister, but I have not forgotten all that I learned. It is also true that the Brothers could cure me if I were to become ill—though I assure you this is next to impossible.'' She paused and then said quietly. ''Your concern touches me.''

Nishima arranged the hem of her robes. ''When you first came to me, you spoke of a desire to serve the Shonto Spiritual Advisor, Brother Shuyun. If you go to care for the sick, you will be more removed from Brother Shuyun than you are presently. Does this not concern you?''

Shimeko nodded reflexively. ''I do not know, Lady Nishima, I. . . . There are sick who I may offer help to. In a time such as this, it seems that I must do what I am able.'' She shrugged.

''I see. Have the Brothers agreed to accept your assistance, Shimeko-sum?''

The young woman shook her head.

''If they agree to allow you to assist them, I will release you upon one condition—you will send messages to assure me that you are well.''

Shimeko bowed. ''Certainly, my lady.''

Nishima forced a smile. ''You are no doubt anxious to proceed with this matter. Please inform me of the Brothers' decision. Certainly you are welcome to stay with me if this plan is untenable.''

"I thank you, my lady." She met Nishima's eye for the briefest second. "It has been an honor to serve you."

With that she bowed and retreated to the door, receiving a last reassuring smile from the young aristocrat as she went. Shimeko was surprised at the feeling of emptiness this decision left. She had almost embarrassed herself in conversation with Lady Nishima, so touched was she by the woman's concern.

My life will become quite simple again, she thought. I will tend the sick, I will eat and I will sleep. There will not be the turmoil and confusion of my present position. No Sisters will come to me with demands that I can not fullfil and I will not have my heart torn by growing loyalties and attachments that I am not suited to.

Forty-eight

For those that had journeyed north in Lord Shonto's fleet, Denji Gorge was remembered not for its unique beauty but for the days when no one had been certain what would befall those traveling with Seh's Imperial Governor.

The country surrounding the gorge itself had changed so much in the intervening months that it was like returning to another time. Over the Imperial Guard Keep at the gorge's northern end flew the Emperor's banner, and the locks were administered by Imperial Functionaries and guarded by black-clad Imperial Guards. Nowhere could one find signs of the Hajiwara presence. The armor with green lacing had disappeared—unless one looked very carefully at the men who formed Lord Komawara's guard. There, among the armor of night blue, one could find a trim of green on the occasional shoulder piece or sleeve.

All of the earthworks and fortifications constructed over the years had been dismantled and several of the larger manor houses that had been protected by moats were in the process of converting these to decorative ponds or filling them in altogether.

Arrayed along the stone quay of the northern locks were several rows of kneeling guards in purple-laced armor, hands on their thighs, faces and posture rigid. As Lord Shonto's boat bumped up against the quay, the warriors bowed low. Out from among this group emerged a youth of such small stature that it brought a smile to the lips of all who had not previously encountered the Lord Butto Joda.

"I greet you, Lord Butto," Shonto said from the deck. "It is a great honor to be met by such an esteemed company."

Lord Butto gave a half bow. "The honor is mine entirely, Lord Shonto. I bring greetings from my father who asks that you forgive him for not meeting you himself."

"Lord Butto does me great honor. I trust that he is well."

Butto Joda gave a half nod and a smile, acknowledging the question but giving no specific answer—the senior lord of the Butto had not been well for many years.

Steps were set out and Shonto and several of his advisors disembarked.

"Certainly you remember Lord Komawara, General Hojo, and Steward Kamu?"

"I could not forget those who fought so valiantly beside the Butto. I am forever in your debt," he said bowing. "And Brother Shuyun, he travels with you also?"

"Brother Shuyun monitors the progress of the ship bearing the sick through the locks. We are taking care that there is no transfer of disease."

The young lord nodded. "I am less concerned knowing this."

Jaku Katta was delivered to the quay at that moment, his sampan coming alongside the stone wall. The Imperial Guards on the quay bowed low in unison.

"General Jaku," Lord Butto greeted him with a great smile. "I see that my concerns regarding who would control the locks were groundless." He looked around. "There seems to be no delegation from the Imperial Governor of Itsa. New to his position, perhaps the worthy Governor has not yet learned proper protocol for such occasions."

The smiles were polite. The Governor of Itsa was no doubt under orders to detain Shonto but had not the troops to do so. Ignoring the flotilla's passing was the only choice left to the poor man, and his situation was made worse by the fact that Imperial Guard on the canal were loyal to Jaku Katta. An appeal to the larger Houses of Itsa for assistance would have been futile as the most powerful family in the province was the Butto—sworn ally of Lord Shonto.

The group walked slowly along the quay in the direction of the gorge, the line of Butto guards bowing in turn as the party passed. On a lookout that had recently been a Hajiwara military position, mats and cushions had been

spread. Calypta and willow trees coming newly into leaf
shaded the lookout from the early afternoon sun so that
no awning or pavilion was necessary.

The great gorge stretched out to the south, the surface
broken by the breeze and sparkling in the spring sunlight.
Off the gravel bar below the fane of the lost Brothers,
river craft of every type and size swung to anchors, so
close together that fouling of rodes and lines must have
been constant.

Along the eastern cliff more boats huddled, mooring
to unseen irregularities in the rock face and countless
more sailed back and forth or drifted free, unable to find
anchorage or moorings. Smoke rose from many of the
craft and a ragged camp had been erected on the gravel
bar itself, shelters of all shapes and colors arranged in
random patterns.

In contrast to this chaos of refugee craft, a line of ships
in formation passed down the middle of the gorge, the
foremost boats almost at the southern locks—Lord Shonto's flotilla continuing south.

A meal was served by Butto attendants and plum wine,
a gift from Lord Shonto, was poured for the young lord
and his guests.

"It is unfortunate that Prince Wakaro was unable to
join us," Shonto said to Lord Butto.

Setting his wine cup down, the young lord nodded.
"Most unfortunate. I had the honor of entertaining the
Prince on his journey north. He was most kind."

Lifting his cup to Komawara and Jaku in turn, Butto
Joda said, "I have heard tales of your recent exploits,
Lord Komawara, General. It was a bold stroke—a frontal
attack on the barbarians' supply train." He gave a half
bow. "Your reputations have become great. I consider it
an honor to join you in your struggle." He bowed also
to Hojo.

"This barbarian force," the young lord continued,
"has divided, I am told, and a part of it is now in close
pursuit?"

Shonto nodded at Hojo.

General Hojo bowed. "There is a force of about
twenty-five thousand not far behind and they come
slightly closer each day—the number of refugee craft
fleeing south is slowing our progress." Hojo stroked the

gray hair of his beard, staring out over the gorge. "This is becoming a cause of some concern."

Butto Joda nodded. "I have considered this situation myself. I have taken the liberty of allowing no boats to pass through the southern locks for six days past. River craft accumulate in the gorge at an alarming rate, but the canal south is now open for many rih. In a letter, Lord Shonto suggested that we prepare this set of locks so that, once your fleet has passed, it would take engineers of great skill to restore them to use. These measures, General Hojo, should improve the speed at which you travel and, at the same time, impede the progress of your pursuers." He held up his cup. "This is excellent wine. Does it come from Seh?"

Shimeko had slept three nights on the deck to be away from the endless coughing and the odors of the sick. Although she had often treated the sick before, she had been too young to minister to those stricken by the plague during the previous outbreak. It was a frightening disease, so she spent as much time out in the fresh air as her duties would allow.

Upwind, and not far off, a small boat sailed a parallel course and aboard it, standing at the rail as she did herself, Shimeko could see Initiate Brother Shuyun. The distance was such that, had they attempted to speak, they could not have heard each other over the wind and boat sounds nor could the other's expression be seen. To the former nun this distance seemed great—as great as the distance between her present life and her days as a Botahist nun. Did she still hope he was the Teacher and would help her find tranquillity of purpose again?

She looked off to the south where the locks awaited them. She was a healer now and though it was a simple life, as she had hoped, the confusion she had felt in Lady Nishima's service had not disappeared.

Earlier the plague ship had passed the fane of the Brothers of the Eightfold Path—the Faceless Lovers. It had been difficult to view the figures, for she did not want to be seen looking at something so unseemly. Even so, she had managed a glance or two. Thoughts of Lady Nishima with Brother Shuyun would not leave her in peace.

* * *

   The wind moved the pine branches in slow circles, constantly spoiling Rohku Tadamori's view of the advancing army. The young guard officer had abandoned his blue-laced armor in favor of the brown and green garb of the huntsmen and this clothing helped to camouflage him where he lay. The forest floor was cooled by occasional rain and the consistent wind out of the east, and Tadamori found that his muscles were growing stiff.

   The *small army,* as it was becoming known, traveled at a pace that was impressive. Even those born of the desert could learn the handling of rafts, and the crude sails the pirates had fabricated from bamboo cloth were surprisingly efficient with such a fair wind. Horsemen still rode along the bank but they led strings of the barbarian ponies which were able to cover much more ground without riders. Constant changing of mounts for the riders was required, but this was not difficult.

   There was no doubt in Tadamori's mind that the small army was gaining on Lord Shonto's flotilla. Occasional refugees were being overtaken by the barbarians now, and the Shonto guard did not like to contemplate what might happen to them—especially the women.

   The huntsman who was Tadamori's companion touched his arm and cocked his head toward the passing army. Among the hundreds of rafts one came into view bearing banners, some gold and crimson. Tadamori and his companion had hidden themselves atop a hill overlooking the canal from the west, but they were still half a rih from the bank—close enough to assess the army but not able to see who its leaders might be.

   The question in the minds of the two men of Wa was: does the Khan lead this expeditionary force? If the great chieftain had taken it upon himself to pursue the retreating army, then Lord Shonto might consider a battle. It was believed likely that the Khan was the only force that held the various tribes together. Brother Shuyun's barbarian servant was utterly convinced that without the Khan the natural rivalry between the tribes would soon lead to the dissolution of the great army if not an outright war between the factions.

   Rohku reached up and stopped the branch from blocking his view. It was difficult to say. Almost certainly that was the Khan's banner, but then the Emperor's banner was seen over all of Wa, above Imperial Keeps and palaces of government. This might be the banner of the desert chieftain, but the Khan himself might be here only in spirit. It would be the worst foolishness for the men of Wa to destroy their army fighting this force and find the Khan was not present. Foolish indeed.

It had been seven years since the Supreme Master had set foot on the land of Wa. Normally his arrival was heralded by celebration and ceremony and pilgrims would come from across the Empire just to kneel outside the temple grounds in which he resided. On this journey, however, the Supreme Master came quietly, if not quite secretly. His ship arrived in Yankura without gaining any notice, and the head of the Botahist Brotherhood boarded a smaller boat that bore him swiftly to the Jade Temple.

Peering out a slit between the curtains the Supreme Master watched the activity of the Floating City. The canals and docks and quays teemed with people in motion, for Yankura was the center of shipping and commerce in the Empire of Wa and it appeared never to rest. Such lack of tranquillity, the monk thought, how can they live such lives? Even more to the point, how did Brother Hutto live in the midst of this? It was not conducive to the contemplation of Botahara's words, there was no doubt of that.

Botahara's words were more on the Supreme Master's mind recently—His true words. The blossoming of the Udumbara, the missing scrolls—these matters disturbed even his sleep. And now news of this barbarian invasion. He had returned to Wa as soon as word had arrived on the first ship of spring.

There was about to be war with an army that did not even know the words of the Perfect Master, a dynasty might fall, civil war was almost certain, and the Shonto House seemed likely to finally suffer the fate that overtook all other Houses—extinction.

Small river craft of all description lay alongside the quay, loading cargo from the great stone warehouses. In the midst of this a ragged child wriggled out of an open port and was spotted by a river man who sent up a shout. Jumping to the next boat, the child was barely able to grab the rail. Shouts echoed the alarm as the child pulled himself up onto the deck. Scrambling over stacked boxes, he leaped an open hatch and dodged a burly sailor. Holding something in his robe, he made another impossible jump to the quay where it seemed certain he would disappear into the clutter and the uncaring crowd.

The Supreme Master watched in fascination. Suddenly a man appeared from behind a pile of sacks and the child ran into him head-on, allowing one of his pursuers to grab him by the hair. A wild struggle ensued until the much larger man landed a blow that drove the child to his knees, and a series of punches and kicks left the child an unmoving pile of rags on the stones.

The scene was lost to view then and the Supreme Master slumped back against the cushions, fixed in his mind was the image of triumph on the man's face as he beat the child to the ground. *And this is what I have come to,* the old monk thought, *a brutal, violent land.*

The Lake of the Seven Masters was not large enough to develop much swell except in storm winds; still it was not as calm as a canal, and Lady Nishima steadied herself by clutching the frame of the port. The fane of the Brothers of the Eightfold Path was quickly falling astern. Nishima could see the cliff that appeared almost to have been carved with shadows and light—carved into the form of a man and woman in the act of love.

She moved away from the port and returned to kneeling on the carpet. After a moment, she lay down and cradled her head on her arm, pressing her eyes closed, the image returning as she did so. The boat rocked her as she lay there, making her feel like a child, though she knew the ache she felt was not the ache of a child.

Forty-nine

Jaku Tadamoto, followed by officers and engineers, strode along the top of the earthworks. Stopping suddenly, he let his eye follow the line of the newly built defenses which ran between two steep hills broken only in its center by the Grand Canal. The earthworks swept up at each end following the curve of the hills and provided a surprising degree of symmetry to the entire composition.

Only a day north and west of the Imperial Capital, the position had been chosen after long deliberation. Tadamoto's eye examined the plain that stretched out for several rih north of the hills. It was there that the battle would take place—the fortifications were only built to ensure that.

Despite all the discussion that had led to this decision Tadamoto was not entirely convinced this was the best course. The Emperor wanted to be certain that Shonto could not reach the Capital where there was every possibility that the population would rise up to support him. It was also true that the Imperial Capital would be a difficult, if not impossible, position to defend. After all, the Capital was not a fortified city but an enormous sprawl without continuous walls or towers and festooned with gates and canals.

And so Tadamoto had been sent north of the city to create these defenses. But who would the battle be with? That was the question in the young colonel's mind. There were two armies hurrying south on the canal—one appearing to pursue the other. Once they encountered the Imperial Army, what would occur? The situation was so confused and unclear that anything the Emperor did was undoubtedly a gamble.

What if Shonto had agreements with this Khan the Emperor had thought was his own toy? Would the rebel army suddenly join the army of the desert, creating a force double the size of the army Tadamoto had raised?

Recent reports indicated that Shonto was rushing down the canal as fast as an army could be moved. This, despite the fact that his own letters claimed he did everything to slow the barbarians' advance so that the Emperor could raise an army. What was Shonto thinking?

Turning south, Jaku looked out over the encampment that was slowly filling with the newly recruited troops. Beyond that lay the commandeered mansion that would be the residence of the Son of Heaven. As he trusted no one and felt everyone to be less capable than himself, the Emperor had made it known that he would assume command of the Imperial Army himself. There was no doubt that the Yamaku would survive or fall according to the decisions made on this field, and the Emperor did not intend to let another take control of his fate.

Tadamoto continued toward the canal. A continuous flow of refugees passed by, both day and night, swelling the population of the Capital and straining the ability of the city to support such an influx. Crime was growing at alarming rates and the Imperial Guard were hard pressed to deal with this, preparing for war as they were.

A messenger approached Tadamoto's guard and was allowed through. He bowed and knelt before his commander. Tadamoto nodded for the man to speak.

"We have brought the merchant, Colonel Jaku, as you requested. He is under guard in your quarters."

Somehow the capture of Shonto's vassal-merchant had been kept a secret and even now Tanaka's name was never used. *Merchants* were as common as street women and a reference to one meant nothing. Tadamoto was not sure what part Tanaka might play in events, if any, but it seemed prudent to have the old man present. He was someone Shonto respected and there were few of whom that could be said.

A hundred paces more brought Tadamoto to the canal bank. Although most of the flowers had been swept from the trees this far south, farther north the Plum Blossom Wind was still blowing, for the boats of refugees were decorated with white and the canal still bore petals south toward the sea.

Turning in a slow circle, Tadamoto surveyed the scene one last time. When his gaze fell on the mansion where the Emperor would dwell, the question that had bothered him all morning flared up: who from the Imperial Court would accompany the Son of Heaven? He whispered a silent prayer. Let the gods spare Osha that indignity—that she be brought along like a common camp woman.

Fifty

Here, above the clouds
Mountain paths
Lead always to the unexpected.
Rush ahead
And see it with the eyes of a child

Lord Shonto Shokan

They had ascended and descended so often that Shokan no longer knew how high in the mountains they were. The type of vegetation that grew seemed to be an indicator but was affected by too many other factors to be relied upon entirely.

The lord lay in the darkness, looking up at the stars. The world he traveled in was so strange that he was surprised to see constellations he recognized floating overhead—the Two Sisters were peaking over the shoulder of a mountain now.

It was not as cold as usual, which might be a sign that they were at a lower elevation. Whatever the reason he was thankful for it.

A few feet away Quinta-la slept, wrapped in a fur. Since they had left the village in the valley she had refused to teach him new words in her language but insisted he teach her words in his own tongue. He was not sure what had led to her decision to learn the tongue of the lowlanders, but she approached this task with an earnestness that Shokan could not help but find charming—almost comic. Even so, Quinta-la was learning at a pace that surprised the men from the Empire.

Closing his eyes, Shokan felt sleep hovering close by. Earlier in the evening he had bathed in a hot spring—an experience almost worth the days of walking. It had been a large pool, one of several etched out into the rock by ten thousand years of moving water. The dwellers had a different sense of propriety—the women bathed with the men and no one seemed to care.

Quinta-la had slipped into the pool beside him and continued her language inquiry without being self-conscious about the naturalness of their state. Shokan smiled. He had fallen into the strange world of a story; at least for now.

The litter was lifted carefully over the river boat's rail and set gently on the deck where it was secured against movement. Sister Sutso stood by, her hand to her mouth. Stepping forward, she opened the curtain a hand's width and was surprised to find the Prioress awake, her lively eyes turned to a half-open curtain on the litter's opposite side.

"Excuse me, Prioress," Sutso said pulling the curtain closed. "I did not mean to intrude. Excuse me."

The dry voice filtered through the curtain. "How far to the river, child?"

"Perhaps seven rih, Prioress," the senior nun's secretary answered. "This creek is quite narrow and not straight. We will be some time,"

"It is a day to be enjoyed, Sister Sutso. A shame the trees have lost their blossoms, but the new leaves are beautiful, are they not?" Before Sutso could agree, the Prioress went on. "Have you heard the most recent news?"

Sutso shook her head. The Prioress took delight in surprising her and usually succeeded. "I have not, Prioress."

"He arrived in Yankura, three days ago; the Brotherhood's Supreme Master. We cannot tarry. Are Sister Gatsa and her companions content with our pilgrimage?"

"They speak of little else, Prioress." The faction lead by Sister Gatsa had been told that the Prioress was on a pilgrimage to Monarta. The fact that the Prioress had sent a message to the Brotherhood demanding that they open the grounds to the Sisters had caused a hum of discussion—so much so in fact that no one had yet thought to wonder if Monarta was their true destination.

The Prioress did not speak for a moment, but Sutso was used to this and waited. One could never be sure when the Prioress slept and when she was awake.

"War could sweep away the prize for which we have lived all these lives. That fool of an Emperor has gone off with his toy army?"

"He has, Prioress."

"May the hand of Botahara guide us. Pray for fair winds, Sutso-sum, the currents are against us."

The officer was awakened in the night and found he was dizzy and disoriented when he sat up. Imperial Guards, he seemed to remember gambling and Imperial Guards . . . and rice wine. His men—the men Lord Butto had left at the northern end of Denji Gorge to be certain the locks were filled—were billeted in the Imperial Guard Keep. Not perhaps the best idea.

"Captain?" The voice came from outside the door to his tiny room.

"What is it?" he said, unable to sound civil.

"Barbarians, Captain. Many barbarians—they are only two rih off."

The officer was on his feet. "Botahara save us! Alert the Imperial Guards."

"The Guards will muster immediately, Captain. Your armor is being readied. I have a lamp."

The Captain opened his door a crack and a lamp was passed in. He began pulling on the clothing that would go under his armor. "What hour?"

"The owl, Captain."

"Huh. And we hoped these barbarians did not even know of Denji Gorge."

A clatter in the hall announced the arrival of his armour, and he threw open the door to his attendants. He could hear men shouting now, the sound of men running.

It could not be a large barbarian force, or Lord Shonto's patrols would have known of it, he reasoned. They would not allow functioning locks to fall into barbarian hands, of that he was certain.

* * *

Shimeko had taken up chanting again, not because she had found her faith but because the chant was like a curtain between one's heart and the world. The smell of smoldering maji was thick in the converted hold of the ship. Maji cleansed the air and inhibited the spread of disease, but it stung the eyes despite its health-giving properties. She lifted the head of a young man and fed him his drug cake a small piece at a time. He was the only soldier on board, a cavalry man in Lord Shonto's army.

"You must make the effort to chew, Inara-sum," Shimeko chided him. "Come, just a little."

The young man made a tiny nod and moved his jaw in a feeble effort. He was racked by the cough that marked the disease then, and Shimeko had to wait some time for him to recover enough to take a sip of water and then she fed him another piece of drug cake—the Brothers' great secret.

"That is better, Inara-sum. You will be well before you know it if you make an effort."

He shook his head a little. "You would be less concerned, honored Sister," he whispered hoarsely, "if you had seen the army that pursues us."

"I do not want to hear this talk. All of your focus must be given to becoming well. Let Lord Shonto and his able staff worry about barbarian armies. You fight your own battle."

The young man nodded weakly.

Most of the sick were slowly recovering, but this boy-man was getting weaker and this concerned the former nun greatly. Of all the patients on the ship this man was without doubt the most devout follower of Botahara and he was the only one who did not seem to respond to the Brother's ministrations. It was as if he was resisting the treatment in some way.

Shimeko was chilled by the conversations she had overheard between this young man and the Brothers—talk of completion and rebirth. This obsession with the size of the barbarian army also unsettled her. It had obviously had a great impact on his young mind. *He is choosing to die,* Shimeko thought. Her recent crisis of faith made this realization extremely disturbing.

Completing her rounds, Shimeko bowed to Brother So-tura and made her way up to the deck. It was a dark night, thin clouds covering the stars. She took many lungfuls of the clear air and walked to the rail, leaning over it and staring down into the black water. They were back in the canal now, south of Denji Gorge. The fleet proceeded at a faster pace, for the canal was almost free of the boats of the refugees which had been detained in Denji Gorge until Shonto's fleet passed.

The evening was warm, full of the scents of spring, the sounds. Had she heard a nightingale earlier?

"Do you fare well, Shimeko-sum?" a whisper came to her out of the dark. A woman's voice.

The quiet swirl of an oar in the water. There in the dark, the shape of a boat and someone sitting to paired oars.

"Morima-sum?"

"Yes. I have come to be sure these fool monks have not let you become ill."

Shimeko had to stay absolutely still to hear—even the noise of her robe moving would mask the words. "I remain well, but you should not come so close, Sister. It is unwise."

Shimeko was not sure if she heard a chuckle or if it was merely the bubble of oars in the water. "You have left your Teacher to come serve the sick, Shimeko-sum, or perhaps it was his bidding?"

The younger woman felt herself relax a little in resignation. It was as Morima said, they would never let her be.

"What is it you wish to know, Morima-sum?"

The sound of oars, unmistakable this time.

"I wish to know what is truth and what is merely a fabric of lies, Aco . . . Shimeko-sum. But the Sisters have other concerns. They wish to know if this young monk is the one so many await. Recently rumors have been whispered—Lady Nishima . . . she is an attractive woman." A pause. "You were her secretary, Shimeko-sum."

The former nun resisted the urge to hang her head in her hands. She shook her head in the darkness. *A woman's cry of ecstasy. . . .*

"Shimeko-sum?"

She said nothing. The swirl of oars holding a boat in position. Again. And yet again.

"May you find tranquillity of purpose, my young seeker," the voice whispered and the dark form disappeared into the shadow of the canal bank.

Fifty-one

The river boats of Shonto's fleet passed slowly by on the constant east wind and on almost every craft warriors lined the rail, bowing low to their liege-lord. Shonto sat on a wooden dock under a blue silk awning and though his retainers bowed as they passed, the lord was hidden from sight behind screens of bamboo and Shonto banners.

Aboard the passing ships there was an uncommon silence, almost funereal in its pervasiveness and emotional weight. News had spread very quickly.

Kneeling before Shonto were the lord's senior advisors, several ranking officers, and sundry allies. Dressed in robes of blue over which he wore a surcoat in the same colour bearing only the shinta blossom in a circle, Shonto was an imposing figure. A powerful man in more than just position.

As was the lord's custom, he allowed the silence to last longer than one would expect, like a Botahist Master who gave his students time to attain the proper state of tranquillity so that they would be better prepared to learn. The lord's retainers were used to this and all others present remained respectfully quiet and still.

"General Hojo," Shonto said at last, "could you explain the situation."

The senior general bowed and composed himself before addressing the council. "It was artfully done, Sire. Our own patrols monitored the progress of the small barbarian army which made its way down the canal and the western bank, but the companies that took the locks at Denji Gorge were from the main barbarian force and made their way secretly through the country east of the canal."

Hojo paused to collect his thoughts. "The locks were

to be filled in with stone by workers from Lord Butto's fief and this task was to be watched over by Imperial Guards and Butto House Guards. The attacking barbarian forces were large and unexpected. We do not know details, but the locks and positions of defense at either end of the gorge are in barbarian hands; losses are unknown. This gives the Khan access to large numbers of river craft, for many of the refugees had not yet locked out of the gorge. We expect the small barbarian army to increase its speed as a result.''

The banners fluttered in a small gust and conversation waited until this noise stopped. Both Jaku Katta and Lord Butto sat calmly, showing no sign that it had been their troops guarding the locks. Shonto sat quietly for a moment, watching a hawk soar high over the canal.

"It appears that we have few courses left open to us. If we turn and fight the small army pursuing us, even were we to win, our own force would be reduced substantially. Yet if we continue south, we must meet the Imperial Army. Commanded by whom?'' Obviously the lord was thinking aloud and no one attempted to answer.

Shonto put his fingertips together, staring at nothing. "No matter who commands the Emperor's forces, I would prefer to meet them with an army at my back rather than as a ragtag company of survivors." He turned to Jaku Katta. "General Jaku, who do you imagine will command the Emperor's army?''

Jaku bowed and returned to a sitting position, hands on his thighs. "There are several generals who served the Yamaku in the Interim Wars who could be called from retirement, Lord Shonto. At least three are worthy commanders and still young enough to wage such a campaign, but none of these are favored by the Emperor. My own brother, Tadamoto-sum, is the acting commander of the Guard, but he has no experience in warfare. I have given this much thought, Sire, and I believe that the Emperor will act as his own commander of forces. The Son of Heaven trusts few and of the few he trusts he doubts their abilities.'' Jaku bowed again.

Shonto nodded. "Huh. I have allowed myself to hope that the commander of the Imperial Army might be convinced to betray his Emperor. . . . Difficult, yeh?'' Shonto shrugged. "I believe we must go on. Somehow the armies must be joined or the barbarians cannot be defeated. The armies cannot stand alone, no matter what the cost." Looking around the gathering, Shonto said, "I will hear other opinions of this matter."

Lord Komawara bowed. "If the barbarians are to be defeated, I agree, Sire. Our army must be kept whole until we meet the Emperor's force. The Son of Heaven must realize what we face. He will certainly fall without our support. All possibilities will be open for discussion then."

Shonto nodded to the young lord. The fact that Komawara had actually spoken first was not lost on the others.

"It is impossible to know what will happen when we meet the Emperor, if indeed it is the Emperor, Sire," Kamu said. "I would prefer not to leave a matter of such import so open to the whims of fate and situation. Can we not approach the Emperor now? If he realizes he will lose his throne without our support, as Lord Komawara has said, the Emperor should welcome discussion."

"I agree with Steward Kamu, Lord Shonto," Lord Butto said. "We should not wait to begin discussions with the Son of Heaven. We are in a position of power—the Emperor cannot continue to sit on his throne without our help."

Jaku Katta shook his head. "Excuse me for saying so, but I have had quiet contact with the Palace. The Emperor believes the entire barbarian army is represented by the mere fraction—the small army—that pursues us. The Son of Heaven will not be willing to listen until he realizes the true peril. To approach the Palace now would be to no avail."

General Hojo stroked his beard as he did when lost in thought. His bow was barely perfunctory, though no one appeared to notice. "The suggestion that Prince Wakaro approach his father comes to mind again. Perhaps the Prince could be an envoy in his father's court."

Shonto frowned. "I suspect that having received no response from the Emperor to his letters has led the Prince to reconsider his offer. Even a son of the Emperor can lose favor at court. Certainly we could send the Prince to the Capital, but I believe it would be a course of futility. The Prince may serve a purpose among us yet. We should keep him close.

"It is only a matter of days until we arrive in the Capital. If we are to have another course, we must decide now. Consider this. Our enemy is showing himself more resourceful than we had previously thought possible. After the clumsy attack on Rhojo-ma I did not consider him a general of note. But now. . . . This barbarian chieftain has stopped our destruction of crops which will allow him to feed his army, and he has seized the locks at Denji Gorge from formidable warriors. As Soto wrote: we cannot rely on this Khan to make a mistake. If we do not raise a force of sufficient size to challenge this desert army, then retreat may be our only recourse. It is not beyond question that we would allow this Khan to take the Imperial Capital—and then he will sit upon the throne he so desires."

Fifty-two

The boat that bore the Emperor to war had sails of crimson silk, a hull ornate with carvings and gilt, a dragon's head on its prow, and sixty men to man the oars should the Son of Heaven lose the favor of the Wind Goddess. On the decks beautiful women played music while other women of equal beauty danced, their long sleeves swaying with the intricate movements of their hands. The Emperor did not go to war as did other men.

Tadamoto waited at the dock that had been prepared for the Emperor's arrival. Banners rustled in the wind, and guards knelt in curving rows forming the shape of a dragon fan. The petals of fresh flowers had been strewn across new mats laid out on the dock, and a guard stood at the end of this fragrant path holding a gray stallion of famous lineage.

An Emperor who rode a horse rather than a sedan chair, who led his own army, turned his back on the religion of Botahara, and in whose hand a sword was more than a sign of office. Tadamoto shook his head—he served an Emperor who would go down in history as defying the pattern, there was no doubt.

Shonto's army was only days away, certainly less than seven, moving by both day and night and reportedly burning any craft that hindered its progress. With the rebel lord's army came Tadamoto's elder brother and this must lead to a reckoning that the young colonel could not think about with ease. Tadamoto had begun to sleep poorly and felt the effects of this more each day.

A sudden strengthening of the wind caused the Emperor's boat to heel slightly and pick up speed, a white wave appearing at the bow as though the dragon on the prow rode forward on a cloud. Willow trees billowed in the breeze, hissing like angry old women waving their arms at truant children.

Straining to overcome the distance, Tadamoto searched the deck of the Emperor's boat for a familiar form—seeking among the flowing silk robes of the dancers, among those who watched. He could not find her there and he was both disappointed and relieved. If Osha was in the Emperor's retinue, then there would be a chance for her and Tadamoto to speak—with the first battle just over the horizon he would welcome such an opportunity—but he neither wanted her in danger nor in the Emperor's company.

With sails dropping and sailors swarming to smother them, the boat fetched the dock just as she lost all way, as perfectly executed as one could imagine. Like everyone within sight, Tadamoto bowed his head to the ground. The Emperor showed no sign of disembarking, however, at least not until the melody and dance was complete. All waited.

At last the performance ended and the Emperor rose and made his way among the bowing retainers to the stairs. As he stepped onto the dock, the Emperor spoke Tadamoto's name and gestured for the colonel to walk with him.

"Shonto's army has reached Chin-ja?"

Tadamoto nodded. "It has, Emperor. They progress at speed."

"And this rumor is unquestionably true, then?"

Tadamoto lowered his voice. "The Prince's banner flies beside the shinta blossom." Saying this he cast the briefest glance over his shoulder at the women on the Emperor's boat.

"We both have known betrayal, Tadamoto-sum. It is a great sadness." They walked a few steps further, the Emperor lost in thought. "You will be the new Commander of my Guard, Colonel Jaku," the Emperor said suddenly. "May you erase the shame your brother has brought to your name."

Tadamoto bowed. "I shall strive to be worthy of this honor, Sire."

"See that you do." They approached the guard holding the Emperor's horse. "Ride with me, Colonel, I wish to inspect our defenses."

Fifty-three

After days of haste Lord Shonto's flotilla lay against the bank, only the current moving the hulls, causing them to tug lightly on their lines. The lengthening day had worn on to dusk, the sun setting behind the western mountains—the colors of an autumn hillside washed into the sky.

Shonto and Nishima walked along the bank, followed at a discreet distance by guards. In the near distance other men in Shonto blue had established a perimeter, keeping the refugees and the curious at bay.

"Are you concerned about the safety of Master Myochin, Uncle?" Nishima asked. Lord Shonto seemed withdrawn, quieter than usual. He had sent a party to the home of his former gii Master, who lived nearby, and they had returned without the old man. Myochin Ekun the legendary master of the board, blind from birth yet six times champion of Wa.

Shonto waved to the small creek mouth that opened across the canal. "I have left guards and archers in the woods. Eku-sum's home is difficult to find. There is no path to lead one there and the barbarians keep most of their force on the canal's opposite side. If there is trouble, my guards will hide Master Myochin in the hills." Shonto shook his head. "He would not leave his home, saying he has nothing even the poorest barbarian would desire. He is getting very old. In a note Eku-sum had a servant write, he suggested that I would soon have an opportunity to perform a move no gii player could ever choose—I could sacrifice an Emperor." Shonto smiled. "He will never cease to offer me lessons."

They walked a little farther along the bank, saying little.

"Do you not find this strange that they would suddenly

give up the chase?'' Nishima asked. It was the subject
on everyone's mind. The small army had ceased to pursue Shonto's flotilla.

''Perhaps, but they are not really such a large force
and we draw near the Capital. If a large Imperial army
suddenly appeared, the small army would be at risk.
Twenty-five thousand is almost a third of the Khan's army.
He is wise not to risk them. It is also true that they have
accomplished their main purpose: in the wake of the
small army crops are growing which will allow the Khan
to feed his entire army very soon.''

Nishima nodded. ''So we have stopped to rest our
forces.''

Shonto nodded. ''That, and for other reasons. The
Emperor has moved north of the Capital with his army.
If we were to meet that force before the Emperor has
seen the true size of the desert army, the Son of Heaven
may be led to foolish actions. We cannot allow a battle
between ourselves and the Emperor. As it stands, our
combined force is likely less than the Khan's. I will risk
no more men.''

They came to a stand of plum trees, the canal bank
almost white with decaying petals. The leaves were
quickly reaching their mature size, opening like blossoms. Long shadows stretched out onto the surface of the
canal and in the warm light the water took on the color
of burnished copper. The thinnest sliver of a crescent
moon floated overhead.

Coming to a tree trunk that curved out almost hori-
zontally over the water, Shonto stopped and leaned
against it. Nishima circled its base and leaned against the
opposite side beside her uncle. They stayed like that, side
by side facing opposite directions, without speaking for
some minutes.

Shonto reached down and plucked a new strand of
grass and twirled it distractedly. ''We will be forced south
again within days. The large barbarian army moves more
quickly now that they have true river craft and river men
to sail them. Once we meet the Emperor's force, I cannot
predict what will happen. Any agreement we make with
the Emperor at that time will be illusory, only respected
as long as there is the common threat of this Khan and
his army. If we defeat the Khan, Akantsu will turn on us

if he is able." Shonto wound the blade of grass around his finger like a ring. "The Emperor is not a man whose actions can easily be foreseen. He may retreat once he sees the barbarian army in its true strength; it is impossible to say. I must tell you now that the safety of the Empire will take precedence over the interests of the Shonto House." The lord fell silent for a moment. A soft breeze rustled the leaves of the plum grove.

"If the worst befalls us, it is my plan to retreat into the mountains. You should know this—one cannot predict who will survive a battle."

Nishima took a long breath. "If we must run, why to the mountains? Ika Cho would seem to offer better possibilities for raising an army? The mountains are not hospitable to those not born there."

"The Emperor holds Ika Cho and Shokan-sum has fled. I have reason to believe we would find friends in the mountains."

Nishima looked up at her uncle's face. He would always surprise her—friends in the mountains? She wanted to ask but knew that if he had wanted her to know more he would have continued.

"I had thought you bore the news of Shokan-sum's retreat into the pass with great poise. Is there hope for him, then?"

Shonto nodded. "I know nothing for certain, but his situation is certainly no worse than our own." The lord tossed the blade of grass like a dart and it was swept away on the breeze. "In the coming battle the forces of Wa will lose if there are factions holding back, hoping to save their troops to win a civil war after the barbarians are vanquished. The army of the desert is too large. We can only hope to meet it with total commitment and intelligent selection of the battle ground. If you are forced to go into the mountains, do not become separated from Shuyun-sum. He will be as valuable as a thousand guards. Do not forget. The Shonto have fled the Empire before and lived in the wilds. If Botahara smiles upon us, Shokan-sum will not find his way through the mountains before this war is decided. Let the Yamaku know that the Shonto are beyond their reach, waiting."

Nishima laid her hand on Shonto's arm. "Uncle, I do not doubt your wisdom, but neither do I doubt the wis-

dom of the people of Wa. They will not allow the Yamaku to call themselves Emperors after this war, no matter what the outcome.''

. Placing his hand over his daughter's, Shonto squeezed.
''I hope you are correct, Nishi-sum. May the people of
Wa not disappoint you.''

The last trace of sunset disappeared before Shimeko's
eyes, but the sky retained a hint of the darkest blue among
the myriad stars and the crescent moon. The young
woman leaned against the rigging of the plague ship,
forcing an appearance of calm over herself. Although Botahist monks were notoriously observant, she hoped they
would not notice her despair. The fact that, commonly,
she was almost entirely ignored by them would no doubt
work in her favor.

A short distance down the bank the last embers of a
funeral pyre were glowing like the molten colors of the
sunset. Inara-sum, the young Shonto soldier, had attained completion. Death, the former nun realized,
should hardly shake her as it did. As a devout follower
of the Way, the young man could only look forward to
returning a step closer to Perfection. Yet. . . . Shimeko
did not feel the conviction necessary to keep grief at bay.

The growing belief that Inara's funeral had been seen
as a celebration by the Brothers caused a constriction
inside her. The young man's death was somehow regarded as a triumph. The Brothers' attitude was frightening to her, seemed almost monstrous. *They had
celebrated his death because he believed with such conviction,* she realized. And this war would bring death to
thousands of Botahara's followers. Would the Brothers
celebrate that?

News was traveling quickly now—news of the atroci-
ties committed by the invaders. She had been watching
the faces of the refugees as they passed, frightened, unable to believe what was occurring. The faces had begun
to haunt her dreams.

With an effort Shimeko forced a calm over her mind
and focused on her situation.

The plague ship was moored to trees and held close to
the canal bank. No other ships lay within a half rih of it
and the long lines of refugees gave the ship flying the

plague banner a wide berth. Turning as casually as she was able, Shimeko surveyed the deck. Other than the single man guarding the gangway, only sleeping river men could be seen.

In one graceful motion Shimeko slipped over the side, lowering herself easily into the water which rose to mid-thigh. Two quiet steps brought her to the bank and several more put her among the trees. She stopped then to be sure there was no sudden movement on board ship, no sign that she had been observed, but there was nothing.

I will not be missed now until morning, she thought, and by then I will be far to the north—and on my way from all the things that cause my turmoil. May Botahara forgive me.

Fifty-four

The Plum Blossom Winds gave way to the fitful breezes of late spring and the nights and mornings saw the occasional fog from cold air descending the mountainsides into the lowlands after the sun set. Although this mist slowed the flotilla that bore Lord Shonto south, the barbarian army suffered the same, putting off the inevitable day of battle—though only briefly.

A day's march north of the Imperial Army's position, Shonto landed his force and spent several days engaged in the final preparations for battle. Reconnaissance parties were sent both north and south to gather information about both hostile armies and a constant stream of riders came and went bearing reports and orders.

The main body of the army of the desert had rejoined the smaller force and they continued their push into the inner provinces. Skirmishes between barbarian patrols and the companies Shonto sent north became more and more frequent as the armies vied to control the lands that lay between them.

Accompanied by General Hojo, Lord Taiki, and Prince Wakaro, Shonto rode among the troops, speaking to the various company commanders, making his presence known. An army caught between two enemy forces needed the reassurance of a confident commander and, in this capacity, Lord Shonto lifted spirits wherever he passed.

The army itself was a patchwork affair made up of the well-armed and trained retainers of various lords, Imperial Guards, and the recruits who had arrived with every variety of weapon and armor—many of them looking like patchwork themselves.

Horses were being exercised and fed on green pasture, many a man squared off against another with swords, and archers loosed their arrows on makeshift targets. More than one wager had been laid on these various contests and officers were alert to see that no disputes erupted into real violence—with men from all regions of the Empire such things were not unknown. Despite the activity in the encampment there was also an air of something being amiss—laughter that was too loud, many a young man deliberately alone with his thoughts, men looking suddenly embarrassed when Shonto approached as though the lord might read what was in their minds by the looks on their faces.

Prince Wakaro turned to Lord Shonto as they rode. "I can't help but wonder about these men, Lord Shonto." He tugged at a braid in his horse's mane. "Are they afraid? I myself cannot find words to describe what I feel. I don't even know if it is fear."

Shonto stroked the neck of his mount with a leather gloved hand. "Anticipation of a battle wears away at men, Prince, until they reach a point where they want a decision to be made: either they will live or die, but they will stand no more of this existence, suspended somewhere between life and death. At a certain point battle comes as a relief."

The Prince looked up at Lord Shonto who surveyed the army with an experienced eye. He was coming to respect this man whom his father considered the Yamaku's greatest enemy, and this he found unsettling.

Shonto waved his hand to encompass the entire encampment. "Your opinion, Lord Taiki."

Taiki brought his horse up and looked slowly around. "It is an army, Lord Shonto. There have been better and there have been far worse. Battle experience is lacking among the young, and I do not know that we will have more than one battle in which to gain this. The other armies, I'm sure, suffer from this same weakness," he hurried to add. "The barbarians, however, fight in a land that is so different from their own that I cannot believe this does not unsettle them. Retreat must also look daunting, should they fail in their purpose. Such factors must be weighed in a battle."

"I agree, Lord Taiki. Numbers are not the only measure of an army."

Three riders in blue came at a gallop through the encampment. As they approached, Shonto recognized Rohku Saicha followed by Shonto House Guards. They pulled up before Lord Shonto and dismounted to bow low before the Imperial Prince and their liege-lord.

"Captain Rohku?" Shonto said, nodding to his retainer.

"There is a party from the Emperor approaching, Sire, under a flag of truce." He pointed south. "They come by fast boat."

"Send for General Hojo, Kamu, and Brother Shuyun. We will ride to meet them. Prince, Lord Taiki, will you meet the Emperor's emissary with me?"

The two men nodded though Shonto thought the Prince showed a tightening around the jaw that had not appeared even during discussions of the coming battle.

The three set off at a canter, followed by their guards. Men in the encampment bowed low as the Prince and Lord Shonto passed and stared after them as they went. Rumor went quickly through the encampment. *The Emperor has sent his minions to bargain with Lord Shonto.* Did this mean there was hope of an alliance?

Just south of the encampment a decked boat that boasted thirty oarsmen swung to an anchor in the middle of the canal. Off its stern the Emperor's banner fluttered in the breeze as did the banner of a senior official and the green flag of truce. Beneath a plum tree, mats had been spread, and it appeared that men had chosen this spot to drink wine and perhaps compose a poem-sequence, for there was no armor worn but by the guards standing at a distance. Those who knelt upon the mats drank from wine bowls and laughed cheerfully.

"Lord Shinzei," Prince Wakaro said quietly to Shonto. "The Emperor's favorite talking bird."

Shonto pulled his horse up and dismounted. Several more Shonto guards had joined them and others had taken up positions close by and stood with hands on their swords.

Rohku Saicha rode up in haste. "Lord Shonto, General Hojo comes now. Kamu is across the canal and Brother Shuyun has been called to the plague ship."

Shonto nodded. "We will do without them, then." Shonto turned and saw men riding toward him at a gallop. "General Hojo is here." Then turning to the Emperor's son, "Prince Wakaro, does this talking bird have power to speak for the Emperor?"

"I would be shocked if that were so. No, this will be an offer from the Emperor. Shinzei will have no power to negotiate. He is but the first move of the game and, as is common, the most expendable piece. Though I doubt he will realize this."

Hojo rode up and dismounted bowing quickly.

"General Hojo," Shonto said, "please approach the Emperor's emissaries and ask them the purpose of their embassy. Or perhaps they have come merely to enjoy the fine day and the view?"

Hojo bowed quickly and set off toward Lord Shinzei and his party.

A moment later he returned. "They will speak to Lord Shonto only, Sire. They do not have concerns about who accompanies you."

Shonto nodded. "And they expect the Prince and me to attend them?" Shonto cast a glance over his shoulder. What happened here would be known by everyone in his army within the hour. What fools did the Emperor send that they would allow such a situation to develop?

Shonto looked back at the Emperor's men and shook his head. "Take them prisoner, bind them, and bring them to my boat." He mounted his horse abruptly, leaving the Prince and Lord Taiki hurrying to follow. They rode off at a canter toward the boats that carried Shonto's family and senior advisors. Much of the activity of the camp had come to a halt and men tried not to be seen watching.

Shonto's own boat was protected by a bamboo fence forming a large open space on the canal's eastern bank. Riding past the sentries, Shonto dismounted and left his horse to a guard. He stormed up the gangway of his boat, throwing gloves and surcoat at a servant. Mounting the stairs to the upper deck, he took up a position under the awning on the stern.

Kamu appeared suddenly. "Sire, excuse me, my attentions were drawn elsewhere . . ."

Shonto waved a hand to cut the old man off. "That guard who is a kick boxer—is he still in our service?"

"He is, Lord Shonto."

"Bring him to me." Shonto turned to Lord Taiki and

Prince Wakaro as they came up onto the deck looking unsure if they should have followed. "Please, join me." Shonto said pleasantly. He gestured to cushions. The two men took the offered positions and an awkward silence ensued.

They did not have long to wait, for Hojo appeared with his charges moments later. A boat ran up on the canal bank and the bound men were assisted onto the land with some degree of concern for their dignity.

Kamu appeared with a young guard and Shonto nodded to have the man brought forward, speaking to him privately and demonstrating several hand signals. "Turn Lord Shinzei over to this guard," Shonto said to Kamu.

The Emperor's emissaries padded up the stairs then and guards requested that they kneel. Shonto sat regarding them for a moment.

"We come under a flag of truce—emissaries of the Son of Heaven. Be certain that this will not be forgotten, Lord Shonto." Shinzei spoke Shonto's name with as much disdain as he could muster.

Shonto gave a hand signal to the young guard who spun quickly and kicked Shinzei in the diaphragm, doubling him over on the deck.

When the lord's struggle to breathe had begun to subside, Shonto nodded and the man was pulled roughly back to a kneeling position. His voice perfectly calm and pleasant, Shonto addressed Lord Shinzei. "Perhaps you can relate the purpose of your visit, Lord Shinzei. Or was this merely an outing to drink wine and enjoy the fine spring weather?"

Shinzei visibly collected himself, trying to gain control of his breathing. "The Emperor of Wa has sent me to demand the immediate surrender of Prince Wakaro, Jaku Katta, Lord Shonto, and all senior advisors and officers of the same."

Shonto waited for a moment and then signaled the young guard who again doubled the kneeling aristocrat over on the deck. His recovery this time was lengthy, the others in his party staring down at the deck, afraid to move. At last, the emissary was set back on his knees, managing not to collapse.

"My liege-lord," Kamu explained quietly, "is addressed as Lord Shonto or Sire, Lord Shinzei."

Shinzei nodded, unable to hide the pain he felt or to maintain his dignity in such a situation. As a favorite of the Emperor he encountered nothing but deference in all of his dealings.

"Lord Shinzei," Shonto began again, his voice remaining calm. "I am well informed on the size and state of the Emperor's army. It is no larger, and certainly less experienced, than my own. You cannot afford arrogance. Not two days north on the canal a barbarian army that, despite our efforts, numbers eighty-five thousand men is moving toward the Imperial Capital. In my estimate, their chieftain is four, perhaps five days away from the throne he seeks—your lord's throne, Lord Shinzei. Already it grows late for the alliance that we require."

Shonto looked at the man kneeling before him and shook his head. "Take this message to your Emperor. If he will provide written pardons for myself, my family, and all who support me, I will consent to join forces with him to face the barbarian threat. If the Emperor will not agree to this, I will allow him to face the barbarian army alone. It is a simple choice—to retain his throne or to be overthrown, perhaps it is a choice between life and death. Be very clear when you explain this point to Akantsu, Lord Shinzei—it is important that he understands his position."

Shonto nodded to Hojo who signaled the guards to take the Emperor's men away. "General," Shonto said to Hojo as the captives were led down the stairs, "put them on horses with their hands bound behind them and trot them through the camp on the return to their boat. Then throw them on the ground before their fine ship and leave them to be unbound by their own guard. Show them not a single sign of respect."

Hojo bowed and hurried off.

Shonto signaled for cha and once it arrived, his spirits lifted noticeably.

"Excuse me for saying so, Lord Shonto," Prince Wakaro said in a soothing voice, "but this will infuriate the Emperor."

Shonto smiled. "But it will lift the morale of our own army to the very skies. We would only dare treat the Emperor's advisors this way if there was no doubt of the outcome of the battle. It will give your father cause to

think also, Prince. The next battle we fight will not require swords—it will be a battle of wills and I have answered his opening with a message which says the Shonto
have nothing to lose, while the Emperor has everything.''

The army of Shonto Motoru moved south as soon as
the fog lifted the morning after Lord Shinzei had paid
his visit. The bulk of the army went by land though some
ships were still in use and these paced the army as it
went. Open fields bordered the canal in this area and
stretched east to foothills and west toward distant mountains, jagged against the horizon.

Many of the ''rebel army'' rode horses, though companies of foot soldiers marched among the mounted
troops. Despite the patchwork nature of this force, Shonto's officers and the officers of his allies had marshaled it
into a tight formation, better to impress the watching
patrols of the Emperor.

Shuyun stood beside his liege-lord at the rail of a river
craft. Before his arrival in Wa, he had never seen an army
and he found the sight both impressive and very sad. In
the next few days many of the men before him would die.
The words of Brother Hitara came back to him; *"War
brings no soul to perfection."* My Order has bound me
to serve this man and now I am at war also—a follower
of Botahara, Shuyun thought, a poor follower.

Something the monk had never anticipated was the
sound of men going to war. There was silence in the
ranks, but the sounds of men and beasts tramping over
the land was ominous, disturbing, like the pulse of a
dying man—the strength of its rhythm came from fear.
Unspoken fear.

''There are no reports of a new outbreak of the disease?'' Shonto asked Shuyun.

The two men stood at the rail of Shonto's ship watching the army as it moved.

Shuyun shook his head. ''I have sent men out among
the refugees and to the villages. The plague seems to be
under control. We have had only one report of a woman
of Shimeko-sum's description, but this was not certain
and whoever it was made an effort to avoid contact with
others.''

"Huh." Shonto tried to turn the hemp shroud, the muscles in his forearm bunching into knots. "Nishima-sum told me this young woman was a person of education and intelligence but caught in a crisis of the spirit."

Shuyun nodded. "I believe Lady Nishima was correct, Sire."

"Perhaps she seeks a monastery or wishes to live the life of a hermit."

"Perhaps." Shuyun seemed lost in thought. The dull pounding of the army on the land kept calling his attention. "She seeks escape, I believe, Sire."

Shonto let go of the shroud and shaded his eyes against the sun, staring off toward the south. The Emperor's position would not become visible until the next day at the earliest, but it was common to see people standing with their gaze focused on the horizon as though meditating upon a distant point.

"It is a fine balance we must achieve, Brother," Shonto said suddenly. "If we meet the Emperor's force before the barbarian army is seen for its true size, then we risk the Emperor making a foolish mistake. If we do not arrive at the Imperial Army's position soon, we will not have time to join the two armies into an effective force. Once we have committed a piece, we cannot retrieve it. There can be no mistakes."

"May Botahara guide us, Lord Shonto." Shuyun had watched his lord carefully since he had come into his service and though it could be said that Shonto always kept much to himself, Shuyun was noticing a change. The lord often shared information that was not truly necessary for others to know, yet at the same time the monk was convinced there was some knowledge that Shonto was keeping entirely to himself. If asked, Shuyun could not have explained why he felt this.

"Once we reach the Emperor's position, I will move the members of my household to the northeast of the probable battlefield. When battle has been engaged, you will join Lady Nishima. Be prepared to run toward the mountains, Shuyun-sum. Leave everyone else behind if they cannot keep your pace." Shonto turned to regard his Spiritual Advisor. "If the Shonto army falls and I cannot escape, Lady Nishima must be protected at all costs. I charge you with this, Brother Shuyun. Do not fail.''

Shuyun gave a half bow in response. ''Perhaps Lady Nishima should be closer to the mountains now?''

Shonto shook his head. ''There is danger whichever course we choose, Shuyun-sum.'' The lord shrugged. ''Perhaps it is the selfish path, but I wish to keep Nishima-sum close for now.''

The river men dropped the sail behind Shonto and Shuyun as the breeze had come up and was moving the ship ahead of the marching army.

Shonto waved a hand out toward the patch of dark blue uniforms among the men on horseback. Shuyun could see Shonto pull his focus away from the knowledge he was hiding. ''I am concerned about Lord Butto and these Hajiwara men in Lord Komawara's guard. Lord Butto has not spoken of it, but certainly it must weigh upon him.''

Shuyun leaned out over the rail looking down into the water. ''I have considered this matter also. Lord Komawara believes that their sworn oath binds these Hajiwara men and that all of my lord's allies are safe from any plans for vengeance. Perhaps that is true, but men have been known to word their oaths in ways that are understood to mean different things to different people. I would keep the Butto and the Komawara companies separate on any battlefield.''

''Huh.'' Shonto shook his head. ''Within our own ranks to have such concerns. . . .'' He left the thought unfinished.

Fifty-five

Fog persisted in the morning so it was not until the sun was high that Lord Shonto was able to move his army south again. Even after the fog had cleared, the sky was covered with a high, thin mist that filtered a weakened sunlight down to the earth.

Several of Shonto's advisors had voiced the concern that the Emperor might move his army north under cover of darkness and surprise Shonto's force in the morning when the fog lifted, but this turned out to be a groundless fear. Patrols reported that the Emperor kept his army behind earthworks that had been dug into the side of hills on either side of the canal.

Shonto sat under an awning on the stern of his ship, giving no sign that he was only hours away from meeting his enemy. He pored over a scroll with great focus of attention; a secretary knelt in attendance and Kamu also waited at hand. Sitting only a few paces off, a servant played a quiet melody on the harp. Occasionally the lord would look up and give his attention to a passage of the tune and then, with a nod to the musician, return to his reading.

Finally Shonto rolled the scroll and set it aside. Reaching for a cup of cha, he sipped and found it cold and returned the cup to the table.

"It is an interesting position, don't you think?" Shonto said to his steward. With some care he unrolled a map and placed four jade paperweights, carved in the shape of the shinta blossom, on the corners. He waved a hand at the map and Kamu moved closer to look on.

"The Emperor has split his position to either side of the canal." The lord tapped the spot with his finger. "What is your opinion of that?"

Despite his age and apparent frailty Kamu had once

been both a swordsman of great reputation and a senior officer in the Shonto armies. Stewards of Great Houses seldom had such a depth of knowledge in military matters and Lord Shonto did not let this expertise go to waste.

"The Emperor must believe it is his function to stop an army from descending on the Capital, therefore he blocks the canal. In truth, I believe he could position his army anywhere and the Khan would not pass it by. This division of his forces . . ." Kamu shook his head. "The Emperor makes a foolish mistake. The bridge that connects them across the canal . . . it is too vulnerable to fire rafts."

Shonto nodded. "I suspect our Emperor has not blocked the canal to stop the barbarian advance but to stop our army from passing. No doubt the Son of Heaven would like to keep the Shonto between his own army and that of the Khan."

Shonto ran his finger up the line of the canal. "And I certainly do not wish to spoil the Emperor's view of the barbarian army." Moving his finger to a hill east and slightly north of the Emperor's position, the lord said. "We will concentrate our troops on this slope. The Khan will array his forces here—there is no other choice." Shonto traced an arc east from the canal north of the Emperor's position.

"That will form a triangle." Shonto said, tracing the three sides with each army being a point. "If the Khan is an intelligent man, he will not wait but will attack both positions at once—the barbarian army is large enough to do this. If the Khan waits, there is a possibility that Akantsu and I can reach an understanding. Once the Emperor sees the army of the desert with his own eyes it is my hope that he will be more willing to listen to our arguments. We shall see."

Shonto stared at the map for a moment more without speaking. "If the Emperor will join forces with us, Kamu-sum, we will have two choices. Fight the barbarian army with a force perhaps two-thirds its size, or retreat to the southeast. If we choose to retreat, we will see if you are correct. Will the lure of an undefended Capital be more than the Khan can resist? If so, there is a chance that we can raise an army large enough to be

sure of defeating the barbarians. A battle now is a difficult decision. Such a fight is likely to be inconclusive
and, at worst, could result in the annihilation of the armies of Wa. It is a great risk, Kamu-sum, a great risk
indeed.''

A guard approached, bowing and waiting to be acknowledged. Kamu gestured and the man came forward
to speak quietly to the steward. The old man nodded.

''Sire,'' he said turning back to his liege-lord, ''our
forward scouts can see the Emperor's position.''

Shonto nodded. ''I will take a fast boat. Have a horse
ready at our forward position. And I will speak with
General Hojo and our senior commanders.'' The lord
rose suddenly. ''Well, steward Kamu, the endgame is
always the most interesting, is it not?''

Late in the day Shonto's army came upon the plain that
lay before the Emperor's army. Patrols reported the barbarians only half a day behind now and the rear of the
Shonto columns were under constant observation from
barbarian patrols. Due to sheer numbers, the barbarians
had taken control of the shifting lands between the two
armies and they tracked the Shonto army as silently and
relentlessly as a predatory animal.

Shonto was still not in armor as he rode before his
army though he wore a sword in his sash—the sword the
Emperor had given to him. A group of concerned Shonto
guards stayed close by, eyes turned to the earthworks that
sheltered the Imperial Army.

''The Emperor will wait,'' Shonto said to his senior
advisors. ''He will not undertake to accomplish with
swords what he hopes can be done by words. It is good
to remember that he hates the Shonto because he fears
us.''

Shonto stood up in his stirrups, looked around the horizon, and then shook his head. ''Excuse me for saying
so, Prince Wakaro, but the Emperor is not the general
your grandfather was. His position is untenable.''

Wakaro gave an almost imperceptible shrug. He was
the only man in Shonto's party who wore full battle armor and he was no doubt suffering some embarrassment
at not demonstrating the acceptable bravado in the face
of the enemy. Having tied his helmet to his saddle, the

Prince's streak of white hair was at the mercy of the breeze and waved like an ominous flag. The Prince was struggling to maintain his Imperial dignity and this was made more difficult by his lack of skill with horses—appearing far worse than it was by proximity to the men of Seh; riders of the first order.

Shonto nodded to the hill upon which he proposed to establish his own army. "What is our assessment of that position?"

Lord Komawara spurred his horse forward three paces and bowed from the saddle. "Lord Toshaki and I have ridden and walked every section of the hill, Lord Shonto. It is not defendable from all directions due to the small size of our force, but it is a reasonable position in which to weather an attack form the west and north. It is certainly more defensible than the Emperor's earthworths," Komawara said with disdain. "The slope is steep at the base and rolls off to a series of benches halfway up the flank. The crest is thickly wooded. Considering this is not a battleground of our choosing, we could do much worse."

Shonto looked over at Hojo, who nodded agreement.

"We will secure that position and move our forces there in the dark," Shonto said. "Light fires to guide the way. Tomorrow we will witness the arrival of the barbarian army, and our Emperor shall have the same pleasure."

Shonto turned his horse to face his advisors. Lord Taiki and Butto Joda had become friends over the past days and sat on horses side by side. Jaku Katta, General Hojo, Lord Komawara, young Toshaki and Shuyun formed a loose group. Only the Prince and his captain rode apart—outsiders, Yamaku; of questionable loyalty.

"We will move our forces to the hill and then set a pavilion on the plain between the Emperor's position and our own. I will attempt to establish contact with the Emperor at the earliest possible moment." Shonto looked into the faces of the men before him. "In the history of Wa no foreign enemy has ever penetrated the inner provinces. It is impossible to separate the clouds that cover the future, but it is beyond doubt that a loss to the army of the desert would mean the loss of the Capital, if not the Empire. If the Khan is an intelligent general, he would pursue our army to the southern borders, for our army is the basis of all our hopes for the future. We do not know which action in the days to come will be a deciding action. We must never forget that anything we do could be the single act that changes the course of history. Do not lose courage, not for an instant. History will turn on the events of these next days and it will be shaped by each of us. Do not lose courage.''

Nishima lay awake long into the night. She had crossed the small plain that men were referring to as the ''battlefield'' in the dark and found the experience disturbing in the extreme. The fires illuminated rows of armed men who marked the way in the dark and fog—an eerie spectacle of yellow-red light reflecting off armor and weapons and faces distorted by the light and darkness.

As Lady Okara had insisted that she did not want a sedan chair, Nishima and Kitsura had gone on foot when Nishima would rather have ridden. Her experience with horses was limited, for ladies of breeding were not supposed to ride, but in the unsettled years after the Interim Wars Lord Shonto had thought it prudent that she master the basics of riding.

A large pavilion had been pitched on a ledge dug into the hillside, just inside the sheltering edge of the wood, and this had been divided with hangings into three rooms for the ladies from the Capital. Mats and rugs made it comfortable and lamps and a few other furnishings created an impression of order and security—all seeming a great sham to Nishima.

In an attempt to gain some sense of tranquility, Nishima had turned to the poetry of Lady Nikko.

Sky
Torn to rags and tatters.
Earth
A ruin of storm shattered trees.
The riches of summer have been scattered
To the four directions.
The first days of Autumn arrive
Like invading armies

Wisdom is more fragile
Than a young girl's love,
Lost between one generation and the next.
These boys drop stones into the village well
To break each morning's ice
Never asking, "How long until the well is filled?"

In Itsa peasants work the family fields
Season after season without rest
Until the soil bears nothing
But thistle and scrub

The moon drifts toward winter
Each night colder than the last,
Soon women will sell winter clothing
For a few sticks of firewood

From A Journey to Itsa
by Lady Nikko

Not precisely the reassurance Nishima was looking for. She set the scroll down.

Earlier it had been decided that Lady Okara would be taken south toward the Capital by Shonto guards who would shed their blue livery. Skirting the Emperor's army would be difficult, for he sent patrols out into the countryside, but there was no doubt in anyone's mind that Lady Okara's reputation would protect her from all but the barbarians. She was anxious to see her island home again and Lord Shonto was equally anxious to have the great painter out of harm's way.

Nishima knew the parting in the morning would be difficult. Oka-sum had risked so much for her, for so little return, Nishima felt. Poor Oka-sum, the young aristocrat thought, I tore her from her solitude and cast her into the center of a war that may see the fall of our Empire. May Botahara protect her.

The thin fabric of the tent seemed impossibly fragile to a woman who had spent most of her life surrounded by substantial walls, and the reality that pressed against this material was not the wild beauty of the world but the coarse brutality of men. She longed to have Shuyun come and lie beside her. It was not entirely a desire to be protected by someone stronger, for Nishima knew that wars could bring down even the mightiest, but a desire to comfort and be comforted in the face of the utter uncertainty of the world.

It was close to dawn before she managed to fall into a fitful sleep.

Fifty-six

S honto walked along the path that had been dug into the side of the hill, followed by his guards. The gray light of early morning had become the gray light of a foggy day. Reports from outriders indicated that this propensity for morning fog diminished only a few rih south, indicating that one did not have to stray far from the mountains to rid oneself of this weather.

Leave it to the Emperor to pick a battlefield commonly enshrouded in fog, Shonto thought. He had risen before first light and met with his advisors. After much discussion it had been decided that Prince Wakaro would bear an offer to his father, and though the Prince had gone off showing a brave face, Shonto did not expect him to return. Even if the Emperor answered Shonto's letter, the lord did not expect the bearer of the response to be Prince Wakaro. It is a sad family that cannibalizes its own, Shonto told himself, but Imperial families seemed to suffer this ill too commonly.

Though the fog muffled sound and played tricks on the ears, there was no doubt that an army moved upon the plain. The sounds of voices, the stamp and whinny of horses, the clanking of weapons and armor filtered up through the layers of mist to the men of Wa perched on their hillsides. This will open the Emperor's eyes, Shonto thought. I would give much to be standing beside him as the fog clears.

Guards in armor laced in the darkest blue appeared through the mist, bowing to Lord Shonto as he passed. A few paces later he came upon Lord Komawara staring out into the featureless gray.

"Can Komawara eyes part the mists?" Shonto asked.

Komawara turned and bowed low. His face lit with half a smile. "Komawara eyes fail this test as miserably as most others, Lord Shonto. But when I traveled in the desert with Brother Shuyun, he taught me not to rely on my eyes as other men do. I cannot claim to have attained the skill of the Botahist-trained in this, but I am learning. It seems to be a matter of focus."

Shonto stopped at the young lord's side and looked out into the mist as Komawara did. "What do your other senses tell you, Lord Komawara?"

Komawara listened for a few seconds before answering. "An army gathers on the plain, Sire, I have heard the pounding of mallets on wood indicating that tents have been raised. Horses are being pastured," he pointed to the north. "I smell fires burning and there is a tang of tar in this odor. They burn the ships now. This close to the Capital the barbarians would appear to have no expectation to return north. I hear the sounds of armor being cleaned and weapons being honed. I hear the sounds of men who are not entirely confident. So far from home—if their chieftain has misjudged the strength of this vast Empire they have crossed, they will never return to their lands, to their people."

Shonto nodded. "You have crossed swords with the men of desert, Lord Komawara, is it possible that we can win a battle against such superior numbers?"

There was a long silence then and Shonto found himself straining to hear the sounds that drifted up from the plain.

"It would depend on the place and the commander, Lord Shonto. When we attacked their supply rafts, we had the advantage of surprise and they thought they had been set upon by an entire army. I do not believe it is foolish pride to say that the men of Wa are stronger warriors. The reports from the battle for Rhojo-ma would indicate this to be true. A confident army with superior position would likely prevail—at great cost—despite smaller numbers. Confidence comes from the men's faith in their commander, Sire."

"And the Emperor? Can he meld the two armies into a force that will bear the blow this Khan will deliver?"

Komawara shrugged. "The Emperor is unknown to me, Sire. If he abandoned his position on the west side of the canal, burned the bridge, and concentrated his force and our own on the eastern hillside, the Emperor's position would be improved. But I cannot say that he could inspire the confidence required to beat a foe who is stronger in numbers. It is impossible to know.''

Shonto turned and looked back toward his own position, hidden in the fog. Noises similar to those heard emanating from the enemy position echoed here.

"We will see," Shonto said quietly.

The sound of armored men approaching caused both lords to turn around. A moment later Kamu materialized out of the fog followed by guards.

He bowed low. "A rider has arrived from the north bearing news, Sire." Kamu paused for a second to catch his breath. "Lord Shonto Shokan has come down from the mountains with a small force. He hurries to join you, Sire."

Shonto remained calm at this, compared to the obvious excitement that his steward barely contained. "We must get word to him. He must not risk capture. There is no reason for him to hurry. His presence here with a small force will hardly be the deciding factor. We must warn him to stay well clear and approach from the southeast. He must take no risk of capture, Kamu-sum, absolutely none. Send messengers immediately."

The steward bowed quickly and was gone.

Prince Wakaro did not know whether to feel relief or not. The ride through the fog toward the perimeter of his father's defenses was a terrifying endeavor. Even his guard wearing the armor of the Imperial Guard was little comfort. The men of the Imperial Army knew that Jaku Katta and his rebel followers still wore their black uniforms and all the insignias of rank.

They had found a guard in the fog and finally been escorted through the lines. The feared arrow did not find him and the Prince was relieved to the point of developing a small tremor. He was not sure if Shonto or his followers would have condescended to wear armor in such situations, but the Prince had decided he did not care. To die of an arrow shot by some nervous, unknown archer did not seem like a dignified death.

He and his men stood surrounded by Imperial Guards, and though they had not been shown the courtesy due an Imperial Prince they had been treated well enough and

even allowed to retain their swords. The Prince realized
he had stopped trying to predict his father's reaction to
this embassy from Lord Shonto—an embassy led by his
own son.

Perhaps he should have refused Shonto's request that
he approach the Emperor, but the Prince felt that what
Shonto had said was true. This was a decisive moment
in history, and he did not want to be known for all time
as the prince who contributed to the fall of the Empire.
So he tried to swallow his fear.

Lord Komawara had told Wakaro that he had been
frightened before the attack on the barbarian supply rafts
and there was something about Komawara that made the
Prince believe the young lord would never stoop to lies.

A guard officer appeared then and it took a moment
for the Prince to realize it was Jaku Tadamoto. The young
guardsman seemed to have aged many years in the past
few months.

"If it is convenient, Prince Wakaro, could you accompany me?" Tadamoto asked in the refined tones of a
scholar. How did the men of the Imperial Guard respond
to a commander who sounded and looked like a historian
or a poet? A few weeks earlier the thought would never
have occurred to him and it surprised him.

Nodding, the Prince fell into step beside the young
colonel who deferred to the Imperial Prince in voice only.
It was no time to demand that proper etiquette be followed, Wakaro decided.

They made their way along a deep trench behind one
level of the earthworks. Bundles of arrows stood against
the trench wall and, on a dirt shelf, archers stood looking
out onto the fogbound plain. Prince Wakaro had become
more intimate with fear recently and this had increased
his sensitivity to it. He could feel the fear among these
men.

They mounted a wooden stairway that brought them
up a level. The effort was causing the Prince to sweat
under his heavy armor, and he pulled off his helmet and
tucked it under his arm as he often saw guards do, for
there was no one on his staff to reach out and take this
burden from him.

They progressed through various rings of guards until
the sound of banners rustling in the frail breeze told

Wakaro that the Emperor would be near at hand. Indeed, only a few paces farther along and they were stopped by guards. Wakaro stood trying to hold together the shreds of his failing courage. I have seen the barbarian army, the Prince reminded himself. Any death I find here will be more charitable than the death I would find on the battlefield. Stories of what the barbarians did to captured enemies had reached Wakaro through his guards. His dreams had not been the same since.

A guard appeared out of the fog and gave a hand signal. Tadamoto motioned the Prince forward. A few paces along and a small pavilion took shape before the Prince. He knelt and bowed to his father who did not offer even a nod in response.

"I am told you are a messenger for the Shonto?" the Emperor said, his voice betraying tight control—a sign of anger that the Prince dreaded.

"Despite all appearances, Sire," Wakaro said, ashamed at the quaver in his voice, "I remain the Emperor's loyal servant. The truth of this will be revealed as the fog lifts. An army of unprecedented size is before us. If the Imperial Army does not join with the forces of Lord Shonto, the Empire will be lost."

The Emperor stared at his son until the young man looked down. "You have a message from your master?" the Emperor said at last.

Wakaro reached into his sash and removed the carefully folded letter. He passed this to Tadamoto who set it on the edge of the small dais.

The Emperor looked down at it for a moment as thought the letter itself was an insult to his dignity. He picked it up suddenly, tearing it open without even glancing at the seal. After casting a final, cold eye upon his son, the Emperor turned his attention to Shonto's letter. He looked up in a moment. "This does not differ from the message Lord Shinzei conveyed," the Emperor said, his face flushing with anger.

Wakaro could only nod. He kept his eyes cast down.

The Emperor threw the letter in his son's face, startling the Prince so that he almost fell backward.

"Colonel Jaku. Take this man out of my sight," the Emperor said as though dismissing an annoying servant.

"He is charged with treason and we are at war. Deal with him accordingly."

The Prince reared up, stumbling to his feet. He felt Jaku Tadamoto's hand on his sword arm and then other hands gripped him also. "I have not lied!" the Prince cried out. "I do not support your enemies. The enemy is a barbarian army that has armed itself using Imperial gold." He was dragged backward, the Emperor disappearing in the fog. "Father! You will see that I tell the truth. In just a few hours. Father!" Jerked off his feet, the Prince hit his head against something hard. He sank completely into the fog then; it swirled close about him obscuring everything, even his thoughts.

Swimming up to the surface of the fog, ever so slowly, the Prince came back to the world. He lay on his side on a surface that was soft and uneven. Nausea passed through him like a wave rushing onto the shore though it did not break but only dissipated in the smallest ripple. Two more waves moved him and he felt for a moment that he had washed ashore and was swept back and forth by the rhythms of the sea.

Finally the Prince opened his eyes. A thick, straw mat was the surface under him.

"Sire?"

It was a soft voice, not at all hostile. Wakaro tried to nod.

"Can you hear me, Sire?"

Tadamoto, Jaku Tadamoto: Wakaro recognized the voice now. He moved his head, a definite nod, he was certain.

"If you wish, I will help you to sit."

After a moment of consideration Wakaro shook his head. I must have more time, he thought. The fog will lift and then I will be vindicated. His eyes focused on a second guard who stood a few paces off. In his hands this man held a sword laid across folds of white silk. The Prince closed his eyes again.

After a few moments had passed, the voice came again. "Sire? I will do everything to preserve your dignity, but you must assist me in this."

"I am more concerned with my life, Colonel," Wakaro said, words coming with difficulty into a dry mouth.

'I am prepared to give you time to make your preparations and also your own sword. In this I defy the orders of my Emperor. Please, Prince Wakaro, I offer you the path of dignity. It is the honorable way."

The Prince shook his head softly.

"Tadamoto-sum?" he whispered, using the familiar form. "If you will grant me one request . . . I will cooperate in any way you wish."

Tadamoto did not answer immediately. "It is not my place to grant requests, Prince Wakaro. I risk the Emperor's displeasure in what I do now."

Displeasure, Wakaro thought, the word striking him like a blow. He fought to control growing panic. "I wish only to be given until the fog lifts to make my preparations. It is a small thing," he said, trying not to let his voice be reduced to the whimper that was threatening. The Prince propped himself up on his elbow then, looking up at the young guard colonel. He prayed it was compassion he saw there.

Tadamoto crouched at the edge of the mat, looking down at the Prince. Very deliberately he nodded once, then rose and walked away, leaving the Emperor's son under the eye of several guards.

The days had fallen into a pattern of fog in the morning which then lifted at virtually the same hour each afternoon. The Prince knelt on his mat facing the north, searching for the first sign of the barbarian army. The rest of the Imperial Army encampment was hidden from view by a roll in the hill and some low bushes. Undoubtedly, the Prince had been carried to the top of the hill on the canal's eastern bank.

Faint signs of blue began to appear overhead and the Prince felt his hope rise. The guard, holding what Wakara realized was a ceremonial white robe, still stood, unmoving, at his back. Had the Prince known how to pray to Botahara, he would not have hesitated to do so.

The fog seemed to have learned considerable cruelty in the last few hours, for it kept showing signs of thinning and then blowing in as dense as it had ever been. Then the plain before the Imperial Army began to appear, a few paces at a time, the green grasses trampled but still vivid against the white of the mists.

Finally a barbarian sentry appeared, riding a dark horse. Colored banners took form, waving among the tendrils of white—gold and Imperial Crimson, and blue and spring green. Wakaro offered up an awkward prayer of thanks to powers unknown and unnamed.

The mist disappeared more quickly by the moment. A man cleared his throat at the Prince's back causing the young man to tear his eyes away from the scene being revealed before him. Jaku Tadamoto had returned.

"May I assist you with your armor, Sire? It would be my honor."

The Prince pointed out at the army that was slowly coming to light. "It is as I said, Colonel. Once I had seen this, I could not chose another course. The Empire is in grave danger. You *need* Shonto Motoru."

Tadamoto nodded. "May I begin with your shoulder pieces, Sire?"

Turning back to the north, the Prince saw that more of the army of the desert was coming into view. Fingers began working at the lacing on his shoulder pieces. *But it is there before them to see, the Prince thought. Could they not see?*

Tadamoto and a guard were lifting the heavy body armor over Wakaro's head when the guard happened to look up.

"Botahara save us. Colonel!" He pointed to the plain.

Tadamoto turned to look as the armor slipped over the Prince's head. He froze in position for a second and then stood up to full height, the Prince completely forgotten.

The barbarian encampment was a vast, teeming sprawl, dark against the new green, like a bloodsucker Tadamoto had once found undulating on a rush beside a pond.

"I am not a traitor, Tadamoto-sum," the Prince said as calmly as he was able, as though the sanity of his tone would make the young guard realize how mad this entire situation was. "I described this army in detail in a letter to my father. I have tried to warn him of this for some weeks. I have committed no act of treason."

Tadamoto stood staring for a moment longer. "I will speak to the Son of Heaven." He turned and hurried off, leaving the Prince to struggle against a fit of shaking that suddenly racked him.

Tadamoto made his way quickly down the path to the Emperor's pavilion. Bowing to the guard, he gave a password reserved for dire emergencies that would allow him immediately into the Emperor's presence. A guard announced his commander and Tadamoto was brought forward.

The Emperor sat in the same place under the small pavilion of crimson silk. Like everyone else, he stared out at the clearing plain as though transfixed. After a moment he spoke to Tadamoto though he did not take his eyes off the sight before him.

"Did he die well, Tadamoto-sum?"

Jaku cleared his throat. "I allowed him time to make his preparations, Sire. And then this . . ." The young officer waved a hand toward the barbarian army. "Prince Wakara wrote the truth, Sire. . . ."

The Emperor turned to Tadamoto, his face suddenly drained of blood. "He aided a rebel lord. I will have no traitors in my House, Colonel Jaku. Carry out your orders." And with that he returned his attention to the north.

Tadamoto stood for an awkward second, then, despite being entirely ignored, bowed stiffly and retreated. *This is a murder,* Tadamoto thought, a coldhearted murder.

Fifty-seven

The army of the barbarians and the two armies of Wa faced each other across the open fields in chilling silence. The men on either side stared out over the green grass and wondered if their death was somehow, mysteriously, taking form among the indistinguishable faces of the enemy.

After the shock of seeing the barbarian army for the first time, Akantsu II sent an embassy to speak with the representatives of Lord Shonto. Appointed to speak for the Emperor, Jaku Tadamoto rode out on a gray horse accompanied by two guards. The Son of Heaven demanded that Jaku Katta, former commander of the Imperial Guard, come forward for Lord Shonto and made it known that no other would be acceptable.

Having already helped an Imperial Prince to die that morning, Tadamoto felt like a man being slowly torn apart, for there was no doubt in his mind that Katta was also on the Emperor's list of those who would fall upon their own swords.

To Tadamoto's left the barbarian army prepared for battle at a pace that could almost be described as leisurely and this did not raise the young colonel's confidence. The Emperor would not discuss the barbarian army, and when Tadamoto dared to push him the Son of Heaven finally answered; "I am well aware that the army is larger than previously reported, Colonel." Beyond that the Son of Heaven would say nothing, knowing full well who had assured him that the barbarian force was small.

How had he been so misinformed? Tadamoto asked himself again, realizing he would quite possibly never know. But what had happened with those fools he had

sent north? Katta had told the truth, he reminded himself
for the thousandth time that day. Katta had told the truth
and his own brother had not listened.

Jaku Katta and his two guards appeared now, coming
down the last run-out of the slope that protected the
Shonto position. Neither party displayed flags of truce
nor did they carry banners, as would have been common under the circumstances. It was still hoped that
the barbarians did not realize the armies of Wa acted
separately.

The two groups rode slowly forward, like two patrols
meeting and pausing to speak for a time. Katta stopped
his horse first and made Tadamoto approach him. The
younger brother shook his head at this tactic. With his
tongue Tadamoto tried to work some moisture into his
mouth. So much depended on this one conversation. . . .
And Tadamoto was still not certain why the Emperor had
demanded that Katta should speak for the Shonto. All of
the Emperor's choices seemed to be selected to cause
Tadamoto confusion and test his loyalty.

The evening before Tadamoto had played gii with
Shonto's vassal-merchant, Tanaka, a practice he had taken
up in the last few days. The old merchant had played a
wily game, forcing the distracted Tadamoto into a foolish
mistake. When the game was surely won, the old man
had surrendered and pushed back from the board. Tanaka
had answered the colonel's expression of surprise with a
shrug. "I can see a course that will win you the game,
Colonel, so I have surrendered my force to you, hoping
thereby to gain your good will. In the days when I played
this game with Lord Shonto, I often did the same. He is
a gii master of some reputation, as you know. My alter-
native was to risk losing everything." The old man spread
his hands in a gesture that seemed to say: *the choice is
yours.*

The brothers motioned for their respective guards to
stop and rode forward, Katta waiting for Tadamoto to
bow and when he did not the elder brother smirked. No
one dismounted.

"Brother," Katta said, and Tadamoto answered his
brother's nod with the same gesture.

A moment of silence. Tadamoto thought his brother

looked much the same as when they had parted months
before, though now Katta had some color on his face
from time in the sun, making Tadamoto wonder what
things had passed in his brother's life since they had last
spoken.

"Lord Shonto has asked me to inquire after Prince
Wakaro. The Prince has not returned to us."

"The Prince is the concern of the Emperor only."
Tadamoto said, the half-lie coming with difficulty. "Lord
Shonto should not trouble himself."

Katta looked into his younger brother's eyes then, and
Tadamoto found himself looking down at the leather reins
in his hands, adjusting his grip on them.

Katta shook his head with some sadness. "The Emperor demands much of his servants, Tadamoto-sum. It
is a sad thing. I will inform Lord Shonto."

Tadamoto swallowed. Perhaps this ability to look into
the souls of others was a characteristic of all opportunists, and womanizers, too, for that matter, the young colonel thought.

Katta cocked his head to the barbarian army. "I did
not lie, Tadamoto-sum. The Emperor thinks I have betrayed him, but I have merely put the safety of Wa first.
There lies the end of our Empire as we have known it.
We must not allow this to happen, Tadamoto-sum, don't
you agree?"

Tadamoto looked into his brother's gray eyes then,
wondering if there was truly some shred of honor behind
the words or if this was merely part of another elaborate
plot. "I have come with a message from the Son of
Heaven." Tadamoto almost referred to his brother as
General Jaku, for he still wore his Imperial Guard uniform and insignia. "You may tell Lord Shonto that the
Emperor will accept the surrender of the lord's army immediately. There will be no pardons for rebels. If Lord
Shonto wishes to show his great loyalty to the Empire,
he will resign his command upon receiving this message.
We will speak only to those who come to arrange the
surrender. No other emissaries will be recognized."
Tadamoto reached into his sash and removed a letter,
thrusting it toward his brother. "This is the message, in-
scribed so that there shall be no misunderstanding. Please,
deliver it to your lord."

Katta looked down at the paper in his brother's hand but made no move to accept it. "The Emperor assumes that Lord Shonto will surrender his life to the Emperor rather than allow Wa to fall. Hear me, Tado-sum, Lord Shonto will retreat in the darkness and leave you to face the barbarians alone. We will retreat toward Yankura and raise the army needed to oust these barbarian chieftains.

"This Khan, you know who he is. The Emperor paid him gold to help bring down the Shonto. He is a half-caste—born in the desert to a woman of Seh. But he is more than that. His mother was born to the House of Tokiko. He has Imperial blood in his veins, this Khan. For many years he lived in Wa, after his mother was rescued from the tribe that had abducted her. If this man takes the throne, his claim could be recognized. The barbarians think that they come to make Wa their own, but I do not believe it is to be so. This Khan does not care for their prophesies or claims or vendettas. He will make himself Emperor with the barbarian army at his back, but he will be an Emperor of Wa. The barbarian army will be split and spread across the Empire, made ineffectual, and this Khan will become a man of Wa.

"But he does not love us, Tadamoto-sum. The half-castes are barbarians to the men of Seh. His life before he returned to the desert was not such that he has gained respect for the men of Wa. He would be a danger on our throne and I cannot say what his reign would bring."

Katta stopped, glancing up for a second at his brother's eyes. Whatever he saw there seemed to give him hope. "Tado-sum. Akantsu is not a man of honor. You know this. What befell Prince Wakaro? Was it just?" Softly Katta pounded his fist on his armored thigh. "Lord Shonto has spent the last months slowing the barbarians' advance, allowing the Emperor to build an army. And yet Lord Shonto knew of the Emperor's plot against him. Knew that the Emperor would be unlikely to make peace with him even in the face of an invasion. Look at this!" Katta waved a hand at the army of the desert. "We can save the Empire, Tado-sum. The Jaku name can go down in history as the Shonto name did in the past—as saviours of Wa.'' Katta lowered his voice. "Exchange guards with me. Tell them it is the Emperor's wish. Return to your master with my men as though they were your own. Take them into the presence of the Emperor as witness of what was spoken here. They are the best swordsmen I have, and utterly loyal. They will not fail. Surrender the Imperial army to Lord Shonto and there will still be a chance that we can win against this Khan.''

Tadamoto still held out the Emperor's letter. It was an impossible scheme. Tadamoto knew he was being watched with great interest by the Emperor's officers. There was no chance that he and his brother could simply exchange guards—it would not go unnoticed. And even if it were possible, these guards would not be allowed, armed, into the Emperor's presence. Tadamoto knew that he was the only one who was allowed near to the Emperor wearing a sword. Yet he was loyal—loyal to the Emperor even while he had grown to hate Yamaku Akantsu.

"Brother,'' Katta said, reaching out and taking the letter. "Motion your guards forward. It is worth any risk to save the Empire.''

Tadamoto shook his head. "Even in time of war they will not be allowed into the Emperor's presence carrying weapons of any sort.''

"You carry a sword, brother. It can be snatched from your sash at the correct moment. These men understand what needs to be done. They have made their peace with Botahara. Once the Emperor falls, you must take control of the army. I know you have many loyal men in the guard, Tado-sum. They will support you. Tomorrow the Khan will have prepared his forces for the battle. There is no time, Tadamoto-sum.''

Shaking his head, the younger brother reined his horse back, his gaze fixed on his brother's gray eyes. "You do not understand loyalty, Katta-sum. You think it is something one owes to another, but it is not so. Loyalty to principles is the essence of all honor.'' Tadamoto looked down at the reins in his hands again. "It is this difference that has led to this—meeting across the field of battle as we do. What you ask . . . it is impossible. I do not believe the Emperor will waver in his position. If you think Lord Shonto can save the Empire by retreating to raise an army, then it is a course you must recommend. But if the Khan pursues you . . . ?'' Tadamoto looked into his brother's face a last time, shook his head, and turned his horse back toward the Emperor's position.

Fifty-eight

An Empire away
From distant battles
Yet there is no peace for the spirit.

When letters come,
White rice paper bearing the Dragon seal,
Old men walk out alone into rain swept fields.

Fog lay around the base of the hill and the thousand
fires of the barbarian army illuminated the mist, causing it to glow like a fabric of mystical origin. Shonto
stood looking out toward the plain, his hand resting
lightly on the trunk of a tree. Two paces away Kamu
stood watching in silence. Lord Shonto had spoken very
little since sending for the steward, but this did not seem
to matter to Kamu—his lord had requested his presence
and it was possible that nothing more than that would be
asked for. The old man did not feel it was his place to
question.

Earlier in the evening Shonto had requested that his
armor be brought and had then inspected it meticulously,
knowing full well that Kamu had done the same. The
steward did not take offense at this, for he knew that
Shonto's inspection was a ritual only, something to occupy the mind. Even so, the old warrior was gratified
that his lord had found the armor to be without flaw.

Now Shonto was lost in silent thought. Everyone wondered if the battle would be joined the next day, after the
fog cleared. It depended on the Khan, for the men of Wa
would not take the offensive.

"Shokan-sum," Shonto said suddenly, "have we word
of his progress?"

Kamu cleared his throat. "The countryside is full of

barbarian patrols, Sire. I instructed Lord Shonto's guides to bring him to us with all possible caution. I apologize, Sire, his present location is not known to me.''

Shonto moved his hand as though he brushed away an insect though Kamu knew it was the apology his lord waved off.

Silence returned. Occasional music and singing would drift up from below—sometimes the haunting scales of a barbarian flute and sometimes the familiar tunes favored by the soldiers of Wa. Neither side seemed inclined to the drunken, boisterous singing often heard in camps. Somehow Kamu had expected it from the barbarians—curious.

Shonto shifted his position, running his hand down the smooth, white bark of the birch. ''I wonder about this Emperor, Kamu. . . . Is it possible that he will sacrifice his Empire? Is Akantsu so certain I will surrender before allowing the loss of the Imperial Capital? He takes a great risk.''

Kamu ran his hand through gray hair. ''Undoubtedly he knows Lord Shonto is more loyal to the Empire than the Yamaku—who are only loyal to their own ambitions. If the Khan is defeated and my lord is part of the command that routs these invaders, the Emperor believes he will lose his throne for his part in bringing the barbarians into Wa. Akantsu must think that he can only survive if both Lord Shonto and the Khan fall. He will not sacrifice his House to save the Empire.''

Shonto nodded. ''If I were to surrender my force to the Emperor, would he fight or would he retreat?''

Kamu kneaded the stump of his missing arm and shifted his weight subtly from foot to foot. ''Sire, I . . . I cannot say what is in the mind of the Emperor of Wa.'' Kamu considered carefully before speaking his next words. ''If Akantsu stands against the barbarian on this field and does not triumph, the Imperial Army will be shattered. The barbarian army is formidable.'' The old steward whispered his last sentence. ''Certainly the Emperor would be a fool if he did not retreat and attempt to increase his force.''

Shonto nodded. ''He would be a fool. I agree. The question is really very simple: who will sacrifice their House to save the Empire? Thank you, Kamu-sum.''

* * *

The former commander of the Imperial Guard, Jaku
Katta, sat on a rock with his back against a tree and
examined a sketch which showed the relative positions
of the armies in the field. A lamp hung from a branch to
the general's right and several guards knelt on the edge
of the circle of light. The fires of the barbarian army
glowed in the mist gathered below, and overhead stars
appeared to be immersed in liquid, points of light dif-
fused by a high veil of the thinnest clouds.

Jaku looked up from his map and stared into the darkness. It is hopeless, he thought, the Emperor could hardly
have chosen a worse field. Considering the number of
ideal positions farther north, it was almost a betrayal of
the Empire to have chosen this site to face the invading
army. Fool! Jaku thought. If he had only listened. . . .

Rolling the map with some care, Jaku created a calm
to replace his anger. His teachers had taught that anger
and fear destroyed one's ability to reason, dulled the reactions, and this was a time that would demand the very
best of the former kick boxer.

Jaku set the map aside. If only Tadamoto would reconsider his proposal. A dead Emperor would change the
world—as surely as the change from winter to summer.
Shonto could defeat this Khan, Jaku had no doubt of that,
and the Jaku family would retain a position at court, for
who would sit upon the throne but a member of the
Shonto family—the son or Lady Nishima.

Tado-sum, the kick boxer sent his thoughts out to his
brother, *why do you stay loyal to this man*?

There was no doubt in Jaku's mind that it would be
worth the life of his brother to kill the Yamaku Emperor.
He was not certain that his brother would agree, however.

What will Shonto do? Jaku asked himself again. He
must retreat, the guardsman thought, it is the only wise
choice. Akantsu was such a fool! Both armies had to be
preserved if they ever hoped to stand against the barbarians.

Jaku believed it would take the Khan another day to
ready his attack, which could allow the armies of Wa a
chance to slip away. But if the Khan had any idea of what
really transpired in the camps of his enemy, he would

attack the next day. Pray that this chieftain does not understand what transpires here, Jaku thought.

As any good general, Jaku tried to consider all the possibilities, no matter how unpleasant. Defeat of the forces of Wa on this plain would put the Jaku on the run—if they survived. Nitashi or Ika Cho would be the provinces most likely to remain autonomous if the Empire fell—at least for a while. An army might be raised there. Whichever province Jaku chose, he knew that he must make his way there by the fastest method—by boat, unquestionably. Yankura would be his destination if the armies of Wa suffered defeat. From there he could go either north or south—Ika Cho or Nitashi. He would not decide before reaching Yankura. Much would depend on what occurred in the next few days—on who survived.

Calling for an inkstone and paper, Jaku shifted so he could write by the light of the lamp. Considering the uncertainty of the future, custom indicated that he must compose the required poems. There were still many hours before a battle would begin—if there was a battle at all.

A servant brought steaming bowls of cha to the two ladies who sat on grass mats looking out over the scene to the south. They were as far away from the sight of the armies as they could manage and still be within the protective perimeter of Shonto's defenses.

Once the servant had returned to the darkness, the conversation resumed.

"Do you remember, when we journeyed north on the canal," Nishima said, "my spirits fell low and you lectured me . . ."

"I never lecture, cousin," Kitsura interrupted.

"*Encouraged* me, then," Nishima said, slowly turning her bowl, steam rising into the air, the swirls barely visible in the starlight. "You said it was truly surprising that, considering our family histories, we had never been forced to flee before. Excuse me for saying so, cousin, but I'm not certain I truly believed that. Yet here we are. If the Emperor does not come to his senses, my uncle will take our force where? South, perhaps, or east. And will the Khan take the Capital then? I believe so. Strange to think—the capital of Wa in the hands of a barbarian chieftain." She sipped her cha.

Kitsura did the same. The night was warm for the time of year and without a breeze. A waning moon would not appear until very late and the stars were suspended in a haze. The lights of the Capital glowed in the south for the nightly fog did not spread south of the hills upon which the armies camped.

"I hope my family have escaped south." Kitsura said quietly. "Our estates in Nitashi should be out of reach of barbarian armies for a while." There had been no word from the Omawara family for many days and Kitsura's worst fear was that the Emperor had moved against them.

Nishima reached out and touched her cousin's arm. "I am certain they have slipped away and have been unable to send word. Your family have been well informed of the true situation, thanks to the diligence of their own daughter. The Omawara have had warning long before any other family in the Capital. Do not despair, cousin, I am sure they are safely away."

Kitsura nodded—a smile of thanks for her cousin's reassurance. They sat quietly, sipping their warm cha, the aroma of the herbs blending with the complex scents of spring in Wa.

Tadamoto sat across the board from the vassal-merchant and stared at the arrangement of pieces as though he contemplated his next move, but in truth his mind was elsewhere.

Tanaka cleared his throat quietly.

Tadamoto looked up and then realized that it was indeed his turn to play. "Excuse me, Tanaka-sum, I am not a worthy opponent this evening. I apologize."

"There is no need to apologize, Colonel Jaku. Please. This battle will decide the fate of the Empire." Tanaka tried a reassuring smile. "Your brother's proposal? It unsettled you?"

Without ever intending to, Tadamoto had spent much of the evening explaining the present situation to the Shonto merchant—had even told him of the Prince's death and his meeting with his brother. It was quite likely that Tanaka was the only man Tadamoto knew who was, beyond a shadow of a doubt, not an informer for the Emperor—a man to be valued for that alone. The young colonel had also come to appreciate the merchant's opinions and the unassuming manner in which they were proposed.

"Katta unsettles me simply by being Katta. He demands much." Out of frustration Tadamoto finally exchanged a piece, a move he had explored several times though he could not remember if he had decided it was a good move or bad.

Tanaka nodded. "Your brother said the same thing of the Emperor, yeh?" The merchant responded by taking a swordsman. "It seems you are caught between two men who have the same requirements but different ends in sight, Colonel." Tanaka's face contorted in a small grimace. "Most difficult."

Tadamoto stared down at the board again. Tanaka was forming a substantial attack, there was no doubt, though Tadamoto could not quite see where the effort would be concentrated. To the right side of the colonel's keep his position was weaker and to the left the board was more complex, so he moved his *Emperor* to the left, hoping the complexity would shield it.

Tanaka contemplated the shift in focus Tadamoto's move created. There was no evidence that he was having trouble concentrating nor did he appear very concerned with the situation just beyond the walls. Tadamoto had been expecting the merchant to ask what would become of him on the eve of the battle but was beginning to realize that Tanaka had no intention of asking him. This response had added to Tadamoto's feeling of anxiety and he suffered from an urge to explain the merchant's situation to him just to be rid of the tension.

"I had the honor of watching Master Myochin Ekun play gii on several occasions—years ago now. He played against my liege-lord. Those were instructive matches, Colonel Jaku, two formidable masters of gii. I must say, those were humbling matches also." Tanaka moved a *dragon ship* into the center of the fray. "Master Myochin won almost invariably—but then he had the advantage of being blind."

Tadamoto looked up at the merchant, wondering if this was meant as humor, but Tanaka stared at the board, his palms together, fingers pushing under his chin, his look serious.

"It is an unusual advantage, Tanaka-sum, one which most people would choose to be spared."

"No doubt that is true, Colonel, but the game that Master Myochin plays exists entirely within, he does not even need a board. He has also never seen any of his opponents—they are only differentiated by their styles of play. Master Myochin plays gii—we play . . ." he waved at the contest in progress, "a game on a board with another who intimidates us or is our friend or rival or lover. Our game is always caught up in the world—we cannot escape this—and it lacks . . . purity." Tanaka shrugged.

Tadamoto moved a *swordmaster* to counter the *dragon ship,* no longer caring if he made intelligent moves. "I had never considered this before, but what you say is . . . fascinating."

Tanaka removed Tadamoto's *swordmaster* with a *guard commander* and the young colonel stared at the position. His *swordmaster* had been well covered, and obviously so. Tanaka was offering a sacrifice and there seemed to be no choice but to take it. He looked further but was not sure where Tanaka's attack would concentrate. He took the *guard commander* with a *foot-soldier* and Tanaka answered without a second's contemplation, taking the *foot-soldier* with his *dragon boat* and pinning Tadamoto's own *dragon boat* in the process.

The young colonel threw up his hands and then pushed over his *Emperor* in surrender.

"The Commander of the Imperial Guard defeated by a *guard commander.*" He smiled, the tension in his face disappearing for an instant. "It could not have been more artfully done, Tanaka-sum." He gave a half bow to his opponent. "I congratulate you. For a man with the affliction of sight you play remarkably well."

Tanaka nodded, bowing lower than his opponent. "You are too kind, Colonel. Like any Emperor, I will sacrifice a guard commander without hesitation to win a battle."

Tadamoto stood abruptly, jarring the gii table as he did so, knocking some of the pieces to the floor. He looked down at the older man, his face hard with controlled anger. "You presume too much, merchant. Your instruction is neither asked for nor acceptable." Tadamoto waved toward the door. "I have much to prepare for."

Tanaka gave a low bow and rose. He was shorter than Tadamoto by half a head, so stood looking up at the younger man. "Loyalty to principles, Colonel, those were the words you used. What principles is your Emperor loyal to? Ask yourself that, for if you serve him you are, without choice, loyal to those same principles."

Tadamoto waved toward the door again, glaring at the merchant as he did so.

Tanaka turned and took a step but stopped. "There is more at stake than the honor of Colonel Jaku Tadamoto. Will you sacrifice the Empire for that?"

"Guard!" Tadamoto called and the door burst open immediately. "Take this man to his quarters, by force if necessary."

The guard bowed, but Tanaka proceeded out the door without further resistance, casting a final glance over his shoulder and though the look on the merchant's face was truly unreadable, Tadamoto felt it was an accusation.

The door closed and Tadamoto was alone. He found himself staring down at the gii board, the pieces in disarray. For a moment he could not find the *guard commander* Tanaka had sacrificed, and this was disturbing. Then he saw it and replaced it carefully on the gii board, as superstitious as any soldier on the eve of a battle.

Tadamoto slumped down on a cushion and stared at nothing. How long he sat like that he did not know, but he was eventually interrupted by a tap on the door.

"Enter," he called.

The face of an Imperial Guard appeared. "A message, Colonel, from the Emperor."

Tadamoto nodded and the guard entered, setting a small stand bearing a letter within his commander's reach. Waiting until the guard had closed the door behind him, Tadamoto picked up the letter, barely glancing at the seal as he broke it. He unfolded the pale yellow paper and found the clear hand of the Emperor's principal secretary. A single vertical line of characters:

Shonto will surrender his army to you at sunrise.

Tadamoto tried to read the message again to be sure he had not made a mistake, but his eyes would not focus.

Shonto would surrender? Shonto would allow his House to come to an end in an attempt to save the Empire?

Tadamoto set the paper back on the stand, staring at it dumbly. He felt no joy at this news, he realized. In truth, he felt deep sadness.

Nishima paced back and forth across the small room in her tent, unable to maintain even a facade of patience or inner peace. After her conversation with Kitsura, she had sent servants to find Brother Shuyun, reasoning that a meeting with her family's Spiritual Advisor under the present circumstances would be completely natural.

A lamp flickered on a low table where Nishima had tried to write earlier—tried to create some order out of the turmoil she felt within. It had been an unsuccessful attempt. She could not find words that even approximated what she felt.

"Excuse me, Lady Nishima," her servant's voice came from close outside the tent.

"Please enter," she answered quickly, her heart lifting.

A maid pulled back the flap of the door. She bore a tray.

"Excuse me, my lady. An Imperial Guard messenger brought these." She nodded down at letters, bound together by a silk cord, lying on the silver tray.

"Please," Nishima waved at the table and the servant placed the tray there, bowing as she left. Nishima was struck by how drawn and pale the woman's face was. Her future is as uncertain as anyone's, the aristocrat thought.

Kneeling by the table she unknotted the cord, careful to choose the letter intended to be read first. Unfolding the crisp paper revealed a blade of spring grain and Jaku Katta's indifferent hand struggling down the page. Her view, she realized, had changed, for she had once convinced herself that the general's brushwork had qualities that could be admired—as she had once felt about the general himself.

> Plum blossoms
> Cover the land
> In a shroud of white.
> Morning in the fields

Grain shoots struggle up
Into the season's warmth

I am not daunted by the sunrise

"He is impossible," Nishima whispered. Jaku cannot accept that a mere woman can resist his efforts. She tossed the letter onto the table and found that the second letter was sealed with the Jaku family symbol and beside this a line of characters read:

If circumstances require.

She was appalled. It is his death poem, she realized, and he has sent it to *me*. Presumptuous fool! On the verge of calling for a servant to have the letter returned, Nishima realized that Jaku might indeed die the next day. He was apparently estranged from his brother—who would he leave his final words to?

It is a small thing, she told herself. In all likelihood the guardsman will survive—it will be a cuckolded husband who brings about the Black Tiger's end—and then I will have the poem returned without comment.

She put the two poems into her sleeve and sat watching the lamp flame flicker. From beyond the thin wall of her tent the sound of a soldier's flute rose up, as light and uncertain as the flight of a butterfly. Listening not as a musician but with her heart, Nishima found the music very beautiful, evoking an image of a fragile, solitary spirit.

A rustling of the tent fabric and a soft voice. "Lady Nishima? Please excuse my intrusion."

It was Shuyun. She rose quickly to her feet and crossed toward the opening.

"Ah. My servants found you, Brother," she said quietly. "Please enter."

Shuyun slipped in through the opening. "I met no servants, Lady Nishima," he said.

He has come of his own will, Nishima thought, and this gladdened her heart. She reached out and took his hand, drawing him into the room.

"You cannot address me as Lady Nishima here,

Shuyun-sum, it is not permissible." She smiled and received a smile in return.

"You sit alone, Nishima-sum. I am concerned."

She shrugged, lowering herself to a cushion. "How can one sleep? Tomorrow the world I know will change utterly. Many, many will die, perhaps some that are close to me. I feel separated from my emotions in the face of this." Nishima reached over and turned down the flame on the lamp. "When my mother died, I remember feeling much like this, as though the shock of what had occurred rendered me incapable of feeling for some time. I remember doing all the things that were required of me, appearing very controlled to everyone, but inside . . . Botahara save me.

"It was more than just the loss of my mother. A time was over suddenly and I felt that I had never given it the attention required to properly appreciate it. Everything had changed. It was as though I had been traveling in a safe canal and suddenly found myself at sea—a sea of uncertainty. I had never truly appreciated the canal and it was past."

She looked up, searching for understanding and felt the monk's warm hand squeeze her own. She smoothed a crease in her robe. "I look back at my recent journeys on the canal and think that I understand things that seemed impossible to untangle before. I realize, now, that Jaku Katta is truly the tiger, driven by instincts he can neither understand nor control, and Lord Komawara, whom I thought impossibly parochial, is thoughtful and noble and quietly very brave. Kitsura-sum and I are often spoiled and compete with each other just as we did when we were children, and my uncle is working tirelessly to preserve an Empire that the Shonto have shaped longer than any Imperial dynasty." She caught the monk's eye again. "And you, my friend . . . are out of place in this world, in the House of a great lord. Yet I sense that you are not at peace within your own Order either. Where is your place, Shuyun-sum? You . . . you look so troubled."

He shook his head. "I have been in a council. Lord Shonto did not want to wake you immediately." Shuyun took a controlled breath. "I'm sure he would rather speak to you himself, but . . . Lord Shonto has agreed to sur-

render his army to the Emperor. We will join the refugees fleeing to Yankura in a few hours.''

Nishima pressed her forehead with her hand, remaining like that for some time. Then she moved forward
until she pressed her cheek against Shuyun's neck and he
held her.

''What will become of us,'' Nishima whispered.
''Whatever will become of us.''

Fifty-nine

All preparations were made in the dark or the dim light of covered lamps. It was crucial that the barbarians saw nothing untoward or they might react in ways no one could predict. Nishima heard more than saw her tent come down in the dark. She was standing in the midst of total chaos, Kitsura clinging to her arm as though she feared Nishima would evaporate into the darkness at any second.

The two women were dressed in men's hunting costumes, the better for riding, and perhaps the thought of this unsettled Lady Kitsura even more—she had less experience with horses than her cousin.

Although she had spoken a few words with her uncle, the meeting had not been private and Nishima still did not know the reason for Shonto's sudden decision to surrender his army to the Emperor. Some part of her wanted to believe it was a ruse of the gii Master, an apparent sacrifice that opened the gate of an elaborate trap.

Yankura was the destination everyone mentioned or the Islands of Konojii, but Shonto had said neither to her, so she was uncertain of their direction.

The great lord met with his advisors now, planning the move of the army to the Emperor's position. The Emperor was expecting the surrender of the Shonto along with the army but this was not to be so. All of those the Emperor named in his scroll would flee with the Shonto; Jaku Katta, Lord Komawara, and all of the Shonto family retainers and senior advisors. The oaths of the Shonto House Guard would never allow them to join the Yamaku. It would not be a small party able to move quickly, and this concerned Nishima.

"There is a hint of gray in the east, cousin," Kitsura

said, her voice curiously high-pitched. "Should we not be on our way?"

Turning to the east, Nishima could see no signs of light. "We have time yet, Kitsu-sum. Be patient."

Servants bustled about, sorting clothing and other goods, packing trunks and bags. Much would be left behind, Nishima realized, but this did not seem important. She was concerned for her staff, and this thought brought an image of Shimeko to her mind. Where had she disappeared to, Nishima wondered? Such a troubled soul but someone Nishima had developed an affection for. I should never have allowed her aboard that infernal ship, Nishima thought.

Her last memory of the plague ship was of it passing along a side canal toward a Botahist Monastery. The land there was so flat it seemed to be setting out across the fields, sails full and drawing, the terrifying green banner waving against the blue sky.

"May Botahara protect her," Nishima whispered.

"Cousin?"

"I am reduced to mumbling. Please excuse me."

She felt Kitsura's grip tighten on her arm for a moment in reassurance.

Lord Taiki rode toward the two torches, their copper light reflecting dully off black lacquered armor in the darkness and fog. Clearing his throat so that his presence would be known, Taiki whispered to a guard. "Give the signal."

A lamp opened quickly, three times, and a torch dipped once in reply, leaving an arc of flame hanging in the air for the briefest instant.

They continued forward. Shapes took form in the fog— riders in black.

"Colonel Jaku? I am the emissary of Lord Shonto Motoru." Taiki spoke quietly.

"Come forward, Lord Taiki."

A pace apart Taiki stopped and looked at the young man illuminated in the torch light. He wore an unadorned helmet and his face-mask hung open revealing a fine-boned silhouette. The green eyes could not be seen and Taiki was surprised that he would think of this.

"I have orders to conduct Lord Shonto through the lines into the presence of the Emperor, Lord Taiki."

Taiki took a long breath. "Lord Shonto slipped away with his family and senior advisors, Colonel Jaku."

Silence.

Taiki saw Tadamoto reach out and take a plait of his horse's mane into his gloved hand. "And my brother, Katta?"

"He has disappeared also along with Lord Komawara."

"I see. My Emperor's instructions were very clear: if I sense treachery, I am to cut you down and retreat."

Taiki controlled his urge to rest a hand on his sword hilt. "There is no treachery, Colonel. Lord Shonto warned the Emperor of this invasion months ago. He has done everything within his power to prepare the Empire for this war. Lord Shonto was ignored. He has now given up his army for the defense of the Empire. Do you expect him to forfeit his life as well?" Taiki realized he had raised his voice and forced his next words in the most reasonable tones. "There is no treachery, Colonel Jaku. Only a desire to save Wa. I am prepared to move our force, retreat or attack or prepare for battle as we are. I will surrender command to whomever you appoint. Do not fear, Colonel Jaku, we will not risk a war between our own army and the forces of the Emperor with a barbarian army standing ready. I await your instructions."

The sounds of clattering armor and horses stamping and calling out to each other carried across the empty field. The barbarians were stirring.

"Bring your men in an organized file down the southwest slope of your hill and form them into ranks behind the position of the Imperial Army. This must be done quickly, Lord Taiki, it is our intention to retreat under cover of morning fog. We must move south. This position is not favorable."

"You will surrender the Capital, then?"

Tadamoto did not answer. "It is the Emperor's will that you retain command of Shonto's army for now," he said. "By the hour of the hare we will have begun moving south. Further orders will be sent to you."

Jaku Tadamoto turned his horse and moved back into

the darkness, the torches borne by his guard were quickly consumed by the fog.

Shonto knelt on cushions set out on a flat section of stone projecting from the side of the hill. Lamps had been hung in the trees nearby, but the apparent tranquility of the scene was belied by the sounds of an army moving in the darkness around them.

"No news could be more welcome, Lord Taiki," Shonto said, his voice calm. "It was my fear that the Emperor would make a stand upon this field, and I would have committed my troops to a slaughter. General Hojo will assist you in moving the army, Lord Taiki, and then will join my party. You have much to do, may Botahara be with you." Shonto bowed low.

"Sire. I take on this duty out of loyalty to the Empire and because you wish it," Lord Taiki said, carefully keeping emotion out of his voice. "The Emperor does not command the smallest part of my loyalty. When the Khan is defeated . . ."

Shonto held up his hand. "When the Khan is defeated, there will be much to do to restore the Empire. The commander of an Imperial Army cannot speak of civil war. Choose your words with care, Lord Taiki, even in this company. The Emperor trusts few men."

Taiki hesitated and then bowed, touching his forehead to the cool earth. He retreated three paces and rose to his feet, the company bowing to him as he turned and walked beyond the circle of light.

Shonto nodded to General Hojo who hurried after Taiki lest the lord become lost to him in the darkness.

"Kamu-sum, is our party ready to travel?"

Kamu bowed quickly. "They will be, Lord Shonto, before the hour of the hare, if need be."

Shonto gave a tight smile. "Please see to our preparations."

Kamu bowed, slipping off into the night as quietly as a Botahist monk.

Lord Komawara bowed then. Like the others present he wore full armor, his helmet tucked under his arm. "May I see to my troops, Sire? I can offer some small assistance to Lord Taiki before we depart."

Shonto nodded. "We must be gone soon after sunrise, Lord Komawara. Do what you can, but we cannot wait."

As had Lord Taiki, Komawara touched his head to the ground before retreating and hurrying off.

"General Jaku, no doubt you wish to do the same."

Jaku nodded.

Shonto gave the guardsman a half bow. "An hour after the sunrise."

Jaku, too, bowed low and disappeared into the darkness.

Shonto was left facing Lord Butto who, like Lord Taiki, was not seen as part of Shonto's rebellion and would join the Imperial Army.

Butto Joda bowed low and returned to a kneeling position, a boy in armor laced in purple.

He is no boy, Shonto reminded himself, he is a formidable strategist and ruthless when necessary.

Shonto nodded, acknowledging the young lord.

"Sire, if I may presume. . . . No one would expect you to go north. If you traveled the edge of the foothills you would come to my fief. It would be an easy thing to hide there. The Butto hunting lodge is secluded and not uncomfortable. I would send word ahead of you. And, Lord Shonto, the mountains could be a last resort. Even if Akantsu can defeat this Khan, he will look for you to go south or to cross the Inner Sea to the islands. You have assisted the Butto in the past, Lord Shonto, and now sacrifice much for the sake of our Empire. I would risk the displeasure of the Son of Heaven without hesitation if I could assist you in any way."

Shonto was silent a moment. "This is a generous offer, Lord Butto. The future is so unclear, I would hesitate to earn anyone the Yamaku's enmity. The Emperor may retain his throne yet. Do not endanger your House as I have mine. The Yamaku will not be a dynasty like the Mori—their ascendancy will not last. Do not be concerned, Lord Butto, the Shonto have survived far worse than this. We are practiced in the art of waiting." He gave the young lord a brief smile. "Lord Taiki will need your assistance, may Botahara walk beside you."

Lord Butto bowed again. "May the Perfect Master watch over your House, Lord Shonto." Bowing low again, the tiny figure backed away and hurried off.

Shonto sat alone but for his guard who kept their distance, kneeling in perfect silence.

A whisper came from beyond the lamp light. "Uncle?"

Shonto smiled. "Lady Nishima. Please, do not be shy."

As she stepped into the light, Shonto was confronted with the sight of his daughter dressed in the clothes of a boy.

"Like Princess Shatsima, I am ready to flee to the wilds if that is your wish, Sire."

Shonto smiled, despite the gravity of the situation. "I am certain that Shatsima never looked so lovely nor faced her exile with such courage. You do honor to your House, Lady Nishima."

She came and perched on the edge of the stone. "I am certain Princess Shatsima not only exhibited but also felt more courage, Uncle." She waved a hand in the direction the Shonto army moved. "It shames me to feel such trepidation when I am not among those who will join the battle."

Shonto shook his head. "After Rohku Tadamori witnessed the fall of Rhojo-ma, he told his father that he would rather die in a thousand battles than stand by and watch others give their lives. It is a common thing to feel. There is little comfort in this knowledge, but I am certain that you would enter the battle as willingly as any man of arms, were that your part to play. Those who do not wield a sword will yet be called upon, Nishi-sum. An act of bravery may be asked of each of us before this war is over."

Nishima nodded her head, sadly it seemed. "I pray I am equal to it, Sire."

"We all have the same prayer, Nishi-sum, even the bravest."

Nishima waved toward the eastern horizon. "It grows light. Sunrise is not distant now. Is it time?"

"I wait only for the few to return who assist Lord Taiki: Jaku Katta, Hojo, and Lord Komawara. They will not be long."

The blaring of horns and the clashing of metal shook the air suddenly and Nishima and Shonto turned to look out toward the field.

"Botahara save us," Nishima whispered. "What is that?"

"An army preparing for battle. The Khan grows impatient to sit upon his throne."

"Will he attack today, then?"

"The army he seeks will be gone when the fog clears. Then this barbarian chieftain will be tested. Will he pursue the Emperor's army or will he choose to ascend the throne and declare himself Emperor of Wa? It is the question our Emperor would give half his wealth to have answered."

"No one can know, Uncle, this Khan is a great mystery. Who is he? From where did he come?"

Shonto looked at his daughter then, raising an eyebrow; "I have not told you? Jaku Katta has admitted many things now that there is no question of regaining the Emperor's favor. This Khan is your very distant cousin, Lady Nishima, a half-barbarian with Tokiko blood in his veins. He has almost as much claim to the throne as do the Yamaku or the Fanisan or the Omawara."

"Uncle, this is not possible! How can you tease at a time such as this?"

"It is the truth, Nishi-sum. His mother was of the House of Tokiko, married to a lord of Seh. Barbarian raiders abducted her and she bore a son in the desert." Shonto waved toward the north. "And now he comes to claim his birthright."

Nishima looked out into the still, dark night, where the fires of the barbarian camp glowed in the mist. "So it is he who has lived in the wilds, like Shatsima, waiting to reclaim his throne." Nishima pressed her fingers to her chin. "It is as Hakata said. During times of upheaval, when history is created daily, miracles become commonplace."

The horns echoed off the hills again and a stillness answered as the moving army paused to listen. There was no answer from the opposing camp who prepared their retreat.

Shonto reached out and took his daughter's hand. "Join Kamu-sum and Brother Shuyun, now. I will wait a while to see that all has gone well. Stay close to Brother Shuyun, Nishima-sum, he is charged with your safety."

Nishima sat for a second and then spoke in a small voice. "May I not wait with you?"

Shaking his head, Shonto squeezed her hand. "The less experienced riders should not come last. Watch over your cousin, she will find this an ordeal, I fear."

Nishima sat saying nothing, then put her arms around Shonto. Neither spoke for a moment, then Nishima released him, touching his cheek as she turned to go.

The body armor was slipped over the Emperor's head by attendants and the lacings tightened.

"Enter, Colonel," the Son of Heaven said to Tadamoto who hovered outside the entrance to the tent.

Tadamoto knelt and bowed his head to the ground, moving forward awkwardly in his armor.

"Do not keep me in suspense, Colonel. If I desire suspense, I attend a play."

"Excuse me, Emperor." Tadamoto shifted his helmet under his arm. "Lord Taiki has delivered the army of Lord Shonto Motoru, Sire, but the Shonto have fled with their advisors and other members of the rebellion."

The Emperor nodded, considering the information. "It was to be expected," the Emperor said with some finality. "Motoru will remain treacherous to the very end."

Tadamoto shifted and felt the weight of his sword against his thigh. The guardsman closed his eyes for a second, the words of both Tanaka and his brother coming back to him.

I am not loyal to his principles, Tadamoto thought. *There are no guards present—I am the only armed man in this room. It would be easy. But what would ensue?*

"Will Taiki deliver up this army as he has said, or is this a trap, Colonel?"

Tadamoto placed a gloved hand on his sword.

This man. . . .

"I believe that Taiki will bring us the army and is prepared to take orders in the coming war. His loyalty to the Emperor is, however, in question."

"Once we have our march in order, Colonel Tadamoto, I will transfer the command of the Shonto army to you. After the river is crossed, we will have time to deal with the disloyal."

The disloyal, Tadamoto thought. *I remain loyal to my principles.*

The Emperor's shoulder pieces were laced into place. "Is there light, Tadamoto-sum?"

"The sky is turning gray."

The Emperor nodded. "Then let us leave this barbarian to wonder. He will take the Capital, I'm certain. We move south toward Yankura."

Tadamoto nodded and retreated from the tent. Osha, he thought, I must send word to Osha.

He stepped outside to find the sky light, hinting at blue, and the fog hanging in the valley being swept away by a breeze from the north. The army of the desert could be seen in the mist, wavering, as though it lay at the bottom of a moving stream.

"Komawara. Is he not with you?" General Hojo asked Jaku Katta.

"I have not seen him since we left your company, General Hojo."

"We wait only for him." Hojo stood holding the bridle of his own horse. He kept looking north as they spoke. The barbarian position was becoming visible and the fog threatened to clear. "This will expose the Emperor's retreat," Hojo said. "The Wind Goddess will bring ruin upon us if this continues."

Jaku nodded. He dismounted. "What will the Khan do?"

Hojo did not answer. The two warriors stood looking out over the field as the sky became fully light. Horses were heard coming down the path behind them, and the two generals turned in time to bow to Lord Shonto.

They were within the protection of the trees just below the base of the hill so their view was imperfect.

"Can you see the Imperial Army?" Shonto asked. "Are they in the earthworks still?"

Hojo dropped the reins of his horse to the ground and picked his way some distance down the slope, stepping over fallen trees and bramble. Leaning out from behind the base of a tree, he scanned the Emperor's position.

Pulling himself back he shouted up the hill. "The Imperial Army appears to be retreating from their position, but this operation is not complete."

"Damn fool," Shonto said. "If this mist clears, they will be caught on an open field. Better to stay behind their earthworks and pray they can hold until dark."

Shonto came up closer to Jaku but did not dismount. Mist pushed up the hill from the valley then, enveloping Hojo in white. The lord motioned his guard forward. "Do not leave General Hojo alone in this fog."

Five guards dismounted and stumbled down the slope, disappearing before they had gone a dozen steps.

Again a braying of horns and a clash of arms, then again, and once more. The shout of hundred thousand went up, an inhuman din, and the sound of a charge shook the earth.

"General Hojo!" Shonto shouted.

There was no answer. All that could be heard was the pounding of hooves, the crying of men.

Suddenly the mist cleared, snaking off around the sides of the hill, and there, on the field, was the barbarian army in full charge.

Hojo turned and ran awkwardly up the embankment followed by his guard. "They break ranks," he said breathlessly, "the few that remain. It will be a slaughter."

"It is a rout!" Shonto shouted. "Damn that fool Emperor! Damn him for eternity. They will fall upon Lord Taiki from behind." He spurred his horse. "Come, we must save what we can. If these armies are broken, the barbarians will take the Empire."

The others were quick to follow, whipping their horses up the hillside in pursuit of their liege-lord. They came up to the shoulder of the hill in moments and Shonto stopped to survey the scene.

The first wave of barbarian warriors washed across the earthworks, taking the few who tried to stand and throwing them back like bits of flotsam. Men of Wa were on the wooden bridge spanning the canal trying to escape to the western bank, but many fell to arrows and a fire ship was bearing down on the bridge.

Standing in his stirrups, Shonto watched with an air of detachment, the gii Master surveying the board, weighing possibilities coldly. "The banners of this Khan, do you see them?"

There was a second's silence and then Hojo pointed. "There."

In the rear of the army the gold and crimson banners fluttered in the cool north wind.

"He made no offer to accept a surrender," Jaku said bitterly.

Shonto nodded, turning to Hojo. "Send guards to warn Kamu and our household. They must leave everything and move as quickly as possible."

Shonto wheeled his horse to the south and set off at a gallop, the sounds of battle growing dim as they descended the long slope of the hill. A different scene faced them as they broke out of the trees: the army of Lord Taiki was formed up, ready to march, but was not on the move, and the army of the Emperor was forming ranks to the west. Over the crest of the hill upon which the earthworks had been established men poured in disarray.

Pointing toward the Imperial Army, Jaku said, "They do not even realize what has happened."

"The barbarians will crest the hill soon enough," Hojo said, "then all will know."

"The Emperor's army will break and run," Shonto said. "Our own forces will take the blow. We must do what we are able. General Jaku, General Hojo, you will organize the rearguard action and we will march south and take our losses." He waved them forward and the small group set off at speed.

A shout went up from Lord Taiki's army before Shonto's party reached them, and men turned to the north where the vanguard of the barbarian army appeared. On the crest of the hill the army of the desert hesitated, banners fluttering, the men of Wa in flight before them. The soldiers of the Imperial Army stood looking back as the Khan's army grew, crimson riders appearing under a cloud of gold silk banners.

The Khan had taken the field and was, for the first time, seeing the distant Imperial Capital rising up above the mist. Barbarian warriors collected below the banners of their chieftain like the dark crest of a wave forming on the hillside. Like a wave crest it gathered weight and grew in size until it must rush down and spread itself across the shore. The din of horns assaulted the ears three times, and each time the barbarians answered the call with a shout and a clash of arms.

With a final shout the army of the desert surged down the hillside. The men of the Imperial Army stood looking on for a few seconds and then they broke and ran, the panic washing through the unformed ranks like wind through wheat.

Shonto's party closed with Taiki's army, standing its ground still, and a guard raised the blue silk and shinta blossom on a staff to a shout of elation from the men. A rider in Komawara blue raced along the edge of the troops, pulling open his face mask-as he came.

Hojo waved a hand at this rider. "The mystery of Lord Komawara . . . he stayed to fight with his men."

Shonto's guard met the rider with drawn swords, but Shonto waved them aside and Komawara pulled up his horse before the lord.

"The barbarians split their force to attack, Lord Shonto. My men are ready to ride out to meet them. Lord Butto will join me."

Shonto looked up the slope to the charging army and nodded to Komawara. "Their force is large, Lord Komawara. You may slow them, but be prepared to fall back quickly. General Hojo will prepare our defense. Where is Lord Taiki?"

Komawara waved a gloved hand to the south. "At the head of the army, Sire."

"May Botahara protect you," Shonto said and waved his guard to follow, setting out toward the south.

Komawara spun his mount and raced off, closing his face-mask as he went and tightening his helmet cord.

The crest of the barbarian wave broke upon the rear of the fleeing Imperial Army first, riding down the foot-soldiers. A conch sounded in the rear of Lord Shonto's force and the Komawara banner shook free in the breeze, fluttered for an instant and then the north wind faltered and died. The conch sounded again and riders in darkest blue and riders in purple set off with a shout to meet the charging barbarian cavalry.

With the dying of the north wind the cloud of fog halted in its southern retreat, reformed its ghostly ranks, and began to creep north, devouring the heads of the two armies of Wa, then drawing in the bodies.

* * *

Lady Nishima turned to Shuyun who stared off at the hilltop. Dark banners waved on the crest and men massed there in growing numbers.

"Those are the banners of the Khan, Lady Nishima. It would appear that the barbarians have attacked the retreating Imperial Army."

Dark stains on the green fields marked the distant armies of Wa. Horns sounded, their metallic voices borne across the land on the north wind.

Nishima looked back toward the hill they had recently departed. "Where is my father?" she said, keeping panic from her voice with an effort.

Kitsura rode up then, one hand on the reins and the other holding tight to the saddle.

"Can you see, Brother?" she asked. "What occurs?"

Rolling across the green land, the shout of the barbarian army struck like the first breath of winter.

"Botahara save us," Kitsura whispered.

The dark mass of the army of the desert poured down the slope of the hill. Nishima tore her eyes away, looking back the way they had come, searching for the signs of blue.

Near at hand a single rider jumped a low stone wall, coming toward them at a gallop from the direction of Lord Taiki's army.

"A messenger," Shuyun said.

Kamu appeared, galloping his horse down the line of Shonto retainers, his empty sleeve blowing in the wind like a banner. He stopped beside Lady Nishima, staring out toward the beginning battle.

"We cannot tarry, Lady Nishima, Brother. We must make haste," he said.

Nishima nodded. "What has become of Lord Shonto?"

The rider who came toward them waved then and no one made a move to make haste as Kamu had suggested. They waited, transfixed by the terrible scene unfolding before them.

His horse in a lather, the rider, a Shonto House Guard, reined in before Kamu, pulling open his face-mask as he did so. "I come from Lord Shonto. Our lord orders that you leave everything and flee with all haste. The barbarians have carried the attack to us."

''Where is he?'' Nishima said, the fear she felt breaking through. ''Where is Lord Shonto?''

''He has joined the army, Lady Nishima, to direct the defense.''

Nishima turned her face away, covering her eyes with her hand.

Shuyun pointed to the north, east of the hill that had been the Shonto encampment. Barbarian riders were emerging from behind a stand of trees not far off. Turning in his saddle, Shuyun surveyed the field in all directions, then he reached over and took the reins from Kitsura's hands, pulling them over the head of her mount.

''The north wind is dying,'' Shuyun said, ''The fog will hold for some time now. Lady Nishima?'' he said with some gentleness. ''Lord Shonto is a capable man surrounded by able warriors. We must look to ourselves.'' He tugged at the reins of Kitsura's mare. ''Steward Kamu, the fog clears first in the east. May Botahara protect you.''

''You must have guards, Brother,'' Kamu protested. ''I cannot let the Ladies Nishima and Kitsura go off unprotected.''

''We will be more likely to slip away undetected the fewer we are.''

''I will go with Brother Shuyun, Kamu-sum,'' Nishima said. ''Do not be concerned. In the fog Brother Shuyun can see where others are blind. Brother.''

The monk turned his horse and led the two ladies south, disappearing into the cloud of white.

Lord Komawara elected to charge the barbarians, knowing from his experience that they could be thrown into confusion by a direct attack. To his left he could see the small form of Butto Joda, riding a massive stallion and outdistancing his apprehensive guard. Jaku Katta held a position to the lord's right. Arrows whistled overhead, passing both north and south.

The opposing armies met with a clash of steel that rang across the field. Komawara took his first man from the saddle with a blow from his pommel. He caught a fleeting glimpse of Jaku Katta, his sword flashing and barbarian riders falling back before the great warrior.

He fought another, one of his Hajiwara guards knee to

knee with him as they both battled forward. It soon became obvious to Komawara that the momentum of their
charge was being overcome. The Hajiwara guard toppled
from the saddle and he saw two barbarians on foot pounce
on him.

A shout came from Komawara's left and he saw Lord
Butto spur toward him. "We must fall back while there
are enough of us to win through."

Komawara looked around quickly and realized that,
among the fallen barbarians, the field was strewn with
men in Komawara colors and the Butto purple. He tore
his conch from his saddle as Lord Butto fought to protect
him. Sounding the retreat, he dropped the conch to the
ground and went to the aid of Butto Joda. Lieutenant
Narihira appeared at Lord Butto's side, unhorsing a barbarian and disarming another who retreated.

The three fell back, more barbarian raiders appearing
with each passing moment.

"There is no end of them," Butto shouted.

"They are like the swarming of the Butto across my
lord's fief," Narihira answered.

Butto Joda almost fell from his horse as he aimed a
blow at the Komawara guard who wore the green lacing
on his sleeve, but Narihira turned this aside. Komawara
drove his horse between the two men as the first tongue
of mist drifted past them. In a moment they were completely enveloped, the sounds of swords ringing came out
of the mist around them, but they could see no others.
Barbarians appeared before them, charging immediately.
They were separated in the ensuing fight and lost their
way, no longer certain which direction was a retreat,
which a futile charge.

Despite the number of his guards the Emperor of Wa
kept his hand on his sword hilt. His army was in retreat
before a vastly superior force and at the crest of the hill
that his army had recently abandoned he could see the
gold banners of the Great Khan waving in the fitful
breeze. The banners slowly descended the hill which told
the Emperor more about what happened in the battle than
any number of reports. The Khan had a perfect view of
the situation—the scene of his triumph.

Colonel Jaku Tadamoto rode through the Emperor's guard, bowing from the saddle.

"Colonel?"

"Lord Taiki's army is holding ranks thus far, Sire, though they are cut off from us now. Our troops have broken rank, Emperor, the barbarian army sweeps all before it."

The Emperor nodded, his reaction unreadable behind the frozen features of his black face-mask. "Gather what troops remain and retreat toward the Capital. If we can slip out across the lake, we may yet save some part of this frightened army. What direction does Lord Taiki go?"

"It is difficult to know, Emperor: south, generally."

The Emperor reached up and tightened his helmet cord. "Offer what resistance you can to cover our retreat, Colonel." The Emperor turned and spurred his horse toward the canal where his boat waited.

Tadamoto sat his horse watching the Emperor go. I did not tell him that many say they saw the Shonto banner at the head of Lord Taiki's army, Tadamoto thought—no doubt he will find out soon enough.

It was quickly obvious to Lord Taiki that they could not be certain of their direction in the fog and the relief he had felt at returning command of the army to Lord Shonto quickly gave way to apprehension. The knowledge that they would face a barbarian army of one hundred thousand if they were still on the field when the fog cleared kept them moving all the same.

In council with Lord Taiki, Shonto had decided to go what they hoped was southwest to meet the canal which would take them to the Capital—perhaps the only destination they could be certain of.

The sounds of battle surrounded them and companies of riders would appear and disappear like apparitions. Neither General Hojo, nor the Lords Butto and Komawara, nor Jaku Katta had been heard from since the fog returned and not one member of their party found their way back to the main body of Shonto's army. The worst was feared, though no one would give voice to this, but Lord Taiki became more pessimistic about their fate by the moment.

Despite moving across level ground the army progressed at the pace of an old man on foot, a result of their uncertainty of direction, no doubt.

"This fog is both a blessing and a curse, Lord Shonto," Taiki said. Like everyone else, he found himself constantly searching the mist around him, looking for signs of the enemy or for a landmark that might tell them where they were. Patrols could not be sent out, for they would never find the army again and this made the commanders doubly blind.

"It is a blessing, do not doubt it. We should have been swept from the field, but the Khan has lost us as we have lost him. Pray it holds until we are beyond his reach. We will march by night. If we can find our way across the river, we may escape, Lord Taiki. It is the most we can hope for."

The ringing of steel sounded before them where Shonto had placed his strongest swordsmen. A rider in blue pushed through toward Lord Shonto and Taiki.

"We have met a barbarian party, Sire," he shouted as he came. "Reinforcements are being called for."

"What numbers? How large a party?"

The man rode up then, bowing from his saddle. "Large, Sire. It is impossible to tell."

Shonto turned and gave orders to an officer and there was a flurry of movement around them. Horns blared to their right, sounding far too close. Riders appeared suddenly and Taiki drew his sword at the same time as Shonto.

"They are Lord Komawara's men!" someone shouted and Taiki heard a voice thank Botahara—his voice. But then he realized these men fought barbarians.

Shonto cursed beside him. "We have ridden into the heart of the battle, Lord Taiki. Fall back in that direction." The lord waved his sword. "We must hold our force together." His words were lost in the chaos. Arrows whistled and fell among the men near him. Like any lord of Seh, Taiki did not flinch or try to cover himself.

Barbarian warriors engaged the guards around the two lords. Butto purple could be seen in the mist now, riders hard pressed and few. Taiki saw Shonto cross swords with a barbarian. The lord of the Shonto fighting like a common warrior, Taiki thought, and then he, too, was fighting for his life. More arrows fell, shot by which side Taiki could not tell. Lord Toshaki Yoshihira unseated a man to Taiki's left, shouting that he had seen the canal bank. Arrows flew and men fell around him.

Taiki took a barbarian's helmet off with a blow and then finished the stunned rider with a perfectly aimed cut. He looked around for Lord Shonto but could find him nowhere. Shouts were heard now: *the canal, they had found the canal.*

They waited in the mist, absolutely still. Nishima had lost track of the times Shuyun had made them do this, or ordered them to turn suddenly, or reverse direction all together.

"What is it, Brother? What do you hear?" Kitsura whispered.

Nishima leaned close to her cousin. "Say nothing. Shuyun-sum can sense chi at some distance. Do not destroy his focus."

Kitsura's beautiful face was pale, frightened, yet she struggled to maintain a semblance of dignity even so. She nodded at Nishima's words.

Riders had passed close to them several times and they often heard the barbarians' horns and the clash of swords. Shuyun looked up at the sky which showed some signs of the lightest blue.

"The fog is clearing to the east, we are forced toward the canal."

He tugged at the reins of Kitsura's mare and Nishima moved her horse to stay close beside him. They went perhaps a hundred feet and the mist grew thicker again. Shuyun motioned for an abrupt turn to the left, then stopped them again. Riders could be heard close by, many riders by the sounds. Kitsura mumbled the Bahitra. The riders passed.

Leading them another hundred feet, Shuyun suddenly stopped, his eyes closed. A man coughed somewhere nearby though Nishima did not know from what direction this sound came.

Shuyun spoke and his voice sounded strange, distant. "Do not move from this spot no matter what occurs."

He handed the reins of Kitsura's mare to Lady Nishima, pressing her hand as he did so.

Moving his horse forward the monk slipped into the mist. Kitsura reached out and gripped her cousin's sleeve. The sound of something of weight striking the ground came to them and then a riderless horse appeared before them, causing their own horses to shy, throwing Kitsura to the ground.

Shuyun appeared then, dismounting quickly and helping Kitsura to rise.

"Are you injured, Lady Kitsura?"

She shook her head. "No. . . ." Moving her arm in an arc, she tried to smile. "No, I am unharmed. The ground is soft." She remounted with the monk's assistance.

Without further hesitation they moved off, more quickly now. The fog was clearing, there was no doubt.

As the mist pushed back, Shuyun pressed the horses into a canter. Soon the sounds of battle seemed to recede and they stopped infrequently now.

There was a shout to their right. "Ride," Shuyun called out. "Stop for nothing." Saying this, he whipped Kitsura's mount with his reins and turned toward the sound of horses bearing down.

The circle of their world had drawn itself out to half a rih and in their entire world Nishima could see no moving figure. At a low stone wall time was lost while Nishima jumped both horses over, one at a time. Kitsura climbed over, one fall being enough for the day.

They rode on, seeing no one, and finally Nishima pulled their horses up, looking back over her shoulder.

"Brother Shuyun said to stop for nothing," Kitsura panted.

Nishima shook her head. "But he is alone. How many were there, did you see?"

Kitsura shrugged. "I cannot see through fog, cousin. I think the Capital is showing through the mist, look."

Off to their left the white walls of the city reflected the afternoon sun.

"I am entirely turned around, Kitsu-sum." She wiped her brow with a sleeve in a most unladylike action, causing her cousin to laugh.

"It is not a time for laughter, cousin," Nishima scolded.

"Excuse me, Nishi-sum, I . . . excuse me." She forced her face into seriousness though her eyes still retained a sparkle.

The sound of a horse running over soft ground came from behind them and they both turned to see a rider jump a ditch.

"It is Brother Shuyun, cousin," Kitsura said, "I am certain."

Nishima pressed her horse forward to meet the monk. When he stopped, she rode up beside him embracing him from her saddle. Kitsura examined a tree in the distance and the beauty of the Capital appearing from the shroud of mist.

Waving toward the north and west where the fog was clearing, Shuyun pulled free of Nishima's arms. She released him reluctantly and turned to look.

Among the tendrils of dissipating mist the Imperial Army straggled over the fields, making their way toward the Capital in small groups, many on foot, having shed their armor to make better speed. Spread out over many rih, the silent, defeated soldiers of Wa retreated.

"Where is my father in all of this?" Nishima asked.

Shuyun shook his head. He pointed east and Nishima turned to see a large force off in the distance moving toward the river. "Lord Taiki's army?" she said.

"Barbarians." Shuyun said quietly. "That line of retreat is cut off. The Khan will force us all into the Capital."

They began to move again. A flowing ditch was used to water the horses and Shuyun stopped them then to let the horses graze for a time.

Sitting on the bank in the warm spring sun it seemed to Nishima that there could hardly be a war only a few rih away. She closed her eyes and tried to make herself believe it was all a dream, but when she opened them the retreating army told her the dream was true.

Taking her reins from Shuyun as they remounted, Kitsura said, "There is no fog for me to become lost in, Brother. I must learn to ride while I may."

A group of horsemen converged with them and though Nishima's tendency was to avoid them Shuyun thought that they wore the midnight blue of the Komawara and this proved to be true.

"We became separated from our lord in the fog and confusion of battle," an officer, one Narihira Chisato explained. One of the men was obviously injured, though not bleeding. Shuyun forced him to dismount and examined his injuries—broken ribs and terrible bruises. The injured man's companions made a bundle of his armor and strapped it behind his saddle.

"Was there news of my father, Lord Shonto?" Nishima asked, almost afraid of what she might be told.

The officer turned back toward the scene of the battle as though searching for the answer to Nishima's question. "Lord Shonto joined Lord Taiki," he said, still looking out over the field, "no doubt regaining control of the army. We charged the barbarians then, Lady Nishima, to protect the retreat. Since that time we have seen no sign of Lord Shonto's force." He waved toward the thousands whose paths converged on the Capital. "All we have spoken to are from the Emperor's army which was routed before they could retreat. The Son of Heaven has fled, surrendering the field to the barbarian pretender. It is a black day, Lady Nishima. The north wind blew out of the desert and brought ruin upon us." The man shook his head sadly and said no more.

The small party continued in silence, pushing their tired mounts on toward the Imperial city. As if the gods of wind and weather had not caused enough pain for one day, the western sky was lit with a sunset that caused the heart to ache.

"It is a sign of the end of a glorious empire," one warrior whispered. The others glared at him and he bowed, whispering apologies.

Darkness came slowly, the colors of the sunset lingering after the stars appeared in the east. The lights of the Capital flickered to life and the night finally turned dark. Seven Imperial Guards joined them and nothing was asked or offered about the identities of the riders without armor.

Nishima and Kitsura pulled cowls over their heads and the darkness masked them well enough. Both were careful not to speak and the Komawara guard formed a protective wall between the guardsmen and the others. Little was said, at any rate, each alone with their thoughts.

The Empire had fallen; that was enough to occupy the mind.

Sixty

The northern gate to the Imperial Capital was open and the bridge that crossed the canal to it had not yet been destroyed. A party of Imperial Guards were stationed at the entrance, or had merely taken it upon themselves to stand guard, it was not clear which.

Lady Nishima's party was challenged as they rode up though it seemed to be mainly for the sake of form—so many fled to the Capital. One of the Imperial Guards in Nishima's company identified himself as the Great Khan come looking for a good inn and in the ensuing laughter they slipped into the city of the Emperor.

The streets and canals were choked with the soldiers of the Imperial Army and panicked residents and refugees attempting to make their way toward the city's eastern gates and the Lake of the Lost Dragon. No organized defense was in evidence and robbery and looting had begun in plain view.

"Where is the Imperial Guard?" Kitsura whispered. "Will the Emperor not defend the city? Has he fled?"

Nishima shrugged, looking about, alarmed by what she saw. The guardsmen who had accompanied them into the city immediately went their separate ways and only Shuyun and the three Komawara guards remained. Among the thousands jostling in the streets this seemed little protection.

As they progressed into the city, Nishima's fear began to recede. She realized that the looting was not widespread and that, generally, people were proceeding in an organized way and often offered assistance to others. She began to relax and smiled at her cousin who looked truly frightened.

Many of the soldiers were headed in the direction of the Island Palace, as was a large part of the population.

Rumors said the Emperor had not fled and that the defense was being organized from the palace.

Although horses were seldom used in the Capital, a city of canals and narrow streets, they were common that evening as the retreating army arrived. The city was not designed for transport by horse, however, and they soon encountered a footbridge too narrow to pass.

Shuyun turned into a tight alley which led out onto an avenue that ran along the edge of a major canal.

"Where shall we go, Shuyun-sum?" Nishima asked. Until then there had been little hope of going anywhere but where the crowds went.

"I do not know, my lady." Shuyun answered. "your family residence will have been taken by Imperial Guards some time ago. Perhaps Lady Kitsura's family have not left the city and we could find rest there for the evening. If we want news of what has happened in the field, I suggest we go toward the palace though your name cannot be spoken there."

Nishima looked toward Kitsura. "I would like news of my family, cousin, but I understand your concern for Lord Shonto. My own family is more likely to be safe. Let us go to the palace gates at least and find out what we can."

Nishima gave her cousin a smile of thanks that dissolved immediately into a look of concern. They followed the canal, walking their tired horses across a bridge where, for the first time in their lives, the two ladies were jostled by the people in the streets.

It was late in the night when they came to the Gate of Serenity and in the square before the gate thousands gathered. A few small fires blazed on the cobbles of the square and soldiers and guards rubbed shoulders with all manner of citizens.

Atop the gate black-clad Imperial Guards stood, ignoring all questions and taunts. A single bell sounded the hour of the owl as though only one bellkeeper in the entire city stayed at his post. The hour rang through the teeming city in a strangely empty way.

Nishima's party dismounted and the Komawara guards took the animals in hand and loosened their saddle girths. One of the men walked off to see what could be learned, but when he returned he shrugged. "You can learn anything you desire here. The Emperor has fled, the Emperor has fallen on his sword. The barbarians are at the gates. The barbarians have gone toward Yankura. Everything is being said, nothing is known.'' He found a wall to place his back against and fell promptly to sleep.

Jaku Tadamoto, Commander of the shattered Imperial Guard, found his way into the city aboard a commandeered sampan, sculled by two riverman his guards had pressed into service. He was not seriously wounded though he was bruised and battered and his once fine armor, a gift from his brother Katta, had saved his life more than once.

Scholars make poor warriors, he told himself over and over again.

The Imperial Army had been shattered and sent fleeing in disarray. The Emperor's decision to take command himself had proven the army's undoing. That and the Emperor's refusal to join forces with Lord Shonto. Had Lord Shonto escaped with his army? Tadamoto wondered. Was there hope for the Empire yet?

A group of Imperial Guards looked on as he passed, yet none made a move to bow to their commander. Tadamoto saw no animosity in their looks. It was as though he had simply lost his rank; there was no anger on their part but neither was there respect.

Scholars make poor warriors, he said to himself again.

He had but one intention now, to go to the Palace and seek out his sovereign if the Emperor was not already on his way to Nitashi. Tadamoto had left his young brother, Yasata, as a guard in the palace—determined that at least one member of the Jaku would survive. They would escape. Tadamoto had a plan and gold enough. Had Osha received his message? Had she fled? He would take Yasata and find her. The three would make their way to the Islands of Konojii. It would be years before this desertborn Khan would cross a sea. It was likely that intrigue would have ended his reign before then—this chieftain did not know what would happen when he entered the Island Palace, could not imagine. He would learn to sleep lightly and listen to whispers.

The rivermen brought the boat alongside a set of stone steps that led to a side gate used by the Imperial Guard.

Tadamoto disembarked stiffly and forced himself to stand erect to ascend the steps. The canal and the quay were thronged with people—all trying to escape the barbarians, no doubt. It was a sad sight and sadder yet when Tadamoto realized that he would soon join them. His future would become as uncertain—was as uncertain now.

A password opened the gate and Tadamoto and his guards entered. They were in a square bordered with quarters for the Imperial Guard.

"Colonel Jaku," a guard said quietly. "I will find attendants to assist you with your armor and to see to your injuries."

Tadamoto shook his head. If he kept moving, the stiffness could be worked out as long as he did not stop again. "I have duties. See to yourself now, but I will need a boat—before dawn, no doubt."

"I will arrange for the boat myself, Colonel."

Tadamoto nodded. He walked toward the central palace buildings. The grounds were quiet, deserted, almost serene in contrast to the streets beyond the walls.

Mounting a set of stairs, Tadamoto passed the hedge-maze where he had been given instructions by the Emperor—instructions and threats, as it always was with the Emperor. Two guards challenged him as he came to one of the great doors to the palace. He identified himself and gave the password needed.

"The Emperor, is he in the Palace?"

"I cannot say, Colonel," one guard answered. "Perhaps the Son of Heaven attends the council in the Great Hall."

"Find my brother, Colonel Jaku Yasata." Tadamoto ordered one of them. "I will need him to attend me in my quarters within the hour."

Inside the palace, Tadamoto was met by near darkness; only a small number of the hall lamps had been lit and these smoked from lack of attention. He removed one and used it to find his way.

Few knew the palace as well as the Commander of the Guard. He took an impossibly narrow set of stairs used by servants and kicked open a door to another hall, saving himself some minutes. The Emperor, Tadamoto was certain, would flee at the first opportunity and Tadamoto did not want that to happen.

* * *

There was a stirring in the square and whispers rippled around the edge. Much pushing occurred at the mouth of the major avenue and then mounted armed men appeared, some in black and others in blue or purple.

"Shonto livery!" one of the Komawara guards exclaimed, rousing the two ladies from a near sleep.

Nishima leapt up from the cobbles, surprised by the pain from riding. "It is General Hojo," she said, and had to be restrained by Shuyun from rushing forward.

"Do nothing," Shuyun whispered in her ear, "until we know what occurs here." He kept a grip on her arm and Nishima leaned against him as others stood and vied for a view. She closed her eyes and felt the monk's warmth. Surprised to find herself fighting back tears, she forced herself to open her eyes and focus on the scene, what little of it she could see.

Jaku Katta and the diminutive Butto Joda rode at Hojo's side. All three were covered in dust and appeared very grim. They rode at the head of a substantial force of armed men, Imperial Guards and Shonto men and a few wearing purple. They stopped before the gate and silence fell in the square as ten thousand held their breath, listening.

Hojo looked up at the guard over the gate. "Open the gate," he called out. "We will speak with the Emperor."

The guard stood frozen in place and then disappeared. There was silence and then Hojo rode up to the gate, drew his sword, and pounded on the wood and bronze with his pommel. The square rang with the sound of his anger.

"Open this gate!" Hojo roared, "or we will have it down and the palace will be open to all."

A guard officer appeared above the gate. "We do not open the gate to rebels," he shouted.

Jaku Katta spurred his horse forward, pulling off his helmet as he did so. "Brother." he called out. "You must open the gate. The barbarians march toward the Capital and the Emperor does nothing. The Yamaku have betrayed Wa. Open the gates! We have an Empire to defend."

There was hesitation above the gates. Other black-uniformed men appeared and there was a hasty council. Suddenly a sword flashed above the gate and then others. The crowd surged forward at this and the Shonto guards pushed them back. The black-uniformed men disappeared and a moment later the gates creaked open and Jaku Yasata appeared.

The crowd surged forward again, shouting. "Bring forth the Emperor." A chant began. "Bring forth the Emperor."

The Shonto men and Imperial Guards pushed the crowd back, but even so Nishima felt herself thrust forward and she struggled to keep her grip on Shuyun and Kitsura.

They were close to a Shonto guard now and Shuyun called out and was recognized. Nishima was squeezed through the wall of guards and found herself face to face with Hojo Masakado.

"Lady Nishima! May Botahara be praised." He almost forgot to bow.

The crowd took this up then and Nishima heard the syllables of her name pass around the square like a chanted prayer, a sound she found deeply disturbing.

"You should not be here, Lady Nishima," Hojo started but then stopped. "Come, we must go in while we may."

Dismounting his horse, Jaku Katta bowed to Lady Nishima, a standing bow but low. "The north wind has brought us together, Lady Nishima, I am grateful."

Nodding Nishima stepped away, looking for Hojo. What of my father? she thought, what has happened to him?

The general had turned toward the gate and Nishima fell into step between him and Butto Joda who performed an awkward bow.

"My father, General, I have had no word of him."

Hojo shook his head. "We were separated on the field. The main force has not reached the city though I do not doubt Lord Shonto has managed an organized retreat. Do not fear, Lady Nishima, your father is wise in the ways of the battlefield."

"And Lord Komawara—what of him?" Kitsura asked.

"Lord Komawara," Hojo said with great warmth. "He is out on the plain yet, harrying the enemy in the dark. Lord Butto tells us that, lost in the fog, Komawara encountered the Great Khan and his guard and engaged them, felling a chieftain and sending the Khan running. Lord Komawara and General Jaku,'' he nodded at the guardsman, ''have become the great warriors of our time, Lady Nishima. Their deeds will make a thousand songs.''

Lady Nishima looked away. What a terrible thing, she thought. Behind her, she heard the whispers of the Komawara guard repeating Hojo's words.

War will destroy all of our souls, Nishima thought.

The Emperor paced the length of his chamber and back again. ''Hopeless fools,'' he muttered, ''they will fall into argument over the correct color robes to wear at the surrender of the Empire.''

A knock rattled the door to his chamber and made the Son of Heaven start. ''Enter,'' he called out.

The face of a kneeling guard appeared. ''We have a boat, Emperor. It is being readied as we speak.

''The palace is completely surrounded, Sire. The people . . .'' he hesitated, ''appear unruly, Emperor.''

''They are calling for my head, is that what you mean?''

The guard said nothing but stared down at the floor before him.

''Knock when the boat is ready.''

Before the door closed, the Emperor had returned to his pacing. Venturing onto the balcony, he looked out over the city. Little could be seen, but the open fires in the squares said much. They will have someone's head before the night is over, the Emperor thought. Anyone's will do—nothing less will satisfy them. Well, he almost smiled, let them have any number of ministers and palace officials.

He paced back into the room and looked down at the armor of an unranked guardsman: the disguise for his escape. It went with the uniform he wore. He crossed the room and knelt on a cushion, staying only a second before morbid curiosity drew him back to the balcony, like a man fascinated by his own fear of heights.

Where was Osha? He had sent for her an hour ago. Were the servants afraid to say that she was gone? Run off like his wife and sons the minute he left the palace to go to war. He shook his head.

From the Gate of Serenity he could hear shouting and

what sounded like a crowd chanting. The words were unclear, but he found the sound unsettling all the same.

A knock sounded at the door again and it opened without the Emperor's command. Osha slipped into the room, looking around, her face like a frightened bird's.

"On the balcony, Osha-sum," came the Emperor's voice. "I am basking in the affection of my loyal subjects—who call out for my death."

Osha moved slowly toward the sound of the Emperor's voice and finally saw him, dressed in the black robes of an Imperial Guard, his dark form blotting out the stars.

"Do not be afraid, it is not your name they chant," the Emperor said.

She did not like the tone of his voice.

The Emperor stood on the balcony, his back to the rail, his arms crossed.

"It warms my heart to see that not everyone has abandoned me, Osha-sum. Loyalty has not fled the palace entirely."

She nodded.

"Here is what you must do," the Emperor said matter-of-factly. "There is no one else I would trust. I will make my escape in moments. You must bar the door to this chamber when I leave and open it to no one. Force them to break it down. I should be out of their reach by then. I had the robes of a servant brought for you. A servant will be safe enough."

I am a mistress, Osha thought. She knew what happened to the pampered mistresses of fallen Emperors.

The Emperor pointed at neatly folded cotton robes lying on a small stand. "Quickly. We will throw your robes off the balcony."

Osha nodded. She began unwinding the yards of brocade sash. Looking up, she saw the Emperor watching. I am about to die at the hands of the people he has betrayed and he stares at me as though I am a hired woman. She closed her eyes and continued.

Steeling her nerve as she finished unwinding her sash, Osha asked the question that haunted her. "I hope your officers survived, Sire, so that they may assist you in the future. Colonel Jaku, for one, would be a great loss."

She turned her back to the Emperor and removed her outer robe.

"The Colonel has acted as a loyal subject should—putting himself in the path of the barbarian army so that his Emperor might escape. As for the rest, they turned and ran, trying to save their miserable lives, may they be damned for eternity."

Osha steadied herself as she felt the room spin.

"Osha-sum, shyness does not become a dancer. Do not hide your beauty."

Nishima fell in behind General Hojo as Jaku Katta led the way to the Great Hall. The tramp of soldiers behind her was disquieting and so out of place. She had been in these halls many times, but they had been filled with laughter and music and poetry on those occasions. She felt Kitsura take her sleeve, like a shy child not wanting to be left behind.

"General Hojo, what is it you intend here?" Nishima asked nervously.

Hojo did not slow his pace. "We intend to force this fool Emperor to perform his duties. He cannot leave his throne, as much as it would gladden me if he did," the general said, casting a glance at Jaku. "We cannot fight the barbarians and a civil war as well," Hojo said, pointedly.

Nishima saw Jaku shake his head. "This Emperor, in an attempt to bring down your lord's House, sold our Empire to the barbarian Khan, General Hojo," Jaku said with force. "I have not changed my opinion—the Emperor is a threat to all."

Nishima looked back at Hojo, wondering how he would respond. The two officers had obviously been arguing the point.

"We will let Lord Shonto decide the fate of Emperors, General Jaku. Soldiers will always make decisions with a sword. It is our way, but there are other ways." He said this with finality.

They reached the doors to the Great Hall and the guards stationed there drew their swords. Jaku did the same, followed by the men around him.

"Stand aside," Jaku commanded as he pulled open his

face-mask. ''The Emperor you serve has fallen. You cannot be loyal to a ghost. Stand aside.''

The men hesitated, exchanging glances, and then gave a half bow and laid down their swords. The doors were thrown open and the members of the council turned, their eyes wide. Immediately the officials leapt to their feet and fled in every possible direction, ornate robes flapping, like a flurry of escaping moths. The Dragon Throne was empty.

Hojo stormed into the room while his guard chased down several running officials and dragged them back to him. Nishima remained outside the door, trying to hear what was said. A commotion to her right drew her attention, and she saw Jaku Katta disappearing down the hall with Lord Butto on his heels.

General Hojo came out the door then, an official in tow. ''This man has kindly offered to lead us to the Emperor,'' Hojo said, pushing the man in front of him. Something drew his attention. ''Where do they go?'' Hojo waved his sword down the hall at the backs of retreating Komawara guards.

''They follow General Jaku and Lord Butto,'' Nishima said.

Hojo looked around as though sure he would find Jaku beside him.

Nishima pointed. ''That is the way to the Imperial apartments, General.''

''May the gods take them!'' Hojo swore and set off at a run, followed by the entire company.

Shuyun paced the general. ''Those Komawara guards wear the green lacings on their sleeve—they were Hajiwara men, General.''

Hojo nodded, saving his breath. They came to stairs and the armored men lagged behind. Shuyun looked over his shoulder once and then sprinted ahead. Seeing this, Nishima pushed past General Hojo and the other men exhausted from battle. She ignored the calls of her cousin and the guard, focusing on the sound of Shuyun's running feet just ahead of her.

Tadamoto reached the head of the stairs leading to the Emperor's apartments. From the guards before the Great Hall he had learned that the Emperor was in the Imperial

apartments and, though less than certain he would be
allowed through the halls, Tadamoto had set out. To his
surprise, he had not been challenged once. The Imperial
Guard, their commander realized, had broken and run
just like the army in the field.

Down the long hallway he saw lamps and the black of
guards before a door, indicating the Emperor was not
unprotected. Akantsu is a fine swordsman, Tadamoto reminded himself, he is never entirely unprotected. Loos-
ening his blade in his scabbard, Tadamoto started down
the hall.

As he approached the guards before the Emperor's
chambers, Tadamoto heard the pounding of boots on the
stairs behind. Turning, he saw a single black-clad guard
crest the stairs with a leap and come running down the
hall toward him. Drawing his sword, Tadamoto signaled
the guards, who rose and drew their weapons as well.

Jaku Katta slid to a stop on the polished floor, facing
his brother. He reached up and removed his helmet and
stood regarding Tadamoto.

"It is my hope the gods have brought us here with the
same purpose, brother."

Tadamoto did not lower his sword. "Do not do this,
Katta-sum." He swallowed with difficulty. "Do not stain
our name with this crime."

"He is a traitor, brother. You know this is the truth.
Wa deserves a sovereign who understands honor. Let me
pass."

The sound of running feet in the stairwell.

Jaku did not look back.

"They are my men, Tadamoto-sum. You can do nothing. Stand aside."

The colonel shook his head. "I cannot, brother."

Jaku nodded. Very slowly he tossed his helmet aside
and it rattled on the floor, sliding to a stop against the
wall.

Turning toward the Emperor, Osha removed a second
robe, the sheer silk wafting to the floor like a falling
banner. She could not stop the tears, but she did not sob.
Forcing her feet to move forward, she stepped out into
the cool night.

The Emperor watched her with some interest. He

reached out to her as she approached and she took his hands and pressed them to her, his touch fueling her resolve.

She stood looking at the confusion in the Emperor's face for a second, realizing she could not let the instant pass. "Tadamoto-sum," she whispered, "was my lover."

Saying this, Osha pushed the Emperor, her Sonsa training giving her surprising strength. As he fell back, the Emperor's grip tightened on one of her hands and she grabbed the rail with the other, pulling against his great weight. Groping with one hand, he grasped at the balustrade, cursing her, but Osha let go of the rail and caught this hand before he could save himself. And then, without hesitation, she followed him over the railing, her motion graceful as though she took flight.

Jaku drew his sword and faced his brother who stepped back immediately, his guard faltering. Men were in the hall behind, running. Butto Joda came to a position off to Jaku Katta's right, stepping into the Tiger's line of vision but staying out of reach of his sword.

"General Katta?" the youth said. "General Hojo is correct. This is a decision for Lord Shonto or the Great Council. I beg you reconsider."

Jaku did not appear to hear. Lunging forward, he took the sword from Tadamoto's hands so that it bounced off a post and fell to the floor.

Tadamoto faced the point of his brother's blade, but his attention was drawn back over Katta's shoulder. "Brother . . ." he said, lifting a hand to point.

That second's warning saved Jaku's life. The first Hajiwara guard's blow missed Jaku's neck, the blade cutting through armor and deep into the guardsman's right arm. He raised the sword again as the Black Tiger stumbled aside. Tadamoto leapt in between and took the second blow on the side of his helmet, which drove him to the floor.

Jaku spun and landed a blow one-handed, accounting for one as the other Hajiwara men fell on him. The guardsman retreated, using a post to protect his injured right side. Lord Butto reached for his sword but, unexpectedly, a Hajiwara guard sprang at the young lord and drove the pommel of his sword into Butto's face mask, leaving him limp on the floor.

The two guards before the Emperor's door held their places, swords at the ready. Jaku circled away from these men, unsure who they would side with. Someone else reached the stairhead and started down the hall.

"We will avenge Lord Hajiwara, General," Narihira Chisato hissed, "for it was you who placed him in the path of Lord Shonto with lies and false promises."

The injured Hajiwara man leapt at Jaku. As the guardsman cut him down, Narihira stepped in coolly, sword raised. The Black Tiger fell heavily to the floor and did not move. Narihira raised his sword for the final stroke but found himself propelled across the room, hitting the floor and sliding to the feet of the guards at the Emperor's door. One held the tip of his sword to Narihira's throat, and the Hajiwara guard lay still.

Nishima arrived to see Shuyun literally toss the Hajiwara guard aside and then bend over Jaku Katta, who lay in a growing pool of blood. The monk made a sign to Botahara and rose, looking around.

"Is there no hope, Brother?" Nishima asked. She stood across the room, frozen in place.

Shuyun shook his head. "His spirit has fled, my lady. Jaku Katta is in the hands of the Perfect Master. May Botahara protect him."

Shuyun crossed to Lord Butto who lay unmoving. Removing the youth's helmet, the monk found his eyes open, only whites showing. Coming to stand beside him, Nishima laid her hand on Shuyun's shoulder.

Katta is dead, she thought, trying to make it seem possible. But why do I feel so little now when I believed I felt so strongly before?

"He breathes," Shuyun said. "His life force is strong."

"He was knocked down with a pommel, Brother," one of the Imperial guards said. "He cannot be badly hurt, I'm certain."

"Please, Lady Nishima. . . ." Shuyun took her hand and drew her down. "Watch Lord Butto."

The monk then rose and went to the other fallen men as Hojo and the others came into the hall.

The other Hajiwara guards were dead, but Tadamoto had raised himself to one elbow, and propped himself there with visible effort.

"My brother?" Tadamoto said in a near whisper.

"Who is your brother, Colonel?" Shuyun asked.

"Katta," he said with effort.

"Lie back, Colonel Jaku, you are injured," Shuyun said. Softly he removed the ruin of the guardsman's helmet.

Tadamoto shook him off when the monk reached out to probe the wound.

"My brother . . ." Tadamoto turned and saw the great, still form of Jaku Katta lying against the wall in a dark pool. Sobs racked him and he would let no one near.

Hojo stood looking on. He made a sign to Botahara.

"He intended to kill the Emperor, General Hojo," Shuyun said. The monk motioned at Narihira still lying at the feet of the two Imperial Guards. "It was Jaku Katta the Hajiwara men had vowed revenge against, not Butto Joda."

"The Emperor is inside?" Hojo panted, motioning to the door with his sword.

The two Imperial Guards held their positions.

"We will not harm your Emperor," General Hojo said. "Let us pass."

One guard shook his head, pushing Narihira away with his foot.

Scrambling to his feet, the Hajiwara retainer joined the other party where Shonto guards pushed him to the rear.

Hojo motioned Shonto swordsmen forward.

Lady Nishima turned away and suddenly her cousin came and knelt beside her. The ringing of swords stopped abruptly and Hojo stepped up to the now unguarded door.

"Wait," Tadamoto said, lurching to his feet. Supported by a man in Butto livery, he followed Hojo as he tried the door and found it unbarred.

Entering the room everyone stopped, searching the dim corners, looking for doors. The room was empty.

"He has hidden or made his escape," Hojo said, driving his pommel into a gloved palm.

Waving at the balcony, Tadamoto moved forward. On the balustrade a torn scrap of silk wafted in the light breeze. The guard colonel stepped out onto the balcony, looking around, confused.

One of Hojo's officers peered over the balcony and turned to his commander, inclining his head almost imperceptibly. The general hurried forward and Tadamoto did the same. A white form lay on the stones far below, a dark shadow at its side.

"There is our Emperor," Hojo whispered. Beside him Tadamoto turned slowly and spiralled to the floor.

A Shonto officer pointed out beyond the north gate where a long line of torches snaked its way south.

"And there is Lord Shonto and his army." Hojo said, his voice strangely quiet. "Inform Lady Nishima. She will have some good news this night."

Standing inside the Gate of Serenity, Nishima held tightly to Kitsura's arm. They almost leaned upon each other, their exhaustion was so great.

"Food," Nishima whispered to Kitsura. "I will greet my father and then food and perhaps a bath. If we are to escape or face a barbarian attack, let us do it fed and clean, and perhaps even rested."

"I could sleep upon the cobbles," Kitsura said.

"You did, cousin," Nishima reminded her, but her lightness of mood was entirely false, in her heart she sent up a silent prayer: *bring him to me safely. He is good and wise. Bring him safely.*

The gates were open and soldiers pushed back the crowds outside. They jostled and shouted and still called for the Emperor, his death not yet known, and then, suddenly, they cheered.

"That will be the hero, Komawara," Kitsura said. "Imagine."

Men on horses appeared in the dim light, framed by the great arch under the dark sweep of tile. Three men rode abreast, one in darkest blue, one in gray, and one in Shonto blue. Nishima let out a long sigh and another prayer to powers unnamed—a prayer of thanks.

Outside, the people in the streets fell utterly silent, and then Nishima heard a single voice—the sound of a woman crying. She found herself moving forward, Kitsura trying to restrain her. She shook off her cousin's grip and continued. Komawara was dismounting now and the rider in

Shonto blue also: *her stepbrother, Shokan.* And then she was running. Shokan saw the movement and turned toward her, his face black from dust and streaked with tears. Nishima felt her body stop, as though it obeyed commands from forces more powerful than her will.

Shonto's personal guard came slowly through the gate bearing a bier of lances upon their shoulders and on it lay a form draped with a banner—the blue silk of the shinta blossom. Nishima felt her knees strike the ground. A cry of deepest agony tore at her throat. Then she felt hands lift her, and she pressed her face into the blue lacing of Shokan's armor. Kitsura's arm encircled her shoulder and she heard the soothing voice of Shuyun, chanting a prayer for the dead.

Nishima had not eaten, bathed, or slept. She sat in a strange room in the Imperial Palace turning a cold cup of cha compulsively between her hands. She stared off, deep into her memories, perhaps, and looked as if she would begin to sob again at any second.

Kitsura had left her for a few minutes, lured by a hot bath, and Shuyun was off seeing to the ceremony for her father. There was so little time; they would have to perform the rites before dawn. *They're going to burn him,* she thought, and this realization was like a blow to her heart.

A tap sounded on the door to the room and a maid's face appeared—one of Nishima's own maids!

"Tokiwa," Nishima exclaimed, "how is it that you are here?"

"Steward Kamu brought us, my Lady," she bowed, hesitating, her eyes cast down. "I'm sorry, my Lady."

Nishima nodded. Her mouth formed the words, *thank you,* but no sound came.

"Lord Shonto and Steward Kamu wish to speak with you, Lady Nishima."

"Please bring them to me," she said. Perhaps their company will help, she thought.

The maid disappeared.

Seconds later Shokan and Kamu entered. They bowed and knelt on the mats.

"I have no cushions, I am sorry," Nishima said, her voice small.

Shokan shrugged.

"It lifts my heart to see you safe, Kamu-sum. It is a miracle." She looked into each of the men's faces. Certainly they are able to maintain an appearance of dignity better than I, she thought. I must look a ruin.

"The miracle," Kamu answered, "is Brother Shu-yun's servant, Kalam. He went out into the fog and met a horde of barbarian raiders, sending them off chasing phantoms. He led us and hid us and put his ear to the ground and lured barbarians off into the mist and even drew his sword against his own people. He will be a man of Wa yet."

Nishima's smile was pained.

"Nishi-sum," Shokan said gently, "despite all, we must prepare for the future. There are many things that must be spoken of."

Nishima nodded, a sudden coldness spread through her. "You will not marry me to this Khan, will you, Shokan?" she said, surprised by the edge of hysteria in her voice.

"Sister, I would not marry you to anyone you did not choose."

She turned her tea bowl, still focusing on nothing.

"Nishima, the Lords of Wa and the officials of the government are meeting in the Great Hall as we speak. There is no heir to the throne."

"There are sons, Shokan-sum. Have you forgotten?"

Skokan glanced over at Kamu. "Wakaro is certainly dead, and the others will follow their brother once the people learn that the Yamaku have fallen. They are a despised family, Nishima-sum. No Yamaku will sit upon the Dragon Throne again."

There was silence for a second, but Nishima did not really take this information in. She could not force herself to focus on the conversation.

"If a suitable sovereign is not found, there will be a civil war, Sister."

Nishima looked up. I have lost a father, why have they come to bother me with this, she asked herself? "Shokan-sum, excuse me for saying so, but you are speaking the worst foolishness. The Khan is about to take the throne. In a few hours he will sit in the Yamaku's place. The Empire, I may remind you, has fallen."

Shokan rubbed his palm with his fingers. "If there is not a chosen sovereign, claimants will spring up all over Wa. There will never be a concerted effort to oust the barbarians, for there will be no alliance strong enough. The lords of Wa will war among themselves, making the barbarians' work easy. It will be a generation before we see the enemy gone, perhaps more."

"They are such fools," Nishima said coolly, but there was no conviction in her voice.

"Nishima-sum!" Shokan reached over and took hold of her arm, spilling cha over her hands. "You must listen."

She fixed him with a cold glare and he let go of her hands. "I am listening, brother. What is it you have come to say?"

Shokan took a deep breath.

Nishima realized he waited for eye contact before he spoke and so she looked up, not trying to hide her anger.

"There is one candidate acceptable to all," her stepbrother said, speaking with unnecessary precision. "If you will consent to become our Empress, Nishima-sum, we will avoid civil war."

Nishima started to laugh, but the laugh died in her throat. She began to speak and could not. She stared at her brother as though he had spoken words that, beyond all doubt, confirmed him mad.

"Lady Nishima," Kamu spoke gently. "Thousands of lives may be saved by your decision. There is an entire Empire to think of."

My father is dead. The Empire has fallen. Why will you not leave me in peace? "Kamu-sum," she said as reasonably as she could. "I know nothing of the ways of government. How can you seriously expect me to rule? This is madness," she said, exasperated. Again she began, trying to achieve a tone of reason. "What of Lady Kitsura? The Omawara have as much Hanama blood as the Fanisan. Perhaps she will consent to be your Empress. Please, brother. Speak no more of this . . . I cannot bear it."

"Sister, my father raised me to understand my duty." Shokan's voice was as cool as hers now. "Did he not do the same with you?"

Lady Nishima stared at Shokan. *My father is dead, how can you insult me now? Have I not paid enough?*

"Lord Shonto," she said to her stepbrother, "if I seriously believed that I could play a part in saving Wa, I would not hesitate to do so. But once this crisis is passed and we avoid civil war—then Wa will be saddled with an Empress who knows nothing of the art of ruling. If one day we do oust the barbarians, I would not know where to begin to rebuild an Empire. I would be a worse ruler than the Yamaku." She waved a hand at the door. "Bother me no more with this. We have a lord whose ceremonies must be seen to."

"I will say no more, sister," Shokan answered, "though I would ask you to come to the Great Hall and inform the gathered lords of your own decision. Then you may see the civil war begin with your own eyes."

"Shokan-sum!" Nishima cried. "You do not know what it is you ask. Please do not place this burden upon me." Her hands trembled and she dropped the cha bowl to the mat. "Please, it is my life you ask for." She covered her face with her hands but no tears came.

Oh, father, she thought, *they are not satisfied with one Shonto life, they want another.*

"Sister," Shokan said very softly, "I would spare you this if I could. I would take it upon myself, but I cannot. By midday a barbarian army will be at our gate. We must have a new sovereign and we must have made our escape. If you will not take up this duty, the Empire will dissolve into chaos. Let me tell the gathered lords that you require time to consider. That you will answer in an hour. Let us hold off calamity as long as possible. Sit and ponder the alternatives, Sister. Speak with your Spiritual Advisor. Let me say you will decide within the hour?"

Nishima sat for a long moment, then nodded her head, the tiniest of movements. "I will give you my decision at dawn. Please ask Brother Shuyun if he will attend me."

Kamu looked over at Shokan who nodded toward the door. Bowing, the two men rose and left, closing the door quietly behind them, and making Nishima think that they suddenly felt they should not disturb the grieving daughter. As though they had not thrown her already uncertain life to the wind once again.

She sat unmoving, and then Lady Kitsura entered through a screen. She was dressed in the silk robes of a peer—one of Nishima's robes, in fact.

"There is a bath, Nishi-sum, and your servants have found some of your own robes." Kitsura paused.

Nishima did not look up. "I can accept the fall of the Empire," she said in a flat voice, "more easily than I can believe that my father is gone—he seemed the greater of the two."

Kitsura nodded. Kneeling, she took Nishima's hands. "A bath will help, cousin, truly."

Nishima nodded. Servants came and led her to her bath, leaving her to soak in peace as she preferred. Carefully laid out within view were robes and combs and perfumes, and the box that belonged to her mother decorated with the warisha blossom of the Fanisan House. Nishima closed her eyes. So many had died that day. Jaku was dead, she realized. His death poem was hidden in her hunting costume. I must have it sent to his brother, poor man. She hugged her arms across her breasts and felt the warmth work at knotted muscles. Remembering the teaching of Brother Satake, she began an exercise to relax her muscles and calm her spirit. Her focus was so poor that this was an indifferent success.

A tap on the screen preceded a maid's voice from outside. "Brother Shuyun awaits, my Lady."

Nishima fought back a sudden attack of tears and, when she felt she had mastered them, she stepped out of the bath.

Dressing without too much haste was difficult, but she forced herself to move slowly lest her servants think she rushed to meet a man. "Tokiwa," Nishima said to the maid who waited beyond the screen. "I wish to pray with Brother Shuyun, I do not want to be disturbed for any reason."

"Yes, my Lady."

"Have you laid a bed for me in the adjoining room? I will try to sleep later."

"It has been done, Lady Nishima."

"Thank you, Tokiwa. You may go. I will tie my sash."

She could easily imagine the servant nodding and performing her graceful bow before hurrying off.

Nishima left her hair down and combed it carefully. She tied her sash with particular care.

Slipping into the room, Nishima was disappointed to find Shuyun not present and then she heard his voice whisper her name from the balcony.

Shuyun was standing at the rail, looking out to the north. Nishima came and stood close beside him, resting her hand on his shoulder.

"Upon the fields," he said, pointing off to the distance.

A fire burned there and then Nishima realized that it must be many rih distant—the figures moving around it were so small. The blaze was enormous.

"What is this?" Nishima asked.

Shuyun shook his head. "Even the Kalam does not know."

"They burn the fallen, certainly."

Shuyun shook his head. "Perhaps, but it is not their way, Lady Nishima."

They stood a moment longer and then Nishima took his hand and gently led Shuyun away from the spectacle, back inside. Nishima opened a screen at the room's end where an enormous bed had been made. A single lamp cast a soft glow.

Nishima stopped him at the bed's edge and embraced the monk who returned the caress with more warmth than usual. Nishima guided his hand to the knot on her sash. "Pull," she whispered.

Doing as he was instructed Shuyun felt the knot give and unravel in his hand.

"A Lover's Knot," she said.

The monk almost stepped away, but she held him.

"I am a fallen Brother," he said, an edge of anguish in his voice. "A lost one."

She held him close, afraid he would leave. "Do not despair, Shuyun-sum, I have found you. Please stay with me. Tonight I have need of a friend more than ever." She reached back and took the sash from his hand and let the heavy brocade slip to the floor, uncoiling itself around her feet.

"They have asked me to ascend the throne," she said suddenly, her voice the smallest whisper.

He nodded. "I have been told."

She stepped away, pulling the quilts back on the bed and drawing the monk in after her.

They lay close in the dim light of the lamp. "I must tell them what I will do in a few hours."

They did not speak for some minutes. "I do not think I can bear my father's death, Shuyun-sum. I have not the strength . . . and they want me to be their Empress."

"I believe Lord Shonto will be reborn in only a few days. His spirit will return, though you may never meet it or know it if you do."

Nishima did not answer immediately. "Even so, he is lost to me. I am a selfish, spoiled peer, and it is *my* loss that grieves me though it shames me to say this.

"It is not surprising that I have led you from the path, Shuyun-sum. I am so far from perfection it is a marvel I was not born an ant."

Shuyun smiled. "Be careful what you say, ants have Empresses also. It is a fate that can pursue you from lifetime to lifetime."

The sounds of distant voices reached them, the chanting of the crowd beyond the gates.

"I do not know what answer I should give the lords of Wa. My father warned that an act of bravery might be required of me, yet I do not think I am brave enough. I know nothing of ruling, Shuyun-sum. It seems a sham to ascend a throne that in a few hours will belong to this barbarian Khan."

"I am not certain the barbarian will be long for this throne," Shuyun whispered. "Perhaps only days."

Nishima pulled back so that she could see the monk's face. "Why do you say this?"

"In the mist, when I disappeared and had you and Lady Kitsura wait—do you remember the coughing? The tribesman suffered from the plague, there is no doubt. It will spread among the army of the desert more easily than the wind blows through unshuttered houses. It will be a great tragedy. Tens of thousands will die, and if the Khan takes the city the plague will spread through the Capital. Barbarian patrols have crossed the river and turn back all those who hoped to make their escape. The population of the city is four times what it would be normally."

"Botahara save us." Nishima said. "We will all die—barbarians and people of Wa alike. Is there no escape?"

Shuyun nodded. "For the few, there is hope of escape."

Nishima closed her eyes. "Do the others know of this, the plague?"

"I have told only General Hojo. It is possible that others may guess what the barbarians' fires mean—they must burn the plague-dead and all of their belongings, perhaps even their horses, hoping this will save them. It will not." Shuyun paused. "I regret that General Hojo will not listen to my counsel in this."

Nishima pulled back so that she could touch the monk's cheek, tracing the outline with great tenderness. "What have you counseled?"

"To save Wa, we must save the barbarians. It is the only possibility."

Nishima froze, unable to believe what she had heard. "Even I am aghast at this suggestion. They have murdered the length our Empire."

"And so have we, my lady. You do not know how many refugees have died on the roads and the canal." Shuyun took her hand and pressed it to his heart. She felt the warmth, the tingle of chi. "When the barbarians reach the Capital tomorrow, I could walk out to meet them under a flag of peace. I would offer them an exchange. My Order will save them from the plague if they will lay down their arms. Thousands of lives might be saved."

Nishima propped herself up on one arm. The people of the Capital—the plague would ravage the city, while she escaped. But save invaders? No one would agree to this. She looked out the half open screen, and saw the flicker of the barbarians' pyre, far out on the plain.

Did not Botahara teach compassion? she asked herself. "Is it possible, Shuyun-sum? Will this Khan believe you?" She rolled back, staring up at the ceiling, her hand to her brow. "If not, you would be in great danger." Her mind raced through the possibilities now. "Will the Botahist Brothers perform this task? The barbarians are not followers of the True Path."

"Few are, Nishima-sum." Shuyun pushed her hair back behind her ear. "The Brothers will agree reluctantly. It saddens me to say this, but I believe it is more likely that the barbarians will listen than it is that the lords of Wa will agree to this course."

"But it is our only hope," Nishima said, convinced now that Shuyun was right. "Tens of thousands could be saved—barbarians and people of Wa alike. The lords of Wa must be convinced."

"They will not be. Their hatred of the barbarians is unreachable. Tell them that plague is about to sweep the barbarian army from the Empire and they will not care how many people of Wa will have to die so that this will occur. Sacrifice is their way. To suggest we save the invaders—they will not allow it."

Nishima rolled so that she pressed her cheek close to Shuyun's. "You make my choice difficult," she whispered in his ear.

An act of bravery, he had told her. There had been so many already.

"Shuyun-sum, tell me truthfully—if an Empress commands that this be done, will the lords of Wa obey?"

Shuyun considered for a moment. "Lord Taiki, General Hojo, and your brother control the army. No others have an organized force. Will these three obey a command from the Empress they have placed on the throne? I believe they will, Lady Nishima, though I fear it is not the answer you wish to hear."

Nishima closed her eyes for some time, breathing as Brother Satake had taught her. Oh, father, it is my greatest fear. You ask me to overcome my greatest fear. She felt her heart beating and forced it to calm. *Thousands of lives she told herself, balanced against my own desires and fears.*

Opening her eyes she whispered to the room. "If Hojo and Shokan-sum will agree to your plan, I will ascend the throne though my entire life I have vowed I would not."

She felt Shuyun draw her close. Pressing her eyes closed she said a silent prayer, though it was not to any god. Nishima spoke to Lord Shonto, praying she had chosen correctly. May this be the act of bravery, she thought, and not an act of foolishness.

She whispered close to Shuyun's ear. "What name will I take if I am to ascend the throne of Wa?"

Shuyun drew her closer and said, *"Shigei."*

"I do not know that name."

"It is from the mountain tongue, as is my name. Shuyun—he who bears. Shigei—she who renews. It is the name of a mountain spirit. It is also the name given to fair spring winds and to the scent of new budding leaves. She who renews. Empress Shigei."

Nishima nodded slowly. "I will need the wisdom of your counsel."

"You will have the wisest of counselors, my Empress," he whispered. "You will rule with your heart as well as your reason and your subjects will come to love you as they have few others."

The lamp flickered out and they lay still in the darkness until the gray light of dawn appeared through the half-open screens.

Sixty-one

The sunrise filtered through a long tear in the cloud, somewhere far out over the unseen sea. Among the weeping birch trees on the edge of the Pool of the Sun the Shonto guard had built the pyre. The sound of the three small falls that crossed the pond mixed with the breeze moving through the new leaves and made Nishima think of her father's private garden.

Under the silk banner that he had borne into battle, Lord Shonto Motoru lay hidden from the eyes of those who cared for him. To one side Kamu stood holding the lord's favorite stallion, a sword strapped to the saddle— the same sword the Emperor had given the lord in this very garden.

The death of his ancestor, Shokan had said, *an honorable death.*

Brother Shuyun completed a long prayer, and all present made signs to Botahara. Nishima felt Shokan release her hand as he stepped forward, a surcoat of pure white over his Shonto blue catching the light of the sun.

Removing a tiny ornate scroll from his sleeve he paused to find his voice.

Through a long winter we have awaited
The rebirth of spring.
During the cold nights
We dreamed
Of the plum tree's blossom

Along the shore of an endless canal
Cranes stand among rushes
So still
The harmony of their world
Is left untouched

The boat passes,
White against blue waters,
Its wake causing birds to fly
Rising up among blossom laden trees

Passing on the breeze, the boat
Follows the ribbon of blue,
As narrow and perfect
As the river among the clouds

Shokan and Lord Komawara had begun this poem during a sleepless night and Nishima had completed it that morning—many others would follow.

Stillness and quiet descended as all present offered their silent prayers. Nishima looked around. The more important lords of Wa, those who had not fled the Capital, were present, as were the lords who had followed her father south from Seh. The senior officials of the Palace were present; chancellors, ministers, and sundry advisors had come to pay respects to the Emperor's most powerful lord—the man who had given his life in an attempt to save Wa. Lord Komawara stood beside a recovered Lord Butto, the two so grim that it hurt Nishima to look at them.

She made herself breathe in careful rhythm, for her part of the ceremony was yet to come. Conscious of her new role, Nishima was determined to conduct herself accordingly though certain this would be the most difficult thing she had ever done.

At a nod from Shuyun she stepped forward, and a bowing attendant passed her a small torch, its flame guttering in the breeze. She closed her eyes for a second, certain she would be overcome by the odors of the burning oil. *I release his spirit from this world,* she reminded herself. She bowed low, holding back the sleeve of her white robe, and touched the torch to the pyre. At first nothing seemed to occur, but then the lamp oil caught and the flames rose up, spreading both left and right with a sound like a giant wing beating the air.

She stepped back then and tossed the torch into the flame. As the silk banner caught, she closed her eyes.

"Lady Nishima," the attendant said softly.

She turned and took the handful of white plum petals

she was offered and these she tossed onto the flaming pyre where the rising heat took them and scattered them on the wind.

The fire crackled and roared now, too hot to be near. The mourners stepped back then and she felt Shokan take her arm. Space opened up around them and Nishima felt the distance despite the presence of her brother. Isolation, she thought, a life of isolation. Only that morning her decision had been made known and already she was set apart.

I cannot turn back, she told herself. *Tens of thousands of lives depend on the strength of my resolve.*

But Shokan and Hojo and Lord Taiki had agreed to support Shuyun's plan though they argued against it strongly. In the end they had decided that having Nishima as an Empress was more important. Then had come her first test. She discovered that the lords of Wa and the senior Ministers of the Right and Left had already selected a name for the new Empress. A name from another tongue was not acceptable, they explained; there were traditions.

Nishima had been forced to be utterly firm with them—she would ascend the throne as the Empress Shigei. Their choice was to offer the throne to someone else. They had acquiesced: a name was an important thing, no doubt, but there were certainly other matters of greater consequence.

Once she had ascended the throne, Nishima thought, this tactic would no longer be possible. There would be many more such battles of wills, Nishima thought, many, many more. Fighting them when all she felt was a need to be alone, to have time and peace to heal the wound inside her—that would be the challenge. It would be so easy to give in, but she must not. She would be an Empress and that meant she would not let ambitious counselors gain control of the government.

They ascended a flight of steps and attendants waited there with a sedan chair. Nishima looked at this with dismay.

"I will walk," she said firmly.

"But, Empress," the Minister of the Right said in his most pleasant voice, "it is unseemly for a member of the Imperial family to walk."

''I am not yet an Empress nor a member of the Imperial family. I am Shonto. I will walk.''

Tugging Shokan's arm she skirted the sedan chair and ascended the next stairs as quickly as decorum would allow. The sound of the funeral pyre could still be heard and as they reached the Palace doors she turned to look back. White smoke rose in a high column from the shore of the glittering pond and she thought of her father lifting up to soar among the clouds.

Movement caught her eye beyond the fire. It was the barbarian army gathering beyond the city walls. Botahara save us all, she thought.

It was the shortest and least elaborate investiture in the history of the Empire of Wa. Ceremonial meals were reduced to a few dishes being arranged to symbolize an entire part of a ceremony. Elaborate rituals involving the Imperial Governors of the Empire's nine provinces were not performed, for there was not a single governor in the Capital. Swearing of oaths by lords and officials and the giving of gifts and favors and ranks—all of these things were left to another time—all present hoping there would be such a time. Only the short, final ceremony was to be performed and this was a great relief to the Empress-to-be.

Nishima was borne to the doors of the Great Audience Hall in the sedan chair she had rejected earlier and here she was allowed to step down to a carpet that stretched the length of hall to the steps of the Dragon Throne.

To each side of this knelt the counselors and senior officials and behind these men, instead of the ceremonial guard, stood men in Shonto blue. In truth, many of the members of the Great Council and of the guard had fled the city and those remaining had been forced to make do as best they could. The Major Chancellor, the second most powerful person in the Empire, had escaped some days earlier. To the dismay of the court Nishima had appointed Kamu to this position temporarily. He knelt at the foot of the steps to the dais, his ceremonial robes spreading out around him like a fan, the gold scroll of his office held in his only hand.

As Nishima entered, the assembled officials bowed their heads to the stone and remained there for some moments. A slow chant of great beauty began as the new Empress slowly progressed the length of the hall, the Ministers of the Right and Left following three paces behind on their knees.

Walk beside me, father, Nishima prayed, *I have not the courage.* She felt as though her spirit had wrenched itself free and she both walked on the carpeted floor and floated up to the heights of the hall, watching herself as she progressed, a small uncertain child in the immense hall.

Do not let my spirit escape, she prayed, *not yet.*

Shokan knelt with his forehead pressed to the stone at the end of the first row of officials and this touched some part of her and called her spirit back, for with his face hidden, Shokan looked for all the world like his father. Her father's presence seemed to be there and this gave her strength.

Before the throne a silk cushion had been set and the Ministers of the Right and Left assisted her in kneeling here and then retreated to their places. Nishima's robes spread out around her, Imperial Crimson bearing the five-clawed, golden dragon. At her insistence a tiny shinta blossom had been embroidered on her right sleeve, the flower of the warisha on her left. Kamu knelt three paces off, his head touched to the floor. Nishima bowed to her ancestors on the empty throne.

The chant continued, rising in volume, reverberating in the great hall. The Minister of the Right came forward and laid the sword of office across the arms of the throne and retreated. An ancient bronze gong was brought forward by the Minister of the Left and this was set at the foot of the throne to one side.

There were no words to be spoken by the ascending sovereign—far too many Emperors had been children barely out of the cradle—but the Major Chancellor rose to a kneeling position and recited the sovereign's oath of office. Kamu's voice gained strength and authority with each phrase.

"It is the duty of the Empress to care for her children, the people of the Empire of Wa, to care for the lands and the forests and the waterways. In time of famine the Empress will give food to her charges; in time of war, provide shelter and restore peace to the people who are the children of the Empress. In gratitude the subjects of the

Empress will attend each to their duties, giving their loyalty only to the sovereign of Wa. May Botahara bless the most revered Empress, Shigei, of the Imperial line of the Fanisan House.''

The courtiers rose to their knees, making a sign to Botahara. As the chant came to an end, Nishima bowed once more to the throne. She was to rise and take her place now, but she could not will her legs to move.

This is wrong, Nishima thought. What is it I do? She could not get up.

Kamu opened his mouth to whisper. She saw ''Nishima'' begin to form on his lips, but he stopped himself. She looked over at him, imploring him to help, and he could only stare back, unable to speak or move.

There was utter silence in the hall then, all eyes turned toward her. The carved dragon that curved around the back of the throne seemed also to stare.

I must, Nishima said, *I must.*

Willing herself to rise, Nishima found her feet under her and, with great deliberation, placed a foot upon the first jade step and then the second and finally the third. Two steps to the throne. She lifted the sword of office with both hands and turned to face her court. Stiffly she lowered herself to the cushion on the jade throne. The Great Council of State knelt before her, each official reflected in the polished stone of the floor.

And now I must rule, Nishima thought, and the realization was like waking in a cold room. The warmth of the dream she had lived had vanished and her feelings seemed distant, confused.

As one, the entire assemblage bowed again and then rose to the kneeling position. Kamu took the place of the Major Chancellor on the first step and reached over and sounded the bronze gong. It was not loud in the massive hall, but in seconds it was answered by all the bells on the grounds of the Island Palace and this in turn was echoed by the bells of the city, the bell-keepers having been found or replaced.

It was a sound of great hope and joy and as she looked down the Empress saw tears on the cheeks of the old Shonto steward. No sound could be heard above the great din of the bells, but Nishima could see that he cried freely like an unashamed child and the new Empress felt a tear streak her own cheek in response.

The ringing of bells seemed to be endless, and Nishima sat attempting an appearance of tranquillity. At last the bells ceased and Nishima took a long breath and nodded to Kamu.

He raised himself up as though the increase in height would project his voice farther. "The Empress requests the presence of the following that we may discuss a solution to the problem of the barbarian army gathering beyond the Capital's gate."

The assembled officials looked stunned, but they did not understand the meaning of this and so sat, casting glances to their allies in the hall.

Kamu read a long list including General Hojo, the Lords Butto, Taiki, Komawara, most of the senior lords of Wa who remained in the city, and Initiate Brother Shuyun.

All of those listed filed in through side doors, approaching the dais on their knees and bowing low to their Empress. Lord Komawara and Lord Butto had just come from the city walls and wore armor still, their helmets tucked under one arm.

Nishima nodded again and Kamu turned to the gathering.

"Due to the machinations of the late Yamaku Emperor, a barbarian army sits beyond our walls, their intention being to place their own chieftain upon the throne of Wa. The Empress will hear the advice of her counselors regarding this matter." To the dismay of the gathered officials, Kamu turned to the Botahist monk. "It is the wish of the Empress that the Spiritual Advisor of Lord Shonto Shokan, Brother Shuyun, make his thoughts known." Kamu nodded to Shuyun.

Performing his double bow, first to the Empress and then to the gathered officials and guests, Shuyun sat back, his hands together as though he would meditate.

"Empress," he said, his soft voice surprisingly calm in the hall full of upspoken tension and emotion. "Honored ministers. I have learned that the plague has begun to spread among the army of the Khan. The great fire seen on the fields in the night was an attempt to cleanse the barbarian army of this disease, but plague is among them and cannot be cured with fire.''

Everyone present leaned forward to listen now and Nishima heard the word ''plague'' whispered down the length of the hall. The reaction of the council was obvious—relief, elation, joy. Many made signs to Botahara.

Shuyun continued. ''It is my recommendation, Empress, that we send emissaries to the Khan bearing an offer to bring Botahist Brothers to heal the barbarians, if, in return, the invading army will lay down its arms. Only this will prevent the plague from being spread among the people of the Capital.''

The reaction was not so controlled this time. Nishima heard voices of protest. She looked down at Hojo and the other Shonto allies. They sat in stolid silence. Now you must keep your word, she thought, or we are lost. Shuyun had been right—they would prefer to see any number dead if it would mean the destruction of their enemies.

Nishima gave a subtle hand signal to Kamu.

''The Empress wishes to express great concern for the people who have gathered in the Capital hoping that the sovereign and the Great Council would protect them. Therefore, it is the wish of the Empress that this mission be carried out immediately. Brother Shuyun, you speak the language of the tribes?''

Shuyun nodded.

The very portly Minister of the Right bowed to the throne and Kamu fixed him with a withering glare as he nodded for the man to speak.

The Minister's voice came out very small. ''Certainly a decision such as this should be considered by the senior officials, Major Chancellor.'' He looked directly at Shokan. ''The course Brother Shuyun suggests—saving those who have caused so many such grievous loss—I fear that the very people we hope to save would not choose this course.''

Shokan did not make eye contact with the Minister. He sat looking toward the foot of the throne, his face composed and unreadable.

Nishima started to answer herself but stopped at a look from Kamu. Instead she whispered to the Major Chancellor. ''There is no time for this,'' she almost hissed.

Kamu turned back to the Minister. ''The barbarians prepare their attack as we speak, Minister, there can be

no time lost in lengthy discussion. This embassy will be
carried out immediately. If you wish to join Brother Shuyun, your wisdom and council would be welcome.''

The Minister looked around attempting to gather support, but no one met his eye. To walk out onto the field
before an army of eighty thousand? The Minister shook
his head and then bowed low. His next words came from
a dry mouth. ''Certainly, the wishes of the Empress will
be carried out immediately. We should, however, be proceeding to remove the Empress to safety.''

''I will not leave,'' Nishima's voice rang out in the
hall. All stared open-mouthed. The voice of a woman in
the Great Hall had not been heard in many years, and
what it lacked in volume it made up for in sheer unique-
ness. ''I will not leave until Brother Shuyun has spoken
to the leader of the tribes,'' she said quietly, ''nor shall
any of my council. The safety of the population is your
charge.'' There was no mistaking the strength of her decision. The Minister of the Right cast a final look at
Shokan, bowed and sat back, his dismay obvious to all.

Nishima nodded to Kamu again. ''Brother Shuyun,
please, there is so little time,'' he said.

Nishima rose from her throne, placing the sword across
the arms. Stepping around the throne, she left the hall
by a small door, her heart beating wildly. Shuyun came
after her, followed by Shokan and several other Shonto
allies.

Nishima stepped aside as the hall widened, waving the
others past. ''You must make all haste, Brother,'' she
said, resisting an urge to embrace him before the others.
''I will follow. May Botahara walk beside you.''

The monk bowed then and turned and ran, followed
by the others, each bowing as he passed.

Shonto guards fell into step around her and they passed
through a door into the main hallway of the palace. Everyone in the hall dropped to their knees as she passed,
pressing their foreheads to the floor.

One bowing woman caught her eye as she passed.

''Kitsura-sum? Come with me please.''

Her cousin rose quickly and fell into place three paces
behind. Nishima reached back and pulled her forward by
her sleeve.

''Please, cousin, hurry.''

* * *

The army of the desert had formed outside the Capital's northern walls and this had drawn the foolish and the curious within the city. They came to see a spectacle, but once they had mounted the walls or roofs the sight left them with little to say. The men of Shonto's army who had survived the terrible retreat now busied themselves with improving the city's defenses, though the Capital was never designed to weather a concerted attack, and their attempts were largely futile.

Between the barbarian army and the walls of the city a dais had been erected under a yellow silk awning. Upon this dais a large wooden chair, almost a throne, was placed and, on either side, the gold banners bearing the Khan's crimson dragons hung from standards. Frames of bamboo had been built behind the dais and crimson silk was laced to these frames, creating an effective screen.

It was not clear to anyone in the city if this seat was meant to be the place where the Khan would accept the surrender of the city or if this was merely the position from which he intended to watch the city's fall. Perhaps it was meant to perform either function, but there were many inside the Capital's walls who hoped a peaceful surrender was possible.

Shuyun mounted the steps to the top of the gate he had so recently used to enter the city. Lord Shonto Shokan, Lord Komawara, and General Hojo were only a few paces behind and they all stopped to look out at the army, clearly preparing its attack not far off.

Hojo nodded. "In Denji Gorge, Brother Shuyun, I opposed your plan to scale the walls and was proven wrong. It is my hope to be proven wrong again. If the Khan does not agree to this plan, Brother, I do not think we will move our army out of the city without terrible losses. Our Empress will have no force with which to regain her throne." Hojo looked down at the small monk, the warrior's discomfiture obvious.

Shuyun said nothing for a moment. "Pray to Botahara, General Hojo. I put myself into His hands."

The monk turned and descended the stairs. He was given the green flag of peace and a guard opened a small portal in the city's wall.

Lord Komawara caught up with Shuyun as he was about to pass through. "I would go with you, Brother Shuyun. Perhaps I may be of some assistance."

The monk hesitated for a second, meeting the young lord's eye. Shaking his head, Shuyun reached out and touched Komawara's arm. "It would be my honor, Lord Komawara, but this plan is my own and has little support. It is my desire to risk as few as possible. I thank you."

Komawara bowed, the short double bow he had learned when the two had gone into the desert. Bowing in return, Shuyun stepped through the arch and heard the door close behind him.

Stairs led down to the canal where a sampan tugged at a line. Shuyun stepped aboard and sculled quickly to the other bank where a ruin of stone was all that remained of the bridge that had been torn down at first light.

Tying the sampan to a rock, Shuyun ascended the bank, unfurling his flag of peace as he went. A few paces took him beyond the plum trees that grew along the canal—in leaf now, the glory of spring blossom having been stripped from them by the winds.

The massive army of the desert did not seem distant now, and Shuyun found himself unconsciously performing a breathing exercise to calm his spirit.

So much depends upon me, the monk thought, performing an instinctive sign to Botahara. The green flag fluttered in the light breeze as Shuyun held it high, moving it slowly back and forth so that it would be seen.

He made his way across a green field, walking deliberately but without haste toward the waving banners of the pavilion. Horsemen broke free of the great mass of humanity before Shuyun and galloped out toward him. They stopped at some distance and examined the monk, and then one turned and spurred his horse back toward the barbarian position. The remaining three riders kept their distance, matching Shuyun's pace and not taking their eyes from him.

Fifty paces from the dais Shuyun stopped and waited. As this Khan aspired to the throne of Wa, Shuyun was unsure what protocol might be expected and so decided it was best to wait and see how the barbarian responded

to his presence. He chanted quietly to himself, a prayer
for tranquility of purpose.

Perhaps an hour passed and then there was a sudden
stirring on the perimeter of the barbarian position. Warriors in crimson-laced armor rode out toward the dais,
forming two lines facing in. Every second rider carried
the Khan's golden banner on a lance.

Time passed and then a group of horsemen appeared
at the far end of the path formed by the mounted guards.
In a rustling of many silk banners the riders came forward, their pace unhurried. Shuyun held his position.
Meditation had focused his will and he felt no reaction
to the Khan's approach. He waited.

The riders halted behind the dais and it was a moment
before they emerged. Six armored men appeared from
behind the awning and knelt upon the dais to either side
of the throne. Guards appeared then, kneeling on the
ground in straight rows. One of these took two steps toward Shuyun and waved him forward.

As he walked toward the dais, a man in a robe of
Imperial Crimson and black and gold stepped around the
dais and mounted the throne. All present bowed but for
two guards who watched Shuyun intently as he approached their leader.

Moving closer, Shuyun could see that the men who
knelt on the dais were barbarian chieftains, armored in
the style of warriors of the Empire but with surcoats of
tiger skins and ornate helmets.

The man who sat upon the throne was bearded and
wore his hair pulled back in the style of the desert. His
face was dark and lined like all men who lived in the
harsh world north of the border of Seh, but as Shuyun
came closer he realized this was a young man, older than
Komawara, perhaps, but certainly he had not seen thirty
years.

The face was handsome in its way, and not unpleasant
to look at, with a strong jaw and a full mouth. A few
paces more and Shuyun realized that what he thought was
an ornament was in fact a patch of white hair at the temple—the sign of the Tokiko blood, the same mark that
Prince Wakaro had inherited from his mother.

Sitting with a sword across his knees the Golden Khan

regarded the small monk who approached, contempt obvious on the chieftain's face.

Shuyun walked until a guard signaled him to stop ten paces from the dais. As there was no mat set out, Shuyun decided that he would stand and bowed from that position, placing the butt of the flag standard on the ground at his side.

The Khan sat for some moments staring at the monk and then nodded to one of the chieftains who knelt on the dais.

The man cleared his throat and then addressed Shuyun in the language of the Empire, though heavily accented. "The Khan wishes to know why so few have come forward on such an important occasion. This displeases him."

Shuyun addressed his answer to the Khan, speaking the tongue of the tribes almost without flaw. "I have been charged to speak for the Empress of Wa. It was not thought that more than one was required—our message is simple."

The Khan looked at Shuyun for a moment and then spoke himself, his voice deep and strong and at ease in the language of the tribes. "The ringing of bells— Akantsu no longer possesses the throne?"

Shuyun shook his head.

The Khan cast a glance at one of his chieftains. "Who sits the throne now, monk—Shonto's daughter?"

Shuyun nodded again. "The Empress Shigei," he answered quietly.

Shaking his head, the Khan spat out, "The council of Wa are fools if they believe I will be satisfied to be the consort of a Shonto Empress."

The monk said nothing.

The Khan waved his scabbard at Shuyun. "Komawara—does he still live?"

"He does."

"This man is a formidable swordsman . . . for a man of Seh. He felled a warrior—a chieftain of great deeds, and drove into my own guard before disappearing into the fog. My warriors call him the Cloud Rider." The Khan fixed Shuyun with a long stare from which the monk did not flinch. "I will have Lord Komawara's head brought to me when the Empress formally surrenders the

Capital. Have her come to me in person to offer me her throne. I am told she is a great beauty, this Shonto daughter. Is this true?''

Shuyun said nothing but stood returning the Khan's stare.

''I have not come to arrange the surrender of the Empire,'' he said softly. ''I have come to save you from the plague, which is silently killing the men of your army as we speak.''

The Khan glanced at the men around him and then addressed Shuyun, changing to the language of Wa.

''We cleansed our army with fire, monk, unless you have been sent to carry the disease to us again as the nun was sent among us bringing disease to every man who touched her and a thousand more besides.''

Tesseko, Shuyun thought, *Botahara protect you.*

Shuyun nodded to one of the men sitting to the Khan's left. ''That man,'' he said, still speaking in the language of the tribes, ''he has contracted the plague. Look at the flush on his face. He struggles to control his cough, but he will not succeed for much longer.'' The other chieftains cast uncertain glances at the man Shuyun singled out. ''You cannot cleanse the plague by fire, it is among you and can only be stopped by the ministrations of my own Order. You may take the throne, but it will not be yours for more than a few days.'' Shuyun let his words have their effect, seeing the arrogance of the men around the Khan quickly dissolve. There was no honor or profit in death by disease.

''The Empress has sent me to offer you your lives, for you will certainly lose them if you do not listen. In return she asks only that you lay down your arms. Your safe conduct to the northern border is guaranteed.''

The Khan pointed the tip of his sheathed sword at Shuyun. ''I sent an emissary to the walls of Rhojo-ma before it fell. He carried a flag of peace as you do now—and this man was murdered with an arrow because the lords of Seh did not like to hear the truth of their own blunders. Does the Empress expect to save her throne with a simple lie? She must believe I am some barbarian huntsman who has never seen the inside of a city's walls. When I have taken all of Wa and sit upon the Dragon Throne she will know differently—will become one of my con-

cubines willingly. I had hoped to begin my reign by sparing the Imperial Capital.'' The Khan shrugged. He
looked over at the chieftain who had first spoken and
nodded.

The chieftain hesitated for the briefest second, then
rose, drawing his sword. The guards who knelt nearby
did the same. Shuyun reached up and tore the banner
from his staff, lifting it to a guard position, pushing himself into a meditative state.

The guards spread out to either side and then one leapt
forward, aiming a blow at Shuyun's hands, but the monk's
staff moved in a blur and the man lay still on the green
field.

The men hesitated then and Shuyun pounced upon their
doubt. ''Your Khan will sacrifice you to the plague so
that he may sit upon the throne for the last few days of
his life. The Brotherhood can save you. . . .''

Another man lunged at Shuyun, but his attack was
thwarted brutally as another guard cut him down, then
turned on the man beside him. The barbarian chieftains
leapt off the dais and joined the struggle. Shuyun saved
the man who sided with him from a sword blow that
would have meant his end. Suddenly the chieftains and
the guards rushed him at once.

The flag staff hummed as it cut the air. Shuyun disarmed a man and rendered another unconscious. A barbarian stepped inside his guard and Shuyun was forced
to drop the staff. He clutched the man's sword as Komawara had seen in the desert and deflected the blow,
driving another man back with what appeared to be a
blow that never landed. Another barbarian warrior was
dealt with in this manner, and suddenly the attack came
to a halt. The barbarian warriors stood staring at the
monk as though he were a ghost.

A cough escaped one of the chieftains and then, as all
stood frozen, this man stepped forward and drove the
point of his sword into the Khan where he stood before
the wooden throne. The man who had gathered the tribes
sagged slowly to his knees, staring forward at Shuyun,
his eyes losing focus. A guard stepped forward and
plunged his own point into the Khan's chest so that he
fell back and to the side, his body limp.

No one moved to avenge this action, and the chieftain

who had struck the first blow was suddenly racked with
a fit of coughing. The others took a step away. Several
fled then and horses were heard at a gallop.

When the man had recovered, he turned to Shuyun.
"That is the end of the man who brought us here to die
in a strange land for his greater glory. The others may
do as they choose, but my own people will lay down their
arms, Brother. How will I know that the army of Lord
Shonto will not fall upon us once we are defenseless?"

Shuyun did not answer for a second, and then he
reached into his robe and pulled out the jade pendant on
its chain. "I will swear by the Botara denu. The Empress
will give you safe passage to the border of Seh." Shuyun
gestured to the ground. "Bring your weapons here. Separate the sick from the well and the monks of my Order
will come. Do not cleanse again with fire, it will save
no one. Tomorrow Brothers will begin to arrive. Others
must come from there." Shuyun gestured toward the
Mountain of the Pure Spirit. "It will take some few
days."

The chieftains looked on, saying nothing. An occasional glance was cast toward the Khan, but it was obvious the men were stunned into inaction by what had
happened. Shuyun took a step forward, then hesitated.
"I would see to your Khan," he said quietly. No one
moved, so the monk knelt beside the fallen leader. Immediately, he made a sign to Botahara. "His spirit has
fled," Shuyun said. Pulling the robe off the man's shoulder, he exposed the skin and pointed there to three small
lesions. "Your chieftain had the plague and did not yet
know it," Shuyun said and then rose slowly.

"I will return at sunrise. The Imperial army will not
be allowed onto these fields, but do not be alarmed if
you see small patrols of armed riders. We must be certain
that the plague is not spread." Shuyun bowed then and
turned back toward the city. As he went, he chanted a
long prayer of thanksgiving.

A great cry went up suddenly behind him and the monk
spun around. The sounds of clashing steel echoed across
the open ground and Shuyun almost covered his eyes.
The barbarian fought among themselves. He could see the
great army of the desert, a seething mass of horses and
men writhing like a great dying beast.

Footsteps sounded behind him, but Shuyun did not turn. Komawara and Hojo arrived at his side and still others stopped nearby.

"What has happened, Brother," Hojo asked, great wonder in his voice.

"Step away, General, Lord Komawara, I have been in contact with the plague." The others did as Shuyun asked. "The Khan is dead, killed by one of his own chieftains. They war among themselves now—those who would lay down their arms and be cured and those who would avenge the death of their leader."

"At least they expend their energies upon each other," Hojo said.

"It is the saddest of days, General. The Kalam has always maintained that most of the tribesmen followed the Khan against their will." He pointed out toward the raging battle. "The innocent are dying in numbers as great as those who came to murder and burn."

Komawara waved toward the city. "We must retreat to the walls, Shuyun-sum. There is nothing we can do and it is possible they may turn against us yet."

Reluctantly Shuyun turned and followed the young lord back toward the city.

Shonto guards held boats at the canal and Shuyun waited while the others were whisked across the canal to the open door, the sound of battle echoing off the walls. He would need to bathe himself in the appropriate herbs and destroy his clothing.

The monk stood among the trees, unable to block the sounds of the fighting from his ears. He knelt upon the grass but an attempt to chant came to nothing so he was left, battered by the sounds of the terrible battle.

I have accomplished that which any warrior of Wa would have willingly sacrificed his life to achieve—I have caused the enemy to destroy themselves. Botahara forgive me, I meant only to heal them and save the people of the Capital.

Shonto guards spread out around Shuyun suddenly, keeping their distance, staring out at the raging struggle. A light step stopped three paces away.

"Shuyun-sum?" the Empress said softly. "Even a self-less act of charity may bring about utter calamity. Know-

ing this cannot stop us from being charitable. These
tribesmen have their own karma which even the Teacher
may not control."

Someone came forward then and set the monk's trunk
a few paces away. Shuyun looked up to see the Kalam,
his face drawn as though in pain.

"Shimeko-sum," Shuyun whispered. "It was she who
carried the plague to the tribes."

The Empress slowly sank to her knees, covering her
mouth as she did do. "She could not have done such a
thing . . . not knowingly."

Shuyun shook his head sadly. "She could hardly have
acted so out of ignorance. The Botahist trained. . . ."
He left the sentence unfinished.

"I cannot think what karma this will bring," Nishima
said. "Life after life after life. . . ."

Shuyun nodded.

"Excuse my interruption, Empress." General Hojo
stood some distance off. "This is not a secure place. The
battle is spreading over the fields. We must allow Shuyun
to perform his purification so that we may all find safety
inside the walls."

The Empress nodded. "Shuyun-sum. Only you tried
to save the tribes. Do not forget the purity of your intent.
All others would have let them die, taking the population
of the Capital with them. Your purpose was pure."

"Thank you for your council, Empress," Shuyun said.

The woman in crimson robes stopped as she rose. "No
one can hear our words, Shuyun-sum. Please, do not
banish Nishi-sum from the world entirely. I—I must exist
somewhere," she said, her voice growing small, "in your
company, if I may." She retreated then and guards surrounded her quickly.

Shuyun went to his trunk and opened the lid.

By the time Shuyun entered the Capital, the barbarian
tribes had divided themselves into distinct camps and,
for the most part, the fighting had ceased although it
flared up again for brief moments between one group and
another.

Shonto guards escorted the monk into the nearby
guardhouse where he found the Empress accompanied by
Lady Kitsura. Lord Komawara, Lord Shonto Shokan,

Hojo, the Kalam, and Rohku Saicha had appeared, taking charge of the Empress' personal guard.

All bowed low to Shuyun as he entered and he found this disturbing, considering the results of his recent action.

"We have a boat awaiting in the nearest canal, Empress. It is a short walk. I apologize, we have no sedan chair," Hojo said.

"Apologize only when you have a sedan chair, Masakado-sum," Nishima said. "I will have the council pass an edict ordering all sedan chairs in the Capital be put to the torch." She nodded toward the door.

Guards formed a tight circle around the Empress, Kitsura and Shuyun, and the monk found himself hemmed in and close to his sovereign.

Out in the avenue two long lines of warriors held back the jostling crowds. Shuyun saw the black of Imperial Guards, Shonto blue, Butto purple—the remains of Lord Shonto's army assuring the safety of the woman they had placed on the throne.

Once the Empress was seen, the people bowed low and a whisper passed down the street like a cool breeze. Both the name of the Empress and his own became almost a chant. Suddenly flower petals of all colors were strewn before the party as they made their way to the quay.

Lord Butto stood at the head of the stairs where several boats were moored, and he knelt and bowed low as the Empress approached. Quickly the small group embarked, Kitsura and Shuyun into the same craft as the Empress, the others into boats both before and behind.

Shuyun felt Nishima breathe a sigh of relief as the boats gained the center of the canal. The banks were thick with the thousands who had hoped to flee the war, and had come to its very center. They began to cheer suddenly, their respect for their new sovereign momentarily overcome by their relief at being delivered from the barbarian army.

Shuyun heard his name chanted now as he had heard the crowds chant Komawara's name for the many lives he had taken in battle. He felt a warm hand take his own and looked over to see his young Empress turned toward him—a look of understanding, of compassion.

The lords of Wa were wise, he found himself thinking. Here sits the woman deserving to rule the Empire. And yet her subjects will never understand that she has given up her own peace so that theirs would be assured.

Sixty-two

In a small audience hall near the Imperial Apartments the Empress had gathered her closest advisors, which meant the only functionary of the Empire's government present was the Major Chancellor, Kamu.

It was late and the sounds of movement on the fields outside the city had finally ceased. For the second time an enormous fire burned outside the city as the barbarians burned all those who had fallen that day. At last light it appeared the barbarian army had split utterly and though this had caused a flood of relief throughout the Capital, anxiety had not disappeared. Everyone waited to be sure the barbarians would not reform their vast army under a new leader. First light would see crowds gathered on the northern walls, there was no doubt of that.

General Hojo bowed low. "The barbarian army has split into three parts," he began, addressing his remarks to the Major Chancellor.

Nishima almost grimaced and waved a gold silk fan at the Shonto officer. "Masakado-sum, please, I cannot bear this custom. We are not in a council of state . . . do not speak to Kamu-sum as though I were not present." She tried a small smile.

"Excuse me, Empress," the soldier said bowing. He returned to the kneeling position and took a second to gather his thoughts. "Since the fall of the Khan this morning, the barbarian army has split. One company, the easternmost tribes according to Kalam, have begun to move north, some on the canal but many by foot and on horse. This is perhaps a fourth part of those who survived the battle between the tribes. A much smaller group has broken off and makes its way northeast—we are not certain of their intent, Empress, but Brother Shuyun has suggested they may make their way toward the temples

on the Mountain of the Pure Spirit. They know the Botahist Brothers possess a cure for their disease. The third
group—the majority by far—remain in the fields north of
the city, awaiting the healers we have promised."

Nishima nodded at this. "What is your advice, General Hojo. Large armed parties wandering through our
lands is a matter for concern."

Hojo considered a moment. "Combining all the men
who remain from the Imperial Army and our own, Empress, gives us a force of perhaps thirty thousand men.
Certainly enough to meet the threat of any of the three
barbarian armies, though hardly enough men to deal with
them all at once. The barbarians outside the city have
disarmed, but we cannot leave them unwatched. If they
do not receive assistance soon . . ." Hojo shrugged.
"Thirty thousand barbarian warriors, well armed or not
is a significant force. They will also need to be fed."
Hojo stroked his graying beard. "The companies making
their way toward the Botahist temples are of concern. We
have sent messages to the Brothers so that they will be
prepared, but still it would be best if these barbarians
could be reasoned with, though I would prefer to send
out a force of some size to emphasize the prudence of
finding a solution that does not require swords.

"The army moving north is of greater concern to me,
Empress. It is both larger and its intent less clear. Do
they plan to take Seh and hold it as their own? Is it their
wish to simply return to the desert? The Kalam believes
they hope to escape the plague and do not trust the people of the Empire sufficiently to lay down their weapons.
Brother Shuyun is certain the plague will begin to show
its hand among these men very soon. We have sent patrols out to warn any citizens who are on the barbarian's
path, but who knows what dying men might do? If the
Botahist Brothers agree to minister to the barbarians, then
perhaps we will be able to take some number of Brothers
north in the wake of the retreating barbarians in hopes
that the men of the desert will see the futility of what
they do and allow the Brothers to help them." Hojo
bowed and fell silent.

Nishima nodded. "I thank you, General." She looked
around at the others, raising an eyebrow as they had often
seen her father do.

Komawara touched his head to the mats. "Empress. I agree entirely with General Hojo. May I suggest that with the force that travels north we might send the Kalam? He is of an eastern tribe himself and may gain their trust more easily than the leader of a well armed force."

Nishima looked over to Shuyun who sat between Komawara and the tribesman. "Brother?"

Shuyun bowed low before speaking. "I will ask the Kalam, Empress, if I may?"

She nodded and the monk spoke quietly to the tribesman who responded in a whisper. Shuyun turned back to Nishima. "The Kalam asks me to say that he will do anything within his power to serve the Empress."

Nishima gave a half bow to the tribesman who touched his forehead to the floor in return, his embarrassment obvious.

"General Hojo, we remain in a state of war, so I do not feel the need to consult the Great Council in this matter. Who would you suggest to carry out each of these tasks? We must send no one who is bent on revenge upon the tribes—we have had a thousand years of raids and war because of a barbarian vendetta, let us do nothing to fuel their anger."

Hojo looked over at Kamu as though the two consulted silently. "I would send Lord Butto to pursue the barbarian army north on the canal. The lord has his own interests to consider there and I must say, Lady Ni . . . Empress, that he is a young man of great political skills. Kamu-sum has made the same assessment.

"Certainly Lord Taiki would be the correct choice to defend the temples, his devotion has been great since Brother Shuyun saved the life of his son. If I remain in the Capital, I will see to the barbarians beyond the walls, with Brother Shuyun's counsel, if he will be so kind."

Nishima looked at Shuyun who nodded. Lord Butto and Lord Taiki were out in the fields patrolling beyond the barbarian encampment. "General Hojo, I will leave this in your hands. I wish to be kept constantly informed. We must restore peace and security to the Empire before we can begin to address the other ills the Yamaku have left us."

Nishima turned to Kamu who consulted a small scroll.

"The matter of the Brothers, Empress," he said. The young sovereign turned to Shuyun.

"I have spoken to the Primate of the Imperial Capital, Empress." Shuyun said. "Brother Hutto and the Supreme Master of the Botahist Order sailed from Yankura recently. They should arrive in the Capital very soon, perhaps tomorrow."

"The Supreme Master?" Nishima opened her fan. "Does he not sequester himself on an island in the sea?"

"He does, Empress." Shuyun answered. "Events in the Empire may have convinced him his presence would be required."

"How are we best to proceed to gain their support?" Nishima asked.

"I would speak with the Supreme Master and Brother Hutto myself, Empress, if that is acceptable."

Nishima nodded. "I will concern myself with this matter no more, Brother Shuyun, if I know that it is in your capable hands." She turned back to the Shonto steward. "Kamu-sum?"

"There is a shortage of grain in the Capital, Empress, and many other things as well. Crowds have begun to gather at the gates of the palace asking for food. As of yet they have been orderly, but if they grow desperate this will change."

"They must be fed," Nishima said. "Certainly we did not destroy all the grain in the Empire as we came down the canal?"

Kamu nodded in response to this, glancing over at Hojo, whose face remained grave but whose eyes smiled. "There is perhaps someone more suited to dealing with this matter than any present, if you will excuse me for saying so," he hastened to add, addressing his remark to all present. Turning back to Nishima; "We have had word from Tanaka, Empress. He comes from Yankura even now."

Nishima greeted this news with a great smile, something her retainers had not seen in recent days. "The barbarians did not find him after all!" she said happily. "Colonel Tadamoto was mistaken."

"No, they did not," Hojo said. "Our good merchant is unscathed, or so he says. There is certainly food in the Empire despite the attempts of many to hide it away.

Tanaka will know the best method to bring it forth, and he will not empty the Imperial Treasury to accomplish it, either.''

Nishima looked over at Shokan who shook his head in mock dismay. ''My steward, my senior general, my guard captain, and now my merchant. Will you leave my personal servants at least, and perhaps my gardener? But what do I say? Anything for my Empress.''

''Lord Shonto,'' Nishima said gravely. ''I wish only to borrow Tanaka-sum—for indeed I shall raise his rank so that he is addressed as he deserves, as my father always addressed him. In a brief time I'm sure he will have rooted out all of the corruption in my government. For this service I will pay you well, brother—and I shall pay Tanaka-sum well also. As to your gardener . . .'' Nishima said, as though this thought had not occurred to her. She moved her head back and forth, weighing the idea. ''Perhaps not at this time, thank you.''

Shokan nodded.

Nishima turned to Kamu who became serious immediately. ''My list is without end, Empress, but may I suggest that we have all done much this day. Brother Shuyun must prepare for his meeting with the senior members of his Order, for their cooperation is crucial to the peace we have arranged. We have, after all, pledged the Brotherhood's assistance without consulting them. This may please them less than we hope, Empress.''

Nishima tapped the edge of the low dais with her fan. ''You are no doubt correct, Major Chancellor. There are so many matters to consider and so many who have risked so much in these last days, yet I can hardly begin to think of this until we are assured of peace and the plague is contained.'' She nodded to all present. ''I thank you. Brother Shuyun, I wish to discuss your coming audience with your superiors, if it is convenient.''

Nishima rose and everyone bowed their heads to the mat as she left.

Nishima did not feel a desire to live in the apartments that had been the quarters of the Yamaku nor was she comfortable with the thought of moving into the abandoned rooms of the Hanama Emperors—ghosts or no— they had fallen to bad luck in the end and Nishima did

not want be reminded of that. Fortunately the palace had
any number of rooms to choose from and she was soon
settled, if only temporarily, in apartments meant for vis-
iting relatives of the Emperors. These apartments had
been left in the Hanama style, uncluttered, almost austere in their simplicity and Nishima had the rugs she had
brought from Seh spread over the straw-matted floors.
With her own servants and retainers about, her situation
did not feel as strange as she expected. Occasionally she
even forgot that her father was no longer part of this
present in which Nishima found herself, though these
moments were brief.

A warm evening had arrived, creeping silently up the
river from the sea, and with it came cloud. The sound of
falling rain seemed comforting to the new Empress as
though it formed a protective barrier from the world beyond. Outside her rooms a terrace with small trees situated carefully about it looked out to the west. The soft
cadence of the spring rain on the terrace stones and the
leaves of trees—a sound in harmony with the mood of
the young aristocrat.

Nishima wore her own familiar robes, avoiding Imperial finery, though her clothing was of white—not of her
choosing. She sat near a partially open screen that led
onto the terrace and rubbed a resin stick over the black-
ened surface of her inkstone. A bead curtain of water
drops had formed from the rain as it ran off the tile roof,
and this caught the light from her lamp and glittered like
strings of bronze colored jewels.

So many things had occurred in the past two days that
Nishima did not feel as though she were part of it somehow—her life was changing more rapidly than she was
able to change herself, there was little question of that.
Only the day before she had been lost in the fog with
Kitsura and Shuyun and the Empire had been poised on
an edge, about to slide into the abyss of the complete
unknown. That morning Lady Nishima Fanisan Shonto
had lit a torch to the pyre of Lord Shonto Motoru. She
closed her eyes tightly. And now, miraculously, the Empire had been delivered. A half-barbarian chieftain who
had been destined for the throne had fallen to the sword
of one of his own followers . . . and Nishima had as-

cended the throne left empty by the passing of the Yamaku. Ascended against her most profound desires.

"I am the Empress," she whispered, as though saying
these words aloud would force her mind to accept this
information, help her understand the truth, for she did
not feel like an Empress, she was sure of that.

Certainly she had heard the crowds repeating her name
as though it were a litany. Nishima could not remember
an experience that had left her feeling so cold, so isolated.

Closing her eyes she tried to conjure up another time,
and an image of walking along the cliffs above the sea
on the Shonto fief came to her. She could see the bleached
copper grasses, their color so carefully complimenting
the blues of the summer sea and the whites of the lazy,
drifting clouds that spread across the far horizon. The
breeze was soft and warm, welcoming her to the shore.

Eyes still closed, Nishima rubbed her inkstone, reaching out to that time, trying to hold it—but she could not.
The chanting of the crowd came back, mixed with the
sound of the funeral pyre as it began to blaze.

Opening her eyes Nishima picked up her brush, dipped
it in ink and with great care selected a piece of mulberry
paper.

> The wind blows
> And the grasses bow to my passing,
> Perfect golden grasses
> What do they know of my thoughts?
> Or of the heart
> They have torn asunder.

For some time Nishima sat looking at the lines she had
written, wondering, for they seemed to have come un-
bidden, as poetry often did. The rain washed the world
outside her rooms.

A knock sounded then and Nishima swirled her brush
in water and set it on its rest. "Please enter," she called
out.

A woman bowed low in the opening and then rose.
The round, girlish face of Lady Kento appeared, looking
more serious than Nishima had ever seen it.

"Kento-sum!" Nishima broke into a smile. "It lifts

my spirits to see you. Miracle after miracle has occurred this day. How is it you are here?''

Kento bowed. ''It is a brief story, Empress, and less interesting than one might think especially to one who has experienced what the Empress has these past months.'' Kento cast a glance over her shoulder. ''I would certainly tell my tale though at the moment Lord Shonto awaits your favor.''

''Cha and a tale you must certainly tell me. Please, invite Shokan-sum to join me.''

Nishima set a small jade paperweight on the edge of her poem and moved her cushion a pace away from the table. The screen slid aside and Shokan knelt in the opening, head bowed low. Even my stepbrother must offer obeisance, Nishima thought, for an Empress has no equals—how very sad.

''Shokan-sum, please, enter.'' Nishima gestured to a second cushion as her brother rose.

The lord had the powerful build of his father and a similar talent for making his presence felt in a room, even when he was not the center of the situation. Dressed in rich robes of white with the blue edges of under-robes showing at his sleeves and neck and hem, Shokan struck Nishima as a handsome figure. The sadness she could see in his face and the white robes of mourning only added to his nobility.

Taking his place, Shokan regarded his sister with a look of concern. ''It has been a day that will occupy the historians for a hundred years. May I say that the Empress has begun her reign auspiciously, showing both skill and wisdom.''

''You may say that but only if you will stop calling me Empress with each breath. We are in the privacy of my rooms. *Nishima*, please, Shokan-sum, *Nishi* would be preferred though I hold little hope that you will breach this foolish etiquette to such a degree, no matter how much I desire it.''

Shokan gave a half bow. ''Excuse me for saying so, Empress, but these formalities have been the tradition in the Imperial Palace for our entire history. It is difficult for me to ignore that.''

Nishima stared at him in exasperation. ''In the Great

Council," she said with deadly seriousness, "I shall insist upon referring to you as *Shoki-sum*."

The young lord broke into a smile and bowed low—the name Nishima had called him as a child. "The Empress has proffered a most convincing argument . . . excuse me—Nishima-sum."

"Nishi-sum."

"Nishi-sum," Shokan said, his voice suddenly thick.

Reaching out, Nishima took her brother's hand. They were silent for a moment.

"He saved my life, Shokan-sum—my life and my mother's also," Nishima said, addressing what was unspoken in both their minds. "It is wrong to say this, but he was more dear to me than my true father who was distant and formal. Your father—our father, did not just save the Fanisan House from destruction, he brought me into your family. I treasure the time I spent in his company, treasure it. . . ."

"You were his delight, Nishi-sum," Shokan said, his voice subdued though under control now. "It was you who were closest to his heart, who brought him joy."

Nishima looked down, she brushed her fingers over the shinta blossom embroidered in white on Shokan's sleeve.

The two sat, not speaking, listening to the rain, each lost in their own memories, comforted by the other's presence.

A bell sounded the hour of the owl and both stirred. Nishima looked up at her brother. "You are the senior lord of the Shonto now, Shokan-sum. You are a lord of great influence and wealth. I shall have to consider who it would be best for you to wed. We have alliances to think of, entire provinces of young women to consider."

Shokan smiled again. "Entire provinces . . . it gives me hope, Nishi-sum. Perhaps, with your guidance, I shall not live my life a lonely man."

Nishima laughed and squeezed his hand. "Your adventures are not as secret as you may think, brother. Never forget that every young woman in the Capital pours out her heart to Kitsu-sum. And I have recently been told that you have come from the mountains in the company of young woman of the mountain race." She looked up slyly at her brother. "This cannot be true?"

Shokan shook his head. "Quinta-la."

"Quinta-la?"

"She has been sent by her elders. . . . I confess I do not know why, but she has come to the lowlands for some reason . . . perhaps she is an emissary from her people. Certainly she has come to learn all she can, there is little doubt of that."

"You have not asked her?" Nishima said, surprised.

Shokan smiled. "I have, but convincing a dweller to speak of something they are not inclined to discuss is more difficult than one might think. There is also a language problem—we understand each other imperfectly."

Nishima nodded. "Shuyun-sum speaks their tongue. Perhaps we can arrange to have them meet. I would be most curious to meet . . . Quinta-la?—to meet her myself."

"Anticipating the Empress' desire, I asked Quinta-la to wait nearby—Nishima-sum," he added.

"You have left her waiting this entire time?"

"The dwellers are very patient, sister."

"Still . . . we cannot leave her waiting like this. She is your guest, brother."

"Guest is perhaps not the word she would use herself, Nishima-sum, but certainly, I will call for her."

A maid was summoned and sent to ask Quinta-la to join them. Almost immediately the maid returned, accompanied by a young woman who bowed her head to the floor, obviously nervous, perhaps even frightened.

"You may rise and come forward, Quinta-la," Shokan said, speaking slowly and with exaggerated clarity. Nishima thought Shokan's voice warmed perceptibly when he spoke to this young woman.

Quinta-la was dressed in the robes of her people, too warm, Nishima thought, for the weather. She was very small but well formed and appeared healthy and strong. Delicate of feature could hardly be said of this woman from the mountains, but despite the roundness of her face she was fair and her mouth was beautifully formed. Nishima immediately wanted to see her smile.

"Empress," Shokan said, "it is my honor to introduce Khosi Quinta-la."

Nishima nodded.

"Quinta-la, the Empress of Wa."

The young woman bowed stiffly.

"We are honored that you would come so far, Quinta-la-sum. There is so little commerce between our peoples," Nishima said.

"La is an honorific, sister," Shokan said quietly making Nishima smile at her mistake.

Shokan gave the dweller a tiny nod.

"The honor is mine, Empress, entirely," Quinta-la said in the studied manner of a child reciting lines. "You live in a lovely village."

"You are kind," Nishima said with all seriousness. She had never heard the Capital or the Island Palace referred to as a village.

Shokan shrugged. "My language lessons have not all been successful."

Cha was brought by servants and Nishima felt a pang when she realized it would not be correct for her to serve this herself—they were entertaining a guest from what amounted to a sovereign nation.

Though the mountains in which Quinta-la dwelt were contained within the Empire, only the mountain people lived there and the people of Wa did not think of the lands beyond the foothills as being their own. Only a few passes were used by the lowlanders and there was a lake here or a spring there that, due to its ease of access, was thought of as part of the Empire proper.

A servant ladled the cha into bowls, retreating a few steps when she was done and sitting absolutely still.

"I am told there are many springs in the mountains and some are very hot and healthful," Nishima said, sipping her cha.

Quinta-la smiled and darted a glance at Shokan. The lord said the word he had learned for the springs and the young dweller nodded.

"Hot," she agreed. "Shokan-li red like an Emperor's flag." She said gesturing to the lord and then touching her own chest.

Nishima cast a look at her brother who sipped his cha deliberately.

"I see," Nishima said. "I hope my brother has found suitable quarters for you?"

Shokan said another word in the mountain language and Quinta-la smiled again, which pleased Nishima. "Dragons and clouds, Empress."

"One of the rooms the Yamaku decorated," Shokan said. "She likes the painted screens."

A tap on the door frame preceded Lady Kento's reappearance. "Excuse me, my Lady. Were you expecting your Spiritual Advisor?"

"Of course. Please bring him to us." Nishima turned to Shokan. "Please, brother, I'm sure Quinta-la would enjoy an opportunity to speak her own language. Stay a while. Shuyun-sum is your Spiritual Advisor now, Shokan-li. He is a remarkable young man. Someone you would do well to know."

The lord gave a half bow. "Brother Shuyun is dedicated to the Empress, there is little question of that," Shokan said and smiled, "like so many others who traveled the canal from Seh in your company."

Shuyun appeared in the doorway, saving Nishima from having to answer. "Please Brother Shuyun, be at your ease."

At the sound of the monk's name Quinta-la's eyes went wide. She turned half around toward the approaching Brother but then prostrated herself on the rug, causing the monk to stop as though he confronted a terrible sight.

"Quinta-la," Shokan said, "please. This is unseemly. You are in the presence of the Empress."

Unaffected by the lord's entreaties the young woman remained facedown on the rug, mumbling rapidly in her own language.

Nishima looked over to Shuyun, her question unspoken.

"I do not understand, Empress." Turning to Shokan he asked, "This is the young woman from the mountains?"

Shokan nodded as he tugged gently on Quinta-la's sleeve.

Shuyun spoke softly to the woman in her own tongue. Her mumbling stopped, but she did not answer nor did she move from her position on the floor. Whispering again Shuyun reached out and touched the girl's wrist, causing a shiver to pass through her.

"Will you not rise up, Quinta-la?" Shuyun said. There was no response. "You are making the Empress and Lord Shonto most uncomfortable and I myself am somewhat disturbed. Please, will you not rise?"

A whisper so low it could almost have been a sigh escaped the young woman.

Nishima raised an eyebrow at the monk.

"She says she is not worthy, Empress," Shuyun said his face showing the tiny signs of strain that Nishima had come to recognize.

"Excuse me, Brother, Empress," Shokan said, "I had no reason to expect anything like this. I apologize."

Shuyun spoke again in the woman's tongue, a bit more forcefully this time, and very slowly she rose to a kneeling position where she sat with her eyes cast down.

"Will Quinta-la not explain this?" Nishima asked the monk.

Shuyun spoke a few words in the mountain language but the young woman only closed her eyes and remained silent.

"Quinta-la," Shokan said. "The Empress would like you to answer Brother Shuyun's question. Will you not?"

The young woman from the mountains opened her mouth as if to speak but no words came forth. After several seconds of effort she managed, "Cah Shu-yung."

Nishima looked up at Shuyun, but it was Shokan who translated. "The bearer."

The monk nodded.

"Do you understand this, Shuyun-sum?" Nishima asked. The young woman's reaction disturbed her deeply, though she was not sure why. Nishima realized she felt an inexplicable anger toward Quinta-la.

"I do not, my lady, I apologize. The bearer: that is my name, taken from the mountain tongue, as you know. What it means to Quinta-la or why she has reacted in this way, I cannot say."

"When I traveled in the mountains, Brother," Shokan said, "I met a woman—an elder of Quinta-la's village, perhaps of her people. It was my impression at the time that this woman was considered a seer among her people. They were somewhat afraid of her, though in awe would perhaps be a better description. I sensed no animosity toward her. It was very unusual. As I do not speak their tongue nor understand their ways, I did not know what to think of this woman. Alinka-sa, for that was her name, questioned me about the situation in the Empire. She also asked about you, Brother Shuyun. She knew you by name.''

Shuyun sat for a moment, his face unreadable even to Nishima who believed she was learning the tiny signs that betrayed what he truly felt. ''Alinka-sa,'' he said quietly. ''Sa is an honorific: a sign of the greatest possible respect. There is no equivalent in our language.

''Alinka means ginkyo, more specifically, the leaf of the ginkyo. This tree, though common to us, does not grow in the mountains and is thought to be almost a legend to the mountain people. Alinka is also the word for fan. I remember our fortunes being cast in your garden, my Lady,'' Shuyun said to Nishima. ''The coins of Kowan-sing have descended to us from the same race that Quinta-la's people call their ancestors. The meaning of Alinka is somewhat similar to the prime Kowan; the fan: *that which is hidden.* In our world it also means temptation or desire. To know the future is one of our greatest desires.'' Shuyun turned to Shokan. ''This woman, Lord Shonto, did she speak of what was to come?''

Shokan shook his head. ''No, Brother. If she saw the future, she did not tell me of her vision.'' The lord fell silent, lost in thought. Finally he looked up at Nishima. ''If she knew of our father's fall, she said nothing to me though now I am left to wonder. She released me from my debt—the debt I owed her people for rescuing me in the snows—but I do not know why.''

Cha had grown cold in everyone's bowls and Nishima suddenly remembered the servant kneeling nearby. She gestured to the maid to leave.

Shokan looked up, slight embarrassment showing. ''Excuse me, I was lost in my thoughts.'' He glanced over at Quinta-la. ''Perhaps it would be wise for me to take Quinta-la back to her rooms for now. Alone she may speak of this.''

Nishima gave a slight nod and Shokan bowed accordingly, touching Quinta-la's sleeve. She prostrated herself before Shuyun once again and backed to the door at Shokan's urging, forgetting to bow to the Empress entirely.

Nishima looked over at Shuyun. She wanted to speak of what had happened with Quinta-la, but she could not. What she might learn frightened her.

''Must everything change?'' she asked quietly instead.

"Botahara taught that change was inevitable and to resist it. . . ." He did not complete the quotation. "Sadly, it appears to be so, Nishima-sum. You are an Empress now. A great empire is dependent upon your wisdom."

She almost asked the question that grew in her mind but could not. *I have become an Empress, Shuyun-sum, and what of you? What have you become?*

She reached out and took his hands in hers. I cannot bear it she thought. Let us not speak of it. Warm arms encircled her and she pushed her cheek up against Shuyun's own. Nishima closed her eyes and the image of Quinta-la, prostrated on the floor, came to mind.

That young woman was far more in awe of Shuyun than of the Empress of Wa, Nishima thought. She had been worshipful.

Sixty-three

Sister Sutso walked slowly beside the sedan chair bearing the Prioress. The scale of the halls that led through the Imperial Palace was more impressive than the largest temple she had seen and the materials and design infinitely richer.

Palace officials, Imperial Guards, lords and ladies, and soldiers in blue passed the Sisters or stood aside to let the party by, though it was hardly necessary, the halls were so wide. Looking into the faces of the people she saw, Sutso realized there was a mood in the palace that she could not quite describe. Elation and sadness seemed to dwell under the same roof and the people who inhabited the palace appeared to be caught up in both at once.

She glanced back and found Sister Gatsa watching the passage of two ladies of high birth. Gatsa-sum looks no less regal than they, Sutso thought, perhaps more: would they look as regal dressed in the plain robes of the Botahist nuns? Of all the nuns in the party Gatsa certainly looked the least out of place here.

Morima, on the other hand, looked terribly lost and at odds with all around her. Sutso cast a look at the large nun who brought up the rear of their party. Morima's appearance may not have been due entirely to her present situation, however—the nun's crisis had not yet passed and Sutso had begun to wonder if it ever would. It was a surprise to Sutso that Morima-sum had been invited at all.

Sutso resisted an urge to open the curtain to assure herself that the Prioress was well. The pretense that the Prioress was stronger than she actually was must be maintained, especially here.

The Empress had summoned the Sisters the previous evening after the Sisterhood had sent their official bless-

ing to the new sovereign. It was only upon their arrival
in the palace that they had learned the Supreme Master,
Brother Hutto, and other senior members of the Botahist
Brotherhood were to attend the same audience as the Sisters.

Only the Prioress had taken this information calmly,
smiling her beatific smile and closing her eyes as though
she would sleep and dream dreams of great peace and
beauty. May Botahara walk beside her, Sutso thought.

Outside the palace wall the barbarian army, or part of
it, had lain down their arms and now they waited,
watched from a distance by patrols from Lord Shonto's
army. Rumors flew through the city. It was said that Lord
Shonto's Spiritual Advisor, Brother Shuyun, had gone out
into the field and defeated the Golden Khan in single
combat and the tribes had then battled among themselves, some retreating north, others surrendering. This
young Initiate monk had become an even greater object
of speculation among the Sisters. Sutso knew the Prioress' hopes regarding this young man and this worried the
Prioress' secretary. She was concerned with the effect it
might have if the Prioress' hopes were dashed entirely.
Desire, Sutso thought, it is as Botahara said. And the
Prioress is so much closer to Perfection than any I know.

The official who led them turned to the right into a hall
that ended in a set of double doors. Shonto guards knelt
in two rows before the doors and two young neophyte
monks swung incense burners before them.

The guards and the neophytes all bowed as the Sisters
passed. The official had the doors opened, and gestured
for them to enter.

Beyond the heavy doors was an audience hall of me-
dium size, no doubt, by Palace standards, though it was
as large as the largest hall of the priory. The entrance to
the great room was not at the end opposite the dais, as
Sutso expected, but to one side of the hall. Perhaps a
dozen senior Brothers knelt in a row directly across from
the opened doors and as Sutso entered she saw a single
ancient monk sitting to her right, opposite the dais.
Brother Nodaku, she thought, the Supreme Master of the
Botahist Brotherhood. The identities of the others she
could not guess.

As the official directed them to silk cushions laid out

on the polished wooden floor, the Brothers bowed. Sutso returned this gesture and then tapped lightly on the sedan chair that bore her superior.

"Open my curtains, child," came the dry voice of Sister Saeja.

Sutso slid the silk curtains aside and found the Prioress propped up on her pillows. The old woman bowed to the Supreme Master and then his party who all did the same in return. Sutso moved a cushion and knelt close to her superior. The official who had brought them to the hall retreated and the doors were closed behind him. No one spoke—no one showed a sign of the surprise or resentment they felt at being forced into this situation. All waited patiently.

A door opened to one side of the dais and an official wearing the dragon fan of the Empress' staff entered. He shuffled quickly to a place directly before the dais and bowed to the assembled followers of Botahara.

"Supreme Master," he said with great dignity. "Prioress, Sisters, Brothers: the Major Chancellor of the Empire of Wa." He bowed again and moved off to one side.

Sutso watched as an old man with one arm entered. He wore the elaborate ceremonial robes of his station but somehow did not seem to belong in them. Despite his age this man would have looked more at home on horseback. To add truth to this, Sutso noticed that the man's face showed signs of having recently been exposed to the wind and sun.

Kamu, Sutso realized. This is the Shonto steward. A capable man by all reports and completely loyal to the Shonto. She wondered how many other key positions in the government were now filled by Shonto retainers. The Yamaku nightmare had come true.

Kamu bowed to all present and took up a place kneeling just before the dais as his position dictated. He produced a scroll from his empty sleeve and unrolled it with obvious skill against his thigh using his only hand.

"I regret to say that the Empress will not join us. As you might imagine, the situation in the Empire at the moment requires much of her attention." It was the closest thing to an apology one received from a sovereign. People of lesser position in the same situation would be expected to apologize for arriving when the Empress had

pressing business elsewhere—despite the fact that they
had been summoned.

Kamu consulted the scroll. "The Empress has instructed me to assure you that the attitude of the previous
Imperial Family toward the Botahist Orders will not continue. The Empress Shigei is a devout follower of Botahara and, as you know, the Shonto have long employed
Spiritual Advisors of the Botahist faith and, until recently, the Empress' personal secretary was a former Sister. There will be no untoward taxes upon property held
by either Order and the Yamaku laws restricting public
religious ceremonies will be rescinded." Kamu lowered
the scroll.

Brother Hutto, the Primate of Yankura, bowed to the
Chancellor. "May Botahara smile upon the Empress
Shigei and her line. May the Perfect Master walk beside
the Daughter of Heaven in these difficult times."

Kamu acknowledged this with a half bow.

Sister Gatsa took her cue. "It was with great joy that
we received the news of the investiture of the Empress,
Major Chancellor. Botahara has answered our prayers for
a sovereign who will protect the followers of the Way. In
our prayers we will ask Botahara to bless the Empress
Shigei and the reign of the Fanisan House. May we also
express our regrets for the Empress' recent loss. Our
prayers will not fail to ask the Perfect Master to look
with favor upon the spirit of Lord Shonto Motoru who
was a great lord and a friend to the Botahist Orders."
She cast a cold glance toward Brother Hutto as if to say,
that is fair speech, Brother.

Kamu nodded to Gatsa. "Both your blessings and your
prayers are welcome in this troubled time. It is the desire
of the Empress to make the Empire secure again so that
all may travel the roads and canals safely and all may
come freely to the temples of your Orders with the blessing of the sovereign. This is the desire of the Empress,
though it is a great task and one which cannot be accomplished without the contributions of many."

Ah, Sutso thought, they have summoned us to ask for
money. She did not smile. This new Imperial family may
be easier to deal with than the Sisters had hoped. Money
was never given without expectations of return.

"The Empress has asked Lord Shonto's Spiritual Advisor, Initiate Brother Shuyun, to speak of the needs of the Empire.''

Kamu nodded over toward a screen which opened immediately. Sutso's eyes moved there as did the gaze of everyone in the room. A small monk, almost a boy, entered. If not for his pendant chain she would certainly have mistaken him for a Neophyte. She glanced over at the Prioress, but the old woman did not notice. Her focus was on the young monk, and nothing else. The old woman made a sign to Botahara.

Sutso turned back in time to see Shuyun complete his bows and kneel before the dais, facing the Supreme Master. She glanced over at the head of the Brotherhood and then back to the boy who sat so calmly across from him. It is impossible to say whose eyes are more ancient, Sutso thought, and she felt the smallest surge of wonder.

Shuyun gave a half nod to Kamu and then began to speak. His voice was as soft as the wing of a butterfly. ''It is a great honor to be here among those who are charged with the protection of the Way. If I may quote the Perfect Master to those who have studied His Words longer than I have lived this life: Lord Botahara said that the beginning of wisdom was compassion. And so I was instructed by my teachers.'' He gave a half bow to Brother Sotura who sat with the other senior monks.

The words Brother Shuyun speaks have been chosen for simplicity, Sutso thought, though not as a child selects from a limited vocabulary but as an artist chooses the simplest lines and yet renders complexity.

''I do not claim to have achieved wisdom, but I am learning compassion and therefore I have made a beginning. Recently Botahara tested my compassion in a manner I would never have expected. It was written in the sacred scrolls that compassion could not be limited to one's family or to one's fellow villagers. True compassion would encompass strangers. True compassion would be extended to one's enemies. Remembering this, I was able to act as Botahara had written. I was able to act compassionately toward the enemies of Wa.'' Shuyun looked at each face in turn, holding everyone's gaze for a second. It was an act of some disrespect from one so young, yet no one seemed to notice.

Touching his palms together as though he would pray,

Shuyun continued. "Among the barbarians outside the gates of the Capital the plague has begun to work its terrible destruction. In return for laying down their arms, I promised that we, the followers of Botahara, those who practice compassion, would heal them of this disease." He let his words hang in the air. "The Empress has asked that you assist me in this endeavor," he said simply.

Silence in the hall. And though many looks were exchanged, no one spoke a word. Finally, after a long awkward moment, the Supreme Master deigned to speak.

"These are not followers of the Way, Brother Shuyun. You have promised much without the consent of the seniors of your Order. Initiate monks do not speak for the Botahist Brotherhood. Even Initiates who have the ear of the Empress. You may have learned something of compassion, but you have certainly forgotten much of humility."

Before Shuyun could respond, the Prioress spoke, her voice rasping out into the tension that charged the air. "We will assist you Brother Shuyun, in any way within our power, but the cure for the plague is the guarded secret of the Brotherhood." She looked over at the Supreme Master, an eyebrow raised.

He did not respond to her but kept his attention on Shuyun as though the head of the Sisterhood had not spoken. "Brother Shuyun, we would do much to assist the new sovereign. It is our sworn duty to minister to the followers of the Way. But caring for barbarian invaders who have put many followers of the true path to the sword. . . . This will not be a popular act of charity among the people of the Empire, let me assure you. The Empress asks much of us." The ancient monk turned his attention to Kamu, dismissing the Initiate who sat opposite him.

"Major Chancellor, the Empress understands the ways of the Empire, as do her advisors who have many years of experience in such matters. It is difficult for me to believe that the Council of the Empire expects Botahist Brothers to cure barbarians when so many of our own faith are in need of our ministrations. . . ."

Sister Sutso did not miss the fact that the Supreme Master let the sentence hang in the air, the implications clear. *What coin is the Empress willing to exchange for such a service?* And the Sisterhood has nothing to bargain with in this exchange, she thought. Only the Brothers will gain concessions from the throne and we will sit silently and bear witness to this. What a moment of triumph for the Brothers.

Kamu did not respond or even acknowledge that he had been spoken to but only looked over to Shuyun.

"Prioress?" came the soft voice of the Initiate. "Do you mean what you say: in any way within your power?"

"Yes, Brother Shuyun, but we do not know the secret of the cure."

"I know the cure," Shuyun said simply.

"I forbid it!" the Supreme Master almost shouted. "I forbid it! You break the laws of the Botahist Order."

Shuyun stared at the old man who had gone red with anger.

"If I act according to the word of Botahara, how is it possible to break the laws of our Order? I act according to the dictates of compassion, Supreme Master."

"Where have you learned such arrogance, Shuyun-sum?" Brother Sotura asked quietly. "The well-being of all who follow the Way must be considered here. Do not attempt to make decisions that are beyond your ability. Pride, Brother Shuyun, will hinder you on your path. Please apologize to the Supreme Master and let the Major Chancellor speak."

Sister Sutso's heart sank as she watched Shuyun bow in deference to this monk. But then Sister Saeja spoke. "They do not know who you were in your previous life, Brother Shuyun. It is unheard of that a Brother with your skill so young cannot be identified." Sutso could hear the controlled excitement in her superior's voice. "Do you know what this means, Brother?"

Shuyun turned back to the woman propped up in her sedan chair. "It could mean many things, Prioress Saeja. How quickly can you gather the Sisters to minister to the barbarians?"

"You will be expelled from our Order," the Supreme Master said loudly. "Stripped of your sash and pendant."

"Immediately, Brother," Sister Saeja answered quickly. "Some will come this very day. Two hundred will arrive tomorrow. Three hundred more in three days, if you require it.''

''Expelled from our Order,'' the Supreme Master said with finality. ''The light of Botahara will be hidden from you.''

Shuyun nodded. ''May Botahara walk beside you, Prioress.'' Saying this he lifted the pendant on its gold chain over his head.

''You will be shunned by all who follow the Way.''

''Shuyun-sum,'' Sotura said, his voice rising. ''Think what you do. . . .''

Sotura watched as Shuyun dropped the pendant and chain into the palm of one hand. The young monk stared at the gold and jade in his hand with a look of deep sadness.

''You will be cursed by the Perfect Master,'' the Supreme Master intoned.

Shuyun looked up at these last words. With a look of great regret he set the pendant on the floor and the chain slid out of his hand to make a pile beside it.

''I will be blessed by Botahara,'' Shuyun said, and Sutso felt the conviction of these words, saw even the Supreme Master hesitate when he heard them.

Shuyun rose slowly to his feet so that he stood above all the senior members of his Order. Sotura watched as he did the unthinkable: Shuyun *pointed* at the Supreme Master.

''Pray that the compassion of Botahara encompasses you, Brother, for if it does you may yet be returned to the wheel.''

Brother Sotura was on his feet, lightning quick. Three blindingly fast strides toward the young monk and then suddenly he stepped back off balance for an instant as though he had been struck. Shuyun stood with his hand raised, palm out, yet he had not touched the senior Brother.

''Forgive me Sotura-sum,'' Shuyun said quietly, his voice full of compassion. ''Separate yourself from those who have lost the Way. Do you remember the lesson you taught when I was but a child? The butterfly enclosed in your chi strong fist?'' Shuyun reached into his sleeve and removed something. When he opened his hand a white blossom lay upon his palm. ''Brother Sotura, your Order has lost compassion—the beginnings of wisdom. To find the True Path you must leave them.''

The Senior Brother stood looking at the blossom in Shuyun's hand. "You did not touch me . . ." he said.

Shuyun nodded once.

Brother Sotura looked up from the blossom into the eyes of his former student. The chi quan Master's face was deeply troubled.

Sister Sutso heard a noise to her right and then a thin hand gripped her shoulder. The Prioress stepped out of her chair and came to her knees beside Sutso. The secretary turned and saw the Prioress was crying. The old woman bowed her head to the floor and began to chant the prayer of thanksgiving.

Shuyun turned at the sound of this and Sutso thought she saw a look of horror cross the Botahist mask. The young monk turned back to his former teacher, holding his gaze for a second, and then almost fled from the hall.

Sutso looked down at her superior who still bowed her head to the floor, and then she realized that others did the same—both Sisters and Brothers.

Botahara help me, she thought, *have I been in the presence of the Teacher and not known?*

Sixty-four

The Empress of Wa stood alone on a balcony looking north across the small part of her vast Empire that could be seen from the Island Palace. The morning's rain had let up, leaving the air clear and the sky hung with retreating clouds that twisted slowly in a clearing breeze. The shadows cast by the clouds flowed slowly across the fields and flanks of distant mountains creating an ever changing pattern no artist could hope to capture.

The barbarian encampment spread in mottled grays and browns across the green grass and came by turns into shadow and light. Outside the protective circle maintained by the Shonto soldiers, people from the Capital and surrounding areas had begun to gather. Nishima could see knots of them collecting here and there, staring with fascination toward the encampment. Many brought food, Nishima had been told, and she was surprised to hear this for there was still little enough to be had in the Imperial Capital.

This sudden generosity did not necessarily indicate a great change in the attitude of the people of Wa toward their invaders: the rumor was spreading that the Shonto Spiritual Advisor, the gifted monk who had defeated the barbarian army, was the Teacher so long awaited. Only the Shonto soldiers and the fear of plague kept the people away from the man they hoped was the one foretold.

Nishima felt a deep uneasiness when she looked down at the gathering crowds as though they were another force intended to keep her and Shuyun apart.

For three days now the monk had been away tending to the barbarians and Nishima had grown more and more restive as though each day took him farther away and made his return less likely. She paced across the short balcony to its end, stopped, and looked out again. Forcing herself to give up the futile searching of tiny figures moving through the barbarian encampment, Nishima fixed her gaze on the northeast.

Kamu had said that the barbarian army that traveled there would begin to raise a dust cloud once the wind dried the land, but there was no sign of this yet nor of Lord Taiki's pursuing force. This part of the shattered barbarian army had razed a village the previous day though the villagers had fled before the tribesmen descended. Nishima pressed her fingers to her temple. No one was really certain of the purpose of these barbarians, loose upon the land as they were. The suggestion that they made their way toward the Botahist temples on the Mountain of the Pure Spirit still appeared the most likely explanation. Obviously these barbarians could not know that the Brothers would never succumb to force, nor would they be likely to simply offer a cure.

Shuyun had said that the plague would take hold among the fleeing barbarians by the third day so that only a few would remain strong when they arrived at their probable destination. Lord Taiki, she hoped, would convince these to surrender.

Her attention was taken by a line of men on foot who passed the Shonto soldiers who guarded the barbarian. Botahist Brothers, Nishima realized. A growing number were leaving their Order to come serve the one said to be the Teacher—to practice compassion rather than politics.

The Botahist Brotherhood, her advisors surmised, were locked in internal struggle. They had stripped Shuyun of his pendant and turned their backs on him, and only after this rash decision had they realized their error. They had alienated the new sovereign, surrendering the advantage of Imperial favor to the Sisterhood—and they might have forced the Teacher from their Order.

Nishima shook her head. As her father often noted, Brother Satake would never have acted so foolishly had he become the leader of the Botahist Brotherhood. It made her wonder if it was not as Shimeko said—the Brotherhood had become decadent.

A full report of the meeting between Shuyun and the Seniors of the Botahist Orders had been supplied by Kamu. He spoke of Shuyun's actions and speech with

pride. The Brothers made few miscalculations as great
as that. It must have been impossible for them to imagine
that a young Initiate could act independently, ignoring
their gravest threats, offering one of the Order's greatest
secrets to their rivals. Only a few months away from Jinjoh Monastery and Initiate Brother Shuyun had rebelled
against them—far more openly than Satake-sum ever had.
In part, Nishima viewed this as almost a personal triumph, but it also filled her with fear. Brother Shuyun
appeared to be under no one's spell.

Shokan was utterly convinced that the Brotherhood
would recant their refusal to assist the barbarians and
would scramble to preserve some shred of the advantage
they had surrendered when the Sisters offered their ser-
vices to Shuyun and the throne. It was perhaps a sign of
how fractured their Order had become that this had not
yet occurred.

A knock on the screen that led from the balcony startled Nishima, and a Shonto guard appeared at her response. "The audience, Empress," he said, keeping his
eyes cast down.

Nishima took a last look out to where Shuyun minis-
tered to the army of the desert and then left the room she
had begun to use so that she might look out over the
barbarian encampment. Her guard fell into step around
her immediately.

She had managed to break the tradition of the sedan
chair, though this shocked more than just a few officials.
To ameliorate this somewhat, she agreed to use the chair
for ceremonies—the struggle now was focused on se-
mantics—which events could be considered ceremonial?
There was, Nishima was sure, a definite move afoot to
broaden the strict definition of the word.

As Shokan had suggested, Nishima tried to view the
situation with humor, but it was difficult. The officials of
the Island Palace were completely obsessed with tradition and ceremony and matters too trivial to believe. It
was obvious that the running of the Empire had not been
their concern for a very long time—not since the days of
the later Hanama Emperors. This would have to change,
if it meant replacing every senior member of the government.

She descended a massive set of stairs, courtiers and

officials bowing as she passed. A private audience hall
off Nishima's official rooms was their destination. Until
Nishima had peopled the Great Council to her liking,
there were still a number of things that needed to be done
beyond the view of the officials. Their interference in
certain things would not be helpful. Nishima was beginning to realize that she had learned more than she ever
realized about leading men from years of watching her
father. There was no one more skilled than Lord Shonto
at winning loyalty and achieving ends through the efforts
of others. It was the intention of the new Empress to
bend Imperial protocol as much as possible so that she
could run her administration upon the Shonto model—
something she knew was effective.

Returning the Empire to a state of stability was her
immediate task and to do this she would need the assistance of many. Shokan and Kamu had pointed out that
rewarding those who had followed her father from Seh,
and supported him when it meant defying the Emperor,
was the beginning. Let it be said that the new Empress
understood and rewarded loyalty. It was the Shonto way.

She had been informed that there were rebellions in
Chou, and a Yamaku cousin there had declared himself
Emperor and began to gather an army—a fool's rebellion,
Hojo assured her, but it indicated that speed was necessary to establish the validity of her rule beyond contest-
ing. The previous day a report had come that the Yamaku
Imperial family dwelt no more on this plane, caught by
the people who fled the barbarian invasion. It was a sad
thing and, though Hojo had breathed a sigh of relief,
Shokan had told Nishima privately that this was not as
significant as others hoped. Pretenders could easily arise
claiming to be Yamaku sons or daughters or cousins—
even distant relatives of the Hanama might make claims,
for that was the basis of Nishima's own. Imperial blood
was not terribly rare among the peers of Wa.

They reached the rooms that Nishima had made her
own and the Empress nodded to bowing Shonto guards
as she passed. The audience hall was empty and Nishima
took her place on the low dais, arranging her robes with
care—white over crimson. She was glad that she had not
met resistance from Shokan or the others to this. It was
customary for those who performed great deeds for the

sake of the Empire to receive their rewards in great ceremony, but Nishima did not feel such a ceremony was appropriate at this time. Perhaps when the Empire was more settled. The people she would speak with this day were not courtiers or officials of the Palace. They would not demand that the smallest of their actions receive public recognition. As callous as it sounded, some part of Nishima knew that to strengthen the ties to those who had supported her father she needed to treat each as a private favorite of the Empress. This knowledge embarrassed her somewhat, but it did not stop her from acting accordingly.

I have a rule to consolidate and legitimize, Nishima told herself, but may I not walk too far down the path of the cold manipulator. Botahara save me from that.

Kamu entered and knelt before the dais, bowing his head to the mat. The Empress nodded to her Major Chancellor. The officials of the palace were no doubt still stinging from Kamu's appointment but, along with the other stands she had made, this was having its desired effect—the officials were realizing that they would not rule the Empress.

"Kamu-sum. It is my hope that the constant whispers of the Palace officials do not make the performance of your duties too difficult."

"The buzzing of flies, Empress. I have long since learned to ignore such things."

"Perhaps it is another of your many skills that I may one day acquire myself, for I confess this buzzing sometimes drives me to the ends of my patience."

The old man smiled, the great wrinkled raincloud of his face creasing in a thousand small lines. "Patience was not something I learned in my youth, Empress, it grew slowly as the years passed. Thus it was that, in my younger years, I fought more duels than perhaps even Lord Komawara." Kamu gestured to his empty sleeve. "Here is my great teacher of patience, Empress, otherwise I may have been too foolish by nature to have ever acquired this most valuable of traits. But you are wiser than I, my Lady," he hurried to add, embarrassed suddenly by what he implied.

Nishima hid a small shudder. "Let us hope that I may learn from you, Kamu-sum. I would certainly live with my loss less skillfully and with less grace than my Chancellor.''

Kamu looked down, perhaps embarrassed. He consulted a scroll.

''I am ready to begin,'' Nishima said, giving her father's steward a small smile.

''Lord Butto Joda of the province of Itsa, Empress,'' Kamu said. ''The lord readies himself to go north in pursuit of the barbarian who retreat along the great canal.''

Nishima nodded. Kamu clapped his hand upon his thigh once, producing a surprisingly loud sound, and the doors to the hall opened. It was a small hall, chosen intentionally so that those arriving for their audience would not have to traverse a vast room on their knees to approach the sovereign. But despite its size it was a room of some beauty. The posts here were not lacquered but left a rich natural red-brown, and the sweep of the ceiling beams that supported the massive tile roof gave the otherwise static space a feeling of motion. Painted screens of courtiers walking in the Palace gardens decorated one wall, and Nishima was thankful they were not scenes of battle.

The small figure of Lord Butto bowed in the doorway and then approached the dais. At an appropriate distance he stopped and bowed again.

''Lord Butto, please be at your ease,'' Kamu said quietly. The old man withdrew then, slipping quietly out through a screen. Nishima was paying Lord Butto the ultimate compliment of favor and trust—meeting the sovereign of the Empire privately.

Nishima turned her attention to the young lord kneeling before her. Like a boy, Nishima thought, all of his features are small though his eyes are very fine. But belying this look of youth was the lord's great poise. He was as sure of himself as many of her officials. Here will be a great man, the Empress found herself thinking, trapped for now in the body of a child. She smiled warmly.

''Lord Butto,'' she began, and was surprised to find her voice become thick with emotion. She paused for a few seconds. ''Lord Butto,'' she began again, ''it is my honor to express to you and the Butto House the gratitude of the government and the people of Wa. In the recent turmoil in the Empire you have shown the greatest wisdom and exemplary judgment, placing the interests of the Province of Itsa and the Empire of Wa before those of your House. To have fought beside my father against the invading barbarian army, and to have risked being judged a rebel House for this, displayed both courage and conviction. In the subsequent battles, Lord Butto, your courage did not falter nor did the warriors of your House ever shrink from their duty.'' Nishima took a long breath. ''If there is anything within the power of an Empress to provide, you have but to ask.''

Lord Butto stared down at the floor.

The young warrior looked up, meeting his Empress' eyes for a second. ''Empress. It was my greatest honor to ride at the side of Lord Shonto Motoru as he fought, unsupported by the Imperial government, to stay the barbarian invasion. It is a tale equal to any in our long history and shall be told for a thousand years. The Butto name shall ever be sung in that tale, though in truth my part was small. What greater gift could I ask? I am honored by your words, as is the Butto House.''

Nishima bowed low in response. ''You are fair spoken, Sire, and your words touch me. Please, Lord Butto, accept these tokens of our regard.'' She clapped her hands twice.

Shonto guards appeared, carrying a saddle of beautiful leather. It was not decorated with silver or stones but was a saddle a warrior would choose, perfectly made of the finest materials. Upon the right side below the pommel a shinta blossom was embossed and on the left the flower of the warisha. Resting upon the seat was a bridle, also of leather, but with silk reins woven of crimson and blue. An armor chest was borne forth on a pole and set beside the saddle. Guards opened the lid and revealed a suit of armor laced in Butto purple and trimmed in the same pattern of crimson and blue.

Finally, a guard carrying a silk cushion, upon which rested a warrior's helmet, emerged and laid this before Lord Butto.

''It is my father's helmet, Lord Butto,'' Lady Nishima said. ''May the crimson and blue always remind you of the gratitude and loyalty of the Shonto and of the Fanisan

House. May the shinta blossom and the warisha symbolize the growing bonds between our families and the great esteem in which you are held." Servants set a low table beside the Empress and from this she removed a brush.

"Lord Butto, Itsa Province needs a governor of great wisdom to repair the ravages of the invasion. I would offer this position first to you, for there is no other I would trust more." This was a formality only, for the governorship of Itsa had been offered to Lord Butto, in private by Kamu, so that he could have refused without rebuffing the Empress.

Lord Butto bowed again. "Empress, this is a great honor for the Butto House. I accept and hope only that I may prove myself worthy of your great trust."

"Lord Butto," Nishima said warmly, "of this there is no doubt." With a flourish Nishima signed the scroll of investiture, making Butto Joda the Imperial Governor of Itsa.

A memory of the Emperor speaking to his new governor of Seh in the Palace garden appeared in Nishima's mind and she hesitated before setting the brush down.

Pushing this thought from her mind, she forced herself to continue.

"You will pursue the retreating barbarian army, Lord Butto?"

"I set out in the morning, Empress."

Nishima nodded. "May Botahara go with you, Lord Butto."

The young man bowed low. "I thank you, Empress," he almost whispered.

Kamu had returned almost silently, nodding to Lord Butto who retreated back to the great doors. The old man gave Nishima a smile of reassurance and then looked at his scroll. "General Hojo Masakado," he said, clapping his hand to his thigh once.

The senior Shonto general knelt in the open doorway and came forward at a gesture from Kamu.

Nishima noted that Hojo looked rather less at ease here than she had seen him appear before a battle. The General wore robes of white embroidered in the palest shades with falling cherry blossoms—a man in mourning for his liege-lord.

With his gray beard neatly trimmed and his hair drawn

back Hojo was a man of great presence despite his lack
of ease in such formal surroundings. This man will be
less happy in the new Empire, Nishima thought, for if
Botahara smiles upon us the Shonto will have little need
of his warrior's skills.

"Masakado-sum," Nishima said as Kamu retreated
again. "Were I a great poet, I could not find words that
would convey my gratitude or do you the honor you de-
serve." Nishima felt her heart begin to break as she
looked at the face of the man kneeling before her. These
are the men who loved my father, she thought, glancing
over at Kamu's retreating back. These are the people who
share my loss and have walled their feelings away for the
sake of the Empire and their new Empress. She remembered both these men from her arrival in the Shonto
house—massive, intimidating strangers they had been
then. But how quickly that had changed. They teased me
as a child and indulged me and adored me as though I
were a member of their own families. She closed her eyes
tightly and took three slow breaths.

"General, your loyalty to Lord Shonto Motoru and the
Shonto House and its causes has been as unwavering as
the loyalty of Fugimori to his outcast prince—as constant
as the seasons. Without your wisdom and bravery, my
lord's effort to slow the barbarian advance would have
faltered, I have no doubt. Anything you ask of me I will
grant, Hojo Masakado-sum, for the Empire's debt to you
is great."

"*Empress,*" Hojo began but his voice came out a
whisper and he cleared his throat before beginning again.
"Empress, I have served two Shonto Lords and it is my
wish to serve a third. I believe this is what I am meant
to do. If I may, I will go with Lord Shonto Shokan."

"But this is a small thing, General—it is your present
position. Is there no other favor an Empress may grant?"

Hojo shook his head. "I thank you, Empress. I am
honoured by your words—that is enough."

"Masakado-sum, my father would never see you go
unrewarded and I cannot change the tradition of my family." As before, she clapped twice and a Shonto guard
appeared carrying a small stand upon which sat a single
scroll. This was set before Hojo.

"It is the deed for a house in the Capital near to the

home of your liege-lord, General—a property I have been told you admire. This, so you may visit the Capital often and so come to the Palace that I may not lose the pleasure of your company.'' Before Hojo could respond, a second guard appeared bearing a sword in both his hands as though it were a valuable artifact.

Nishima beckoned the guard to her and, to his great surprise, took the sword into her own hands. With the grace of a Sonsa she rose and descended from the dais. Holding the sword in both her hands, she offered it to Hojo who was so taken aback he hesitated for a moment.

"It was my father's favored weapon," Nishima said as though to reassure him.

"My Lady, it is the *Mitsushito*," Hojo said, still not reaching for it. An Empress did not descend from her dais to offer a soldier a gift from her own hands—it was unheard of.

"So it is, Masakado-sum. My brother and I hope that you will accept it." She held it out again.

Hojo took it gently from her hands, and Nishima saw him close his eyes. She thought tears would appear, but the general was a warrior and maintained control with effort. Nishima reached out for a second, touching his hard wrist, and then she returned to the dais, unable to bear his discomfort any longer.

Hojo bowed but no words came, and he retreated even before Nishima had called an end to their audience.

Nishima sat for a few moments before she would continue. Nodding to Kamu, she again followed a breathing exercise taught to her by Brother Satake.

"Captain Rohku Saicha," Kamu said quietly.

Nishima nodded. The Captain of the Shonto Guard approached. He wore the light duty armor she often saw him in and carried his helmet under his arm. A white sash was worn for Lord Shonto and in this he wore no sword, making Nishima realize that the Shonto Captain had not been granted permission to wear a sword in the presence of the Empress. A grievous oversight with a man so proud.

Except for the white sash and the missing sword Rohku had been dressed exactly so when he had argued against Nishima's decision to journey to Seh.

What a position I placed this poor man in, she thought.

"Saicha-sum," Nishima said, "Though unintentional I assure you, I have paid you a terrible insult." Clapping her hands a guard appeared, for the second time bearing a sheathed sword. "Of my father's extensive collection of blades there were only three that he chose to carry into battle. The Mitsushito I have given to General Hojo. This is a Kentoka, Saicha-sum. It is my wish that you will wear it in my presence."

Rohku Saicha set his helmet gently on the floor and took the sword in both his hands. "My Lady, I did not for a moment believe you had lost trust in me but only focused on affairs of the Empire and struggled with grief. I will wear this always for your protection."

Nishima nodded. "That is my hope, Captain Rohku, for I have spoken long with my brother of this very matter. Too many rulers have been deposed by disloyal guard commanders and in an unsettled Empire this is a matter of grave concern. Lord Shonto has suggested, if you would agree, that you take command of the Imperial Guard, Saicha-sum, and, if you do, I will sleep easily. It is a choice left entirely to you. If it is your wish to stay with the Shonto, it would be with my blessing." Nishima found her mouth suddenly dry. She had said *Shonto* as though they were another family—not her own.

Nishima watched the captain's face as he considered this offer. Neither she nor Shokan had been sure of his decision. Certainly she had proven a difficult charge in the past, but Nishima needed someone she could trust completely and that left very few with the proper experience—it was not enough to be a warrior or a great general, a guard captain must be born suspicious, and yet reveal this to no one. He must have the mind of an assassin for this was how security was created without weaknesses.

"Empress, I am concerned for Lord Shonto. . . . He is my liege-lord and my charge. It is difficult for me to abandon him."

"If your heart cannot, Saicha-sum, then you must stay with Shokan-sum. I will say only this—your lord has said that Shonto security could best be served by making the Imperial household completely safe. Please consider this. I will accept either decision in your own time."

Nishima waited, trying to read the look of the captain,

but he kept his face hidden by staring at the floor, cradling his sword across his knees.

"Saicha-sum. My father chose to ride into the midst of a battle. You did not make this choice for him. An arrow—in a battle there is no way to guard against an arrow. No one bears responsibility for Lord Shonto Motoru's death."

Rohku nodded. "Thank you, my Lady." He did not look up.

Nishima had more to say, more praise for the guard captain for his part in the war against the barbarian and compliments for his son as well but she thought these things better said at another time.

She gave a signal to Kamu, who watched through a crack in the screen and the Major Chancellor returned, clearing his throat and then nodding to Rohku who retreated.

"Kamu-sum, if giving rewards is this difficult, how will I survive making even the slightest criticism?"

"Empress, if I may say . . . this is a difficult thing you do. These men supported your father while the rest of the Empire watched the Yamaku attempt to bring about his fall. They fought a barbarian army of a size never before seen with a small force and acquitted themselves in a manner that can only be cause for awe. They have become figures in our history." Kamu gestured out at the empty hall. "This audience signals an end of sorts. How will these warriors live up to the reputations that have been created? The captain who knelt before you will be a greater figure in history than all but a few lords who live in our Empire today. Hojo Masakado-sum will be mentioned in the same breath as the Emperor Jirri. I believe that they no longer know who they are, Lady Nishima. Until only a few days ago they were the men who resisted a barbarian invasion against impossible odds. Their lives had no other purpose. And now?

"You are releasing them from the purpose that has guided them, Empress. They do not know where they will go or who they will be. Not one had previously thought of himself as becoming a character of importance in our history. You praise them, Empress, and rightly so, but also you send them into the unknown. How does one act as a living historical figure, a legend?"

Nishima nodded. "I do not know, Kamu-sum," she said quietly. "In this matter I know as little as they."

Kamu smiled. "My Lady, excuse me for saying so, but Lord Shonto always said that you have long denied your place in our Empire."

Nishima nodded slowly. "If you will lecture me regularly with quotations from my father, I will give you the wealth of a province in return, Kamu-sum."

"Excuse me, Empress, I did not mean to step out of my place."

Nishima looked up at this remark, unable to hide her distress. "Kamu-sum, I did not intend to criticize. To hear my father's words spoken by a true friend. . . . It breaks my heart and is a comfort at the same time." Nishima looked over at the peaceful scene depicted in the screens. "Please, Kamu-sum, ask Lady Kento if she will join me for my meal."

Kamu bowed low and retreated almost silently.

Nishima rose from the dais and crossed the room. There was no balcony, but unshuttered windows looked out to the west as did her own rooms. The sprawling barbarian camp could not be seen from here and this bothered her. What does he do now? Nishima wondered. What are his thoughts of me? More and more the last days she had begun to admit the true question to herself. *How long will he stay?* Shuyun is no longer a Botahist monk, she told herself, but this provided little comfort. He is something more, she was forced to admit. Who am I to interfere with the course that has been set for him? It was not a question she could answer.

A knock behind her brought Lady Kento into the hall, followed by servants bearing tables and trays.

"Kento-sum," Nishima smiled at her lady-in-waiting and then held up her hand to stop the woman from her deep bow. "If you address me or treat me as an Empress in any way, I shall throw myself off the balcony."

Kento gave a slight nod. "As you wish, my lady, though may I point out that this room has no balcony?"

"I shall throw myself from the spiritual heights I have attained, then. With such a small distance to fall, I shall not risk much injury." She smiled again and then gestured suddenly to the painted screens. "We have been invited to join these fine and generous people."

Kento broke into a broad smile. "Have we, indeed? How kind of them."

Like girls playing at make-believe the two women moved their tables closer to the screen and ate their entire meal as though they were in the company of the people depicted in the painting. Many received absurd names and Nishima and Kento gossiped about them shamelessly, attributing the most shocking behavior to one and all.

In the midst of this a letter arrived from Kitsura that contained a poem, written in a mock romantic style, which made the women almost howl with laughter. The guards outside the doors must have wondered what their Empress and her lady-in-waiting could be doing.

It was as though a dam had burst in Nishima's spirit and released a flood in the form of laughter, though it was not necessarily joy at this river's source.

Only toward the end of the meal did the tone of the conversation become sober.

"When Lord Shonto was declared a rebel lord," Kento explained, "the Imperial Guards broke down the doors to the house and took the servants to be questioned. I had escaped before they arrived. The gates were guarded by the Emperor's men and it was not until it became apparent that the battle had been lost that they abandoned their post. Our own brave guards returned to the house as soon as it seemed possible to do so, Lady Nishima. I cannot criticize them—no one was certain what transpired in the Capital and if they had come out of hiding too soon. . . . Less was lost than I had feared though more than I hoped. Even so, the house will soon be much as it always was." Kento toyed with her cup, looking down as she spoke. "There for your pleasure whenever the Palace does not enhance your harmony, my Lady."

"Kento-sum, I would move back tomorrow if I could, but it is truly Shokan-sum's home now." Nishima reached out and touched the woman's sleeve. "But Kento-sum, you are a lady-in-waiting to one Nishima Fanisan Shonto, presently masquerading as an Empress. You would be welcome to join me here, though I can say little to recommend this place." The corners of Nishima's mouth turned down. "It is devoid of humor and joy, bound by senseless conventions, inhabited by men and women whose concerns and thoughts,'' Nishima gestured at the painted figures, ''have a depth not unlike our present companions'.''

''Lady Nishima,'' Kento said, ''I do not presume to involve myself in matters of the Empire, but as to this campaign we must wage against convention and . . .'' she searched for a word, ''the stultification of the spirit, I will take up my sword by your side.''

Nishima clasped her companion's hand. ''Kento-sum, you lift my spirit. I will make you the unofficial Minister of Joy, and for this service you will earn my undying gratitude.''

''To begin, in my new capacity, I believe we should find a husband for your cousin. This will make her more joyful, I'm certain.''

''Kitsura-sum?''

''Of course. She does not grow younger, my lady,'' Kento thought for a second, ''though it does appear she grows fairer. A husband, unquestionably. She will be searching for a consort for you even as we speak. This is self-defense.''

''Huh,'' Nishima said—her father's response. ''Who would be suitable, do you think?''

Kento replaced her cup on the table. ''Your brother is certainly the most appropriate of the lords I know, my lady.''

''But Shokan-sum has known Lady Kitsura all her life,'' Nishima protested weakly.

''Does he not find her enchanting?''

Nishima weighed this for a second. ''It would seem unlikely that he is the only man in the Empire unaffected by her charms. Certainly he does not confide such things to me.''

''If not Lord Shonto, then perhaps Lord Komawara?''

''Really, Kento-sum, that is not likely.''

''But Lady Nishima, consider—Lord Komawara is the hero of the barbarian war. Certainly he will be rewarded richly for this; larger estates, Imperial Favor, a governorship one day. Every young woman in the Empire will be burning incense and chanting his name at sunrise each first day of the month. I have only met him briefly, but is he not noble and kind and quick of mind? So everyone says.''

Nishima smiled. "Less than a year ago our brave hero was thought to be the most provincial lord in the Capital."

"In less time one can change from a lady into an Empress, my lady. I have seen it myself."

Nishima laughed with delight.

"Then he was thought provincial, Lady Nishima, but now he is viewed as having been an innocent—noble of spirit, perhaps even pure."

"Botahara save us!"

Kento laughed now. "You do not seem disposed to let Lord Komawara go, so I return to Shokan-sum."

A bell sounded and Nishima threw up her hands, relieved to end this conversation. "I must return to my duties. I will meet with the hero of the barbarian war this very hour. It is my belief that, offered anything he would desire, rather than ask for Kitsura's hand, a sword, a suit of fine armor, and the greatest horse in the Empire will satisfy Lord Komawara."

"Certainly the Empress knows best," Kento said humbly.

Nishima favored her with a look of exasperation.

Returning to her dais as the servants cleaned away all signs of the meal, Nishima sat considering the words of both Kamu and Lady Kento. It seemed to be true—the men who followed her father and fought the barbarians when the odds were impossible had become heroes on a scale that one found only in scrolls of ancient history and tales of times beyond history. To think, she said to herself, Komawara has become the object of desire for the women of the Empire. *Komawara*.

Kamu entered and bowed, kneeling before and to one side of the dais as his office required. "A letter has come from Lady Okara, Empress." He took it from his empty sleeve and went to place it on the edge of the dais, but Nishima intercepted it. As always, she was surprised by the simplicity of the great painter's hand. Nishima slipped the letter into her sleeve pocket—my reward for completing my duties, she thought.

She raised an eyebrow at Kamu.

"Colonel Jaku Tadamoto, Empress."

Nishima nodded. Ah, yes, the brother of Katta. Tadamoto had been the subject of a lengthy debate among Nishima's advisors.

As one known to have had the ear of the Yamaku Emperor, Tadamoto certainly warranted exile from the inner provinces, or at least the Capital. Yet his case was not that simple. Jaku Tadamoto had corresponded with his brother Jaku Katta when the Black Tiger was ostensibly a Shonto ally and, according to Katta, was the man who had convinced the Emperor to raise an army when the barbarians invaded. Many thought him a man loyal to the throne, even though he had grown to despise the Emperor. In the end, Tadamoto had tried to stop his brother from committing regicide and then had thrown himself between Katta and a sword blow that was intended to end Katta's life. This Tadamoto was a man of many contradictions, Nishima realized. Rohku Saicha was of the belief that the young colonel's knowledge of the machinations of the Imperial Government alone made him too valuable to lose.

Nishima did not yet know what should be done with this man. She was not ready to trust him, yet there was no evidence that he was a threat.

Shonto guards entered and stationed themselves close about the dais just as the doors at the hall's end opened.

A man in the black uniform of the Imperial Guard knelt in the opening. When he rose, Nishima felt a catch in her breath. She had seen Tadamoto before, the night of the Emperor's death, but he had been injured and in a daze and she had been much occupied with other things. She was surprised to find that he looked so much like his brother Katta.

But Tadamoto was Katta refined. His features were certainly not weak, but they were significantly less strong than his older brother's. His presence was also unlike his brother's. Where Katta was all instinct and desire and strength, Tadamoto appeared to be a person deep in thought, caught up in things that had little connection with the everyday world. In truth he looked like a scholar, handsome and sincere. And then there were the famous Jaku eyes: and here the difference was profound. Unlike the cold, gray gaze of his famous brother, Tadamoto's eyes were the green of the earth—warm and verdant.

He bowed low before the dais and knelt with his hands

resting on his thighs. Nishima could read nothing on his face except perhaps a sense of sadness, which was so common among her subjects that it seemed normal. *Here is one who has learned to wall his true self away,* she thought, and she wondered if life in the Palace would soon make her the same.

"Colonel Jaku Tadamoto," Kamu stated formally. The old steward stayed in his place for this audience.

Nishima hesitated a second, trying to catch the young man's eye, but she could not. He seemed like a man defeated—incongruous in one so young.

"Colonel Tadamoto," Nishima said softly, for gentleness seemed the tone needed here. "I hope you received my letter?" She had sent him the death poem, unopened, that Jaku Katta had entrusted to her.

He stirred himself to speak but did not look up. "I did, Empress. I am in your debt."

"Certainly that is not so, Colonel. General Katta was an ally of my father when few believed there was a barbarian threat at all." She paused but saw no reaction. "Colonel Jaku, may I express my regrets at your loss."

Tadamoto nodded. "You are very kind Empress. I thank you."

"If there is anything that I may do.. . . . You are the brother of my father's ally."

"Empress, I was the loyal servant of the late Emperor. I accepted the surrender of Lord Shonto's army and would certainly have fought my own brother's forces if I had been so ordered. In the end Katta-sum and I crossed swords." She saw his shoulders sag.

"Loyalty, Colonel, is something the Shonto understand. Honor and loyalty cannot be split apart, but that is not so with love. One can honor one's liege-lord but not love him—I have seen it many times. One can love one's own brother, but honor may not allow you to act in a manner that would indicate loyalty. I must ask you, Colonel—were you loyal to the throne or to the man, Yamaku Akantsu?"

Tadamoto hesitated for some seconds. "I began with loyalty to both, Empress, but I could not maintain my loyalty to the man. In the end, I am not certain that I remained loyal to the throne, for how can one be loyal to the throne when the man who possesses it has thrown the Empire into ruin? What is the loyal act then?''

"When you went to the rooms of the Emperor the night he died, what did you intend?''

Tadamoto shook his head, pain written across his face. "In truth, my lady, I do not know. To face him, to face the Emperor with his treachery, his betrayal of his office. I do not know beyond that. I do not know.''

Nishima regarded the young man before her. "What you have said is wise, Tadamoto-sum. Loyalty to the throne and loyalty to the person who sits upon that throne are synonymous—until the sovereign betrays his office. I do not criticize you, Jaku Tadamoto-sum, for you acted from intentions that were honorable. Few would have acted with more wisdom.''

Tadamoto bowed. "These are comforting words, Empress.''

"My father's vassal-merchant has spoken highly of you, Colonel. Tanaka-sum believed that you suffered much from the Emperor's betrayal of his office. Tanaka-sum is a man whose judgment I value.''

"He is a remarkable man, Empress. If the Emperor had been as wise as your merchant, the Empire would have been well governed, indeed.''

This almost made Nishima smile. "I have no doubt that would be so, Colonel. I have many questions, Colonel Tadamoto, if you don't mind. Many things have occurred that are not entirely clear to me.''

"I am the servant of my Empress,'' he replied like a reflex.

"As you are aware, no one knows the circumstances under which the Emperor died. The woman who was found with him—she was his mistress?''

Tadamoto took a long breath before answering. "Yes, Empress.''

"She was a Sonsa dancer, was she not? I believe I saw her dance in a program created for Lady Okara's paintings.''

"That is correct, Empress.''

"How very sad,'' Nishima said, obviously touched by yet another death. "She was a beautiful dancer.''

"Very beautiful, my lady.''

"Did they go to their end together? A lovers' ending?"

Tadamoto took a long unsteady breath as though he fought down physical pain.

"Are you well, Colonel? You were badly injured."

"I am well, Empress." He paused again. "There were signs in the room that the Emperor was about to escape. A suit of Imperial Guard armor. The Emperor himself was dressed as a guard without rank. Those who guarded him said a boat was being prepared to leave the Capital." Tadamoto stopped again and Nishima wondered if he indeed spoken the truth when he said he was well. "It is my belief that Osha-sum pushed the Emperor from the balcony and he dragged her after him. I do not believe that she intended to make her end with the Emperor."

Nishima was quiet for a moment. "But she was his lover, Colonel. Do you know something that my advisors are not aware of?"

Tadamoto sat stiffly, controlling pain, certainly, but Nishima realized now that it was not physical pain. He met her eye briefly and Nishima herself looked away.

"She did not love him, Empress," he said quietly but with great certainty.

Nishima gave a single nod. "I see. Her family, where are they?"

"I do not know, Empress," he moved a hand in the tiniest gesture. "The Empire is in chaos, everywhere. It is difficult to know where anyone might be."

"Sadly true, Colonel. Someone must see to her ceremony. Is there someone you might suggest? Did she have friends in the Capital?"

Tadamoto clasped his hands together on his knees. "I would see to Osha-sum's final needs if that would be acceptable, Empress." He fought to keep his tone even, but it was not a successful battle.

"That would be acceptable, certainly." She looked at Kamu who gave a small nod.

Nishima gave Tadamoto a moment to recover his surface of calm. "I will tell you honestly, Colonel Jaku, that my advisors do not agree on what should be done about you. Most of those who supported the Yamaku do not pose this problem—they will be exiled to far corners of the Empire and their power stripped away. Opportunists are not to be trusted. But you, Colonel, there are some who believe you were loyal to Wa and to the throne and, as I have said, the Shonto value loyalty. You are also a man renowned for your intellect and knowledge of the court and its intrigues. Was it you who convinced the Emperor to restore order to the roads and canals?''

Tadamoto nodded.

"Why?''

"The dynasties that provided stability have invariably held the throne longest, my Lady. It is as though history has passed its own judgment, sweeping away those Imperial families that do not care for their charges, though often not quickly enough, I fear.''

Nishima produced a fan from her sleeve and tapped it in slow rhythm against her palm. "If you were offered a position in the new government, Colonel, would you accept it?''

Tadamoto did not hide his surprise, though his deep sense of sadness did not lift. "I am honored that you would ask, Empress.'' Language failed him for a moment and Nishima spoke to cover his lapse.

"You have suffered great losses, Colonel. You have sacrificed love for loyalty to principles. Your brother. . . .'' She did not complete the thought. "If the principles of the sovereign were the principles you were loyal to, it is unlikely that you would find yourself in this position again, Colonel. Let us speak of this when you have dealt with the other matters that occupy you. If you will swear loyalty to me, Colonel, I will not require guards to be present when next we speak.''

Tadamoto's head rose, Nishima could see the surprise in his green eyes. The look on his face said that he had not expected the world to ever bestow another act of kindness upon him. "Empress, I have knelt before the ruler of Wa more often than I am able to count, yet only today have I heard words of wisdom and compassion. I will swear loyalty, Empress—I would lay down my life that your rule may not falter, for the people of Wa need wisdom and compassion no less than they need food and water.''

Nishima gave the scholar a half bow. "We will speak again, Colonel Tadamoto. If you would offer the benefits

of your experience to Captain Rohku Saicha of my guard,
I would be in your debt.''

"Empress, I will be in your debt, always." Bowing
low, Tadamoto retreated from the room.

"She who renews," Kamu said softly, "renews honor
and hope."

Nishima pretended she did not hear, but Kamu's words
gave her pleasure. "This Sonsa dancer was his lover,"
Nishima said.

Kamu nodded.

"Have I let compassion blind me, Kamu-sum? I fear
it is my weakness.''

"I believe, as you have said, that Jaku Tadamoto was
an honorable man torn between honor and loyalty and
love. In a lifetime of service to the Shonto I have never
once felt so torn." He made a sign to Botahara that would
have been out of place if Nishima had not known him so
long. It was for her father and she did the same.

"May I suggest that, once you have spoken to Lord
Komawara, it would be appropriate to speak with others
tomorrow or at a later date."

"You coddle me, Chancellor," she said.

"Not at all, Empress. One cannot rebuild an Empire
in a day and, if driven to the point where one's tranquillity is destroyed, one can do no good at all.''

"You sound now like Brother Satake."

"It is a compliment I shall always cherish, Empress.''

She smiled. "I will meet with Lord Komawara, please,
Major Chancellor.''

Kamu slapped his thigh once and then retreated, the
Shonto guards in his wake.

The doors opened and Lord Komawara, dressed in
white robes, knelt with his head touching the floor. His
hair has grown back sufficiently, Nishima thought, and
then smiled at the triviality of this.

The hero of Wa came forward stiffly as though he suffered from the performance of his deeds. The agony she
had seen in his face at her father's funeral had not faded
and there was no doubt in Nishima's mind that this pain
had no physical cause. So shaken was Nishima by what
she saw that she could not speak immediately. The hero
of Wa, she thought, his spirit destroyed by the horror of
his own deeds. Suddenly she was ashamed of what she

had said to Lady Kento—*a sword, a suit of fine armor, and the greatest horse in the Empire will satisfy Lord Komawara.* I have given up the life I dreamed of, Nishima thought, but, Botahara save him, Komawara has sacrificed his soul.

"Lord Komawara," Nishima began, intending to express the gratitude of the Empire, but suddenly she found it was a pose she could not continue. Her voice quavering unexpectedly, Nishima said, "Your spirit, Samyamusum, it is like a stone in water. How has this happened?"

"Have you not heard, Empress?" he answered, his voice as cool as rain, "I have become a great hero. To accomplish this I have written no poetry, played not a song, nor proposed laws indicating great wisdom. Instead I have become the greatest butcher in ten generations. And so I am honored throughout the Empire."

Nishima put her hand to her face. It will be easier to rebuild an Empire than to heal the wounds of this man, she thought. Oh, father, look what we have done.

"Samyamu-sum," she said as gently as she could, "what may I do?"

A bitter smile passed across his face like the shadow of a quick flying bird. "I am told Lord Butto prepares to pursue the barbarians who retreat north. I would accompany Lord Butto, Empress."

"Do you not feel you have done enough? Will you not leave this to others now?"

Komawara moved his shoulders. "But Empress, there is not a warrior in all of Wa more suited to this than I. There is not a trace of my humanity that has not been washed away, washed away by the blood of others."

"Lord Komawara, I would ask you to stay in the Capital. Please, you have done more than any sovereign has a right to ask." Shuyun, she thought, perhaps he would know what to do for this man. But Shuyun could not be reached and Komawara knelt before her asking to be sent back to war—sent to search for his own death, she was sure.

"Empress," Komawara said firmly, meeting her eye, "it would be better if you gave me a blade, as you have the others, and sent me north."

She felt her face grow hot at this but forced herself to

meet his gaze. He did not look away. Are you unreachable, then, Nishima asked silently. Is there no trace of
the young man I knew that I can appeal to. "Lord Komawara," Nishima began, "I will not order you to stay
in the Capital . . . but I will beg you to remain."

"Empress," Komawara said, taken aback by this.
"You cannot say such a thing. You do not understand—
it is what I am intended to do."

Nishima shook her head, a tight gesture. "I will beg
you. I do beg you. I will bow my head to the mat before
you. . . ."

"My Lady, you cannot!"

Nishima stepped down off the dais into the space between them, placed her hands on the floor, and began to
bow.

Komawara leaned forward and caught her shoulders.
"You are the Empress. This is beneath you."

Nishima came back to her knees facing him, catching
his hands. "If I let you go, you might find the death you
are seeking or you will complete the destruction of your
spirit. I could not bear it, Samyamu-sum, I could not
bear it."

As though overcome by turmoil he did not speak for a
moment. "Lady Nishima, I am of no use to you
here. . . ."

She felt a tear streak her cheek at these words and he
stopped at the sight of this. "I will stay. If it is your
wish, I will stay."

Nishima squeezed his hands. "I know you have seen
terrible things. . . ."

He shook his head as though there were something he
tried to cast off. "No," he said, and the word came out
like a moan. "I have *done* terrible things. You should not
even touch my hands."

Hearing this, she took the hand that wielded his sword
and raised it to her lips and then pressed it against her
cheek. "You have a fine and noble spirit—we will find
it," she said, "I do not know how, but we will."

"I do not know myself, Empress," he said in a hoarse
whisper.

Nishima returned his hand gently to his lap. "I do
know how we will begin," she said suddenly. Turning

back to the dais she removed the brush, inkstone, and brush-stand from the table.

She pressed the inkstone into his hands. "This belonged to my mother," she said.

"Lady Nishima, I could not accept this."

She stopped him as he tried to return it, saying firmly, "I am not above begging."

"But it is a treasure."

"Nonsense," she said with a sly smile, "I gave Hojo a palace and Lord Butto a province. You can certainly accept a much used inkstone."

It did not bring a smile to his lips, but there was something different about his eyes for a second as though whatever haunted them had released its grip briefly.

She held out the brush-stand on the palm of her hand—a swan, delicately carved of jade. "This was a gift from my adopted father."

Almost timidly, Komawara took it up, turning it slowly from side to side.

"And this brush," she said pushing it into his hands, "is a gift from a woman who might have been a poet had not duty forced her into other pursuits. If you write poems to me, I will answer them."

"Empress, you have more important things to do than trade verses with a poet of little ability."

"I remember your poem in my father's garden, Samyamu-sum. Do not speak to me of your lack of skill. And I have nothing I would rather do. Will you not help me keep a tiny part of my former life alive?"

Looking down at Nishima's writing implements, he nodded. "I thank you, Empress." Komawara did not look less distraught, but she thought the hard edge of bitterness and the struggle with suppressed rage were less evident.

Sadness is not destructive to the soul, she told herself. We all have reasons for sadness.

"Everything that can be restored to you, Samyamu-sum, I will restore, ten times over."

He nodded. "Thank you, Empress." His discomfort was acute, Nishima could see, but she was also sure she could see signs that he responded to her words. He cares for me, this young man, she realized. And this touched her.

"You have duties," Komawara said, quietly, bowing low. Nishima thought it best not to protest and let him go, clutching her mother's inkstone. When the doors closed, she sat staring at them for a moment before rising and crossing to the windows again. She expected Kamu to enter; when he didn't, she remembered that this was the last of her official duties.

The day's interviews had not been what she had expected. She had been so young during the Interim War that she had been shielded from its effects—had not seen the cost. I thought I would give out accolades and rewards. The faces of Tadamoto and Komawara were not easily erased from her thoughts. They were too young. Not hardened veterans like Hojo.

She wished Kamu had returned. His council had been wise. Another who must be thanked for his part in this mad war, she thought. Touching the frame of the window, she felt Lady Okara's letter in her sleeve and took it out. Returning to the cushion on the dais, Nishima broke the seal and read.

My Empress:

Upon hearing the news of your ascension my heart sang, for I knew the Empire would need the wisdom of your open heart if it was to heal. If I do not presume too much, my heart then became heavy for I was aware of your desire for a life of contemplation and art. This is a great sacrifice you have made, and greater so for it is no small talent that you have been given. How is it that fate would call a great artist to govern the Empire?

It is my belief, Empress, that Wa requires your artist's soul to heal from the betrayal of the Yamaku and from the loss and ruin of the war. Art, true art is a force for compassion and tranquillity. Let us have an Empire ruled by compassion rather than greed and warfare. Let us have art in the fabric of our lives.

And then, Empress, came the sad news of your great loss. Motoru-sum was an old and trusted

friend and his passing is a loss to all of Wa. May
Botahara protect his soul.

> *Out of the gray winter mists*
> *An Empire in blossom*
> *Spring*
> *Drawn from the pigments of the soul.*

May Botahara walk beside you,
Okara

Nishima folded the letter with great care, and then offered a prayer asking Botahara to protect all those she loved.

Sixty-five

Brother Sotura moved slowly through the barbarian encampment, and though he searched with a practiced eye there were no signs that Shuyun had made even the slightest error.

He is a marvel, Sotura thought. He was never taught to manage an outbreak of plague such as this, and yet. . . . The tribesmen the senior monk saw appeared well, if somewhat underfed.

Tents off to the west housed the sick. Sotura made his way in that direction, receiving many bows from the barbarian warriors who lazed about in the warm sun. Among some crude shelters he found a Botahist Sister praying with three tribesmen. She is making converts here, he thought, not sure why this bothered him.

Nearby, men cooked by a dung fire, apparently impervious to the smoke and the smell. Horses were being moved about the area and staked where there was less-trampled grass. Nowhere was there evidence of weapons—skinning knives were all the monk saw. Quiet, Sotura realized, it is so strangely quiet here. And it was true any who spoke did so in subdued tones; there was no laughter, no calling out. A military camp and it was as silent as a temple.

The population of the camp thinned noticeably as Sotura approached the tents of the sick, but there were tribesmen standing guard here, watching him warily.

Why would they guard the tents of the sick, Sotura wondered and then realized the answer. It was Shuyun—some would brave the plague to meet the Teacher.

Many Brothers of the Faith had forsaken their vows to come to Shuyun and minister to the barbarians, so the tribesmen who stood guard did not question Sotura as a stranger in the camp.

The sound of men coughing came to the monk as he stepped over ropes guying a barbarian tent. A Sister hurried past and Brother Sotura spoke to her. "Brother Shuyun, Sister—where may I find him?"

She stopped and eyed him carefully, suspiciously even, and then pointed toward a tent across an open area. He bowed his thanks. To Sotura's surprise he found himself nervous as he crossed the sward.

Four barbarian warriors bearing staffs guarded the tent and stopped Sotura as he approached. Speaking in their tongue, he asked for Brother Shuyun.

"The Master is at his labors, Brother," one warrior answered. "If you require instructions it is best to speak to Sister Morima."

Morima! Sotura almost said aloud, she has become Shuyun's shadow.

"I have come with a message from the Botahist Brotherhood. It is important that I speak with Brother Shuyun."

The tribesmen exchanged glances. "I will ask," one offered and retreated toward the tent. In the dim light inside the door Sotura saw the man gesturing to a young Sister. She stared out at Brother Sotura for a second and then hurried off.

A moment later Shuyun appeared, drying his hands on a scrap of cotton. If he was surprised to find his former teacher, he did not show it.

"Brother Sotura," Shuyun said, bowing low. "This is a surprise and an honor. Please." Shuyun gestured off to one side and ushered the senior monk away from the tent, out of hearing of the young Sister.

A breeze ruffled the heavy fabric of the tents and overhead a plague banner fluttered on a tall staff, adding its staccatto to the eerie silence of the encampment. Once assured of privacy Shuyun did not hesitate, as though matters of great importance required his attention. Yet he was unfailingly polite.

"Do you truly bear a message, Brother Sotura, or have you found compassion in your soul?"

Sotura gave a small frown, not easily adjusting to being addressed as though an equal. "I do bear a message, Shuyun-sum—a message of compassion." He met the younger man's eye. "The Supreme Master will send our

Brothers to meet the barbarians who ride toward the Mountain of the Pure Spirit. We will offer to heal them if they, too, will lay down their weapons."

Shuyun gave the senior monk a deep bow. "May Botahara chant your name, Sotura-sum."

Sotura remained impassive. "I was also instructed to give you this." He held out his clenched fist. Shuyun hesitated for a moment, then extended his open hand. He half expected Sotura to release a small blue butterfly into his palm, but instead he felt the cool weight of a jade pendant and chain.

"Never before has one been returned, Shuyun-sum. It is my hope that you will not refuse."

The young monk looked down at the pendant in his palm. "Why, Brother?"

"Many felt the Supreme Master may have acted in some haste," Sotura said, embarrassed to be admitting fallibility on the part of his Order. "We have swayed him in this matter." Sotura waved a hand at the camp. "Think of the other Brothers who have followed you here. If they see you wearing your pendant, Brother Shuyun, it will cause them to reconsider their decision. I am concerned for their souls, Shuyun-sum—for theirs and yours."

The younger monk broke into a smile that seemed to arise from joy. "Your concern would be better focused elsewhere, Brother. Those who have come here to cure the barbarians of the plague live the word of the Perfect Master." He held the pendant up by its chain so that it hung between them. "No stone can change that."

"Brother Shuyun," Sotura said, his voice carrying an edge of desperation, "they come because they believe you are the Teacher. What do you tell them?"

Shuyun reached out and took the senior monk's hand, lowering the pendant into it and then closing Sotura's fingers, holding the Master's hand thus as though expressing great affection. "I tell them I do not believe I am the Teacher."

Sotura shook his head in confusion. "If this is true, what will you do? You have turned your back on the Botahist faith."

"But the Teacher is among us, Sotura-sum. I will go to him and hear the Word from one who has attained that which we can only dream of."

Sotura reached out and gripped the younger monk's shoulder, staring steadily into his eyes. "Do you know where the Teacher dwells?"

Shuyun nodded.

"Where?"

Shuyun shook his head slowly. "When the Teacher wishes you to find him, he will send you a message, Brother Sotura."

Sotura gave Shuyun a gentle shake. "You have had such a message?" he almost demanded.

"I believe I have, Brother." Shuyun, stepped back so that Sotura released him.

The older monk stared down at the grass for a moment. "How can this be true, Brother? Why has he not sent for the Supreme Master, for Brother Hutto?"

"Their karma is their own, Brother," Shuyun said with great gentleness, his face full of concern. "Ask why he has not sent for you, Sotura-sum. It is the question that will lead you to wisdom." Saying so, he bowed to the senior Brother and returned to the tent where he labored to heal the enemies of Wa.

The following day Shuyun was interrupted in his work by Sister Morima. She stood silhouetted by the sun as Shuyun bowed over a young tribesman who lay on blankets on the grass.

"Brother Shuyun?"

Like all the Botahist-trained in the encampment, she still called him *Brother* though the tribesman called him the Master.

He looked up, squinting. Though he could not see her against the light, he knew and was glad that Sister Morima had returned to her previous appearance of good health. Her step had grown light as she went about her work—her crisis of spirit had been resolved by an act of compassion.

"Sister?"

"On the edge of the encampment," she waved to the south. "The Prioress, Sister Saeja, has come. She asks for you, Brother, and will come to you if you will allow her to enter the camp."

Shuyun said a few words to the tribesman and then rose quickly. "I will go to her, Sister." He hurried off across the encampment, nodding to the many bows he received.

Emerging from the edge of the camp, he saw that a small pavilion had been erected on the invisible border maintained by the Shonto guards. He set out toward this immediately, unprepared for the reaction. There was a surge among the people who had been gathering around the encampment. He heard his name over and over and people offering prayers of thanksgiving. The soldiers were not caught off guard by this, appeared to have anticipated it, in fact, so the crowd was restrained.

Steeling himself, he moved forward. Looking at the press of the crowd and the hope in the faces Shuyun thought, this will become my life, I cannot turn away. Approaching the Sisters, Shuyun noticed some of the faces he had seen in the Palace. The one with the strong jaw and the haughty manner, the small one who tended the Prioress.

When Shuyun was three paces away, the Sisters knelt and bowed low. The Prioress stayed in her sedan chair this time but managed a bow all the same.

Before Shuyun could speak, the dry rasp of the Prioress' voice broke in. "It is our shame to admit that we do not know how to address you."

"I would be honored if you would call me Shuyun-sum, Prioress," Shuyun said without hesitation.

The ancient woman considered this for a moment but then rejected it as inadequate. "Master Shuyun, we seek the Teacher," she said simply.

Shuyun looked into the ancient eyes and saw the hope there and it saddened him. "He will be found by few, Prioress," Shuyun said, his voice carrying a note of concern.

The Sisters exchanged uneasy glances.

"Master Shuyun," the old woman said, the hope in her eyes replaced by growing uncertainty, "are you the one who was spoken of?"

Shuyun slowly shook his head, sorry that he must do so.

The Sister took a long breath, her face growing soft, like a child whose hopes have been dashed—who would dissolve into tears. "Then how is it that you have powers unheard of in all our history?"

Shuyun looked down at the grass and when he raised his head his eyes seemed moist, his voice almost overcome with awe. "I am the bearer, Prioress. I will serve Him."

There was a long silence then, the nuns not taking their eyes from the monk as though he were a myth come to life. "The few who will find the Teacher . . . who?" the Prioress asked, her question tentative as though she feared the answer.

"I am not certain, Prioress."

The Prioress nodded. "Master Shuyun, will you not take one of us with you?"

Shuyun looked down again, but only for a brief second, and then he raised his head, saying, "If I may, I will send word to Sister Morima, Prioress. I will ask her to join me, if it is possible."

In some of the faces Shuyun saw a hint of anger, resentment, but the Prioress smiled suddenly, like the sun emerging from behind a cloud. "I have not been wrong in all things, at least. Botahara bless you, Brother. I will pray for you."

"Prioress?" Shuyun said, deeply serious. "Shimekosum—the one whom you called Sister Tesseko—it is her soul in need of your prayers."

The Prioress paused for a second, her face grave. And then she nodded once and the smile returned.

The Empress sat on the balcony overlooking the vast barbarian army. She had finished reading a letter written by Tanaka—a report on the state of the Imperial Treasury. The situation was not as desperate as her worst fears had whispered it might be. Hojo had secured so much of the Palace when the Yamaku fell that few officials were able to slip away with stolen fortunes. Over many years Tanaka had made an exhaustive study of corruption in the Imperial Government, though it had never been his intention. The Yamaku way of governing had forced him to it. Tanaka had paid for information, bought influence when necessary, bribed Ministers and bureaucrats. As a result he had a long list of those who could not be trusted and was quickly purging the civil service. It was an irony her father would have appreciated, Nishima thought.

The Empress smiled. She had talked with Shokan regarding Tanaka and discovered the poor man was consumed by guilt. He had given Colonel Tadamoto a detailed list (though incomplete) of Shonto holdings and now felt he had betrayed every trust he had ever been given. As this ploy had quite possibly kept the merchant alive, Shokan applauded it as wisdom. But Tanaka was not reassured and suffered all the same.

Duty, Nishima thought. He thinks he has failed in his duty, though absolutely no harm came of his action and much good—he preserved his very valuable life. It occurred to her to send the merchant a charter, raising him to a minor peerage, and citing his betrayal of Shonto trust as the reason for this. She was not sure he would see the humor in this, however.

A knock on the frame of the open screens drew her attention inside.

Lady Kento knelt in the opening.

"Kento-sum," Nishima said, smiling, for pleasure came to her easily that day.

"My Lady. Captain Rohku is satisfied with the security in the block of your apartments, the private Audience Halls, and the Imperial guest chambers. He feels it is perfectly safe for the Empress to move through these areas without guards."

"This is good news indeed, Kento-sum. I was going mad being followed everywhere. Please commend the Guard Commander for his diligence."

"And, Empress, Lady Kitsura has arrived."

"Please, do not keep her waiting."

Lady Kento bowed and disappeared.

Nishima quickly rolled the scroll and pushed her work table to one side. She gazed out over the fields again. A message had arrived from Shuyun earlier that morning. He would come to the Palace that evening and Nishima looked forward to this visit with both excitement and dread. *How long will he stay?* she asked herself again. The question had become a litany.

Kitsura appeared, bowing in the opening to the inner rooms.

"Kitsu-sum, you are as welcome as the arrival of spring and as lovely."

"Empress, it is good to see you well." The eleventh

day of mourning had passed and the only white Kitsura wore was a sash, in memory of those who were lost during the recent turmoil and for Lord Shonto, of course. Her robe was deep green embroidered with a pattern of gold-edged sea shells.

"You have seen your family, I am told. I trust they are well?"

"It is kind of you to inquire, cousin. They are indeed well. My family send their highest regards to the Empress."

Nishima leaned over and squeezed her cousin's arm. "Kitsu-sum, your father—how is he truly?"

Kitsura gave her cousin a tight smile, thanking her for her concern, and began to turn a ring on a finger. "It is true that he is less well than he appeared when I left for Seh, but he is a miracle, truly, Nishi-sum. Speaking of your ascension, he told me that Wa has lost a great artist but gained a greater Empress. I think he wanted you to hear that."

"Lord Omawara is too kind." Nishima felt her heart go out to her cousin, for she had twice lost a father and knew what it meant. She did not press the matter further.

"Cha, Kitsu-sum?" Nishima asked, moving the conversation away from the area that caused her cousin pain. "Or shall we sample some of the Palace's fine wines. There is a trove of rare vintages, I am told. Shokan-sum has said the wine cellar is of greater value than the treasury."

"Cha would be lovely, cousin, thank you—though I would gladly sample your rare wines another time."

Nishima clapped for a servant and asked for cha.

"I was able to speak with Lady Kento when I arrived," Kitsura said casually. "She is determined to find you a suitable husband, Nishima-sum."

"Me!" Nishima said, taken aback. "It is you she is searching for."

"As I suspected," Kitsura said, laughing. "I tease, cousin. She said nothing of husbands for you." Kitsura tried not to look too pleased with herself. "Who has my Empress chosen for her loyal and humble servant."

"Your Empress has not yet decided," Nishima answered, shaking her head at how easily she had been tricked. "It will depend on how loyal and humble the Lady Kitsura is able to demonstrate herself to be."

Kitsura laughed. "I fear for the happiness of my marriage, cousin."

They both laughed.

"I will admit that we had not progressed beyond the obvious choices: Shokan-sum and Lord Komawara." Nishima eyed her cousin as she said this, wondering what her reaction might be, but Kitsura showed no sign of what she felt.

Cha arrived and Nishima shooed the servant out so that she might complete the preparations herself.

"The hero of Wa, Empress? I did not realize you thought me that loyal and humble." She considered for a moment. "Though I would have to live in Seh, far from my beloved Empress."

". . . and the pleasures of the Palace," Nishima added, ladling cha into bowls.

Kitsura's face turned suddenly serious. "Meeting Lord Komawara here in the Palace garden only last autumn, I would never have believed his name would one day be on everyone's lips. People kneel down and bow to him in the streets—peers! I have seen it. Lord Toshaki, who almost forced Lord Komawara into a duel in Seh, is now his shadow. And all the young women of the Empire are mad to meet him. Your first social events will be attended by more lovesick young women than either of us can imagine." She held out open hands and shrugged. "Our shy Lord Komawara. Who ever could have guessed?" Kitsura sipped her cha. "Of course I tell all the women who ask that I—that we—saw this in him from the beginning. I admit that I am a most shameless liar, Empress."

Nishima stared into her bowl of cha. "Does this mean that you will accept Lord Komawara, Lady Kitsura?"

Kitsura laughed, but Nishima thought it was somewhat forced. "I believe our young hero must make his own choices, Empress."

Nishima looked out over the barbarian camp. "Lord Komawara has suffered a serious wound to his spirit, Lady Kitsura. I am not quite sure what can be done for him."

"I can think of a number of things," Kitsura smiled, "if I am not being too bold."

"I was thinking of something more spiritual, Lady Kitsura."

"He is a warrior, Nishima-sum. A spiritual cure may not be what is required."

Nishima shaded her eyes and looked out toward the mountains. Was that a dust cloud? She had received news that morning: the Brothers had met the wandering barbarian army and, with Lord Taiki's assistance, convinced them to lay down their arms. Shokan had been right, the Brotherhood were scrambling to recover from their mistake.

The barbarian force retreating north on the canal was not faring so well. They were dying in numbers, leaving a trail of burial mounds behind them. There would not be a handful left when they crossed the border into their own lands. It was a terrible thing. The Kalam had returned to the Capital the previous day, sent by Lord Butto. He was convinced the barbarian army would not surrender. Imagine such pride, Nishima thought.

Kitsura was speaking again, and Nishima had not been listening.

". . . everyone says it is so, Nishi-sum. Is this true?"

"I'm sorry Kitsu-sum, my thoughts wandered. Please excuse me."

Kitsura looked at Nishima with some concern but must have been reassured by what she saw, for her concern faded. "Brother Shuyun? Is it true, as everyone says, that he is the Teacher?"

Nishima took a moment to ladle more cha and stir up the embers of the burner. It was the question she had been avoiding for days, though somehow late at night it became more persistant and troubled her both waking and dreaming.

"I do not know, Kitsura-sum. Brother Shuyun denies it, but Tesseko, may Botahara rest her soul, believed he might be the Teacher and not yet know."

"What is your own belief, Nishi-sum? What does your heart tell you?"

"My heart?" Nishima said, with the tiniest hint of resentment in her voice. "I am an Empress, cousin, I am not governed by my heart."

Kitsura was quiet for a moment, watching her cousin

who stared out toward the fields, her mood suddenly changed.

"Excuse me, Kitsu-sum," she said turning back, catching Kitsura looking at her closely. "Please accept my apology. It is unworthy of me to become bitter because of the part I have chosen to play."

Kitsura reached out and took Nishima's hand. Her skin was so perfect and soft. "Where will Shuyun go now? Will he go with Lord Shonto?"

Nishima shook her head. "Shokan-sum has released him."

Kitsura pressed Nishima's hand. "Then surely he will stay with you."

Nishima squeezed her eyes closed.

"Cousin?"

Nishima wanted to give a neutral answer, but she could not and she felt Kitsura move closer. A hand rested on her shoulder, stroking her gently. Then Kitsura came still closer and embraced her. They stayed like that for some time.

"If you marry, Kitsu-sum, you must promise to remain in the Capital. I cannot bear to lose anyone else."

"You have my word," Kitsura whispered. "Shuyun-sum is out among the barbarians?"

"He returns this evening."

"What may I do, cousin?"

"Nothing. You have done so much already. Often, when we traveled on the canal and in Seh, you were my strength. I have not forgotten."

"Do you know," Kitsura said, and Nishima could hear the smile in her voice, "Okara-sum told me that we must learn not to compete with one another?"

"Us, cousin?"

Kitsura nodded. "But, of course, now you are the Empress and therefore have won everything. There is nothing left to compete for."

Nishima did not smile. "I feel that becoming the Empress has meant more loss than gain."

Kitsura nodded.

"Okara-sum is wise, cousin."

"I agree," Kitsura said after a few seconds, "I agree entirely."

Gently they disentangled.

"I am certain that sovereigns are not supposed to require such coddling," Nishima said.

"They require nothing but, cousin. Have you not read the histories? You are the exception in that you don't require such treatment all the time."

The tea had grown cold and what was in the cauldron was too strong. "I will call for more," Nishima said.

"Thank you, cousin, but—I know it is improper to excuse one's self from the presence of the sovereign. . . . My father often awakes in the late afternoon and is strong enough for a visitor."

"You must take him my warmest regards."

Kitsura bowed low and with a squeeze of her cousin's hand slipped into the inner rooms.

Nishima stood and paced across the balcony. She sat on the rail for a moment, looking out over the encampment, but then rose and returned to her work table suddenly. Rubbing a resin stick over her inkstone Nishima began to breathe in rhythm.

When Shokan heard that Nishima had given her mother's inkstone to Komawara, he sent her a stone that had belonged to Lord Shonto. She recognized it immediately. The inkstone was very old and had seen much use and she adored it.

Nishima added a few drops of water. Shuyun would not come for some hours. As she had not yet received a poem from Lord Komawara, she decided to force a response. The Empress would write to him.

By the time dusk arrived, Nishima was pleased with the poem she had composed. But after making many drafts she chose to send one that showed less skill than the final version. She did not want to intimidate him entirely. And then she laughed at her own vanity. A few moments later, however, she convinced herself that she was simply being considerate of Komawara's present state. In the future, when the lord had begun to heal, this would not be required of her.

Nishima read the poem a last time. She hoped her memory for the verse Komawara had composed in her father's garden so long ago was correct.

Distant horizons glimpsed in the autumn garden
Casting the ancient coins
Among the mist-lilies and new friendships.
   The Boat setting forth
   Into uncertain winds
   As unwavering as the constant heart.

Does the Open Fan of temptation
Appear to you
Spread against a white sky?
   We all stare into green water
   Seeking the passing cloud
   Knowing it appears only to the tranquil soul.

Calling for a lamp and wax Nishima folded and sealed the poem, then hesitated before she stamped the soft wax. After a moment of consideration she chose the shinta blossom rather than the five clawed dragon circling the sun—she had asked Komawara to help keep a part of her former life alive, after all.

The sun had sunk into a line of clouds above the distant mountains, appeared briefly in a blaze of copper between the cloud and the peaks, and then dissolved into embers, leaving the clouds glowing like hot coals. Nishima turned and watched the scene slowly fade.

A maid knocked on the frame to the opening, bowing low.

"Yes," Nishima said, distracted.

"Brother Shuyun, Empress."

Nishima returned from her brooding immediately, trying to hide her pleasure from the maid. "Please, I will see him here." Quickly she reached over to the cushion Kitsura had used and pulled it closer.

Although it was hardly expected of an Empress, Nishima could not stop herself from staring at the opening, waiting for a glimpse of the monk. She could barely wait to see his face, as though the answer to the question that had become her litany might be seen there even before they spoke.

Coming through the opening, kneeling, Shuyun bowed immediately, hiding his face. The last light of the day lit the room in a warm, golden light and when the monk rose, his features appeared softer, less severe than Nishima had come to expect. And the light seemed to illuminate him, light him from within.

Something has occurred, Nishima thought. Look at him—he has had a revelation. A feeling akin to panic began to rise inside her and she struggled not to give in to it.

"Shuyun-sum," she said, trying to give her voice warmth, but the words came out of a constricted throat and sounded so. "Please join me."

Shuyun came forward with the grace that always delighted her, and though his manner was as serious as usual, she sensed a lightness in him that she had not seen before. To her surprise, Shuyun reached out and took her hand in his own. For a moment she found herself carefully scrutinized by those eyes that seemed at once ancient and innocent.

"You are well, my lady?"

Nishima nodded, her voice suddenly deserting her. She did not take her gaze away from his eyes, still looking for the answer to her question.

Shuyun took her hand between both of his suddenly and she felt a warm tingle of chi-flow. "Has something distressed you?"

With effort she found her voice. "I am well, truly. Learning to govern has taken some toll, perhaps." She made a gesture as though dismissing this as minor. "The barbarians have been cured?"

"The healing takes some time, Nishi-sum. It will be many days yet. But it is not too soon to consider what will be done with them when they are well."

Although the conversation led away from the discussion she desired, Nishima found herself taking it up with some relief—the news she feared would be delayed. "Kamu-sum has begun the arrangements. We will send the barbarians north up the canal, returning them to their own lands."

Shuyun nodded. "Excuse me for saying so, but I believe we should do more. We must establish regular commerce with the tribes and open relations. We must send ambassadors and gifts when chieftains are named and allow the barbarians to trade across our border more freely. If we do not . . ." Shuyun bent his head toward the barbarian army, quickly disappearing in the growing darkness. "We shall have another Khan one day."

"I am sure you are correct, Brother." Nishima responded. "It will be difficult to convince the Council that this is the path of wisdom—the anger toward the barbarians is great—but I will speak to my advisors. There must be a way to convince the Council."

"May I also suggest, Nishima-sum, that the Kalam could become an ambassador between the tribes and Wa."

This surprised Nishima and she felt herself drawn further away from the true questions that she must ask. "Is it not true that he is obliged stay with you until death ends his servitude?"

"It is true, Tha-telor is a strict law, but so much has changed in the world now. I have spoken to the Kalam at length and he has agreed to act as I have suggested, if it is the wish of the Empress." Very quietly Shuyun continued. "The Kalam realizes now that he cannot follow me on my journey."

Nishima let out a long breath, looking down at his hands around her own. "In your eyes I see that you have made decisions, Shuyun-sum." Nishima said quietly. "You will make a journey?"

Shuyun stroked her hand. "What you see, Nishi-sum, is tranquillity of purpose. Though I have been told to seek it all my life, it is only now that I have found it. I will seek the Teacher. It is my place to serve him, as it is yours to rule an Empire."

Nishima felt her senses swirl into confusion—it was like numbness creeping through her body, but it was not lack of feeling—it was too much. Too much and all at once and she could not sort those feelings or control them. The reaction was not unfamiliar, for it felt as though she had learned of yet another death.

"Will we never meet again?" she managed to say.

"I do not know, Nishi-sum," the monk answered. Nishima could hear how gentle his tone had become. He reached out and took her into his arms, but she remained limp as though this last blow had robbed her of all remaining strength.

"You are not the Teacher, then? You know this?"

Nishima felt Shuyun's head nod, close beside her own.

"When I first met Quinta-la, when she prostrated herself and recited a prayer in her own language. Later I realized some of what she said: *he who bears the Word*. Among the mountain people there is a seer—an ancient woman. Your brother spoke to her. She questioned him about me.

"In the ancient scroll that speaks of the coming of the Teacher it also says that one will come bearing the Word. Botahist scholars have long agreed that this was another reference to the Teacher, but it is not so." Nishima felt the monk take a long breath. "It is a reference to me, Nishima-sum. I will bear the Teacher's Word. He has sent for me. He sent for me some time ago and I did not realize it."

Part of Nishima wanted to offer an argument, dispute the logic of what he said but another part of her believed he could not be wrong in this matter.

He walked out into the fields alone and stopped the barbarian invasion, Nishima told herself. Among the senior Brothers he inspires both awe and fear and the Sisters have followed him since the day he arrived in Wa. And now he goes to meet one who has attained perfection—as though Botahara has been reborn. It is no wonder that I have become unimportant in his life. How could I think that he would stay with me?

"It is without question, then," Nishima said, trying to keep the feeling that she had been slighted out of her words, "you must leave to seek the Teacher."

"Perhaps I have not yet achieved perfect tranquillity of purpose," Shuyun said, his voice tender, "for I do not know how to leave when my heart is here with you."

Nishima reached up and put her arms around him now, holding him close. "Then you must stay until you know." *He wants me to release him,* she told herself in a flash of insight.

Shuyun reached up and traced the curve of her neck with a finger. He did not speak as she expected him to. Stars were beginning to appear in the sky, and even in the west the light was all but gone. Nishima began to feel a deep sadness rising out of the confusion of her emotions, overcoming all else.

It was completely dark before they spoke again and it was Shuyun who broke the silence. "I wish to take a gift to the Teacher, but the gift I desire is not within my power."

"If it is something I may provide, Shuyun-sum, you have but to name it," Nishima said without hesitation.

"Then I would ask you to write a poem."

"This is the gift you will take to the Teacher?" She pulled back slightly so she could see his face in the light of the lamp.

He smiled. "Yes. It is the gift he will desire, I am certain."

"Shuyun-sum, this man is the living evidence of the Way. He is as close to being a god as one can come. Certainly he does not want a poem from me."

Shuyun touched his forehead against her own. "A poem from you is what he desires," the monk said firmly.

"But what would I write? What words could I send to the Teacher?"

"It does not matter. Write about the sunset or becoming Empress or about your garden. It only matters that it is from you and that it is signed Nishima-sum."

"Really, Shuyun-sum, this is an unusual request, to say the least."

"Have I asked too much of you?"

This stopped Nishima for a second. "No. If it is a poem you desire, I will attempt to write a poem worthy of one who has reached perfection—as impossible as that may be."

Shuyun pressed her close to him and then, to her surprise, released her, waving toward her writing table.

"You don't expect me to do this now? Really, Shuyun-sum, I must have time to think."

"You do not need time to think. Three lines would be adequate. I would venture that one would be enough." He smiled again and she began to wonder if he was serious. This did not seem like an occasion for humor to her.

Throwing up her hands in resignation, Nishima turned to the table and began to prepare her ink. As she did so, she felt Shuyun's fingers begin to explore the intricacies of the fastenings that held her hair in place. Though this made concentration almost impossible, Nishima did not want to ask him to stop, for to her it was a sign that he felt some sense of intimacy as she always he hoped he would.

Her hair fell about her shoulders and cascaded down her back, bringing a smile to her face.

"You are not focused," Shuyun said close to her ear. "Your teacher would be disappointed."

"You are not helping, I must tell you."

He laughed. "I will leave and let you work in peace."

"You certainly will not! You must sit close to me and try not to be too much of a distraction."

"I can be as still as a stone," he said, and she felt the smile in his voice.

"Well that may be more than is required." It took a great deal of will power, but Nishima removed a piece of mulberry paper from a folder and dipped her brush in ink.

> *Even a few years without change*
> *Lull the mind*
> *And then in a day*
> *The world changes utterly.*
> *Heroes appear*
> *And legends come to life.*
> *Things immutable are transformed:*
> *War turns to peace, despair becomes joy*
> *The living die*
> *And are born again.*

"You are finished?" Shuyun asked.

"Finished? I have hardly begun."

"Let me see," the monk said and then leaned forward to read over her shoulder. "Nishi-sum, it is perfect."

"It is perfectly awful. I will need hours to make this a poem."

"No. Do not change a word. That is the poem I will take to the Teacher. You must sign it as I said."

"But Shuyun-sum, I would be ashamed to have anyone see this. And now you ask me to sign it in a familiar form. This seems most unconventional."

Shuyun put a hand on her shoulder. "The Teacher is not as other men. Do not judge him according to the standards of the Empire. Please, sign."

Shaking her head, Nishima did as he asked, wondering

if the culture of the Botahist monks was perhaps more different than she had formerly imagined. She blew gently on the ink until it dried.

"Now you must fold it as gateway," Shuyun instructed.

Through resisting, Nishima did as she was asked, handing it to Shuyun as she finished. "I hope your Teacher will not think me as poor an Empress as I am a poet."

Shuyun smiled, putting the poem into his sleeve pocket.

The night was growing cool, as nights usually did in the late spring. Nishima reached out, touching Shuyun's wrist, then slid her hand up his sleeve past the elbow, feeling the warmth there.

"Now you must do a favor for me," she said.

"I am your servant," he answered, his tone serious.

Rising, Nishima drew the monk up with her and, taking him in tow, she walked into the inner room. She opened a screen and entered the sleeping room. There was no lamp lit here and only the starlight through the open shojis gave the scene light.

Releasing Shuyun's hand, she undid the complex knot at her back and unwound her sash. When she had done this, the monk helped her remove her outer robes until she wore only a single layer of silk. She felt the questions that consumed her being pushed aside by growing desire. When she reached out to untie Shuyun's sash, her fingers were not inclined to obey and her breath was short.

Pulling back the quilts, they almost tumbled into bed. Nishima slipped out of her robe almost immediately and pressed herself as close to him as she could manage.

"If you did not spend the night resisting me," Nishima said close to his ear, "I'm certain you would not be in such a hurry to leave. You might spend a few days more, at least."

"I fear that this is so," Shuyun answered.

They lay close for a moment more and Nishima realized that she was not alone in having lost her breath. She kissed the soft place at the corner of his eye and his mouth found hers. For the first time, he returned her kiss. Nishima thought she felt a strange sensation, almost vertigo, and then she realized that a kiss became endless and her skin was alive to the touch as it had never been before. Strong currents of emotion and energy and chi seemed to flow through her. For a second she felt panic begin to touch her, but it was swept away by a wave of tenderness and she abandoned herself to the feeling without hesitation.

Much later, Nishima lay bathed in the warmth of her companion.

"I do not want to sleep. I want to say everything that is in my heart though I do not know where to begin to find the words."

Shuyun kissed her neck. "There are no words. Everything has been said."

Despite her desire to stay awake, Nishima could not and she fell into an untroubled, dreamless sleep.

A breeze moved her hair and this finally awoke her. It was early morning, but completely light. She lay completely still for a moment, lost in memories and pleasure, and then turned to find her lover.

But Shuyun was not there. Where . . . she began to ask herself when awareness came. Burying her face in the quilt she lay very still, as though moving would alter everything for ever. If she could just not move. . . .

A bell sounded and Nishima opened her eyes to the light. On a table at the bedside lay a brocade bag containing something angular. She sat up and found the most delicate blue seashell on top of this and in the cup of the shell a bit of white paper had been placed so that it could not blow away. On this was written a single character which meant *she who renews*. My heart will break, she found herself thinking, my heart will surely break.

Setting the shell upon the pillow, Nishima took the brocade bag and opened it, finding a plain wooden box inside.

It is the blossom of the Udumbara, she realized. For a moment she did not know what to do but then, with great care, she set the box aside and rose from the bed. She found her robes and slipped them on, belting them loosely. Taking up the box in both hands, Nishima went out onto the balcony.

She perched herself on the rail with her back against

a pillar and forced herself to be calm. Performing a
breathing exercise taught to her by Brother Satake helped.

Finally, when her spirit was as calm as she could make
it, when the pang of Shuyun's leaving was a sweet sadness not a sorrow, she opened the box.

To her great surprise she did not find a sacred blossom
inside but a white butterfly, tinged with the faintest purple. It fanned its wings slowly and then, in a single motion, took to the air. It circled about the balcony once,
then rose on a current, descended again, and then fluttered off into the garden where it was soon lost from
sight. Nishima watched long after it had gone, hoping
for a last glimpse, but it did not reappear and she leaned
her head back against the pillar and closed her eyes.

My heart is both broken and full of joy, she told herself. *I do not know whether to cry or laugh.*

Opening her eyes she realized that a perfect paper
shinta blossom lay on the silk of the wooden case and
she set the case on the rail and took it up. After a moment of searching, she found the key and began to unfold
the blossom. In the heart of the paper flower she found
a single line of characters written in Shuyun's beautiful
flowing hand.

*Beyond the future lies a future in which we cannot be
separated.*

She thought of the butterfly flying out of the case and
she smiled.

"Things are never what one expects," Nishima said
to herself, and she laughed. She laughed until tears ran
down her cheeks.

The guards led the Empress along a path paved in
stones. They stopped at a simple wooden gate under a
small arch and tile roof. Very quickly, one of the guards
passed through the gate and when he returned four other
guards came with him. This man nodded to the senior
officer who in turn knelt and bowed to the Empress. The
garden was secure.

Nishima went through the open gate and heard it close
behind her.

It is a day for partings, she told herself.

A few steps into the garden Nishima stopped to look out to the north over the large encampment of the tribes. She knew he was not there, but still her eyes searched for a moment among the thousands of tiny figures before she turned away.

A few more paces brought her to the shrine and she knelt on a mat that had been placed for her. Into the face of an uncut stone had been chiseled the name character *Shimeko*.

Nishima offered up a silent prayer to Botahara and then one also to the Teacher.

We will never know, Nishima thought, *we will never know if you fell into their hands without intending to or whether you chose to take your terrible weapon out among our enemies so that others might live. When I think of your fate, Shimeko-sum, I am gripped by its horror. Among all the brave, all the heroes of this pointless war, you alone went into battle without armor, without protection. Only you risked the destruction of your spirit. May Botahara rest you and protect your soul.*

Nishima offered up a long prayer for forgiveness and then rose and went to her duties.

Sixty-six

They had slipped out of the city at dawn, all three in disguise, and set out across country until they found the narrow road they sought. Only then did they throw back their hoods to the sunlight—a warrior, a monk, and a barbarian tribesman.

There was no indication that they hurried to an appointed time or place—in truth, their pace seemed almost leisurely. They stopped, it appeared, whenever whim struck and often finished their day's travel before sunset. In a time when a significant portion of the population of Wa were on the roads and canals, returning or moving to places where they would begin their lives again, these three travelers hardly stood out. Except that they did not seem to be driven to reach their destination as others did.

Of course the area the three traveled through was not flooded with refugees the way the northern canal and roads were aswarm with people returning to homes, or even the way the roads to the south and the west were filled with people seeking places to begin anew. The three set their course north by east and encountered few as they went.

Shuyun knelt cross-legged on a mat by the edge of the stream. He had spent an hour in meditation upon the sunlight falling through the leaves as the wind moved among the trees. He watched the beauty of the movement and patterns as though they were dance.

Two dozen paces up the stream bank Komawara sat bent over a letter, reading. Shuyun had seen the lord take this same paper from his sleeve several times, to pore over it as he did now, but Komawara did not speak of this and Shuyun felt it would be the worst manners to inquire.

Shuyun was certain he saw the beginnings of healing in Komawara, just a glimmer, but there, nonetheless. He carries wounds as deep as any cut by a sword, Shuyun thought. One cannot expect him to heal overnight.

What Nishima had done, the gifts that she had given the young lord, showed great wisdom, Shuyun thought. There was no question in Shuyun's mind that Nishima was the ruler that Wa needed in this time. Thinking of the Empress brought a sense of warmth and joy. She was my teacher, he thought, though she did not know it.

He turned his attention back to the light dappling the ferns and the forest floor across the stream. *The Illusion,* he had been taught and it had taken some time to learn what that truly meant. He had labored under so many misapprehensions—it made him wonder what was truly written in the scrolls of Botahara.

The sound of the lightest of footsteps sounded in the soft undergrowth and Shuyun turned to find the Kalam bearing bowls of cha. With a bow, the tribesman set one on the edge of Shuyun's mat and then turned and took a second bowl to Komawara.

Shuyun caught the lord's eye then and waved an invitation. Folding his letter, Komawara came and found a place on the corner of the monk's mat. Yes, there it was, around the eyes and the mouth, signs that Komawara was emerging through the bitterness and anger.

Shuyun noticed that the lord did not carry a sword in his sash, and had not during their journey—highly unusual for a warrior of Seh. Of course, Komawara did keep a blade strapped to his saddle, but Shuyun had not seen him touch it yet. The Kalam removed the sword at each stop and kept it close at hand for the lord's use. There were brigands abroad in Wa, and many inclined to honesty were being forced to this life. But all the same Komawara chose not to carry a blade.

"We might reach the foot of the mountain this afternoon, Brother, it is not as far off as it appears."

Shuyun nodded. "Yes. In the morning I must proceed alone, Samyamu-sum, though I will miss your company."

"I fear my company has been poor, Shuyun-sum. I apologize for this."

Shuyun met the lord's gaze for a moment, searching

his eyes. "Lord Komawara, do you suggest that one who will serve the Teacher would speak anything but the truth?" he said, his tone mock-serious.

Komawara grinned. "Please excuse me, Brother. I meant to imply no such thing. But, in truth, I think my company has been less than joyful."

"Perhaps, but it has given me great joy even so. After our other journeys together, this one has certainly been the most pleasant."

Komawara gave a short laugh. "What, Brother, you did not feel great joy climbing the walls of Denji Gorge in the darkness? The legends will no doubt say that you did."

Shuyun grimaced. "It is your legend, Lord Komawara, that will speak of fearlessness."

"Huh," Komawara sipped his cha. "That is one of the many things I fear, Brother. On the walls of Denji Gorge I was as terrified as I can remember being, yet no song will tell that part of the tale." And then quieter. "No play will show the regret I feel for the lives I have taken."

Shuyun stared at the lord's face, watching the anguish return. "I have taken a life as well, Samyamu-sum. Lord Botahara was once a great general. The spirit can rise above all things—it is possible. Do not think that your soul will carry this stain forever—it can be cleansed. You are not a simple warrior, Samyamu-sum, able to follow the way of the sword without question. It is the terrible thing about war; it sends the most innocent into the field and strips their souls bare of this innocence. We have both seen it. Lord Shonto, Lady Nishima, Jaku Katta, you—we have all played parts in this terrible war. None have escaped unscathed.

"Duty requires much of us all. Of some it requires a life of drudgery. To rise above that is as difficult as it is to rise above what you have done in the performance of your duties. Yet souls of great enlightenment have arisen from the poorest circumstances. I have faith that you will rise above this, Samyamu-sum, though it may be as difficult as all the other feats you are celebrated for."

Komawara took a long breath. "Thank you, Shuyun-sum. It is my hope that you are right, as you have been in so many other matters."

The Kalam came and sat on a rock a pace away, sipping his cha silently. The three stayed like that into the afternoon, preserving their company as long as possible.

The next morning found the three travelers at the base of the Mountain of the Pure Spirit. They rode along a road that wound through a woods of birch and pine and golden slip maple.

They did not speak as they rode, for there was little left to be said. They had survived their travels in the desert and the war fought the length of the Grand Canal—words could not begin to say what these things meant. Riding out with Shuyun on the beginning of his journey said all that was required.

At length they came to a shrine at the road's edge. The road narrowed here and began to rise more steeply. As though this was a sign, Shuyun stopped and turned his horse so that he faced his companions.

"I must go alone from here, Samyamu-sum."

The monk could see the young lord struggling as he had often watched the Kalam do—looking for the correct words. In this case, Shuyun thought, none would be found.

"May Botahara journey at your side, Samyamu-sum," Shuyun said.

With an effort, Komawara managed to speak in a whisper. "May Botahara chant your name, Brother."

Shuyun reached out and touched the lord's arm. "He has, Lord Komawara. He has." The monk smiled.

Turning to the Kalam, he spoke to the tribesman in the language of the desert, the tribesman bobbing his head at almost every word. The monk reached into his sleeve then and removed something that he placed in the Kalam's hand. The final words Shuyun said left the tribesman utterly still and silent.

With a bow that the others returned, Shuyun turned his horse and began to climb up into the trees. At a point where he was about to disappear into the woods, Shuyun turned his horse and waved once to his companions. And then he was gone from sight.

It was a small gesture, but it gladdened Komawara's heart more than he could have guessed.

The lord and the tribesman turned their horses back the way they had come, riding knee to knee. It was sev-

eral rih before Komawara's curiosity got the better of
him.

"If I may ask," the lord said, "what was Shuyun-
sum's gift?"

The barbarian dug into a pouch at his waist and held
out his hand. On his palm lay a deep blue stone, the kind
one might find in the bed of river—smooth and regular
in shape.

"It is the soul of a butterfly, Lord Komawara," the
Kalam said with apparent awe. "Brother Shuyun said to
me I would one day see that this was so."

"Then that is no doubt true," Komawara responded
and the two men rode on through the late spring day, lost
in their own thoughts.

Shuyun gave his horse to three monks that he met, and
this unexpected generosity allowed him to pass on without also giving them his name. The road wound up
through the trees, past temples and monasteries belonging to both the Sisterhood and the Order to which Shuyun
had once belonged. There were many shrines and, like
all good seekers, Shuyun stopped at each one and offered
a prayer.

Rather than sleep in the lodgings provided for seekers
near the monasteries and temples Shuyun slept out under
the sky, wrapped in the single blanket in which, during
the day, he carried a bowl and a few things required for
him to act as a healer.

With each step up the sacred mountain the monk felt
he was breaking free of the earth, rising up onto a different plane. Summer clouds sailed in from the ocean
and occasionally one seemed to attach itself to the mountain, clinging there until it stretched itself out in the wind
like a torn banner, then it would break its bond and sail
free.

They come to me, Shuyun laughed to himself, the
Gatherer of Clouds. Like the Brother in the ancient play,
it is my place to gather together the nebulous, the am-
biguous. I will dispel the Illusion, if only for a few.

On the second day Shuyun came to the shrine he
sought—the place where Botahara had given up his army
and renounced all property, the place mentioned in the
scroll Shuyun had received from Brother Hitara. Here the

monk found a place on a large rock and began to fast
and meditate. The shrine was just above the tree line and
only a few of the most hardy trees survived here. Though
few in number, these mountain pines were very old and
each had been given a name, for they had been there a
thousand years before when the Perfect Master had
walked over these very stones.

Many seekers came to this shrine but few spoke to
Shuyun, for most had taken vows of silence and assumed
the same of others.

On the third day of Shuyun's fast, the monk he awaited
appeared at last. Seeing Shuyun, he approached, bowing
in the manner of the Botahist Brothers.

"May the Perfect Master walk beside you, Brother Hitara," Shuyun said.

"May the Teacher greet you by name, Brother Shuyun."

The monk Shuyun had met in the desert perched on
the edge of the rock.

"It is my hope, Brother Hitara, that you have come to
show me the Way."

"Only the Teacher can do that, Brother—the Teacher
and his bearer. But I will guide you some short distance."

Shuyun gave a deep bow in answer. They set off, passing between two tall stones set like gate posts on the stark
landscape. The gray bones of the mountain were exposed
here and interrupted only occasionally by dusky-green
lichen beds.

As they passed the western shoulder of the peak itself,
Shuyun was given a view of the Empire stretching off
into the distance. He was above the clouds now and could
see the masses of white, each trailing a shadow across
the land, as they rolled off toward the western horizon.
The Grand Canal was a silver thread pulled straight across
the landscape and the Imperial Capital was a mound of
white stones, stark against the greens of the land and the
blues of the lake. Shuyun stopped for a moment, and
Brother Hitara walked on a few paces to leave him in
peace.

It was an easy thing to fill himself with the presence
of Nishima and he did so now—her humor, her tenderness, her open spirit. Raising his hand at last as though

he waved to someone far off, the monk turned and followed Hitara.

"Good-bye, my teacher," he whispered, "I go to meet
another."

At dusk they had passed around the shoulder of the
mountain and Shuyun felt that they were in the mountains
proper now, for there was no sight of the Empire. They
made a camp after dark and meditated on the stars until
a moon appeared and then they continued, walking a narrow ridge that twisted and rolled like a stem of lintel
vine. By daylight they had gone many rih.

Brother Hitara was also fasting, so they stopped only
occasionally to drink. The late-spring sun beat down, but
the air remained cool and there was always a breeze from
the sea, making their relentless pace bearable. Toward the
end of the second day Shuyun realized that only his
Botahist-trained memory would allow him to retrace their
route, so twisted was it, so devoid of distinguishing
marks.

Working down a scree slope late in the day, Brother
Hitara began to search along the face of a cliff. After
some searching he located a break in the rock that could
not be seen from even a few feet away. Through this they
came upon a ledge wide enough for two to walk abreast.
It wound up around the side of the cliff, its slope gradual,
disappearing into a white cloud that clung to the mountain side. The stone here appeared to have seen so many
generations of men pass along it that it was worn completely smooth.

Hitara stood gazing along the pathway with a look of
satisfaction as though reassured somehow that it was still
here or that he had been able to find it. "You must not
wear your sandals here, Brother Shuyun—for you this is
the beginning of the Way. Give a prayer of thanks each
time your sole touches the stone, for few have walked
this path."

"Brother Hitara," Shuyun said. "My gratitude cannot
be expressed."

Hitara looked at him oddly then, almost quizzically.
"Brother Shuyun, certainly the honor is mine. I have
taken some small part in the completion of a prophesy.
With each breath I thank Botahara for this. Few can say

as much." He raised his hands to encompass the whole world. "What more can I ask of this life?"

He knelt down and kissed the smooth stone that began the path, then rose and bowed to Shuyun. "We shall meet again, Brother Shuyun. May the Teacher bless you."

"I must thank you for delivering His message, though I confess it took some months before I realized.

"It grows dark, Brother, will you not make camp with me until morning?" Suddenly Shuyun felt it odd to be abandoned. The path he had sought for so long seemed more daunting than he had imagined.

Hitara waved up the slope. "The moon will light my way, Brother Shuyun, for I have many tasks to perform. I would suggest you wait until daylight before you proceed, however. The Way is narrow." Bowing again, Hitara began to make his way lightly up the loose rock.

Finding a flat stone, Shuyun sat and began to meditate. Later, in the moonlight, he chanted, his voice echoing among the mountains as though he were a hundred men.

At the first hint of light he rose and removed his sandals. Like Hitara, he knelt and kissed the stone before placing a foot upon it. If there had been water, he would have bathed his feet.

The pathway led up the shoulder of the mountain until it entered a draw between that mountain and the next. Shuyun passed over the ridge that lay here, glad to find a stream of cool water. The path then followed the narrow ridge, the stone sloping off on both sides into green valleys far below. To his right Shuyun could see a small lake the color of turquoise.

At the end of the day the monk found a tiny rivulet of water that wound down the steep mountainside. A rough stone shrine stood here and Shuyun spent the night as he had before, in prayer.

He set out again at dawn and followed the narrow path as it wound its way deeper into the ancient mountains. Here and there a twisted pine sprang up impossibly from the desert of stone, and now and then he found a pond of clear water. Nowhere did he see signs that others had passed this way, no remains of fires or camps, yet the pathway remained as obvious and clear as a road in the

Capital. Who has passed this way? Shuyun asked himself. How could there have been so many?

On the third day, the sixth of his fast, he came into a hanging valley suspended between three mountains, and here there was enough accumulation of soil that both grass and trees grew—tall narrow firs of a type Shuyun had never seen. Rounding a massive boulder Shuyun surprised a Botahist Sister. Immediately she recovered. She smiled and bowed, making signs of welcome, but she said nothing. In a basket she gathered the cones of the pine trees and some small plant that Shuyun did not know. Obviously, she had taken a vow of silence, so the monk smiled and passed her by, following the pathway.

This valley is my destination, he realized, the awareness surfacing in him as though it was knowledge he had always possessed. The Teacher is here.

He skirted the shore of a tiny lake, and walked through a stand of trees. Here, without warning he came upon a small, roughly built house surrounded by a fence of unplaned boards.

Two Brothers knelt at the gate and they bowed low when Shuyun came into view, showing less surprise at the arrival of a stranger than had the foraging Sister. One rose immediately and slipped through the gate.

The Order's missing Brothers, Shuyun said to himself. Brother Hitara is one of these. The great mystery to the Botahist Brotherhood. They came to serve the Teacher. But how did they know? How did they find Him? Had they received messages like the one Shuyun had received from Hitara? Knowing where the Brothers had come did not solve the mystery.

Realizing the remaining monk did not intend to speak, Shuyun turned and gazed out over the lake, breathing in the scents of the valley that drifted on the cool breeze. It was a fine perfume.

I have found Him, Shuyun thought, feeling his spirit lift as though it took wing on the breeze. We have waited a thousand years. . . .

"Brother Shuyun." It was a woman's voice.

The monk turned to find a Sister regarding him with obvious interest. She was older, though nowhere near as old as the Prioress, and her bearing was that of a woman Shuyun's age.

"May you be welcome in our home," she said in a voice as youthful as her movement. "It is a place of great peace."

"I feel that I have arrived, Sister, but I do not know where."

When the woman smiled, the wrinkles at the corners of her eyes made them appear delightfully mischievous and Shuyun could not help but smile at this contrast.

"This valley, this lake, they have no names." She waved up the slope behind the house. "Nor is this mountain named. It is the home of the Teacher, kept ready for hundreds of years. And now he has come. Please, Brother, walk with me."

Shuyun followed her into a garden, stretching his time sense as he stepped through the gate to make the moment last. A gravel path led to the porch of the house but the nun did not go there. She took a second path, that wound among trees Shuyun could not name, and came to a second gate. She opened this gently, peering inside, then held it wide for her guest.

"He awaits you, Brother."

Shuyun was suddenly light-headed and he forced control over himself with great discipline. When he passed through the gate, the nun did something he did not expect—she reached out and touched him. It was not a gesture of affection or reassurance, she simply wanted to touch him. *I am the bearer of the Word,* Shuyun thought. I am part of a prophesy.

Stepping through the gate, Shuyun swept the garden with his gaze but saw no one. He stood for a moment, offering up a prayer, and then he began to walk along the path, his bare feet alive in every nerve as though the holiness of the earth flowed like chi.

The garden was small, large stones set among trees and unusual shrubs. The elevation no doubt imposed limits on what could be grown, giving the garden a sense of sparseness. All the same, this was a garden of great artistry and Shuyun drank in every detail.

Rounding a boulder, he found a man sitting on a cushion on a low, flat stone that formed a natural dais. Before this was an area of raked gravel. Shuyun stopped suddenly, unable to proceed.

The Teacher bent over a scroll. He dressed in the man-

ner of Shuyun's own Order including a pendant and purple sash. He was not as old as many monks Shuyun had
known and this was a surprise, though it should not have
been. The Teacher appeared to have seen perhaps
seventy-five years in this lifetime, though Shuyun was
sure that was at least ten short of the truth. He was of
average size with little about him, physically, to mark
him. Perhaps his eyes were wider apart than most and
his cheekbones higher, making his face appear less round
than common among the people of Wa.

The Teacher looked up and smiled at Shuyun, a smile
like the Prioress Saeja's—full of compassion, though
touched by humor and the perspective of great age—many
lifetimes in this case.

"Welcome," the Teacher said, his voice melodic. In
that single word Shuyun was certain he heard an echo of
both Lord Shonto and Lady Nishima.

Gesturing as he began to roll the scroll, the Teacher
invited Shuyun to come forward.

Unsure of what was expected, Shuyun chose to walk,
though he knelt and bowed three paces from the rock
dais.

For several minutes the Teacher did not take his eyes
off the young monk before him and his expression of
great pleasure did not change. Somehow Shuyun felt like
a favored son returning after a long absence.

"Brother Shuyun, it is with great joy that we welcome
you into our home."

"The honor is mine entirely . . . Brother Satake."

The older man's face lit up in a great smile. "Motoru-
sum would never have told you."

"He did not, Brother."

The Teacher laughed. "You will be most welcome. I
only regret that I will stay but a short time."

Not quite sure what was meant by this, Shuyun
searched for something to say. "I bring you a gift,
Brother Satake," Shuyun said. He felt his spirit calming
as though he were in the presence of someone he had
known a very long time.

"It is most kind, Brother Shuyun, though I have need
of nothing."

"It is a poem, Brother."

"Ah! A poem is always welcome."

Reaching into his sleeve, Shuyun found the mulberry paper. He leaned forward to place it on the dais, but Satake reached out and took it from his hand. Slowly the Teacher unfolded it and read, the look on his face made Shuyun believe that never had the Teacher received anything that delighted him more. He finished reading, and then he laughed his laugh of great joy.

"Nishi-sum, Nishi-sum," he said, as though the Empress were there in the garden with them. Brother Satake looked up. "This gift brings me great joy, Brother Shuyun. I thank you. She is well?"

Shuyun nodded.

"How I miss her at times," the Teacher said with feeling.

Shuyun nodded. "I fear I shall say the same."

The Teacher regarded him again, unembarrassed, it seemed, to do this. "It has been many centuries since a follower of the Eightfold Path walked the roads of Wa, Brother Shuyun."

Shuyun broke away from the man's gaze with some effort. "I am not sure what the Eightfold Path is, Brother Satake, but I have wandered far from the path taught by my Order."

The Teacher's face became grave. "You rode to war beside my former charge, Motoru-sum; were stripped of your pendant and ejected from your Order; met the barbarian threat; and took an Empress as your lover—all in the few months since you left Jinjoh Monastery?"

Shuyun did not know what to answer. Though the charges were most serious, the Teacher's tone seemed to lighten with each word.

Satake laughed suddenly. "I spent decades accomplishing less, Brother." He smiled his beautiful smile. "Perhaps only Botahara has lived more fully before finding His true purpose." The Teacher laughed again. "Nishi-sum, Nishi-sum," he said as though he chastised a favored child, "my own bearer."

Brother Satake regarded Shuyun again and the humor in the man's eyes seemed to shine through. "Here we have labored on other pursuits, Brother." He gestured to the scroll he had been reading. "We true-copy Botahara's great work."

Shuyun looked up, certain he had let his surprise show. "How, Brother?"

He was not sure this question did not bring a glint of pleasure to the old man's eyes. "There are Faithful even among the Botahist Brothers, Shuyun-sum. Even among the hypocrites and liars. The scrolls have been in the possession of the faithful for some years.

"So we have labored. It is a task more difficult than one would think, for the language has changed and grown—but my special knowledge of the past has allowed us to come near to the end of this. The Word of Botahara as it must be known." He smiled at Brother Shuyun. "And the word of Satake as I have written it." He hefted the scroll he had been reading as if demonstrating its weight. "The word you will bear. Your way will be hard, Brother, never doubt it."

Shuyun stared openly at the scroll in Satake held. *The hand of Botahara, so close I could reach out and touch it.*

Suddenly his face became serious. "You have not yet stopped the sand, Brother Shuyun."

"I have not, Brother Satake," Shuyun admitted. "I confess that I am afraid."

The Teacher nodded, understanding in his eyes. "As was I, Brother Shuyun." He set the scroll down gently and wrapped it in brocade. "Tell me what it is you have learned from your teachers, the Shonto."

Yes, Shuyun thought, it is as I believed. Nishima was my teacher as was her father. "I have learned much, Brother Satake . . . and perhaps I have learned nothing. I do not know."

The Teacher did not answer but gave his full attention to the young monk, waiting.

Shuyun stared down at the gravel for a moment as though studying the patterns there, looking for order among the randomness of the world. "It is the Illusion, Brother Satake: what I was taught did not ring of truth. The world, it is not illusion, it is a plane on which our spirits take form. I was taught that believing in the Illusion would lead to great sorrow, and that joy and pleasure were not real—things meant only to trap us in an endless cycle of rebirth into the world of Illusion." He looked up suddenly. "But I now believe this was wrong. Joy and pleasure are as real as pain and sorrow and one must learn what they have to teach, just as a Neophyte Brother must learn the Form. The Illusion exists in the minds of those who do not truly believe they can progress beyond that plane onto another, who do not know that there is a lesson to be learned. To progress beyond the world one must give it up, finally. It will not disappear the day this is done—one must still come to completion before one leaves it behind. The world will exist for all the souls to come. But one must break free of the Illusion, perceive the path to the next plane. I say this though I have not done so, Brother Satake."

The Teacher smiled and Shuyun felt like a student who had pleased his Master. "You have other duties, Brother. Your time will come." He waved toward the mountains. "When I am no longer among you, Shuyun-sum, you must go to the faithful. The mountain people await you as the tribes of the desert await the rains. It will be the beginning of your long task, Brother Shuyun. Your path will eventually lead you among the hypocrites and liars—some whom you will know by name." He looked up at a passing cloud. "You will be the Bearer, Shuyun-sum, you will be the Gatherer." He smiled upon Shuyun, a smile of great peace. "Botahara will walk beside you."

I have gone to the base of the Sacred Mountain
And watched him ride up among the clouds,
He of the tranquil soul.

Turning back then,
My soul was a raging torrent
But tonight I dream of dark eyes
Above the fan's edge.

If peace can restore an Empire
Will it not a man's spirit?

　　　　　　　　　　　Lord Komawara Samyamu,
　　　　　　　　　　　Consort to the Empress Shigei

　　　　　　　　　The End

DAW

New Dimensions in Fantasy

Sean Russell

☐ **THE INITIATE BROTHER (Book 1)**   UE2466—$4.99
In this powerful debut novel rich with the magic and majesty of
the ancient Orient, one of the most influential lords of the Great
Houses is marked for destruction by the new Emperor and
must use every weapon at his command to survive—including
a young Botahist monk gifted with powers not seen in the world
for nearly a thousand years.

☐ **GATHERER OF CLOUDS (Book 2)**   UE2536—$5.50
Initiate Brother Shuyun, spiritual adviser to Lord Shonto, receives a shocking message: the massive army of the Golden
Khan is poised at the border, and Lord Shonto is caught
between it and his own hostile Emperor's Imperial Army. Yet
even as this trap closes, Brother Shuyun faces another crisis.
For in the same scroll that warned of the invasion was a sacred
Udumbara blossom—a sign his order has awaited for a mil-
lennium. . . .

Elizabeth Forrest

☐ **PHOENIX FIRE**   UE2515—$4.99
As the legendary Phoenix awoke, so, too, did an ancient Chi-
nese demon—and Los Angeles was destined to become the
final battleground in their millennia-old war. Now, the very earth
begins to dance as these two creatures of legend fight to break
free. And as earthquake and fire start to take their toll on the
mortal world, four desperate people begin to suspect the terror
that is about to engulf mankind.

DAW

Tad Williams

Memory, Sorrow and Thorn

THE DRAGONBONE CHAIR: Book 1
- [ ] **Hardcover Edition**   0-8099-003-3—$19.50
- [ ] **Paperback Edition**   UE2384—$5.99

A war fueled by the dark powers of sorcery is about to engulf the long-peaceful land of Osten Ard—as the Storm King, undead ruler of the elvishlike Sithi, seeks to regain his lost realm through a pact with one of human royal blood. And to Simon, a former castle scullion, will go the task of spearheading the quest that offers the only hope of salvation . . . a quest that will see him fleeing and facing enemies straight out of a legend-maker's worst nightmares!

STONE OF FAREWELL: Book 2
- [ ] **Hardcover Edition**   UE2435—$21.95
- [ ] **Paperback Edition**   UE2480—$5.99

As the dark magic and dread minions of the undead Sithi ruler spread their seemingly undefeatable evil across the land, the tattered remnants of a once-proud human army flee in search of a last sanctuary and rallying point, and the last survivors of the League of the Scroll seek to fulfill missions which will take them from the fallen citadels of humans to the secret heartland of the Sithi.

—and coming in March 1993—

TO GREEN ANGEL TOWER: Book 3
- [ ] **Hardcover Edition**   UE2521—$25.00

In this concluding volume of the best-selling trilogy, the forces of Prince Josua march toward their final confrontation with the dread minions of the undead Storm King, while Simon, Miriamele, and Binabek embark on a desperate mission into evil's stronghold.

DAW

Melanie Rawn

THE DRAGON PRINCE NOVELS